LOCKED ROOMS

A Mystery Guild Lost Classics Omnibus

LOCKED ROOMS

A Mystery Guild Lost Classics Omnibus

CONTENTS

CONTENTS

THE THREE COFFINS

LOCKED ROOMS:
A Mystery Guild Lost Classics Omnibus

THE THREE COFFINS

by

John Dickson Carr

Mystery Guild
Garden City, New York

Published by DELL PUBLISHING CO., INC.
750 Third Avenue, New York, N.Y. 10017

Copyright © 1935 by John Dickson Carr

Dell ® TM 681510, Dell Publishing Co., Inc.
Reprinted by arrangement with
Harper & Brothers
New York, New York
ISBN: 978-0-7394-9089-1
Printed in U.S.A.

1st
COFFIN

THE PROBLEM OF THE SAVANT'S STUDY

THE THREAT 1

To the murder of Professor Grimaud, and later the equally incredible crime in Cagliostro Street, many fantastic terms could be applied—with reason. Those of Dr. Fell's friends who like impossible situations will not find in his casebook any puzzle more baffling or more terrifying. Thus: two murders were committed, in such fashion that the murderer must not only have been invisible, but lighter than air. According to the evidence, this person killed his first victim and literally disappeared. Again according to the evidence, he killed his second victim in the middle of an empty street, with watchers at either end; yet not a soul saw him, and no footprint appeared in the snow.

Naturally, Superintendent Hadley never for a moment believed in goblins or wizardry. And he was quite right— unless you believe in a magic that will be explained naturally in this narrative at the proper time. But several people began to wonder whether the figure which stalked through this case might not be a hollow shell. They began to wonder whether, if you took away the cap and the black coat and the child's false-face, you might not reveal nothing inside, like a man in a certain famous romance by Mr. H. G. Wells. The figure was grisly enough, anyhow.

The words "according to the evidence" have been used. We must be very careful about the evidence when it is not given at first-hand. And in this case the reader must be told at the outset, to avoid useless confusion, on whose evidence he can absolutely rely. That is to say, it must be assumed that *somebody* is telling the truth—else there is no legitimate mystery, and, in fact, no story at all.

Therefore it must be stated that Mr. Stuart Mills at Professor Grimaud's house was not lying, was not omitting or adding anything, but telling the whole business exactly as he saw it in every case. Also it must be stated that the three independent witnesses of Cagliostro Street (Messrs. Short and Blackwin, and Police-constable Withers) were telling the exact truth.

Under these circumstances, one of the events which led

up to the crime must be outlined more fully than is possible in retrospect. It was the keynote, the whiplash, the challenge. And it is retold from Dr. Fell's notes, in essential details exactly as Stuart Mills later told it to Dr. Fell and Superintendent Hadley. It occurred on the night of Wednesday, February 6th, three days before the murder, in the back parlour of the Warwick Tavern in Museum Street.

Dr. Charles Vernet Grimaud had lived in England for nearly thirty years, and spoke English without accent. Except for a few curt mannerisms when he was excited, and his habit of wearing an old-fashioned square-topped bowler hat and black string tie, he was even more British than his friends. Nobody knew much about his earlier years. He was of independent means, but he had chosen to be "occupied" and made a good thing of it financially. Professor Grimaud had been a teacher, a popular lecturer and writer. But he had done little of late, and occupied some vague unsalaried post at the British Museum which gave him access to what he called the low-magic manuscripts. Low magic was the hobby of which he had made capital: any form of picturesque supernatural devilry from vampirism to the Black Mass, over which he nodded and chuckled with childlike amusement—and got a bullet through the lung for his pains.

A sound common-sense fellow, Grimaud, with a quizzical twinkle in his eye. He spoke in rapid, gruff bursts, from deep down in his throat; and he had a trick of chuckling behind closed teeth. He was of middle size, but he had a powerful chest and enormous physical stamina. Everybody in the neighbourhood of the Museum knew his black beard, trimmed so closely that it looked only like greying stubble, his shells of eye-glasses, his upright walk as he moved along in quick short steps, raising his hat curtly or making a semaphore gesture with his umbrella.

He lived, in fact, just round the corner at a solid old house on the west side of Russell Square. The other occupants of the house were his daughter Rosette, his housekeeper, Mme Dumont, his secretary, Stuart Mills, and a broken-down ex-teacher named Drayman, whom he kept as a sort of hanger-on to look after his books.

But his few real cronies were to be found at a sort of club they had instituted at the Warwick Tavern in Museum Street. They met four or five nights in a week, an unofficial conclave, in the snug back room reserved for that purpose. Although it was not officially a private room, few outsiders from the bar ever blundered in there, or were made welcome if they did. The most regular attendants of the club were fussy baldheaded little Pettis, the authority on ghost stories; Mangan, the newspaperman; and Burnaby, the artist; but Professor Grimaud was its undisputed Dr. Johnson.

He ruled. Nearly every night in the year (except Saturdays and Sundays, which he reserved for work), he would set out for the Warwick accompanied by Stuart Mills. He would sit in his favourite cane armchair before a blazing fire, with a glass of hot rum and water, and hold forth autocratically in the fashion he enjoyed. The discussions, Mills says, were often brilliant, although nobody except Pettis or Burnaby ever gave Professor Grimaud serious battle. Despite his affability, he had a violent temper. As a rule they were content to listen to his storehouse of knowledge about witchcraft and sham witchcraft, wherein trickery hoaxed the credulous; his child-like love of mystification and drama, wherein he would tell a story of mediaeval sorcery, and, at the end, abruptly explain all the puzzles in the fashion of a detective story. They were amusing evenings, with something of the rural-inn flavor about them, though they were tucked away behind the gas-lamps of Bloomsbury. They were amusing evenings—until the night of February 6th, when the premonition of terror entered as suddenly as the wind blowing open a door.

The wind was blowing shrewdly that night, Mills says, with a threat of snow in the air. Besides himself and Grimaud, there were present at the fireside only Pettis and Mangan and Burnaby. Professor Grimaud had been speaking, with pointed gestures of his cigar, about the legend of vampirism.

"Frankly, what puzzles me," said Pettis, "is your attitude towards the whole business. Now, I study only fiction; only ghost stories that never happen. Yet in a way I believe in ghosts. But you're an authority on attested happenings—things that we're forced to call facts unless we can refute 'em. Yet you don't believe a word of what you've made the most important thing in your life. It's as though Bradshaw wrote a treatise to prove that steam-locomotion was impossible, or the editor of the Encyclopaedia Britannica inserted a preface saying that there wasn't a reliable article in the whole edition."

"Well, and why not?" said Grimaud, with that quick, gruff bark of his wherein he hardly seemed to open his mouth. "You see the moral, don't you?"

" 'Much study hath made him mad,' perhaps?" suggested Burnaby.

Grimaud continued to stare at the fire. Mills says that he seemed more angry than the casual gibe would have warranted. He sat with the cigar exactly in the middle of his mouth, drawing at it in the manner of a child sucking a peppermint-stick.

"I am the man who knew too much," he said, after a pause. "And it is not recorded that the temple priest was ever a very devout believer. However, that is beside the point. I am interested in the causes behind these superstitions. How did the superstition start? What gave it impetus, so that the gullible could believe? For example! We are speaking of the vampire legend. Now, that is a belief which prevails in Slavonic lands. Agreed? It got its firm grip on Europe when it swept in a blast out of Hungary between 1730 and 1735. Well, how did Hungary get its proof that dead men could leave their coffins, and float in the air in the form of straw or fluff until they took human shape for an attack?"

"Was there proof?" asked Burnaby.

Grimaud lifted his shoulders in a broad gesture.

"They exhumed bodies from the churchyards. They found some corpses in twisted positions, with blood on their faces and hands and shrouds. That was their proof. . . . But why not? Those were plague years. Think of all the poor devils who were buried alive though believed to be dead. Think how they struggled to get out of the coffin before they really died. You see, gentlemen? That's what I mean by the causes behind superstitions. That's what I am interested in."

"*I also,*" said a new voice, "*am interested in it.*"

Mills says that he had not heard the man come in, although he thought he felt a current of air from the opened door. Possibly they were startled by the mere intrusion of a stranger, in a room where a stranger seldom intruded and never spoke. Or it may have been the man's voice, which was harsh, husky, and faintly foreign, with a sly triumph croaking in it. Anyhow, the suddenness of it made them all switch round.

There was nothing remarkable about him, Mills says. He stood back from the firelight, with the collar of his shabby black overcoat turned up and the brim of his shabby soft hat pulled down. And what little they could see of his face was shaded by the gloved hand with which he was stroking his chin. Beyond the fact that he was tall and shabby and of gaunt build, Mills could tell nothing. But in his voice or bearing, or maybe a trick of gesture, there was something vaguely familiar while it remained foreign.

He spoke again. And his speech had a stiff, pedantic quality, as though it were a burlesque of Grimaud.

"You must forgive me, gentlemen," he said,—and the triumph grew, "for intruding into your conversation. But I should like to ask the famous Professor Grimaud a question."

Nobody thought of snubbing him, Mills says. They were all intent; there was a kind of wintry power about the man, which disturbed the snug firelit room. Even Grimaud, who sat dark and solid and ugly as an Epstein figure, with his cigar halfway to his mouth and his eyes glittering behind the thin glasses, was intent. He only barked:

"Well?"

"You do not believe, then," the other went on, turning his gloved hand round from his chin only far enough to point with one finger, "that a man can get up out of his coffin; that he can move anywhere invisibly; that four walls are nothing to him; and that he is as dangerous as anything out of hell?"

"I do not," Grimaud answered, harshly. "Do you?"

"Yes. I have done it. But more! I have a brother who can do much more than I can, and is very dangerous to you. *I* don't want your life; he does. But if *he* calls on you. . . ."

The climax of this wild talk snapped like a piece of slate exploding in the fire. Young Mangan, an ex-footballer, jumped to his feet. Little Pettis peered round nervously.

"Look here, Grimaud," said Pettis, "this fellow's stark mad. Shall I—" He made an uneasy gesture in the direction of the bell, but the stranger interposed.

"Look at Professor Grimaud," he said, "before you decide."

Grimaud was regarding him with a heavy, graven contempt. "No, no, no! You hear me? Let him alone. Let him talk about his brother and his coffins—"

"Three coffins," interposed the stranger.

"Three coffins," agreed Grimaud, with bristling suavity, "if you like. As many as you like, in God's name! Now perhaps you'll tell us who you are?"

The stranger's left hand came out of his pocket and laid a grubby card on the table. Somehow the sight of that prosaic visiting-card seemed to restore sane values; to whirl the whole delusion up the chimney as a joke; and to make of this harsh-voiced visitor nothing but a scarecrow of an actor with a bee under his shabby hat. For Mills saw that the card read: *Pierre Fley. Illusionist.* In one corner was printed *2B Cagliostro Street W.C. 1.*, and over it was scribbled *Or c/o Academy Theatre.* Grimaud laughed. Pettis swore and rang the bell for the waiter.

"So," remarked Grimaud, and ticked the card against his thumb. "I thought we should come to something like that. You are a conjuror, then?"

"Does the card say so?"

"Well, well, if it's a lower professional grade, I beg your pardon," nodded Grimaud. A sort of asthmatic mirth whistled in his nostrils. "I don't suppose we might see one of your illusions?"

"With pleasure," said Fley, unexpectedly.

His movement was so quick that nobody anticipated it. It looked like an attack, and was nothing of the kind—in a physical sense. He bent across the table toward Grimaud, his gloved hands twitching down the collar of his coat, and twitching it back up again before anybody else could get a glimpse of him. But Mills had an impression that he was grinning. Grimaud remained motionless and hard. Only his jaw seemed to jut and rise, so that the mouth was like a contemptuous arc in the clipped beard. And his color was a little darker, though he continued to tick the card quietly against his thumb.

"And now, before I go," said Fley, curtly, "I have a last question for the famous professor. Some one will call on you one evening soon. I also am in danger when I associate with my brother, but I am prepared to run that risk. Some one, I repeat, will call on you. Would you rather I did— or shall I send my brother?"

"Send your brother," snarled Grimaud, getting up suddenly, "and be damned!"

The door had closed behind Fley before anybody moved or spoke. And the door also closes on the only clear view we have of the events leading up to the night of Saturday, February 9th. The rest lies in flashes and glimpses, to be interpreted in jig-saw fashion as Dr. Fell later fitted together the charred fragments between the sheets of glass. The first deadly walking of the hollow man took place on that last-named night, when the side streets of London were quiet with snow and the three coffins of the prophecy were filled at last.

THE DOOR 2

There was roaring good-humour that night round the fire in Dr. Fell's library at Number 1 Adelphi Terrace. The doctor sat ruddy-faced and enthroned in his largest, most comfortable, and decrepit chair, which had sagged and cracked across the padding in the only way a chair can be made comfortable, but which for some reason makes wives go frantic. Dr. Fell beamed with all his vastness behind the eye-glasses on the black ribbon, and hammered his cane on the hearth rug as he chuckled. He was celebrating. Dr. Fell likes to celebrate the arrival of his friends; or, in fact, anything else. And tonight there was double cause for revelry.

For one thing, his young friends, Ted and Dorothy Rampole, had arrived from America in the most exuberant of good spirits. For another his friend Hadley—now Superintendent Hadley of the C.I.D., remember—had just concluded a brilliant piece of work on the Bayswater forgery case, and was relaxing. Ted Rampole sat at one side of the hearth, and Hadley at the other, with the doctor presiding between over a steaming bowl of punch. Upstairs the Mesdames Fell, Hadley, and Rampole were conferring about something, and down here the Messieurs Fell and Hadley were already engaged in a violent argument about something else, so Ted Rampole felt at home.

Sitting back lazily in the deep chair, he remembered old days. Across from him Superintendent Hadley, with his clipped moustache and his hair the colour of dull steel, was smiling and making satiric remarks to his pipe. Dr. Fell flourished the punch ladle in thunder.

They seemed to be arguing about scientific criminology, and photography in particular. Rampole remembered hearing echoes of this, which had roused the ribald mirth of the C.I.D. During one of his absent-minded intervals of pottering about after a hobby, Dr. Fell had been snared by his friend the Bishop of Mappleham into reading Gross, Jesserich, and Mitchell. He had been bitten. Now Dr. Fell has not, it may be thankfully stated, what is called the scientific brain. But his chemical researches left the roof on the house, since, fortunately, he always managed to smash the apparatus before the experiment had begun; and, beyond setting fire to the curtains with a Bunsen burner, he did little damage. His photographic work (he said) had been very successful. He had bought a Davontel microscopic camera, with an achromatic lens, and littered the place with what resembled X-ray prints of a particularly dyspeptic stomach. Also, he claimed to have perfected Dr. Gross' method of deciphering the writing on burnt paper.

Listening to Hadley jeer at this, Rampole let his mind drift drowsily. He could see the firelight moving on crooked walls of books, and hear fine snow ticking the window panes behind drawn curtains. He grinned to himself in sheer amiability. He had nothing in the excellent world to irk him—or had he? Shifting, he stared at the fire. Little things popped up like a jack-in-the-box to jab you when you were most comfortable.

Criminal cases! Of course there was nothing to it. It had been Mangan's ghoulish eagerness to enrich a good story. All the same—

"I don't give a hoot *what* Gross says," Hadley was declaring, with a flap of his hand on the chair-arm. "You people always seem to think a man is accurate just because he's thorough. In most cases the letters against burnt paper don't show up at all. . . ."

Rampole cleared his throat pacifically. "By the way," he said, "do the words 'three coffins' mean anything to you?"

There was an abrupt silence, as he had hoped there would be. Hadley regarded him suspiciously. Dr. Fell blinked over the ladle with a puzzled air, as though he vaguely associated the words with a cigarette or a pub. Then a twinkle appeared in his eye.

"Heh," he said, and rubbed his hands. "Heh-heh-heh!

Making peace, hey? Or do you by any chance mean it? What coffins?"

"Well," said Rampole, "I shouldn't exactly call it a criminal case—" Hadley whistled.

"—but it's a queer business, unless Mangan was stretching things. I know Boyd Mangan quite well; he lived on the other side for a couple of years. He's a damned good fellow who's knocked about the world a lot and has a too-Celtic imagination." He paused, remembering Mangan's dark, slovenly, rather dissipated good looks; his slow-moving ways despite his excitable temperament; his quick generosity and homely grin. "Anyhow, he's here in London working for the *Evening Banner* now. I ran into him this morning in the Haymarket. He dragged me into a bar and poured out the whole story. Then," said Rampole, laying it on with a trowel, "when he learned I knew the great Dr. Fell—"

"Rats," said Hadley, looking at him in that sharp, watchful way of his. "Get down to cases."

"Heh-heh-heh," said Dr. Fell, highly delighted. "Shut up, will you, Hadley? This sounds interesting, my boy. Well?"

"Well, it seems that he's a great admirer of a lecturer or writer named Grimaud. Also he has fallen hard for Grimaud's daughter, and that makes him a still greater admirer of the old man. The old man and some of his friends have a habit of visiting a pub near the British Museum, and a few nights ago something happened which seems to have shaken up Mangan more than the antics of a casual lunatic would warrant. While the old man was talking about corpses getting up out of their graves, or some such cheerful subject, in walked a tall queer-looking bird who began babbling some nonsense about himself and his brother really being able to leave their graves and float in the air like straw." (Here Hadley made a disgusted noise and relaxed his attention, but Dr. Fell continued to look curiously at Rampole.) "Actually, it seems to have been some sort of threat against this Professor Grimaud. At the end this stranger made a threat that his brother would call on Grimaud before long. The odd part was that, though Grimaud didn't turn a hair, Mangan swears he was actually scared green."

Hadley grunted. "That's Bloomsbury for you. But what of it? Somebody with a scary old-womanish mind—"

"That's the point," growled Dr. Fell, scowling. "He

isn't. I know Grimaud quite well. I say, Hadley, you don't know how queer it is unless you know Grimaud. H'mf. Ha. Go on, son. How did it end?"

"Grimaud didn't say anything. In fact, he turned it into a joke and an anti-climax that punctured the lunacy pretty well. Just after this stranger had gone, a street musician came up against the door of the pub and struck up 'The Daring Young Man on the Flying Trapeze.' The whole crowd of them burst out laughing, and sanity was restored. Grimaud smiled and said, 'Well, gentlemen, our revived corpse will have to be even nimbler than that if he expects to float down from *my* study window.'

"They dismissed it at that. But Mangan was curious to find out who this visitor, this 'Pierre Fley,' was. Fley had given Grimaud a card with the name of a theatre on it. So the next day Mangan followed it up in the guise of getting a newspaper story. The theatre turned out to be a rather broken-down and disreputable music-hall in the East End, staging nightly variety. Mangan didn't want to run into Fley. He got into talk with the stage-door keeper, who introduced him to an acrobat in the turn before Fley. This acrobat calls himself—Lord knows why—'Pagliacci the Great,' although he's actually an Irishman and a shrewd one. He told Mangan what he knew.

"Fley is known at the theatre as 'Loony.' They know nothing about him; he speaks to nobody and ducks out after every show. But—this is the point—he is *good*. The acrobat said he didn't understand why some West End manager hadn't tumbled to it long before, unless Fley was simply unambitious. It's a sort of super-conjuring, with a specialty in vanishing-tricks. . . ."

Hadley grunted again, derisively.

"No," insisted Rampole, "so far as I can gather it isn't just the old, old stuff. Mangan says he works without an assistant, and that all his props together can go into a box the size of a coffin. If you know anything about magicians, you'll know what a whale of an incredible thing that is. In fact, the man seems hipped on the subject of coffins. Pagliacci the Great once asked him why, and got a jump he didn't expect. Fley turned round with a broad grin and said: 'Three of us were once buried alive. Only one escaped.' Pagliacci said: 'And how did you escape?' To which Fley answered, calmly: 'I didn't, you see. I was one of the two who did not escape.' "

Hadley was tugging at the lobe of his ear. He was serious now.

"Look here," he said, rather uneasily, "this may be a little more important than I'd thought. The fellow's crazy, right enough. If he's got any imaginary grudge— You say he's an alien? I might give the Home Office a call and have him looked up. Then, if he tries to make trouble for your friend . . ."

"*Has* he tried to make trouble?" asked Dr. Fell.

Rampole shifted. "Some sort of letter has come for Professor Grimaud in every post since Wednesday. He has torn 'em up without saying anything, but somebody told his daughter about the affair at the pub, and she has begun to worry. Finally, to cap the whole business, yesterday Grimaud himself began to act queerly."

"How?" asked Dr. Fell. He took away the hand with which he had been shading his eyes. His little eyes blinked at Rampole in startling sharpness.

"He phoned Mangan yesterday, and said: 'I want you to be at the house on Saturday evening. Somebody threatens to pay me a visit.' Naturally, Mangan advised warning the police, which Grimaud wouldn't hear of. Then Mangan said: 'But hang it, sir, this fellow's stark mad and he may be dangerous. Aren't you going to take *any* precautions to defend yourself?' To which the professor answered: 'Oh yes, by all means. I am going to buy a painting.' "

"A what?" demanded Hadley, sitting up.

"A painting to hang on the wall. No, I'm not joking. It seems he did buy it: it was a landscape of some sort, weird business showing trees and gravestones, and a devil of a huge landscape that it took two workmen to carry upstairs. I say 'devil of a landscape' advisedly; I haven't seen it. It was painted by an artist named Burnaby, who's a member of the club and an amateur criminologist. . . . Anyhow, that's Grimaud's idea of defending himself."

To Hadley, who was again eyeing him suspiciously, he repeated his words with some violence. They both turned to look at Dr. Fell. The doctor sat wheezing over his double chins, his big mop of hair rumpled and his hands folded on his cane. He nodded, staring at the fire. When he spoke, the room seemed to grow less comfortable.

"Have you got the address of the place, my boy?" he asked, in a colourless voice. . . . "Good. Better warm up your car, Hadley."

"Yes, but look here—!"

"When an alleged lunatic threatens a sane man," said Dr. Fell, nodding again, "then you may or may not be disturbed. But when a sane man begins to act exactly like the lunatic, then I know *I'm* jolly well disturbed. It may be nothing at all. But I don't like it." Wheezing, he hoisted himself up. "Come on, Hadley. We'll go and have a look at the place, even if we only cruise past."

A sharp wind bit through the narrow streets of the Adelphi; the snow had stopped. It lay white and unreal on the terrace, and in the Embankment gardens below.

In the Strand, bright and deserted during the theatre hour, it was churned to dirty ruts. A clock said five minutes past ten as they turned up into Aldwych. Hadley sat quiet at the wheel, his collar turned up. At Dr. Fell's roar for more speed, Hadley looked first at Rampole and then at the doctor piled into the rear seat.

"This is a lot of nonsense, you know," he snapped. "And it's none of our business. Besides, if there has been a visitor, he's probably gone by now."

"I know," said Dr. Fell. "That's what I'm afraid of."

The car shot into Southampton Row. Hadley kept hooting the horn as though to express his own feelings —but they gathered speed. The street was a bleak canyon, opening into the bleaker canyon of Russell Square. On the west side ran few foot-tracks and even fewer wheelmarks. If you know the telephone box at the north end, just after you pass Keppel Street, you will have seen the house opposite even if you have not noticed it. Rampole saw a plain, broad, three-storied front, the ground floor of stone blocks painted dun, and red brick above. Six steps led up to a big front door with a brass-edged letter-slot and brass knob. Except for two windows glowing behind drawn blinds on the ground floor over the areaway, the whole place was dark. It seemed the most prosaic house in a prosaic neighbourhood. But it did not remain so.

A blind was torn aside. One of the lighted windo went up with a bang just as they idled past. A fig climbed on the sill, outlined against the crackling b hesitated, and leaped. The leap carried him far beyond the spiked area rails. He struck the paveme one leg, slipped in the snow, and pitched out acr kerb nearly under the wheels of the car.

Hadley jammed on his brakes. He was out of

as it skidded against the kerb, and had the man by the arm before the latter had got to his feet. But Rampole had caught a glimpse of the man's face in the headlights.

"Mangan!" he said. "What the devil—!"

Mangan was without a hat or overcoat. His eyes glittered in the light like the glassy bits of snow streaking his arms and hands.

"Who's that?" he demanded, hoarsely. "No, no, I'm all right! Let go, damn it!" He yanked loose from Hadley and began to wipe his hands on his coat. "Who—Ted! Listen. Get somebody. Come along yourself. Hurry! He locked us in—there was a shot upstairs; we just heard it. He'd locked us in, you see. . . ."

Looking behind him, Rampole could see a woman's figure silhouetted against the window. Hadley cut through these incoherent words.

"Steady on. Who locked you in?"

"*He* did. Fley. He's still in there. We heard the shot, and the door's too thick to break. Well, are you coming on?"

He was already running for the front steps, with Hadley and Rampole after him. Neither of the latter had expected the front door to be unlocked, but it swung open when Mangan wrenched the knob. The high hallway inside was dark except for a lamp burning on a table far at the rear. Something seemed to be standing back there, looking at them, with a face more grotesque than any they might have imagined on Pierre Fley; and then Rampole saw it was only a suit of Japanese armour decked out in its devil mask. Mangan hurried to a door at the right, and turned the key that was in the lock. The door was opened from inside by the girl whose silhouette they had seen at the window, but Mangan held her back with his arm extended. From upstairs they could hear a heavy banging noise.

"It's all right, Boyd!" cried Rampole, feeling his heart rise in his throat. "This is Superintendent Hadley—I told you about him. Where is it? What is it?"

Mangan pointed at the staircase. "Carry on. I'll take care of Rosette. He's still upstairs. He can't get out. For God's sake be careful!"

He was reaching after a clumsy weapon on the wall as they went up thick-carpeted stairs. The floor above was dark and seemed deserted. But a light shone down from a

niche in the staircase to the next floor, and the banging had changed to a series of thuds.

"Dr. Grimaud!" a voice was crying. "Dr. *Gri*maud! Answer me, will you?"

Rampole had no time to analyze what seemed the exotic, thick atmosphere of this place. He hurried after Hadley up the second staircase, under an open archway at its top, and into a broad hallway which ran the breadth of the house instead of the length. It was panelled to the ceiling in oak, with three curtained windows in the long side of this oblong opposite the staircase, and its thick black carpet deadened every footstep. There were two doors —facing each other from the narrow ends of the oblong. The door far down at their left was open; the door at their right, only about ten feet from the staircase, remained closed despite the man who was beating on it with his fists.

This man whirled round at their approach. Although there was no illumination in the hallway itself, a yellow light streamed through the arch from the niche on the staircase—from the stomach of a great brass Buddha in the niche—and they could see everything clearly. Full in the glow stood a breathless little man who was gesturing uncertainly. He had a big goblin-like shock of hair on his big head, and peered behind big spectacles.

"Boyd?" he cried. "Drayman? I say, is that you? Who's there?"

"Police," said Hadley, and strode past him as he jumped back.

"You can't get in there," said the little man, cracking the joints of his fingers. "But we've got to get in. The door's locked on the inside. Somebody's in there with Grimaud. A gun went off— He won't answer. Where's Madame Dumont? Get Madame Dumont! That fellow's still in there, I tell you!"

Hadley turned round snappishly.

"Stop dancing and see if you can find a pair of pliers. The key's in the lock; we'll turn it from the outside. I want a pair of *pliers*. Have you got 'em?"

"I—I really don't know where—"

Hadley looked at Rampole. "Hop down to the toolbox in my car. It's under the back seat. Get the smallest pliers you can find, and you might bring along a couple of heavy spanners. If this fellow is armed—"

Rampole turned round to see Dr. Fell emerge through

the arch, wheezing heavily. The doctor did not speak, but his face was not so ruddy as before. Going downstairs three at a time, Rampole blundered for what seemed hours before he found the pliers. As he returned he could hear Mangan's voice behind the closed door in the downstairs room, and the hysterical tones of a girl. . . .

Hadley, still impassive, eased the pliers gently into the keyhole. His powerful hands clamped, and began to turn towards the left.

"There's something moving in there—" said the little man.

"Got it," said Hadley. "Stand back!"

He drew on a pair of gloves, braced himself, and threw the door inward. It flapped back against the wall with a crash that shook tinglings from the chandelier inside. Nothing came out, although something was trying to come out. Except for that, the bright room was empty. Something, on which Rampole saw a good deal of blood, was painfully trying to drag itself on hands and knees across the black carpet. It choked, rolled over on its side, and lay still.

THE FALSE FACE 3

"Stay in the door, two of you," Hadley said, curtly. "And if anybody's got weak nerves, don't look."

Dr. Fell lumbered in after him, and Rampole remained in the doorway with his arm extended across it. Professor Grimaud was heavy, but Hadley did not dare wrench. In that effort to crawl to the door there had been a hemorrhage which was not altogether internal, although Grimaud kept his teeth clenched against the blood. Hadley raised him up against one knee. His face had a bluish tinge under the mask of blackish-grey stubble; his eyes were closed and sunken; and he was still trying to press a sodden handkerchief to the bullet hole in his chest. They heard his breath sink thinly. Despite a draught, there was still a sharp mist of powder-smoke.

"Dead?" muttered Dr. Fell.

"Dying," said Hadley. "See the colour? He got it through the lung." He whirled round towards the little man in the doorway. "Phone for an ambulance. Quick! There's not a chance, but he may be able to say something before—"

"Yes," said Dr. Fell, with a kind of fierce sombreness; "that's the thing we're most interested in, isn't it?"

"If it's the only thing we can do," Hadley answered, coolly, "yes. Get me some sofa pillows from over there. Make him as comfortable as we can." When Grimaud's head lolled on one pillow, Hadley bent close. "Dr. Grimaud! *Dr. Grimaud!* Can you hear me?"

The waxy eyelids fluttered. Grimaud's eyes, only half open, moved in a queer, helpless, puzzled way, like a small child's in a face that you would have described as "knowing" or "civilized." He could not seem to understand what had happened. His glasses hung down on a cord from the dressing-gown; he made a weak twitching of his fingers as though he would try to raise them. His barrel chest still rose and fell slightly.

"I am from the police, Dr. Grimaud. Who did this? Don't try to answer if you can't. Nod your head. Was it the man Pierre Fley?"

A faint look of comprehension was succeeded by an even more puzzled expression. Then, distinctly Grimaud shook his head.

"Who was it, then?"

Grimaud was eager; too eager, for it defeated him. He spoke for the first and last time. His lips stuttered in those words whose interpretation, and even the exact wording itself, was so puzzling afterwards. Then he fainted.

The window in the left-hand wall was a few inches up, and a chill draught blew through. Rampole shivered. What had been a brilliant man lay inert on a couple of pillows, spilled and torn like a sack; with something rattling like clockwork inside it to show that it lived, but no more. There was too much blood in the bright, quiet room.

"My God!" Rampole said, uncontrollably, "isn't there anything we can *do?*"

Hadley was bitter. "Nothing, except get to work. 'Still in the house?' Fine lot of dummies!—oh, myself included." He pointed to the partly open window. "Of course the fellow was out of there before we were even inside the house. He certainly isn't here now."

Rampole looked round. The sharp tang of powdersmoke was blowing away, from his vision as well as from the room. He saw the place for the first time in focus.

It was a room some fifteen feet square, with walls panelled in oak and thick black carpet on the floor. In the left-hand wall (as you stood at the door) was the window with its brown velvet draperies blowing. On either side of the window stretched high bookshelves with marble busts along the top. Just out from the window, so as to get the light from the left, stood a great flat-topped desk heavy in claw-footed carving. A padded chair was pushed back from it; at the extreme left was a lamp of mosaic glass, and a bronze ash-tray over which a dead cigar had smoldered to long ash. The blotter, on which a closed calfskin book had been put down, was clean except for a tray of pens and a pile of note-slips held down by a curious little figure—a buffalo carved in yellow jade.

Rampole looked across the room at the side directly opposite the window. In that wall was a great stone fireplace, flanked also by shelves and busts. Above the fireplace, two fencing-foils hung crossed behind a blazoned shield of arms which Rampole did not (then) examine. Only on that side of the room had furniture been disarranged. Just before the fire, a long brown-leather sofa had been knocked awry, and a leather chair rolled back in a twisted-up hearth rug. There was blood on the sofa.

And finally, towards the rear wall of the room facing the door, Rampole saw the painting. Between the bookshelves in this wall there was a vast cleared space where cases had recently been removed; removed within the last few days, for the marks of their bases were still indented in the carpet. A place on the wall had been made for the painting which Grimaud would now never hang. The painting itself lay face upwards on the floor not far from where Grimaud himself lay—and it had been slashed across twice with a knife. In its frame it was fully seven feet broad by four feet high: a thing so big that Hadley had to trundle it out and switch it round in the cleared space down the centre of the room before he could prop it up for a look.

"And that," said Hadley, propping it against the back of the sofa, "is the painting he bought to 'defend himself' with, is it? Look here, Fell, do you think Grimaud was just as mad as this fellow Fley?"

Dr. Fell, who had been owlishly contemplating the window, lumbered round. "As Pierre Fley," he rumbled, and pushed back his shovel-hat, "who *didn't* commit the crime. H'm. I say, Hadley, do you see any weapon?"

"I do not. First there isn't any gun—a high-calibre automatic is what we want—and now there isn't any knife with which this thing was cut to blazes. Look at it! It looks like an ordinary landscape to me."

It was not, Rampole thought, exactly ordinary. There was a sort of blowing power about it, as though the artist had painted in a fury and caught in oils the wind that whipped those crooked trees. You felt bleakness and terror. Its motif was sombre, with a greenish tint underlying greys and blacks, except for low white mountains rising in the background. In the foreground, through the branches of a crooked tree, you could see three headstones in rank grass. Somehow it had an atmosphere like this room, subtly foreign, but as hard to identify as a faint odour. The headstones were toppling; in one way you looked at it, there was an illusion that this was because the grave mounds had begun to heave and crack across. Even the slashes did not seem to disfigure it.

Rampole started a little as he heard a trampling of feet up the staircase in the hall. Boyd Mangan burst in, thinner and more dishevelled than Rampole remembered. Even his black hair, which clung to his head in wirelike scrolls, looked rumpled. He took a quick look at the man on the floor, the heavy brows shading his eyes, and then began to rub a parchment-like cheek. Actually he was about Rampole's age, but the slanting lines drawn under his eyes made him look ten years older.

"Mills told me," he said. "Is he—?" He nodded quickly at Grimaud.

Hadley ignored this. "Did you get the ambulance?"

"Chaps with a stretcher—coming now. The whole neighbourhood's filthy with hospitals, and nobody knew where to telephone. I remembered a friend of the professor's who's got a nursing-home round the corner. They're—" He stood aside to admit two uniformed attendants, and behind them a placid little clean-shaven man with a bald head. "This is Dr. Peterson—er—the police. And that's your—patient."

Dr. Peterson sucked in his cheek and hurried over. "Stretcher, boys," he said, after a brief look. "I won't dig for it here. Take him easy." He scowled and stared curiously round as the stretcher was carried out.

"Any chance?" asked Hadley.

"He might last a couple of hours; not more, and probably less. If he hadn't had the constitution of a bull he'd be dead already. Looks as though he's made a further lesion in the lung trying to exert himself—torn it across." Dr. Peterson dived into his pocket. "You'll want to send your police surgeon round, won't you? Here's my card. I'll keep the bullet when I get it. I should guess a thirty-eight bullet, fired from about ten feet off. May I ask what happened?"

"Murder," said Hadley. "Keep a nurse with him, and if he says anything have it taken down word for word." As the doctor hurried out, Hadley scribbled on a leaf of his notebook and handed it to Mangan. "Got your head about you? Good. I wish you'd phone the Hunter Street police station with these instructions; they'll get in touch with the Yard. Tell 'em what happened if they ask. Dr. Watson is to go to the address of this nursing-home, and the rest are to come on here. . . . Who's that at the door?"

The man at the door was the small, thin, top-heavy youth who had been pounding there to begin with. In full light Rampole saw a big goblin-like shock of dark red hair. He saw dull brown eyes magnified behind thick gold-rimmed glasses, and a bony face sloping outwards to a large and loose mouth. This mouth wriggled with a sonorous precision of utterance, showing wide-spaced teeth with an upward movement of the lip like a fish. The mouth looked flexible from much speaking. Every time he spoke, in fact, he had the appearance of thinly addressing an audience, raising and lowering his head as though from notes, and speaking in a penetrating singsong towards a point over his listeners' heads. You would have diagnosed a Physics B.Sc. with Socialist platform tendencies, and you would have been right. His clothes were of a reddish-check pattern, and his fingers were laced together before him. His earlier terror had changed to inscrutable calm. He bowed a little, and replied without expression:

"I am Stuart Mills. I am, or was, Dr. Grimaud's secretary." His big eyes moved round. "May I ask what has happened to the—culprit?"

"Presumably," said Hadley, "he escaped through the window while we were all so sure he couldn't get out. Now, Mr. Mills—"

"Pardon me," the sing-song voice interposed, with a sort of aerial detachment about it. "He must have been a very

extraordinary man if he did that. Have you examined the
window?"

"He's right, Hadley," said Dr. Fell, wheezing heavily.
"Take a look! This business is beginning to worry me. I
tell you in all sincerity that, if our man didn't leave here
by way of the door . . ."

"He did not. I am not," announced Mills, and smiled,
"the only witness to that. I saw it all from start to finish."

". . . then he must have been lighter than air to leave
by the window. Open the window and have a look.
H'mf, wait! We'd better search the room first."

There was nobody hidden in the room. Afterwards,
growling under his breath, Hadley eased the window
up. Unbroken snow—stretching flat up to the window-
frame itself—covered all the wide sill outside. Rampole
bent out and looked round.

There was a bright moon in the west, and every detail stood out sharp as a wood-cut. It was a good fifty feet
to the ground; the wall fell away in a drop of smooth, wet
stone. Just below there was a back yard, like that of all
the houses in this row, surrounded by a low wall. The
snow lay unbroken in this courtyard, or any other as far
as they could look, and along the tops of the walls. Below
in the whole side of the house there were no windows whatever. The only windows were on this top floor; and the
nearest one to this room was in the hallway to the left, a
good thirty feet away. To the right, the nearest window
would have been in the adjoining house, an equal distance
away. Ahead there lay a vast chessboard of adjoining back
yards from houses lining the square, so that the nearest
house was several hundred yards away. Finally, there
stretched above this window a smooth upward run of
stone for some fifteen feet to the roof—whose slope
afforded neither hold for the fingers nor for the attaching
of a rope.

But Hadley, craning his neck out, pointed malevolently.
"All the same, that's it," he declared. "Look there!
Suppose he first hitched a rope to a chimney or something,
and had it dangling outside the window when he paid his
visit. Then he kills Grimaud, swings out, climbs up over
the edge of the roof, crawls up to untie the rope from the
chimney, and gets away. There will be plenty of tracks of
that, right enough. So—"

"Yes," said Mills' voice. "That is why I must tell you that there aren't any."

Hadley looked round. Mills had been examining the fireplace, but now he regarded them with his wide-spaced teeth showing in an impassive smile, though his eyes looked nervous and there was sweat on his forehead.

"You see," he continued, lifting his hand with the forefinger raised, "as soon as I perceived that the man in the false face had disappeared—"

"The *what?*" said Hadley.

"The false face. Do I make myself clear?"

"No. We must see whether we can't extract some sense presently, Mr. Mills. In the meantime, what is this business about the roof?"

"There are no tracks or marks of any nature on it, you see," the other answered, with a bright expression of his eyes as he opened them wide. This was another trick of his, smiling and staring as though with inspiration, even if it sometimes seemed rather a half-witted inspiration. He raised his forefinger again. "I repeat, gentlemen: when I saw that the man in the false face had evidently disappeared, I foresaw difficulties for myself—"

"Why?"

"Because I myself had this door under observation, and I should have been compelled to asseverate that the man had not come out. Very well. It was therefore deducible that he must have left (a) by way of a rope to the roof, or (b) by means of climbing up inside the chimney to the roof. This was a simple mathematical certainty. If PQ = pq, it is therefore quite obvious that $PQ = pq + p\beta + qa + a\beta$."

"Is it indeed?" said Hadley, with restraint. "Well?"

"At the end of this hallway which you see—that is to say, which you could see if the door were open," pursued Mills, with unshakable exactitude, "I have my workroom. From there a door leads to the attic, and thence to a trap-door opening out on the roof. By raising the trap-door I could see clearly both sides of the roof over this room. The snow was not marked in any fashion."

"You didn't go out there?" demanded Hadley.

"No. I could not have kept my footing if I had. In fact, I do not at the moment see how this could be done even in dry weather."

Dr. Fell turned a radiant face. He seemed to resist a

desire to pick up this phenomenon and dangle him in the air like an ingenious toy.

"And what then, my boy?" he enquired, affably. "I mean, what did you think when your equation was shot to blazes?"

Mills remained smiling and inflexibly profound. "Ah, that remains to be seen. I am a mathematician, sir. I never permit myself to think." He folded his arms. "But I wished to call this to your attention, gentlemen, in spite of my firm statement that he did not leave by the door."

"Suppose you tell us exactly what did happen here tonight," urged Hadley, passing a hand across his forehead. He sat down at the desk and took out his notebook. "Easy, now! We'll lead up to it gradually. How long have you worked for Professor Grimaud?"

"For three years and eight months," said Mills, clicking his teeth. Rampole saw that, in the legal atmosphere of the notebook, he was compressing himself to give brief answers.

"What are your duties?"

"Partly correspondence and general secretarial duties. In greater ratio to assist him in preparing his new .work, *The Origin and History of Middle-European Superstitions, Together with* . . ."

"Quite so. How many people live in this house?"

"Besides Dr. Grimaud and myself, four."

"Yes, yes, well?"

"Ah, I see! You wish their names. Rosette Grimaud, his daughter. Madame Dumont, who is housekeeper. An elderly friend of Dr. Grimaud, named Drayman. A general maid whose last name I have never yet been told, but whose first name is Annie."

"How many were here tonight when this happened?"

Mills brought the toe of his shoe forward, balanced himself, and studied it, another trick of his. "That, obviously, I cannot say with certainty. I will tell you what I know." He rocked back and forth. "At the conclusion of dinner, at seven-thirty, Dr. Grimaud came up here to work. This is his custom on Saturday evenings. He told me he did not wish to be disturbed until eleven o'clock; that is also the inviolable custom. He said, however,"— quite suddenly beads of sweat appeared on the young man's forehead again, though he remained impassive— "he said, however, that he might have a visitor about half-past nine."

"Did he say who this visitor might be?"

"He did not."

Hadley leaned forward. "Come, now, Mr. Mills! Haven't you heard of any threat to him? Didn't you hear what happened on Wednesday evening?"

"I—er—I had previous information of it, certainly. In fact, I was at the Warwick Tavern myself. I suppose Mangan told you?"

Uneasily, but with startling vividness, he sketched out the story. Meanwhile, Dr. Fell had stumped away and was going through an examination he several times made that night. He seemed most interested in the fireplace. Since Rampole had already heard an outline of the tavern incident, he did not listen to Mills; he watched Dr. Fell. The doctor inspected the blood-stains splashing the top and right arm of the disarranged sofa. There were more blood-stains on the hearth, though they were difficult to follow against the black carpet. A struggle there? Yet, Rampole saw, the fire-irons were upright in their rack, in such a position that a struggle before the hearth must have sent them clattering. A very small coal fire had been nearly smothered under a drift of charred papers.

Dr. Fell was muttering to himself. He reared up to examine the escutcheon. To Rampole, no student of heraldry, this presented itself as a divided shield in red and blue and silver: a black eagle and crescent moon in the upper part, and in the lower a wedge of what looked like rooks on a chessboard. Though its colours were darkened, it glowed with barbaric richness in a queerly barbaric room. Dr. Fell grunted.

But he did not speak until he began to examine the books in the shelves at the left of the fireplace. After the fashion of bibliophiles, he pounced. Then he began to yank out book after book, glance at the title-page, and shoot it back in again. Also, he seemed to have pounced on the most disreputable-looking volumes in the shelves. He was raising some dust, and making so much noise that it jarred across Mills' sing-song recital. Then he rose up and waved books at them in excited intentness.

"I say, Hadley, I don't want to interrupt, but this is very rummy and very revealing. Gabriel Dobrentei, 'Yorick és Eliza levelei,' two volumes. 'Shakspere Minden Munkái,' nine volumes in different editions. And here's a name—" He stopped. "H'mf. Ha. Do you know anything about these, Mr. Mills? They're the only books in the lot that haven't been dusted."

Mills was startled out of his recital. "I—I don't know. I believe they are from a batch that Dr. Grimaud meant for the attic. Mr. Drayman found them put away behind others when we removed some bookcases from the room last night to make room for the painting to be hung. . . . Where was I, Mr. Hadley? Ah yes! Well, when Dr. Grimaud told me that he might have a visitor tonight, I had no reason to assume it was the man of the Warwick Tavern. He did not say so."

"What, exactly, did he say?"

"I—you see, after dinner I was working in the big library downstairs. He suggested that I should come upstairs to my workroom at half-past nine, sit with my door open, and—and 'keep an eye on' this room, in case . . ."

"In case?"

Mills cleared his throat. "He was not specific."

"He told you all this," snapped Hadley, "and you still did not suspect who might be coming?"

"I think," interposed Dr. Fell, wheezing gently, "that I may be able to explain what our young friend means. It must have been rather a struggle. He means that in spite of the sternest convictions of the youngest B.Sc., in spite of the stoutest buckler emblazoned with $x^2 + 2xy + y^2$, he still had enough imagination to get the wind up over that scene at the Warwick Tavern. And he didn't want to know any more than it was his duty to know. Is that it, hey?"

"I do not admit it, sir," Mills returned, with relief, nevertheless. "My motives have nothing to do with the facts. You will observe that I carried out my orders exactly. I came up here at precisely half-past nine—"

"Where were the others then? Steady, now!" urged Hadley. "Don't say you can't reply with certainty; just tell us where you *think* they were."

"To the best of my knowledge, Miss Rosette Grimaud and Mangan were in the drawing-room, playing cards. Drayman had told me that he was going out; I did not see him."

"And Madame Dumont?"

"I met her as I came up here. She was coming out with Dr. Grimaud's after-dinner coffee; that is to say, with the remnants of it. . . . I went to my workroom, left my door open, and drew out the typewriter desk so that I could face the hallway while I worked. At exactly"—he shut his eyes, and opened them again—"at exactly fifteen minutes to ten I heard the front-door bell ring. The electric bell is on the second floor, and I heard it plainly.

"Two minutes later, Madame Dumont came up from the staircase. She was carrying one of those trays on which it is customary to place visiting-cards. She was about to knock at the door when I was startled to see the—er—the tall man come upstairs directly after her. She turned round and saw him. She then exclaimed certain words which I am unable to repeat verbatim, but whose purport was to ask why he had not waited downstairs; and she seemed agitated. The—er—tall man made no reply. He walked to the door, and without haste turned down the collar of his coat and removed his cap, which he placed in his overcoat pocket. I think that he laughed, and that Madame Dumont cried out something, shrank back against the wall, and hurried to open the door. Dr. Grimaud appeared on the threshold in some evident annoyance; his exact words were, 'What the devil is all this row about?' Then he stood stockstill, looking up at the tall man; and his exact words were, 'In God's name, who are *you*?' "

Mills' sing-song voice was hurling the words faster; his smile had become rather ghastly, although he tried to make it merely bright.

"Steady, Mr. Mills. Did you get a good look at this tall man?"

"A fairly good look. As he came up under the arch from the staircase, he glanced down in my direction."

"Well?"

"The collar of his overcoat was turned up, and he wore a peaked cap. But I am endowed with what is called 'long sight,' gentlemen, and I could distinctly observe the conformation and colour of the nose and mouth. He was wearing a child's false face, a species of mask in papier-maché. I have an impression that it was long, of a pinkish colour, and had a wide-open mouth. And, so far as my observation went, he did not remove it. I think I am safe in asserting—"

"You are generally right, are you not?" asked a cold voice from the doorway. "It was a false face. And, unfortunately, he did not remove it."

THE IMPOSSIBLE 4

She stood in the doorway, looking from one to the other of them. Rampole received the impression of an extraordinary woman without knowing why he felt it. There was nothing remarkable about her, except a certain brilliance and vividness of the black eyes, which had a sanded, reddish look as though of smart without tears. She seemed all contradiction. She was short, and of sturdy figure, with a broad face, rather high cheekbones, and a shiny skin: yet Rampole had a curious impression that she could have been beautiful if she had tried. Her dark brown hair was coiled loosely over her ears, and she wore the plainest of dark dresses slashed with white across the breast: yet she did not look dowdy.

Poise, strength, carriage, what? The word "electric" is meaningless, yet it conveys the wave that came with her; something of crackle and heat and power, like a blow. She moved towards them, her shoes creaking. The prominent dark eyes, turned a little upwards at the outer corner, sought Hadley. She was rubbing the palms of her hands together before her, up and down. Rampole was conscious of two things—that the killing of Professor Grimaud had struck her with a hurt from which she would never recover, and would have left her stunned and crying if it had not been for one other wish.

"I am Ernestine Dumont," she said, as though interpreting the thought. "I have come to help you find the man who shot Charles."

She spoke almost without accent, but with a certain slur and deadness. The palms of her hands continued to brush up and down.

"When I heard, I could not come up—at first. Then I wished to go with him in the ambulance to the nursing-home, but the doctor would not let me. He said the police would wish to speak with me. Yes, I suppose that was wise."

Hadley rose and moved out for her the chair in which he had been sitting.

"Please sit down, madame. We should like to hear your

own statement in a moment. I must ask you to listen carefully to what Mr. Mills is saying, in case you should be required to corroborate . . ."

She shivered in the cold from the open window, and Dr. Fell, who had been watching her sharply, lumbered over to close it. Then she glanced at the fireplace, where the fire had smouldered nearly out under the mass of burnt papers. Realizing Hadley's words over the gap, she nodded. She looked at Mills absent-mindedly, with a sort of vacant affection which showed almost in a smile.

"Yes, of course. He is a nice poor fool boy, and he means well. Do you not, Stuart? You must go on, by all means. I will—look."

Mills showed no anger, if he felt any. His eyelids flickered a few times, and he folded his arms.

"If it gives the Pythoness any pleasure to think so," he sang, imperturbably, "I have no objection. But perhaps I had better continue. Er—where was I?"

"Dr. Grimaud's words when he saw the visitor, you told us, were, 'In God's name, who are *you?*' Then?"

"Ah yes! He was not wearing his eye-glasses, which were hanging down by their cord; his sight is not good without them, and I am under the impression that he mistook the mask for a real face. But before he could raise the glasses, the stranger made so quick a movement that I was rather confused, and he darted in at the door. Dr. Grimaud made a movement to get in front of him, but he was too quick, and I heard him laughing. When he got inside—" Mills stopped, apparently puzzled. "This is most extraordinary. I am under the impression that Madame Dumont, although she was shrinking back against the wall, closed the door after him. I recall that she had her hand on the knob."

Ernestine Dumont blazed.

"What do you wish to be understood by that, little boy?" she asked. "You fool, be sure you know what you are saying. Do you think I would willingly have had that man alone with Charles?— He kicked the door shut behind him. Then he turned the key in the lock."

"One moment, madame. . . . Is that true, Mr. Mills?"

"I wish it clearly understood," Mills sang, "that I am merely trying to give *every* fact and even every impression. I meant nothing. I accept the correction. He did, as the Pythoness says, turn the key in the lock."

"That is what he calls his little joke, 'the Pythoness,' " Mme Dumont said, savagely. "Ah, bah!"

Mills smiled. "To resume, gentlemen: I can well believe that the Pythoness was agitated. She began to call Dr. Grimaud's Christian name, and to shake the knob of the door. I heard voices inside, but I was some distance away, and you will perceive that the door is thick." He pointed. "I could distinguish nothing until, after an interval of about thirty seconds, during which it is deducible that the tall man removed his mask, Dr. Grimaud called out, to the Pythoness, rather angrily: 'Go away, you fool. I can handle this.' "

"I see. Did he seem—afraid, or anything of the sort?"

The secretary reflected. "On the contrary, I should have said that he sounded in a sense relieved."

"And you, madame: you obeyed and went away without further—?"

"Yes."

"Even though," said Hadley, suavely, "I presume it is not usual for practical jokers to call at the house in false faces and act in such a wild way? You knew, I suppose, of the threat to your employer?"

"I have obeyed Charles Grimaud for over twenty years," said the woman, very quietly. The word "employer" had stung her hard. Her reddish, sanded eyes were intent. "And I have never known a situation which he could *not* handle. Obey! Of course I did; I would always obey. Besides, you do not understand. You have asked me nothing." The contempt changed to a half-smile. "But this is interesting— psychologically, as Charles would say. You have not asked Stuart why *he* obeyed, and caused no fuss. That is merely because you think he would have been afraid. I thank you for the implied compliment. Please go on."

Rampole had a sensation of watching a supple wrist on a swordsman. Hadley seemed to feel this, too, although he addressed the secretary.

"Do you remember, Mr. Mills, the time at which this tall man went into the room?"

"It was at ten minutes to ten. There is a clock on my typewriter desk, you see."

"And when did you hear the shot?"

"At exactly ten minutes past ten."

"You mean to say that you watched the door all that time?"

"I did, most assuredly." He cleared his throat. "In spite of what the Pythoness describes as my timidity, I was the first to reach the door when the shot was fired. It was still locked on the inside, as you gentlemen saw— you yourselves arrived very shortly afterwards."

"During the twenty minutes while these two were together, did you hear any voices, movements, sounds of any kind?"

"At one point I was under the impression that I heard voices raised, and something which I can only describe as resembling a bumping sound. But I was some distance away. . . ." He began to rock again, and stare, as he met Hadley's cold eye. The sweat broke out again. "Now I am aware, of course, that I am under the necessity of telling what must seem an absolutely incredible story. Yet, gentlemen, I *swear* . . . *!*" Quite suddenly he lifted a plump fist and his voice went high.

"That is all right, Stuart," the woman said, gently. "I can confirm you."

Hadley was suavely grim. "That would be just as well, I think. One last question, Mr. Mills. Can you give an exact outward description of this caller you saw? . . . In a moment, madame!" he broke off, turning quickly. "In good time. Well, Mr. Mills?"

"I can state accurately that he wore a long black overcoat, and a peaked cap of some brownish material. His trousers were darkish. I did not observe his shoes. His hair, when he took off the cap—" Mills stopped. "This is extraordinary. I do not wish to be fanciful, but now that I recall it, his hair had a dark, painted, *shiny* look, if you understand me, almost as though his whole head were made of papier-maché."

Hadley, who had been pacing up and down past the big picture, turned on him in a way that brought a squeak from Mills.

"Gentlemen," cried the latter, "you asked me to tell you what I saw. And that is what I saw. It is true."

"Go on," said Hadley, grimly.

"I believe he was wearing gloves, although he put his hands in his pockets and I cannot be absolutely certain. He was tall, a good three or four inches taller than Dr. Grimaud, and of a medium—er—anatomical structure. That is all I can definitely assert."

"Did he look like the man Pierre Fley?"

"Well—yes. That is to say, in one way yes, and another no. I should have said this man was even taller than Fley, and not quite so thin, but I would not be prepared to swear it."

During this questioning, Rampole had been watching Dr. Fell out of the tail of his eye. The doctor, his big cloak humped and his shovel-hat under one arm, had been lumbering about the room with annoyed digs of his cane at the carpet. He bent down to blink at things until his eye-glasses tumbled off his nose. He looked at the painting, along the rows of books, at the jade buffalo on the desk. He went down wheezingly to look at the fireplace, and hoisted himself up again to study the coat of arms over it. Toward the last he seemed to become blankly amiable— and yet always, Rampole saw, he was watching Mme Dumont. She seemed to fascinate him. There was something rather terrible in that small bright eye, which would swing round the second he had finished looking at something. And the woman knew it. Her hands were clenched in her lap. She tried to ignore him, but her glance would come round again. It was as though they were fighting an intangible battle.

"There are other questions, Mr. Mills," said Hadley, "particularly about this Warwick Tavern affair and that painting. But they can wait until we get things in order. . . . Would you mind going down and asking Miss Grimaud and Mr. Mangan to come up here? Also Mr. Drayman, if he has returned? . . . Thanks. Stop a bit! Er—any questions, Fell?"

Dr. Fell shook his head with broad amiability. Rampole could see the woman's white knuckles tighten.

"*Must* your friend walk about in that way?" she cried, abruptly, and in the shrillness of the voice she pronounced the *w* as *v*. "It is maddening. It is—"

Hadley studied her. "I understand, madame. Unfortunately, that is his way."

"Who are you, then? You walk into my house—"

"I had better explain. I am the superintendent of the Criminal Investigation Department. This is Mr. Rampole. And the other man, of whom you may have heard, is Dr. Gideon Fell."

"Yes. Yes, I thought so." She nodded, and then slapped the desk beside her. "Well, well, well! Even so, must you forget your manners? Must you make the room freezing with your open windows, even? May we not at least have a fire to warm us?"

"I don't advise it, you know," said Dr. Fell. "That is, until we see what papers have already been burnt there. It must have been rather a bonfire."

Ernestine Dumont said, wearily: "Oh, why must you be such fools? Why do you sit here? You know quite well who did this. It was the fellow Fley, and you know it. Well, well, well? Why don't you go after him? Why do you sit here when I tell you he did it?"

There was a look about her, a trance-like and gypsyish look of hatred. She seemed to see Fley go down a trap on a gallows.

"Do you know Fley?" Hadley snapped.

"No, no, I never saw him! I mean, before this. But I know what Charles told me."

"Which was what?"

"Ah, *zut!* This Fley is a lunatic. Charles never knew him, but the man had some insane idea that he made fun of the occult, you understand. He has a brother who is"— she gestured—"the same, you understand? Well, Charles told me that he might call here tonight at half-past nine. If he did, I was to admit him. But when I took down Charles' coffee-tray at half-past nine, Charles laughed and said that if the man had not arrived by then he would not come at all. Charles said: 'People with a grudge are prompt.'" She sat back, squaring her shoulders. "Well, he was wrong. The door bell rang at a quarter to ten. I answered it. There was a man standing on the step. He held out a visiting-card, and said, 'Will you take this to Professor Grimaud and ask if he will see me?'"

Hadley leaned against the edge of the leather sofa and studied her.

"What about the false face, madame? Didn't you think that a little odd?"

"I did not *see* the false face! Have you noticed there is only one light in the downstairs hall? Well! There was a street lamp behind him, and all I could see was his shape. He spoke so courteously, you understand, and handed in the card, that for a second I did not realize . . ."

"One moment, please. Would you recognize that voice if you heard it again?"

She moved her shoulders as though she were shifting a weight on her back. "Yes! I don't know—yes, yes! But it did not sound right, you see; muffled up in that mask, I think now. Ah, why are men such—!" She leaned back in the chair, and for no apparent reason tears brimmed over her eyes. "I do not see such things! I am real, I am honest! If some one does you a hurt, good. You lie in wait for him and kill him. Then your friends go into court and swear you were somewhere else. You do not put on a painted mask, like old Drayman with the children on Guy Fawkes night; you do not hand in visiting-cards like this horror of a man, and go upstairs and kill a man and then vanish out of a window. It is like the legends they told us when I was a girl. . . ." Her cynical poise cracked across in hysteria. "Oh, my God, Charles! My poor Charles!"

Hadley waited, very quietly. She had herself in hand in a moment; she also was as still, and as foreign and inexplicable, as the big painting which faced her in tortured sombreness across the room. The gust of emotion left her relieved and watchful, though she breathed hard. They could hear the scraping noise of her finger nails on the chair-arms.

"The man said," Hadley prompted, " 'Will you take this to Professor Grimaud and ask if he will see me?' Very well. Now at this time, we understand, Miss Grimaud and Mr. Mangan were downstairs in the drawing-room near the front door?"

She looked at him curiously.

"Now that is a strange thing to ask. I wonder why you ask it? Yes—yes, I suppose they were. I did not notice."

"Do you remember whether the drawing-room door was open or shut?"

"I don't know. But I should think it was shut, or I should have seen more light in the hall."

"Go on, please."

"Well, when the man gave me the card, I was going to say, 'Step in, please, and I will see,' when I *did* see. I could not be faced with him alone—a lunatic? I wished to go up and get Charles to come down. So I said, 'Wait there and I will see.' And I very quickly slammed the door in his face, so that the spring-lock caught and he could not get in. Then I went back to the lamp and looked at the card. I still have it; I had no chance to deliver it. And it was blank."

"Blank?"

"There was no writing or printing on it at all. I went up

to show it to Charles, and plead with him to come down. But the poor little Mills has told you what happened. I was going to knock at the door, when I heard somebody come upstairs behind me. I looked round, and there he was coming big and thin behind me. But I will swear, I will swear on the Cross, that I had locked that door downstairs. Well, I was not afraid of him! No! I asked him what he meant by coming upstairs.

"And still, you understand, I could not see the false face, because his back was to that bright light on the stairs, which shows up all this end of the hall and Charles's door. But he said, in French, 'Madame, you cannot keep me out like that,' and turned down his collar and put his cap in his pocket. I opened the door because I knew he would not dare face Charles, just as Charles opened it from inside. Then I saw the mask, which was a pinkish colour like flesh. And before I could do anything he made a horrible jump inside, and kicked the door shut, and turned the key in the lock."

She paused, as though she had got through the worst part of the recital, and could breathe more easily now.

"And then?"

She said, dully: "I went away, as Charles ordered me to do. I made no fuss or scene. But I did not go far. I went a little way down the stairs, where I could still see the door to this room, and I did not leave my post any more than poor Stuart did. It was—horrible. I am not a young girl, you understand. I was there when the shot was fired; I was there when Stuart ran forward and began to pound the door; I was even there when you people began to come upstairs. But I could not stand it. I *knew* what had happened. When I felt myself going faint, I had just time to get to my room at the foot of that flight when I was—ill. Women sometimes are." The pale lips cracked across her oily face in a smile, shakily. "But Stuart was right; nobody left that room. God help us both, we are telling the truth. However else that horror left the room, he did not leave by the door. . . . And now please, please, will you let me go to the nursing-home to see Charles?"

THE JIG-SAW WORDS 5

It was Dr. Fell who answered. He was standing with his back to the fireplace, a vast black-caped figure under the fencing-foils and shield of arms. He seemed to fit there, like a baron out of feudalism, with the bookshelves and white busts towering on either side of him. But he did not look like a very terrible Front de Bœuf. His eye-glasses were coming askew on his nose as he bit off the end of a cigar, turned, and expectorated it neatly into the fireplace.

"Ma'am," he said, turning back with a long challenging sound in his nose, like a battle cry, "we shall not detain you very long. And it is only fair to say that I don't in the least doubt your story, any more than I doubt Mills'. Before getting down to business, I will prove that I believe you. . . . Ma'am, do you remember what time to-night it stopped snowing?"

She was looking at him with hard, bright, defensive eyes. She had evidently heard of Dr. Fell.

"Does it matter? I think it was about half-past nine. Yes! I remember, because when I came up to collect Charles's coffee-tray I looked out of the window and I noticed that it had stopped. Does it matter?"

"Oh, very much, ma'am. Otherwise we have only half an impossible situation. . . . And you are quite right. H'mf. Remember, Hadley? Half-past nine is about the time it stopped. Right, Hadley?"

"Yes," admitted the superintendent. He also looked at Dr. Fell suspiciously. He had learned to distrust that blank stare over the several chins. "Granting that it was half-past nine, what then?"

"Not only had it stopped snowing a full forty minutes before the visitor made his escape from this room," pursued the doctor, with a meditative air, "but it had stopped fifteen minutes before the visitor even arrived at this house. That's true, ma'am? Eh? He rang the door-bell at a quarter to ten? Good. . . . Now, Hadley, do you remember when *we* arrived at this house? Did you notice that, before you and Rampole and young Mangan went charging in,

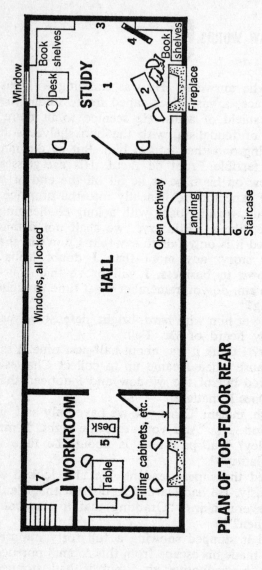

PLAN OF TOP-FLOOR REAR

1. Where Grimaud's body was found.
2. Disarranged sofa, chairs, and hearth rug.
3. Cleared space against wall, where painting was to have been hung.
4. Painting itself, propped up lengthwise against bookshelves.
5. Where Mills sat.
6. Where Mme Dumont stood.
7. Door leading to staircase communicating with trap in roof.

there wasn't a single footprint on the flight of steps leading up to the front door, or even the pavement leading up to the steps? You see, I did. I remained behind to make sure."

Hadley straightened up with a kind of muffled roar. "By God! that's right! The whole pavement was clean. It—" He stopped, and swung slowly round to Mme Dumont. "So this, you say, is your evidence of why you believe madame's story? Fell, have you gone mad, too? We hear a story of how a man rang the door-bell and walked through a locked door fifteen minutes after the snow had stopped, and yet—"

Dr. Fell opened his eyes. Then a series of chuckles ran up the ridges of his waistcoat.

"I say, son, why are you so flabbergasted? Apparently he sailed out of here without leaving a footprint. Why should it upset you to learn that he also sailed in?"

"I don't know," the other admitted, stubbornly. "But, hang it, it does! In my experience with locked-room murders, getting in and getting out are two very different things. It would throw my universe off balance if I found an impossible situation that worked sensibly both ways. Never mind! You say—"

"Please listen. I say," Mme Dumont interposed, pale but with the bunched muscles standing out at the corners of her jaws, "that I am telling the absolute truth, so help me God!"

"And I believe you," said Dr. Fell. "You mustn't let Hadley's stern Scotch common-sense overawe you. He will believe it, too, before I'm through with him. But my point is this. I have shown you, haven't I, that I have strong faith in you—if I can credit what you have said? Very well. I only want to warn you not to upset that faith. I should not dream of doubting what you have already told me. But I fancy I shall very strongly doubt what you are going to tell me in a moment."

Hadley half-closed one eye. "I was afraid of that. I always dread the time when you begin to trot out your damned paradoxes. Seriously, now—"

"Please go on," the woman said, stolidly.

"Humph. Harrumph. Thanks. Now, ma'am, how long have you been Grimaud's housekeeper? No, I'll change that. How long have you been with him?"

"For over twenty-five years," she answered. "I was more than his housekeeper—once."

She had been looking at her interlocked fingers, which she moved in and out; but now she lifted her head. Her eyes had a fierce, steady glaze, as though she wondered how much she dared tell. It was the expression of one peering round a corner at an enemy, ready for instant flight.

"I tell you that," she went on quietly, "in the hope that you will give me your word to keep silent. You will find it in your alien records at Bow Street, and you may make unnecessary trouble that has nothing to do with this matter. It is not for myself, you understand. Rosette Grimaud is my daughter. She was born here, and there had to be a record. But she does not know it—nobody knows it. Please, please, can I trust you to keep silent?"

The glaze over her eyes was changing to a different one. She had not raised her voice, but there was a terrible urgency in it.

"Why, ma'am," said Dr. Fell, a wrinkle in his forehead, "I can't see that it's any of our business. Can you? We shall certainly say nothing about it."

"You mean that?"

"Ma'am," the doctor said, gently, "I don't know the young lady, but I'll bet you a tanner you're worrying yourself unnecessarily, and that you've both been worrying yourselves unnecessarily for years. She probably knows already. Children do. And she's trying to keep it from *you*. And the whole world goes skew-whiff because we like to pretend that people under twenty will never have any emotions, and people over forty never had. Humph. Let's forget it. Shall we?" He beamed. "What I wanted to ask you, Where did you first meet Grimaud? Before you came to England?"

She breathed hard. She answered, but vaguely, as though she were thinking of something else.

"Yes. In Paris."

"You are a Parisienne?"

"Er—what—? No, no, not by birth! I am of the provinces. But I worked there when I met him. I was a costumier."

Hadley looked up from jotting in his notebook. " 'Costumier'?" he repeated. "Do you mean a dressmaker, or what?"

"No, no, I mean what I say. I was one of the women who made costumes for the opera and the ballet. We worked in the Opéra itself. You can find record of that! And, if it will save you time, I will tell you that I was never married and my maiden name was Ernestine Dumont."

"And Grimaud?" Dr. Fell asked, sharply. "Where was he from?"

"From the south of France, I think. But he studied at Paris. His family are all dead, so that will not help you. He inherited their money."

There was an air of tension which these casual questions did not seem to warrant. Dr. Fell's next three questions were so extraordinary that Hadley stared up from his notebook, and Ernestine Dumont, who had recovered herself, shifted uneasily, with a wary brilliance in her eyes.

"What is your religious faith, ma'am?"

"I am a Unitarian. Why?"

"H'm, yes. Did Grimaud ever visit the United States, or has he any friends there?"

"Never. And he has no friends that I know of there."

"Do the words 'seven towers' mean anything to you, ma'am?"

"No!" cried Ernestine Dumont, and went oily white.

Dr. Fell, who had finished lighting his cigar, blinked at her out of the smoke. He lumbered out from the hearth and round the sofa, so that she shrank back. But he only indicated the big painting with his cane, tracing out the line of the white mountains in the background of the picture.

"I won't ask you whether you know what this represents," he continued, "but I will ask you whether Grimaud told you why he bought it. What sort of charm was it supposed to contain, anyhow? What power did it have to ward off the bullet or the evil eye? What sort of weight could its influ . . ." He stopped, as though recalling something rather startling. Then he reached out, wheezing, to lift the picture off the floor with one hand and turn it curiously from side to side. "Oh, my hat!" said Dr. Fell, with explosive absent-mindedness. "O Lord! O Bacchus! Wow!"

"What is it?" demanded Hadley, jumping forward. "Do you see anything?"

"No, I don't see anything," said Dr. Fell argumentatively. "That's just the point. Well, madame?"

"I think," said the woman, in a shaky voice, "that you are the strangest man I ever met. No. I do not know what that thing is. Charles would not tell me. He only grunted and laughed in his throat. Why don't you ask the artist? Burnaby painted it. He should know. But you people will never do anything sensible. It looks like a picture of a country that does not exist."

Dr. Fell nodded sombrely. "I am afraid you are right, ma'am. I don't think it does exist. And if three people were buried there, it might be difficult to find them—mightn't it?"

"Will you stop talking this gibberish?" shouted Hadley; and then Hadley was taken aback by the fact that this gibberish had struck Ernestine Dumont like a blow. She got to her feet to conceal the effect of those meaningless words.

"I am going," she said. "You cannot stop me. You are all crazy. You sit here raving while—while you let Pierre Fley escape. Why don't you go after him? Why don't you *do* something?"

"Because you see, ma'am . . . Grimaud himself said that Pierre Fley did not do this thing." While she was still staring at him, he let the painting fall back with a thump against the sofa. The scene out of a country which did not exist, and yet where three gravestones stood among crooked trees, brought Rampole's mind to an edge of terror. He was still looking at the painting when they heard footsteps on the stairs.

It was a heartening thing to see the prosaic, earnest, hatchet face of Sergeant Betts, whom Rampole remembered from the Tower of London case. Behind him came two cheerful plainclothes men carrying the photographic and fingerprint apparatus. A uniformed policeman stood behind Mills, Boyd Mangan, and the girl who had been in the drawing room. She pushed through this group into the room.

"Boyd told me you wanted me," she said, in a quiet but very unsteady voice. "But I insisted on going over with the ambulance, you see. You'd better get over there as quick as you can, Aunt Ernestine. They say he's—going."

She tried to be efficient and peremptory, even in the way she drew off her gloves; but she could not manage it. She had those decided manners which come in the early twenties from lack of experience and lack of opposition. Rampole was rather startled to see that her hair was a heavy blond colour, bobbed and drawn behind the ears. Her face was squarish, with somewhat high cheek bones; not beautiful, but disturbing and vivid in the way that makes you think of old times even when you do not know what times. Her rather broad mouth was painted dark red, but in contrast to this, and to the firm shape of the whole face, the long hazel eyes were of an uneasy gentleness. She looked round quickly, and shrank back towards Mangan with her fur coat drawn tightly round. She was not far from sheer hysteria.

"Will you please hurry and tell me what you want?" she cried. "Don't you realize he's *dying?* Aunt Ernestine . . ."

"If these gentlemen are through with me," the woman said, stolidly, "I will go. I meant to go, as you know."

She was docile all of a sudden. But it was a heavy docility, with a half challenge in it—as though there were limits. Something bristled between these two women, something like the uneasiness in Rosette Grimaud's eyes. They looked at each other quickly, without a direct glance; they seemed to burlesque each other's movements, to become abruptly conscious of it, and stop. Hadley prolonged the silence, as though he were confronting two suspects with each other at Scotland Yard. Then:

"Mr. Mangan," he said, briskly, "will you take Miss Grimaud down to Mr. Mills' room at the end of the hall? Thank you. We shall be with you in a moment. Mr. Mills, just a second! Wait. . . . Betts!"

"Sir?"

"I want you to do some important work. Did Mangan tell you to bring ropes and a flashlight? . . . Good. I want you to go up on the roof of this place and search every inch of it for a footprint or a mark of any kind, especially over this room. Then go down to the yard behind this place, and both adjoining yards, and see if you can find any marks there. Mr. Mills will show you how to get to the roof. . . . Preston! Is Preston here?"

A sharp-nosed young man bustled in from the hall—the Sergeant Preston whose business it was to poke for secret places and who had discovered the evidence behind the panel in the Death Watch case.

"Go over this room for any secret entrance whatever, understand? Tear the place to bits if you like. See if anybody could get up the chimney. . . . You fellows carry on with the prints and pictures. Mark out every blood stain in chalk before you photograph. But don't disturb that burnt paper in the fireplace. . . . Constable! Where the hell's that constable?"

"Here, sir."

"Did Bow Street phone through the address of a man named Fley—Pierre Fley? . . . Right. Go to wherever he lives and pick him up. Bring him here. If he's not there, wait. Have they sent a man to the theatre where he works? . . . All right. That's all. Hop to it, everybody."

He strode out into the hall, muttering to himself. Dr. Fell, lumbering after him, was for the first time imbued with a ghoulish eagerness. He poked at the superintendent's arm with his shovel-hat.

"Look here, Hadley," he urged, "you go down and attend to the questioning, hey? I think I can be of much more service if I stay behind and assist those duffers with their photographs . . ."

"No, I'm hanged if you spoil any more plates!" said the other, with heat. "Those film packs cost money, and, besides, we need the evidence. Now, I want to talk to you privately and plainly. What's all this wild mumbo-jumbo about seven towers, and people buried in countries that never existed? I've seen you in these fits of mystification before, but never quite so bad. Let's compare notes. What did you . . . yes, yes. What is it?"

He turned irascibly as Stuart Mills plucked at his arm.

"Er—before I conduct the sergeant up to the roof," said Mills, imperturbably, "I think I had better tell you that in case you wish to see Mr. Drayman, he is here in the house."

"Drayman? Oh yes! When did he get back?"

Mills frowned. "So far as I am able to deduce, he did not get back. I should say he had never left. A short time ago I had occasion to look into his room . . ."

"Why?" enquired Dr. Fell, with sudden interest.

The secretary blinked impassively. "I was curious, sir. I discovered him asleep there, and it will be difficult to rouse him; I believe he has taken a sleeping draught. Mr. Drayman is fond of taking them. I do not mean that he is an inebriate or a drug-user, but quite literally that he is very fond of taking sleeping draughts."

"Rummiest household *I* ever heard of," declared Hadley, after a pause, to nobody in particular. "Anything else?"

"Yes, sir. There is a friend of Dr. Grimaud's downstairs. He has just arrived, and he would like to see you.

I do not think it is anything of immediate importance, but
he is a member of the circle at the Warwick Tavern. His
name is Pettis—Mr. Anthony Pettis."

"Pettis, eh?" repeated Dr. Fell, rubbing his chin. "I
wonder if that's the Pettis who collects the ghost stories and
writes those excellent prefaces? H'm, yes. I dare say. Now,
how would he fit into this?"

"I'm asking you how anything fits into it," insisted
Hadley. "Look here. I can't see this fellow now, unless he's
got something important to tell. Get his address, will you,
and say I'll call on him in the morning? Thanks." He
turned to Dr. Fell. "Now carry on about the seven towers
and the country that never existed."

The doctor waited until Mills had led Sergeant Betts
down the big hall to the door at the opposite end. A subdued mutter of voices from Grimaud's room was the only
noise. The bright yellow light still streamed from the
great arch of the staircase, illuminating the whole hall. Dr.
Fell took a few lumbering steps round the hall, looking up
and down and then across at the three brown-draped windows. He pulled back the drapes and made certain that
these three windows were all firmly locked on the inside.
Then he beckoned Hadley and Rampole towards the
staircase.

"Scrum," he said. "A little comparing of notes, I
admit, will be advisable before we tackle the next witnesses. But not for a second about the seven towers. I'll
lead up to those gradually, like Childe Roland. Hadley,
a few disjointed words—the only real evidence we have,
because it comes from the victim—may be the most important clue of all. I mean those few mutterings from
Grimaud just before he fainted. I hope to heaven we all
heard 'em. Remember, you asked him whether Fley had
shot him. He shook his head. Then you asked him who had
done it. What did he say?— I want to ask each of you in
turn what you thought you heard."

He looked at Rampole. The American's wits were
muddled. He had a strong recollection of certain words,
but the whole was confused by a too-vivid picture of a
blood-soaked chest and a writhing neck. He hesitated.

"The first thing he said," Rampole answered, "sounded
to me like *hover*—"

"Nonsense," interrupted Hadley. "I jotted it all down
right away. The first thing he said was *Bath* or 'the bath,'

though I'm hanged if I see——"

"Steady now. Your own gibberish," said Dr. Fell, "is a little worse than mine. Go on, Ted."

"Well, I wouldn't swear to any of it. But then I did hear the words *not suicide,* and *he couldn't use rope.* Next there was some reference to a *roof* and to *snow* and to a *fox.* The last thing I heard sounded like *too much light.* Again, I wouldn't swear it was all in consecutive order."

Hadley was indulgent. "You've got it all twisted, even if you have got one or two of the points." He seemed uneasy, nevertheless. "All the same, I'm bound to admit that my notes don't make much better sense. After the word *bath,* he said *salt and wine.* You're right about the rope, although I heard nothing about suicide. Roof and snow are correct; *too much light* came afterwards; then *got gun.* Finally, he did say something about a fox, and the last thing—I barely heard it because of that blood—was something like *Don't blame poor* . . . And that's all."

"O Lord!" groaned Dr. Fell. He stared from one to the other. "This is terrible. Gents, I was going to be very triumphant over you. I was going to explain what he said. But I am beaten by the staggering size of your respective ears. I never heard all that out of the gabble, although I dare say you're within some distance of the truth. Wow!"

"Well, what's your version?" demanded Hadley.

The doctor stumped up and down, rumbling. "I heard only the first few words. They make tolerably good sense if I'm right—*if* I'm right. But the rest is a nightmare. I have visions of foxes running across roofs in the snow, or——"

"Lycanthropy?" suggested Rampole. "Did anybody mention werewolves?"

"No, and nobody's going to!" roared Hadley. He struck his notebook. "To put everything in order, Rampole, I'll write down what you thought you heard for comparison. . . . So. We now have:

"Your list. *Hover. Not suicide. He couldn't use rope. Roof. Snow. Fox. Too much light.*

"My list. *Bath. Salt. Wine. He couldn't use rope. Roof. Snow. Too much light. Got gun. Don't blame poor—*

"There we are. And, as usual, with your own brand of cussedness, Fell, you're most confident about the most senseless part. I might rig up an explanation that could fit together all the latter part, but how the devil does a dying man give us a clue by talking about baths and salt and wine?"

Dr. Fell stared at his cigar, which had gone out.

"H'mf, yes. We'd better clear up a little of that. There are puzzles enough as it is. Let's go gently along the road. . . . First, my lad, what happened in that room after Grimaud was shot?"

"How the hell should I know? That's what I'm asking you. If there's no secret entrance—"

"No, no, I don't mean how the vanishing-trick was worked. You're obsessed with that business, Hadley; so obsessed that you don't stop to ask yourself what *else* happened. First let's get clear the obvious things for which we can find an explanation, and go on from there. Humph. Now, then, what clearly did happen in that room after the man was shot? First, all the marks centred round the fireplace—"

"You mean the fellow climbed up the chimney?"

"I am absolutely certain he didn't," said Dr. Fell, testily. "That flue is so narrow that you can barely get your fist through. Control yourself and think. First, a heavy sofa was pushed away from in front of the fireplace; there was a good deal of blood on the top, as though Grimaud had slipped or leaned against it. The hearth rug was pulled or kicked away; there was blood on that; and a fireside chair was shoved away. Finally, I found spots of blood on the hearth and even in the fireplace. They led us to a huge mass of burnt papers that had nearly smothered the fire.

"Now, consider the behaviour of the faithful Madame Dumont. As soon as she came into that room, she was very terribly concerned about that fireplace. She kept looking at it all the time, and nearly grew hysterical when she saw I was doing so, too. She even, you recall, made the foolish blunder of asking us to light a fire—even though she must have known that the police wouldn't go fooling about with coals and kindling to make witnesses comfortable on the very scene of a crime. No, no, my boy. Somebody had tried to burn letters or documents there. She wanted to be certain they had been destroyed."

Hadley said, heavily: "So she knew about it, then? And yet you said you believed her story?"

"Yes. I did and do believe her story—about the visitor and the crime. What I don't believe is the information she gave us about herself and Grimaud. . . . Now think again what happened! The intruder shot Grimaud. Yet Grimaud, although he is still conscious, does not shout for help, try to stop the killer, make a row of any kind, or even open the door when Mills is pounding there. But he does do something. He does do something, with such a violent exertion that he tears wide open the wound in his lung: as you heard the doctor say.

"And I'll tell you what he did do. He knew he was a goner and that the police would be in. He had in his possession a mass of things that *must be* destroyed. It was more vital to destroy them than to catch the man who shot him or even save his own life. He lurched back and forth from that fireplace, burning this evidence. Hence the sofa knocked away, the hearth rug, the stains of blood. . . . You understand now?"

There was a silence in the bright bleak hall.

"And the Dumont woman?" Hadley asked, heavily.

"She knew it, of course. It was their joint secret. And she happens to love him."

"If this is true, it must have been something pretty damned important that he destroyed," said Hadley, staring. "How the devil do you know all this? What secret could they have had, anyway? And what makes you think they had any dangerous secret at all?"

Dr. Fell pressed his hands to his temples and ruffled his big mop of hair. He spoke argumentatively.

"I may be able to tell you a little of it," he said, "although there are parts that puzzle me beyond hope. You see, neither Grimaud nor Dumont is any more French than I am. A woman with those cheekbones, a woman who pronounces the silent 'h' in honest, never came from a Latin race. But that's not important. They're both Magyar. To be precise: Grimaud came originally from Hungary. His real name is Károly, or Charles, or Grimaud Horváth. He probably had a French mother. He came from the principality of Transylvania, formerly a part of the Hungarian kingdom but annexed by Rumania since the war. In the late 'nineties or early nineteen hundreds, Károly Grimaud Horváth and his two brothers were all sent to prison. Did I tell you he had two brothers? One we haven't seen, but the other now calls himself Pierre Fley.

"I don't know what crime the three brothers Horváth had committed, but they were sent to the prison of Siebenturmen, to work in the salt-mines near Tradj in the Carpathian Mountains. Charles probably escaped. Now, the rather deadly 'secret' in his life can't concern the fact that he was sent to prison or even that he escaped before finishing the sentence; the Hungarian kingdom is broken up, and its authority no longer exists. More probably he did some black devilry that concerned the other two brothers; something pretty horrible concerning those three coffins, and people buried alive, that would hang him even now if it were discovered. . . . That's all I can hazard at the moment. Has anybody got a match?"

THE SEVEN TOWERS 6

In the long pause after this recital, Hadley tossed a match-box to the doctor and eyed him malevolently.

"Are you joking?" he asked. "Or is this black magic?"

"Not about a thing like this. I wish I could. Those three coffins . . . Dammit, Hadley!" muttered Dr. Fell, knocking his fists against his temples, "I wish I could see a glimmer—something. . . ."

"You seem to have done pretty well. Have you been holding out information, or how do you know all that? Stop a bit!" He looked at his notebook. " 'Hover.' 'Bath.' 'Salt.' 'Wine.' In other words, you're trying to tell us that what Grimaud really said was, 'Horváth,' and 'salt-mine'? Take it easy, now! If that's your basis, we're going to have a lot of star-gazing on our hands to twist round the rest of those words."

"This assumption of rage," said Dr. Fell, "shows that you agree with me. Thankee. As you yourself shrewdly pointed out, dying men do not commonly mention bath salts. If your version is correct, we might as well all retire to a padded cell. He really said it, Hadley. I heard him. You asked him for a name, didn't you? Was it Fley? No. Who was it, then? And he answered, Horváth."

"Which *you* say is his own name."

"Yes. Look here," said Dr. Fell. "If it will salve your wounds, I will cheerfully admit that it wasn't fair detective work, and that I didn't show you the sources of my information from that room. I'll show you them presently, although Lord knows I tried to show them to you at the time.

"It's like this. We hear from Ted Rampole about a queer customer who threatens Grimaud, and significantly talks about people 'buried alive.' Grimaud takes this seriously; he has known that man before and knows what he is talking about, since for some reason he buys a picture depicting three graves. When you ask Grimaud who shot him, he answers with the name 'Horváth' and says something about salt-mines. Whether or not you think that's odd of a French professor, it is rather odd to find up over his mantelpiece the device of a shield graven thus: *coupé, a demi-eagle issuant sable, in chief a moon argent . . .*"

"I think we may omit the heraldry," said Hadley, with a sort of evil dignity. "What is it?"

"It's the arms of Transylvania. Dead since the war, of course, and hardly very well known in England (or France) even before that. First a Slavic name, and then Slavic arms. Next those books I showed you. Know what they were? They were English books translated into the Magyar. I couldn't pretend to read 'em—"

"Thank God."

"—but I could at least recognize the complete works of Shakespeare, and Sterne's *Letters from Yorick to Eliza,* and Pope's *Essay on Man.* That was so startling that I examined 'em all."

"Why startling?" asked Rampole. "There are all sorts of funny books in anybody's library. There are in your own."

"Certainly. But suppose a scholarly Frenchman wants to read English. Well, he reads it in English, or he gets it translated into French. But he very seldom insists on getting its full flavour by first having it translated into Hungarian. In other words, they weren't *Hungarian* books; they weren't even French books on which a Frenchman might have been practising his Magyar; they were English. It meant that whoever owned those books, his native language was Hungarian. I went through all of 'em, hoping to find a name. When I found *Károly Grimaud Horváth, 1898* faded out on one flyleaf, it seemed to put the tin hat on it.

"If Horváth was his real name, why had he kept up this pretence for so long? Think of the words 'buried alive,' and 'salt-mines,' and there is a gleam. But, when you ask him who shot him, he said Horváth. A moment like that is probably the only time when a man isn't willing to talk about himself; he didn't mean himself, but somebody else named Horváth. While I was thinking of that, our excellent Mills was telling you about the man called Fley at the public house. Mills said that there seemed something very familiar about Fley, although he had never seen him before, and that his speech sounded like a burlesque of Grimaud's. Was it Grimaud he suggested? Brother, brother, brother! You see, there were three coffins, but Fley mentioned only two brothers. It sounded like a third.

"While I was thinking about this, there entered the obviously Slavic Madame Dumont. If I could establish Grimaud as coming from Transylvania, it would narrow down our search when we tried to find out his history. But it had to be done delicately. Notice that carved figure of a buffalo on Grimaud's desk? What does that suggest to you?"

"It doesn't suggest Transylvania, I can tell you that," the superintendent growled. "It's more like the Wild West —Buffalo Bill—Indians. Hold on! Was that why you asked her whether Grimaud had ever been in the United States?"

Dr. Fell nodded guiltily. "It seemed an innocent question, and she answered. You see, if he'd got that figure in an American curio shop— H'm. Hadley, I've been in Hungary. I went in my younger and lither days, when I'd just read *Dracula*. Transylvania was the only European country where buffaloes were bred; they used 'em like oxen. Hungary was full of mixed religious beliefs; but Transylvania was Unitarian. I asked Madame Ernestine, and she qualified. Then I threw my hand grenade. If Grimaud had been innocently associated with salt-mines, it wouldn't matter. But I named the only prison in Transylvania where convicts were used to work the salt-mines. I named the Siebenturmen—or the Seven Towers—without even saying it was a prison. It almost finished her. Now perhaps you will understand my remark about the seven towers and the country that does not now exist. And for God's sake will somebody give me a match?"

"You've got 'em," said Hadley. He took a few strides round the hall, accepted a cigar from the now bland and beaming Dr. Fell, and muttered to himself: "Yes—so far as it goes, it seems reasonable enough. Your long shot about the prison worked. But the whole basis of your case, that these three people are brothers, is pure surmise. In fact, I think it's the weakest part of the case. . . ."

"Oh, admitted. But what then?"

"Only that it's the crucial joint. Suppose Grimaud didn't mean that a person named Horváth had shot him, but was only referring to himself in some way? Then the murderer might be anybody. But if there are three brothers, and he did mean that, the thing is simple. We come back to the belief that Pierre Fley *did* shoot him, after all, or Fley's brother did. We can put our hands on Fley at any time, and as for the brother—"

"Are you sure you'd recognize the brother," said Dr. Fell, reflectively, "if you met him?"

"How do you mean?"

"I was thinking of Grimaud. He spoke English perfectly, and also passed perfectly for a Frenchman. I don't doubt he did study at Paris, and that the Dumont woman did make costumes at the Opéra. Anyhow, there he went stumping round Bloomsbury for nearly thirty years, gruff, good-natured, harmless, with his clipped beard and his square bowler, keeping a check on a savage temper and placidly lecturing in public. Nobody ever saw a devil in him—though somehow I fancy it must have been a wily, brilliant devil. Nobody ever suspected. He could have shaved, cultivated tweeds and a port-wine complexion, and passed for a British squire, or anything else he liked. . . . Then what about this third brother? He's the one who intrigues me. Suppose he's right here somewhere in our midst, in some guise or other, and nobody knows him for what he really is?"

"Possibly. But we don't know anything about the brother."

Dr. Fell, struggling to light his cigar, peered up with extraordinary intentness.

"I know. That's what bothers me, Hadley." He rumbled for a moment, and then blew out the match with a vast puff. "We have two theoretical brothers who have taken French names: Charles and Pierre. Then there's a third. For the sake of clearness and argument, let's call him Henri—"

"Look here. You're not going to tell me you know something about him also?"

"On the contrary," returned Dr. Fell, with a sort of ferocity, "I'm going to emphasize just how little we know about him. We know about Charles and Pierre. But we haven't even the merest hint about Henri, *although* Pierre appears to be forever talking about him and using him as a threat. It is, 'My brother who can do much more than I can.' 'My brother who wants your life.' 'I am in danger when I associate with him.' And so on. But no shape comes out of the smoke, neither man nor goblin. Son, it worries me. I thing that ugly presence is behind the whole business, controlling it, using poor half-crazy Pierre for his own ends, and probably as dangerous to Pierre as to Charles. I can't help feeling that this presence staged the whole scene at the Warwick Tavern; that he's somewhere close at hand and watchful; that—" Dr. Fell stared round, as though he expected to see something move or speak in the empty hall. Then he added: "You know, I hope your constable gets hold of Pierre and keeps hold of him. Maybe his usefulness is over."

Hadley made a vague gesture. He bit at the end of his clipped moustache. "Yes, I know," he said; "but let's stick to the facts. The facts will be difficult enough to dig out, I warn you. I'll cable the Rumanian police tonight. But if Transylvania's been annexed, in the fuss and uproar there may be few official records left. The Bolshies were storming through there just after the war, weren't they? Um. Anyhow, we want facts! Come on and let's get after Mangan and Grimaud's daughter. I'm not entirely satisfied with *their* behaviour, by the way. . . ."

"Eh? Why?"

"I mean, always provided the Dumont woman is telling the truth," Hadley amended. "You seem to think she is. But, as I've heard the thing, wasn't Mangan here tonight at Grimaud's request, in case the visitor should drop in? Yes. Then he seems to have been rather a tame watch-dog. He was sitting in a room near the front door. The door-bell rings—if Dumont's not lying—and enter the mysterious visitor. All this time Mangan doesn't show any curiosity; he sits in the room with the door shut, pays no attention to the visitor, and only kicks up a row when he hears a shot and suddenly finds that the door has been locked. Is that logical?"

"Nothing is logical," said Dr. Fell. "Not even— But that can wait."

They went down the long hall, and Hadley assumed his most tactful and impassive manner when he opened the door. It was a room somewhat smaller than the other, lined with orderly books and wooden filing cabinets. It had a plain rag carpet on the floor, hard business-like chairs, and a sickly fire. Under a green-shaded hanging-lamp, Mills' typewriter desk was drawn up directly facing the door. On one side of the machine neat manuscript sheets lay clipped in a wire basket; on the other side stood a glass of milk, a dish of dried prunes, and a copy of Williamson's *Differential and Integral Calculus.*

"I'll bet he drinks mineral water, too," said Dr. Fell, in some agitation. "I'll swear by all my gods he drinks mineral water and reads that sort of thing for fun. I'll bet—" He stopped at a violent nudge from Hadley, who was speaking to Rosette Grimaud across the room. Hadley introduced the three of them.

"Naturally, Miss Grimaud, I don't wish to distress you at this time—"

"Please don't say anything," she said. She was sitting before the fire, so tense that she jumped a little. "I mean —just don't say anything about *that.* You see, I'm fond of him, but not so fond that it hurts terribly unless somebody begins to talk about it. Then I begin to think."

She pressed her hands against her temples. In the firelight, with her fur coat thrown back, there was again a contrast between eyes and face. But it was a changing contrast. She had her mother's intense personality shaped into blond, square-faced, rather barbaric Slavic beauty. Yet in one moment the face would be hard and the long hazel eyes gentle and uneasy, like the curate's daughter. And in the next moment the face would be softened and the eyes brilliantly hard, like the devil's daughter. Her thin eyebrows turned a little upwards at the outer corners, but she had a broad humorous mouth. She was restless, sleek, and puzzling. Behind her stood Mangan in gloomy helplessness.

"One thing, though," she went on, pounding her fist slowly on the arm of the chair—"one thing I've got to know, though, before you start your third degree." She nodded towards a little door across the room, and spoke breathlessly. "Stuart's—showing that detective of yours up to the roof. Is it true, *is* it true what we hear about a man getting in—and out—and killing my father—without— without—?"

"Better let me handle this, Hadley," said Dr. Fell, very quietly.

The doctor, Rampole knew, was firmly under the impression that he was a model of tact. Very often this tact resembled a load of bricks coming through a skylight. But his utter conviction that he was doing the thing handsomely, his vast good-nature and complete naïveté, had an effect that the most skilled tact could never have produced. It was as though he had slid down on the bricks himself to offer sympathy or shake hands. And people instantly began to tell him all about themselves.

"Harrumph!" he snorted. "Of course it's not true, Miss Grimaud. We know all about how the blighter worked his trick, even if it was done by somebody you never heard of." She looked up quickly. "Furthermore, there'll be no third degree, and your father has a fighting chance to pull through. Look here, Miss Grimaud, haven't I met you somewhere before?"

"Oh, I know you're trying to make me feel better," she said, with a faint smile. "Boyd has told me about you, but—"

"No, I mean it," wheezed Dr. Fell, seriously. He squinted at memory. "H'm, yes. Got it! You're at London University, aren't you? Of course. And you're in a debating circle or something? It seems to me I officiated as chairman when your team debated Woman's Rights in the World, wasn't it?"

"That's Rosette," assented Mangan, gloomily. "She's a strong feminist. She says—"

"Heh-heh-heh," said Dr. Fell. "I remember now." He was radiant, and pointed with a vast flipper. "She may be a feminist, my boy, but she has startling lapses. In fact, I remember that debate as ending in the most beautiful and appalling row I ever heard outside a Pacifist meeting. You were on the side for Women's Rights, Miss Grimaud, and against the Tyranny of Man. Yes, yes. You entered very pale and serious and solemn, and stayed like that until your own side began to present their case. They went on something awful, but you didn't look pleased. Then one lean female carried on for twenty minutes about what woman needed for an ideal state of existence, but you only seemed to get madder and madder. So when your turn came, all you did was rise to proclaim in silvery ringing tones that what woman needed for an ideal existence was less talking and more copulation."

"Good God!" said Mangan, and jumped.

"Well, I felt like it—then," said Rosette, hotly. "But you don't need to think . . ."

"Or perhaps you didn't say copulation," ruminated Dr. Fell. "Anyway, the effect of that terrible word was beyond description. It was as though you had whispered, 'Asbestos!' to a gang of pyromaniacs. Unfortunately, I tried to keep a straight face by swallowing water. This, my friends, is a practice to which I am unaccustomed. The result had the general aspect, to eye and ear, of a bomb exploding in an aquarium. But I was wondering whether you and Mr. Mangan often discussed these subjects. They must be enlightening talks. What was the argument about this evening, for instance?"

Both of them began to speak at once, chaotically. Dr. Fell beamed, and they both stopped with a startled expression.

"Yes," nodded the doctor. "You understand now, don't you, that there's nothing to be afraid of in talking to the police? And that you can speak as freely as you like? It'll be better, you know. Let's face the thing and clear it up sensibly now, among ourselves, hey?"

"Right," said Rosette. "Has somebody got a cigarette?"

Hadley looked at Rampole. "The old blighter's done it," he said.

The old blighter was again lighting his cigar while Mangan fumbled in his haste to produce cigarettes. Then Dr. Fell pointed.

"Now, I want to know about a very rummy thing," he continued. "Were you two kids so engrossed in each other that you didn't notice anything tonight until the rumpus started? As I understand it, Mangan, Professor Grimaud asked you here tonight to be on the lookout for possible trouble. Why didn't you? Didn't you hear the door-bell?"

Mangan's swarthy face was clouded. He made a fierce gesture.

"Oh, I admit it's my fault. But at the time I never gave it a thought. How was I going to know? Of course I heard the door-bell. In fact, we both spoke to the fellow—"

"You *what?*" interrupted Hadley, striding past Dr. Fell.

"Certainly. Otherwise you don't think I'd have let him get past me and upstairs, do you? But he said he was old Pettis—Anthony Pettis, you know."

THE GUY FAWKES VISITOR 7

"Of course we know now that it wasn't Pettis," Mangan pursued, lighting the girl's cigarette with an angry snap of his lighter, "Pettis must be all of five feet four inches tall. Besides, now that I think back on it, it wasn't even a very exact imitation of his voice. But he sang out and spoke in words Pettis always uses. . . ."

Dr. Fell scowled. "But didn't it strike you as queer that even a collector of ghost stories should walk about dressed up like a Fifth of November Guy? Is he addicted to pranks?"

Rosette Grimaud looked up with a startled expression. She held out her cigarette level and motionless, as though she were pointing, and then twitched to look at Mangan. When she turned back again there was a narrow flash of those long eyes, a deepness of breathing like anger or cruelty, or enlightenment. They had shared a thought—and Mangan was much the more disturbed by it. He had the air of one who is trying to be a good fellow and at peace with the world, if the world would only let him. Rampole had a feeling that this secret thought did not concern Pettis at all, for Mangan stumbled before he could recapture Dr. Fell's question.

"Pranks?" he repeated, and passed a hand nervously over his wiry black hair. "Oh! Pettis? Good Lord, no! He's as correct and fussy as they make 'em. But, you understand, we didn't see his face. It was like this:

"We'd been sitting in that front room since just after dinner—"

"Stop a bit," interrupted Hadley. "Was the door to the hall open?"

"No. Hang it all," said Mangan in a defensive tone, and shifted, "you don't sit in a draughty room on a snowy night with the door standing open; not without central heating, you don't. I knew we could hear the bell ring if it did ring. Besides—well, honestly, I didn't expect anything to happen. The professor gave us the impression at dinner that it was a hoax, or that it had been adjusted somehow; anyway, that he had been inclined to get the wind up over nothing. . . ."

Hadley was looking at him with hard, bright eyes. "You got that impression, too, Miss Grimaud?"

"Yes, in a way. . . . I don't know! It's always hard to tell," she answered, with a faint anger (or rebellion?), "whether he's annoyed or amused or just pretending both. My father has a queer sense of humour, and he loves dramatic effects. He treats me as a child. I don't think I ever in my life saw him frightened, so I don't know. But for the past three days he's been acting so dashed queerly that when Boyd told me about the man in that pub—" She lifted her shoulders.

"In what way was he acting queerly?"

"Well, muttering to himself, for instance. And suddenly roaring out over trifles, which he seldom does. And then again he would laugh too much. But most of all it was those letters. He began to get them in every post. Don't ask me what was in them; he burnt all of them. They were in plain penny envelopes. . . . I shouldn't have noticed at all if it hadn't been for a habit of his." She hesitated. "Maybe you'll understand. My father is one of those people who can never get a letter in your presence without your instantly knowing what it's about or even who it's from. He'll explode, 'Damned swindler!' or, 'Now, there's impudence for you!' or, genially, 'Well, well, here's a letter from old So-and-so!'—in rather a surprised tone, as though he expected somebody in Liverpool or Birmingham to be at the other side of the moon. I don't know if you understand . . . ?"

"We understand. Please go on."

"But when he got these notes, or whatever they were, he didn't say anything at all. He didn't move a muscle. Yet, you see, he never openly destroyed one except yesterday morning at the breakfast table. After he'd glanced at it he crumpled it up, got up from his chair, and went over in a thoughtful sort of way and threw it in the fire. Just at that second Au—" Rosette glanced quickly at Hadley, seemed to discover her own hesitation, and blundered into confusion. "Mrs.—Madame—oh, I mean Aunt Ernestine! Just at that second she asked him if he would have some more bacon. Suddenly he whirled round from the fire and yelled, 'Go to hell!' It was so unexpected that before we had recovered our wits he'd stamped out of the room, muttering that a man couldn't have any peace. He looked devilish. That was the day he came back with that painting. He was good-humoured again; he banged about, chuckling, and helped the cabman and somebody else cart it upstairs. I—I don't want you to think—" Evidently the memories were crowding back again to this complex Rosette; she began to think, and that was bad. She added, shakily, "I don't want you to think I don't like him."

Hadley ignored the personal. "Did he ever mention this man at the public house?"

"Off-handedly, when I asked him. He said it was one of the quacks who often threatened him for jeering at— the history of magic. Of course I knew it wasn't merely that."

"Why, Miss Grimaud?"

During a pause she looked at him unwinkingly.

"Because I felt that this was the real thing. And because I have often wondered whether there was anything in my father's past life which might bring something like that on him."

It was a direct challenge. During a long silence they could hear muffled creakings and flat, heavy footsteps shaking on the roof. Some change moved and played like firelight on her face—fear, or hatred, or pain, or doubt. That illusion of the barbaric had returned—as though the mink coat should have been a leopard-skin coat. Crossing her legs, she leaned back voluptuously, wriggling into the chair. She tilted her head against the back of the chair, so that the firelight gleamed on her throat and in her half-shut eyes. She regarded them with a faint, fixed smile; the cheek bones were outlined in shadow. All the same, Rampole saw that she was trembling. Why, incidentally, should her face seem broader than it was long?

"Well?" she prompted.

Hadley appeared mildly surprised. "Bring something on him? I don't quite understand. Had you any reason to think so?"

"Oh, no reason! I don't think so, really. Just these fancies—" The denial was quick, but the sharp rise and fall of her breast had quietened. "Probably it's living with my father's hobby. And then my mother—she's dead, you know; died when I was quite a kid—my mother was supposed to have second-sight." Rosette raised her cigarette again. "But you were asking me . . . ?"

"About tonight, first of all. If you think it would be

helpful to go into your father's past, the Yard will certainly act on your suggestion."

She jerked the cigarette away from her lips.

"But," pursued Hadley in the same colourless voice, "let's get on with the story Mr. Mangan was telling. You two went to the drawing-room after dinner, and the door to the hall was shut. Now, did Professor Grimaud tell you what time he expected a dangerous visitor?"

"Er—yes," said Mangan. He had taken out a handkerchief and was mopping his forehead. Seen sideways in the firelight, there were many small wrinkles across the forehead of the thin, hollowed, sharp-angled face. "That was another reason why I didn't tumble to who it might be. He was too early. The professor said ten o'clock, and this fellow arrived at a quarter to."

"Ten o'clock. I see. You're sure he said that?"

"Well—yes! At least, I think so. About ten o'clock. Wasn't it, Rosette?"

"I don't know. He didn't say anything to me."

"I—see. Go on, Mr. Mangan."

"We had the radio on. That was bad, because the music was loud. And we were playing cards in front of the fire. All the same, I heard the door-bell, I looked up at the clock on the mantel, and it said a quarter to ten. I was getting up when I heard the front door open. Then I heard Mrs. Dumont's voice saying something like, 'Wait, I'll see,' and a sound as though the door slammed. I called out, 'Ahoy there! Who is it?' But the radio was making such a row that I naturally stepped over and shut it off. And just afterwards we heard Pettis—naturally we both thought it was Pettis—call out: 'Hullo, children! It's Pettis. What's all this formality about seeing the Governor? I'm going up and break in on him.' "

"Those were his exact words?"

"Yes. He always called Dr. Grimaud the Governor; nobody else had the nerve to; except Burnaby, and he calls him Pop. . . . So we said, 'Righto,' as you do, and didn't bother any more about it. We both sat down again. But I noticed that it was getting near ten o'clock and I began to be watchful and jumpy, now that it was coming towards ten o'clock . . ."

Hadley drew a design on the margin of his notebook.

"So the man who called himself Pettis," he mused, "spoke to you through the door without seeing you? How did he know you two were there, do you think?"

Mangan frowned. "He saw us through the window, I suppose. As you come up the front steps you can see straight into the front room through the nearest window. I always notice it myself. In fact, if I see anybody in the front room I usually lean across and tap on the window instead of ringing the bell."

The superintendent was still drawing designs, meditatively. He seemed about to ask a question, but checked himself. Rosette regarded him with a sharp, unwinking gaze. Hadley merely said:

"Go on. You were waiting for ten o'clock—"

"And nothing happened," Mangan insisted. "But, a funny thing, every minute past ten o'clock I got more nervous instead of more relieved. I told you I didn't really expect the man would come, or that there would be any trouble. But I kept picturing that dark hall, and the queer suit of armour with the mask out there, and the more I thought of it the less I liked it. . . ."

"I know exactly what you mean," said Rosette. She looked at him in a strange, rather startled manner. "I was thinking the same thing. But I didn't want to talk about it in case you called me a fool."

"Oh, I have these psychic fits, too. That," Mangan said bitterly, "is why I get the sack so often, and why I shall probably get the sack for not phoning in this story tonight. News editor be damned. I'm no Judas." He shifted. "Anyway, it was nearly ten past ten when I felt I couldn't stand it any longer. I slammed down the cards and said to Rosette, 'Look here, let's get a drink and turn on all the lights in the hall—or do something.' I was going to ring for Annie, when I remembered it was Saturday and her night out. . . ."

"Annie? That's the maid? Yes. I'd forgotten her. Well?"

"So I went over to open the door, and it was locked on the outside. It was like . . . like this! You have some conspicuous object in your bedroom, like a picture or an ornament, that's so common you never fully notice it. Then one day you walk in and have a vague feeling that there's something wrong with the room. It irritates and disturbs you, because you can't imagine why. Then all of a sudden a gap jumps up, and you see with a shock that the object has been removed. Understand? I felt just like that. I *knew* something was wrong, I felt it ever since that fellow had sung out from the hall, but it never hit me with a smash until I found that door locked. Just as I began idiotically yanking at the knob, we heard the shot.

"A firearm indoors makes a devil of a noise, and we heard it even up at the top of the house. Rosette screamed——"

"I did not!"

"Then she pointed at me and said what I'd been thinking, too. She said, 'That wasn't Pettis at all. He's got in.' "

"Can you fix the time of that?"

"Yes. It was just ten minutes past ten. Well, I tried to break the door down." In spite of staring at that memory, a wry and mocking gleam of mirth twinkled in Mangan's eyes. It was as though he hated to speak, but could not help commenting. "I say, have you ever noticed how easy it is to break down doors in the stories? Those stories are a carpenter's paradise. They're an endless trail of doors smashed down on the slightest pretext, even when somebody inside won't answer a casual question. But try it on one of these doors! . . . That's about all. I banged my shoulder-bone against it for a while, and then I thought about getting out through the window and in again through the front door or the area door. I ran into you, and you know what happened."

Hadley tapped the notebook with his pencil. "Was it customary for the front door to be unlocked, Mr. Mangan?"

"O Lord! I don't know! But it was the only thing I could think of. Anyhow, it *was* unlocked."

"Yes, it was unlocked. Have you anything to add to that, Miss Grimaud?"

Her eyelids drooped. "Nothing—that is, not exactly. Boyd has told you everything that happened just as it happened. But you people always want all kinds of queer things, don't you? Even if they don't seem to bear on the matter? This probably has nothing to do with the matter at all, but I'll tell you. . . . A little while before the door-bell rang, I was going over to get some cigarettes from a table between the windows. The radio was on, as Boyd says. But I heard from somewhere out in the street, or on the pavement in front of the door, a loud sound like—like a thud, as though a heavy object had fallen from a big height. It wasn't an ordinary street noise, you see. Like a man falling."

Rampole felt himself stirring uneasily. Hadley asked:

"A thud, you say? H'm. Did you look out to see what it was?"

"Yes. But I couldn't see anything. Of course, I only pulled the blind back and peeped round the side of it, but I can swear the street was empt—" She stopped in full flight. Her lips fell open a little and her eyes were suddenly fixed. "Oh, my *God!*" she said.

"Yes, Miss Grimaud," said Hadley without inflection, "the blinds were all down, as you say. I especially noticed that, because Mr. Mangan got entangled with one when he jumped out. That was why I wondered how the visitor could have seen you through any window in that room. But possibly they weren't drawn down all the time?"

There was a silence, except for faint noises on the roof. Rampole glanced at Dr. Fell, who was propped back against one of the unbreakable doors with his chin in his hand and his shovel-hat tilted over his eyes. Then Rampole looked at the impassive Hadley, and back to the girl.

"He thinks we're lying, Boyd," said Rosette Grimaud, coolly. "I don't think we'd better say anything more."

And then Hadley smiled. "I don't think anything of the kind, Miss Grimaud. I'm going to tell you why, because you're the only person who can help us. I'm even going to tell you what did happen. —Fell!"

"Eh?" boomed Dr. Fell, looking up with a start.

"I want you to listen to this," the superintendent pursued, grimly. "A while ago you were having a lot of pleasure and mystification out of saying that you believed the stories—apparently incredible—told by Mills and Mrs. Dumont; without giving any reasons why you believed them. I'll return the compliment. I'll say that I believe not only their story, but the story told by these two also. And, in explaining why, I'll also explain the impossible situation."

This time Dr. Fell did come out of his abstraction with a jerk. He puffed out his cheeks and peered at Hadley as though prepared to leap into battle.

"Not all of it, I admit," pursued Hadley, "but enough to narrow down the field of suspects to a few people, and to explain why there were no footprints in the snow."

"Oh, *that!*" said Dr. Fell, contemptuously. He relaxed with a grunt. "You know, for a second I hoped you had something. But that part is obvious."

Hadley kept his temper with a violent effort. "The man we want," he went on, "made no footprints on the pavement or up the steps because he never walked on the pavement or up the steps—after the snow had stopped. He was in the house all the time. He had been in the house for some time. He was either (a) an inmate; or (b) more probably somebody who had concealed himself there, using a key to the front door earlier in the evening. This would explain all the inconsistencies in everybody's story. At the proper time he put on his fancy rig, stepped outside the front door on the swept doorstep, and rang the door-bell. It explains how he knew Miss Grimaud and Mr. Mangan were in the front room when the blinds were drawn—he had seen them go in. It explains how, when the door was slammed in his face and he was told to wait outside, he could simply walk in—he had a key."

Dr. Fell was slowly shaking his head and rumbling to himself. He folded his arms argumentatively.

"H'mf, yes. But why should even a slightly cracked person indulge in all that elaborate hocus-pocus? If he lived in the house, the argument isn't bad: he wanted to make the visitor seem an outsider. But if he really came from outside, why take the dangerous risk of hanging about inside long before he was ready to act? Why not march straight up at the right time?"

"First," said the methodical Hadley, checking it off on his fingers, "he had to know where people were, so as to have no interference. Second, and more important, he wanted to put the finishing touches on his vanishing trick by having no footprints whatever, anywhere, in the snow. The vanishing-trick would be everything to the crazy mind of—brother Henri, let's say. So he got in while it was snowing heavily, and waited until it had stopped."

"Who," Rosette asked in a sharp voice, "is brother Henri?"

"He's a name, my dear," Dr. Fell returned, affably. "I told you that you didn't know him. . . . Now, Hadley, here's where I enter a mild, firm objection to this whole rummy affair. We've talked glibly about snow starting and stopping, as though you could regulate it like a tap. But I want to know how in blazes a man can tell WHEN snow is going to start or stop? That is, a man seldom says to himself, 'Aha! On Saturday night I will commit a crime. On that night, I think, it will commence to snow at exactly 5:00 P.M., and leave off at exactly 9:30 P.M. This will afford me ample time to get into the house, and be prepared with my trick when the snowfall ends.' Tut, tut! Your explanation is rather more staggering than your problem. It's much easier to believe that a man walked on snow without leaving a footprint than to believe he knew precisely when he would have it to walk on."

The superintendent was irritable. "I am trying," he said, "to get to the main point of all this. But if you must fight about that— Don't you see it explains away the last problem?"

"What problem?"

"Our friend Mangan here says that the visitor threatened to pay his visit at ten o'clock. Mrs. Dumont and Mills say nine-thirty. Wait!" He checked Mangan's outburst. "Was A lying, or B? First, what sane reason could either have for lying *afterwards* about the time he *threatened* to come? Second, if A says ten o'clock and B says nine-thirty, then, innocent or guilty, one of the two should have learned beforehand the time at which the visitor really would arrive. And which was right about the time he did arrive?"

"Neither," said Mangan, staring. "It was between 'em. At 9:45."

"Yes. That's a sign that neither lied. It's a sign that the visitor's threat to Grimaud was not definite; it was 'nine-thirty or ten o'clock or thereabouts.' And Grimaud, who was trying pretty desperately to, act as though the threat hadn't scared him, nevertheless took very good care to mention both times in order to make sure everybody was there. My wife does the same thing with invitations to bridge parties. . . . Well, but *why* couldn't brother Henri be definite? Because, as Fell says, he couldn't turn off the snow like a tap. He could risk a long gamble on there being snow tonight, as there's been for several nights; but he had to wait until it stopped even if he waited until midnight. He didn't have to wait so long. It stopped at half-past nine. And then he acted exactly as such a lunatic would—he waited fifteen minutes so that there could be no argument afterwards, and rang the bell."

Dr. Fell opened his mouth to speak, looked shrewdly at the intent faces of Rosette and Mangan, and stopped.

"Now, then!" said Hadley, squaring his shoulders. "I've shown you two that I believe everything you say, because I want your help on the most important thing this tells us. . . . The man we want is no casual acquaintance. He knows this house inside out—the rooms, the routine, the habits of the occupants. He knows your phrases and nick-names. He knows how this Mr. Pettis is accustomed to address not only Dr. Grimaud, but *you;* hence he's no casual business friend of the professor whom you haven't seen. So I want to know all about everybody who's a frequent enough visitor to this house, everybody who is close enough to Dr. Grimaud, to answer the description."

She moved uneasily, startled. "You think—somebody like that. . . . Oh, it's impossible! No, no, no!" (It was a queer echo of her mother's voice.) "Not anybody like that, anyhow!"

"Why do you say that?" Hadley asked, sharply. "Do you know who-shot your father?"

The sudden crack of the words made her jump. "No, of course not!"

"Or have any suspicion?"

"No. Except," her teeth gleamed, "I don't see why you should keep looking outside the house. That was a very nice little lesson in deduction you gave, and thanks awfully. But if the person had come from *inside* the house, and acted as you said, then it would really be reasonable, wouldn't it? It would apply much better."

"To whom?"

"Let's see! Well . . . that's your business, isn't it?" (He had somehow stirred a sleek tiger cat, and she was enjoying it.) "Of course, you haven't met the whole household. You haven't met Annie—or Mr. Drayman, come to think of it. But your other idea is utterly ridiculous. In the first place, my father has very few friends. Outside of the people in this house, there are only two who fit the qualifications, and neither of them could possibly be the man you want. They couldn't be in the mere matter of their physical characteristics. One is Anthony Pettis himself; he's no taller than I am, and I'm no Amazon. The other is Jerome Burnaby, the artist who did that queer picture. He has a deformity; a slight one, but it couldn't be disguised and anybody could spot it a mile away. Aunt Ernestine or Stuart would have known him instantly."

"All the same, what do you know about them?"

She lifted her shoulders. "Both are middle-aged, well-to-do, and potter after their hobbies. Pettis is bald-headed and fastidious. . . . I don't mean he's old-womanish: he's what the men call a good fellow, and he's clever as sin. Bah! Why won't they *do* something with themselves!" She clenched her hands. Then she glanced up at Mangan, and a slow, calculating, drowsily pleasant expression came into her look. "Burnaby—yes, Jerome has done something with himself, in a way. He's fairly well known as an artist, though he'd rather be known as a criminologist. He's big and bluff; he likes to talk about crime and brag about his athletic prowess of old. Jerome is attractive in his way. He's very fond of me, and Boyd is horribly jealous." Her smile widened.

"I don't like the fellow," said Mangan, quietly. "In fact, I hate him like poison—and we both know it. But at least Rosette's right about one thing. He'd never do a thing like that."

Hadley scribbled again. "What is this deformity of his?"

"A club foot. You can see how he couldn't possibly conceal it."

"Thank you. For the moment," said Hadley, shutting up his notebook, "that will be all. I should suggest that you go along to the nursing-home. Unless . . . er—any questions, Fell?"

The doctor stumped forward. He towered over the girl, peering down at her with his head a little on one side.

"Just one last question," he said, brushing aside the black ribbon of his eye-glasses as he would a fly. "Harrumph! Ha! Now! Miss Grimaud, why are you so certain that the guilty person is this Mr. Drayman?"

THE BULLET 8

He never received any answer to that question, although he received some illumination. It was all over before Rampole realized what had happened. Since the doctor had spoken with the greatest casualness, the name "Drayman" had made no impression on Rampole, and he was not even looking at Rosette. Uneasily, he had been wondering for some time what had happened to change the gusty, garrulous, beaming Mangan he used to know into this shuffling figure who backed and deprecated and talked like a fool. In the past Mangan had never talked like a fool, even when he talked like an idiot. But now—

"You *devil!*" cried Rosette Grimaud.

It was like a screech of chalk on a blackboard. Rampole whirled round to see high cheek bones gone still higher as her mouth widened, and a blaze that seemed to take the colour from her eyes: It was only a glimpse; she had flung herself past Dr. Fell, the mink coat flying, and out into the hall, with Mangan after her. The door slammed. Mangan reappeared for a moment, said to them, "Er—sorry!" and quickly closed the door once more. He looked almost grotesque in the doorway, his back bent and his head lowered, so that it seemed all wrinkled forehead and nervous dark eyes shining intensely. His hands were extended, with palms turned down, as though he were trying to quiet an audience. "Er—sorry!" he said, and closed the door.

Dr. Fell remained blinking at it.

"She's her father's daughter, Hadley," he wheezed, and shook his head slowly. "Harrumph, yes. She goes just so far under hard emotional pressure; very quiet, powder packed into a cartridge; then some little thing jars the hair trigger, and—h'm. I'm afraid she's morbid in the real sense, but maybe she thinks she has reason to be. I wonder how much she knows?"

"Oh, well, she's a foreigner. But that's not the point. It seems to me," said Hadley, with some asperity, "that you're always making a wild shot like a trick rifleman and knocking the cigarette out of somebody's mouth. What was that business about Drayman, anyhow?"

Dr. Fell seemed bothered.

"In a minute, in a minute. . . . What did you think of her, Hadley? And Mangan?" He turned to Rampole. "My ideas are a little mixed. I'd got the impression, from what you said, that Mangan was a wild Irishman of the type I know and like."

"He was," said Rampole. "Understand?"

"As to what I think of her," Hadley said, "I think she could sit here as cool as you please, analyzing her father's life (she's got a damned good head on her, by the way); and yet at this moment I'll bet she's in tears and hysterics, rushing across there, because she didn't show him enough consideration. I think she's fundamentally sound. But she's got the Old Nick in her, Fell. She wants a master in both senses. She and Mangan will never hit it off until he has sense enough to punch her head or take her own advice at the London University debate."

"Ever since you have become superintendent of the C.I.D.," declared Dr. Fell, squinting at him, "I have detected in you a certain raffish air which pains and surprises me. Listen, you old satyr. Did you honestly believe all that rubbish you talked, about the murderer sneaking into this house to wait until the snowstorm had stopped?"

Hadley permitted himself a broad grin. "It's as good an explanation as any," he said, "until I can think of a better. And it keeps their minds occupied. Always keep witnesses' minds occupied. At least I believe their story. . . . We're going to find something in the way of footprints on that roof, don't you worry. But we'll talk about that later. What about Drayman?"

"To begin with, I had stuck in my mind an odd remark made by Madame Dumont. It was so odd that it jumped out of the sentence. Not a calculated remark; she cried it out at the time she was most hysterical, when she could not understand why even murderers acted out so silly a charade. She said (if you wish to kill somebody), 'You do not put on a painted mask, like old Drayman with the children on Guy Fawkes night.' I filed away the suggestion of this Guy Fawkes spectre, wondering what it meant. Then, all unintentionally, I phrased a question about Pettis—when speaking to Rosette—with the words, 'dressed up like a Fifth of November Guy?' Did you notice her expression, Hadley? Just my suggestion that the visitor was dressed like that gave her the hint, but it startled her as much as it pleased her. She didn't say anything; she was thinking. She hated the person she was thinking of. What person?"

Hadley stared across the room. "Yes, I remember. I could see she was hinting at somebody she suspected or wanted us to suspect; that was why I asked her flat out. She practically made me see it was somebody in this house. But to tell you the truth,"—he rubbed his hand across his forehead—"this is such a rum crowd that for a second I thought she was hinting at her own mother."

"Not by the way she dragged in Drayman. 'You haven't met Annie—or Mr. Drayman, come to think of it.' The important news was in the postscript. . . ." Dr. Fell stumped round the typewriter desk, peering malevolently at the glass of milk. "We must rout him out. He interests me. Who is this Drayman, this old friend and hanger-on of Grimaud, who takes sleeping draughts and wears Fifth of

November masks? What's his place in the household; what's he doing here, anyway?"

"You mean—blackmail?"

"Rubbish, my boy. Did you ever hear of a schoolmaster being a blackmailer? No, no. They're much too worried about what people might find out about *them*. The academic profession has its faults, as I know for my sins; but it doesn't produce blackmailers. . . . No, it was probably only a kindly impulse of Grimaud to take him in, but—"

He paused as a rush of cold air blew his cloak. A door across the room, evidently communicating with a staircase to the attic and the roof, opened and shut. Mills popped in. His mouth was bluish and a large wool muffler was wound round his neck; but he looked warm with satisfaction. After refreshing himself with a pull at the glass of milk (impassively, with head thrown back in a way which somehow suggested a sword-swallower), he put out his hands to the fire.

He chattered: "I have been watching your detective, gentlemen, from a point of vantage at the top of the trap-door. He has caused a few landslides, but. . . . Excuse me! Didn't you have a commission of some description for me to execute? Ah yes. I am anxious to lend assistance, but I fear I forgot—"

"Wake up Mr. Drayman," the superintendent said, "if you have to slosh him with water. And . . . Hullo! Pettis! If Mr. Pettis is still here, tell him I want to see him. What did Sergeant Betts discover up there?"

Betts answered for himself. He looked as though he had taken a header in a ski-jump; he breathed hard, stamped and slapped the snow from his clothes as he shook his way towards the fire.

"Sir," he announced, "you can take my word for it that not even a bird's lit on that roof anywhere. There's no mark of any kind in any place. I've covered every foot of it." He stripped off his sodden gloves. "I had myself tied on a rope to each of the chimneys, so I could get down and crawl straight along the gutters. Nothing round the edges, nothing round the chimneys, nothing anywhere. If anybody got up on that roof tonight, he must have been lighter than air. Now I'll go down and have a look at the back garden . . ."

"But—!" cried Hadley.

"Quite so," said Dr. Fell. "Look here, we'd better go

down and see what your bloodhounds are doing in the other room. If the good Preston—"

Sergeant Preston, fuming a little, pulled open the door to the hall as though he had been summoned. He looked at Betts and back to Hadley.

"It's taken me a little time, sir," he reported, "because we had to pull out all those bookcases and shove 'em back again. The answer is nothing! No secret entrance of any kind. Chimney's solid and no funny business about it; flue's only about two or three inches wide, and goes up on an angle at that. . . . Is that all, sir? The boys have finished."

"Fingerprints?"

"Plenty of prints, except— You raised and lowered that window yourself, didn't you, sir? With your fingers on the glass up near the top of the frame? I recognized your prints."

"I am generally careful about things like that," snapped Hadley. "Well?"

"Nothing else on the glass. And all the woodwork of that window, frame and sill, is high-gloss varnish that'd take a glove-smudge as clear as a print. There's nothing, not even a smudge. If anybody went out there, he must have stood back and dived out head first without touching anything."

"That's enough, thanks," said Hadley. "Wait downstairs. Get after that back garden, Betts. . . . No, wait, Mr. Mills. Preston will fetch Mr. Pettis, if he's still there. I should like to speak to you."

"It would seem," said Mills, rather shrilly, when the other two had gone, "that we return to doubts about my own story. I assure you I am telling the truth. Here is where I sat. See for yourself."

Hadley opened the door. Ahead of them the high, sombre hallway ran thirty feet to the door opposite—a door brilliantly illuminated by the glow from under the archway.

"I don't suppose there's any possibility of a mistake?" muttered the superintendent. "That he really didn't go in, or something like that? A lot of funny business might go on in a shuffle at the doorway; I've heard of its being done. I don't suppose the woman was up to any funny business, dressing up in a mask herself, or— No, you saw them together, and anyway. . . . *Hell!*"

"There was absolutely none of what you describe as

funny business," said Mills. Even in his perspiring earnestness he handled the last two words with distaste. "I saw all
three of them clearly and wide apart. Madame Dumont was
in front of the door, yes; but towards the right. The tall man
was towards the left, and Dr. Grimaud separating them.
The tall man really did go in; he closed the door behind
him; and he did not come out. It is not as though the oc-
currence took place in half-light. There was no possibility
of ever mistaking that man's gigantic stature."

"I don't see how we can doubt it, Hadley," said Dr. Fell,
after a pause. "We've got to eliminate the door also." He
wheeled round. "What do you know about this man Drayman?"

Mills' eyes narrowed. His sing-song voice had a guarded
quality.

"It is true, sir, that he offers a subject for intelligent
curiosity. Hurrum! But I know very little. He has been
here some years, I am informed; in any event, before I
arrived. He was forced to give up his academic work
because he had gone almost blind. He is still almost blind,
in spite of treatment, although you would not deduce this
from the—er—aspect of his eyes. He appealed to Dr.
Grimaud for help."

"Had he some sort of claim on Dr. Grimaud?"

The secretary frowned. "I cannot say. I have heard
it mentioned that Dr. Grimaud knew him at Paris, where
he studied. That is the only bit of information I have,
except one remark which Dr. Grimaud made when he
had, let us say, imbibed a convivial glass." A superior
kind of smile curved round Mills' mouth without opening
it; his eyes narrowed, and gleamed in drowsy satire. "Hum!
He stated that Mr. Drayman had once saved his life, and
described him as the best damned good fellow in the
world. Of course, under the circumstances . . ."

Mills had a jerky trick of putting one foot before the
other, rocking, and tapping the toe of one shoe with the
heel of the other. With his jerky movements, tiny figure,
and big shock of hair, he was like a caricature of Swinburne. Dr. Fell looked at him curiously. But Dr. Fell only
said:

"So? And why don't *you* like him?"

"I neither like nor dislike him. But he does nothing."

"Is that why Miss Grimaud doesn't like him, either?"

"Miss Grimaud does not like him?" said Mills, opening his eyes and then narrowing them. "Yes, I had fancied that. I watched, but I could not be certain."

"H'mf. And why is he so interested in Guy Fawkes night?"

"Guy Fa— Ah!" Mills broke off in his surprise, and uttered a flat bleat of laughter. "I see! I did not follow. You see, he is very fond of children. He had two children of his own, who were killed—by the falling of a roof, I believe, some years ago. It was one of those foolish, petty tragedies which we shall eliminate when we build the bigger, greater, more spacious world of the future." At this point in the recital Dr. Fell's face was murderous, but Mills went on: "His wife did not survive long. Then he began to lose his sight. . . . He likes to help the children in all their games, and has himself a somewhat childish mind in spite of certain mental qualities." The fish lip lifted a little. "His favourite occasion seems to be the Fifth of November, which was the birthday of one of his unfortunate progeny. He saves up throughout the year to buy illuminations and trappings, and builds a Guy for a procession to—" A sharp knocking at the door was followed by the appearance of Sergeant Preston.

"There's nobody downstairs, sir," he reported. "That gentleman you wanted to see must have left. . . . A chap from the nursing-home just brought this over for you."

He handed over an envelope and a square cardboard box like a jeweller's box. Hadley ripped open the letter, glanced down it, and swore.

"He's gone," snapped Hadley, "and not a word. . . . Here, read this!"

Rampole looked over Dr. Fell's shoulder as the latter read.

For Superintendent Hadley:
    Poor Grimaud died at 11:30. I am sending you the bullet. It's a thirty-eight, as I thought. I tried to get in touch with your police surgeon, but he was out on another case, and so I am sending it to you.
    He was conscious just before the end. He said certain things which can be attested by two of my nurses and myself; but he might have been wandering and I should be careful of them. I knew him pretty well,

but I certainly never knew he had a brother.

First he said he wished to tell me about it; then he spoke exactly as follows:

"It was my brother who did it. I never thought he would shoot. God knows how he got out of that room. One second he was there, and the next he wasn't. Get a pencil and paper, quick! I want to tell you who my brother is, so that you won't think I'm raving."

His shouting brought in the final hemorrhage, and he died without saying anything else. I am holding the body subject to your orders. If there is any help I can give, let me know.

E. H. Peterson, M. D.

They all looked at each other. The puzzle stood rounded and complete; the facts stood confirmed and the witnesses vindicated; but the terror of the hollow man remained. After a pause the superintendent spoke in a heavy voice. " 'God knows,' " repeated Hadley, " 'how he got out of that room.' "

2nd
COFFIN

THE PROBLEM OF CAGLIOSTRO STREET

THE BREAKING GRAVE 9

Dr. Fell walked over aimlessly, sighed, and settled himself down in the largest chair. "Brother Henri—" he rumbled. "H'mf, yes. I was afraid we should get back to Brother Henri."

"Damn Brother Henri," said Hadley in a flat voice. "We're going after Brother Pierre first. He knows! Why haven't I had any message from that constable? Where's the man who was to pick him up at that theatre? Have the whole blasted lot of them gone to sleep and—"

"We mustn't get the wind up about this thing," interposed the other, as Hadley began to stamp and declaim rather wildly. "That's exactly what Brother Henri would want us to do. Now that we've got Grimaud's last statement, we've at least got one clue. . . ."

"To what?"

"To the words he spoke to *us*, the ones we couldn't make any sense of. The unfortunate point is that they may not help us now that we can hazard a theory as to what they mean. With this new evidence, I'm afraid we were listening to Grimaud running up a blind alley. He wasn't telling us anything; he was only trying to ask us a question."

"What's all this?"

"Don't you see that's exactly what he must have been doing? Last statement: 'God knows how he got out of that room. One second he was there and the next he wasn't.' Now let's try to sort out the words from that invaluable notebook of yours. You and friend Ted have slightly different versions; but we'll begin with the words on which you both agree and which we must assume to be correct. Put aside the first puzzlers—I think we can now feel safe in saying that the words were 'Horváth' and 'salt-mine.' Put aside also the terms on which you do not agree. What words are found in both lists?"

Hadley snapped his fingers. "I begin to— Yes! The words are, 'He couldn't use rope. Roof. Snow. Fox. Too much light.' Well, then! If we try to make a composite statement; fit together the words and the sense of both statements; we have his meaning as something like this: 'God knows how he got out. He couldn't use a rope, either up on the roof or down in the snow. One second he was there, and the next he wasn't. There was too much light for me to miss any move he made—' Stop a bit, though! What about. . . ."

"And now," said Dr. Fell, with a disgusted grunt, "you can begin to fit in the differences. Ted heard, 'not suicide.' That goes into the picture as an assurance to accord with the other expressions. 'This isn't suicide; I didn't kill myself.' You heard, 'Got gun'; which isn't difficult to tie up with the sentence out of the other statement, 'I never thought he would shoot.' BAH! All the clues whirl straight round in a circle and become questions. It's the first case I ever heard of in which the murdered man was just as inquisitive as everybody else."

"But what about the word 'fox'? That doesn't fit anywhere."

Dr. Fell regarded him with a sour twinkle in his eye.

"Oh, yes, it does. It's the easiest part of all—though it may be the trickiest, and we mustn't jump to conclusions about applying it. It's a matter of how words strike the ear when they're not spelled out. If I'm using the word-association test (that damned thing) on various people, and I suddenly whisper, 'Fox!' to a horseman, he will probably answer, 'Hounds!' But if I use the same word on a historian, he is likely to yell . . . quick! What?"

"Guy," said Hadley, and swore. After a lurid interval he demanded: "Do you mean that we come back to some babbling about a Guy Fawkes mask, or the resemblance to a Guy Fawkes mask?"

"Well, everybody else has been doing a tall amount of babbling about it," the doctor pointed out, scratching his forehead. "And I'm not surprised it struck the eye of somebody who saw it at somewhat closer quarters. Does that tell you anything?"

"It tells me to have a little talk with Mr. Drayman," said the superintendent, grimly. He strode towards the door, and was startled to find the bony face of Mills poked out in eager listening against the thick glasses.

"Steady, Hadley," Dr. Fell interposed as the superintendent gave indications of an explosion. "It's a queer thing about you: you can be steady as the Guards when riddles are flying, but you never seem able to keep your shirt on when we get within sight of the truth. Let our young friend stop. He should hear all this, if only to hear the end of it." He chuckled. "Does that make you suspicious of Drayman? Pfaa! On the contrary, it should be just the opposite. Remember, we haven't quite finished putting the pieces in our jig saw. There's one last bit we haven't accounted for, and it was a bit you heard yourself. That pink mask suggested Drayman to Grimaud, just as he seems to have been suggested to several others. But Grimaud knew whose face was behind the mask. Therefore we have a fairly sensible explanation of those final words you noted down, *'Don't blame poor—'* He seems to have had a great liking for Drayman, you know." After a silence, Dr. Fell turned to Mills, "Now go and fetch him up here, son."

When the door had closed, Hadley sat down wearily and took from his breast pocket the frayed cigar he had not yet lighted. Then he ran a finger round under his collar with that malevolent, broken-necked expression which people have when worry makes them think the collar is too tight.

"More trick marksmanship, eh?" he suggested. "More deductive tight-rope work, and the daring young man on the—um!" He stared at the floor, and then grunted with annoyance. "I must be losing my grip! It's no good getting fantastic notions like the one I just had. Have you got any concrete suggestions?"

"Yes. Later, if you'll permit it, I am going to apply Gross's test."

"Apply what?"

"Gross's test. Don't you remember? We were arguing about it tonight. I'm going to collect very carefully all the mass of burnt and half-burnt paper in that fireplace, to see whether Gross's test will bring out the writing. Be quiet, will you?" he roared, as Hadley made scornful noises. "I don't say all of it, or even half of it, will come out. But I should get a line here and there to give me a hint about what was more important to Grimaud than saving his own life. Purph! Hah! Yes."

"And how do you work this trick?"

"You'll see. Mind, I don't say that thoroughly burnt paper will come out satisfactorily. But there'll be something, especially in the charred parts sandwiched in and only scorched black, that *will* come out. . . . Aside from that, I haven't a suggestion, unless we ask—yes, what is it?"

Sergeant Betts, not quite so plastered with snow this time, made his report woodenly. He looked out the door behind him before he closed it.

"I've been all over that back-garden, sir. And the two adjoining ones, and the tops of all the walls. There's no footprint or any kind of mark. . . . But I believe we've caught a fish, Preston and I. As I was coming back through the house, down the stairs comes running a tallish old bloke, plunging away with his hand on the banister rail. He ran over to a clothes closet, and banged about as though he wasn't familiar with the place, until he got on his overcoat and hat, and then made for the door. He says his name's Drayman and that he lives here, but we thought—"

"I think you'll find that his sight isn't any too good," said Dr. Fell. "Send him in."

The man who entered was, in his own way, an impressive figure. His long, quiet face was hollowed at the temples; his grey hair grew far back on the skull, giving him a great height of narrow and wrinkled forehead. His bright blue eyes, which did not seem at all dimmed despite the wrinkles round them, looked gentle and puzzled. He had a hooked nose, and deep furrows running down to a kindly, uncertain mouth; and his trick of wrinkling the forehead, so that one eyebrow was slightly raised, made him look more uncertain still. Despite his stoop he was still tall; despite his bony frailty he was still powerful. He looked like a military man gone senile, a well-brushed man gone slovenly. There was nothing of humour in the face, but a great deal of muddled and apologetic good-nature. He wore a dark overcoat buttoned up to the chin. Standing in the doorway, peering hard at them from under tangled eyebrows, he held a bowler hat pressed against his chest, and hesitated.

"I am sorry, gentlemen. I am honestly very sorry," he said. His deep voice had a curious quality as though the man were unused to speech. "I know I should have come to see you before going over there. But young Mr. Mangan woke me up to tell me what had happened. I felt I had to go over and see Grimaud, to see whether there might be anything I could do—"

Rampole had a feeling that he was still dull-witted and uncertain from sleep or sleeping-drugs; that the bright stare of his eyes might have been so much glass. He moved over, and one hand found the back of a chair. But he did not sit down until Hadley asked him to do so.

"Mr. Mangan told me—" he said, "Dr. Grimaud—"

"Dr. Grimaud is dead," said Hadley.

Drayman remained sitting as bolt upright as his stoop would allow, his hands folded across his hat. There was a heavy silence in the room, while Drayman shut his eyes and opened them again. Then he seemed to stare a long way off, and to breathe with heavy, whistling sluggishness.

"God rest his soul," Drayman said, very quietly. "Charles Grimaud was a good friend."

"Do you know how he died?"

"Yes. Mr. Mangan told me."

Hadley studied him. "Then you will understand that to tell everything, *everything* you might happen to know, will be the only way to help us catch the murderer of your friend?"

"I— Yes, of course."

"Be very certain of that, Mr. Drayman! More certain than you are. We wish to know something of his past life. You knew him well. Where did you first know him?"

The other's long face looked muddled; an illusion as though the features had got out of line. "In Paris. He took his doctorate at the university in 1905, the same year I . . . the same year I knew him." Facts seemed to elude Drayman; he shaded his eyes with his hand, and his voice had a querulous note like a man asking where somebody has hidden his collar studs. "Grimaud was very brilliant. He obtained an associate professorship at Dijon the year afterwards. But a relative died, or something of the sort, and left him well provided for. He—he gave up his work and came to England shortly afterwards. Or so I understand. I did not see him until years afterwards. Was that what you wished to know?"

"Did you ever know him before 1905?"

"No."

Hadley leaned forward. "Where did you save his life?" he asked, sharply.

"Save his life? I don't understand."

"Ever visit Hungary, Mr. Drayman?"

"I—I have travelled on the Continent, and I may have been in Hungary. But that was years ago, when I was young. I don't remember."

And now it was Hadley's turn to pull the trigger in trick marksmanship.

"You saved his life," he stated, "near the prison of Siebenturmen, in the Carpathian Mountains, when he was escaping. *Didn't you?*"

The other sat upright, his bony hands clenched across the bowler. Rampole had a feeling that there was more dogged strength in him now than there had been for a dozen years.

"Did I?" he said.

"There's no use going on with this. We know everything —even to dates, now that you've supplied them. Károly Horváth, as a free man, wrote the date in a book in 1898. With full academic preparation behind, it would have taken him four years at least to get his doctorate at Paris. We can narrow down the time of his conviction and escape to three years. With that information," said Hadley, coolly, "I can cable to Bucharest and get the full details within twelve hours. You had better tell the truth, you see. I want to know all you know of Károly Horváth—and his two brothers. One of those two brothers killed him. Finally, I'll remind you that withholding information of this kind is a serious offence. Well?"

Drayman remained for a little time with his hand shading his eyes, his foot tapping the carpet. Then he looked up. They were startled to see that, though his puckered eyes kept their blue glassiness, the man was gently smiling.

"A serious offence," he repeated, and nodded. "Is it, indeed? Now, frankly, sir, I don't give a damn for your threats. There are very few things which can move or anger or terrify a man who can see you only in outline, as he sees a poached egg on his plate. Nearly all the fears of the world (and its ambitions, too) are caused by shapes— eyes and gestures and figures. Young people can't understand this, but I had hoped you would. You see, I am not precisely blind. I can see faces and the morning sky, and all those objects which the poets insist blind men should rave about. But I cannot *read,* and the faces I cared most to see have been for eight years blinder than mine. Wait until your whole life is built on those two things, and you will learn that not much can move you when they go." He nodded again, staring across the room. His forehead wrinkled. "Sir, I am perfectly willing to give you any information you wish, if it will help Charles Grimaud. But I don't see the sense of raking up old scandal."

"Not even to find the brother who killed him?"

Drayman made a slight gesture, frowning. "Look here, if it will help you, I can honestly tell you to forget such an idea. I don't know how you learned it. He did have two brothers. And they were imprisoned." He smiled again. "There was nothing terrible about it. They were imprisoned for a political offence. I imagine half the young fire-eaters of the time must have been concerned in it. . . . Forget the two brothers. They have both been dead a good many years."

It was so quiet in the room that Rampole heard the last collapsing rattle of the fire and the wheezing breaths of Dr. Fell. Hadley glanced at Dr. Fell, whose eyes were closed. Then Hadley regarded Drayman as impassively as though the latter's sight had been sharp.

"How do you know that?"

"Grimaud told me," said the other, accentuating the name. "Besides, all the newspapers from Budapest to Brasso were shouting about it at the time. You can easily verify all this." He spoke simply. "They died of bubonic plague."

Hadley was suave. "If, of course, you could prove this beyond any doubt . . ."

"You promise that there would be no old scandal raked up?" (That bright blue stare was difficult to meet. Drayman twisted and untwisted his bony hands.) "If I tell you exactly, and you receive the proof, will you let the dead rest?"

"It depends on your information."

"Very well. I will tell you what I saw myself." He reflected—rather uneasily, Rampole thought. "It was in its own way a horrible business. Grimaud and I never spoke of it afterwards. That was agreed. But I don't intend to lie to you and say I've forgotten it—any detail of it."

He was silent for so long a time, tapping his fingers at his temple, that even the patient Hadley was about to prompt him. Then he went on:

"Excuse me, gentlemen. I was trying to remember the exact date, so that you can verify everything. The best I can do is to say it was in August or September of nineteen hundred . . . or was it nineteen one? Anyhow, it occurs to me that I might begin, with perfect truth, exactly in the style of the contemporary French romances.

I might begin, 'Towards dusk of a cool September day in the year 19— a solitary horseman might have been seen hurrying along a road,' and what a devil of a road!—'in a rugged valley below the southeastern Carpathians.' Then I should launch into a description of the wild scenery and so on. I was the horseman; it was coming on to rain, and I was trying to reach Tradj before dark."

He smiled. Hadley stirred in some impatience, though Dr. Fell opened his eyes; and Drayman was quick to take it up.

"I must insist on that sort of novelesque atmosphere, because it fitted into my mood and explains so much. I was at the romantic Byronic age, fired with ideas of political liberty. I rode horseback instead of walking because I thought I cut a good figure; I even took pleasure in carrying a pistol against (mythical) brigands, and a rosary as a charm against ghosts. But if there weren't either ghosts or brigands, there should have been. I know that I several times got the wind up about both. There was a sort of fairy-tale wildness and darkness about those cold forests and gorges. Even about the cultivated parts there was something queer. Transylvania, you see, is shadowed in on three sides by mountains. It startles an English eye to see a rye-field or a vineyard going straight up the side of a steep hill; the red-and-yellow costumes, the garlicky inns, and even, in the bleaker parts, hills made of pure salt.

"Anyhow, there I was going along a snaky road in the bleakest part, with a storm blowing up and no inn for miles. People saw the devil lurking behind every hedge in a way that gave me the creeps, but I had a worse cause for the creeps. Plague had broken out after a hot summer, and was over the whole area like a cloud of gnats, even in the chilly weather. In the last village I passed through—I've forgotten its name—they told me it was raging at the salt-mines in the mountains ahead. But I was hoping to meet an English friend of mine, also a tourist, at Tradj. Also I wanted a look at the prison, which got its name after seven white hills, like a low range of mountains, just behind. So I said I meant to go on.

"I knew I must be getting near the prison, for I could see the white hills ahead. But, just as it was getting too dark to see at all, and the wind seemed to be tearing the trees to pieces, I came down into a hollow past the three graves. They had been freshly dug, for there were still footmarks round them; but no living person was in sight."

Hadley broke across the queer atmosphere which that dreaming voice was beginning to create.

"A place," he said, "just like the one in the painting Dr. Grimaud bought from Mr. Burnaby."

"I—I don't know," answered Drayman, evidently startled. "Is it? I didn't notice."

"Didn't notice? Didn't you see the picture?"

"Not very well. Just a general outline—trees, ordinary landscape—"

"And three headstones . . . ?"

"I don't know where Burnaby got his inspiration," the other said, dully, and rubbed his forehead. "God knows *I* never told him. It's probably a coincidence; there were no headstones over these graves. They wouldn't have bothered. There were simply three crosses made of sticks.

"But I was telling you. I sat there on my horse, looking at those graves, and with a not very pleasant feeling. They looked wild enough, with the greenish-black landscape around and the white hills beyond. But it wasn't that. If they were prison graves, I wondered why they had been dug so far away. The next thing I knew my horse reared and nearly threw me. I slewed round against a tree; and, when I looked back, I saw what was wrong with the horse. The mound of one grave was upheaving and sliding. There was a cracking noise; something began to twist and wriggle; and a dark-coloured thing came groping up out of the mound. It was only a hand moving the fingers—but I don't think I have ever seen anything more horrible."

THE BLOOD ON THE COAT 10

"By that time," Drayman went on, "there was something wrong with me as well. I didn't dare dismount, for fear the horse would bolt; and I was ashamed to bolt, myself. I thought of vampires and all the legends of hell coming up out of the twilight. Frankly, the thing scared me silly. I remember battering round on that horse like a teetotum, trying to curb it with one hand while I got out my revolver. When I looked back again, the thing had climbed clear out of the grave and was coming towards me.

"That, gentlemen, was how I met one of my best friends. The man reached down and seized a spade, which somebody who dug the grave must have left there and forgotten. And still he came on. I yelled in English, 'What do you want?'—because I was so fuddled that I couldn't remember a word in any other language. The man stopped. After a second he answered in English, but with an outlandish accent. 'Help,' he said, 'help, milord; don't be afraid,' or something of the sort, and threw down the spade. The horse was quieter, but I wasn't. The man was not tall, but very powerful; his face was dark and swollen, with little scaly spots which gave it a pinkish look in the twilight. And down came the rain while he was still standing there waving his arms.

"He stood in the rain, crying out to me. I won't try to reproduce it, but he said something like, 'Look, milord, I am not dead of plague like those two poor devils,' and pointed at the graves. 'I am not infected at all. See how the rain washes it off. It is my own blood which I have pricked out of my skin.' He even stuck out his tongue to show how it was blackened with soot, and the rain made it clean. It was as mad a sight as the figure and the place. Then he went on to say that he was not a criminal, but a political offender, and was making his escape from the prison."

Drayman's forehead wrinkled. He smiled again.

"Help him? Naturally I did. I was fired by the idea. He explained things to me while we laid plans. He was one of three brothers, students at the University of Klausenburg, who had been arrested in an insurrection for an independent Transylvania under the protection of Austria; as it was before 1860. The three of them were in the same cell, and two had died of the pestilence. With the help of the prison doctor, also a convict, he had faked the same symptoms— and died. It wasn't likely that anybody would go very close to test the doctor's judgment; the whole prison was mad with fear. Even the people who buried those three would keep their heads turned away when they threw the bodies into pine coffins and nailed on the lids. They would bury the bodies at some distance from the prison. Most of all, they would do a quick job of nailing the lids. The doctor had smuggled in a pair of nail-cutters, which my resurrected friend showed me. A powerful man, if he kept his nerve and didn't use up too much air after he had been buried, could force up the lids with his head enough to wedge the nail-cutters into the loose space. Afterwards a powerful man could dig up through loose ground.

"Very well. When he found I was a student at Paris, conversation became easy. His mother had been French, and he spoke the language perfectly. We decided that he had better make for France, where he could set up a new identity without suspicion. He had a little money hidden away, and there was a girl in his native town who——"

Drayman stopped abruptly, like one who remembers that he has gone too far. Hadley merely nodded.

"I think we know who the girl was," he said. "For the moment, we can leave 'Madame Dumont' out of this. What then?"

"She could be trusted to bring the money and follow him to Paris. It wasn't likely that there would be a hue and cry—in fact, there wasn't any. He passed as dead; even if Grimaud was frightened enough to tear away from that neighbourhood before he would even shave or put on a suit of my clothes. We excited no suspicion. There were no passports in those days, and he posed on the way out of Hungary as the English friend of mine I had been expecting to meet at Tradj. Once into France . . . you know all the rest. Now, gentlemen!" Drayman drew a curiously shuddering breath, stiffened, and faced them with his hard blank eyes. "You can verify everything I have said——"

"What about that cracking sound?" interjected Dr. Fell, in an argumentative tone.

The question was so quiet, and yet so startling, that Hadley whirled round. Even Drayman's gaze groped towards him. Dr. Fell's red face was screwed up absently, and he wheezed as he poked at the carpet with his stick.

"I think it's very important," he announced to the fire, as though somebody had contradicted him. "Very important indeed. H'mf. Ha. Look here, Mr. Drayman, I've got only two questions to ask you. You heard a cracking sound—of the lid wrenching on the coffin, hey? Yes. Then that would mean it was a fairly shallow grave Grimaud climbed out of?"

"Quite shallow, yes, or he might never have got out."

"Second question. That prison, now . . . was it a well or badly managed place?"

Drayman was puzzled, but his jaw set grimly. "I do not know, sir. But I do know it was under fire at that time from a number of officials. I think they were bitter against the prison authorities for letting the disease get started—it interfered with the usefulness of the workmen at the mines. By the way, the dead men's names were published; I saw them. And I ask you again, what's the good of raking up old scandals? It can't help you. You can see that it's not any particular discredit to Grimaud, but—"

"Yes, that's the point," rumbled Dr. Fell, peering at him curiously. "That's the thing I want to emphasize. It's not discreditable at all. Is it anything to make a man bury all traces of his past life?"

"—but it might become a discredit to Ernestine Dumont," said Drayman, raising his voice on a fiercer note. "Can't you see what I'm implying? What about Grimaud's daughter? And all this digging into the mess rests on some wild guess that one or both of his brothers might be alive. They're dead, and the dead don't get out of their graves. May I ask where you got such a notion as that one of Grimaud's brothers killed him?"

"From Grimaud himself," said Hadley.

For a second Rampole thought Drayman had not understood. Then the man shakily got up from his chair, as though he could not breathe. He fumbled to open his coat, felt at his throat, and sat down again. Only the glassy look of his eyes did not alter.

"Are you lying to me?" he asked—and it was with a shaky, querulous, childish tone coming through his gravity. "Why do you lie to me?"

"It happens to be the truth. Read this!"

Very quickly he thrust out the note from Dr. Peterson. Drayman made a movement to take it; then he drew back and shook his head.

"It would tell me nothing, sir. I—I— You mean he said something before he . . . ?"

"He said that the murderer was his brother."

"Did he say anything else?" asked Drayman, hesitating. Hadley let the man's imagination work, and did not reply. Presently Drayman went on: "But I tell you it's fantastic! Are you implying that this mountebank who threatened him, this fellow he had never seen before in his life, was one of his brothers? I suppose you are. I still don't understand. From the first moment I learned he had been stabbed . . ."

"Stabbed?"

"Yes. As I say, I—"

"He was shot," said Hadley. "What gave you the idea that he had been stabbed?"

Drayman lifted his shoulders. A wry, sardonic, rather despairing expression crept over his wrinkled face.

"I seem to be a very bad witness, gentlemen," he said in an even tone. "I persist with the best intentions, in telling you things you don't believe. Possibly I jumped to conclusions. Mr. Mangan said that Grimaud had been attacked and was dying; that the murderer had disappeared after slashing that painting to pieces. So I assumed—" He rubbed the bridge of his nose. "Was there anything else you wished to ask me?"

"How did you spend the evening?"

"I was asleep. I— You see, there are pains. Here, behind the eyeballs. I had them so badly at dinner that instead of going out (I was to go to a concert at the Albert Hall), I took a sleeping-tablet and lay down. Unfortunately, I don't remember anything from about half-past seven to the time Mr. Mangan woke me."

Hadley was studying his open overcoat, keeping himself very quiet, but with a dangerous expression like a man about to pounce.

"I see. Did you undress when you went to bed, Mr. Drayman?"

"I beg your— Undress? No. I took off my shoes, that's all. Why?"

"Did you leave your room at any time?"

"No."

"Then how did you get that blood on your jacket? . . . Yes, that's it. Get up! Don't run away, now. Stand where you are. Now take off your overcoat."

Rampole saw it when Drayman, standing uncertainly beside his chair and pulling off the overcoat, moved his hand across his own chest with the motions of a man groping on a floor. He was wearing a light gray suit, against which the stain splashed vividly. It was a darkish smear running from the side of the coat down across the right pocket. Drayman's fingers found it and stopped. The fingers rubbed it, then brushed together.

"It can't be blood," he muttered, with the same querulous noise rising in his voice. "I don't know what it is, but it can't be blood, I tell you!"

"We shall have to see about that. Take off the coat,

please. I'm afraid I must ask you to leave it with us. Is
there anything in the pockets you want to take out?"

"But—"

"Where did you get that stain?"

"I don't know. I swear to God I don't know, and I can't
imagine. It isn't blood. What makes you think it is?"

"Give me the coat, please. Good!" He watched sharply
while Drayman with unsteady fingers removed from the
pockets a few coppers, a concert ticket, a handkerchief, a
paper of Woodbine cigarettes, and a box of matches.
Then Hadley took the coat and spread it across his knees.
"Do you have any objection to your room being searched?
— It's only fair to tell you I have no authority to do it, if
you refuse."

"No objection at all," said the other, dully. He was
rubbing his forehead. "If you'd only tell me how it happened, Inspector! I don't know. I've tried to do the right
thing . . . yes. The right thing. . . . I didn't have anything
to do with this business." He stopped, and smiled with
such sardonic bitterness that Rampole felt more puzzled
than suspicious. "Am I under arrest? I have no objection
to that, either, you know."

Now, there was something wrong here: and yet not
wrong in the proper way. Rampole saw that Hadley shared
his own irrational doubts. Here was a man who had made
several erratic misstatements. He had told a lurid tale which
might or might not be true, but which had a vaguely
theatrical, pasteboard flimsiness about it. Finally, there
was blood on his coat. And yet, for a reason he could not
determine, Rampole was inclined to believe his story—or,
at least, the man's own belief in his story. It might have
been his complete (apparent) lack of shrewdness; his utter
simplicity. There he stood, looking taller, more shrunken
and bony in his shirt sleeves, the blue shirt itself faded to
a dingy white, the sleeves tucked up on corded arms, his
tie askew and the overcoat trailing from one hand. And
he was smiling.

Hadley swore under his breath. "Betts!" he called,
"Betts! Preston!" and tapped his heel impatiently on the
floor until they answered. "Betts, get this coat to the
pathologist for analysis of this stain. See it? Report in the
morning. That's all for tonight. Preston, go down with
Mr. Drayman and have a look round his room. You have
a good idea what to look for; also keep an eye out for

something in the mask line. I'll join you in a moment. . . . Think it over, Mr. Drayman. I'm going to ask you to come down to the Yard in the morning. That's all."

Drayman paid no attention. He blundered out in his batlike way, shaking his head and trailing the overcoat behind him. He even plucked Preston by the sleeve. "Where could I have got that blood?" he asked, eagerly. "It's a queer thing, you know, but where could I have got that blood?"

"Dunno, sir," said Preston. "Mind that doorpost!"

Presently the bleak room was quiet. Hadley shook his head slowly.

"It's got me, Fell," he admitted. "I don't know whether I'm coming or going. What do you make of the fellow? He seems gentle and pliable and easy enough; but you can keep pounding him like a punching-bag, and at the end of it he's still swinging gently in the same old place. He doesn't seem to care a rap *what* you think of him. Or what you do to him, for that matter. Maybe that's why the young people don't like him."

"H'm, yes. When I gather up those papers from the fireplace," grunted Dr. Fell, "I'm going home to think. Because what I think now . . ."

"Yes?"

"Is plain horrible."

With a gust of energy Dr. Fell surged up out of the chair, jammed his shovel-hat down over his eyes, and flourished his stick.

"I don't want to go jumping at theories. You'll have to cable for the real truth. Ha! Yes. But it's the story about the three coffins I don't believe—although Drayman may believe it, God knows! Unless our whole theory is blown to blazes, we've got to assume that the two Horváth brothers aren't dead. Hey?"

"The question being . . ."

"What happened to them. Harrumph, yes. What I think might have happened is based on the assumption that Drayman believes he's telling the truth. First point! I don't believe for a second that those brothers were sent to prison for a political offense. Grimaud, with his 'little money saved,' escapes from prison. He lies low for five years or more, and then suddenly 'inherits' a substantial fortune, under an entirely different name, from somebody we haven't heard of. But he slides out of France to enjoy it without comment. Second point, supporting! Where's the dangerous secret in Grimaud's life, if all this is true? Most people would consider that Monte Cristo escape as merely exciting and romantic; and, as for his offense, it would sound to English ears about as hideous and blasting an infamy as pinching a Belisha beacon or pasting a policeman in the eye on boat-race night. Dammit, Hadley, it won't do!"

"You mean—?"

"I mean," said Dr. Fell in a very quiet voice, "Grimaud was alive when he was nailed up in his coffin. Suppose the other two were alive, too? Suppose all three 'deaths' were faked exactly as Grimaud's was faked? Suppose there were two living people in those other coffins when Grimaud climbed out of his? But they couldn't come out . . . because he had the nail-cutters and didn't choose to use 'em. It wasn't likely that there would be more than one pair of cutters. Grimaud had 'em, because he was the strongest. Once he got out, it would have been easy for him to let the others out, as they had arranged. But he prudently decided to let them lie buried, because then there would be nobody to share the money that all three had stolen. A brilliant crime, you see. A brilliant crime."

Nobody spoke. Hadley muttered something under his breath; his face was incredulous and rather wild as he got up.

"Oh, I know it's a black business!" rumbled Dr. Fell; "a black, unholy business that would turn a man's dreams sick if he'd done it. But it's the only thing that will explain this unholy case, and why a man *would* be hounded if those brothers ever climbed up out of their graves. . . . Why was Grimaud so desperately anxious to rush Drayman away from that spot without getting rid of his convict garb as soon as he could? Why would he run the risk of being seen from the road, when a hideaway near a plague grave would be the last place any native would venture? Well, those graves were very shallow. If, as time went on, the brothers found themselves choking to death . . . and still nobody had come to let them out . . . they might begin to shriek and batter and pound in their coffins. It was just possible Drayman might have seen the loose earth trembling or heard the last scream from inside."

Hadley got out a handkerchief and mopped his face.

"Would any swine—" he said in an incredulous voice,

which trailed away. "No. We're running off the rails, Fell. It's all imagination. It can't be! Besides, in that case they wouldn't have climbed up out of their graves. They'd be dead."

"Would they?" said Dr. Fell, vacantly. "You're forgetting the spade."

"What spade?"

"The spade that some poor devil in his fear or hurry left behind when he'd dug the grave. Prisons, even the worst prisons, don't permit *that* sort of negligence. They would send back after it. Man, I can see that business in every detail, even if I haven't one shred of proof to support it! Think of every word that crazy Pierre Fley said to Grimaud at the Warwick Tavern, and see if it doesn't fit. . . . Back come a couple of armed, hard-headed warders looking for that discarded spade. They see or hear what Grimaud was afraid Drayman would see or hear. They either tumble to the trick or else they act in common humanity. The coffins are smashed open; the two brothers are rolled out, fainting and bloody, but alive."

"And no hue and cry after Grimaud? Why, they'd have torn Hungary apart looking for the man who had escaped and—"

"H'mf, yes. I thought of that too, and asked about it. The prison authorities would have done just that . . . if they weren't being so bitterly attacked that their heads were in danger at the time. What do you think the attackers would have said if it became known that, through carelessness, they allowed a thing like that to happen? Much better to keep quiet about it, hey? Much better to shove those two brothers into close confinement and keep quiet about the third."

"It's all theory," said Hadley, after a pause. "But, if it's true, I could come close to believing in evil spirits. God knows Grimaud got exactly what he deserved. And we've got to go on trying to find his murderer just the same. If that's the whole story—"

"Of course it's not the whole story!" said Dr. Fell. "It's not the whole story even if it's true, and that's the worst part. You talk of evil spirits. I tell you that in some way I can't fathom there's a worse evil spirit than Grimaud; and that's X, that's the hollow man, that's brother Henri." He pointed out with his stick. "Why? Why does Pierre Fley admit he fears him? It would be reasonable for Grimaud to fear his enemy; but why does Fley even fear his brother and his ally against the common antagonist? Why is a skilled illusionist afraid of illusion, unless this gentle brother Henri is as rattlebrained as a criminal lunatic and as clever as Satan?"

Hadley put his notebook in his pocket and buttoned up his coat.

"*You* go home if you like," he said. "We've finished here. But I'm going after Fley. Whoever the other brother is, Fley knows. And he's going to tell, I can promise you that. I'll have a look round Drayman's room, but I don't anticipate much. Fley is the key to this cipher, and he's going to lead us to the murderer. Ready?"

They did not learn it until the next morning; but Fley, as a matter of fact, was already dead. He had been shot down with the same pistol that killed Grimaud. And the murderer was invisible before the eyes of witnesses, and still he had left no footprint in the snow.

THE MURDER BY MAGIC 11

When Dr. Fell hammered on the door at nine o'clock next morning, both his guests were in a drowsy state. Rampole had got very little sleep the night before. When he and the doctor returned at half-past one, Dorothy had been hopping with eagerness to hear all the details, and her husband was not at all unwilling to tell them. They equipped themselves with cigarettes and beer, and retired to their room, where Dorothy piled a heap of sofa pillows on the floor like Sherlock Holmes, and sat there with a glass of beer and a sinister expression of wisdom while her husband stalked about the room, declaiming. Her views were vigorous but hazy. She rather liked the descriptions of Mme Dumont and Drayman, but took a violent dislike to Rosette Grimaud. Even when Rampole quoted Rosette's remarks to the debating society, a motto of which they both approved, she was not mollified.

"All the same, you mark my words," said Dorothy, pointing her cigarette at him wisely, "that funny-faced blonde is mixed up in it somehow. She's a wrong un, old boy. I mean she wants ber-lud. Bah! I'll bet she wouldn't even make a good—um—courtesan, to use her own terms. And if I had ever treated you the way she treats Boyd Mangan, and you hadn't landed me a sock under the jaw, I'd never have spoken to either of us again . . . if you see my meaning?"

"Let's omit the personal," said Rampole. "Besides, what's she done to Mangan? Nothing that I can see. And you don't seriously think she would kill her father, even if she hadn't been locked in the front room?"

"N-no, because I don't see how she could have put on that fancy costume and fooled Mrs. Dumont," said Dorothy, with an expression of great profundity in her bright dark eyes. "But I'll tell you how it is, Mrs. Dumont and Drayman are both innocent. As for Mills—well, Mills does sound rather a prig, but then your view is highly coloured because you don't like science or the Vision of the Future. And you'll admit he does sound as though he's telling the truth?"

"Yes."

She smoked reflectively. " 'M. I'm getting tremendous ideas. The people I'm most suspicious of, and the ones against whom it'd be easiest to make out a case, are the two you haven't seen—Pettis and Burnaby."

"*What?*"

"Like this. The objection to Pettis is that he's too small, isn't it? I should have thought Dr. Fell's erudition would have got it like a shot. I was thinking of a story. . . . I can't remember where I've read it, but it comes in one shape or another into several mediaeval tales. J'you remember? There's always an enormous figure in armour, with its vizor down, who rides in a tournament and smacks everybody flat. Then along comes ye mightiest knight to joust against it. Down he rides with a bang, hits the tall champion's helmet squarely in the middle of the vizor, and to everybody's horror knocks the head clean off. Then up pipes a voice from inside the shell, and they discover it belongs to a handsome young lad who's not tall enough to fill up the suit of armour. . . ."

Rampole looked at her. "Beloved," said he, with dignity, "this is pure drivelling. This is beyond all question the looniest idea which . . . Look here, are you seriously trying to tell me Pettis might walk about with a dummy head and shoulders rigged up on him?"

"You're too conservative," she said, wrinkling her nose.

"*I* think it's a jolly-good idea. And do you want confirmation? Right! Didn't Mills himself comment on the shiny look about the back of the head, and say it looked as though the whole head were made of papier-maché? What have you got to say to that?"

"I say it's a nightmare. Haven't you any more practical idea?"

"Yes!" said Dorothy, wriggling. She had obviously just been struck with the inspiration, but she passed it off as an old one. "It's about the impossible situation. *Why* didn't the murderer want to leave any footprints? You're all going after the most horribly complicated reasons. And, anyway, they generally end in your thinking that the murderer just wants to have some fun with the police. Rats, darling! What's the only real reason, the first reason anybody would think of outside a murder case, why a man mightn't want to leave any footprints? Why, because the footprints would be so distinctive that they'd lead straight to him! Because he had a deformity or something which would hang him if he left a footprint. . . ."

"And—?"

"And, you tell me," she said, "this chap Burnaby has a club foot."

When, towards daylight, Rampole at last fell asleep, he was haunted by images in which Burnaby's club foot seemed even more sinister than the man who wore a dummy head. It was all nonsense; but it was a disturbing kind of nonsense to mingle in a dream with the puzzle of the three graves.

He struggled out of bed when Dr. Fell knocked at the door towards nine o'clock on Sunday morning; he shaved and dressed hastily, and stumbled down through a silent house. It was an unearthly hour for Dr. Fell (or anybody else) to be stirring, and Rampole knew some fresh deviltry had broken overnight. The hallways were chilly; even the great library, where a roaring fire had been lighted, had that unreal look which all things assume when you get up at daybreak to catch a train. Breakfast—for three—was set out in the embrasure of the bay window overlooking the terrace. It was a leaden day, the sky already moving with snow. Dr. Fell, fully dressed, sat at the table with his head in his hands and stared at a newspaper.

"Brother Henri—" he rumbled, and struck the paper. "Oh yes. He's at it again. Hadley just phoned with more

details, and he'll be here any minute. Look at this for a
starter. If we thought we'd got a hard problem on our
hands last night—oh, Bacchus, look at *this* one! I'm like
Drayman—I can't believe it. It's crowded Grimaud's
murder clean off the front page. Fortunately, they haven't
spotted the connection between 'em, or else Hadley's given
'em the word to keep off. Here!"

Rampole, as coffee was poured out for him, saw the
headlines. "MAGICIAN MURDERED BY MAGIC!" said
one, which must have given great pleasure to the writer.
"RIDDLE OF CAGLIOSTRO STREET." " 'THE
SECOND BULLET IS FOR YOU!' "

"Cagliostro Street?" the American repeated. "Where in
the name of sanity is Cagliostro Street? I thought I'd heard
of some funny street names, but this one—"

"You'd never hear of it ordinarily," grunted Dr. Fell.
"It's one of those streets hidden behind streets, that you
only stumble on by accident when you're looking for a
short-cut, and you're startled to find a whole community
lost in the middle of London. . . . Anyway, Cagliostro
Street is not more than three minutes' walk from Grimaud's
house. It's a little cul-de-sac behind Guilford Street, on the
other side of Russell Square. So far as I remember, it has a
lot of tradesmen's shops overflowing from Lamb's Conduit
Street, and the rest lodging-houses. . . . Brother Henri left
Grimaud's place after the shooting, walked over there, hung
about for a little time, and then completed his work."

Rampole ran his eye down the story:

The body of the man found murdered last night
in Cagliostro Street, W. C. 1, has been identified as
that of Pierre Fley, a French conjuror and illusionist.
Although he had been performing for some months
at a music-hall in Commercial Road, E.C., he took
lodgings two weeks ago in Cagliostro Street. About
half-past ten last night, he was found shot to death
under circumstances which seem to indicate that a
magician was murdered by magic. Nothing was seen
and no trace left—three witnesses testify—although
they all distinctly heard a voice say, *"The second
bullet is for you."*

Cagliostro Street is two hundred yards long, and
ends in a blank brick wall. There are a few shops
at the beginning of the street, closed at that time,

although a few night lights were burning, and the pavements were swept in front of them. But, beginning some twenty yards on, there was unbroken snow on the pavement and the street.

Mr. Jesse Short and Mr. R. G. Blackwin, Birmingham visitors to London, were on their way to visit a friend with lodgings near the end of the street. They were walking on the right-hand pavement, and had their backs to the mouth of the street. Mr. Blackwin, who was turning round to make sure of the numbers on the doors, noticed a man walking some distance behind them. This man was walking slowly and rather nervously, looking round him as though he expected to see some one near. He was walking in the middle of the street. But the light was dim, and, aside from seeing that he was tall and wore a slouch-hat, neither Mr. Short nor Mr. Blackwin noticed anything else. At the same time, P. C. Henry Withers—whose beat was along Lamb's Conduit Street—reached the entrance to Cagliostro Street. He saw the man walking in the snow, but glanced back again without noticing him. And in the space of three or four seconds the thing happened.

Mr. Short and Mr. Blackwin heard behind them a cry that was nearer a scream. They then heard some one distinctly say the words, "The second bullet is for you," and a laugh followed by a muffled pistol-shot. As they whirled round, the man behind staggered, screamed again, and pitched forward on his face.

The street, they could see, was absolutely empty from end to end. Moreover, the man was walking in the middle of it, and both state that there were no footprints in the snow but his own. This is confirmed by P. C. Withers, who came running from the mouth of the street. In the light from a jeweller's window, they could see the victim lying face downward, his arms spread out, and blood jetting from a bullet-hole under his left shoulder blade. The weapon—a long-barrelled .38 Colt revolver, of a pattern thirty years out of date—had been thrown away some ten feet behind.

Despite the words they had all heard, and the gun lying at some distance, the witnesses thought because of the empty street that he must have shot himself. They saw that the man was still breathing, and carried him to the office of Dr. M. R. Jenkins near the end of the street, while the constable made certain there were no footprints anywhere. The victim, however, died, without speaking, not long afterwards.

Then occurred the most startling disclosures. The man's overcoat round the wound was burnt and singed black, showing that the weapon must have been pressed against his back or held only a few inches away. But Dr. Jenkins gave it as his opinion— later confirmed by the police—that suicide was not possible. No man, he stated, could have held any pistol in such a way as to shoot himself through the back at that angle, and more especially with the long-barrelled weapon which was used. It was murder, but an incredible murder. If the man had been shot from some distance away, from a window or door, the absence of a murderer and even the absence of footprints would mean nothing. But he was shot by some one who stood beside him, spoke to him, and vanished.

No papers or marks of identification could be found in the man's clothes, and nobody seemed to know him. After some delay he was sent to the mortuary—

"But what about the officer Hadley sent round to pick him up?" Rampole asked. "Couldn't he identify the man?"

"He did identify him, later," growled Dr. Fell. "But the whole hullabaloo was over by the time he got there. He ran into the policeman, Hadley says, when Withers was still making inquiries from door to door. Then he put two and two together. Meantime, the man Hadley had sent to the music-hall also in quest of Fley had phoned through that Fley wasn't there. Fley had coolly told the theatre manager he had no intention of doing his turn that night, and walked out with some sort of cryptic remark. . . . Well, to identify the body at the mortuary they got hold of Fley's landlord in Cagliostro Street. And, to make sure it was the same person, they asked for somebody from the music-hall to come along. An Irishman with an Italian name, who was also on the bill but couldn't do his turn that night because of some sort of injury, volunteered. Harrumph, yes. It was

Fley, and he's dead, and we're in a hell of a mess. Bah!"

"And this story," cried Rampole, "is actually true?"

He was answered by Hadley, whose ring at the bell was belligerent. Hadley stamped in, carrying his briefcase like a tomahawk, and released some of his grievances before he would even touch bacon and eggs.

"It's true, right enough," he said, grimly, stamping his heels before the fire. "I let the papers splash it out so we could broadcast an appeal for information from anybody who knew Pierre Fley or his —— —— —— brother Henri. By God! Fell, I'm losing my mind! That damned nickname of yours sticks in my head, and I can't get rid of it. I find myself referring to brother Henri as though I knew that was his real name. I find myself getting imaginary pictures of brother Henri. At least we soon ought to know what his real name is. I've cabled to Bucharest. Brother Henri! Brother Henri! We've picked up his trail again, and lost it again. Bro—"

"For Lord's sake go easy!" urged Dr. Fell, puffing uneasily. "Don't rave; it's bad enough now. I suppose you've been at it nearly all night? And got some more information? H'mf, yes. Now sit down and console the inner man. Then we can approach in—humph—a philosophic spirit, hey?"

Hadley said he wanted nothing to eat. But, after he had finished two helpings, drunk several cups of coffee, and lighted a cigar, he mellowed into a more normal mood.

"Now, then! Let's begin," he said, squaring himself determinedly as he took papers from the briefcase, "by checking over this newspaper account point by point— as well as what it doesn't say. Hum! First, as to these chaps Blackwin and Short. They're reliable; besides, it's certain neither of them is brother Henri. We wired Birmingham, and found they've been well known in their district all their lives. They're prosperous, sound people who wouldn't go off the handle as witnesses in a thing like this. The constable, Withers, is a thoroughly reliable man; in fact, he's painstaking to the extent of a vice. If those people say they didn't see anybody, they may have been deceived, but at least they were telling the truth as they knew it."

"Deceived . . . how?"

"*I don't know,*" growled Hadley, drawing a deep breath and shaking his head grimly, "except that they must have been. I had a brief look at the street, although I didn't go through Fley's room. It's no Piccadilly Circus for illumination, but at least it's not dark enough for any man in his five wits to be mistaken about what he saw. Shadows —I don't know! As to footprints, if Withers swears there weren't any, I'll take his word for it. And there we are."

Dr. Fell only grunted, and Hadley went on:

"Now, about the weapon. Fley was shot with a bullet from that Colt .38, and so was Grimaud. There were two exploded cartridge-cases in the magazine, only two bullets, and bro—and the murderer scored with each. The modern revolver, you see, ejects its shells like an automatic; but this gun is so old that we haven't a ghost of a chance of being able to trace it. It's in good working order, it fires modern steel-jacket ammunition, but somebody has kept it hidden away for years."

"He didn't forget anything, Harry didn't. Well. Did you trace Fley's movements?"

"Yes. He was going to call on Henri."

Dr. Fell's eyes snapped open. *"Eh?* Look here, you mean you've got a lead about—"

"It's the only lead we have got. And," said Hadley, with bitter satisfaction, "if it doesn't produce results within a couple of hours I'll eat that briefcase. You remember, I told you over the phone that Fley had refused to perform and walked out of the theatre last night? Yes. My plainclothes officer got the story both from the theatre-manager, fellow named Isaacstein, and from an acrobat named O'Rourke, who was friendlier with Fley than anybody else and identified the body later.

"Saturday, naturally, is the big night down Limehouse way. The theatre runs continuous variety from one in the afternoon until eleven at night. Business was booming in the evening, and Fley's first night turn was to begin at eight-fifteen. About five minutes before then, O'Rourke—who had broken his wrist and couldn't go on that night—sneaked down into the cellar for a smoke. They have a coal furnace for hot-water pipes there."

Hadley unfolded a closely written sheet.

"Here is what O'Rourke said, just as Somers took it down and O'Rourke later initialled.

"The minute I got through the asbestos door and downstairs, I heard a noise like somebody smashing up kindling-wood. Then I did get a jump. The fur-

nace door was open, and there was old Loony with a
hatchet in his hand, busting hell out of the few
properties he owned and shoving them all in the fire.
I said, 'For cat's sake, Loony, what are you doing?'
He said, in that queer way of his, 'I am destroying
my equipment, Signor Pagliacci.' (I use the name of
Pagliacci the Great, you understand, but then he always talked like that, so help me!) Well, he said,
'My work is finished; I shall not need them any
longer'—and, zingo! in went his faked ropes and the
hollow bamboo rods for his cabinet. I said, 'Loony,
great goddelmighty, pull yourself together.' I said,
'You go on in a few minutes, and you're not even
dressed.' He said: 'Didn't I tell you? I am going to
see my brother. He will do something that will settle
an old affair for both of us.'

"Well, he walked over to the stairs and then
turned around sharp. Loony's got a face like a white
horse, Lord pity me for saying it, and it had a queer
creepy look with the fire from the furnace shining on
it. He said, 'In case anything happens to me after he
has done the business, you will find my brother in
the same street where I myself live. That is not where
he really resides, but he has taken a room there.'
Just then down comes old Isaacstein, looking for
him. He couldn't believe his ears when he heard
Loony refuse to go on. There was a row. Isaacstein
bawled, 'You know what'll happen if you don't go
on?' And Loony says, as pleasant as a three-card man,
'Yes, I know what will happen.' Then he lifts his hat
very courteously, and says, 'Good night, gentlemen.
I am going back to my grave.' And up the stairs this
lunatic walks without another word."

Hadley folded up the sheet and replaced it in his
briefcase.

"Yes, he was a good showman," said Dr. Fell, struggling to light his pipe. "It seems a pity brother Henri had
to . . . what then?"

"Now, it may or may not mean anything to track
Henri down in Cagliostro Street, but we're sure to get
his temporary hideout," Hadley went on. "The question occurred to me, where was Fley *going* when he was
shot? Where was he walking to? Not to his own room.

He lived at number 2B, at the beginning of the street, and he was going in the other direction. When he was shot he was a little over halfway down, between number 18 on his right and number 21 on his left—but in the middle of the street, of course. That's a good trail, and I've sent Somers out on it. He's to turn out every house past the middle, looking for *any* new or suspicious or otherwise noticeable lodger. Landladies being what they are, we shall probably get dozens, but that doesn't matter."

Dr. Fell, who was slouched as far down in the big chair as the bulk of his weight would allow, ruffled his hair.

"Yes, but I shouldn't concentrate too much on any end of the street. Rip 'em all up, say I. You see, suppose Fley was running from somebody, trying to get away from somebody, when he was shot?"

"Running away into a blind alley?"

"It's *wrong!* I tell you it's all wrong!" roared the doctor, hoisting himself up in the chair. "Not merely because I can't see anywhere a chink or glimmer of reason (which I freely admit), but because the simplicity of the thing is so maddening. It's no matter of hocus-pocus within four walls. There's a street. There's a man walking along it in the snow. Scream, whispered words, bang! Witnesses turn, and murderer gone. Where? Did the pistol come flying through the air like a thrown knife, explode against Fley's back, and spin away?"

"Rubbish!"

"I know it's rubbish. But I still ask the question," nodded Dr. Fell. He let his eye-glasses drop and pressed his hands over his eyes. "I say, how does this new development affect the Russell Square group? I mean, considering that everybody is officially under suspicion, can't we eliminate a few of those? Even if they were telling us lies at Grimaud's house, they still weren't out hurling Colt revolvers in the middle of Cagliostro Street."

The superintendent's face was ugly with sarcasm. "Now there's another bit of luck for us, kindly notice. I forgot that! We could eliminate one or two—if the Cagliostro Street business had occurred a little later, or even a little earlier. It didn't. Fley was shot at just ten-twenty-five. In other words, about fifteen minutes after Grimaud. Brother Henri took no chances. He anticipated exactly what we would do: send out a man to pick up Fley as soon as the alarm was given. Only brother Henri (or somebody) anticipated us in both ways. He was there with his little vanishing-trick."

" 'Or somebody'?" repeated Dr. Fell. "Your mental processes are interesting. Why 'or somebody'?"

"That's what I'm getting at—the unfortunate, un-observed fifteen minutes just after Grimaud's murder. I'm learning new wrinkles in crime, Fell. If you want to commit a couple of shrewd murders, don't commit one and then hang about waiting for the dramatic moment to pull off the other. Hit once—and then hit again instantly, while the watchers are still so muddled by the first that nobody, including the police, can definitely remember who was where at a given time. Can we?"

"Now, now," growled Dr. Fell, to conceal the fact that he couldn't. "It ought to be easy to work out a time-table. Let's see. We arrived at Grimaud's . . . when?"

Hadley was jotting on a slip of paper. "Just as Mangan jumped out the window, which couldn't have been more than two minutes after the shot. Say ten-twelve. We ran upstairs, found the door locked, got the pliers, and opened the door. Say three minutes more."

"Isn't that allowing a small margin of time?" Rampole interposed. "It seemed to me we were doing a good deal of tearing around."

"People often think so. In fact," said Hadley, "I thought so myself until I handled that Kynaston knifing case (remember, Fell?), where a damned clever killer depended for his alibi on the tendency of witnesses always to *over*-estimate time. That's because we think in minutes rather than seconds. Try it yourself. Put a watch on the table, shut your eyes, and look again when you think a minute is up. You'll probably look thirty seconds too soon. No, say three minutes here!" He scowled. "Mangan phoned, and the ambulance was round very quickly. Did you notice the address of that nursing-home, Fell?"

"No. I leave these sordid details to you," said Dr. Fell, with dignity. "Somebody said it was just round the corner, I remember. Humph. Ha."

"In Guilford Street, next to the Children's Hospital. In fact," said Hadley, "backed up against Cagliostro Street so closely that the back garden must be in line. . . . Well, say five minutes to get the ambulance to Russell Square. That's ten-twenty. And what about the next five minutes, the time just before the second murder, and the equally important five or ten or fifteen minutes afterwards? Rosette Grimaud, alone, rode over in the ambulance with her father, and didn't return for some time. Mangan, alone, was downstairs doing some telephoning for me, and didn't come upstairs until Rosette returned. I don't seriously consider either of 'em, but take it all for the sake of argument. Drayman? Nobody saw Drayman all this time and for a long while afterwards. As to Mills and the Dumont woman—h'm. Well, yes; I'm afraid it does clear them. Mills was talking to us all the earlier part of the time, until at least ten-thirty anyhow, and Madame Dumont joined him very shortly; they both stayed with us for a while. That tears it."

Dr. Fell chuckled.

"In fact," he said, reflectively, "we know exactly what we did before, no more and no less. The only people it clears are the ones we were sure were innocent, and who had to be telling the truth if we made any sanity of the story. Hadley, it's the cussedness of things in general which makes me raise my hat. By the way, did you get anything last night out of searching Drayman's room? And what about that blood?"

"Oh, it's human blood, right enough, but there was nothing in Drayman's room that gave a clue to it—or to anything else. There were several of those pasteboard masks, yes. But they were all elaborate affairs with whiskers and goggle eyes: more the sort of thing that would appeal to a kid. Nothing, anyway, in the—the plain pink style. There was a lot of stuff for kids' amateur theatricals, some old sparklers and pinwheels and the like, and a toy theatre. . . ."

"Penny plain and twopence coloured," said Dr. Fell, with a wheeze of reminiscent pleasure. "Gone forever the glory of childhood. Wow! The grandeur of a toy theatre! In my innocent childhood days, Hadley, when I came trailing clouds of glory to the view (a thesis, by the way, which might have been open to considerable debate on the part of my parents); in my childhood days, I say, I owned a toy theatre with sixteen changes of scenery. Half of 'em, I am pleased to say, were jail scenes. Why does the young imagination run so strongly to jail scenes, I wonder? Why—"

"What the hell's the matter with you?" demanded Hadley, staring. "Why the sentimentality?"

"Because I have suddenly got an idea," said Dr. Fell, gently. "And, oh, my sacred hat, what an idea!" He remained blinking at Hadley. "What about Drayman? Are you going to arrest him?"

"No. In the first place, I don't see how he could have done it, and I couldn't even get a warrant. In the second place—"

"You don't believe he's guilty?"

"H'm," grunted Hadley, with an innate caution about doubting anybody's innocence. "I don't say that, but I think he's likely to be less culpable than anybody else. Anyhow, we've got to get a move on! Cagliostro Street first, then to interview several people. Finally—"

They heard the door-bell ring, and a sleepy maid-servant tumbled down to answer it.

"There's a gentleman downstairs, sir," said Vida, poking her head into the room, "who says he wants to see either you or the superintendent. A Mr. Anthony Pettis, sir."

THE PICTURE 12

Dr. Fell, rumbling and chuckling and spilling ashes from his pipe like the Spirit of the Volcano, surged up to greet the visitor with a cordiality which seemed to put Mr. Anthony Pettis much more at his ease. Mr. Pettis bowed slightly to each of them.

"You must excuse me, gentlemen, for intruding so early," he said. "But I had to get it off my mind, and couldn't feel easy until I did. I understand you were—um—looking for me last night. And I had an unpleasant night of it, I can tell you." He smiled. "My one criminal adventure was when I forgot to renew a dog license, and my guilty conscience was all over me. Every time I went out with that confounded dog I thought every policeman in London was eyeing me in a sinister way. I began to slink. So in this case I thought I'd better hunt you out. They gave me this address at Scotland Yard."

Dr. Fell was already stripping off his guest's overcoat, with a gesture that nearly upset Mr. Pettis, and hurling him into a chair. Mr. Pettis grinned. He was a small, neat, starched man with a shiny bald head and a startlingly booming voice. He had prominent eyes, looking more shrewd with a wrinkle of concentration between them, a humorous mouth and a square cleft chin. It was a bony face—imaginative, ascetic, rather nervous. When he spoke he had a trick of sitting forward in his chair, clasping his hands, and frowning at the floor.

"It's a bad business about Grimaud," he said, and hesitated. "Naturally I'll follow the formula of saying I wish to do everything I can to help. In this case it happens to be true." He smiled again. "Er—do you want me sitting with my face to the light, or what? Outside novels, this is my first experience with the police."

"Nonsense," said Dr. Fell, introducing everybody. "I've been wanting to meet you for some time; we've written a few things on the same lines. What'll you drink? Whisky? Brandy and soda?"

"It's rather early," said Pettis, doubtfully. "Still, if you insist—thanks! I'm very familiar with your book on the supernatural in English fiction, Doctor; you're a great deal more popular than I shall ever be. And it's sound." He frowned. "It's very sound. But I don't entirely agree with you (or Dr. James) that a ghost in a story should always be malignant. . . ."

"Of course it should always be malignant. The more malignant," thundered Dr. Fell, screwing his own face up into a tolerably hideous leer, "then the better. I want no sighing of gentle airs round *my* couch. I want no sweet whispers o'er Eden. I want BLOOD!" He looked at Pettis in a way which seemed to give the latter an uncomfortable idea that it was his blood. "Harrumph. Ha. I will give you rules, sir. The ghost should be malignant. It should never speak. It should never be transparent, but solid. It should never hold the stage for long, but appear in brief vivid flashes like the poking of a face round a corner. It should never appear in too much light. It should have an old, an academic or ecclesiastical background; a flavour of cloisters or Latin manuscripts. There is an unfortunate tendency nowadays to sneer at old libraries or ancient ruins; to say that the really horrible phantom would appear in a confectioner's shop or at a lemonade stand. This is what they call applying the 'modern test.' Very well; apply the test of real life. Now, people in real life honestly *have* been frightened out of their five wits in old ruins or churchyards.

Nobody would deny that. But, until somebody in actual life really does scream out and faint at the sight of something at a lemonade stand (other, of course, than that beverage itself), then there is nothing to be said for this theory except that it is rubbish."

"Some people would say," observed Pettis, cocking one eyebrow, "that the old ruins were rubbish. Don't you believe that good ghost stories can be written nowadays?"

"Of course they can be written nowadays, and there are more brilliant people to write 'em . . . if they would. The point is, they are afraid of the thing called Melodrama. So, if they can't eliminate the melodrama, they try to hide it by writing in such an oblique, upside-down way that nobody under heaven can understand what they are talking about. Instead of saying flat out what the character saw or heard, they try to give Impressions. It's as though a butler, in announcing guests at a ball, were to throw open the drawing-room doors and cry: 'Flicker of a top-hat, vacantly seen, or is it my complex fixed on the umbrella stand faintly gleaming?' Now, his employer might not find this satisfactory. He might want to know who in blazes was calling on him. Terror ceases to be terror if it has to be worked out like an algebra problem. It may be deplorable if a man is told a joke on Saturday night and suddenly bursts out laughing in church next morning. But it is much more deplorable if a man reads a terrifying ghost story on Saturday night, and two weeks later suddenly snaps his fingers and realizes that he ought to have been scared. Sir, I say now——"

For some time an irritated superintendent of the C.I.D. had been fuming and clearing his throat in the background. Now Hadley settled matters by slamming his fist down on the table.

"Easy on, will you?" he demanded. "We don't want to hear any lecture now. And it's Mr. Pettis who wants to do the talking. So——" When he saw Dr. Fell's puffings subside into a grin, he went on, smoothly, "As a matter of fact, it is a Saturday night I want to talk about; last night."

"And about a ghost?" Pettis inquired, whimsically. Dr. Fell's outburst had put him entirely at his ease. "The ghost who called on poor Grimaud?"

"Yes. . . . First, just as a matter of form, I must ask

you to give an account of your movements last night.
Especially between, say, nine-thirty and ten-thirty?"

Pettis put down his glass. His face had grown troubled
again. "Then you mean, Mr. Hadley—after all, I *am*
under suspicion?"

"The ghost said he was you. Didn't you know that?"

"Said he was. . . . Good God, no!" cried Pettis, spring-
ing up like a bald-headed jack-in-the-box. "Said he
was me? I mean—er—said he was—hang the grammar! I
want to know what you're talking about? What do you
mean?" He sat down quietly and stared as Hadley explained. But he fussed with his cuffs, fussed with his tie,
and several times nearly interrupted.

"Therefore, if you'll disprove it by giving an account
of your movements last night . . ." Hadley took out his
notebook.

"Nobody told me about this last night. I was at
Grimaud's after he was shot, but nobody told me," said
Pettis, troubled. "As for last night, I went to the theatre:
to His Majesty's Theatre."

"You can establish that, of course."

Pettis frowned. "I don't know. I sincerely hope so.
I can tell you about the play, although I don't suppose
that's much good. Oh yes; and I think I've still got my
ticket stub somewhere, or my program. But you'll want
to know if I met anybody I knew. Eh? No, I'm afraid
not—unless I could find somebody who remembered
me. I went alone. You see, every one of the few friends
I have runs in a set groove. We know exactly where he
is at most times, especially Saturday evenings, and we
don't try to change the orbit." There was a wry twinkle
in his eye. "It's—it's a kind of respectable Bohemianism, not to say stodgy Bohemianism."

"That," said Hadley, "would interest the murderer.
What are these orbits?"

"Grimaud always works . . . excuse me; I can't get
used to the idea that he's dead . . . always works until
eleven. Afterwards you could disturb him as much as
you liked; he's a night owl; but not before. Burnaby
always plays poker at his club. Mangan, who's a sort of
acolyte, is with Grimaud's daughter. He's with her
most evenings, for that matter. I go to the theatre or
the films, but not always. I'm the exception."

"I see. And after the theatre last night? What time did you get out?"

"Near enough to eleven or a little past. I was restless. I thought I might drop in on Grimaud and have a drink with him. And—well, you know what happened. Mills told me. I asked to see you, or whoever was in charge. After I had waited downstairs for a long time, without anybody paying any attention to me,"—he spoke rather snappishly—"I went across to the nursing-home to see how Grimaud was getting on. I got there just as he died. Now, Mr. Hadley, I know this is a terrible business, but I will swear to you—"

"Why did you ask to see me?"

"I was at the public house when this man Fley uttered his threat, and I thought I might be of some help. Of course I supposed at the time it was Fley who had shot him; but this morning I see in the paper—"

"Just a minute! Before we go on to that, I understand that whoever imitated you used all your tricks of address, and so on, correctly? Good! Then who in your circle (or out of it) would you suspect of being able to do that?"

"Or wanting to do it," the other said, sharply.

He sat back, being careful about the knife-crease of his trousers. His nervousness was clearly giving way before the twistings of a dry, curious, insatiable brain; an abstract problem intrigued him. Putting his fingertips together, he stared out of the long windows.

"Don't think I'm trying to evade your question, Mr. Hadley," he said, with an abrupt little cough. "Frankly, I can't think of anybody. But this puzzle bothers me apart from the danger, in a way, to myself. If you think my ideas suffer from too much subtlety, or from too much plain damned nonsense, I'll put it up to Dr. Fell. Let's suppose, for the sake of argument, that I am the murderer."

He looked mockingly at Hadley, who had straightened up.

"Hold on! I am not the murderer, but let's suppose it. I go to kill Grimaud in some outlandish disguise (which, by the way, I *would* rather commit a murder than be seen wearing). Hum! I indulge in all the rest of the tomfoolery. Is it likely that, after all these things, I would blatantly sing out my real name to those young people?"

He paused, tapping his fingers.

"That's the first view, the short-sighted view. But the very shrewd investigator would answer: 'Yes, a clever murderer might do just that. It would be the most effective way of bamboozling all the people who had jumped to the first conclusion. He changed his voice a very little, just enough so that people would remember it afterwards. He spoke as Pettis because he wanted people to think it *wasn't* Pettis.' Had you thought of that?"

"Oh yes," said Dr. Fell, beaming broadly. "It was the first thing I did think of."

Pettis nodded. "Then you will have thought of the answer to that, which clears me either way. If I were to do a thing like that, it isn't my voice I should have altered slightly. If the hearers accepted it to begin with, they might not later have the doubts I wanted them to have. *But,*" he said, pointing, "what I should have done was to make one slip in my speech. I should have said something unusual, something wrong and obviously not like myself, which later they would have remembered. And this the visitor didn't do. His imitation was too thorough, which seems to excuse me. Whether you take the forthright view or the subtle one, I can plead not guilty either because I'm not a fool or because I am."

Hadley laughed. His amused gaze travelled from Pettis to Dr. Fell, and he could keep his worried expression no longer.

"You two are birds of a feather," he said. "I like these gyrations. But I'll tell you from practical experience, Mr. Pettis, that a criminal who tried anything like that would find himself in the soup. The police wouldn't stop to consider whether he was a fool or whether he wasn't. The police would take the forthright view—and hang him."

"As you would hang me," said Pettis, "if you could find contributory evidence?"

"Exactly."

"Well—er—that's frank, anyhow," said Pettis, though he seemed acutely uneasy and startled at the reply. "Er—shall I go on? You've rather taken the wind out of my sails."

"Go on, certainly," urged the superintendent, with an affable gesture. "We can get ideas even from a clever man. What else have you to suggest?"

Whether or not that was a deliberate sting, it had a result nobody had expected. Pettis smiled, but his eyes had a fixed quality and his face seemed to become more bony.

"Yes, I think you can," he agreed. "Even ideas you should have had yourselves. Let me take one instance. You—or somebody—got himself quoted at some length in all the papers this morning, about Grimaud's murder. You showed how the murderer was careful to ensure unbroken snow for his vanishing-trick, whatever it was. He could be sure that it would snow last night, lay all his plans accordingly, and gamble on waiting until the snow stopped for the working of his scheme. In any event, he could reasonably depend on there being some snow. Is that correct?"

"I said something of the sort, yes. What of it?"

"Then I think you should have remembered," Pettis answered, evenly, "that the weather forecast said he could do nothing of the kind. Yesterday's weather forecast announced that there would be no snow at all."

"Oh, Bacchus!" boomed Dr. Fell, and brought his fist down on the table after a pause in which he blinked at Pettis. "Well done! I never thought of it. Hadley, this changes things altogether! This—"

Pettis relaxed. He took out a cigarette-case and opened it. "Of course, there is an objection. I mean, you can make the obvious retort that the murderer knew it was bound to snow because the weather forecast said it wouldn't. But in that case *you'd* be the one who took subtlety to the edge of comedy. I can't follow it so far. Fact is, I think the weather forecast comes in for as many untrue jeers as the telephone service. It dropped a brick in this instance, yes . . . but that doesn't matter. Don't you believe me? Look up last night's papers and see."

Hadley swore, and then grinned.

"Sorry," he said. "I didn't mean to touch you on the raw, but I'm glad I did. Yes, it does seem to alter matters. Blast it, if a man intended to commit a crime that depended on snow, he'd certainly treat the forecast with some sort of consideration." Hadley drummed on the table. "Never mind; we'll come back to that. I seriously ask for ideas now."

"That's all, I'm afraid. Criminology is more in Burnaby's line than in mine. I only happened to notice," Pettis admitted, with a jeering look at his own clothes, "so as to decide whether I ought to wear overshoes. Habit! . . . As

to the person who imitated my voice, why try to implicate
me? I'm a harmless enough old codger, I assure you. I
don't fit into the rôle of gigantic nemesis. The only reason
I can think of is that I'm the only one of the group who
has no definite orbit on Saturday night and might not be
able to prove an alibi. But as to who could have done it
. . . Any good mimic could have pulled it off; still, who
knew just how I addressed those people?"

"What about the circle at the Warwick Tavern? There
were others besides the ones we've heard about, weren't
there?"

"Oh yes. There were two other irregulars. But I can't
see either as a candidate. There's old Mornington, who
has had a post at the Museum for over fifty years; he's
got a cracked tenor that would never pass for me. There's
Swayle, but I believe he was speaking on the wireless last
night, about ant life or something, and should have an
alibi. . . ."

"Speaking at what time?"

"Nine forty-five or thereabouts, I believe, although
I wouldn't swear to it. Besides, neither of them ever
visited Grimaud's house.—And casual drifters at the
pub? Well, some may have listened or sat down at the
back of the room, though nobody ever joined the conversation. I suppose that's your best lead, even if it's a
very thin one." Pettis took out a cigarette and closed the
case with a snap. "Yes. We'd better *decide* it was an unknown quantity, or we shall be in all kinds of quicksand,
eh? Burnaby and I were Grimaud's only close friends. But
I didn't do it, and Burnaby was playing cards."

Hadley looked at him. "I suppose Mr. Burnaby really
was playing cards?"

"I don't know," the other admitted, with flat candour.
"But I'll give you odds he was, all the same. Burnaby's no
fool. And a man would have to be rather an outstanding
fathead to commit a murder on the one night when his
absence from a certain group would be certain to be
noticed."

Clearly this impressed the superintendent more than
anything Pettis had yet said. He continued to drum on the
table, scowling. Dr. Fell was occupied with some obscure,
cross-eyed meditation of his own. Pettis looked curiously
from one to the other of them.

"If I have given you food for thought, gentlemen—?"

he suggested, and Hadley became brisk.

"Yes, yes! No end! Now, about Burnaby: you know he painted the picture which Dr. Grimaud bought to defend himself?"

"To defend himself? How? From what?"

"We don't know. I was hoping you might be able to explain it." Hadley studied him. "The taste for making cryptic remarks seems to run in his family. Do you know anything about his family, by the way?"

Pettis was evidently puzzled. "Well, Rosette is a very charming girl. Er—though I shouldn't say she had a taste for making cryptic remarks. Quite the contrary. She's a little too modern for my taste." His forehead wrinkled. "I never knew Grimaud's wife; she's been dead some years. But I still don't see—"

"Never mind. What do you think of Drayman?"

Pettis chuckled. "Old Hubert Drayman is the most unsuspicious man I ever met. So unsuspicious that some people think it hides a deep and devilish cunning. Excuse me, but have you got him on the carpet? If you have, I should forget it."

"We'll go back to Burnaby, then. Do you know how he came to paint that picture, or when he did it, or anything about it?"

"I think he did it a year or two ago. I remember it particularly, because it was the biggest canvas at his studio; he used it as a screen or a partition, turned up endways, whenever he needed one. I asked him once what it was intended to represent. He said, 'An imaginative conception of something I never saw.' It had some French name, *Dans l'Ombre des Montagnes du Sel,* or something of the sort." He stopped tapping the still unlighted cigarette on the case. His curious, restless brain was probing again. "Hullo! Now that I remember it, Burnaby said, 'Don't you like it? It gave Grimaud a hell of a turn when he saw it.'"

"Why?"

"I paid no attention. I naturally supposed it was some joke or piece of bragging; he laughed when he said it, and Burnaby's like that. But the thing had been lying about the studio, collecting dust, for such a long time that I was surprised when Grimaud came charging in on Friday morning and asked for it."

Hadley leaned forward sharply. "You were there then?"

"At the studio? Yes. I'd dropped in early for some reason or other—I forget what. Grimaud came stumping in . . ."

"Upset?"

"Yes. N-no. Say excited." Pettis reflected, studying Hadley covertly. "Grimaud said, with that machine-gun snap of his, 'Burnaby, where's your salt-mountain picture? I want it. What's your price?' Burnaby looked at him in a queer way. He came hobbling over and pointed to the picture and said, 'The thing's yours, man, if you want it; take it.' Grimaud said, 'No, I have a use for it and I insist on buying it.' Well, when Burnaby named some fool price like ten shillings, Grimaud quite solemnly got out a cheque-book and wrote a cheque for ten shillings. He would say nothing except that he had a place on the wall where it ought to go, in his study. That's all. He took the picture downstairs, and I got him a cab to take it away in. . . ."

"Was it wrapped up?" asked Dr. Fell, sharply; so sharply that Pettis jumped a little.

Dr. Fell had been showing more interest, not to say fierce concentration, in this recital than in anything Pettis had yet said. The doctor was bending forward with his hands clasped over his stick, and Pettis regarded him curiously.

"I wonder why you ask that?" he said. "It's what I was just going to mention—the fuss Grimaud made about wrapping it. He asked for paper, and Burnaby said, 'Where do you think I'd get a sheet of paper big enough to go round that? Why be ashamed of it? Take it as it is.' But Grimaud insisted on going downstairs and getting yards of brown paper off one of those rolls in somebody's shop. It seemed to annoy Burnaby a good deal."

"You don't know whether Grimaud went straight home with it?"

"No . . . I think he was going to have it framed, but I'm not sure."

Dr. Fell sat back with a grunt and let the subject go without more questions, in spite of Pettis's hints. Although Hadley kept on questioning for some time, nothing of importance was elicited so far as Rampole could see. On the personal side Pettis spoke guardedly; but there was, he said, little to conceal. There had been no friction in Grimaud's household, and none in the immediate circle except an antagonism between Mangan and Burnaby.

Burnaby, although nearly thirty years older, had a strong interest in Rosette Grimaud, at once lazy and jealous. Dr. Grimaud had said nothing about this; if anything, he encouraged it, although so far as Pettis could observe he made no objection to Mangan.

"But I think you'll find, gentlemen," concluded Pettis, as he rose to go when Big Ben was striking ten, "that all these are side issues. It would be difficult to associate the *crime passionel* with any of our group. As to the financial side of affairs, I can't tell you much, either. Grimaud was fairly well-to-do, I should think. His solicitors, I happen to know, are Tennant and Williams of Gray's Inn. . . . By the way, I wonder if you'd all have lunch with me on a dreary Sunday? I'm just at the other side of Russell Square, you know; I've had a suite of rooms at the Imperial for fifteen years. You're investigating in that neighbourhood, and it might be handy; besides, if Dr. Fell feels inclined to discuss ghost stories—?"

He smiled. The doctor cut in to accept before Hadley could refuse, and Pettis left with a much more jaunty air than he had worn at his entrance. Afterwards they all looked at each other.

"Well?" growled Hadley. "Straightforward enough, it seemed to me. Of course we'll check it up. The point, the impressive point, is: why should *any* of them commit a crime on the one night when absence would be bound to be noticed? We'll go after this chap Burnaby, but he sounds out of it, too, if only for that reason. . . ."

"And the weather forecast said it wouldn't snow," said Dr. Fell, with a kind of obstinacy. "Hadley, that shoots everything to blazes! It turns the whole case upside down somehow, but I don't see . . . Cagliostro Street! Let's go on to Cagliostro Street. Anywhere is better than this darkness."

Fuming, he stumped over after his cloak and shovel-hat.

THE SECRET FLAT 13

London, on the morning of a grey winter Sunday, was deserted to the point of ghostliness along miles of streets.

And Cagliostro Street, into which Hadley's car presently turned, looked as though it would never wake up.

Cagliostro Street, as Dr. Fell had said, contained a thin dingy overflow of both shops and rooming-houses. It was a backwater of Lamb's Conduit Street—which itself is a long and narrow thoroughfare, a shopping centre of its own, stretching north to the barrack-windowed quiet of Guilford Street, and south to the main artery of traffic along Theobald's Road. Towards the Guilford Street end on the west side, the entrance to Cagliostro Street is tucked between a stationer's and a butcher's. It looks so much like an alley that you would miss it altogether if you were not watching for the sign. Past these two buildings, it suddenly widens to an unexpected breadth, and runs straight for two hundred yards to a blank brick wall at the end.

This eerie feeling of streets in hiding, or whole rows of houses created by illusory magic to trick you, had never deserted Rampole in his prowlings through London. It was like wondering whether, if you walked out your own front door, you might not find the whole street mysteriously changed overnight, and strange faces grinning out of houses you had never seen before. He stood with Hadley and Dr. Fell at the entrance, staring down. The overflow of shops stretched only a little way on either side. They were all shuttered, or had their windows covered with a folding steel fretwork, with an air of defying customers as a fort would defy attackers. Even the gilt signs had an air of defiance. The windows were at all stages of cleanliness, from the bright gloss of a jeweller's farthest down on the right, to the grey murkiness of a tobacconist's nearest on the right: a tobacconist's that seemed to have dried up worse than ancient tobacco, shrunk together, and hidden itself behind news placards headlining news you never remembered having heard of. Beyond there were two rows of flat three-story houses in dark red brick, with window-frames in white or yellow, and drawn curtains of which a few (on the ground floor) showed a sportive bit of lace. They had darkened to the same hue with soot; they looked like one house except where iron railings went to the front doors from the lone line of area rails; they sprouted with hopeful signs announcing furnished rooms. Over them the chimney-pots stood up dark against a heavy grey sky. The snow had melted to patches of grey slush, despite a sharp wind that was swooping through the entrance and chasing a discarded newspaper with flaps and rustlings round a lamp-post.

"Cheerful," grunted Dr. Fell. He lumbered forward, and there were echoes of his footsteps. "Now, let's get this all straight before we attract attention. Show me where Fley was when he was hit. Stop a bit! Where did he live, by the way?"

Hadley pointed at the tobacconist's near which they were standing.

"Up over that place; just at the beginning of the street, as I told you. We'll go up presently—although Somers has been there, and says there's nothing at all. Now, come along and get roughly the middle point of the street . . ." He went ahead, pacing off a yard at a stride. "The swept pavements and the marked street ended somewhere about here; say, more or less, a hundred and fifty feet. Then unmarked snow. A good distance beyond that, nearer to another hundred and fifty . . . *here*."

He stopped and turned round slowly.

"Halfway up, centre of the roadway. You can see how broad the road is; walking there, he was a good thirty feet from any house on *either* side. If he'd been walking on the pavement, we might have constructed some wild theory of a person leaning out of a window or an areaway, with the gun fastened to the end of a pole or something, and—"

"Nonsense!"

"All right, nonsense; but what else can we think?" demanded Hadley, with some violence, and made a broad gesture with his briefcase. "As you said, yourself, here's the street; it's plain, simple, and impossible! I know there was no hanky-panky like that, but what *was* there? Also, the witnesses didn't see anything; and, if there had been anything, they must have seen it. Look here! Stay where you are, now, and keep facing the same direction." He paced again to a point some distance farther on, and turned after inspecting the numbers. Then he moved over to the right-hand pavement. "Here's where Blackwin and Short were when they heard the scream. You're walking along there in the middle of the street. I'm ahead of you. I whirl around—so. How far am I from you now?"

Rampole, who had drawn off from both of them, saw Dr. Fell standing big and alone in the middle of an empty rectangle.

"Shorter distance this time. Those two chaps," said the doctor, pushing back his shovel-hat, "were not much more than thirty feet ahead! Hadley, this is even rummier than I thought. He was in the middle of a snow desert. Yet they whirl round when they hear the shot . . . h'm . . . h'mf. . . ."

"Exactly. Next, as to lights. You're taking the part of Fley. On your right—a little distance ahead, and just beyond the door of number 18—you see a street lamp. A little distance behind, also on the right, you see that jeweller's window? Right. There was a light burning in that; not a bright one, but still it was there. Now, can you explain to me how two people, standing where I'm standing now, could possibly be mistaken about whether they saw anybody near Fley?"

His voice rose, and the street gave it a satiric echo. The discarded newspaper, caught again by an eddy of the wind, scuttled along with a sudden rush; and the wind tore with a hollow roar among chimney-pots as though it blew through a tunnel. Dr. Fell's black cloak flapped about him, and the ribbon on his eye-glasses danced wildly.

"Jeweller's—" he repeated, and stared. "Jeweller's! And a light in it. . . . Was there anybody there?"

"No. Withers thought of that and went to see. It was a show-light. The wire fretwork was stretched across both the window and the door; just as it is now. Nobody could have got in or out of there. Besides, it's much too far away from Fley."

Dr. Fell craned his neck round, and then went over to look owlishly into the protected window. Inside were displayed velvet trays of cheap rings and watches, an array of candlesticks, and in the middle a big round-hooded German clock with moving eyes in its sun of a face, which began to tinkle eleven. Dr. Fell stared at the moving eyes, which had an unpleasant effect of seeming to watch with idiot amusement the place where a man had been killed. It lent a touch of the horrible to Cagliostro Street. Then Dr. Fell stumped back to the middle of the street.

"But that," he said—obstinately, as though he were continuing an argument—"that is on the right-hand side of the street. And Fley was shot through the back from the *left* side. If we assume, as apparently we must assume, that the attacker approached from the left . . . or at least the flying pistol travelled over from the left . . . I don't know! Even granting that the murderer could walk on snow without leaving a footprint, can we at least decide where he came from?"

"He came from here," said a voice.

The rising of the wind seem to whirl the words about them, as though they came from empty air. For one second in that gusty half-light Rampole experienced a worse shock than he had known even in the days of the Chatterham Prison case. He had a mad vision of flying things, and of hearing words from an invisible man exactly as the two witnesses had heard the hollow murderer whisper the night before. For one second, then, something took him by the throat—before he turned and, with a drop of anticlimax, saw the explanation. A thick-set young man with a reddish face and a bowler pulled down on his forehead (which gave him a somewhat sinister air) was coming down the steps from the open door of number 18. The young man grinned broadly as he saluted Hadley.

"He came from here, sir. I'm Somers, sir. You remember, you asked me to find out where the dead one, the Frenchie, was going when he was killed? And to find out what landlady had any sort of rum lodger that might be the man we're looking for? . . . Well, I've found out about the rum lodger, and it oughtn't to be difficult to find him. He came from *here.* Excuse my interrupting you."

Hadley, trying not to show that the interruption had been unpleasantly startling, growled a pleased word. His eyes travelled up to the doorway, where another figure stood hesitating. Somers followed the glance.

"Oh no, sir. That's not the lodger," he said, and grinned again. "That's Mr. O'Rourke; chap from the music-hall, you know, who identified the Frenchie last night. He's been giving me a bit of help this morning."

The figure detached itself from the gloom and came down the steps. He looked thin despite his heavy overcoat; thin and powerful, with the quick smooth steps carried on the ball of the foot which mark the trapeze or high-wire man. He was affable, easy, and bent slightly backwards as he spoke, like a man who wants room for his gestures. In looks he was rather swarthily reminiscent of the Italian: an effect that was heightened by a luxuriant black moustache with waxed ends, which curled under his hooked nose. Beneath this a large curved pipe hung from one corner of his mouth, and he was puffing with evident enjoyment. His wrinkled eyes had a humorous blue gleam; and he pushed back an elaborate fawn-coloured hat as he introduced himself. This was the Irishman with the Italian pseudonym; he spoke like an American, and in point of fact was, he explained, a Canadian.

"O'Rourke's the name, yes," he said. "John L. Sullivan O'Rourke. Does anybody know what my middle name is? You know, the name of the—" He squared back and took a hard right-hander at the empty air—"the greatest of 'em all? *I* don't. My old man didn't, when he named me. *L.* is all I know. I hope you don't mind my butting in. You see, I knew old Loony—" He paused, grinned, and twisted his moustache. "I see, gents! You're all looking at this soup-strainer of mine. Everybody does. It's on account of that goddam song. You know. The management thought it'd be a good idea if I got myself up like the fellow in the song. Oh, it's real! Look"—he pulled—"nothing phony about it, see? But I was telling you, excuse my butting in. I'm damn sorry for old Loony. . . ." His face clouded.

"That's all right," said Hadley. "Thanks for all the help as it is. It saves me seeing you at the theatre—"

"I'm not working, anyway," said O'Rourke, gloomily. He thrust his left hand out of a long overcoat sleeve. The wrist was wound into a cast and bandaged. "If I'd had any sense I'd have followed Loony last night. But here! Don't let me interrupt. . . ."

"Yes. If you'll come along, sir," Somers interposed, grimly, "I've got something pretty important to show you. *As* well as tell you. The landlady's downstairs getting dressed up, and she'll tell you about the lodger. There's no doubt he's the man you want. But first I'd like you to see his rooms."

"What's in his rooms?"

"Well, sir, there's blood, for one thing," replied Somers. "And also a very queer sort of rope. . . ." He assumed an expression of satisfaction as he saw Hadley's face. "You'll be interested in that rope, and in other things. The fellow's a burglar—at least a crook of some sort, by the look of his outfit. He's put a special lock on the door, so that Miss Hake (that's the landlady) couldn't get in. But I used one of my keys—there's nothing illegal about that, sir; the fellow's evidently cleared out. Miss Hake says he's had the rooms for some time, but he's only used them one or two times since . . ."

"Come *on*," said Hadley.

Somers, closing the door behind, led them into a gloomy hallway and up three flights of stairs. The house was narrow, and had on each floor one furnished flat which ran the whole depth from back to front. The door of the top floor—close up near a ladder which led to the roof— stood open, its extra lock gleaming above the ordinary keyhole. Somers took them into a darkish passage with three doors.

"In here first, sir," he said, indicating the first on the left. "It's the bathroom. I had to put a shilling in the electric meter to get any light—now!"

He pressed a switch. The bathroom was a dingy converted box-room, with glazed paper on the wall in imitation of tile, worn oilcloth on the floor, a top-heavy geyser-bath whose tank had gone to rust, and a wavy mirror hung over a washstand with bowl and pitcher on the floor.

"Effort made to clean the place up, you see, sir." Somers went on. "But you'll still see reddish traces in the bath where the water was poured out. That was where he washed his hands. And over behind this clothes-hamper, now—"

With dramatic satisfaction he swung the hamper to one side, reached into the dust behind, and produced a still-damp face-cloth with sodden patches that had turned to dull pink.

"—he sponged his clothes with that," said Somers, nodding.

"Well done," said Hadley, softly. He juggled the face-cloth, glanced at Dr. Fell, smiled, and put down the find. "The other rooms, now. I'm curious about that rope."

Somebody's personality permeated those rooms like the sickly yellow of the electric lights; like the chilly chemical smell which was not quite obliterated by the strong tobacco O'Rourke smoked. It was a den in more senses than one. Heavy curtains were drawn across the windows in a fairly large front room. Under a powerful light on a broad table lay an assortment of little steel or wire tools with rounded heads and curved ends, (Hadley said, "Lockpicks, eh?" and whistled), an assortment of detached locks, and a sheaf of notes. There was a powerful microscope, a box fitted with glass slides, a bench of chemicals on which six labelled test-tubes were arranged in a rack, a wall of books, and in one corner a small iron safe at the sight of which

Hadley uttered an exclamation.

"If he's a burglar," said the superintendent, "he's the most modern and scientific burglar I've seen in a long time. I didn't know this trick was known in England. You've been dipping into this, Fell. Recognize it?"

"There's a big hole cut right out of the iron in the top, sir," put in Somers. "If he used a blow-pipe, it's the neatest acetylene-cutting job I ever saw. He—"

"He didn't use a blow-pipe," said Hadley. "It's neater and easier than that. This is the Krupp preparation. I'm not strong on chemistry, but I think this is powdered aluminum and ferrous oxide. You mix the powder on top of the safe, you add—what is it?—powdered magnesium, and set a match to it. It doesn't explode. It simply generates a heat of several thousand degrees and melts a hole straight through the metal. . . . See that metal tube on the table? We have one at the Black Museum. It's a detectascope, or what they call a fish-eye lens, with a refraction over half a sphere like the eye of a fish. You can put it to a hole in the wall and see everything that's going on in the next room. What do you think of this, Fell?"

"Yes, yes," said the doctor, with a vacant stare as though all this were of no importance; "I hope you see what it suggests. The mystery, the— But where's that rope? I'm very much interested in that rope."

"Other room, sir. Back room," said Somers. "It's got up in rather grand style, like an Eastern . . . you know."

Presumably he meant divan; or even harem. There was a spurious Turkish floridity and mysteriousness about the rich-coloured couches and hangings; the tassels, gimcracks, and weapon-groups; yet your eye was almost startled into belief by finding such things in such a place. Hadley flung back the curtains. Bloomsbury intruded with winter daylight, making sickly the illusion. They looked out on the backs of the houses along Guilford Street, on paved yards below, and an alley winding up towards the back of the Children's Hospital. But Hadley did not consider that for long. He pounced on the coil of rope that lay across a divan.

It was thin but very strong, knotted at intervals of two feet apart; an ordinary rope except for the curious device hooked to one end. This looked like a black rubber cup, something larger than a coffee-cup, of great toughness and with a grip edge like a car tire.

"Wow!" said Dr. Fell. "Look here, is that—?"

Hadley nodded. "I've heard of them, but I never saw one before and I didn't believe they existed. See here! It's an air-suction cup. You've probably seen the same sort of thing in a child's toy. A spring toy-pistol fires at a smooth card a little rod with a miniature suction-cup in soft rubber on the end. It strikes the card, and the suction of the air holds it."

"You mean," said Rampole, "that a burglar could force that thing against the side of a wall, and its pressure would hold him on the rope?"

Hadley hesitated. "That's how they *say* it works. Of course, I don't—"

"But how would he get it loose again? That is, would he just walk away and leave it hanging there?"

"He'd need a confederate, naturally. If you pressed the edges of this thing at the bottom, they would let the air in and destroy the grip. Even so, I don't see how the devil it could have been used for—"

O'Rourke, who had been eyeing the rope in a bothered way, cleared his throat. He took the pipe out of his mouth and cleared his throat again for attention.

"Look, gents," he said in his hoarse, confidential voice. "I don't want to butt in, but I think that's all bunk."

Hadley swung round. "How so? Do you know anything about it?"

"I'll make you a little bet," nodded the other, and poked at the air with his pipe-stem for emphasis, "that this thing belonged to Loony Fley. Give it to me for a second and I'll see. Mind, I don't *swear* it belonged to Loony. There are plenty of queer things in this joint. But—"

He took the rope, and ran his fingers gently along it until he reached the middle. Then he winked and nodded with satisfaction. He twirled his fingers, and then suddenly held his hands apart with the air of a conjuror. The rope came in two pieces.

"Uh-huh. Yes. I thought it was one of Loony's trick ropes. See this? The rope's tapped. It's fitted with a screw in one side and a thread in the other, and you can twist it together just like a screw in wood. You can't see the joint; you can examine the rope all you like, and yet it won't come apart under any pressure. Get the idea? Members of the audience tie the illusionist, or whatdyecallum—tie him up tight in his cabinet. This joint of the rope goes across his hands. The watchers outside can hold the ends of the rope tight to make sure he don't try to get out of it. See? But he unscrews the thing with his teeth, holds the rope taut with his knees, and all kinds of hell start to pop inside the cabinet. Wonder! Mystification! Greatest show on earth!" said O'Rourke, hoarsely. He regarded them amiably, put the pipe back in his mouth, and inhaled deeply. "Yes. That was one of Loony's ropes, I'll bet anything."

"I don't doubt that," said Hadley. "But what about the suction-cup?"

Again O'Rourke bent slightly backwards to give room for his gestures.

"We-el, Loony was as secretive as they make 'em, of course. But I haven't been around with magic acts and the rest of that stuff without keeping my eyes peeled. . . . Wait a minute; don't get me wrong! Loony had tricks that were GOOD, and I mean good. This was just routine stuff that everybody knew about. Well. He was working on one. . . . You've heard of the Indian rope trick, haven't you? Fakir throws a rope up in the air; it stands upright; boy climbs up it—whoosh! he disappears. Eh?"

A cloud of smoke whirled up and vanished before his broad gesture.

"I've also heard," said Dr. Fell, blinking at him, "that nobody has ever yet seen it performed."

"Sure! Exactly! That's just it," O'Rourke returned, with a sort of pounce. "That's why Loony was trying to dope out a means of doing it. God knows whether he did. I think that suction-cup was to catch the rope somewhere when it was thrown up. But don't ask me how."

"And somebody was to climb up," said Hadley, in a heavy voice; "climb up, and disappear?"

"We-el, a kid—!" O'Rourke brushed the idea away. "But I'll tell you this much: that thing you've got won't support a full-grown man's weight. Look, gents! I'd try it for you, and swing out the window, only I don't want to break my goddam neck; and besides, my wrist is out of kilter."

"I think we've got enough evidence just the same," said Hadley. "You say this fellow's bolted, Somers? Any description of him?"

Somers nodded with great satisfaction.

"We shouldn't have any difficulty in pulling him in, sir. He goes under the name of 'Jerome Burnaby,' which is probably a fake; but he's got a pretty distinctive appearance—and he has a club foot."

THE CLUE OF THE CHURCH BELLS 14

The next sound was the vast, dust-shaking noise of Dr. Fell's mirth. The doctor did not only chuckle; he roared. Sitting down on a red-and-yellow divan, which sagged and creaked alarmingly, he chortled away and pounded his stick on the floor.

"Stung!" said Dr. Fell. "Stung, me bonny boys! Heh-heh-heh. Bang goes the ghost. Bang goes the evidence. Oh, my eye!"

"What do you mean, stung?" demanded Hadley. "I don't see anything funny in getting our man dead to rights. Doesn't this pretty well convince you that Burnaby's guilty?"

"It convinces me absolutely that he's innocent," said Dr. Fell. He got out a red bandana and wiped his eyes as the amusement subsided. "I was afraid we should find just this sort of thing when we saw the other room. It was a little too good to be true. Burnaby is the Sphinx without a secret; the criminal without a crime—or at least this particular sort of crime."

"If you would mind explaining . . . ?"

"Not at all," said the doctor, affably. "Hadley, take a look around and tell me what this whole place reminds you of. Did you ever know of any burglar, any criminal at all, who ever had his secret hideaway arranged with such atmospheric effect, with such romantic setting? With the lockpicks arranged on the table, the brooding microscope, the sinister chemicals and so on? The real burglar, the real criminal of any kind, takes care to have his haunt looking a little more respectable than a churchwarden's. This display doesn't even remind me of somebody playing at being a burglar. But if you'll think for a second you'll see what it does remind you of, out of a hundred stories and films. I know that," the doctor explained, "because I'm so fond of the atmosphere, even the theatrical atmosphere, myself. . . . It sounds like somebody playing detective."

Hadley stopped, rubbing his chin thoughtfully. He peered round.

"When you were a kid," pursued Dr. Fell, with relish, "didn't you ever wish for a secret passage in your house?— and pretend that some hole in the attic *was* a secret passage, and go crawling through it with a candle, and nearly burn the place down? Didn't you ever play the Great Detective, and wish for a secret lair in some secret street, where you could pursue your deadly studies under an assumed name? Didn't somebody say Burnaby was a fierce amateur criminologist? Maybe he's writing a book. Anyhow, he has the time and the money to do, in rather a sophisticated way, just what a lot of other grown-up children have wished to do. He's created an *alter ego.* He's done it on the quiet, because his circle would have roared with laughter if they had known. Relentlessly the bloodhounds of Scotland Yard have tracked down his deadly secret; and his deadly secret is a joke."

"But, sir—!" protested Somers, in a kind of yelp.

"Stop a bit," said Hadley, meditatively, and gestured him to silence. The superintendent again examined the place with a half-angry doubt. "I admit there's an unconvincing look about the place, yes. I admit it has a movie-ish appearance. But what about that blood and this rope? This rope is Fley's, remember. And the blood . . ."

Dr. Fell nodded.

"H'mf, yes. Don't misunderstand. I don't say these rooms mightn't play a part in the business; I'm only warning you not to believe too much in Burnaby's evil double life."

"We'll soon find out about that. And," growled Hadley, "if the fellow's a murderer I don't care how innocent his double life as a burglar may be. Somers!"

"Sir?"

"Go over to Mr. Jerome Burnaby's flat—yes, I know you don't understand, but I mean his other flat. I've got the address. H'm. 13A Bloomsbury Square, second floor. Got it? Bring him here; use any pretext you like, but see that he comes. Don't answer any questions about this place, or ask any. Got that? And when you go downstairs, see if you can hurry up that landlady."

He stalked about the room, kicking at the edges of the

furniture, as a bewildered and crestfallen Somers hurried out. O'Rourke, who had sat down and was regarding them with amiable interest, waved his pipe.

"Well, gents," he said, "I like to see the bloodhounds on the trail, at that. I don't know who this Burnaby is, but he seems to be somebody you already know. Is there anything you'd like to ask *me?* I told what I knew about Loony to Sergeant, or whatever he is, Somers. But if there's anything else . . . ?"

Hadley drew a deep breath and set his shoulder back to work again. He went through the papers in his briefcase.

"This is your statement—right?" The superintendent read it briefly. "Have you anything to add to that? I mean, are you positive he said his brother had taken lodgings in this street?"

"That's what he said, yes, sir. He said he'd seen him hanging around here."

Hadley glanced up sharply. "That's not the same thing, is it? Which did he say?"

O'Rourke seemed to think this a quibble. He shifted. "Oh, well, he said that just afterwards. He said, 'He's got a room there; I've seen him hanging around.' Or something. That's the honest truth, now!"

"But not very definite, is it?" demanded Hadley. "Think again!"

"Well hell's bells, I *am* thinking!" protested O'Rourke in an aggrieved tone. "Take it easy. Somebody reels off a lot of stuff like that; and then afterwards they ask you questions about it and seem to think you're lying if you can't repeat every word. Sorry, partner, but that's the best I can do."

"What do you know about this brother of his? Since you've known Fley, what has he told you?"

"Not a thing! Not one word! I don't want you to get the wrong idea. When I say I knew Loony better than most people, that don't mean I know anything about him. Nobody did. If you ever saw him, you'd know he was the last person you could get confidential with over a few drinks, and tell about yourself. It would be like treating Dracula to a couple of beers. Wait a minute!—I mean somebody who looked like Dracula, that's all. Loony was a pretty good sport in his own way."

Hadley reflected, and then decided on a course.

"The biggest problem we have now—you'll have guessed

that—is an impossible situation. I suppose you've seen the newspapers?"

"Yes." O'Rourke's eyes narrowed. "Why ask me about that?"

"Some sort of illusion, or stage trick, must have been used to kill both those men. You say you've known magicians and escape artists. Can you think of any trick that would explain how it was done?"

O'Rourke laughed, showing gleaming teeth under the elaborate moustache. The wrinkles of amusement deepened round his eyes.

"Oh, well! That's different! That's a lot different. Look, I'll tell you straight. When I offered to swing out the window on that rope, I noticed you. I was afraid you were getting ideas. Get me? I mean about me." He chuckled. "Forget it! It'd take a miracle man to work any stunt like that with a rope, even if he had a rope and could walk without leaving any tracks. But as for the other business . . ." Frowningly O'Rourke brushed up his moustache with the stem of his pipe. He stared across the room. "It's this way. I'm no authority. I don't know very much about it, and what I do know I generally keep mum about. Kind of"—he gestured—"kind of professional etiquette, if you get me. Also, for things like escapes from locked boxes, and disappearances and the rest of it . . . well, I've given up even talking about 'em."

"Why?"

"Because," said O'Rourke, with great emphasis, "most people are so damned disappointed when they know the secret. Either, in the first place, the thing is so smart and simple—so simple it's funny—that they won't believe they could have been fooled by it. They'll say, 'Oh, hell! don't tell us that stuff! I'd have seen it in a second.' Or, in the second place, it's a trick worked with a confederate. That disappoints 'em even more. They say, 'Oh, well, if you're going to have somebody to help—!' as though anything was possible then."

He smoked reflectively.

"It's a funny thing about people. They go to see an illusion; you tell 'em it's an illusion; they pay their money to see an illusion. And yet for some funny reason they get sore because it isn't *real* magic. When they hear an explanation of how somebody got out of a locked box or a roped sack that they've examined, they get sore because it *was* a trick. They say it's farfetched when they know how they were deceived. Now, it takes BRAINS, I'm telling you, to work out one of those simple tricks. And, to be a good escape-artist, a man's got to be cool, strong, experienced and quick as greased lightning. But they never think of the cleverness it takes just to fool 'em under their noses. I think they'd like the secret of an escape to be some unholy business like real magic; something that nobody on God's earth could ever do. Now, no man who ever lived can make himself as thin as a post-card and slide out through a crack. No man ever crawled out through a keyhole, or pushed himself through a piece of wood. Want me to give you an example?"

"Go on," said Hadley, who was looking at him curiously.

"All right. Take the second sort first! Take the roped and sealed sack trick: one way of doing it." [1] O'Rourke was enjoying himself. "Out comes the performer—in the middle of a group of people, if you want him to—with a light sack made out of black muslin or sateen, and big enough for him to stand up in. He gets inside. His assistant draws it up, holds the sack about six inches below the mouth, and ties it round tightly with a long handkerchief. Then the people watching can add more knots if they want to, and seal his knots and theirs with wax, and stamp 'em with signets . . . anything at all. Bang! Up goes a screen round the performer. Thirty seconds later out he walks, with the knots still tied and sealed and stamped, and the sack over his arm. Heigh-ho!"

"Well?"

O'Rourke grinned, made the usual play with his moustache (he could not seem to leave off twisting it), and rolled on the divan.

"Now, gents, here's where you take a poke at me. There's dublicate sacks, exactly alike. One of 'em the performer's got all folded up and stuck inside his vest. When he gets into the sack, and he's moving and jerking it around, and the assistant is pulling it up over his head— why, out comes the duplicate. The mouth of the other black sack is pushed up through the mouth of the first; six inches or so; it *looks* like the mouth of the first. The assistant grabs it round, and what he honest-to-God ties is the mouth of the duplicate sack, with such a thin edge of the real one included so that you can't see the joining. Bang!

[1] See the admirable and startling book by Mr. J. C. Cannell.

On go the knots and seals. When the performer gets behind his screen, all he does is shove loose the tied sack, drop the one he's standing in, stick the loose sack under his vest, and walk out holding the duplicate sack roped and sealed. Get it? See? It's simple, it's easy, and yet people go nuts trying to figure out how it was done. But when they hear how it *was* done, they say, 'Oh, well, with a confederate—!' " He gestured.

Hadley was interested in spite of his professional manner, and Dr. Fell was listening with a childlike gaping.

"Yes, I know," said the superintendent, as though urging an argument, "but the man we're after, the man who committed these two murders, couldn't have had a confederate! Besides, that's not a vanishing-trick. . . ."

"All right," said O'Rourke, and pushed his hat to one side of his head. "I'll give you an example of a whopping-big vanishing-trick. This is a stage illusion, mind. All very fancy. But you can work it in an outdoor theatre, if you want to, where there's no trapdoors, no wires from the flies, no props or funny business at all. Just a stretch of ground. Out rides the illusionist, in a grand blue uniform, on a grand white horse. Out come his gang of attendants, in white uniforms, with the usual hoop-la like a circus. They go round in a circle once, and then two attendants whisk up a great big fan which—just for a moment, see?—hides the man on the horse. Down comes the fan, which is tossed out in the audience to show it's O.K.; but the man on the horse has vanished. He's vanished straight from the middle of a ten-acre field. Heigh-ho!"

"And how do you get out of that one?" demanded Dr. Fell.

"Easy! The man's never left the field. But you don't see him. You don't see him because that grand blue uniform is made of paper—*over* a real white one. As soon as the fan goes up, he tears off the blue one and stuffs it under the white. He jumps down off the horse, and just joins in the gang of white-uniformed attendants. Point is, nobody ever takes the trouble to *count* them attendants beforehand, and they all exit without anybody ever seeing. That's the basis of most tricks. You're looking at something you don't see, or you'll swear you've seen something that's not there. Hey presto! Bang! Greatest show on earth!"

The stuffy, gaudily coloured room was quiet. Wind rattled at the windows. Distantly there was a noise of church bells, and the honking of a taxi that passed and died. Hadley shook his notebook.

"We're getting off the track," he said. "It's clever enough, yes; but how does it apply to this problem?"

"It don't," admitted O'Rourke, who seemed convulsed by a noiseless mirth. "I'm telling you—well, because you asked. And to show you what you're up against. I'm giving you the straight dope, Mr. Superintendent: I don't want to discourage you, but if you're up against a smart illusionist, you haven't got the chance of a snowball in hell; you haven't got the chance of *that*." He snapped his fingers. "They're trained to it. It's their business. And there ain't a prison on earth that can hold 'em."

Hadley's jaw tightened. "We'll see about that when the time comes. What bothers me, and what's been bothering me for some time, is why Fley sent his brother to do the killing. Fley was the illusionist. Fley would have been the man to do it. But he didn't. Was his brother in the same line?"

"Dunno. At least, I never saw his name billed anywhere. But—"

Dr. Fell interrupted. With a heavy wheeze, he lumbered up from the couch and spoke sharply.

"Clear the decks for action, Hadley. We're going to have visitors in about two minutes. Look out there!—but keep back from the window."

He was pointing with his stick. Below them, where the alley curved out between the blank windows of houses, two figures shouldered against the wind. They had turned in from Guilford Street; and, fortunately had their heads down. One Rampole recognized as that of Rosette Grimaud. The other was a tall man whose shoulder lunged and swung as he walked with the aid of a cane; a man whose leg had a crooked twist and whose right boot was of abnormal thickness.

"Get the lights out in those other rooms," said Hadley, swiftly. He turned to O'Rourke. "I'll ask you a big favour. Get downstairs as quickly as you can; stop that landlady from coming up and saying anything; keep her there until you hear from me. Pull the door shut after you!"

He was already out into the narrow passage, snapping off the lights. Dr. Fell looked mildly harassed.

"Look here, you don't mean we're going to hide and overhear terrible secrets, do you?" he demanded. "I've not got what Mills would call the anatomical structure for such tomfoolery. Besides, they'll spot us in a second. This place is full of smoke—O'Rourke's shag."

Hadley muttered profanities. He drew the curtains so that only a pencil of light slanted into the room.

"Can't be helped; we've got to chance it. We'll sit here quietly. If they've got anything on their minds, they may blurt it out as soon as they get inside the flat and the door is shut. People do. What do you think of O'Rourke, by the way?"

"I think," stated Dr. Fell, with energy, "that O'Rourke is the most stimulating, enlightening, and suggestive witness we have heard so far in this nightmare. He has saved my intellectual self-respect. He is, in fact, almost as enlightening as the church bells."

Hadley, who was peering through the crack between the curtains, turned his head round. The line of light across his eyes showed a certain wildness.

"Church bells? What church bells?"

"Any church bells," said Dr. Fell's voice out of the gloom. "I tell you that to me in my heathen blindness the thought of those bells has brought light and balm. It may save me from making an awful mistake. . . . Yes, I'm quite sane." The ferrule of a stick rapped the floor and his voice became tense. "Light, Hadley! Light at last, and glorious messages in the belfry."

"Are you sure it's not something else in the belfry? Yes? Then for God's sake will you stop this mystification and tell me what you mean? I suppose the church bells tell you how the vanishing-trick was worked?"

"Oh no," said Dr. Fell. "Unfortunately not. They only tell me the name of the murderer."

There was a palpable stillness in the room, a physical heaviness, as of breath restrained to bursting. Dr. Fell spoke in a blank, almost an incredulous voice which carried conviction in its mere incredulity. Downstairs a back door closed. Faintly through the quiet house they heard footsteps on the staircase. One set of footsteps was sharp, light, and impatient. The other had a drag and then a heavy stamp; there was the noise of a cane knocking the banisters. The noises grew louder, but no word was spoken. A key scraped into the lock of the outer door, which opened and closed again with a click of the spring-lock. There was another click as the light in the hallway was snapped on.

Then—evidently when they could see each other—the two burst out as though they had been the ones who held in breath to suffocation.

"So you've lost the key I gave you," a man's thin, harsh, quiet voice spoke. It was mocking and yet repressed. "And you say you didn't come here last night, after all?"

"Not last night," said Rosette Grimaud's voice, which had a flat and yet furious tone; "not last night or any other night." She laughed. "I never had any intention of coming at all. You frightened me a little. Well, what of it? And now that I *am* here, I don't think so much of your hideout. Did you have a pleasant time waiting last night?"

There was a movement as though she had stepped forward, and been restrained. The man's voice rose.

"Now, you little devil," said the man, with equal quietness, "I'm going to tell you something for the good of your soul. I wasn't here. I had no intention of coming. If you think all you have to do is crack the whip to send people through hoops—well, I wasn't here, do you see? You can go through the hoops yourself. I wasn't here."

"That's a lie, Jerome," said Rosette, calmly.

"You think so, eh? Why?"

Two figures appeared against the light of the partly opened door. Hadley reached out and drew back the curtains with a rattle of rings.

"We also would like to know the answer to that, Mr. Burnaby," he said.

The flood of murky daylight in their faces caught them off-guard; so much off-guard that expressions were hollowed out as though snapped by a camera. Rosette Grimaud cried out, making a movement of her raised arm as though she would dodge under it, but the flash of the previous look had been bitter, watchful, dangerously triumphant. Jerome Burnaby stood motionless, his chest rising and falling. Silhouetted against the sickly electric light behind, and wearing an old-fashioned broad-brimmed black hat, he bore a curious resemblance to the lean Sandeman figure in the advertisement. But he was more than a silhouette. He had a strong, furrowed face, that ordinarily might have been bluff and amiable like his gestures; an underhung jaw, and eyes which seemed to have lost their colour with anger. Taking off his hat, he tossed it on a divan with a swash-buckling air that struck Rampole as rather theatrical. His wiry brown hair, patched with grey round the temples, stood up as though released from pressure like a jack-in-the-box.

"Well?" he said with a sort of thin, bluff jocularity, and took a lurching step forward, on the club foot. "Is this a hold-up, or what? Three to one, I see. I happen to have a sword-stick, though——"

"It won't be needed, Jerome," said the girl. "They're the police."

Burnaby stopped; stopped and rubbed his mouth with a big hand. He seemed nervous, though he went on with ironical jocularity. "Oh! The police, eh? I'm honoured. Breaking and entering, I see."

"You are the tenant of this flat," said Hadley, returning an equal suavity, "not the owner or landlord of the house. If suspicious behaviour is seen. . . . I don't know about suspicious, Mr. Burnaby, but I think your friends would be amused at these—Oriental surroundings. Wouldn't they?"

That smile, that tone of voice, struck through to a raw place. Burnaby's face became a muddy colour.

"Damn you," he said, and half raised the cane, "what do you want here?"

"First of all, before we forget it, about what you were saying when you came in here. . . ."

"You overheard it, eh?"

"Yes. It's unfortunate," said Hadley, composedly, "that we couldn't have overheard more. Miss Grimaud said that you were in this flat last night. Were you?"

"I was not."

"You were not. . . . Was he, Miss Grimaud?"

Her colour had come back; come back strongly, for she was angry with a quiet, smiling poise. She spoke in a breathless way, and her long hazel eyes had that fixity, that luminous strained expression, of one who determines to show no emotion. She was pressing her gloves between the fingers, and in the jerkiness of her breathing there was less anger than fear.

"Since you overheard it," she answered, after a speculative pause while she glanced from one to the other, "it's no good my denying it, is there? I don't see why you're interested. It can't have anything to do with—my father's death. That's certain. Whatever else Jerome is," she showed her teeth in an unsteady smile, "he's not a murderer. But since for some reason you *are* interested, I've a good mind to have the whole thing thrashed out now.

Some version of this, I can see, is going to get back to Boyd. It might as well be the true one. . . . I'll begin by saying, yes, Jerome was in this flat last night."

"How do you know that, Miss Grimaud? Were you here?"

"No. But I saw a light in this room at half-past ten."

THE LIGHTED WINDOW 15

Burnaby, still rubbing his chin, looked down at her in dull blankness. Rampole could have sworn that the man was genuinely startled; so startled that he could not quite understand her words, and peered at her as though he had never seen her before. Then he spoke in a quiet, common-sense tone which contrasted with his earlier one.

"I say, Rosette," he observed, "be careful now. Are you sure you know what you're talking about?"

"Yes. Quite sure."

Hadley cut in briskly. "At half-past ten? How did you happen to see this light, Miss Grimaud, when you were at your own home with us?"

"Oh no, I wasn't—if you remember. Not at that time. I was at the nursing-home, with the doctor in the room where my father was dying. I don't know whether you know it, but the back of the nursing-home faces the back of this house. I happened to be near a window, and I noticed. There was a light in this room; and, I think, the bathroom, too, though I'm not positive of that . . ."

"How do you know the rooms," said Hadley, sharply, "if you've never been here before?"

"I took jolly good care to observe when we came in just now," she answered, with a serene and imperturbable smile which somehow reminded Rampole of Mills. "I didn't know the rooms last night; I only knew he had this flat, and where the windows were. The curtains weren't quite drawn. That's how I came to notice the light."

Burnaby was still contemplating her with the same heavy curiosity.

"Just a moment, Mr.—Inspector—er—!" He humped his shoulder. "Are you sure you couldn't have been mistaken about the rooms, Rosette?"

"Positive, my dear. This is the house on the left hand side at the corner of the alley, and you have the top floor."

"And you say you saw *me?*"

"No, I say I saw a light. But you and I are the only ones who know about this flat. And, since you'd invited me here, and said you would be here . . ."

"By God!" said Burnaby, "I'm curious to see how far you'll go." He hobbled over, with a trick of pulling down the corner of his mouth each time he lunged on the cane; he sat down heavily in a chair, and continued to study her out of his pale eyes. That upstanding hair gave him somehow a queerly alert look. "Please go on! You interest me. Yes. I'm curious to see how far you have the nerve to go."

"Are you really," said Rosette, in a flat voice. She whirled round; but her resolution seemed to crack and she succeeded in looking only miserable to the point of tears. "I wish I knew myself! I—I wish I knew about *you!* . . . I said we'd have this out," she appealed to Hadley, "but now I don't know whether I want to have it out. If I could decide about him, whether he's really sympathetic, and just a nice bluff old—old—"

"Don't say friend of the family," snapped Burnaby. "For Lord's sake don't say friend of the family. Personally, I wish I could decide about you. I wish I could decide whether you think you're telling the truth, or whether you're (excuse me for forgetting my chivalry for a moment!) a lying little vixen."

She went on steadily: "—or whether he's a sort of polite blackmailer. Oh, not for money!" she blazed again. "Vixen? Yes. Bitch if you like. I admit it. I've been both—but why? Because you've poisoned everything with all the hints you've dropped . . . if I could be sure they were hints and not just my imagination; if I could even be sure you were an honest blackmailer! . . ."

Hadley intervened. "Hints about what?"

"Oh, about my father's past life, if you must know." She clenched her hands. "About my birth, for one thing, and whether we mightn't add another nice term to bitch. But that's not important. That doesn't bother me at all. It's this business about some horrible thing—about my father— I don't know! Maybe they're not even hints. But . . . I've got it in my head somehow that old Drayman is a blackmailer. . . . Then, last night, Jerome asked me to come over here—why, why? I thought: well, is it because that's the night Boyd always sees me, and it will tickle Jerome's vanity no end to choose just that night? But I don't and I didn't —please understand me!—want to think Jerome was trying a little blackmail himself. I do like him; I can't help it; and that's what makes it so awful. . . ."

"We might clear it up, then," said Hadley. "Were you 'hinting,' Mr. Burnaby?"

There was a long silence while Burnaby examined his hands. Something in the posture of his bent head, in his slow heavy breathing, as though he were bewilderedly trying to make up his mind, kept Hadley from prompting him until he raised his head.

"I never thought—" he said. "Hinting. Yes. Yes, in strict accuracy, I suppose I was. But never intentionally, I'll swear. I never thought—" He stared at Rosette. "Those things slip out. Maybe you mean only what you think is a subtle question. . . ." He puffed out his breath in a sort of despairing hiss, and shrugged his shoulders. "To me it was an interesting deductive game, that's all. I didn't even think of it as prying. I swear I never thought anybody noticed, let alone taking it to heart. Rosette, if that's the only reason for your interest in me—thinking I was a blackmailer, and afraid of me—then I'm sorry I learned. Or am I?" He looked down at his hands again, opened and shut them, and then looked slowly round the room. "Take a look at this place, gentlemen. The front room especially . . . but you'll have seen that. Then you know the answer. The Great Detective. The poor ass with the deformed foot, dreaming."

For a second Hadley hesitated. .

"And did the Great Detective find out anything about Dr. Grimaud's past?"

"No. . . . If I had, do you think I'd be apt to tell you?"

"We'll see if we can't persuade you. Do you know that there are bloodstains in that bathroom of yours, where Miss Grimaud says she saw a light last night? Do you know that Pierre Fley was murdered outside your door not long before half-past ten?"

Rosette Grimaud cried out, and Burnaby jerked up his head.

"Fley mur . . . Blood-stains! No! Where? Man, what do you mean?"

"Fley had a room in this street. We think he was coming

here when he died. Anyhow, he was shot in the street outside here by the same man who killed Dr. Grimaud. Can you prove who you are, Mr. Burnaby? Can you prove, for instance, that you are not actually Dr. Grimaud's and Fley's brother?"

The other stared at him. He hoisted himself up shakily from the chair.

"Good God! man, are you mad?" he asked, in a quiet voice. "Brother! Now I see! . . . No, I'm not his brother. Do you think if I were his brother I should be interested in . . ." He checked himself, glanced at Rosette, and his expression became rather wild. "Certainly I can prove it. I ought to have a birth certificate somewhere. I—I can produce people who've known me all my life. Brother!"

Hadley reached round to the divan and held up the coil of rope.

"What about this rope? Is it a part of your Great Detective scheme, too?"

"That thing? No. What is it? I never saw it before. Brother!"

Rampole glanced at Rosette Grimaud, and saw that she was crying. She stood motionless, her hands at her sides and her face set; but the tears brimmed over her eyes.

"And can you prove," Hadley continued, "that you were not in this flat last night?"

Burnaby drew a deep breath. Relief lightened his heavy face.

"Yes, fortunately I can. I was at my club last night from eight o'clock—or thereabouts; maybe a little earlier—until past eleven. Dozens of people will tell you that. If you want me to be specific, ask the three I played poker with the whole of that time. Do you want an alibi? Right! There's as strong an alibi as you're ever likely to get. I wasn't here. I didn't leave any blood-stains, wherever the devil you say you found some. I didn't kill Fley, or Grimaud, or anybody else." His heavy jaw came out. "Now, then, what do you think of *that?*"

The superintendent swung his batteries so quickly that Burnaby had hardly finished speaking before Hadley had turned to Rosette.

"You still insist that you saw a light here at half-past ten?"

"Yes! . . . But, Jerome, truly, I never meant—!"

"Even though, when my man arrived here this morning,

the electric meter was cut off and the lights would not work?"

"I . . . Yes, it's still true! But what I wanted to say—"

"Let's suppose Mr. Burnaby is telling the truth about last night. You say he invited you here. Is it likely that he invited you here when he intended to be at his club?"

Burnaby lurched forward and put a hand on Hadley's arm. "Steady! Let's get this straightened out, Inspector. That's what I did. It was a swine's trick, but—I did it. Look here, have I *got* to explain?"

"Now, now, now!" struck in the quiet, rumbling, deprecating tones of Dr. Fell. He took out the red bandana and blew his nose with a loud honking noise, to attract attention. Then he blinked at them, mildly disturbed. "Hadley, we're confused enough as it is. Let me put in a soothing word. Mr. Burnaby did that, as he expressed it himself, to make her jump through a hoop. Hurrum! Excuse my bluntness, ma'am, but then it's all right because that particular leopard wouldn't jump, eh?— About the question of the light not working, that's not nearly so ominous as it sounds. It's a shilling meter, d'ye see. Somebody was here. Somebody left the lights burning, possibly all night. Well, the meter used up a bob's worth of electricity, and then the lights went out. We don't know which way the switches were turned, because Somers got here first. Blast it, Hadley, we've got ample proof that there *was* somebody here last night. The question is, who?" He looked at the others. "H'm. You two say that nobody else knew of this place. But—assuming your story to be straight, Mr. Burnaby; and you'd be a first-class fathead to lie about a thing so easily checked up as that story—then somebody else must have known of it."

"I can only tell you I wasn't likely to speak of it," insisted Burnaby, rubbing his chin. "Unless somebody noticed me coming here . . . unless . . ."

"Unless, in other words, I told somebody about it?" Rosette flared again. Her sharp teeth bit at her under lip. "But I didn't. I—I don't know why I didn't"—she seemed fiercely puzzled—"but I never mentioned it to anybody. There!"

"But you have a key to the place?" asked Dr. Fell.

"I had a key to the place. I lost it."

"When?"

"Oh, how should I know? I never noticed." She had

folded her arms and was walking round the room with excited little movements of her head. "I kept it in my bag, and I only noticed this morning, when we were coming over here, that it was gone. But one thing I insist on knowing." She stopped, facing Burnaby. "I—I don't know whether I'm fond of you or whether I hate you. If it was only a nasty little fondness for detective work, if that's all it really was and you didn't mean anything, then speak up. What do you know about my father? Tell me! *I* don't mind. They're the police, and they'll find out anyway. Now, now, don't act! I hate your acting. Tell me. What's this about brothers?"

"That's good advice, Mr. Burnaby. You painted a picture," said Hadley, "that I was going to ask about next. What did you know about Dr. Grimaud?"

Burnaby, leaning back against the window with an unconsciously swaggering gesture, shrugged his shoulders. His pale grey eyes, with their pin-point black pupils, shifted and gleamed sardonically.

He said: "Rosette, if I had ever known, if I had ever suspected, that my detective efforts were being interpreted as . . . Very well! I'll tell you in a few words what I'd have told you long ago, if I had known it worried you at all. Your father was once imprisoned at the salt-mines in Hungary, and he escaped. Not very terrible, is it?"

"In prison! What for?"

"For trying to start a revolution, I was told. . . . My own guess is for theft. You see, I'm being frank."

Hadley cut in quickly. "Where did you learn that? From Drayman?"

"So Drayman knows, does he?" Burnaby stiffened, and his eyes narrowed. "Yes, I rather thought he did. Ah! Yes. That was another thing I tried to find out, and it seems to have been construed into . . . And, come to think of it, what do *you* fellows know about it, anyhow?" Then he burst out. "Look here, I'm no busybody! I'd better tell you if only to prove it. I was dragged into the thing; Grimaud wouldn't let me alone. You talk about that picture. The picture was the cause rather than the effect. It was all accident—though I had a bad time persuading Grimaud of that. It was all on account of a damned magic-lantern lecture."

"A what?"

"Fact! A magic-lantern lecture. I ducked into the thing

to get out of the rain one night; it was out in North London somewhere, a parish hall, about eighteen months ago." Wryly Burnaby twiddled his thumbs. For the first time there was an honest and homely expression on his face. "I'd like to make a romantic story out of this. But you asked for the truth. Right! Chap was lecturing on Hungary: lantern-slides and plenty of ghostly atmosphere to thrill the church-goers. But it caught my imagination; by George, it did!" His eyes gleamed. "There was one slide—something like what I painted. Nothing effective about it; but the story that went with it, about the three lonely graves in an un-hallowed place, gave me a good idea for a nightmare. The lecturer inferred that they were vampires' graves, you see? I came home and worked like fury on the idea. Well, I frankly told everybody it was an imaginative conception of something I never saw. But for some reason nobody be-lieved me. Then Grimaud saw it . . ."

"Mr. Pettis told us," Hadley remarked, woodenly, "that it gave him a turn. Or that you said it did."

"Gave him a turn? I should say it did! He hunched his head down into his shoulders and stood as quiet as a mummy, looking at it. I took it as a tribute. And then, in my sinister innocence," said Burnaby, with a kind of leer, "out I came with the remark, 'You'll notice how the earth is cracking on one grave. He's just getting out.' My mind was still running on vampires, of course. But he didn't know that. For a second I thought he was coming at me with a palette knife."

It was a straightforward story Burnaby told. Grimaud, he said, had questioned him about that picture; questioned, watched, questioned again, until even a less imaginative man would have been suspicious. The uneasy tension of being always under surveillance had set him to solve the puzzle in ordinary self-defence. A few pieces of hand-writing in books in Grimaud's library; the shield of arms over the mantelpiece; a casual word dropped . . . Burnaby looked at Rosette with a grim smile. Then, he continued, about three months before the murder Grimaud had collared him and, under an oath of secrecy, told him the truth. The "truth" was exactly the story Drayman had told Hadley and Dr. Fell last night: the plague, the two dead brothers, the escape.

During this time Rosette had been staring out of the window with an incredulous, half-witted blankness which ended in something like a tearfulness of relief.

"And that's *all?*" she cried, breathing hard. "That's all there is to it? That's what I've been worrying about all this time?"

"That's all, my dear," Burnaby answered, folding his arms. "I told you it wasn't very terrible. But I didn't want to tell it to the police. Now, however, that you've insisted . . ."

"Be careful, Hadley," grunted Dr. Fell in a low voice, and knocked against the superintendent's arm. He cleared his throat. "Harrumph! Yes. We have some reason to believe the story, too, Miss Grimaud."

Hadley took a new line. "Supposing all this to be true, Mr. Burnaby: you were at the Warwick Tavern the night Fley came in first?"

"Yes."

"Well, then? Knowing what you did, didn't you connect him with that business in the past? Especially after his remarks about the three coffins?"

Burnaby hesitated, and then gestured. "Frankly, yes. I walked home with Grimaud on that night—the Wednesday night. I didn't say anything, but I thought he was going to tell me something. We sat down on either side of the fire in his study, and he took an extra large whisky, a thing he seldom does. I noticed he seemed to be looking very hard at the fireplace. . . ."

"By the way," Dr. Fell put in, with such casualness that Rampole jumped, "where did he keep his private and personal papers? Do you know?"

The other darted a sharp glance at him.

"Mills would be better able to tell you that than I," he returned. (Something veiled, something guarded, some cloud of dust here?) "He may have had a safe. So far as I know, he kept them in a locked drawer at the side of that big desk."

"Go on."

"For a long time neither of us said anything. There was one of those uncomfortable strains when each person wants to introduce a subject, but wonders whether the other is thinking about it, too. Well, I took the plunge, and said, 'Who was it?' He made one of those noises of his like a dog just before it barks, and shifted round in the chair. Finally he said: 'I don't know. It's been a long time. It may have been the doctor; it looked like the doctor.'"

"Doctor? You mean the one who certified him as dead of plague at the prison?" asked Hadley. Rosette Grimaud shivered, and suddenly sat down with her face in her hands. Burnaby grew uncomfortable.

"Yes. Look here, must I go on with this? . . . All right, all right! 'Back for a little blackmail,' he said. You know the look of the stoutish opera stars, who sing Mephistopheles in 'Faust'? He looked just like that when he turned round towards me, with his hands on the arms of the chair, and his elbows hooked as though he were going to get up. Face reddish with the firelight, clipped beard, raised eyebrows—everything. I said, 'Yes, but actually what can he do?' You see, I was trying to draw him out. I thought it must be more serious than a political offence or it wouldn't carry any weight after so long. He said, 'Oh, *he* won't do anything. He never had the nerve. *He* won't do anything.'

"Now," snapped Burnaby, looking round, "you asked for everything, and here it is. I don't mind. Everybody knows it. Grimaud said, with that barking directness of his, 'You want to marry Rosette, don't you?' I admitted it. He said, 'Very well; you shall,' and began nodding and drumming on the arm of the chair. I laughed and said . . . Well! I said something about Rosette's having preference in another direction. He said: 'Bah! the young one! I'll fix that.' "

Rosette was looking at him with a hard, luminous, inscrutable stare, her eyes nearly closed. She spoke in a tone too puzzling to identify. She said:

"So you had it all arranged, did you?"

"O Lord, don't fly off the handle! You know better than that. I was asked what happened, and here it is. The last thing he said was that, whatever happened to him, I was to keep my mouth shut about what I knew—"

"Which you didn't . . ."

"At your express orders, no." He turned back to the others. "Well, gentlemen, that's all I can tell you. When he came hurrying in on Friday morning to get that picture, I was a good deal puzzled. But I had been told to keep out of it entirely, and I did."

Hadley, who had been writing in his notebook, went on without speaking until he came to the end of the page. Then he looked at Rosette, who was sitting back on the divan with a pillow under her elbow. Under the fur coat she wore a dark dress, but her head was bare as usual; so that the heavy blonde hair and square face seemed to fit with the gaudy red-and-yellow divan. She turned her hand outward from the wrist, shakily.

"I know. You're going to ask me what *I* think of all this. About my father . . . and all." She stared at the ceiling. "I don't know. It takes such a load off my mind, it's so much too good to be true, that I'm afraid somebody's not telling the truth. Why, I'd have admired the old boy for a thing like that! It's—it's awful and terrible, and I'm glad he had so much of the devil in him! Of course if it was because he was a thief"—she smiled in some pleasure at the idea—"you can't blame him for keeping it quiet, can you?"

"That was not what I was going to ask," said Hadley, who seemed a good deal taken aback by this frankly broad-minded attitude. "I do want to know why, if you always refused to come over here with Mr. Burnaby, you suddenly decided on coming this morning?"

"To have it out with him, of course. And I—I wanted to get drunk or something. Then things were so unpleasant, you see, when we found that coat with the blood on it hanging in the closet. . . ."

She stopped as she saw faces change, and jerked back a little.

"When you found *what?*" said Hadley, in the midst of a heavy silence.

"The coat with blood inside it, all stained down the inside of the front," she answered, with something of a gulp. "I—er—I didn't mention it, did I? Well, you didn't give me any chance! The minute we walked in here, you leaped out at us like . . . like . . . Yes, that's it! The coat was hanging up in the coat-closet in the hall. Jerome found it when he was hanging up his own."

"Whose coat?"

"Nobody's! That's the odd part! I never saw it before. It wouldn't have fitted anybody at our house. It was too big for father—and it's a flashy tweed overcoat of the kind he'd have shuddered at, anyway; it would have swallowed Stuart Mills, and yet it isn't quite big enough for old Drayman. It's a new coat. It looks as though it had never been worn before . . ."

"*I see,*" said Dr. Fell, and puffed out his cheeks.

"You see what?" snapped Hadley. "This is a fine state

of affairs now! You told Pettis you wanted blood. Well, you're getting blood—too infernally much blood!—and all in the wrong places. What's on your mind now?"

"I see," replied Dr. Fell, pointing with his stick, "where Drayman got the blood on him last night."

"You mean he wore the coat?"

"No, no! Think back. Remember what your sergeant said. He said that Drayman, half-blind, came blundering and rushing downstairs; blundered round in the clothes-closet getting his hat and coat. Hadley, he brushed close up against that coat when the blood was fresh. And it's no wonder he couldn't understand afterwards how it got there. Doesn't that clear up a good deal?"

"No, I'm damned if it does! It clears up one point by substituting another twice as bad. An extra coat! Come along. We're going over there at once. If you will go with us, Miss Grimaud, and you, Mr. . . ."

Dr. Fell shook his head. "You go along, Hadley. There's something I must see now. Something that changes the whole twist of the case; something that has become the most vitally important thing in it."

"What?"

"Pierre Fley's lodgings," said Dr. Fell, and shouldered out with his cape whirling behind him.

3rd

COFFIN

THE PROBLEM OF SEVEN TOWERS

THE CHAMELEON OVERCOAT 16

Between that discovery and the time they were to meet Pettis for lunch, Dr. Fell's spirits sank to a depth of gloom Rampole would not have believed possible, and which he certainly could not understand.

To begin with, the doctor refused to go straight back to Russell Square with Hadley, although he insisted Hadley should go. He said the essential clue must be at Fley's room. He said he would keep Rampole behind for some "dirty work of a strenuous pattern." Finally, he swore at himself with such heart-felt violence that even Hadley, sometimes sharing the views he expressed, was moved to remonstrate.

"But what do you expect to find there?" insisted Hadley. "Somers has already been through the place!"

"I don't expect anything. I can only say I hope," grumbled the doctor, "to find certain traces of brother Henri. His trademark, so to speak. His whiskers. His . . . oh, my hat, brother Henri, damn you!"

Hadley said that they could forego the Soliloquy in a Spanish Cloister, and could not understand why his friend's rage at the elusive Henri seemed to have grown to the status of a mania. There appeared nothing fresh to inspire it. Besides, the doctor, before leaving Burnaby's lodging-house, held up everybody for some time with a searching examination of Miss Hake, the landlady. O'Rourke had been gallantly keeping her downstairs with reminiscences of his trouping days; but both of them were tall talkers, and it is to be doubted whether he reminisced any more than Miss Hake did.

The questioning of Miss Hake, Dr. Fell admitted, was not productive. Miss Hake was a faded, agreeable spinster with good intentions but somewhat wandering wits, and a tendency to confuse erratic lodgers with burglars or murderers. When she was at last persuaded out of her belief that Burnaby was a burglar, she could give little information. She had not been at home last night. She had been at the moving pictures from eight o'clock until eleven, and at a friend's house in Gray's Inn Road until nearly midnight. She could not tell who might have used Burnaby's room; she had not even known of the murder until that morning. As to her other lodgers, there were three: an American student and his wife on the ground floor, and a veterinary surgeon on the floor above. All three had been out on the night before.

Somers, who had returned from his futile errand to Bloomsbury Square, was put to work on this lead; Hadley set out for Grimaud's house with Rosette and Burnaby, and Dr. Fell, who was doggedly intent on tackling another communicative landlady, found instead an uncommunicative landlord.

The premises over and under the tobacconist's shop at number 2 looked as flimsy as one of those half-houses which stand out from the side of the stage in a musical comedy. But they were bleak, dark-painted, and filled with the mustiness of the shop itself. Energy at a clanking bell at last brought James Dolberman, tobacconist and news agent, materializing slowly from the shadows at the back of his shop. He was a small, tight-lipped old man with large knuckles and a black muslin coat that shone like armour in a cave of fly-blown novelettes and mummified peppermints. His view of the whole matter was that it was no business of his.

Staring past them at the shop window, as though he were waiting for some one to come and give him an excuse to leave off talking, he bit off a few grudging answers. Yes, he had a lodger; yes, it was a man named Fley—a foreigner. Fley occupied a bed-sitting-room on the top floor. He had been there two weeks, paying in advance. No, the landlord didn't know anything about him, and didn't want to, except that he gave no trouble. He had a habit of talking to himself in a foreign language, that was all. The landlord didn't know anything about him, because he hardly ever saw him. There were no other lodgers; he (James Dolberman) wasn't carrying hot water upstairs for anybody. Why did Fley choose the top floor? How should he know? They had better ask Fley.

Didn't he know Fley was dead? Yes, he did; there had been a policeman here asking fool questions already, and taking him to identify the body. But it wasn't any business of his. What about the shooting at twenty-five minutes past ten last night? James Dolberman looked as though he might say something, but snapped his jaws shut and stared even harder at the window. He had been belowstairs in his kitchen with the radio on; he knew nothing about it, and wouldn't have come out to see if he had.

Had Fley ever had any visitors? No. Were there ever any suspicious-looking strangers, any people associated with Fley, hereabouts?

This had an unexpected result: the landlord's jaws still moved in a somnambulistic way, but he grew almost voluble. Yes, there was something the police ought to see to, instead of wasting taxpayer's money! He had seen somebody dodging round this place, watching it, once even speaking to Fley and then darting up the street. Nasty-looking customer. Criminal most likely! He didn't like people who dodged. No, he couldn't give any description of him—that was the police's business. Besides, it was always at night.

"But isn't there anything," said Dr. Fell, who was nearly at the limit of his affability and was wiping his face with the bandana, "you can give as description? Any clothes, anything of that sort? Hey?"

"He might," Dolberman conceded, after a tight-lipped struggle with the window, "he *might* have been wearing a kind of fancy overcoat, or the like. Of a light yellow tweed; with red spots in it, maybe. That's your business. You wish to go upstairs? Here is the key. The door is outside."

As they were stamping up a dark and narrow stairway, through a house surprisingly solid despite its flimsy appearance, Rampole fumed.

"You're right, sir," he said, "in saying that the whole case has been turned upside down. It has been—on a matter of overcoats—and it makes less sense than anything else. We've been looking for the sinister figure in the long black overcoat. And now along comes another figure in a bloodstained tweed coat that you can at least call gay in colour. Which is which, and does the whole business turn on a matter of overcoats?"

Dr. Fell puffed as he hauled himself up. "Well, I wasn't thinking of that," he said, doubtfully, "when I said that the case had been turned upside down—or perhaps I should say wrong way round. But in a way it may depend on overcoats. H'm. The Man with Two Overcoats. Yes, I think it's the same murderer, even if he doesn't happen to to be sartorially consistent."

"You said you had an idea as to who the murderer might be?"

"I know who he is!" roared Dr. Fell. "And do you know why I feel an urge to kick myself? Not only because he's been right under my nose all the time, but *because he's been practically telling me the truth the whole time,* and yet I've never had the sense to see it. He's been so truthful that it hurts me to think of how I disbelieved him and thought he was innocent!"

"But the vanishing-trick?"

"No, I don't know how it was done. Here we are."

There was only one room on the top floor, to which a grimy skylight admitted a faint glow on the landing. The room had a door of plain boards painted green; it stood ajar, and opened on a low cave of a room whose window had evidently not been opened in some time. After fumbling round in the gloom, Dr. Fell found a gas-mantle in a tipsy globe. The ragged light showed a neat, but very grimy, room with blue cabbages on the wall-paper and a white iron bed. On the bureau lay a folded note under a bottle of ink. Only one touch remained of Pierre Fley's weird and twisted brain: it was as though they saw Fley himself, in his rusty evening clothes and top-hat, standing by the bureau for a performance. Over the mirror hung framed an old-fashioned motto in curly script of gilt and black and red. The spidery scrollwork read, *"Vengeance is Mine, Saith the Lord; I Will Repay."* But it was hung upside down.

Wheezing in the quiet, Dr. Fell lumbered over to the bureau and picked up the folded note. The handwriting was flowery, Rampole saw, and the short message had almost the air of a proclamation.

James Dolberman, Esq.

I am leaving you my few belongings, such as they are, in lieu of a week's notice. I shall not need them again. I am going back to my grave.

PIERRE FLEY.

"Why," said Rampole, "this insistent harping on 'I am going back to my grave'? It sounds as though it ought to have a meaning, even if it doesn't. . . . I suppose there really was such a person as Fley? He existed; he wasn't somebody else pretending to be Fley, or the like?"

Dr. Fell did not answer that. He was at the beginning of a mood of gloom which sank lower and lower as he inspected the tattered grey carpet on the floor.

"Not a trace," he groaned. "Not a trace or a bus ticket or anything. Serene and unswept and traceless. His possessions? No, I don't want to see his possessions. I suppose Somers had a look through those. Come on; we'll go back and join Hadley."

They walked to Russell Square through a gloom of mind as well as overcast sky. As they went up the steps, Hadley saw them through the drawing-room window and came to open the front door. Making sure the drawing-room door was closed—there was a mutter of voices beyond—Hadley faced them in the dimness of the ornate hallway. Behind him the devil mask on the suit of Japanese armour gave a fair caricature of his face.

"More trouble, I perceive," said Dr. Fell, almost genially. "Well, out with it. I have nothing to report. I was afraid my expedition would be a failure, but I have no consolation merely from being a good prophet. What's up?"

"That overcoat—" Hadley stopped. He was in such a state that wrath could go no farther; he touched the other side, and ended with a sour grin. "Come in and listen to it, Fell. Maybe it'll make sense to you. If Mangan is lying, I don't see any good reason why he could be lying. But that overcoat . . . we've got it right enough. A new coat, brand new. Nothing in the pockets, not even the usual grit and fluff and tobacco ash that you get when you've worn a coat a little while. But first we were faced with the problem of two overcoats. Now we have what you would probably call the Mystery of the Chameleon Overcoat. . . ."

"What's the matter with the overcoat?"

"It's changed colour," said Hadley.

Dr. Fell blinked. He examined the superintendent with an air of refreshed interest. "I don't imagine by any chance," he said, "that this business has turned your brain, has it? Changed colour, hey? Are you about to tell me that the overcoat is now a bright emerald green?"

"I mean it's changed colour since . . . Come on!"

Tension was thick in the air when he threw open the door on a drawing-room furnished in heavy old-fashioned luxury, with bronze groups holding lights, gilt cornices, and curtains stiff with such an overdose of lace that they looked like frozen waterfalls. All the lights were on. Burnaby lounged on a sofa. Rosette was walking about with quick, angry steps. In the corner by the radio stood Ernestine Dumont, her hands on her hips and her lower lip folded across the upper, amused, or satiric, or both. Finally, Boyd Mangan stood with his back to the fire hopping a little and moving from one side to the other as though it burnt him. But it was excitement, or something else, that burnt him.

". . . I know the damn thing fits me!" he was saying, with an air of fierce repetition. "I know it. I admit it. The overcoat fits me, but it's not my coat. In the first place, I always wear a waterproof; it's hanging up in the hall now. In the second place, I could never afford a coat like that; the thing must have cost twenty guineas if it cost a penny. In the third place—"

Hadley figuratively rapped for attention. The entrance of Dr. Fell and Rampole seemed to soothe Mangan.

"Would you mind repeating," said Hadley, "what you've just been telling us?"

Mangan lit a cigarette. The match-flame gleamed in dark eyes that were a little bloodshot. He twitched out the match, inhaled, and expelled smoke with the air of one who is determined to be convicted in a good cause.

"Personally, I don't see why everybody should want to jump all over me," he said. "It may have been another overcoat, although I don't see why anybody should want to strew his wardrobe all over the place. . . . Look here, Ted, I'll put it up to you." He seized Rampole's arm and dragged him over in front of the fire as though he were setting up an exhibit. "When I got here for dinner last night, I went to hang up my coat—my waterproof, mind you—in the clothes-closet in the hall. Generally you don't bother to turn on the light in there. You just grope round and stick your coat on the first convenient hook. I wouldn't have bothered then, but I was carrying a parcel of books I wanted to put on the shelf. So I switched on the light. And I saw an overcoat, an extra coat, hanging by itself over in the far corner. It was about the same size as the yellow tweed one you've got; just the same, I should have said, only it was black."

"An extra coat," repeated Dr. Fell. He drew in his chins and looked curiously at Mangan. "Why do you say an extra coat, my boy? If you see a line of coats in somebody's house, does the idea of an extra one ever enter your head? My experience is that the least noticed things in a house are coats hanging on a peg; you have a vague idea that one of 'em must be your own, but you're not even sure which it is. Eh?"

"I knew the coats people have here, all the same. *And,*" replied Mangan, "I particularly noticed this one, because I thought it must be Burnaby's. They hadn't told me he was here, and I wondered if he was. . . ."

Burnaby had adopted a very bluff, indulgent air towards Mangan. He was not now the thin-skinned figure they had seen sitting on the divan in Cagliostro Street; he was an elder chiding youth with a theatrical wave of his hand.

"Mangan," he said, "is very observant, Dr. Fell. A very observant young man. Ha-ha-ha! Especially where I am concerned."

"Got any objections?" asked Mangan, lowering his voice to a calm note.

". . . But let him tell you the story. Rosette, my dear, may I offer you a cigarette? By the way, I may say that it wasn't my coat."

Mangan's anger grew without his seeming to know exactly why. But he turned back to Dr. Fell. "Anyway, I noticed it. Then, when Burnaby came here this morning and found that coat with the blood inside it . . . well, the light one was hanging in the same place. Of course, the only explanation is that there were two overcoats. But what kind of crazy business is it? I'll swear that coat last night didn't belong to anybody here. You can see for yourself that the tweed one doesn't. Did the murderer wear one coat, or both, or neither? Besides, that black coat had a queer look about it—"

"Queer?" interrupted Dr. Fell, so sharply that Mangan turned round. "How do you mean, queer?"

Ernestine Dumont came forward from beside the radio, her flat-heeled shoes creaking a little. She looked more withered this morning; the high cheek bones more accentuated, the nose more flat, the eyes so puffed round the lids that they gave her a hooded, furtive appearance. Yet, despite the gritty look, her black eyes still had their glitter.

"Ah, bah!" she said, and made a sharp, somehow wooden gesture. "What is the reason to go on with all this foolishness? Why do you not ask me? I would know more about such things than he. Would I not?" She looked at Mangan and her forehead wrinkled. "No, no, I think you are trying to tell the truth, you understand. But I think

you have mixed it up a little. That is easy, as the Dr.
Fell says. . . . The yellow coat was there last night, yes.
Early in the evening, before dinner. It was hanging on the
hook where he says he saw the black one. I saw it myself."

"But—" cried Mangan.

"Now, now," boomed Dr. Fell, soothingly. "Let's see
if we can't straighten this out. If you saw the coat there,
ma'am, didn't it strike you as unusual? A little queer, hey, if
you knew it didn't belong to anybody here?"

"No, not at all." She nodded towards Mangan. "I did
not see him arrive. I supposed it was his."

"Who did let you in, by the way?" Dr. Fell asked
Mangan, sleepily.

"Annie. But I hung up my things myself. I'll swear—"

"Better ring the bell and have Annie up, if she's here,
Hadley," said Dr. Fell. "This problem of the chameleon
overcoat intrigues me. Oh, Bacchus, it intrigues me! Now,
ma'am, I'm not saying you're not telling the truth any
more than you say it of our friend Mangan. I was telling
Ted Rampole a while ago how unfortunately truthful a
certain person has been. Hah! Incidentally have you
spoken to Annie?"

"Oh yes," Hadley answered, as Rosette Grimaud strode
past him and rang a bell. "She tells a straight story. She
was out last night, and didn't get back until past twelve.
But I haven't asked her about this."

"I don't see what all the fuss is about!" cried Rosette.
"What difference does it make? Haven't you better things
to do than go fooling about trying to decide whether an
overcoat was yellow or black?"

Mangan turned on her. "It makes a lot of difference,
and you know it. I wasn't seeing things. No, and I don't
think she was, either! But somebody's got to be right.
Though I admit Annie probably won't know. God! I don't
know anything!"

"Quite right," said Burnaby.

"Go to hell," said Mangan. "Do you mind?"

Hadley strode over between them and spoke quietly but
to the point. Burnaby, who looked rather white, sat down
on the couch again. The fray and strain of nerves showed
raw in that room; everybody seemed eager to be quiet when
Annie answered the bell. Annie was a quiet, long-nosed
serious-minded girl who showed none of that quality which
is called nonsense. She looked capable; she also looked

hard-worked. Standing rather bent at the doorway, her cap so precise on her head that it seemed to have been stamped there, she regarded Hadley with level brown eyes. She was a little upset, but not in the least nervous.

"One thing I neglected to ask you about last night—er," said the superintendent, not too easy himself. "Hum! You let Mr. Mangan in, did you?"

"Yes, sir."

"About what time was that?"

"Couldn't say, sir." She seemed puzzled. "Might have been half an hour before dinner. Couldn't say exactly."

"Did you see him hang up hat and coat?"

"*Yes*, sir! He never gives them to me, or of course I'd have—"

"But did you look into the clothes-closet?"

"Oh, I see. . . . Yes, sir, I did! You see, when I'd let him in, I went straight back to the dining-room, but then I discovered I had to go downstairs to the kitchen. So I went back through the front hall. And I noticed he'd gone away and left the light on in the clothes-closet so I went down and turned it out. . . ."

Hadley leaned forward. "Now be careful! You know the light tweed overcoat that was found in that closet this morning? You knew about that, did you? Good! Do you remember the hook it was hanging from?"

"Yes, sir, I do." Her lips closed tightly. "I was in the front hall this morning when Mr. Burnaby found it, and the rest came round. Mr. Mills said we must leave it where it was, with that blood on it and all, because the police . . ."

"Exactly. The question, Annie, is about the colour of that coat. When you looked into that closet last night, was the coat a light brown or a black? Can you remember?"

She stared at him. "Yes, sir, I can re— light brown or black, sir? Do you mean it? Well, sir, strictly speaking, it wasn't either. *Because there was no coat hanging from that hook at all.*"

A babble of voices crossed and clashed: Mangan furious, Rosette almost hysterically mocking, Burnaby amused. Only Ernestine Dumont remained wearily and contemptuously silent. For a full minute Hadley studied the set, now fighting-earnest face of the witness: Annie had her hands clenched and her neck thrust out. Hadley moved over towards the window, saying nothing in a markedly violent fashion.

Then Dr. Fell chuckled.

"Well, cheer up," he urged. "At least it hasn't turned another colour on us. And I must insist it's a very revealing fact, although I shall be in some danger of having that chair chucked at my head. H'mf. Hah! Yes. Come along, Hadley. Lunch is what we want. Lunch!"

THE LOCKED-ROOM LECTURE 17

The coffee was on the table, the wine-bottles were empty, cigars lighted. Hadley, Pettis, Rampole, and Dr. Fell sat round the glow of a red-shaded table lamp in the vast, dusky dining-room at Pettis's hotel. They had stayed on beyond most, and only a few people remained at other tables in that lazy, replete hour of a winter afternoon when the fire is most comfortable and snowflakes begin to sift past the windows. Under the dark gleam of armour and armorial bearings, Dr. Fell looked more than ever like a feudal baron. He glanced with contempt at the demitasse, which he seemed in danger of swallowing cup and all. He made an expansive, settling gesture with his cigar. He cleared his throat.

"I will now lecture," announced the doctor, with amiable firmness, "on the general mechanics and development of that situation which is known in detective fiction as the 'hermetically sealed chamber.'"

Hadley groaned. "Some other time," he suggested. "We don't want to hear any lecture after this excellent lunch, and especially when there's work to be done. Now, as I was saying a moment ago—"

"I will now lecture," said Dr. Fell, inexorably, "on the general mechanics and development of the situation which is known in detective fiction as the 'hermetically sealed chamber.' Harrumph. All those opposing can skip this chapter. Harrumph. To begin with, gentlemen! Having been improving my mind with sensational fiction for the last forty years, I can say—"

"But, if you're going to analyze impossible situations," interrupted Pettis, "why discuss detective fiction?"

"Because," said the doctor, frankly, "we're in a detective story, and we don't fool the reader by pretending we're not. Let's not invent elaborate excuses to drag in a discussion of detective stories. Let's candidly glory in the noblest pursuits possible to characters in a book.

"But to continue: In discussing 'em, gentlemen, I am not going to start an argument by attempting to lay down rules. I mean to speak solely of personal tastes and preferences. We can tamper with Kipling thus: 'There are nine and sixty ways to construct a murder maze, and every single one of them is right.' Now, if I said that to me every single one of them was equally interesting, then I should be—to put the matter as civilly as possible—a cock-eyed liar. But that is not the point. When I say that a story about a hermetically sealed chamber is more interesting than anything else in detective fiction, that's merely a prejudice. I like my murders to be frequent, gory, and grotesque. I like some vividness of colour and imagination flashing out of my plot, since I cannot find a story enthralling solely on the grounds that it sounds as though it might really have happened. All these things, I admit, are happy, cheerful, rational prejudices, and entail no criticism of more tepid (or more able) work.

"But this point must be made, because a few people who do not like the slightly lurid insist on treating their preferences as rules. They use, as a stamp of condemnation, the word 'improbable.' And thereby they gull the unwary into their own belief that 'improbable' simply means 'bad.'

"Now, it seems reasonable to point out that the word improbable is the very last which should ever be used to curse detective fiction in any case. A great part of our liking for detective fiction is *based* on a liking for improbability. When A is murdered, and B and C are under strong suspicion, it is improbable that the innocent-looking D can be guilty. But he is. If G has a perfect alibi, sworn to at every point by every other letter in the alphabet, it is improbable that G can have committed the crime. But he has. When the detective picks up a fleck of coal dust at the seashore, it is improbable that such an insignificant thing can have any importance. But it will. In short, you come to a point where the word improbable grows meaningless as a jeer. There can be no such thing as any probability until the end of the story. And then, if you wish the murder to be fastened on an unlikely person (as some of us old fogies do), you can hardly complain because he acted from motives less likely or necessarily less apparent than those of the person first suspected.

"When the cry of 'This-sort-of-thing-wouldn't-happen!' goes up, when you complain about half-faced fiends and hooded phantoms and blond hypnotic sirens, you are merely saying, 'I don't like this sort of story.' That's fair enough. If you do not like it, you are howlingly right to say so. But when you twist this matter of taste into a rule for judging the merit or even the probability of the story, you are merely saying, 'This series of events couldn't happen, because I shouldn't enjoy it if it did.'

"What would seem to be the truth of the matter? We might test it out by taking the hermetically-sealed-chamber as an example, because this situation has been under a hotter fire than any other on the grounds of being unconvincing.

"Most people, I am delighted to say, are fond of the locked room. But—here's the damned rub—even its friends are often dubious. I cheerfully admit that *I* frequently am. So, for the moment, we'll all side together on the score and see what we can discover. Why are we dubious when we hear the explanation of the locked room? Not in the least because we are incredulous, but simply because in some vague way we are *disappointed*. And from that feeling it is only natural to take an unfair step farther, and call the whole business incredible or impossible or flatly ridiculous.

"Precisely, in short," boomed Dr. Fell, pointing his cigar, "what O'Rourke was telling us today about illusions that are performed *in real life*. Lord! gents, what chance has a story got when we even jeer at real occurrences? The very fact that they do happen, and that the illusionist gets away with it, seems to make the deception worse. When it occurs in a detective story, we call it incredible. When it happens in real life, and we are forced to credit it, we merely call the explanation disappointing. And the secret of both disappointments is the same—we expect too much.

"You see, the effect is so magical that we somehow expect the cause to be magical also. When we see that it isn't wizardry, we call it tomfoolery. Which is hardly fair play. The last thing we should complain about with regard to the murderer is his erratic conduct. The whole test is, *can* the thing be done? If so, the question of whether it *would* be done does not enter into it. A man escapes from a locked room—well? Since apparently he has violated the laws of nature for our entertainment, then heaven knows he is entitled to violate the laws of Probable Behaviour! If a man offers to stand on his head, we can hardly make the stipulation that he must keep his feet on the ground while he does it. Bear that in mind, gents, when you judge. Call the result uninteresting, if you like, or anything else that is a matter of personal taste. But be very careful about making the nonsensical statement that it is improbable or far fetched."

"All right, all right," said Hadley, shifting in his chair. "I don't feel very strongly on the matter myself. But if you insist on lecturing—apparently with some application to this case—?"

"Yes."

"Then why take the hermetically sealed room? You yourself said that Grimaud's murder wasn't our biggest problem. The main puzzle is the business of a man shot in the middle of an empty street. . . ."

"Oh, that?" said Dr. Fell, with such a contemptuous wave of his hand that Hadley stared at him. "That part of it? I knew the explanation of that as soon as I heard the church bells. —Tut, tut, such language! I'm quite serious. It's the escape from the room that bothers me. And, to see if we can't get a lead, I am going to outline roughly some of the various means of committing murders in locked rooms, under separate classifications. This crime belongs under one of them. It's got to! No matter how wide the variation may be, it's *only* a variation of a few central methods.

"H'mf! Ha! Now, here is your box with one door, one window, and solid walls. In discussing ways of escaping when both door and window are sealed, I shall not mention the low (and nowadays very rare) trick of having a secret passage to a locked room. This so puts a story beyond the pale that a self-respecting author scarcely needs even to mention that there is no such thing. We don't need to discuss minor variations of this outrage: the panel which is only large enough to admit a hand; or the plugged hole in the ceiling through which a knife is dropped, the plug replaced undetectably, and the floor of the attic above sprayed with dust so that no one seems to have walked there. This is only the same foul in miniature. The principal remains the same whether the secret opening is as small as a thimble or as big as a barn door. . . . As to legitimate classification, you might jot some of these down, Mr. Pettis. . . ."

"Right," said Pettis, who was grinning. "Go on."

"First! There is the crime committed in a hermetically sealed room which really is hermetically sealed, and from which no murderer has escaped because no murderer was actually in the room. Explanations:

"1. It is not murder, but a series of coincidences ending in an accident which looks like murder. At an earlier time, before the room was locked, there has been a robbery, an attack, a wound, or a breaking of furniture which suggests a murder struggle. Later the victim is either accidentally killed or stunned in a locked room, and all these incidents are assumed to have taken place at the same time. In this case the means of death is usually a crack on the head—presumably by a bludgeon, but really from some piece of furniture. It may be from the corner of a table or the sharp edge of a chair, but the most popular object is an iron fender. The murderous fender, by the way, has been killing people in a way that looks like murder ever since Sherlock Holmes' adventure with the Crooked Man. The most thoroughly satisfying solution of this type of plot, which includes a murderer, is in Gaston Leroux's *The Mystery of the Yellow Room* —the best detective tale ever written.

"2. It is murder, but the victim is impelled to kill himself or crash into an accidental death. This may be by the effect of a haunted room, by suggestion, or more usually. by a gas introduced from outside the room. This gas or poison makes the victim go beserk, smash up the room as though there had been a struggle, and die of a knife-slash inflicted on himself. In other variations he drives the spike of the chandelier through his head, is hanged on a loop of wire, or even strangles himself with his own hands.

"3. It is murder, by a mechanical device already planted in the room, and hidden undetectably in some innocent-looking piece of furniture. It may be a trap set by somebody long dead, and work either automatically or be set anew by the modern killer. It may be some fresh quirk of devilry from present-day science. We have, for instance, the gun-mechanism concealed in the telephone receiver, which fires a bullet into the victim's head as he lifts the receiver. We have the pistol with a string to the trigger, which is pulled by the expansion of water as it freezes. We have the clock that fires a bullet when you wind it; and (clocks being popular) we have the ingenious grandfather clock which sets ringing a hideously clanging bell on its top, so that when you reach up to shut off the din your own touch releases a blade that slashes open your stomach. We have the weight that swings down from the ceiling, and the weight that crashes out on your skull from the high back of a chair. There is the bed that exhales a deadly gas when your body warms it, the poisoned needle that leaves no trace, the—

"You see," said Dr. Fell, stabbing out with his cigar at each point, "when we become involved with these mechanical devices we are rather in the sphere of the general 'impossible situation' than the narrower one of the locked room. It would be possible to go on forever, even on mechanical devices for electrocuting people. A cord in front of a row of pictures is electrified. A chessboard is electrified. Even a glove is electrified. There is death in every article of furniture, including a tea-urn. But these things seem to have no present application, so we go on to:

"4. It is suicide, which is intended to look like murder. A man stabs himself with an icicle; the icicle melts! and, no weapon being found in the locked room, murder is presumed. A man shoots himself with a gun fastened on the end of an elastic—the gun, as he releases it, being carried up out of sight into the chimney. Variations of this trick (not locked-room affairs) have been the pistol with a string attached to a weight, which is whisked over the parapet of a bridge into the water after the shot; and, in the same style, the pistol jerked out of a window into a snowdrift.

"5. It is a murder which derives its problem from illusion and impersonation. Thus: the victim, still thought to be alive, is already lying murdered inside a room, of which the door is under observation. The murderer, either dressed as his victim or mistaken from behind for the victim, hurries in at the door. He whirls round, gets rid of his disguise, and instantly comes out of the room *as himself*. The illusion is that he has merely passed the other man in coming out. In any event, he has an alibi; since, when the body is discovered later, the murder is presumed to have taken place some time after the impersonated 'victim' entered the room.

"6. It is a murder which, although committed by somebody outside the room at the time, nevertheless seems to have been committed by somebody who must have been inside.

"In explaining this," said Dr. Fell, breaking off, "I will classify this type of murder under the general name of the Long-Distance or Icicle Crime, since it is usually a variation of that principle. I've spoken of icicles; you understand what I mean. The door is locked, the window too small to admit a murderer; yet the victim has apparently been stabbed from inside the room and the weapon is missing. Well, the icicle has been fired as a bullet from outside—we will not discuss whether this is practical, any more than we have discussed the mysterious gases previously mentioned—and it melts without a trace. I believe Anna Katherine Green was the first to use this trick in detective fiction, in a novel called *Initials Only*.

"(By the way, she was responsible for starting a number of traditions. In her first detective novel, over fifty years ago, she founded the legend of the murderous secretary killing his employer, and I think present-day statistics would prove that the secretary is still the commonest murderer in fiction. Butlers have long gone out of fashion; the invalid in the wheel-chair is too suspect; and the placid middle-aged spinster has long ago given up homicidal mania in order to become a detective. Doctors, too, are better behaved nowadays, unless, of course, they grow eminent and turn into Mad Scientists. Lawyers, while they remain persistently crooked, are only in some cases actively dangerous. But cycles return! Edgar Allan Poe, eighty years ago, blew the gaff by calling his murderer Goodfellow; and the most popular modern mystery-writer does precisely the same thing by calling his arch-villain Goodman. Meanwhile, those secretaries are still the most dangerous people to have about the house.)

"To continue with regard to the icicle: Its actual use has been attributed to the Medici, and in one of the admirable Fleming Stone stories an epigram of Martial is quoted to show that it had its deadly origin in Rome in the first century A.D. Well, it has been fired, thrown, or shot from a crossbow as in one adventure of Hamilton Cleek (that magnificent character of the *Forty Faces).* Variants of the same theme, a soluble missile, have been rock-salt bullets and even bullets made of frozen blood.

"But it illustrates what I mean in crimes committed inside a room by somebody who was outside. There are other methods. The victim may be stabbed by a thin swordstick blade, passed between the twinings of a summer-house and withdrawn; or he may be stabbed with a blade so thin that he does not know he is hurt at all, and walks into another room before he suddenly collapses in death. Or he is lured into looking out of a window inaccessible from below; yet from above our old friend ice smashes down on his head, leaving him with a smashed skull but no weapon because the weapon has melted.

"Under this heading (although it might equally well go under head number 3) we might list murders committed by means of poisonous snakes or insects. Snakes can be concealed not only in chests and safes, but also deftly hidden in flowerpots, books, chandeliers, and walking-sticks. I even remember one cheerful item in which the amber stem of a pipe, grotesquely carven as a scorpion, comes to life a real scorpion as the victim is about to put it into his mouth. But for the greatest long-range murder ever committed in a locked room, gents, I commend you to one of the most brilliant short detective stories in the history of detective fiction. (In fact, it shares the honours for supreme untouchable top-notch excellence with Thomas Burke's, *The Hands of Mr. Ottermole,* Chesterton's, *The Man in the Passage,* and Jacques Futrelle's, *The Problem of Cell 13.)* This is Melville Davisson Post's, *The Doomdorf Mystery*—and the long-range assassin is the sun. The sun strikes through the window of the locked room, makes a burning-glass of a bottle of Doomdorf's own raw white wood-alcohol liquor on the table, and ignites through it the percussion cap of a gun hanging on the wall: so that the breast of the hated one is blown open as he lies in his bed. Then, again, we have . . .

"Steady! Harrumph. Ha. I'd better not meander; I'll round off this classification with the final heading:

"7. This is a murder depending on an effect exactly the reverse of number 5. That is, the victim is presumed to be dead long before he actually is. The victim lies asleep (drugged but unharmed) in a locked room. Knockings on the door fail to rouse him. The murderer starts a foul-play scare; forces the door; gets in ahead and kills by stabbing or throat-cutting, while suggesting to other watchers that they have seen something they have not seen. The honour of inventing this device belongs to Israel Zangwill, and it has since been used in many forms. It has been done (usually by stabbing) on a ship, in a ruined house, in a conservatory, in an attic, and even in the open air—where the victim has first stumbled and stunned himself before the assassin bends over him. So—"

"Steady! Wait a minute!" interposed Hadley, pounding on the table for attention. Dr. Fell, the muscles of whose eloquence were oiling up in a satisfactory way, turned agreeably and beamed on him. Hadley went on: "This may be all very well. You've dealt with all the locked-room situations—"

"All of them?" snorted Dr. Fell, opening his eyes wide. "Of course I haven't. That doesn't even deal comprehensively with the methods under that particular classification; it's only a rough offhand outline; but I'll let it stand. I was going to speak of the other classification: the various means of hocussing doors and windows so that they can be locked on the inside. H'mf! Hah! So, gentlemen, I continue—"

"Not yet you don't," said the superintendent, doggedly. "I'll argue the thing on your own grounds. You say we can get a lead from stating the various ways in which the stunt has been worked. You've stated seven points; but, applied to *this* case, each one must be ruled out according to your own classification-head. You head the whole list, 'No murderer escaped from the room because no murderer was ever actually in it at the time of the crime.' Out goes everything! The one thing we definitely do know, unless we presume Mills and Dumont to be liars, is that the murderer really was in the room! What about that?"

Pettis was sitting forward, his bald head gleaming by the glow of the red-shaded lamp as he bent over an envelope. He was making neat notes with a neat gold pencil. Now he raised his prominent eyes, which seemed more prominent and rather froglike as he studied Dr. Fell.

"Er—yes," he said, with a short cough. "But that point number 5 is suggestive, I should think! Illusion! What if Mills and Mrs. Dumont really didn't see somebody go in that door; that they were hoaxed somehow or that the whole thing was an illusion like a magic-lantern?"

"Illusion me foot," said Hadley. "Sorry! I thought of that, too. I hammered Mills about it last night, and I had another word or two with him this morning. Whatever else the murderer was, he wasn't an illusion and he did go in that door. He was solid enough to cast a shadow and make the hall vibrate when he walked. He was solid enough to talk and slam a door. You agree with that, Fell?"

The doctor nodded disconsolately. He drew in absent puffs on his dead cigar.

"Oh yes, I agree to that. He was solid enough, and he did go in."

"And even," Hadley pursued, while Pettis summoned the waiter to get more coffee, "granting what we know is untrue. Even granting a magic-lantern shadow did all that, a magic-lantern shadow didn't kill Grimaud. It was a solid pistol in a solid hand. And for the rest of the points, Lord knows Grimaud didn't get shot by a mechanical device. What's more, he didn't shoot himself—and have the gun whisk up the chimney like the one in your example. In the first place, a man can't shoot himself from some feet away. And in the second place, the gun can't whisk up the chimney and sail across the roofs to Cagliostro Street, shoot Fley, and tumble down with its work finished. Blast it, Fell, my conversation is getting like yours! It's too much exposure to your habits of thought. I'm expecting a call from the office any minute, and I want to get back to sanity. What's the matter with you?"

Dr. Fell, his little eyes opened wide, was staring at the lamp, and his fist came down slowly on the table.

"Chimney!" he said. "Chimney! Wow! I wonder if—? Lord! Hadley, what an ass I've been!"

"What about the chimney?" asked the superintendent. "We've proved the murderer couldn't have got out like that: getting up the chimney."

"Yes, of course; but I didn't mean that. I begin to get a glimmer, even if it may be a glimmer of moonshine. I must have another look at that chimney."

Pettis chuckled, tapping the gold pencil on his notes. "Anyhow," he suggested, "you may as well round out this discussion. I agree with the superintendent about one thing. You might do better to outline ways of tampering with doors, windows, or chimneys."

"Chimneys, I regret to say," Dr. Fell pursued, his gusto returning as his abstraction left him, "chimneys, I regret to say, are not favoured as a means of escape in detective fiction—except, of course, for secret passages. There they are supreme. There is the hollow chimney with the secret room behind; the back of the fireplace opening like a curtain; the fireplace that swings out; even the room under the hearthstone. Moreover, all kinds of things can be dropped *down* chimneys, chiefly poisonous things. But the murderer who makes his escape by climbing up is very rare. Besides being next to impossible, it is a much grimier business than monkeying with doors or windows. Of the two chief classifications, doors and windows, the door is by far the more popular, and we may list thus a few means of tampering with it so that it seems to be locked on the inside:

"1. Tampering with the key which is still in the lock. This was the favourite old-fashioned method, but its variations are too well-known nowadays for anybody to use it seriously. The stem of the key can be gripped and turned with pliers from outside; we did this ourselves to *open* the door of Grimaud's study. One practical little mechanism consists of a thin metal bar about two inches long, to which is attached a length of stout string. Before leaving the room, this bar is thrust into the hole at the head of the key, one end under and one end over, so that it acts as a lever; the string is dropped down and run under the door to the outside. The door is closed from outside. You have only to pull on the string, and the lever turns the lock; you then shake or pull out the loose bar by means of the string, and when it drops, draw it under the door to you. There are various applications of this same principle, all entailing the use of string.

"2. Simply removing the hinges of the door without disturbing lock or bolt. This is a neat trick, known to most schoolboys when they want to burgle a locked cupboard; but of course the hinges must be on the outside of the door.

"3. Tampering with the bolt. String again: this time with a mechanism of pins and darning-needles, by which the bolt is shot from the outside by leverage of a pin stuck on the inside of the door, and the string is worked through the keyhole. Philo Vance, to whom my hat is lifted, has shown us this best application of the stunt. There are simpler, but not so effective, variations using one piece of string. A 'tomfool' knot, which a sharp jerk will straighten out, is looped in one end of a long piece of cord. This loop is passed round the knob of the bolt, down, and under the door. The door is then closed, and, by drawing the string along to the left or right, the bolt is shot. A jerk releases the knot from the knob, and the string drawn out. Ellery Queen has shown us still another method, entailing the use of the dead man himself— but a bald statement of this, taken out of its context, would sound so wild as to be unfair to that brilliant gentleman.

"4. Tampering with a falling bar or latch. This usually consists in propping something under the latch, which can be pulled away after the door is closed from the outside, and let the bar drop. The best method by far is by the use of the ever-helpful ice, a cube of which is propped under the latch; and, when it melts, the latch falls. There is one case in which the mere slam of the door suffices to drop the bar inside.

"5. An illusion, simple but effective. The murderer, after committing his crime, has locked the door from the outside and kept the key. It is assumed, however, that the key is still in the lock on the inside. The murderer, who is first to raise a scare and find the body smashes the upper glass panel of the door, puts his hand through with the key concealed in it, and 'finds' the key in the lock inside, by which he opens the door. This device has also been used with the breaking of a panel out of an ordinary wooden door.

"There are miscellaneous methods, such as locking a door from the outside and returning the key to the room by means of string again, but you can see for yourselves that in this case none of them can have any application. We found the door locked on the inside. Well, there are many ways by which it could have been done—but it was *not* done, because Mills was watching the door the whole time. This room was only locked in a technical sense. It was watched, and that shoots us all to blazes."

"I don't like to drag in famous platitudes," said Pettis, his forehead wrinkled, "but it would seem plenty sound to say exclude the impossible and whatever remains, however improbable, must be the truth. You've excluded the door; I presume you also exclude the chimney?"

"I do," grunted Dr. Fell.

"Then we come back in a circle to the window, don't we?" demanded Hadley. "You've gone on and on about ways that obviously couldn't have been used. But in this catalogue of sensationalism you've omitted all mention of the only means of exit the murderer *could* have used. . . ."

"Because it wasn't a locked window, don't you see?" cried Dr. Fell. "I can tell you several brands of funny business with windows if they're only locked. It can be traced down from the earliest dummy nail-heads to the latest hocus-pocus with steel shutters. You can smash a window, carefully turn its catch to lock it, and then, when you leave, simply replace the whole pane with a new pane of glass and putty it round; so that the new pane looks like the original and the window is locked inside. But this window wasn't locked or even closed— it was only inaccessible."

"I seem to have read somewhere of human flies . . ." Pettis suggested.

Dr. Fell shook his head. "We won't debate whether a human fly can walk on a sheer smooth wall. Since I've cheerfully accepted so much, I might believe that if the fly had any place to light. That is, he would have to start from somewhere and end somewhere. But he didn't; not on the roof, not on the ground below. . . ." Dr. Fell hammered his fists against his temples. "However, if you want a suggestion or two in that respect, I will tell you—"

He stopped, raising his head. At the end of the quiet, now deserted dining-room a line of windows showed pale light now flickering with snow. A figure had darted in silhouette against them, hesitating, peering from side to side, and then hurrying down towards them. Hadley uttered a muffled exclamation as they saw it was Mangan. Mangan was pale.

"Not something else?" asked Hadley, as coolly as he could. He pushed back his chair. "Not something else about coats changing colour or—"

"No," said Mangan. He stood by the table, drawing his breath in gasps. "But you'd better get over there. Something's happened to Drayman; apoplectic stroke or something like that. No, he's not dead or anything. But he's in a bad way. He was trying to get in touch with you when he had the stroke. . . . He keeps talking wildly about somebody in his room, and fireworks, and chimneys."

THE CHIMNEY 18

Again there were three people—three people strained and with frayed nerves—waiting in the drawing-room. Even Stuart Mills, who stood with his back to the fireplace, kept clearing his throat in a way that seemed to drive Rosette half frantic. Ernestine Dumont sat quietly by the fire when Mangan led in Dr. Fell, Hadley, Pettis, and Rampole. The lights had been turned off; only the bleakness of the snow-shadowed afternoon penetrated through heavy lace curtains, and Mills' shadow blocked the tired gleam of the fire. Burnaby had gone.

"You cannot see him," said the woman, with her eyes fixed on that shadow. "The doctor is with him now. Things all come at once. Probably he is mad."

Rosette, her arms folded, had been pacing about with her own feline grace. She faced the newcomers and spoke with harsh suddenness.

"I can't stand this, you know. It can go on just so long, and then—*Have* you any idea of what happened? Do you know how my father was killed, or who killed him? For God's sake say something, even if you only accuse me!"

"Suppose you tell us exactly what happened to Mr. Drayman," Hadley said, quietly, "and when it happened. Is he in any grave danger?"

Mme Dumont shrugged. "That is possible. His heart . . . I do not know. He collapsed. He is unconscious now. As to whether he will ever come alive again, that I do not know, either. About what happened to him, we have no idea what caused it. . . ."

Again Mills cleared his throat. His head was in the air, and his fixed smile looked rather ghastly. He said:

"If, sir, you have any idea of—um—foul play, or any suspicion that he was murderously set upon, you may dismiss it. And, strangely enough, you will receive confirmation of it from us in—what shall I say—pairs? I mean that the same people were together this afternoon who were together last night. The Pythoness and I," he bowed gravely towards Ernestine Dumont, "were together upstairs in my little workroom. I am given to understand that Miss Grimaud and our friend Mangan were down here. . . ."

Rosette jerked her head. "You had better hear it from the beginning. Did Boyd tell you about Drayman coming down here first?"

"No, I didn't tell 'em anything," Mangan answered, with some bitterness. "After that business of the overcoat, I wanted somebody to give me a little confirmation." He swung round, the muscles tightening at his temples. "It was about half an hour ago, you see. Rosette and I were here alone. I'd had a row with Burnaby—well, the usual thing. Everybody was yelling and fighting about that overcoat affair, and we'd all separated. Burnaby had gone. I hadn't seen Drayman at all; he'd kept to his room this morning. Anyhow, Drayman walked in here and asked me how he could get in touch with you."

"You mean he had discovered something?"

Rosette sniffed. "Or wanted us to think he had. Very mysterious! He came in with that doddering way of his, and as Boyd says, asked where he could find you. Boyd asked him what was up. . . ."

"Did he act as though he might have—well, found something important?"

"Yes, he did. We both nearly jumped out of our shoes. . . ."

"Why?"

"So would you," said Rosette, coolly, "if you were innocent." She twitched her shoulders, her arms still folded, as though she were cold. "So we said, 'What is it, anyhow?' He doddered a little, and said, 'I've found something missing from my room, and it makes me remember something I'd forgotten about last night.' It was all a lot of nonsense about some subconscious memory, though he wasn't very clear on the point. It came down to some hallucination that, while he was lying down last night after he'd taken the sleeping-powder, somebody had come into his room."

"Before the—crime?"

"Yes."

"Who came into his room?"

"That's it! He either didn't know, or wouldn't say, or else the whole thing was a plain dream. Of course that's probably what it was. I won't suggest," said Rosette, still coolly, "the other alternative. When we asked him, he simply tapped his head, and hedged, and said, 'I really can't say,' in that infuriating way of his. . . . Lord! how I hate these people who won't come out and say what they mean! We both got rather annoyed—"

"Oh, he's all right," said Mangan, whose discomfort appeared to be growing. "Only, damn it all, if I hadn't said what I did . . ."

"Said what?" asked Hadley, quickly.

Mangan hunched his shoulders and looked moodily at the fire. "I said, 'Well, if you've discovered so much, why don't you go up to the scene of the 'orrid murder and see if you can't discover some more?' Yes, I was sore. He took me seriously. He looked at me for a minute and said: 'Yes, I believe I will. I had better make sure.' And with that out he went! It was maybe twenty minutes later that we heard a noise like somebody banging downstairs. . . . You see, we hadn't left the room, although—" He checked himself suddenly.

"You might as well go on and say it," Rosette told

him, with an air of surprised indifference. "I don't mind who knows it. I wanted to sneak up after him and watch him. But we didn't. After that twenty minutes, we heard him blundering downstairs. Then, apparently when he'd just got to the last step, we heard a choking sound and a thud—*flap*, like that. Boyd opened the door, and there he was lying doubled up. His face was all congested, and the veins up round the forehead were standing out in a blue colour; horrible business! Of course we sent for the doctor. He hasn't said anything except to rave about 'chimneys' and 'fireworks.' "

Ernestine Dumont still remained stolid, her eyes not moving from the fire. Mills took a little hopping step forward.

"If you will allow me to take up the story," he said, inclining his head, "I think it probable that I can fill the gap. That is, of course, with the Pythoness' permission. . . ."

"Ah, bah!" the woman cried. Her face was in shadow as she looked up, there was about her a rigidity as of whalebone, but Rampole was startled to see that her eyes blazed. "You must always act the fool, must you not? The Pythoness this, the Pythoness that. Very well, I must tell you. I am Pythoness enough to know that you did not like poor Drayman, and that my little Rosette does not like him, either. God! what do you know of human men or sympathy or . . . Drayman is a good man, even if he may be a little mad. He may be mistaken. He may be full of drugs. But he is a good man at the heart, and if he dies I shall pray for his soul."

"Shall I—er—go on?" observed Mills, imperturbably.

"Yes, you shall go on," the woman mimicked, and was silent.

"The Pythoness and I were in my workroom on the top floor; opposite the study, as you know. And again the door was open. I was shifting some papers, and I noticed Mr. Drayman come up and go into the study . . ."

"Do you know what he did there?" asked Hadley.

"Unfortunately, no. He closed the door. I could not even venture a deduction as to what he might be doing, since I could hear nothing. After some time he came out, in what I can only describe as a panting and unsteady condition—"

"What do you mean by that?"

Mills frowned. "I regret, sir, that it is impossible to be more precise. I can only say that I received an impression as though he had been indulging in violent exercise. This, I have no doubt, caused or hastened the collapse, since there were clear evidences of an apoplectic stroke. If I may correct the Pythoness, it had nothing to do with his heart. Er—I might add something which has not yet been mentioned. When he was picked up after the stroke, I observed that his hands and sleeves were covered with soot."

"The chimney again," Pettis murmured, very softly, and Hadley turned round towards Dr. Fell. It gave Rampole a shock to see that the doctor was no longer in the room. A person of his weight and girth can, as a rule, make small success of an effort to fade mysteriously away; but he was gone, and Rampole thought he knew where.

"Follow him up there," Hadley said quickly to the American. "And see that he doesn't work any of his blasted mystification. Now, Mr. Mills—"

Rampole heard Hadley's questions probing and crackling as he went out into the sombre hall. The house was very quiet; so quiet that, as he mounted the stairs, the sudden shrilling of the telephone bell in the lower hall made him jump a little. Passing Drayman's door upstairs, he heard hoarse breathing inside, and quiet footfalls tiptoeing about the room: through the door he could see the doctor's medicine-case and hat on a chair. No lights burned on the top floor; again such a stillness that he could distinctly hear Annie's voice answering the telephone far below.

The study was dusky. Despite the few snowflakes, some faint lurid light, dull red-and-orange with sunset, glimmered through the window. It made a stormy glow across the room; it kindled the colours of the shield of arms, glittered on the crossed fencing-foils above the fireplace, and made vast and shadowy the white busts on the bookshelves. The shape of Charles Grimaud, half-studious, half-barbaric like the room, seemed to move and chuckle here after Charles Grimaud was dead. That vast blank space in the panelled wall, where the picture was to have hung, faced Rampole in mockery. And, standing motionless in his black cloak before the window, Dr. Fell leaned on his cane and stared out into the sunset.

The creaking of the door did not rouse him. Rampole, his voice seeming to make echoes, said:

"Did you—?"

Dr. Fell blinked round. His breath, when he puffed it out with a sort of weary explosiveness, turned to smoke in the sharp air.

"Eh? Oh! Did I what?"

"Find anything."

"Well, I think I know the truth. I think I know the truth," he answered, with a sort of reflective stubbornness, "and tonight I shall probably be able to prove it. H'mf. Hah. Yes. D'ye see, I've been standing here wondering what to do about it. It's the old problem, son, and it becomes more difficult each year I live: when the sky grows nobler, and the old chair more comfortable, and maybe the human heart—" He brushed his hand across his forehead. "What is justice? I've asked it at the end of nearly every case I ever handled. I see faces rise, and sick souls and bad dreams. . . . No matter. Shall we go downstairs?"

"But what about the fireplace?" insisted Rampole. He went over, peered at it, hammered it, and still he could see nothing out of the way. A little soot had been scattered on the hearth, and there was a crooked streak in the coating of soot on the back of the fireplace. "What's wrong with it? Is there a secret passage, after all?"

"Oh no. There's nothing wrong with it in the way you mean. Nobody got up there. No," he added, as Rampole put his hand into the long opening of the flue and groped round. "I'm afraid you're wasting your time; there's nothing up there to find."

"But," said Rampole, desperately, "if this brother Henri—"

"Yes," said a heavy voice from the doorway, "brother Henri."

The voice was so unlike Hadley's that at the moment they did not recognize it. Hadley stood in the doorway, a sheet of paper crumpled in his hand; his face was in shadow, but there was such a dull quietness in his tones that Rampole recognized something like despair. Closing the door softly behind him, Hadley stood in the darkening and went on calmly:

"It was our own fault, I know, for being hypnotized by a theory. It ran away with us—and now we've got to start the whole case afresh. Fell, when you said this morning that the case had been turned upside down, I don't believe you knew just how true it was. It's not only upside down;

it's non-existent. Our chief prop is knocked to blazes. Damn the rotten, impossible . . . !" He stared at the sheet of paper as though he meant to crush it into a ball. "A phone-call just came through from the Yard. They've heard from Bucharest."

"I'm afraid I know what you're going to say," Dr. Fell nodded. "You're going to say that brother Henri—"

"There is no brother Henri," said Hadley. *"The third of the three Horváth brothers died over thirty years ago."*

The faint reddish light had grown muddy; in the cold, quiet study they could hear from far away the mutter of London awaking towards nightfall. Walking over to the broad desk, Hadley spread out the crumpled sheet on the desk so that others could read. The shadow of the yellow jade buffalo lay across it sardonically. Across the room they could see the slashes gaping in the picture of the three graves.

"There's no possibility of a mistake," Hadley went on. "The case is a very well-known one, it seems. The whole cablegram they sent was very long, but I've copied the important parts verbatim from what they read over the phone. Take a look."

No difficulty about information desired [it ran]. Two men now in my personal service were at Siebenturmen as warders in 1900, and confirm record. Facts: Károly Grimaud Horváth, Pierre Fley Horváth, and Nicholas Revéi Horváth were sons of Professor Károly Horváth (of Klausenburg University) and Cécile Fley Horváth (French) his wife. For robbery of Kunar Bank at Brasso, November, 1898, the three brothers were sentenced, January, 1899, to twenty years' penal servitude. Bank watchman died of injuries inflicted, and loot never recovered; believed to have been hidden. All three, with aid of prison doctor during plague scare of August, 1900, made daring attempt at escape by being certified as dead, and buried in plague-ground. J. Lahner and R. Görgei, warders, returning to graves an hour later with wooden crosses for marking, noticed disturbance had taken place on earth at grave of Károly Horváth. Investigation showed coffin open and empty. Digging into other two graves, warders found Pierre

Horváth bloody and insensible, but still alive. Nicholas Horváth had already suffocated to death. Nicholas reburied after absolute certainty made the man was dead; Pierre returned to prison. Scandal hushed up, no chase of fugitive, and story never discovered until end of war. Pierre Fley Horváth never mentally responsible afterwards. Released January, 1919, having served full term. Assure you no doubt whatever third brother dead.

    —ALEXANDER CUZA, Policedirector, Bucharest

"Oh yes," said Hadley, when they had finished reading. "It confirms the reconstruction right enough, except for the little point that we've been chasing a ghost as the murderer. Brother Henri (or brother Nicholas, to be exact) never did leave his grave. He's there yet. And the whole case . . ."

Dr. Fell rapped his knuckles slowly on the paper.

"It's my fault, Hadley," he admitted. "I told you this morning that I'd come close to making the biggest mistake of my life. I was hypnotized by brother Henri! I couldn't think of anything else. You see now why we knew so remarkably little about that third brother, so little that with my cursed cocksureness I put all kinds of fantastic interpretations on it?"

"Well, it won't do us any good just to admit the mistake. How the devil are we going to explain all those crazy remarks of Fley's now? Private vendetta! Vengeance? Now that that's swept away, we haven't a lead to work on. Not one lead! And, if you exclude the motive of vengeance on Grimaud and Fley, what is there left?"

Dr. Fell pointed rather malevolently with his stick.

"Don't you see what's left?" he roared. "Don't you see the explanation of those two murders that we've got to accept now or retire to the madhouse?"

"You mean that somebody cooked up the whole thing to make it look like the work of an avenger?—I'm at the state now," explained the superintendent, "where I could believe nearly anything. But that strikes me as being a good bit too subtle. How would the real murderer ever know we could dig so far into the past? We'd never have done it if it hadn't been, saving your presence, for a few lucky shots. How would the real murderer know we should ever connect Professor Grimaud with a Hungarian criminal, or connect him with Fley or any of the rest of it? It strikes me as a false trail far *too* well concealed." He paced up and down, driving his fist into his palm. "Besides, the more I think of it the more confusing it gets! We had damned good reason to think it was the third brother who killed those two . . . and, the more I think of that possibility, the more I'm inclined to doubt that Nicholas is dead. Grimaud *said* his third brother shot him!—and when a man's dying, and knows he's dying, what earthly reason would he have for lying? Or . . . Stop a bit! Do you suppose he might have meant *Fley?* Do you suppose Fley came here, shot Grimaud, and then afterwards somebody else shot Fley? It would explain a lot of the puzzles—"

"But," said Rampole, "excuse the interruption, I mean, but it wouldn't explain why Fley kept talking about a third brother as well! Either brother Henri is dead or he isn't. Still, if he is dead, what reason have both victims got to lie about him all the time? If he's really dead, he must be one hell of a live ghost."

Hadley shook the briefcase. "I know. That's exactly what I'm kicking about! We've got to take somebody's word for it, and it seems more reasonable to take the word of two people who were shot by him, rather than this cablegram which might be influenced or mistaken for several reasons. Or—h'm! Suppose he really is dead, but the murderer is pretending to be that dead brother come to life?" He stopped, nodded, and stared out of the window. "Now I think we're getting warm. That would explain all the inconsistencies, wouldn't it? The real murderer assumes the rôle of a man neither of the other brothers has seen for nearly thirty years; well? When the murders are committed, and we get on his track—if we do get on his track—we put it all down to vengeance. How's that, Fell?"

Dr. Fell, scowling heavily, stumped round the table.

"Not bad . . . no, not bad, as a disguise. But what about the motive for which Grimaud and Fley were really killed?"

"How do you mean?"

"There has to be a connecting thread, hasn't there? There might be any number of motives, plain or obscure, why a person would kill Grimaud. Mills or Dumont or Burnaby or—yes, anybody *might* have killed Grimaud. Also, anybody might have killed Fley: but not, I must point out, anybody in the same circle or group of people. Why should Fley be killed by a member of Grimaud's group, none of whom had presumably ever seen him before? If these murders are the work of one person, where is the connecting link? A respected professor in Bloomsbury and a tramp actor with a prison record. Where's the human motive that ties those two together in the murderer's mind, unless it is a link that goes back into the past?"

"I can think of one person who is associated with both from the past," Hadley pointed out.

"Who? You mean the Dumont woman?"

"Yes."

"Then what becomes of somebody impersonating brother Henri? Whatever else you decide on, you must decide that she's not doing that. No, my lad. Dumont is not only a bad suspect; she's an impossible suspect."

"I don't see that. Look here, you're basing your whole belief that Dumont didn't kill Grimaud on the grounds that you think she loved Grimaud. No defence, Fell—no defence at all! Remember that she told the whole fantastic story to begin with . . ."

"In coöperation with—Mills," boomed Dr. Fell, with a sardonic leer. He was puffing again. "Can you think of any two less likely conspirators to band together at the dark of the moon and hoodwink the police with their imaginative fairy-tales? She might wear a mask; I mean a figurative mask in life. Mills might wear a mask. But the combination of those two masks, and their activities, is too much. I prefer the one literal false face. Besides, bear in mind that as the double killer Ernestine D. is absolutely O-U-T. Why? Because, at the time of Fley's death sworn to by three good men and true, she was here in this room, talking to us." He pondered, and a twinkle began to appear in his eye. "Or will you drag in the second generation? Rosette is Grimaud's daughter; suppose the mysterious Stuart Mills is really the son of the dead brother Henri?"

About to reply, Hadley checked himself and studied Dr. Fell. He sat down on the edge of the desk.

"I know this mood. I know it very well," he asserted, with the air of one who confirms a sinister suspicion. "It's the beginning of some more blasted mystification, and there's no use arguing with you now. Why are you so anxious for me to believe the story?"

"First," said Dr. Fell, "because I wish to force it into your head that Mills told the truth. . . ."

"You mean, as a point in the mystification, in order to prove later that he didn't? The sort of low trick you played me in that Death Watch case?"

The doctor ignored this with a testy grunt. "And, second, because I know the real murderer."

"Who is somebody we've seen and talked to?"

"Oh yes; very much so."

"And have we got a chance of—?"

Dr. Fell, an absent, fierce, almost pitying expression on his red face, stared for some time at the desk.

"Yes, Lord help us all," he said, in a curious tone, "I suppose you've got to. In the meantime, I'm going home. . . ."

"Home?"

"To apply Gross's test," said Dr. Fell.

He turned away, but he did not immediately go. As the muddy light deepened to purple, and dust-coloured shadows swallowed up the room, he remained for a long time staring at the slashed picture which caught the last glow with its turbulent power, and the three coffins that were filled at last.

THE HOLLOW MAN **19**

That night Dr. Fell shut himself up in the small cubbyhole off the library which was reserved for what he called his scientific experiments and what Mrs. Fell called "that horrible messing about." Now, a liking for messing about is one of the best of human traits, and Rampole and Dorothy both offered to assist. But the doctor was so serious, and so unwontedly troubled, that they left off with an uncomfortable feeling that to make a joke would be bad taste. The tireless Hadley had already gone off to check alibis. Rampole left the matter with only one question.

"I know you're going to try to read those burnt letters," he said, "and I know you think they're important. But what do you expect to find?"

"The worst possible thing," replied Dr. Fell. "The thing that last night could have made a fool of me."

And with a sleepy shake of his head he closed the door.

Rampole and Dorothy sat on opposite sides of the fireplace, looking at each other. The snow was whirling outside, and it was not a night to venture far. Rampole at first had an idea that he ought to invite Mangan out to dinner, to renew old times; but Mangan, when he telephoned, said that obviously Rosette could not go, and he had better remain with her. So the other two, Mrs. Fell being at church, had the library to themselves for argument.

"Ever since last night," commented her husband, "I've been hearing about Gross's method for reading burnt letters. But nobody seems to know what it is. I suppose you mix chemicals or something?"

"I know what it is," she told him, with an air of triumph. "I looked it up while you people were dashing about this afternoon. And what's more, I bet you it won't work even if it is simple. I bet you *anything* it won't work!"

"You read Gross?"

"Well, I read it in English. It's simple enough. It says something like this. It says that anybody who has thrown letters on the fire will have noticed that the writing on the charred fragments stands out quite clearly, usually white or grey against a black background, but sometimes with the colours reversed. Did you ever notice that?"

"Can't say I have. But then I've seen very few open fires before I came to England. Is it true?"

She frowned. "It works with cardboard boxes that have printing on them, boxes of soap flakes or things like that. But regular writing. . . . Anyway, here's what you're supposed to do. You get a lot of transparent tracing-paper and pin it to a board with drawing-pins. As you pick up each of the charred pieces of paper you cover a place on the tracing-paper with gum, press the charred paper down on it. . . ."

"When it's crumpled up like that? It'll break, won't it?"

"Aha! That's the trick, Gross says. You have to soften the fragments. You arrange over and around the tracing-paper a frame two or three inches high, with all the bits under it. Then you stretch across a damp cloth folded several times. That puts the papers in a damp atmosphere, and they straighten out. When they're all flattened out and fixed, you cut out the tracing-paper round each separate fragment. Then you reconstruct them on a sheet of glass. Like a jig-saw puzzle. Afterwards you press a second sheet of glass over the first, and bind the edges, and look through both against the light. But I'll bet you anything you like—"

"We'll try it," said Rampole, impressed and afire with the idea.

The experiments at burning paper were not a complete success. First he got an old letter out of his pocket and touched a match to it. Despite his frantic manœuvring, it soared up into flame, twitched round, sailed out of his hand, and shrank to rest on the hearth as not more than two inches of shrivelled blackness rolled up like an umbrella. Though they got down on their knees and scrutinized it from every angle, no writing was visible. Rampole burnt several more pieces, which sailed apart like gentle sky-rockets and powdered the hearth. Then he began to get mad and burn everything within reach. And, the madder he got, the more convinced he grew that the trick could be worked somehow if he did it properly. Typewriting was tried; he tapped out "Now is the time for all good men to come to the aid of the party" a number of times on Dr. Fell's machine and presently the carpet was littered with floating fragments.

"Besides," he argued, with his cheek against the floor and one eye closed as he studied them, "these aren't charred—they're burnt to hell. They're too far gone to fulfill the conditions. Aha! Got it! I can see 'party' as plain as day. It's much smaller than the actual typing; it seems to be indented on the black; but here it is. Have you got anything out of that handwritten letter?"

Her own excitement was growing as she made a discovery. The words "East 11th Street" stood out in dirty grey letters. With some care, but much powdering of the brittle pieces, they at last deciphered plainly the words, "Saturday night," "ginch," "hangover," and "gin." Rampole got up with satisfaction.

"If those pieces can be straightened out by dampness, then it works!" he declared. "The only thing is whether you could get enough words out of any letter to make sense of it. Besides, we're only amateurs; Gross could get the whole thing. But what does Dr. Fell expect to find?"

This was the subject of an argument which was carried on far into the night.

"And with the case turned upside down," Rampole pointed out, "where do we go now for a motive? That's the crux of the whole business. There's no motive that could connect both Grimaud and Fley with the murderer! By the way, what's become of your wild theories last night, that the guilty person must be either Pettis or Burnaby?"

"Or the funny-faced blonde," she corrected, with a certain emphasis on the term. "I say, you know, what bothers me most is that overcoat changing colour and disappearing and all the rest of it. It seems to lead straight back to that house, or does it?" She brooded. "No, I've changed my mind altogether. I don't think Pettis or Burnaby can be implicated. I don't even think the blonde is. The possible murderer, I'm certain now, can be narrowed down to two other people."

"Well?"

"It's either Drayman or O'Rourke," she said, firmly, and nodded. "You mark my words."

Rampole stifled a strong protest. "Yes, I'd thought of O'Rourke," he admitted. "But you're picking him for just two reasons. First because he's a trapeze man, and you associate a flying escape of some sort with the way this thing was done. But, so far as I can see, it's impossible. Second and more important, you're picking him for the reason that he doesn't seem to have any connection with this case at all; that he's standing around for no good reason, and that's always a suspicious sign. Isn't that so?"

"Maybe."

"Then Drayman . . . yes, Drayman might have been the only one who could now be associated with both Grimaud and Fley in the past. That's a point! H'm. Also, nobody saw him during the whole evening from dinner time until a much later hour—eleven o'clock, anyhow. But I don't believe he's guilty. Tell you what: let's make a rough time-table of last night's events to get this thing straightened out. We'll put in everything, from before dinner on. It'll have to be a very rough time-table, with a lot of guessing on smaller points. We don't know much definitely except the time of the actual murders and a few statements leading up to them, but we can make a stab at it. Our times before dinner are vague too. But let's say . . ."

He took out an envelope and wrote rapidly.

(About) 6:45 Mangan arrives, hangs his coat in the hall closet, and sees a black overcoat hanging there.

(About) 6:48 (give her three minutes) Annie comes from the dining-room, switches off the light in the hall closet left burning by Mangan, and sees no overcoat at all.

(About) 6:55 (this is not specified, but we know it was before dinner), Mme Dumont looks into the hall closet and sees a yellow overcoat.

"I arrange it like that," said Rampole, "because presumably in the very brief time between Mangan's hanging up his own coat and going away, with the light left on, Dumont didn't rush out to look in there before Annie came to turn the light off."

The girl's eyes narrowed. "Oo, wait! How do you know that? I mean, if the light wasn't on, how did she see a yellow coat at all?"

There was a pause while they looked at each other. Rampole said:

"This is getting interesting. And, if it comes to that, why did she look in there, anyhow?" The point is this: If the sequence of times can be established at what I've written, that's reasonable. First, there's a black coat, which Mangan sees. Well, then somebody swipes the black coat just after Mangan goes—for what reason we don't know—and Annie sees nothing. Later the coat is replaced with a light tweed one. That sounds all right. *But,*" he cried, stabbing out with his pencil, "if it worked the other way around, then either somebody is lying or the whole thing is impossible. In that case it doesn't matter what time Mangan arrived, because the whole business must have taken place in a matter of minutes or even seconds. See it? Boyd gets there, hangs his coat up, and walks away. Out comes Dumont, looks in, and walks away. Along comes Annie immediately afterwards, turns out the light, and *she* goes. In that short flash a black overcoat has first turned yellow and then disappeared. Which is impossible."

"Well done!" said the other, beaming. "Then which one was lying? I suppose you'll insist it wasn't your friend—"

"I certainly will. It's the Dumont woman, I'll bet you anything you like!"

"But she's not guilty. That's been proved. Besides, I like her."

"Don't mix me up, now," Rampole urged. "Let's go on with this time-table and see if we can discover anything else. Haa! Where were we? Yes. Dinner we'll put at seven o'clock, because we know it was over at seven-thirty. Hence—

"7:30 Rosette G. and Mangan go to drawing-room.

7:30 Drayman goes upstairs to his room.

7:30 E. Dumont—where she goes is not known, except that she remains in the house.

7:30 Mills goes to downstairs library.

7:30 Grimaud joins Mills in downstairs library, tells him to come upstairs about 9:30, since he expects a visitor then.

"Whoa! Here's a snag. I was just going to write that then Grimaud goes on to the drawing-room, and tells Mangan the visitor is expected at ten o'clock. But that won't do, because Rosette knew nothing about it, and yet she was with Mangan! The trouble is, Boyd didn't say exactly when he was told that. But it isn't important— Grimaud might have taken him aside or something like that. Similarly, we don't know when Madame Dumont was told to expect the visitor at nine-thirty; probably earlier. It amounts to the same thing."

"Are you sure it does?" enquired Dorothy, searching after cigarettes. "H'm! Well, carry on."

"(About) 7:35 Grimaud goes up to his study.

7:35 to 9:30 no developments. Nobody moves. **Heavy snow.**

(About) 9:30 snow stops.

(About) 9:30 E. Dumont collects coffee-tray from Grimaud's study. Grimaud remarks that visitor will probably not come that night. E. Dumont leaves study just as—

9:30 Mills comes upstairs.

"I don't think anything noticeable happened in the next interval. Mills was upstairs, Drayman in his room, and Rosette and Boyd in the front room with the radio on. . . . Wait! I'm forgetting something. A little while before the door-bell rang, Rosette heard a thud from somewhere out in the street, as though somebody had fallen off a high place. . . ."

"How did she hear that if they had the radio on?"

"Apparently it wasn't playing loudly enough to— Yes, it was, though. It made such a racket they could hardly hear the fake 'Pettis's' voice. But put that in order:

"9:45 Door-bell rings.

9:45 to 9:50 E. Dumont goes to answer door; speaks to visitor (failing to recognize voice). She receives card, shuts the door on him, examines card and finds it blank, hesitates, and starts upstairs. . . .

9:45 to 9:50. Visitor, after E. D. has started upstairs, gets inside somehow, locks Rosette G. and Boyd M. in front room, answers their hail by imitating the voice of Pettis—"

"I don't like to keep on interrupting you," cut in Dorothy. "But doesn't it seem to have taken them a terribly long time to sing out and ask who the caller was? I mean, would anybody wait so long? If I were expecting a visitor like that, I know I should have piped up, 'Hullo! who is it?' as soon as I heard the door open."

"What are you trying to prove? Nothing? Sure of that? Don't be so hard on the blonde! It was some time before they expected anybody, remember—and that sniff of yours indicates prejudice. Let's continue, with the still inclusive times of nine forty-five to nine-fifty, the interval between the moment X entered the house and the moment he entered Grimaud's study:

"9:45 to 9:50. Visitor follows E. Dumont upstairs, overtakes her in upper hall. He takes off cap and pulls down coat collar, but does not remove mask. Grimaud comes to the door, but does not recognize visitor. Visitor leaps inside and door is slammed. (This is attested by both E. Dumont and S. Mills.)

9:50 to 10:10. Mills watches door from end of hall; Dumont watches same door from staircase landing.

10:10 Shot is fired.

10:10 to 10:12. Mangan in front room finds door to hall locked, on the inside.

10:10 to 10:12. E. Dumont faints or is sick, and gets to her room. (N. B. Drayman, asleep in his room, does not hear shot.)

10:10 to 10:12. Mangan in front room finds door to hall locked, attempts to break it and fails. He then jumps out window, just as—

10:12 We arrive outside; front door unlocked; we go up to study.

10:12 to 10:15. Door is opened with pliers, Grimaud found shot.

10:15 to 10:20. Investigation, ambulance sent for.

10:20 Ambulance arrives. Grimaud removed. Rosette goes with him in ambulance. Boyd M., at orders from Hadley, goes down stairs to telephone police.

"Which," Rampole pointed out with some satisfaction, "absolutely clears both Rosette and Boyd. I don't even need to set down minute times there. The ambulance-men coming upstairs, the doctor's examination, the body taken down to the ambulance—all that in itself would have taken at least five minutes if they'd moved fast enough to slide down the banisters with that stretcher. By God! it's as plain as print when you write it out! It would have taken a good deal longer before they could get to the nursing-home . . . and yet Fley was shot in Cagliostro Street at just ten twenty-five! Now, Rosette did ride over with the ambulance. Boyd was in the house when the ambulance-men arrived, because he came upstairs with them and went down after them. There's a fairly perfect alibi."

"Oh, you don't need to think I'm so anxious to convict them!—especially Boyd, who's rather nice what little I've seen of him." She frowned. "That's always granting your guess that the ambulance didn't arrive at Grimaud's before ten-twenty."

Rampole shrugged. "If it did," he pointed out, "then it flew over from Guilford Street. It wasn't sent for before ten-fifteen, and even so it's something like a miracle that they had it at Grimaud's in five minutes. No, Boyd and Rosette are out of it. Besides, now that I remember, she was at the nursing-home—in the presence of witnesses—when she saw the light in the window of Burnaby's flat at ten-thirty. Let's put the rest into the record and exonerate anyone else we can.

"10:20 to 10:25. Arrival and departure of ambulance with Grimaud.

10:25 Fley shot in Cagliostro Street.

10:20 to (at least) 10:30. Stuart Mills remains with us in study, answering questions.

10:25 Madame Dumont comes into study.

10:30 Rosette, at nursing-home, sees a light in the window of Burnaby's flat.

10:25 to 10:40. Madame Dumont remains with us in the study.

10:40 Rosette returns from nursing-home.

10:40 Arrival of police at Hadley's call."

Rampole, sitting back to run his eye down the scrawl, drew a long flourish under the last item.

"That not only completes our time-table as far as we need to go," he said, "but it unquestionably adds two more to our list of innocents. Mills and Dumont are out. Rosette and Boyd are out. Which accounts for everybody in the house except Drayman."

"But," protested Dorothy, after a pause, "it's getting even worse tangled up. What happens to your brilliant inspiration about the overcoat? You suggested somebody was lying. It could only have been either Boyd Mangan or

Ernestine Dumont; and both are exonerated. Unless that
girl Annie— But that won't do, will it? Or it shouldn't."

Again they looked at each other. Wryly he folded up
his list and put it into his pocket. Outside, the night wind
whirled by in a long blast, and they could hear Dr. Fell
blundering round his cubbyhole behind the closed door.

Rampole overslept the next morning, partly from ex-
haustion and partly because the following day was so
overcast that he did not open his eyes until past ten o'clock.
It was not only so dark that the lights were on, but a day
of numbing cold. He had not seen Dr. Fell again last
night, and, when he went downstairs to breakfast in the
little back dining-room, the maid was indignant as she set
out bacon and eggs.

"The doctor's just gone up to have a wash, sir," Vida
informed him. "He was up all night on them scientific
things, and I found him asleep in the chair in there
at eight o'clock this morning. I don't know what Mrs.
Fell will say, indeed I don't. Superintendent Hadley's
just got here, too. He's in the library."

Hadley, who was impatiently knocking his heels against
the fender as though he were pawing the floor, asked for
news with some eagerness.

"Have you seen Fell?" he demanded. "Did he go after
those letters? And if so—?"

Rampole explained. "Any news from you?"

"Yes, and important news. Both Pettis and Burnaby
are out. They've got cast-iron alibis."

Wind whooped past along Adelphi Terrace, and the
long window-frames rattled. Hadley continued to paw
the hearth rug. He went on: "I saw Burnaby's three card-
playing friends last night. One, by the way, is an Old
Bailey judge; it'd be pretty difficult to drag a man into
court when the judge on the bench can testify to his innocence. Burnaby was playing poker on Saturday night
from eight o'clock to nearly half-past eleven.—And this
morning Betts has been round to the theatre where Pettis
said he saw the play that night. Well, he did. One of the
bar-attendants at the theatre knows him quite well by sight.
It seems that the second act of the show ends at five
minutes past ten. A few minutes afterwards, during the
interval, this attendant is willing to swear he served Pettis
with a whisky-and-soda in the bar. In other words, he was

having a drink at just about the exact moment Grimaud was shot nearly a mile away."

"I expected something like that," said Rampole, after a silence. "And yet, to hear it confirmed. . . . I wish you'd look at this."

He handed over the time-table he had made last night. Hadley glanced over it.

"Oh yes. I sketched out one of my own. This is fairly sound; especially the point about the girl and Mangan, although we can't swear too closely to time in that respect. But I think it would hold." He tapped the envelope against his palm. "Narrows it down, I admit. We'll have another go at Drayman. I phoned the house this morning. Everybody was a bit hysterical because they've brought the old man's body back to the house, and I couldn't get much out of Rosette except that Drayman was still only half-conscious and under morphia. We—"

He stopped as they heard the familiar, lumbering step with the tap of the cane, which seemed to have hesitated just outside the door as though at Hadley's words. Then Dr. Fell pushed open the door. There was no twinkle in his eye when he wheezed in. He seemed a part of the heavy morning, and a sense of doom pervading that leaden air.

"Well?" prompted Hadley. "Did you find out what you wanted to know from those papers?"

Dr. Fell fumbled after, found, and lit his black pipe. Before he answered he waddled over to toss the match into the fire. Then he chuckled at last, but very wryly.

"Yes, I found out what I wanted to know. —Hadley, twice in my theories on Saturday night I unintentionally led you wrong. *So* wrong, with such a monstrous and dizzying stupidity, that if I hadn't saved my self-respect by seeing the truth of this thing yesterday, I should have deserved the last punishment reserved for fools. Still, mine wasn't the only blunder. Chance and circumstance made an even worse blunder, and they've combined to make a terrifying, inexplicable puzzle out of what is really only a commonplace and ugly and petty murder-case. Oh, there was shrewdness to the murderer; I admit that. But—yes, I've found out what I wanted to know."

"Well? What about the writing on those papers? What was on those papers?"

"Nothing," said Dr. Fell.

There was something eerie in the slow, heavy way he spoke the word.

"You mean," cried Hadley, "that the experiment didn't work?"

"No, I mean that the experiment did work. I mean that there was *nothing* on those papers," boomed Dr. Fell. "Not so much as a single line or scrap or shred of handwriting, not so much as a whisper or pothook of the deadly secrets I told you on Saturday night we might find. That's what I mean. Except—well, yes. There were a few bits of heavier paper, rather like thick cardboard, with one or two letters printed there."

"But why burn letters unless—?"

"Because they weren't letters. That's just it; that's where we went wrong. Don't you see even yet what they were? . . . Well, Hadley, we'd better finish this up and get the whole mess off our minds. You want to meet the Invisible Murderer, do you? You want to meet the damned ghoul and hollow man who's been walking through our dreams? Very well; I'll introduce you. Got your car? Then come along. *I'm going to see if I can't extract a confession.*"

"From—?"

"From somebody at Grimaud's house. Come on."

Rampole saw the end looming, and was afraid of it, without an idea in his whirling head as to what it might be. Hadley had to spin a half-frozen engine before the car would start. They were caught in several traffic blocks on the way up, but Hadley did not even curse. And the quietest of all was Dr. Fell.

All the blinds were drawn on the house in Russell Square. It looked even more dead than yesterday, because death had come inside. And it was so quiet that even from outside they could hear the ringing of the bell when Dr. Fell pressed it. After a long interval Annie, without her cap or apron, answered it. She looked pale and strained, but still calm.

"We should like to see Madame Dumont," said Dr. Fell.

Hadley jerked his head round to look, even though he remained impassive. Annie seemed to speak out of the darkness in the hall as she moved back.

"She is in with the—she's in there," the girl answered, and pointed towards the drawing-room door. "I'll call—" She swallowed.

Dr. Fell shook his head. He moved over with surprising quietness and softly opened the drawing-room door.

The dull brown blinds were drawn, and the thick lace curtains muffled what little light filtered through. Although the room looked vaster, its furniture was lost in shadow; except for one piece of furniture, of gleaming black metal lined with white satin. It was an open coffin. Thin candles were burning around it. Of the dead face Rampole afterwards remembered that from where he stood he could see only the tip of a nose. But those candles alone, or the faint thickness of flowers and incense in the air, moved the scene weirdly from dun London to some place of crags and blasts among the Hungarian mountains: where the gold cross loomed guard against devils, and garlic wreaths kept off the prowling vampire.

Yet this was not the thing they first noticed. Ernestine Dumont stood beside the coffin, one hand gripping its edge. The high, thin candle-light above turned her greying hair to gold; it softened and subdued even the crumpled posture of her bent shoulders. When she turned her head slowly round, they saw that her eyes were sunken and smeared—though she still could not weep. Her breast heaved jerkily. Yet round her shoulders she had wound a gay, heavy, long-fringed yellow shawl, with red brocade and bead embroidery that burnt with a shifting glitter under the light. It was the last touch of the barbaric.

And then she saw them. Both hands suddenly gripped the edge of the coffin, as though she would shield the dead. She remained a silhouette, one hand outspread on either side, under the unsteady candles.

"It will do you good, madame, to confess," said Dr. Fell, very gently. "Believe me, it will do you good."

For a second Rampole thought she had stopped breathing, so easy was every motion to follow in the unearthliness of that light. Then she made a sound as though she were half-coughing, which is only grief before it becomes hysterical mirth.

"Confess?" she said. "So that is what you think, all you fools? Well, I do not care. Confess! Confess to murder?"

"No," said Dr. Fell.

His voice, in that one quiet monosyllable, had a heavy note across the room. And now she stared at him, and now for the first time she began to stare with fright as he moved across towards her.

"No," said Dr. Fell. "You are not the murderer. Let me tell you what you are."

Now he towered over her, black against the candle-light, but he still spoke gently.

"Yesterday, you see, a man named O'Rourke told us several things. Among them was the fact that most illusions either on or off the stage are worked with the aid of a confederate. This was no exception. You were the confederate of the illusionist and murderer."

"The hollow man," said Ernestine Dumont, and suddenly began to laugh hysterically.

"The hollow man," said Dr. Fell, and turned quietly to Hadley, "in a real sense. The hollow man whose naming was a terrible and an ironic jest, even if we did not know it, because it was the exact truth. That is the horror and in a way the shame. Do you want to see the murderer you have been hunting all through this case?—The murderer lies *there*," said Dr. Fell, "but God forbid that we should judge him now."

And with a slow gesture he pointed to the white, dead, tight-lipped face of Dr. Charles Grimaud.

THE TWO BULLETS 20

Dr. Fell continued to look steadily at the woman, who had again shrunk against the side of the coffin as though to defend it.

"Ma'am," he went on, "the man you loved is dead. He is beyond the reach of the law now, and, whatever he has done, he has paid for it. Our immediate problem, yours and mine, is to hush this thing up so that the living may not be hurt. But, you see, you are implicated, even though you took no actual hand in the murder. Believe me, ma'am, if I could have explained the whole thing without bringing you into it at all, I should have done so. I know you have suffered. But you will see for yourself that such a course was impossible if I were to explain the entire problem. So we must persuade Superintendent Hadley that this affair must be hushed up."

Something in his voice, something of the unweary, un-

changing, limitless compassion that was Gideon Fell,
seemed to touch her as gently as sleep after tears. Her
hysteria had gone.

"Do you know?" she asked him, after a pause, and almost eagerly. "Do not fool me! Do you really know?"

"Yes, I really know."

"Go upstairs. Go to *his* room," she said in a dull voice,
"and I will join you presently. I—I cannot face you just
now. I must think, and— But please do not speak to anybody until I come. Please! No, I will not run away."

Dr. Fell's fierce gesture silenced Hadley as they went
out. Still in silence they tramped up the gloomy stairs
to the top floor. They passed no one, they saw no one.
Once more they came into the study, where it was so
dark that Hadley switched on the mosaic lamp at the desk.
After he had made sure the door was closed, Hadley turned
round rather wildly.

"Are you trying to tell me that Grimaud killed Fley?" he
demanded.

"Yes."

"While he was lying unconscious and dying under
the eyes of witnesses in a nursing-home, he went to
Cagliostro Street and—!"

"Not then," said Dr. Fell quietly. "You see, that's what
you don't understand. That's what's led you wrong. That's
what I meant by saying that the case had been turned
not upside down, but *the wrong way round*. Fley was
killed before Grimaud. And, worst of all, Grimaud was
trying to tell us the exact, literal truth. He did tell us the
exact truth, when he knew he was dying beyond hope—
it's one of the good gleams in him—but we chose to misin-
terpret it. Sit down, and I'll see if I can explain it. Once you
have grasped the three essential points, you will need no
deduction and very little elucidation from me. The thing
will explain itself."

He lowered himself, wheezing, into the chair behind
the desk. For a little time he remained staring vacantly
at the lamp. Then he went on:

"The three essential points, then, are these. (1) There
is no brother Henri; there are only two brothers. (2) Both
these brothers were speaking the truth. (3) A question of
time has turned the case wrong way round.

"Many things in this case have turned on a matter of
brief spaces of time, and how brief they are. It's a part of

the same irony which described our murderer as the hollow man that the crux of the case should be a matter of mistaken time. You can easily spot it if you think back.

"Now remember yesterday morning! I already had some occasion to believe there was something queer about that business in Cagliostro Street. The shooting there, we were told by three (truthful) witnesses who agreed precisely and to a second, took place at just ten twenty-five. I wondered, in an idle sort of way, why they corroborated each other with such startling exactitude. In the case of the usual street accident, even the most cool witnesses don't usually take such notice, or are careful to consult their watches, or (even if they do) agree about the time with such uncanny precision. But they were truthful people, and there must have been some reason for their exactitude. The time must have been thrust on them.

"Of course there was a reason. Just across from where the murdered man fell there was a lighted show-window— the only lighted window thereabouts—of a jeweller's shop. It was the most noticeable thing in the foreground. It illuminated the murdered man; it was the first place to which the constable rushed in search of the murderer; it quite naturally focussed their attention. And, facing them from that window, there was an enormous clock of such unusual design that it immediately took the eye. It was inevitable that the constable should look for the time, and natural that the others should also. Hence their agreement.

"But one thing, not apparently important at that time, bothered me a little. After Grimaud was shot, Hadley summoned his men to this house, and instantly dispatched one of them to pick up Fley as a suspect. Now, then, those men arrived here . . . about what time?"

"About ten-forty," said Rampole, "according to a rough calculation. I've got it in my time-table."

"And," said Dr. Fell, "a man was sent immediately to get Fley. This man must have arrived in Cagliostro, Street—when? Between fifteen and twenty minutes after Fley was presumed to have been killed. But in the space of that brief time what has happened? An incredible number of things! Fley has been carried down to the doctor's house, he has died, an examination has been made, a fruitless effort undertaken to identify Fley; and then, 'after some delay' in the words of the newspaper account, the van is sent for and Fley removed to the mortuary. All this! For, when Hadley's detective arrived in Cagliostro Street to pick up Fley, he found the whole business finished—and the constable back making inquiries from door to door. The entire excitement had died down. Which seemed incredible.

"Unfortunately, I was so dense that I didn't see the significance of this even yesterday morning when I saw the clock in the jeweller's window.

"Think back once more. Yesterday morning we had breakfast at my house; Pettis dropped in, and we talked to him—until what time?"

There was a pause.

"Until exactly ten o'clock," Hadley answered, suddenly, and snapped his fingers. "Yes! I remember, because Big Ben was striking just as he got up to go."

"Quite right. He left us, and afterwards we put on our hats and coats and drove *straight* to Cagliostro Street. Now, allow any reasonable margin of time you like for our putting on our hats, going downstairs, driving a short distance on deserted roads Sunday morning—a drive that took us only ten minutes when there was Saturday-night traffic. I think you'll say the whole process can hardly have taken twenty minutes in all. . . . But in Cagliostro Street you showed me the jeweller's shop, and that fancy clock was just striking *eleven*.

"Even then in my musing density it never occurred to me to look at that clock and wonder, just as in their excitement it never occurred to the three witnesses last night. Just afterwards, you recall, Somers and O'Rourke summoned us up to Burnaby's flat. We made quite a long investigation, and then had a talk with O'Rourke. And while O'Rourke was speaking, I noticed that the earlier dead quiet of the day—the quiet when in the street we heard only the wind—had a new sound. I heard church bells.

"Well, what time *do* church bells begin to ring? Not after eleven o'clock; the service has begun. Usually before eleven, for a preparatory bell. But, if I accepted the evidence of that German clock, it must then be a very long time past eleven o'clock. Then my dull mind woke up. I remembered Big Ben and our drive to Cagliostro Street. The combination of those bells and Big Ben— against (hem!) a trumpery foreign clock. Church and

State, so to speak, couldn't both be wrong. . . . In other words, *the clock in that jeweller's window was more than forty minutes fast. Hence the shooting in Cagliostro Street the night before could not have taken place at twenty-five minutes past ten. Actually it must have taken place a short time previous to a quarter to ten. Say, roughly, at nine-forty.*

"Now, sooner or later somebody would have noticed this; maybe somebody has noticed it already. A thing like that would be bound to come out in a coroner's court. Somebody would come forward to dispute the right time. Whether you'd have instantly seen the truth then (as I hope), or whether it would have confused you even more, I don't know. . . . But the solid fact remains that the affair in Cagliostro Street took place some minutes before the man in the false face rang the bell of this house at nine forty-five."

"But I still don't see—!" protested Hadley.

"The impossible situation? No; but I have a clear course now to tell you the whole story from the beginning."

"Yes, but let me get this straightened out. If Grimaud, as you say, shot Fley in Cagliostro Street just before nine forty-five—"

"I didn't say that," said Dr. Fell.

"What?"

"You'll understand if you follow my patient elucidation from the beginning. On Wednesday night of last week— when Fley first appeared out of the past, apparently out of his grave, to confront his brother with rather a terrible threat at the Warwick Tavern—Grimaud resolved to kill him. In the whole case, you see, Grimaud was the only person with a motive for killing Fley. And, my God! Hadley, but he did have a motive! He was safe, he was rich, he was respected; the past was buried. And then, all of a sudden, a door blows open to admit this thin grinning stranger who is his brother Pierre. Grimaud, in escaping from prison, had murdered one of his brothers by leaving him buried alive; he would have murdered the other except for an accident. He could still be extradited and hanged—and Pierre Fley had traced him.

"Now, bear in mind exactly what Fley said when he suddenly flew in to confront Grimaud that night at the tavern. Study *why* he said and did certain things, and you will see that even shaky-minded Fley was very far from being as mad as he liked to pretend. Why, if he were intent merely on private vengeance, did he choose to confront Grimaud in the presence of a circle of friends and speak in just the innuendoes he used? He used his *dead* brother as a threat; and it was the only time he did speak of that *dead* brother. Why did he say, 'He can be much more dangerous to you than I can'? Because the dead brother could hang Grimaud! Why did he say, 'I don't want your life; he does'? Why did he say, 'Shall I have him call on you'? And then why, just afterwards, did he hand Grimaud his card on which his own address was carefully written? The giving of that card, combined with his words and later actions, is significant. What Fley really meant, veiled so that he could throw a scare into Grimaud before witnesses, was just this: 'You, my brother, are fat and rich on the proceeds of a robbery we both committed when we were young. I am poor—and I hate my work. Now will you come and call on me at my address, so that we can arrange this matter, or shall I set the police on you?' "

"Blackmail," said Hadley, softly.

"Yes. Fley had a bee in his bonnet, but Fley was far from being a fool. Now mark how he twisted round his meaning in his last threatening words to Grimaud. 'I also am in danger when I associate with my brother, but I am prepared to run that risk.' And in that case, as always afterwards, he was referring in strict truth to *Grimaud*. 'You, my brother, might also kill me as you killed the other, but I will risk it. So shall I call on you amiably, or will my other dead brother come to hang you?'

"For think of his behaviour afterwards, on the night of his murder. Remember the glee he had of smashing up and getting rid of his illusion-properties? And what words did he use to O'Rourke? Words which, if you look at them squarely in the light of what we now know, can have only one explanation. He said:

"'I shall not need them again. My work is finished. Didn't I tell you? I am going to see my brother. He will do something that will settle an old affair for both of us.'

"Meaning, of course, that Grimaud had agreed to come to terms. Fley meant that he was leaving his old life for good; going back to his grave as a dead man with plenty

of money; but he couldn't be more specific without blowing
the gaff. Still, he knew that his brother was tricky; he'd
had good reason in the past to know it. He couldn't leave
behind him a big warning when he spoke with O'Rourke,
in case Grimaud really meant to pay; but he threw out a
hint:

> " 'In case anything happens to me, you will find
> my brother in the same street where I myself live.
> That is not where he really resides, but he has a
> room there.'

"I'll explain that last statement in just a moment.
But go back to Grimaud. Now, Grimaud never had
any intention of coming to terms with Fley. Fley was
going to die. That wily, shrewd, theatrical mind of
Grimaud's (who, as you know, was more interested in
magical illusions than anybody else we have met) was
determined not to suffer any nonsense from this inconvenient brother of his. Fley must die—but this was
more difficult than it looked.

"If Fley had come to him in private, without anybody
in the world ever being able to associate Fley's name with
his, it would have been simple. But Fley had been too
shrewd for that. He had blazoned forth his own name and
address, and hinted at mysterious secrets concerning
Grimaud, before a group of Grimaud's friends. Awkward!
Now if Fley is found obviously murdered, somebody is
likely to say, 'Hullo! Isn't that the same chap who—?' And
then presently there may be dangerous enquiries; because
Lord knows what Fley may have told *other* people about
Grimaud. The only thing he isn't likely to have confided
to somebody else is his last deadly hold over Grimaud;
and that is the thing about which he must be silenced.
Whatever happens to Fley, however he dies, there are
likely to be enquiries concerning Grimaud. The only thing
to do is frankly to pretend that Fley is after his life; to
send himself threatening letters (not too obviously); to
stir up the household in an ingenious way; finally, to inform everybody that Fley has threatened to call on him
on the night he himself intends to call on Fley. You will see
very shortly just how he planned to work out a very
brilliant murder.

"The effect he intended to produce was this: The murderous Fley should be seen calling on him on Saturday night. There should be witnesses to this. The two should be together alone when Fley goes into his study. A row is heard, the sound of a fight, a shot, and a fall. The door being opened, Grimaud should be found alone—a nasty-looking but superficial wound from a bullet scratched along his side. No weapon is there. Out of the window hangs a rope belonging to Fley, by which Fley is assumed to have escaped. (Remember, it had been predicted that there would be *no* snow that night, so it would have been impossible to trace footprints.) Grimaud says: 'He thought he killed me; I pretended to be dead; and he escaped. No, don't set the police on him, poor devil. I'm not hurt.'— And the next morning Fley would have been found dead in his own room. He would have been found, a suicide, having pressed his own gun against his chest and pulled the trigger. The gun is beside him. A suicide note lies on the table. In despair at thinking he has killed Grimaud, he has shot himself. . . . That, gentlemen, was the illusion Grimaud intended to produce."

"But how did he do it?" demanded Hadley. "And, anyway, it didn't turn out like that!"

"No. You see, the plan miscarried badly. The latter part of the illusion of Fley calling on him in his study when actually Fley would already have been dead in the Cagliostro Street house—I'll deal with in its proper place. Grimaud, with the aid of Madame Dumont, had already made certain preparations.

"He had told Fley to meet him at Fley's room on the top floor over the tobacconist's. He had told Fley to meet him there at nine o'clock on the Saturday night, for a cash settlement. (You recall that Fley, gleefully throwing up his job and burning his properties, left the theatre in Limehouse at about eight-fifteen.)

"Grimaud had chosen Saturday night because that night, by inviolable custom, he remained alone all evening in his study without anyone being allowed to disturb him for any reason whatsoever. He chose that night because he needed to use the areaway door, and go and come by way of the basement; and Saturday night was the night out for Annie, who had her quarters there. You'll remember that, after he went up to his study at seven-thirty, nobody *did* see him until, according to the evidence, he opened the study door to admit the visitor at nine-fifty. Madame Dumont claimed to have spoken to him in the study at nine-thirty, when she gathered up the coffee things. I'll tell you shortly why I disbelieved that statement—the fact is, he was not in the study at all: he was in Cagliostro Street. Madame Dumont had been told to lurk round the study door at nine-thirty, and to come out for some excuse. Why? Because Grimaud had ordered Mills to come upstairs at nine-thirty, you see, and watch the study door from the room down the hall. Mills was to be the dupe of the illusion Grimaud meant to work. But if—as he came upstairs near the study door—Mills had for any reason taken it into his head to try to speak with Grimaud, or see him, Dumont was there to head him off. Dumont was to wait in the archway, and keep Mills away from that door if he showed any curiosity.

"Mills was chosen as the dupe of the illusion: why? Because, although he was so meticulously conscientious that he would carry out his instructions to the tick, he was so afraid of 'Fley' that he would not interfere when the hollow man came stalking up those stairs. It was not only that he must not attack the man in the false face in those dangerous few moments before the man got into the study (as, for instance, Mangan or even Drayman might have done), but also that he must not even venture out of his room. He had been told to stay in that room, and he would. Finally, he had been chosen because he was a very short man, a fact which will presently became clear.

"Now, he was told to go upstairs and watch at nine-thirty. This was because the hollow man was timed to make his appearance only a little afterwards; although, in fact, the hollow man was late. Mark one discrepancy. Mills was told nine-thirty—but Mangan was told ten o'clock! The reason is obvious. There was to be somebody downstairs to testify that a visitor had really arrived by the front door, confirming Dumont. But Mangan might be inclined towards curiosity about this visitor; he might be inclined to challenge the hollow man . . . unless he had first been jokingly told by Grimaud that the visitor would probably not arrive at all, or, if he did arrive, it could not possibly be before ten o'clock. All that was necessary was to throw his mind off, and make him hesitate long enough, for the hollow man to get upstairs past that dangerous door. And, if the worst came to the worst, Mangan and Rosette could always be locked in.

"For everybody else: Annie was out, Drayman had been supplied with a ticket to a concert, Burnaby was unquestionably playing cards, and Pettis at the theatre. The field was clear.

"At some time before nine o'clock (probably about ten minutes) Grimaud slipped out of the house, using the area door up to the street. Trouble had already started. It had been snowing heavily for some time, contrary to rules. But Grimaud did not regard it as serious trouble. He believed he could do the business and return by half-past nine, and that it would still be snowing heavily enough to gloss over any footprints that he would make, and cause no comment on the absence of any footprints the visitor later *should* have made when the visitor would be supposed to have swung down from his window. In any case, his plans had been carried too far for him to back out.

"When he left the house he was carrying an old and untraceable Colt revolver, loaded with just two bullets. The sort of hat he wore I don't know, but his overcoat was a light yellow, glaring tweed with chicken-pox spots. He bought this coat several sizes too large. He bought it because it was the sort of coat he had never been known to wear and because nobody would recognize him in it if he were to be seen. He—"

Hadley intervened.

"Stop a bit! What about that business of the overcoats changing colour? That would come earlier in the evening. What had happened there?"

"Again I've got to ask you to wait until we get to the last illusion he worked; that's a part of it.

"Well, Grimaud's purpose was to call on Fley. There he would speak with Fley amiably for a time. He would say something like: 'You must leave this hovel, brother! You will be comfortably off now; I will see to that. Why not leave these useless possessions behind and come to my house? Let your landlord have the damned things in place of notice!'—Any sort of speech, you see, the purpose being to make Fley write one of his ambiguous notes for the landlord. 'I am leaving for good.' 'I am going back to my grave.' Anything *that could be understood as a suicide note when Fley was found dead with a gun in his hand.*"

Dr. Fell leaned forward. "And then Grimaud would

take out his Colt, jam it against Fley's chest, and smilingly pull the trigger.

"It was the top floor of an empty house. As you have seen, the walls are astonishingly thick and solid. The landlord lived far down in the basement, and was the most incurious man in Cagliostro Street. No shot, especially a muffled shot with the gun held against Fley, could have been heard. It might be some time before the body was discovered; it would certainly not be before morning. And in the meantime, what will Grimaud do? After killing Fley he will turn the same gun on himself to give himself a slight wound, even if he has to imbed the bullet—he had, as we know from that little episode of the three coffins years before, the constitution of an ox and the nerve of hell. Then he would leave the gun lying beside Fley. He would quite coolly clap a handkerchief or cotton wool across this wound, which must be *inside* the coat and across the shirt; bind it with adhesive tape until the time came to rip it open—and go back home to work his illusion, which should prove that Fley came to see him. That Fley shot him, and then returned to Cagliostro Street and used the same gun for suicide, no coroner's jury would afterwards doubt. Do I make it clear so far? It was crime turned the wrong way round.

"That, as I say, was what Grimaud *intended* to do. Had he performed it as he intended, it would have been an ingenious murder; and I doubt whether we should ever have questioned Fley's suicide.

"Now, there was only one difficulty about accomplishing this plan. If anybody—not anybody recognizable as himself, but anybody at all—were seen visiting Fley's house, the fat would be in the fire. It might not appear so easily as suicide. There was only one entrance from the street—the door beside the tobacconist's. And he was wearing a conspicuous coat, in which he had reconnoitred the ground before. (By the way, Dolberman, the tobacconist, had seen him hanging about previously.) He found the solution of his difficulty in Burnaby's secret flat.

"You see, of course, that Grimaud was the likeliest person of all to have known of Burnaby's flat in Cagliostro Street? Burnaby himself told us that, some months before when Grimaud suspected him of having an ulterior motive in painting that picture, Grimaud had not only questioned him—he had *watched* him. From a man who was in such fancied danger, it would have been real watching. He knew of the flat. He knew from spying that Rosette had a key. And so, when the time came and the idea occurred to him, he stole Rosette's key.

"The house in which Burnaby had his flat was on the same side of the street as the house where Fley lived. All those houses are built side by side, with flat roofs; so that you have only to step over a low dividing wall to walk on the roofs from one end of the street to the other. Both men, remember, lived on the top floor. You recall what we saw when we went up to look at Burnaby's flat—just beside the door to the flat?"

Hadley nodded. "Yes, of course. A short ladder going to a trap-door in the roof."

"Exactly. And, on the landing just outside Fley's room, there is a low skylight also communicating with the roof. Grimaud had only to go to Cagliostro Street by the back way, never appearing in the street itself, but going up the alley which we saw from Burnaby's window. He came in the back door (as we saw Burnaby and Rosette do later), he went up to the top floor and thence to the roof. Then he followed the roofs to Fley's lodgings, descended from the skylight to the landing, and could both enter and leave the place without a soul seeing him. Moreover, he knew absolutely that that night Burnaby would be playing cards elsewhere.

"And then everything went wrong.

"He must have got to Fley's lodgings before Fley arrived there himself; it wouldn't do to make Fley suspicious by being seen coming from the roof. But we know that Fley had some suspicions already. This may have been caused by Grimaud's request for Fley to bring along one of his long conjuring-ropes. . . . Grimaud wanted that rope as a piece of evidence to use later against Fley. Or it may have been caused by Fley's knowledge that Grimaud had been hanging about in Cagliostro Street for the past couple of days; possibly seeing him duck across the roofs towards Burnaby's after one reconnoitering, and thereby making Fley believe he had taken a room in the street.

"The two brothers met in that gaslit room at nine. What they talked about we don't know. We may never know. But evidently Grimaud lulled Fley's suspicions; they became pleasant and amiable and forgot old scores; Grimaud jocularly persuaded him to write that note for the landlord. Then——"

"I'm not disputing all this," said Hadley, quietly, "but how do you happen to know it?"

"Grimaud told us," said Dr. Fell. Hadley stared.

"Oh yes. Once I had tumbled to that terrible mistake in times, I could understand. You'll see. But to continue:

"Fley had written his note. He had got into his hat and coat for departure—because Grimaud wished it to be assumed that he had killed himself just after having returned from a journey *outdoors:* his return from the phantom visit to Grimaud, in other words. They were all ready to go. And then Grimaud leaped.

"Whether Fley was subconsciously on his guard; whether he twitched round to run for the door, since he was no match for the powerful Grimaud; whether it happened in the twisting and scuffle—this we do not know. But Grimaud, with the gun against Fley's coat as Fley wrenched round from him, made a hellish mistake. He fired. And he put the bullet in the wrong place. Instead of getting his victim through the heart, he got him under the left shoulder blade: a wound of almost the same sort, although at the back, as the one from which Grimaud later died himself. It was a fatal wound, but far from instantly fatal. The poetic ironies were working to kill these brothers, with interchangeable methods, in precisely the same way.

"Of course Fley went down. He could do nothing else; and it was the wisest course, or Grimaud might have finished him. But Grimaud, for a second, must have lost his nerve in sheer terror. This might have wrecked his whole plan. *Could* a man shoot himself in that spot? If not, God help the murderer. And worse—Fley, not caught quickly enough, had screamed out before the bullet went home, and Grimaud thought he heard pursuers.

"He had sense enough, and guts enough, even in that hellish moment, to keep his head. He jammed the pistol into the hand of the motionless Fley, lying on his face. He picked up the coil of rope. Somehow, in spite of crash and fuddlement, the plan must go on. But he had more sense than to risk the noise of another shot to be heard by people possibly listening, or to waste more time. He darted out of the room.

"The roof, do you see! The roof was his only chance.

He heard imaginary pursuers everywhere; maybe some grisly recollection came back to him of three graves in a storm below the Hungarian mountains. He imagined that they would hear him and track him across those roofs. So he dashed for the trap door at Burnaby's, and down into the dark of Burnaby's flat.

"It was only then that his wits began to recover themselves. . . .

"And, meantime, what has happened? Pierre Fley is fatally hurt. But he still has the ribs of that iron frame which once enabled him to survive being buried alive. The murderer has gone. And Fley will *not* give in. He must get help. He must get to—

"*To a doctor,* Hadley. You asked yesterday why Fley was walking towards the other end of the street, towards the end of a blind alley. Because (as you saw in the newspaper) a doctor lived there: the doctor to whose office he later was carried. He is mortally hurt and he knows it; but he will not be beaten! He gets up, still in his hat and overcoat. The gun has been put into his hand; he rams it in his pocket, for it may be useful. Down he goes, downstairs as steadily as he can, to a silent street where no alarm has been raised. He walks on. . . .

"Have you asked yourself why he was walking in the middle of the street and kept looking so sharply round? The most reasonable explanation is not that he was going to visit anybody; but that he knew the murderer to be lurking somewhere, and he expected another attack. He thinks he is safe. Ahead of him, two men are walking rapidly. He passes a lighted jeweller's, he sees a street lamp ahead on the right. . . .

"But what has happened to Grimaud? Grimaud has heard no pursuit, but he is half-insane with wondering. He does not dare go back to the roof and risk investigation. But stop a moment! If there has been any discovery, he will be able to know by looking for a second out into the street. He can go down to the front door, look out, and peer up the street, can't he? No danger in that, since the house where Burnaby lives is deserted.

"He goes softly downstairs. He opens the door softly, having unbuttoned his coat to wind the coil of rope round him inside that overcoat. He opens the door—full in the glow of a street lamp just beyond that door—and facing him, walking slowly in the middle of the street, is the man he left for dead in the other house less than ten minutes ago. And for the last time those brothers come face to face.

"Grimaud's shirt is a target under that street lamp. And Fley, driven mad with pain and hysteria, does not hesitate. He screams. *He* cries the words, 'The second bullet is for *you!*'—just before he whips up the same pistol and fires.

"That last effort is too much. The hemorrhage has got him, and he knows it. He screams again, lets go of the gun as he tries to throw it (now empty) at Grimaud; and then he pitches forward on his face. That, my lads, is the shot which the three witnesses heard in Cagliostro Street. It was the shot which struck Grimaud in the chest just before he had time to close the door."

THE UNRAVELLING 21

"And then?" prompted Hadley, as Dr. Fell paused and lowered his head.

"The three witnesses did not see Grimaud, of course," said Dr. Fell, wheezing, after a long pause, "because he was never outside the door; never on the steps at all; never within twenty feet of the man who seemed to have been murdered in the middle of a snow desert. Of course Fley already had the wound, which jetted blood from the last convulsion. Of course any deduction from the direction of the wound was useless. Of course there were no fingerprints on the gun, since it landed in snow and in a literal sense had been washed clean."

"By God!" said Hadley, so quietly that he seemed to be making a statement. "It fulfills every condition of the facts, and yet I never thought of it. . . . But go on. Grimaud?"

"Grimaud is inside the door. He knows he's got it in his chest; but he doesn't think it's very serious. He's survived worse things than bullets, and other things (he thinks) *are* more serious.

"After all, he's only got what he was going to give himself—a wound. He could bark out that chuckle of his at such a thing. But his plan has crashed to hell! (How is he to know, by the way, that the clock at the jeweller's will be fast? He doesn't even know that Fley is dead, for there is Fley walking in the street with fire and sting still in him. Luck—by reason of the jeweller's clock—is with him when he thought it had deserted him, but how is he to know it?) All he is sure of is that Fley will never now be found, a suicide, up in that little room. Fley—probably dangerously wounded, yes, but still able to talk—is out in that street with a policeman running towards him. Grimaud is undone. Unless he can use his wits, he's on his way to the hangman, for Fley will not keep silent now.

"All this comes an instant after the shot, the rush of fancies crowding in. He can't stay here in this dark hall. He'd better have a look at that wound, though, and make sure he doesn't leave a trail of blood. Where? Burnaby's flat upstairs, of course. Up he goes, gets the door open, and switches on the lights. Here's the rope wound round him . . . no use for *that* thing now; he can't pretend Fley came to call on him when Fley may now be talking with the police. He flings the rope off and leaves it.

"A look at the wound next. There's blood all over the inside of that light tweed overcoat, and blood on his inner clothes. But the wound is of small consequence. He's got his handkerchief and his adhesive tape, and he can plug himself up like a horse gored in the bull-ring. Károly Horváth, whom nothing can kill, can afford to chuckle at this. He feels as steady and fresh as ever. But he patches himself up —hence the blood in the bathroom of Burnaby's flat—and tries to collect his wits. What time is it? Good God! he's late; it's just on a quarter to ten. Got to get out of here and hurry home before they catch him. . . .

"And he leaves the lights on. When they burnt up a shilling's worth and went out in the later course of the night, we don't know. They were on three-quarters of an hour afterwards, anyhow, when Rosette saw them.

"But I think that his sanity returns as he hurries home. *Is* he caught? It seems inevitable. Yet is there any loophole, any ghost of a fighting chance, however thin? You see, whatever else Grimaud is, he's a fighter. He's a shrewd, theatrical, imaginative, sneering, common-sense black-guard: but don't forget that he's also a fighter. He wasn't all of a black colour, you know. He would murder a brother, but I question whether he would murder a friend or a woman who loved him. In any case, *is* there some way out? There's one chance, so thin that it's almost useless; but the only one. That's to carry through his original scheme and pretend that Fley has called on him and given him that wound *in his own house.* Fley still has the gun. It will be Grimaud's word, and his witnesses' word, that he never left the house all evening! Whereas they can swear that Fley did come to see him—and then let the damned police try to prove anything! Why not? The snow? It's stopped snowing, and Fley won't have left a track. Grimaud has thrown away the rope Fley was supposed to have used. But it's a toss-up, a last daring of the devil, the only course in an extremity. . . .

"Fley shot him at about twenty minutes to ten. He gets back here at a quarter to ten or a little after. Getting into the house without leaving a footprint? Easy! for a man with a constitution like an ox, and only slightly wounded. (By the way, I believe he was really wounded only slightly, and that he'd live now to hang, if he hadn't done certain things; you'll see.) He'll return by way of the steps down to the areaway, and the area door, as arranged. —How? Well, there is a coating of snow on the areaway steps, of course. But the entrance to the areaway steps is beside the next house, isn't it? Yes. And, at the foot of the area steps, the basement door is protected from snow by a projection: the projection of the main front steps overhanging. So that there is no snow exactly in front of the area door. If he can get down there without leaving a mark—

"He can. He can approach from the other direction, as though he were going to the house next door, and then simply jump down the area steps to the cleared patch below. . . . Don't I seem to remember a *thud,* as of some one falling, which some one heard just before the front-door bell rang?"

"But he didn't ring the front-door bell!"

"Oh yes, he did—but from inside. After he'd gone into the house by way of the area door, and up to where Ernestine Dumont was waiting for him. Then they were ready to perform their illusion."

"Yes," said Hadley. "Now we come to the illusion. How was it done, and how do you know how it was done?"

Dr. Fell sat back and tapped his finger tips together as though he were marshalling facts.

"How do I know? Well, I think my first suggestion was the weight of that picture." He pointed sleepily at the big slashed canvas leaning against the wall. "Yes, it was the weight of the picture. That wasn't very helpful, until I remembered something else. . . ."

"Weight of the picture? Yes, the picture," growled Hadley. "I'd forgotten that. How does *it* figure in the blasted business, anyhow? What did Grimaud mean to do with that?"

"H'mf, ha, yes. That's what I wondered, you see."

"But the weight of the picture, man! It doesn't weigh very much. You yourself picked it up with one hand and turned it round in the air."

Dr. Fell sat up with an air of some excitement. "Exactly. You've hit it. I picked it up with one hand and swung it round. . . . Then why should it take two husky men, the cabman and one extra, to carry it upstairs?"

"What?"

"It did, you know. That was twice pointed out to us. Grimaud, when he took it from Burnaby's studio, easily carried it downstairs. Yet, when he returned here with that same painting late in the afternoon, two people had a job carting it up. Where had it picked up so much weight all of a sudden? He didn't have glass put in it—you can see that for yourself. Where was Grimaud all that time, the morning when he bought the picture and the afternoon when he returned with it? It's much too big a thing to carry about with you for pleasure. Why was Grimaud so insistent on having the picture all wrapped up?

"It wasn't a very far-fetched deduction to think that he used that picture as a blind to hide something that the men were carrying up, unintentionally, along with it. Something in the same parcel. Something very big . . . seven feet by four . . . h'm. . . ."

"But there couldn't have been anything," objected Hadley, "or we'd have found it in this room, wouldn't we? Besides, in any case the thing must have been almost absolutely flat, or it would have been noticed in the wrappings of the picture. What sort of object is it that's as big as seven feet by four, and yet thin enough not to be noticed inside the wrappings of a picture; what's as huge a business as that picture, which can nevertheless be spirited out of sight whenever you wish?"

"A mirror," said Dr. Fell.

After a sort of thunderous silence, while Hadley rose from his chair, Dr. Fell went on sleepily: "And it can be spirited out of sight, as you put it, merely by being pushed up the flue of that very broad chimney—where we've all tried to get our fists, by the way—and propped up on the ledge inside where the chimney turns. You don't need magic. You only need to be damnably strong in the arms and shoulders."

"You mean," cried Hadley, "that damned stage trick . . ."

"A new version of the stage trick," said Dr. Fell, "and a very good one which is practical if you care to try it. Now, look round this room. You see the door? What do you see in the wall directly opposite the door?"

"Nothing," said Hadley. "I mean, he's had the book-cases cleared away in a big space on either side. There's blank panelled wall, that's all."

"Exactly. And do you see any furniture in a line between the door and that wall?"

"No. It's cleared."

"So if you were out in that hall looking in, you would see only black carpet, no furniture, and to the rear an expanse of blank oak-panelled wall?"

"Yes."

"Now, Ted, open the door and look out into the hall," said Dr. Fell. "What about the walls and carpet out there?"

Rampole made a feint of looking, although he knew. "They're just the same," he said. "The floor is one solid carpet running to the baseboards, like this one, and the panelling is the same."

"Right! By the way, Hadley," pursued Dr. Fell, still drowsily, "you might drag out that mirror from behind the bookcase over there. It's been behind the bookcase since yesterday afternoon, when Drayman found it in the chimney. It was lifting it down that brought on his stroke. We'll try a little experiment. I don't think any of the house-hold will interrupt us up here, but we can head off any-body who does. I want you to take that mirror, Hadley, and set it up just inside the door—so that when you open the door (it opens inwards and to the right, you see, as you come in from the hall) the edge of the door at its outermost swing is a few inches away from the mirror."

The superintendent with some difficulty trundled out the object he found behind the bookcase. It was bigger than a tailor's swinging mirror; several inches, in fact, higher and wider than the door. Its base rested flat on the carpet, and it was supported upright by a heavy swing-base on the right-hand side as you faced it. Hadley regarded it curiously.

"Set it up inside the door?"

"Yes. The door will only swing open a short distance; you'll see an aperture only a couple of feet wide at the most. . . . Try it!"

"I know, but if you do that . . . well, somebody sitting in the room down at the end of the hall, where Mills was, would see his own reflection smack in the middle of the mirror."

"Not at all. Not at the angle—a slight angle, but enough; a poor thing, but mine own—not at the angle to which I'm going to tilt it. You'll see. The two of you go down there where Mills was while I adjust it. Keep your eyes off until I sing out."

Hadley, muttering that it was damned foolishness, but highly interested in spite of that, tramped down after Rampole. They kept their eyes off until they heard the doctor's hail, and then turned round.

The hallway was gloomy and high enough. Its black-carpeted length ran down to a closed door. Dr. Fell stood outside that door, like an overfat master of ceremonies about to unveil a statue. He stood a little to the right of the door, well back from it against the wall, and had his hand stretched out across to the knob. "Here she goes!" he grunted, and quickly opened the door—hesitated—and closed it. "Well? What did you see?"

"I saw the room inside," returned Hadley. "Or at least I thought I did. I saw the carpet, and the rear wall. It seemed a very big room."

"You didn't see that," said Dr. Fell. "As a matter of fact, you saw the reflection of the panelled wall immediately to the right of the door where you're standing, and the carpet going up to it. That's why it seemed so big a room: you were looking at a double length of reflection. This mirror is bigger than the door, you know. And you didn't see a reflection of the door itself because it opens inwards to the right. If you looked carefully, you might have seen a line of what looks like a shadow just along the top edge of the door. That's where the top edge of the mirror inevitably reflects, being taller, an inch or so of the *inner* top edge of the door. But your attention would

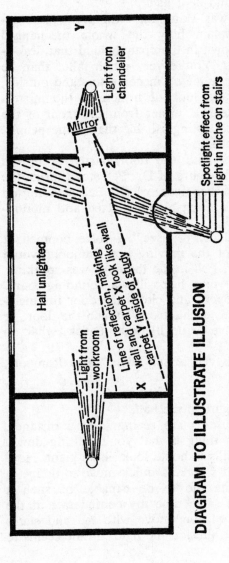

Hall unlighted

Light from workroom

Line of reflection, making wall wall and carpet X look like wall

carpet Y inside of study

X

3

1

2

Mirror

Light from chandelier

Y

Spotlight effect from light in niche on stairs

DIAGRAM TO ILLUSTRATE ILLUSION

1. Man whose own reflection is seen by watcher, but appearing three inches taller than reflection because watcher, thirty feet away, is sitting down on a much lower level of observation.

2. Confederate who opens and shuts door.

3. Watcher.

In testing this illusion, one important point must be observed. No light must fall directly on the mirror, else there will be a reflected dazzle to betray its presence. It will be seen that a spotlight from the niche on the stairs has been caused to fall across the line of the door, but not in a position to catch any reflection. No light is in the hall, and the workroom light does not penetrate far. In the study itself, the light comes from the chandelier in a very high ceiling, thus coming almost directly over the top of the mirror. It will throw, therefore, very little shadow of this mirror into the hall; and such throw as it does throw will be obscured by the counter-shadow of the man standing before the door.

be concentrated on any figures you saw. . . . Did you see me, by the way?"

"No; you were too far over. You had your arm across the door to the knob, and kept back."

"Yes. As Dumont was standing. Now try a last experiment before I explain how the whole mechanism worked. Ted, you sit down in the chair behind that desk— where Mills was sitting. You're very much taller than he is, but it will illustrate the idea. I'm going to stand outside, with this door open, and look at myself in the mirror. Now, you can't mistake ME, either from the front or the rear; but then I'm more distinguishable than some people. Just tell me what you see."

In the ghostly light, with the door partly open, the effect was rather eerie. A figure of Dr. Fell stood inside the door, peering out at another figure of Dr. Fell standing on the threshold and confronting himself—fixed and motionless, with a startled look.

"I don't touch the door, you see," a voice boomed at them. By the illusion of the moving lips Rampole would have sworn that the Dr. Fell inside the door was speaking. The mirror threw the voice back like a sounding-board. "Somebody obligingly opens and closes the door for me— somebody standing at my right. I don't touch the door, or my reflection would have to do likewise. Quick, what do you notice?"

"Why—one of you is very much taller," said Rampole, studying the images.

"Which one?"

"You yourself: the figure in the hall."

"Exactly. First because you're seeing it at a distance, but the most important thing is that you're sitting down. To a man the size of Mills I should look like a giant. Hey? H'mf. Hah. Yes. Now if I make a quick move to dodge in at that door (supposing me to be capable of such a manœuvre), and at the same time my confederate at the right makes a quick confusing move with me and slams the door, in the muddled illusion the figure inside seems to be—?"

"Jumping in front of you to keep you out."

"Yes. Now come and read the evidence, if Hadley has it."

When they were again in the room, past the tilted mirror which Hadley moved back, Dr. Fell sank into a chair, sighing wheezingly.

"I'm sorry, gents. I should have realized the truth long before, from the careful, methodical, exact Mr. Mills' evidence. Let me see if I can repeat from memory his exact words. Check me up, Hadley. H'm." He rapped his knuckles against his head and scowled. "Like this:

> " 'She [Dumont] was about to knock at the door when I was startled to see the tall man come upstairs directly after us. She turned round and saw him. She exclaimed certain words. . . . The tall man made no reply. He walked to the door, and without haste turned down the collar of his coat and removed his cap, which he placed in his overcoat pocket. . . .'

"You see, gents? He had to do that, because the reflection couldn't show a cap and couldn't show a collar turned up when the figure inside must appear to be wearing a dressing-gown. But I wondered *why* he was so methodical about that, since apparently he didn't remove the mask—"

"Yes, what about that mask? Mills says he didn't—"

"Mills didn't see him take it off; I'll show you why as soon as we go on with Mills:

> " 'Madame Dumont cried out something, shrank back against the wall, and hurried to open the door. Dr. Grimaud appeared on the threshold—'

"Appeared! That's precisely what he did do. Our methodical witness is uncomfortably exact. But Dumont? There was the first flaw. A frightened woman, looking up at a terrifying figure while she's standing before the door of a room in which there's a man who will protect her, doesn't *shrink back*. She rushes towards the door to get protection. Anyhow, follow Mills' testimony. He says Grimaud was not wearing his eye-glasses (they wouldn't have fitted behind that mask). But the natural movement of a man inside, I thought, would have been to raise his glasses. Grimaud—according to Mills—stands *stock-still* the whole time; like the stranger, with his hands in his pockets. Now for the damning part. Mills says: 'I am under the impression that Madame Dumont, although she was shrinking back against the wall, closed the door after him. I recall that she had her hand on the knob.' Not a natural action for her, either! She contradicted him—but Mills was right." Dr. Fell gestured.

"No use going on with all this. But here was my difficulty: if Grimaud was alone in that room, if he simply walked in on his own reflection, what became of his clothes? What about that long black overcoat, the brown peaked cap, even the false face? They weren't in the room. Then I remembered that Ernestine's profession had been the making of costumes for the opera and ballet; I remembered a story O'Rourke had told us; and I knew—"

"Well?"

"That Grimaud had burnt them," said Dr. Fell. "He had burnt them because they were made of paper, like the uniform of the Vanishing Horseman described by O'Rourke. He couldn't risk the long and dangerous business of burning real clothes in that fire; he had to work too fast. They had to be torn up and burnt. And bundles of loose, blank sheets of writing-paper—perfectly blank!—had to be burned on top of them to hide the fact that some of it was coloured paper. Dangerous letters! Oh, Bacchus, I could murder myself for thinking such a thing!" He shook his fist. "When there was no blood-trail, no blood-stain at all, going to the drawer in his desk where he did keep his important papers! And there was another reason for burning papers . . . they had to conceal the fragments of the 'shot.' "

"Shot?"

"Don't forget that a pistol was supposed to have been fired in that room. Of course, what the witnesses really heard was the noise of a heavy firecracker—pinched from the hoard Drayman always keeps, as you know, for Guy Fawkes night. Drayman discovered the missing thunderbolt; I think that's how he tumbled to the scheme, and why he kept muttering about 'fireworks.' Well, the fragments of an exploding firecracker fly wide. They're heavy reënforced cardboard, hard to burn, and they had to be destroyed in the fire or hidden in that drift of papers. I found some of them. Of course, we should have realized no bullet had really been fired. Modern cartridges—such as you informed me were used in that Colt revolver—have smokeless powder. You can smell it, but you can't see it. And yet there was a *haze* in this room (left by the firecracker) even after the window was up.

"Ah, well, let's recapitulate! Grimaud's heavy crêpe-paper uniform consisted of a black coat—black like a dressing-gown, long like a dressing-gown, and having at the front shiny lapels which would show like a dressing-gown when you turned down the collar to face your own image. It consisted of a paper cap, to which the false face was attached—so that in sweeping off the cap you simply folded both together and shoved 'em into your pocket. (The real dressing-gown, by the way, was already in this room while Grimaud was out.) And the black 'uniform,' early last evening, had been incautiously hung up in the closet downstairs.

"Mangan, unfortunately, spotted it. The watchful Dumont knew that he spotted it, and whisked it out of that cupboard to a safer place as soon as he went away. She, naturally, never saw a yellow tweed coat hanging there at all. Grimaud had it upstairs here with him, ready for his expedition. But it was found in the closet yesterday afternoon, and she had to pretend it had been there all the time. Hence the chameleon overcoat.

"You can now make a reconstruction of just what happened when Grimaud, after killing Fley and getting a bullet himself, returned to the house on Saturday night. Right at the start of the illusion he and his confederate were in dangerous trouble. You see, Grimaud was late. He'd expected to be back by nine-thirty—and he didn't get there until a quarter to ten. The longer he delayed, the nearer it got to the time he had told *Mangan* to expect a visitor, and now Mangan would be expecting the visitor he had been told to watch. It was touch-and-go, and I rather imagine the cool Grimaud was fairly close to insane. He got up through the basement entrance, where his confederate was waiting. The tweed coat, with the blood inside it, went into the hall closet to be disposed of presently—and it never was, because he died. Dumont eased open the door, rang the bell by putting her hand out, and then went to 'answer' it while Grimaud was getting ready with his uniform.

"But they delayed too long. Mangan called out. Grimaud, with his wits still not functioning well, grew a little panicky and made a blunder to ward off immediate detection. He'd got so far; he didn't want to fail then from the nosiness of a damned penniless kid. So he said that he was Pettis, and locked them in. (You notice that Pettis is the only one with a voice of the same bass quality as Grimaud's?) Yes, it was a spur-of-the-moment error, but his only wish was to writhe like a footballer down a field and *somehow* escape those hands for the moment.

"The illusion was performed; he was alone in his room. His jacket, probably with blood on that, had been taken in charge by Dumont; he wore the uniform over his shirt-sleeves, open shirt, and bandaged wound. He had only to lock the door behind him, put on his real dressing-gown, destroy the paper uniform, and get that mirror up into the chimney. . . .

"That, I say again, was the finish. The blood had begun to flow again, you see. No ordinary man, wounded, could have stood the strain under which he had already been. He wasn't killed by Fley's bullet. He ripped his own lung like a rotted piece of rubber when he tried to—and superhumanly did—lift that mirror into its hiding-place. That was when he knew. Then was when he began to bleed from the mouth like a slashed artery; when he staggered against the couch, knocked away the chair, and reeled forward in his last successful effort to ignite the firecracker. After all the hates and dodgings and plans, the world was not spinning in front of him: it was only slowly going black. He tried to scream out, and he could not, for the blood was welling in his throat. And at that moment Charles Grimaud suddenly knew what he would never have believed possible, the breaking of the last and most shattering mirror-illusion in his bitter life. . . ."

"Well?"

"He knew that he was dying," said Dr. Fell. "And, stranger than any of his dreams, he was glad."

The heavy leaden light had begun to darken again with snow. Dr. Fell's voice sounded weirdly in the chill room. Then they saw that the door was opening and that in it stood the figure of a woman with a damned face. A damned face and a black dress, but round her shoulders was still drawn a red-and-yellow shawl for the love of the dead.

"You see, he confessed," Dr. Fell said in the same low, monotonous tone, "he tried to tell us the truth about his killing of Fley, and Fley's killing of him. Only we did not choose to understand, and I didn't understand until I knew from the clock what must have happened in Cagliostro Street. Man, man, don't you see? Take first his final statement, the statement made just before he died:

" 'It was my brother who did it. I never thought he would shoot. God knows how he got out of that room—' "

"You mean Fley's room in Cagliostro Street, after Fley had been left for dead?" demanded Hadley.

"Yes. And the horrible shock of coming on him suddenly, as Grimaud opened the door under the street light. You see:

" 'One second he was there, and the next he wasn't. . . . I want to tell you who my brother is, so you won't think I'm raving. . . .'

"For, of course, he did not think anybody knew about Fley. Now, in the light of that, examine the tangled, muddled, half-choked words with which—when he heard the statement that he was sinking—he tried to explain the whole puzzle to us.

"First he tried to tell us about the Horváths and the salt-mine. But he went on to the killing of Fley, and what Fley had done to him. *'Not suicide.'* When he'd seen Fley in the street, he couldn't make Fley's death the suicide he pretended. *'He couldn't use the rope.'* Fley couldn't, after that, be supposed to use the rope that Grimaud had discarded as useless. *'Roof.'* Grimaud did not mean this roof; but the other roof which he crossed when he left Fley's room. *'Snow.'* The snow had stopped and wrecked his plans. *'Too much light.'* There's the crux, Hadley! When he looked out into the street, there was too much light from the street lamp; Fley recognized him, and fired. *'Got gun.'* Naturally, Fley had got the gun then. *'Fox.'* The mask, the Guy Fawkes charade he tried to work. But finally, *'Don't blame poor—'* Not Drayman; he didn't mean Drayman. But it was a last apology for the one thing, I think, of which he was ashamed; the one piece of imposture he would never have done. 'Don't blame poor Pettis; I didn't mean to implicate him.' "

For a long time nobody spoke.

"Yes," Hadley agreed, dully. "Yes. All except one thing. What about the slashing of that picture, and where did the knife go?"

"The slashing of the picture, I think, was an extra touch

of the picturesque to help the illusion; Grimaud did it—or so I imagine. As for the knife, I frankly don't know. Grimaud probably had it here, and put it up the chimney beside the mirror so that the invisible man should seem to be doubly armed. But it isn't on the chimney ledge now. I should suppose that Drayman found it yesterday, and took it away—"

"That is the one point," said a voice, "on which you are wrong."

Ernestine Dumont remained in the doorway, her hands folded across the shawl at her breast. But she was smiling.

"I have heard everything you said," she went on. "Perhaps you can hang me, or perhaps not. That is not important. I do know that after so many years it is not quite worth while going on without Charles. . . . I took the knife, my friend. I had another use for it."

She was still smiling, and there was a blaze of pride in her eyes. Rampole saw what her hands were hiding. He saw her totter suddenly, but he was too late to catch her when she pitched forward on her face. Dr. Fell lumbered out of his chair and remained staring at her with a face as white as her own.

"I have committed another crime, Hadley," he said. "I have guessed the truth again."

TO WAKE THE DEAD

The Collier John Dickson Carr series includes:

THE FOUR FALSE WEAPONS

THE ARABIAN NIGHTS MURDER

THE BLIND BARBER

THE CASE OF THE CONSTANT SUICIDES

THE CORPSE IN THE WAXWORKS

THE CROOKED HINGE

DEATH WATCH

THE MAD HATTER MYSTERY

POISON IN JEST

TO WAKE THE DEAD

LOCKED ROOMS:
A Mystery Guild Lost Classics Omnibus

TO WAKE THE DEAD

by

John Dickson Carr

Mystery Guild
Garden City, New York

Macmillan Publishing Company
866 Third Avenue, New York, N.Y. 10022
Collier Macmillan Canada, Inc.

This edition is published by arrangement
with Harper & Row Publishers, Inc.

ISBN: 978-0-7394-9089-1

Printed in the United States of America

Contents

Contents

TO WAKE THE DEAD

Chapter 1

The Crime of Having Breakfast

At just after daybreak on that raw January morning, Christopher Kent stood in Piccadilly and shivered. The air seemed painted grey as though with a brush. He was only a dozen yards from Piccadilly Circus, and the Guinness clock told him that it was twenty minutes past seven. The only thing moving in the Circus was a taxi whose motor clanked with great distinctness; it circled Ares's island and throbbed away down a quiet Regent Street. A wind had begun to blow from the east, shaking the bitter air as you might shake a carpet. Christopher Kent noticed a flake of snow, and then another, blown suddenly past him. He eyed them without animosity, but he was not amused.

At the bank round the corner, he could draw a cheque for whatever he liked. But he had not a penny in his pocket, nor was it likely that he would have one for twenty-four hours more. That was the trouble. He had not eaten since yesterday's breakfast, and he was so hungry that it was beginning to cramp him.

As though by instinct he was almost at the doors of the Royal Scarlet Hotel. It fascinated him. One day later—to

be exact at ten o'clock on the morning of February 1st—
he would walk into that hotel and meet Dan Reaper, as
had been arranged. Then the whole matter under debate
would be over. There would be satisfaction in winning
from Dan; but, at the moment, hunger and light-headed-
ness were turning his earlier amusement to a mood of
sullen anger.

As usual, the events leading to that meeting of the ways
were unreasonable. He was the son of the late Kent's
South African Ales. South African by bringing-up, he had
lived in nearly every country except his own; and he had
not seen England since they had taken him away at the
age of two. Something had always happened to prevent it.
Kent's Ales required attention, though he was nowadays
too lazy to pay much attention to them beyond the drinking. He had other views. Having been brought up on sound
principles by his father, with whose judgments he agreed
on everything except the fascination of business, he had
early acquired a liking for sensational fiction. In the middle twenties he began to write it, and at that trade he
worked like a Kaffir to make the stuff good. But Dan
Reaper was not pleased.

Standing on the more-than-hard London pavement, he
remembered a more pleasant day three months ago, with
iced drinks at hand, and the noise of the surf coming up
from Durban beach. He was arguing, as usual, with Dan.
He remembered Dan's heavy red-brown complexion, his
crisp-moving gestures, his flat positiveness. At fifty Dan
had prospered in a young man's country, and was one of
those who have made Johannesburg a new Chicago.
Though Dan was nearly twenty years older than Kent, they
had been friends for a long time, and enjoyed arguing the
worth or trash of all created things. Dan was a Member of
the Assembly, and was working his way towards becoming
an important man politically. And (again as usual) he was
laying down the law.

"I haven't got time to read novels," Dan said as usual.
"Biographies, histories: yes. That's my line. It's real. I

want something that Repays Study. About the other stuff, I feel like old Mrs. Patterson: 'What's the use? It's all a pack of lies.' But if people must turn out novels, at least they ought to write out of experience—out of a full knowledge of life—like mine, for instance. I sometimes think I could————"

"Yes," said Kent. "I know. I seem to have heard all this somewhere else. Nonsense. The job's a trade, like any other good trade; and it's got to be learned. As for your cursed experience————"

"You don't deny it's necessary?"

"I don't know," Kent had admitted honestly. He remembered studying the colours of blue water and sky through his glass. "One thing has always struck me, when I've read the brief biographical notices of writers tucked away on the back flap of the book. It's astonishing how alike they all are. In nine cases out of ten you'll read, 'Mr. Blank has been lumberman, rancher, newspaperman, miner, and barman in the course of an adventurous life; has travelled through Canada; was for a time—' and so on. The number of writers who have been ranchers in Canada must be overwhelming. One day when I'm asked for a biographical note, I am going to break this tyranny. I am going to write, 'I have *not* been lumberman, rancher, newspaperman, miner, or barman; and, in fact, I never did an honest day's work in my life until I took up writing.' "

This stung Dan on the raw.

"I know you didn't," he retorted grimly. "You've always had all the money you wanted. But you couldn't do an honest day's work. It would kill you."

From there the argument, stimulated by a John Collins or two had taken a sharper and more business-like turn, while Dan grew still more heated.

"I'll bet you a thousand pounds," cried Dan, who had a romantic imagination, "that you couldn't stand up to a test that I've been through myself. Look here, it's an idea. You couldn't start at Johannesburg without a penny in your pocket, say; you couldn't work or beat your way to the coast—Durban, Capetown, Port Elizabeth, anywhere you like—you couldn't work your way to England aboard ship, and turn up to meet me there at a given rendezvous on a date, say, ten weeks from now. I mean, you couldn't do it without cashing a cheque or using your own name to be helped along. Bah!"

Kent did not tell him that the idea, in fiction, was not original. But it interested him.

"I might take you up on that," he said.

Dan regarded him suspiciously; Dan looked for a catch in everything.

"Are you serious? Mind, if you did a thing like that—or tried to do it—it would do you all the good in the world. Teach you what Life is like. And you'd get material for some real books instead of these footling stories about master-spies and murders. But you don't mean it. You'll think better of it to-morrow morning."

"Damn your hide, I believe I do mean it."

"Ho ho!" said Dan, and gurgled into his glass. "All right!" He pointed a heavy finger. "At the beginning of January I've got to go to England on business. Melitta's going with me, and your cousin Rod, and Jenny; and probably Francine and Harvey as well." Dan always travelled like an emperor, with a suite of friends. "I've got to go down to Gay's place in Sussex when we first get there. But on the morning of February 1st, sharp, we're to be in London. Do you think you could make that trip and meet me in my suite at the Royal Scarlet Hotel at ten o'clock on the morning of the first? Think it over, my lad. A thousand pounds you can't—no cheating, mind."

Two more snowflakes curled over in the air and were blown wide by that bitter wind. Kent looked up Piccadilly, figuratively tightening his belt. Well, he had done it. Here he was; or, at least, he would have done it in twenty-four hours more if he could hold out until then. And his chief impression now was that nearly everything Dan had so confidently predicted was wrong.

Experience? Material for books? At the moment he did not know whether to laugh or swear. None of these things had come on adventurous wings. To Dan himself, going out to South Africa in a cattle-boat after the War, there might have come some vision of high adventure or mystic twilights: though Kent doubted this. Exhilaration be hanged. It had been nothing but monotony and work; bone-cracking work, which—if he had not been solidly put together—would have broken him in the first two weeks. His own stubbornness had carried him through. He could have learned as much about human nature from a boarding-house in Johannesburg, and nearly as much about adventure.

But here he was. Nearly a week ago he had landed from the *Volpar* at Tilbury, with a trimmer's pay in his pocket; and had spent most of it in one glorious bust with a couple of messmates. Possibly, with time to lend joke and point, a sense of adventure on the high seas would come in retrospect. At the moment he knew only that he was devilish hungry.

He moved a little closer to the great revolving doors of the Royal Scarlet Hotel, which towered up in white stone over Piccadilly. Inside he could see charwomen finishing their work on the marble floors; carpets were being put down again, silently; and the hush of early morning was disturbed only by the echo of footsteps.

The Royal Scarlet was an imposing but not expensive place. Dan Reaper always preferred to go there, though as a rule he hired half a floor and in the end paid nearly as much as he might have paid at the Savoy. It was the principle of the thing, Dan said, never to let high-priced hotels make you pay for a name. Besides, the manager was a fellow South-African and a friend of his. For Coronation year they were building a top-floor annex which was predicted to be something new in the way of luxury rooms, and which had also attracted Dan.

Christopher Kent moved closer. It was warm inside those glass doors; warm and drowsy; and you might rest even hungry innards in a comfortable chair. Looking through into the lobby, he was conscious of an irrational resentment against Dan—Dan, expansive *père de famille* without any family, Dan, who exulted in going to all kinds of trouble if he could get a ten-shilling article for nine and elevenpence three farthings. At this moment Dan would still be at Gay's house in Sussex, snugly tucked into bed. But he would be here presently, with his suite of friends and employees. Kent ran them over in his mind. Melitta, Dan's wife. Francine Forbes, his niece. Rodney Kent, Christopher's cousin, and Rodney's wife Jenny: Rodney was Dan's political secretary. Harvey Wrayburn, a great friend of the family, would probably have made the trip too. And in another day they would be descending on London. . . .

That was a real cramp in the stomach this time. He would not have thought it possible to be so hungry.

Something white, something that was too large to be a snowflake, caught the corner of his eye. It was drifting down from the sky; it slipped past his shoulder; and automatically he put out his hand for it. It was a little folded card, of the sort they gave you when you were assigned to a room. It said in red letters:

> ### THE
> ### ROYAL SCARLET
> ### HOTEL
>
> Date: 30/1/37.
> Room: 707.
> Charge: 21/6 (Double).
>
> The charge includes room, bath, and breakfast. No responsibility can be accepted for valuables unless they are placed in the manager's safe.

"Room, bath, *and* breakfast—" Kent stared at the card; first the idea occurred to him as a good thing for a story, and then with a rush of hesitant surprise he realised that it might be practical.

He remembered how these things were done. You walked into the dining-room and gave your room-number either to the waiter or to someone sitting at the entrance with a book. Then you were served with breakfast. If he walked in boldly and gave the number of a room certain to be occupied, he could breakfast well—and then walk out again into the void. Why not? How were they to know he wasn't the occupier of the room? It was now barely seven-thirty. The chances were slight that the real occupant of the room would be down so early; and, in any case, it was something that would have to be risked.

The idea appealed to him enormously. Though he had pawned most of his possessions, and needed a haircut, still his suit was presentable; and he had shaved the night before. He pushed through the revolving doors into the foyer, removing his hat and overcoat.

It was a mild enough form of swindle; but Kent suddenly realised that he had never felt so guilty in his life. An empty stomach gives very little assurance; still, he wondered whether they were all looking at him hard or peering at the thoughts in his head. He had to get a grip on himself to prevent himself from hurrying across the foyer as though he were pursued. Only a hall-porter—in the neat dark-blue uniform naturally adopted by any hotel calling itself the Royal Scarlet—seemed to be looking at him. He strolled casually through the foyer, then through a palm-lounge, and into a big dining-room which seemed to be just waking up from sleep.

There were, he was relieved to see, already several people at the tables. If he had been the first there, and a swindler at that, he might have bolted. He almost did bolt at the sight of so many waiters. But he tried to walk with cool assurance, like a man carrying a morning paper. Then a head waiter bowed to him; and the thing was done.

He has afterwards admitted that his heart was in his mouth when the waiter drew out a chair for him at an isolated table.

"Yes, sir?"

"Bacon and eggs, toast, and coffee. Lots of bacon and eggs."

"Yes, sir," said the waiter briskly, and whipped out a pad. "And the number of your room?"

"Seven-o-seven."

It seemed to excite no surprise. The waiter noted it down, tore out a duplicate slip made on carbon-paper underneath, and hurried away. Kent sat back. It was pleasantly warm; the scent of coffee in the air made him a little more light-headed; but he felt like a man unsteadily getting his grip at last. Before he had time to wonder whether it might be snatched away from him, there was put before him a plate of what seemed the finest eggs and the most succulent bacon he had ever seen. A rack of toast and a coffee-service of polished pewter added silver to the already bright colours of the table; the yellow and red-brown of bacon and eggs, against shining white china and cloth, might make a painting of rare quality.

"Banners," he thought, looking at the eggs, " 'banners yellow, glorious, golden, From its roof did float and flow ———,' "

"Sir?" said the waiter.

" 'We fight to the finish, we drink to the dregs,' " quoted Kent recklessly, " 'And dare to be Daniels on bacon and eggs.' That's all, thanks."

Then he dug in. It was difficult at first, for his insides appeared to be opening and shutting like a concertina; but presently a soothing sense of well-being began to creep into him. He sat back drowsily, feeling at peace with the world, and wished for something to smoke. But that would not do. He had had his meal; now he must get out of here before———

Then he noticed the two waiters. One had just come into the dining-room; they were looking towards his table and conferring.

"That's done it," he thought. But he felt almost cheerful.

Getting to his feet with as much dignity as he could, he

started to walk out of the room. Behind the waiters, he noticed, was a hotel-attendant of some sort, wearing the dark-blue uniform. He could guess what that meant even before the attendant stepped out and spoke to him.

"Will you come this way, sir, please?" asked the man, with what seemed a very sinister inflection.

Kent drew a deep breath. That was that, then. He wondered if they put you in jail for this sort of thing. He could imagine Dan Reaper's roars of laughter (and the laughter of everyone else) if they arrived next day and found him in clink for cadging a breakfast; or washing dishes to pay it off. It made him furious, but there was no way out unless he ran for it; and he was not going to do that. He walked as sedately as he could beside the attendant, who led him through the palm-lounge, and then to the lodge of the hall-porter. That dignitary, a burly man with a sergeant-major's moustache and bearing, did not look sinister; he looked polite and disturbed. After glancing round as though he suspected the presence of enemy spies, he addressed Kent with confidential heartiness.

"I'm very sorry to trouble you, sir," he said; "but I wonder if you'd be good enough to help us out of a difficulty? You're the gentleman in 707?"

"Yes, that's right."

"Ah! Well, sir, it's like this. The room you're in—707— was occupied up to yesterday afternoon," again the sergeant-major looked around, "by an American lady who's sailing home in the *Directoire* late to-day. She rang us up late last night; but of course we didn't like to disturb you until you were up and about. The fact is, sir, that when she left here she forgot a very valuable bracelet; pushed it down in the drawer of the bureau, it seems, inside the paper lining, and clean forgot about it. The lady prizes it very highly, she tells us, and doesn't want to go home without it. It's too bad the chambermaid didn't spot it when the room was made up yesterday before you came in; but you know how these things happen. Now, sir, I know it's an imposition on you; but if we found that bracelet right now, we could get it to Southampton in time to catch her boat. I wonder if you'd mind just stepping upstairs with me, and looking in that drawer?"

Kent had begun to feel a trifle ill.

"I'm afraid I have to go out," he said slowly. "But there's no reason why *you* shouldn't go upstairs and look —or the maid, or whoever wants to. You have my full permission, and you could get in with a pass-key."

The hall-porter assumed an even more heavily reluctant air.

"Ah, but that's just the trouble, sir," he pointed out, shaking his head. "Under the circumstances————"

"What circumstances?"

"Your good lady being asleep up there, and having hung a 'quiet' sign on the door," said the porter, with an air of handsome frankness, "you can see we hardly liked————"

"My good lady?"

"Your wife. It would hardly do for us to wake anyone up with a request like that. But I thought if you wouldn't mind going in and explaining to your wife————"

Even as his mind registered the word "sunk," Kent found himself being urged by some hypnotic power in the direction of the nearer of the two lifts.

Chapter 2

The Crime of Murder

THERE were, he afterwards realised, very few courses open to him. No course, in fact, except that of walking sternly and quickly out of the hotel: an action into which his inflamed conscience put an interpretation of guilt bringing about immediate pursuit. Also, with a stomach now lined with good food, he began to take a pleasant interest in the situation. It was like a situation in one of his own books; and it stirred in him the quality of devilment. Apparently he would have to break into the room of a blameless husband and wife, now asleep upstairs—and get away with it somehow. Adventures (he could have told Dan Reaper) are to be found within walls, not on the plain.

Going up in the lift, the hall-porter was affable.

"Have a good night, sir? Sleep well?"

"Pretty well."

"I hope you weren't disturbed by the men in the hall getting ready that second lift. That top floor where you are, you know, is very new; we're quite proud of it; and it isn't quite finished. They haven't finished installing the second lift. They're working double-time to get all that floor ready in time for Coronation. Ah, here we are."

The seventh floor of the Royal Scarlet was constructed on the principle of fewer and larger rooms. It had four wings, of which wing A (immediately to your right as you stepped out of the working lift) was the only one with which Kent ever had any concern. A broad descending staircase faced the two lifts, set side by side, and on the second lift workmen were now tinkering with the mechanism under a powerful light.

Wing A was spacious and luxurious enough, although Kent could have wished for a little of the less frantically modern note in chromium, glass, and murals. To the right of the lifts, a broad corridor ran some distance down before turning again at right angles. Underfoot was a very thick grey carpet; and the walls were decorated in a way which suggested the smoking-room or lounge of a liner. On one side ran a full-length representation of a scene round a prize-ring, and the other side appeared to be composed of a coloured alphabet gone mad. Dim lights illuminated it with a chrysalis effect. It was very new, and not quite out of its smooth rawness; you could almost smell the stream-lining as you could smell the paint.

Kent was growing even more uneasy as he came to face it. Number 707 was in the corner at the turning of the corridor, its door being round the corner and out of sight from the direction of the lifts. Kent, a little ahead of the hall-porter, was the first to see that door. Outside it stood a pair of woman's brown shoes: of what material he could not tell or did not notice. And hanging from the knob was one of those cardboard notices reading, "Quiet is requested for the benefit of those who have retired." But that was not what made him stop dead, instinctively shielding the card with his body. Across the notice had been scrawled, half-writing, half-printing, in red ink:

DEAD WOMAN

In Kent's mind it took on a weird clearness. At the end of this bend in the corridor there was a window, and outside the window a fire-escape; he seemed to notice a dozen things at once. He noted also the linen-closet at the end of the corridor: there was a bright light inside it, and a chambermaid in a blue-and-white uniform. Yet it all concentrated on those words, "Dead Woman," hanging helpfully outside the door.

Surely if the chambermaid had already passed the door, those words would have been noticed? His own voice sounded very queer when he said:

"I'm afraid I haven't got my key."

(Well, should he own up now, or bolt for it?)

"Oh, that's all right, sir," the hall-porter assured him, in a surprisingly natural tone. "We'll have the maid here in half a tick. S-sss-t!"

He was already hurrying down the hall to get the maid. Christopher Kent remained where he stood: he did nothing because he could think of absolutely nothing to do. But one thing he did not like. He put out his hand quickly and reversed the card, so that its inner side (printed in the same way except for that curious note in red ink) was now outwards.

"Here we are, sir," said the hall-porter. The key clicked in the lock and the door opened an inch. Even if the porter had not tactfully stood aside, Kent was instantly in front of him.

"If you'll just wait here a moment—?" he said.

"Of course, sir. No hurry."

Gritting his teeth, Kent slipped in and let the door swing shut after him; it was one of those which automatically lock on closing.

The room inside was almost dark. Heavy cream-coloured blinds had been drawn full down on its two windows, and made opaque blurs against the gloom. Neither window could have been up, for the place smelt heavily stuffy. In the wall to his left he could dimly make out the line of twin beds; and he momentarily expected someone to sit up in one of them and ask him what the devil he was doing there. But nothing stirred, not even the quilted counterpane on either, and he saw that both beds were empty. Nothing stirred, that is, except his own scalp; for he began to realise that the notice on the door was probably true.

A little way out in the big room he could discern a wardrobe trunk, of the sort that stands on end and opens out like a book. It now stood part way open towards him, and something was projecting along the floor from between its leaves. First it was a dark mass; then it had a leg in a grey silk stocking; then a hand. It was a woman's body lying on its side with the head between the leaves of the trunk. Something white was partly draped over the shoulder.

Those interested in such matters have argued what an ordinary man in the street would do if he were thrown into a bad position with a dead person before him; Kent had argued it himself. He did nothing. The time he actually spent in that room he afterwards computed as about three minutes.

First he must bring himself to go and look. His hand was moving uncertainly in the air, and to the right of the door his fingers brushed something which made him draw back. A little table stood there: on the table was a huge pile of neatly-folded bath-towels.

He did not think of turning on a light or raising a blind. In his pocket he had a box of matches, with two or three left. He went over to the woman as quietly as he could, bent down, and hurriedly struck a match. That this was murder he had not doubted from the first. And, after a quick look, he blew out the match with equal haste: swallowing to keep down that feeling of revulsion which creeps on you before you are aware of it.

To the best of his knowledge, he had never seen the woman before. She seemed to be young, and had brown bobbed hair: which was one of the few details of which he could be sure. She was fully dressed, in a dark grey tailored suit and white silk blouse, except that instead of shoes she wore soft black slippers trimmed with fur. Evidently she had been strangled: the murderer having wrapped on his hands, to avoid leaving any marks, the ordinary crumpled face-towel which now lay across her shoulder. But this was not all that had been done. Her face had been heavily beaten or stamped on—undoubtedly after death, for there was not a great deal of blood despite the damage of that vicious afterthought. She was quite cold.

Kent crept across the room. There was a chair near the window and he sat down on the edge of it, though he automatically refrained from touching anything. He said to himself, coolly and half aloud, "My lad, you're in one terrible mess."

He had claimed he had spent that night in the room, with a woman he did not know from Eve. Logically, one thing ought to sustain him: he was in no danger of eventual arrest or hanging. The woman had been dead many hours. He had spent the night at a coffee-stall on the Embankment, and he could prove it by much congenial company; fortunately, his alibi was secure.

But that was only eventually. If he did not wish to spend the next day or so in a cell—to say nothing of being obliged to reveal his real name, losing a thousand-pound wager to Dan, and making himself a laughing-stock—he would have to get out of there somehow. All his stubbornness butted against this mess. Flight? Certainly; why not, if it could be managed? But in decency he could not leave that woman lying there———

There was a discreet knock at the door.

Kent got up quickly, searching for the bureau. One name and address now stood out in his mind as clearly as the lettering on the card. It was the name and address of a man whom he had never met, but with whom he frequently corresponded: Dr. Gideon Fell, number 1 Adelphi Terrace. He must call Dr. Fell. In the meantime, if he could find that infernal bracelet which someone had left behind in the bureau, he might get rid of the hall-porter.

He found the bureau, which was between the two windows; he had to touch things now. Through the sides of the blinds, pale light illuminated it. But he did not find the bracelet, because it was not there. A sense of something even more crooked and dangerous stirred in Kent's brain: he did not exactly suspect the waxed moustaches of the hall-porter, now waiting patiently outside the door, but he thought there must be something wrong besides murder. There was nothing at all in the bureau, whose drawers had each a clean paper lining.

Gingerly lifting a corner of the window-blind, Kent peered out. The windows of the room opened out on a high enclosed air-well faced with white tiles. Something else was wrong as well. A little while ago, the folded card bearing the number 707—the card that had brought him here—had floated down from some high window into his hand. But he had been standing in front of the hotel. Ergo, it had come from someone else's room. . . .

The discreet knock at the door was repeated. This time he thought he could hear the hall-porter cough.

Kent turned round and studied the room. In the wall now on his right there was another door; but this side of the room formed the angle with the two corridors outside. He made a quick and correct calculation. Unless it were a cupboard, that door must open directly into the corridor on the side out of sight of the hall-porter. It did: he drew back the bolt and opened it, now in sight of the men working on the lift. Accept what the gods give; in other words, here goes! Slipping out, he closed the door behind him and made off towards the stairs. Fifteen minutes later, in the midst of a thickening snowstorm, he was ringing the doorbell at number 1 Adelphi Terrace.

"*Aha!*" said Dr. Fell.

The door was opened by the doctor himself. He stood as vast as the door itself, projecting thence like a figurehead on a ship, and beaming out into the snow. His red face shone, as though by the reflection of firelight through the library windows; his small eyes twinkled behind eye-glasses on a broad black ribbon; and he seemed to peer down, with massive and wheezy geniality, over the ridges of his stomach. Kent restrained an impulse to cheer. It was like meeting Old King Cole on his own doorstep. Even before the visitor had mentioned his name or his errand, Dr. Fell cocked his head affably and waited.

His visitor arrived at a decision.

"I'm Christopher Kent," he said, breaking the rule and losing his bet. "And I'm afraid I've come six thousand miles to tell you I've walked into trouble."

Dr. Fell blinked at him. Though his geniality did not lessen, his face had become grave. He seemed to hover in the doorway (if such a manoeuvre were possible), like a great balloon with an ivory-headed stick. Then he glanced round at his own uncurtained library windows. Through them Kent could see a table laid for breakfast in the embrasure of the bay, and a tall, middle-aged man pacing round as though with impatience.

"Look here," said Dr. Fell seriously, "I think I can guess why and who. But I've got to warn you—you see that chap in there? That's Superintendent Hadley of the Criminal Investigation Department; I've written to you about him. Knowing that, will you come in and smoke a cigar?"

"I'd like to."

"Aha!" said Dr. Fell, with a pleased chuckle.

He lumbered into a big room lined to the ceiling with books; and the watchful, cautious, explosive Hadley, whose mental picture Kent had been able to build up already, stared when he heard the visitor's name. Then Hadley sat down quietly, smoothing out his noncommittal face. Kent found himself in a comfortable easy-chair by the breakfast-table, a cup of coffee in his hand, and he told his story with directness. Now that he had decided to lose his bet and let Dan's triumph go hang, there was satisfaction in feeling like a human being again.

"—and that's the whole story," he concluded. "Probably I was a fool to run out of there; but, if I'm going to jail, I'd rather be sent to jail by the head-man than explain to the hotel-staff how I cadged a breakfast. I didn't kill the woman. I never saw her before in my life. And, fortunately, I'm pretty sure I can prove where I was last night. That's the full list of my crimes."

Throughout this Hadley had been regarding him steadily. He seemed friendly enough, if very worried.

"No, it wasn't the thing to do," Hadley said. "But I don't suppose there's any great harm done, if you can prove what you say. And in a way I'm glad you did. (Eh, Fell?) The point is—" He drummed his fingers on his brief-case, and moved forward in the chair. "Never mind about last night. Where were you last Thursday fortnight: the 14th of January, to be exact?"

"On the *Volpar*, from Capetown to Tilbury."

"That ought to be easy enough to prove?"

"Yes. But why?"

Hadley glanced at Dr. Fell. Dr. Fell was sitting back in an enormous chair, several of his chins showing over his collar, and looking in an uneasy fashion down his nose. Over Kent's account of the wager he had made rumbling noises of approval; but now his noises were of a different sort.

"It would not be either striking or original," he observed, clearing his throat, "if I observed that I did not like this. H'mf. Ha. No. The business itself is neither striking nor original. It is not very bizarre. It is not very unusual. It is merely completely brutal and completely unreasonable. Dammit, Hadley———!"

"Look here, what's up?" demanded Kent. He had felt a tension brush that snug and firelit room.

"I know you found a woman in that room," Hadley said. "The news was phoned to me here not five minutes before you arrived. She had been strangled. Then, presumably after death, her face had been so battered as to be almost unrecognisable. You saw her by the light of a match with her head against the floor. Now, Mr. Kent, I assume you're telling the truth." His eyelids moved briefly. "And therefore I'm afraid I've got some bad news for you. If you had got a better look at her, you might have recognised her. The lady was Mrs. Josephine Kent—the wife of your cousin, Mr. Rodney Kent."

He looked from Hadley to Dr. Fell, and saw that neither of them was in the mood for joking.

"Jenny!" he said. "But that's————"

He stopped, because he did not know what he meant himself. It was simply that the two ideas, Jenny Kent and death, would not coincide; one was a stencil that would not go over the other. He tried to build up a picture of her. Small, plump, neat woman; yes. Brown hair; yes. But the description would fit a thousand women. It seemed impossible that it should have been his cousin's wife over whom he had struck a match not half an hour ago; yet why not? That piece of clay beside the trunk would not carry Jenny's extraordinary attractiveness.

Hadley looked hard at him. "There's no doubt it is Mrs. Kent if that's what you're thinking," the superintendent said. "You see, Mr. Reaper's party arrived at the Royal Scarlet last night, and they're occupying that wing on the seventh floor."

"The whole party? Then they were already there when I walked in?"

"Yes. Did you know Mrs. Kent well?"

"I suppose I should have expected that," muttered Kent, reflecting that much trouble could have been saved had he known it. He tried to arrange his thoughts. "Jenny? I don't know," he answered, honestly doubtful. "She wasn't the sort you did know well, and yet everybody in the world liked her. It's difficult to explain. I suppose you could call her 'nice.' Not unpleasantly nice; but you couldn't imagine her on a party or doing anything that wasn't strictly according to Hansard. And she was amazingly attractive without being beautiful: bright complexion, very quiet. Rod worshipped her; they've been married only a year or two, and—" He stopped. "Good God, that's the worst of it! This will just about kill Rod."

The figure of his cousin Rodney was very distinct in his mind then. He sympathised more with Rod than with the woman who was dead, for he had grown up with Rod and liked him very well. To Christopher Kent things had always come easily. To Rodney they came by plodding. Rodney was in simple earnest about everything. He was admirably suited to be Dan Reaper's political secretary; to answer letters with interest and thoroughness; to assemble the facts for Dan's speeches (Rodney Kent's facts could never be questioned); and even to write the sincere prose into which Dan stuck a tail-feather of rhetoric.

"The double room at the hotel, of course." Kent remembered it suddenly. "Rod would have been with her. But where was he? Where was he while she was being murdered? He wasn't there this morning. I tell you, it'll just about kill him————"

"No," said Dr. Fell. "He has been spared that, anyhow."

Again he became aware that both Dr. Fell and Hadley were looking at him.

"We may as well get this over with," the superintendent went on. "You may have wondered how I come to know so much about you and your affairs. I knew about this wager of yours; Mr. Reaper told me. We have been trying to get in touch with you, but nobody knew what ship you would be on or even what name you would use. . . . This isn't the first time I've been in touch with that party. Your cousin, Mr. Rodney Kent, was murdered on the 14th of January in exactly the same way that his wife was murdered last night."

Chapter 3

The Statement of Ritchie Bellowes

Consequently," pursued the superintendent, "I think you can help us." For the first time a human look appeared on his face, the shadow of an exasperated smile. "I've come to *this* duffer for help," he nodded towards Dr. Fell, who scowled, "because it seems to be another of those meaningless cases which delight his heart so much. Here are two young people, a happily married couple. It is universally agreed (at least, it's agreed by everyone I've spoken to) that neither of them had an enemy in the world. They certainly hadn't an enemy in England, for neither of them has ever been out of South Africa up until now. There seems no doubt that they were as harmless a pair as you'd find anywhere. Yet somebody patiently stalks and kills them—one at Sir Gyles Gay's place in Sussex, the other here at the Royal Scarlet Hotel. After killing them, the murderer stands over them and batters their faces with a vindictiveness I've not often seen equalled. Well?"

There was a pause.

"Naturally I'll help all I can," said Kent with bitterness. "But I still can't believe it. It's—hang it, it's indecent! As you say, neither of them had an enemy in— By the way, how is Jenny fixed? I mean, does she need money or anything, for—no, I forgot; she's dead. But haven't you got any idea who did it?"

Hadley hesitated. Then, pushing his finished breakfast-plate to one side, he opened his brief-case on the table.

"There's a fellow we've got in jail: not on a charge of murder, of course, though that's actually why he's there. Fellow named Bellowes. A good deal of the evidence points to him as the murderer of Rodney Kent————"

"Bellowes," said Dr. Fell blankly, "has now become the most important figure in the case, if I understand you properly."

"I don't think you do understand. Whether or not Bellowes killed Rodney Kent, I'm ruddy sure he didn't kill Mrs. Kent, because he's in jail."

A long sniff rumbled in Dr. Fell's nose. The light of battle, never very far away between these two, made them momentarily forget their visitor. Dr. Fell's face was fiery with controversy.

"What I am patiently attempting to point out," he returned, "is that Bellowes's statement, which seemed so ridiculous to you at the time————"

"Bellowes's statement can't be true. In the first place, his finger-prints were in the room. In the second place, when any man, drunk or sober, seriously maintains that he saw a man in the resplendent uniform of a hotel attendant walking about a Sussex country house at two o'clock in the morning————"

"Here!" protested Kent.

"I think," said Dr. Fell mildly, "that we had better enlighten our friend about a few things. H'mf. Suppose you go over the evidence again, Hadley, and ask for any information you want. Speaking for myself, I cannot hear too much of it. It's like one of Lear's nonsense rhymes: it flows so smoothly that for a second you are almost tricked into thinking you know what it means. The hotel attendant in a country house is a difficulty, I admit; but I can't see it's a difficulty that tells against Bellowes."

Hadley turned to Kent. "To begin with," he asked, "do you know Sir Gyles Gay?"

"No. I've heard Dan talk a lot about him, but I've never met him. He's something in the government, isn't he?"

"He used to be. He was under-secretary for the Union of South Africa: that means, I gather, a sort of buffer or liaison-officer between Whitehall and Pretoria. But he retired about a year ago, and it's been less than a year since he took a house at Northfield, in Sussex, just over the border of Kent." Hadley reflected. "Reaper's chief reason for coming to England was to see him, it seems. It was a business-deal: some property in Middelburg that Reaper was either buying or selling for Sir Gyles, and a friendly visit as well. Gay is a bachelor, and seems to have welcomed a lot of company in his new country house."

Again Hadley reflected. Then, as though frankly getting something off his chest, he got up and began to pace about the room, measuring the spots in the carpet while he talked. His voice was as indeterminate as his clipped moustache. But Kent had an impression that his watchfulness never relaxed.

"On Tuesday, January 12th, Reaper and his party went down from London to Northfield; they had arrived in England the day before. They intended to stay there for a little over a fortnight, and return to London on the evening of January 31st—that's actually to-day—in time for Reaper to meet you at the Royal Scarlet *if* you won the wager and appeared to-morrow. Everybody in the party seems to have been speculating about it.

"In the party at Northfield there were six persons. Sir Gyles Gay himself, the host. Mr. and Mrs. Reaper. Miss Francine Forbes, their niece. Mr. Harvey Wrayburn. And your cousin, Mr. Rodney Kent," continued Hadley. He was as formal as though he were giving evidence. "Mrs. Kent was not there. She has two aunts in Dorset—we checked up on them—and she decided to pay them a visit; she had never seen them before, although she had heard about them for years. So she went down there before coming on to Northfield. I suppose you know all the persons in Reaper's party?"

"Oh, yes," said Kent, thinking of Francine.

"And you'll be willing to supply any information I need about them?"

Kent faced him frankly.

"Look here, it's no good saying I don't see your implication. But you'll never find a murderer in that group. It's a funny thing, too: I know most of them better than I knew my own cousin."

"Oh, a murderer—!" said Hadley, with a slow and dry smile, as though he brushed the matter aside as being unimportant. "At the moment we're not finding a murderer; we're merely finding facts.

"Now the facts about the business are simple enough. Nobody was running about the place at the wrong times. No group of people cross each other's trails or contradict each other's stories. But the background is the unusual part of the business, which seems to appeal to Fell.

"The village, Northfield, is an attractive sort of place such as you find frequently in Kent and Sussex. It consists of a village green with a church, a pub, and a dozen or so houses round it. It's rather secluded, set in the middle of all those thousand little lanes designed exactly like a maze for motorcars; it runs to half-timbering and an 'old-world' atmosphere."

Dr. Fell grunted.

"This back-handed lyricism," he said, "is inspired by the fact that Hadley, in spite of being a Scot, is a good Cockney who hates the country, and profoundly resents the circumstance that roads antedated motor-cars."

"That may be," admitted Hadley quite seriously. "But all the same I was looking for a hint in it. Say what you like, it can't be—it wasn't—a very exciting place in the dead of winter. I was just wondering why *all* Reaper's party wanted to go down there for a fortnight and dig in. You'd think they'd prefer to stay in town and see some shows.

"Well, for the past forty years one of the great local characters thereabouts was old Ritchie Bellowes: the father of our chief suspect. He's dead now, but they thought a lot of him. Old Bellowes was both an architect and a practical builder, with a taste for doing a lot of the work with his own hands. He built half the modern houses in the district. He seems to have had a fondness for wood-carving and all sorts of gadgets; but his particular hobby was building replicas of Tudor or Stuart houses so cleverly faked, with beams and floor-boards out of other houses, that the most expert architect would be deceived about the age of the house. It was a sort of village joke, and the old man seems to have had rather a queer sense of humour himself. He loved putting in trick doors and secret passages—stop! I hasten to assure you, from absolute knowledge, that there's no secret passage or the like in the house I'm telling you about.

"This house, the one he built for his own use, was bought by Sir Gyles Gay some months ago. It's a fairly large place—eight bedrooms—and stands at the foot of a lane going down past the church. It's an imitation Queen Anne place, and a really beautiful job if you don't mind something on the heavy and grim style. Some of the windows look straight out across the churchyard, which is hardly my idea of rural grandeur.

"What we have to consider is the position of young Ritchie Bellowes, the old man's son. I tell you quite frankly I'm damned if I see how he fits into this, and I should feel happier if I could. He's a character also. He was born and brought up in that house. From what I've been able to learn, he's had the best of educations, and he's certainly a clever chap. What seems to impress everyone is his phenomenal power of quick observation, drunk or sober: the sort of person before whom you can riffle a pack of cards and he can afterwards name you consecutively every card he saw. As a matter of fact, he gave a little entertainment of this kind, mental tests, before Sir Gyles's guests during the first few days they were at the house.

"He was left very well off when the old man died. Then the dry rot set in. He doesn't seem to have had any actual vices: he was simply plain lazy, added to a slight paralysis in the left arm, and he liked the drink. The slide down the incline was first gradual, and then abrupt. First his business dropped to pieces; the slump hit him and he didn't improve it by the way he squandered money. Then his wife died of typhoid at the seaside, and he caught it too. He kept on quietly drinking. By this time he's become something like the village drunk. He gives no trouble and makes no fuss. Every night of his life he leaves the bar-parlour of the Stag and Glove under his own steam, with great politeness. Finally, he had to sell his favourite fake Queen Anne house —Four Doors, it's called—for whatever it would bring. He's been living in lodgings with a pious widow; and almost haunting the old place since Sir Gyles Gay bought it. That may have been the root of the trouble.

"Now we come to the bare facts about the night of the murder. Exclusive of servants there were six persons in the house. Sir Gyles and his five guests all slept on the same floor. They all occupied separate rooms (Mr. and Mrs. Reaper were in connecting ones); and all the rooms opened on a central passage running the breadth of the house. Like a hotel, you'll say. The household retired together about midnight. So far as I can find out, there had been absolutely nothing unusual, abnormal, or even suspicious about anyone or any event that night; on the contrary, it seems to have been a fairly dull evening. After midnight only one person—according to the testimony—left his room at any time. At about five minutes past two o'clock Mr. Reaper woke up, put on his dressing-gown, turned on the light, and went out in the hall to go to the bathroom. Up to this time it is agreed that no noise or disturbance of any kind had been heard.

"Next, compare this with our knowledge of Bellowes's movements for that night. Bellowes left the Stag and Glove, which is off the village green about two hundred yards from the lane leading to Four Doors, at just ten o'clock: closing time. He had drunk no more than usual that night; six pints of ale, the landlord says. But on the last round he called for whisky, and, when he left, he bought a half-bottle of whisky to take with him. He then seemed to be his usual self. He was seen to walk off along the road towards Porting, the next village, and to branch from there into a lane leading to a wood called Grinning Copse: another favourite haunt of his, where he often sat and drank alone. The 14th was a cold night, with a very bright moon. There we lose sight of him.

"At five minutes past two, then, Reaper at the house opened his bedroom door and walked out into the main passage. Along one wall of this passage—not far outside the door of the room occupied by Rodney Kent—there is a leather-covered sofa. By the moonlight through the window at the end of the passage, Reaper could see a man stretched out on this sofa, asleep and snoring. In that light he didn't recognise the man; but it was Bellowes, unquestionably dead drunk.

"Reaper turned on the lights and knocked at Sir Gyles's door. Sir Gyles knew Bellowes, of course, and seems to have sympathised with him. They both assumed that Bellowes, drunk, had simply come here by instinct, as he had been doing all his life: a key to the house was found in his pocket. Then they noticed that the door to Rodney Kent's room was wide open."

Outside the windows the snow was falling with silent insistence, shadowing this book-lined room. In a sort of hypnosis induced by reaction or firelight, Christopher Kent was trying to fit the person he had always known under warmer skies—ginger-haired, serious-minded Rodney—into this bleak atmosphere of a sham Queen Anne house by a churchyard. During the recital Dr. Fell had not moved, except to ruffle his big mop of grey-streaked hair.

"Well," Hadley went on abruptly, "they found your cousin dead there, Mr. Kent. He was lying at the foot of the bed. He wore his pyjamas and dressing-gown, but he had not yet gone to bed when the murderer caught him.

He had been strangled by hands wrapped in a face-towel; the towel itself, which came from the wash-hand-stand, was lying across his shoulder. (That particular room is furnished in heavy eighteen-sixties style, with marble-topped bureaux and the old massive stuff.) After being strangled, his face had been bashed in by about a dozen blows—our old friend the blunt instrument, of course—but the blunt instrument wasn't found.

"It was a nasty bit of work, because the blows must have been delivered some minutes after his actual death, out of deliberate hatred or mania. But it was not enough to prevent positive identification, so there's no doubt as to the victim. Finally the murderer must have caught him almost as soon as he'd retired to his room, because the medical evidence showed he had been dead nearly two hours. Is all that clear?"

"No," said Dr. Fell. "But go on."

"Stop a bit," interposed Kent. "There's something even more queer here. Rod was thin, but he was as tough as wire. The murderer must have been very quick and very powerful to catch him like that without any noise; or was there a struggle?"

"Not necessarily. No, there was no sign of a struggle. But on the back of his head there was a bad bruise which did not quite break the skin. It might have come from the scrollwork and curves on the footboard of the bed—you know the sort of thing—when he fell. Or the murderer might have stunned him with the instrument that was later used to batter him."

"So you arrested this fellow Bellowes?"

Hadley was irritable. His measurement of the spots in the carpet had now become a matter of painful preciseness.

"Not on a charge of murder. Technically, of housebreaking," he retorted. "Naturally he was the suspect. First of all, his finger-prints were found in the room, round the light-switch: though he says he has no recollection of being in the room and is willing to swear he didn't go in. Second, he is the only person likely to have committed the crime.

He was drunk; he may have suffered from a sense of grievance about the house; he may have come back there and gone berserk————

"Wait!" Hadley interrupted himself, forestalling objection. "I can see all the holes in it, and I'll give you them. If he killed his victim at midnight and then went out and fell asleep on the sofa in the hall, what happened to our blunt instrument? Also, there was no trace whatever of blood on him or on his clothes. Finally, it so happens that his left arm is partially paralysed (one of the reasons why he never took to work), and the doctor is of the opinion that he couldn't have strangled anybody. The drunken motive is also weak. If he had a grievance against anybody, it would have been against Sir Gyles Gay. He would hardly have walked in and—(with malice aforethought, since there was a weapon)—assaulted a complete stranger at random, especially as he didn't make the least noise in doing it. I also admit that nobody in a village where he's been drinking for a good many years has ever found him savage or vindictive, no matter how much he had aboard. But there you are.

"Then there's his statement, which seems a mass of nonsense. He wasn't coherent until the next day, and even in jail he didn't seem to realise what was happening. When he told his story for the first time, Inspector Tanner thought he was still drunk and didn't even bother to write it down; but he repeated it when he was cold sober, and he's stuck to it since.

"According to him—well, here you are."

Opening his brief-case, Hadley took a typewritten sheet from among a sheaf of others and ran his finger down it.

I remember being in Grinning Copse, going there after the pub closed, and I remember drinking most of the bottle I had. I have no idea how long I was there. At one time I thought there was someone talking to me; but I may have imagined this. The last thing I remember distinctly is sitting in the copse on one of the iron seats.

The next thing I knew I was back at Four Doors, sitting on the sofa in the upstairs hall.

I cannot tell you how I got there; but it did not seem strange to find myself there. I thought, "Hullo, I'm home," that's all. Since I was already on the sofa and did not feel like moving, I thought I would just stretch out and take a nap.

At this time I do not think I went to sleep immediately. While I was lying there I saw something; I think I looked round and saw it. It was bright moonlight in the hall; there is a window at the end of the hall, on the south side, and the moon was high then. I do not know how it caught the corner of my eye, but I saw him in the corner there, by the Blue Room door.

I should describe him as a medium-sized man wearing a uniform such as you see in the big hotels like the Royal Scarlet or the Royal Purple. It was a dark blue uniform, with a long coat, and silver or brass buttons; I could not be sure about colours in the moonlight. I think there was a stripe round the cuffs, a dark red stripe. He was carrying a kind of tray, and at first he stood in the corner and did not move.

Question: What about his face?

A.: I could not make out his face, because there seemed to be a lot of shadow, or a hole or something, where his eyes ought to be.

Then he moved out of the corner, and moved or walked down where I could not see him, past my head. His walk also made me think of a hotel attendant.

Q.: Where did he go?

A.: I do not know.

Q.: Did it not surprise you to see a hotel-attendant walking along the hall with a tray in the middle of the night?

A.: No, I did not even think much about it that I remember. I rolled over and went to sleep; or at least I do not remember anything more. Besides, it was not a tray he had; it was more like a salver to carry visiting-cards.

"Which," commented Hadley, slapping the typewritten sheet down on the table, "makes it all the more nonsensical. A salver, mind you! Blast it, Fell, this is either delirium tremens or prophecy or truth. A salver for what? For carrying the weapon? I don't say this fellow Bellowes is guilty; just among the three of us, I don't think he is. But if he's quite sincere in telling this, and if the hotel-attendant isn't the same kind of vision as a brass-buttoned snake, where are we?"

"Well, I'll tell you," said Dr. Fell modestly. He pointed his ivory-headed stick at Hadley, and sighted along it as though it were a rifle. "That toper of yours, you recall, is the same man who can describe a shop-window full of articles after one glance at 'em. A little *causerie* with Ritchie Bellowes, now languishing in clink, is indicated. Dig into that statement; find out what he really saw, or thinks he saw; and we shall probably have a glimmer of the truth."

Hadley considered.

"Of course," he said, "there's the theory that Bellowes committed the first murder while drunk; and that some other person merely used it, used the way of the crime and Bellowes's story about a phantom hotel-attendant, to kill Mrs. Kent later at the Royal Scarlet Hotel————"

"Do you believe that?"

"Frankly, no."

"Thank'e," said Dr. Fell. He wheezed for a moment, regarding Hadley with what can only be called ruddy dignity. "These two murders are the work of one person: anything else, my boy, would be artistically wrong: and I have an unpleasant feeling that someone behind the scenes is managing matters with great artistry." For a time he remained blinking, in a vacant and somewhat cross-eyed fashion, at the hands folded over his stick. " 'Mf. Take this business at the Royal Scarlet last night. All of Reaper's party were present again, I take it?"

"All I know," said Hadley, "is what Betts told me over the phone a few minutes ago. Yes. And Gay himself was with them again—making six persons, just as there were at Four Doors."

"Gay went with 'em to the hotel? Why?"

"Instinct to stick together, I suppose. Gay and Reaper are as thick as thieves."

Dr. Fell looked at him curiously, as though interested by the choice of phrase. But he turned to Kent. "This," rumbled the doctor apologetically, "is hardly what you would be inclined to call fine old English hospitality. I've been looking forward to meeting you, because there are one or two points concerning sensational fiction which I should like to debate with some vehemence. But, frankly, I should like to ask some questions now. These friends of yours—I haven't met any of them, and I want you to describe them for me. Not (heaven forbid) any complicated backgrounds. Just give me one word or phrase about them, the first word or phrase that jumps into your head. Eh?"

"Right," said Kent, "though I still think————"

"Well: Daniel Reaper?"

"Talk and action," replied the other promptly.

"Melitta Reaper?"

"Talk."

"Francine Forbes?"

"Femininity," said Kent, after a pause.

Hadley spoke in a colourless voice. "I understand from talking to Mr. Reaper that you were a good deal interested in the young lady."

"I am," the other admitted frankly. "But we don't get on very well. She is vitally concerned with the importance of new political movements, new theories of all kinds; she *is* The Intelligent Woman's Guide to Socialism, Capitalism, Sovietism, and so on. I'm not. In politics, like Andrew Lang, I never got any farther than being a Jacobite; and I think that, if a man's got the gumption to go out and make himself a fortune, more power to him. Consequently, she regards me as a pig-headed Tory and reactionary. But one of the main reasons why I took up this fool bet was to show her————"

"Heh," said Dr. Fell. "Heh-heh-heh. I see. Next name on our list: Harvey Wrayburn."

"Acrobat."

"Is he?" inquired Dr. Fell, opening his eyes. "I say, Hadley, this is interesting. Do you remember O'Rourke in the Hollow Man case?"

"He's not an acrobat literally," interposed Hadley. "But I think I see what you mean." His eyes narrowed as he regarded Kent. "Very versatile fellow, Fell. He seems to know a good deal about, or to have had some personal experience with, every subject you could mention. He buttonholed me on the subject of crime, and was spouting encyclopaedia after your own heart. He seems a decent sort and," added Hadley, with innate caution about saying this of anyone, "straightforward enough."

"He is," agreed Kent.

"And that's the lot. Now," argued the superintendent, "I don't want to say too much before we've got all our facts. But, by George! a more sterile, harmless lot, as far as suspicion is concerned, I never came across. We've looked up the pasts of all these people. I've talked to them until I'm blue in the face. No one hated or disliked anyone else. No one is financially crooked or even financially crippled. There is not even a hint of a last stand-by in someone's having a love-affair with someone else's wife. There seems to be absolutely no reason why two ordinary young people, whose death would not benefit or even please anyone, should be carefully stalked and murdered. But again —there you are. They were not only murdered: they were battered with patient fury after death. Unless some member of that group is homicidally mad (which I refuse to believe, because I never met a case of it in which signs didn't crop out plainly even when the person was not in a seizure), it makes no sense. What do you make of it?"

"There's just one thing, Hadley. After the man was murdered, you at least had his wife to question. Couldn't she tell you anything to throw any light on it?"

"No. Or she said she couldn't, and I'll swear she was telling the truth; so why should anyone kill her? As I told you, she was with the aunts in Dorset when it happened.

She went half out of her mind, and took to her bed under the soothing hysterics of the aunts. She only got out of the doctor's care long enough to rejoin the rest of the party in London: and on her first night here *she's* murdered. I still ask, what do you make of it?"

"Well, I'll tell you," said Dr. Fell. He puffed out his cheeks, seeming to loom even vaster as he leaned back in the chair. "I can give no assistance at the moment, I regret to say. I can only indicate the things which seem intriguing. I'm interested in towels. I'm interested in buttons. And I'm interested in names."

"Names?"

"Or their permutations," said Dr. Fell. "Shall we get on to the hotel?"

Chapter 4

Hotel-service for Murder

WHEN they were introduced to the manager of the Royal Scarlet Hotel, Kent had expected to meet a suave autocrat in a morning coat, a sort of super head-waiter, of foreign and possibly Semitic extraction. Quite to the contrary, Mr. Kenneth Hardwick was a homely, comfortable, and friendly island product, who wore an ordinary grey suit. Kenneth Hardwick was a grizzled man of middle age, with a strong face, a hooked nose, and a twinkling eye; the keynote of himself, as of his hotel, seemed to be an untroubled efficiency which was shaken by a murder but prepared to deal with it without fuss.

Superintendent Hadley, Dr. Fell, and Kent sat in the manager's private rooms on the seventh floor. The ordinary business office was downstairs; but two rooms on the new floor, in Wing D, had been set apart for him. His living-room, a severe but comfortable place in dark oak, had two windows looking out on the white-tiled air-well. Hardwick sat behind a big desk, where a desk-lamp was burning in the gloom of the day, and tapped a plan of Wing A spread out before him. He constantly put on and took off a pair of eyeglasses, his only sign of perturbation in a business-like recital.

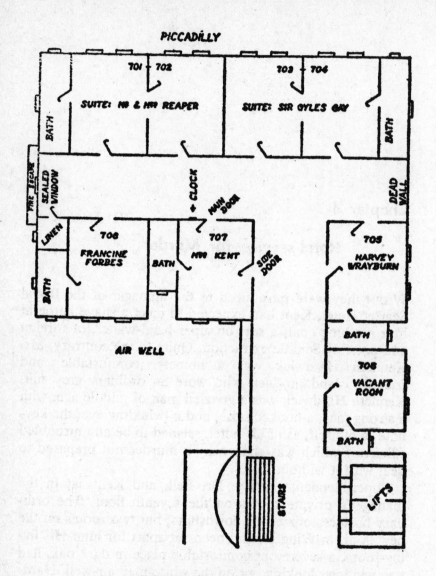

PLAN OF WING A
SEVENTH FLOOR, ROYAL SCARLET HOTEL

"—so," he concluded, "before the other Mr. Kent came here this morning, that was the position. Mr. Reaper booked the rooms for his party six weeks ago, and asked particularly to have the accommodations on this floor. Of course I knew about Mr. Rodney Kent's death two weeks ago, and a bad business it was." He seemed to draw himself together, setting his glasses on more firmly. "Although there was practically nothing about it in the Press, and certainly no hint of anything except—um—a drunken attack. . . ."

"No," said Hadley. "The Home Office have instructed us to keep it out of the public eye. The inquest has been adjourned."

"I see." Hardwick leaned a little farther forward. "Now the position is this, superintendent. Ordinarily I should be a fool if I asked whether this affair could be kept quiet. I had and have no intention of asking that. But what's the situation? If there has been a certain amount of secrecy about Mr. Kent's death, does the same thing apply to Mrs. Kent? Right up to this minute nobody, except those immediately concerned, knows anything about it. Business as usual, you see. This has been easy, because Mr. Reaper's party are the only persons in Wing A; they're more or less cut off———"

"Cut off," repeated Hadley. "Until I get my instructions, it will certainly be kept quiet. Now for details. Just which rooms are these various persons occupying?"

Hardwick pushed the plan across the desk. "I've marked them here," he explained. "You'll see that number 707 says, 'Mr. and Mrs. Rodney Kent.' It was down like that in our books; and it was not changed. That was why, this morning, the staff saw nothing odd in there being a second occupant of the room when someone asked for breakfast."

There was a knock at the door. Sergeant Betts, Hadley's aide-de-camp, came in with a note-book significantly displayed.

"Doctor's just finished, sir," he announced. "He'd like to see you. I've checked up on the other points you asked about."

"Right. Where are the—guests?"

"All in their own rooms. I had a bit of difficulty with Mr. Reaper, but Preston is standing guard in the hall."

Hadley grunted, hitching his chair closer to study the plan. There was a long silence. The light of the desk-lamp shone on Hardwick's face, moulded with attention, a half-smile fixed there. Dr. Fell, a great bandit figure in the black cape, with his shovel-hat in his lap, stared down over Hadley's shoulder. Faintly they were aware of the music of the orchestra from the lounge below, coming up the air-well; but it was a background, a vibration, rather than something actually heard.

"I see," the superintendent began abruptly, "that all the rooms have private bathrooms. And only one of them is unoccupied."

"Yes; number 706 is unoccupied. Nearest the lifts. The workmen are still there, and I was afraid it might disturb anybody who was too close."

"Do you take charge of these arrangements personally?"

"Not ordinarily, no. But in this case, yes; I know Mr. Reaper, and I used to live in South Africa myself."

"Were these rooms assigned some time ago?"

"Oh, yes. The only difference was that the party arrived here a day earlier than they had intended."

"How was that? Do you know?"

"Well, Mr. Reaper rang me up from Northfield yesterday afternoon. He said—their nerves were all on edge, you see—" Hardwick made a slight deprecating gesture; "he felt they had better not stay in the country any longer, and the police had no objection to their coming to London. It was easy enough to fit them in; this is a slack season. As a matter of fact, only one of the rooms had been occupied —707—by a lady who was vacating it yesterday afternoon."

Hadley glanced at Kent. "That's the American lady who said she left a valuable bracelet behind in the bureau of the room?"

"Said?" repeated the manager. "I don't know what you

mean by that exactly. She *did* leave a bracelet in the bureau. Myers, the day hall-porter, found it there at the same time he found—Mrs. Kent."

Christopher Kent stared at him. He had too vivid a recollection of that maplewood bureau, with its sleek-moving drawers and their paper linings, to let this pass.

"Wait. There's a mistake here somewhere," he interposed. "During my little adventure this morning I looked all through that bureau; and I'll swear by anything you like that there was no bracelet in it then."

Hardwick spoke after a pause. The small lines had returned to his forehead; it was as though they were poised there. He looked quickly from one to the other of his guests.

"I don't know what to say. All I know is that I have the bracelet now; a fairly clinching argument. Myers brought it to me when he came to report the other business. Here, have a look at it."

He pulled out a drawer at the left-hand side of his desk. Tearing open a sealed envelope, he put down the bracelet under the light. It was of white gold, set in broad links, and in the centre was one stone of curious design. Square, black, polished and dully gleaming, it had engraved on it two lines in Roman script just large enough to read. *Claudite jam rivos, pueri,* said the inscription, *sat prata biberunt.* Behind Hadley's shoulder Dr. Fell was making vast and seething noises of excitement.

"Yes, it's unusual," Hardwick commented. "That stone —obsidian, black opal, what is it?—looks as though it had been taken out of a ring and set into the bracelet. But the inscription is still more unusual. The remains of a once-passable stock of Latin don't help me. I should render it irreverently as, 'Shut up the liquor, boys; the meadows have had enough to drink'—which seems to be nonsense."

He regarded Dr. Fell with a dry and inquiring grin, which had a sudden keenness in it.

"Oh, Baachus!" growled Dr. Fell, not informatively. "I say, no wonder she wants to get this back! The stone is not intrinsically valuable; but there are several museum-curators who would cut your throat to get it. If it's what I think it is, there must be very few of them extant. As for the inscription, you're not far off. It's a string of metaphors in Virgil's coyest style; his injunction to the shepherds; and a schoolbook softener would render it, 'Cease to sing, lads; recreation enough has been taken.' H'mf. Ha. Yes, I should say this had certainly been taken out of a ring and set into the bracelet. White gold; broad links—nothing there. Only the stone is old. Of course the scheme originated in Greece, and was only copied by the Romans. It's unique! Wow! Dammit, Hadley, you are looking at one of the most ingenious devices of the ancient world."

"Ingenious devices?" demanded Hadley. "Ingenious device for what? You mean it's a poison-stone or bracelet or something?"

"The professional touch," said Dr. Fell with austerity. He stared at it. "No, nothing of that sort; and yet it is as severely practical as one. The Romans were a practical race. Who is the owner of this, Mr. Hardwick?"

The manager looked puzzled. "A Mrs. Jopley-Dunne. I have her address here."

"You don't happen to know her, do you?"

"Yes, quite well. She always stays with us when she is in England."

Wheezing, Dr. Fell sat down again and shook his head. An exasperated Hadley waited for him to speak; but, when the doctor's eye wandered off towards vacancy, Hadley gave it up in favour of more practical matters.

"The bracelet can wait; one thing at a time. Just at the moment, we're following Mr. Reaper's party. At what time did they arrive here?"

"About six o'clock last evening."

"What were they like then? I mean, what was the mood of the party?"

"Definitely glum," said Hardwick, with a gravity which Kent felt was hiding a bleak smile. It did not pass unnoticed by Hadley.

"Go on," said the superintendent. "What happened then?"

"I met them, and took them upstairs. As I told you, I know Mr. Reaper personally. Well, under the circumstances, I advised him to take his friends out and see a show, preferably something funny. You know."

"And did he?"

"Yes; he took six tickets for *She Will When She Won't.*"

"Did they all go?"

"Yes. I don't think Mrs. Kent wanted to go, but she was persuaded. I happened to be leaving my office—downstairs that is—about a quarter past eleven, and I met the party returning from the theatre. They certainly seemed in much better spirits. Mr. Reaper stopped to buy a cigar, and told me that they had all enjoyed the show."

"And then?"

"They went upstairs. At least," said Hardwick, cocking his head on one side and choosing terms carefully, "they got into the lift. I did not see any of them again. The next thing I knew of the business was next morning, when Myers came in to report the discovery of the body." He removed his eyeglasses, put them into their case, and shut it with a snap. For a time he remained looking meditatively at the blotter. "I am not," he added, "going to make any more comments on the ugly nature of this business. You know it; I know it; and it's bad enough to speak for itself." He looked up. "Have you seen that woman's face?"

"Not yet," said Hadley. "Now one question in particular. You say that there were men working on one of the lifts. Were they working all night?"

"Yes."

"Do you know what time they came on and went off duty?"

"Yes."

"Yes. That shift—three men—began at ten last night and worked until eight this morning. They were still there when the body was discovered."

"Suppose some other person—some outsider, someone

not connected with Mr. Reaper's party—had gone into Wing A or come out of it at any time during the night. Those men would have seen him, wouldn't they?"

"I should certainly think so. The wing is lighted all night. A person could have come up or down only by the lift or by the staircase; and the workmen were standing between both."

Hadley gave an interrogative glance at Sergeant Betts, who nodded.

"Yes, sir," agreed the sergeant. "I've got a statement from all three men. They seem straightforward enough and they all tell the same story. They remember Mr. Reaper's party coming upstairs about a quarter past eleven. As a matter of fact, Mr. Reaper stopped and asked them some questions about how the lift worked, and how they were getting on with it. They saw the party separate at the turning of the corridor. Afterwards, they're willing to swear no other person came in or went out of the wing all night."

"So. But is there any other way an outsider could have got in?"

Hadley's question was directed midway between Betts and the hotel-manager. After a pause the latter shook his head.

"Unlikely," he said.

"Why?"

"Look at your plan. I don't say it's impossible, but you're the judge of that." Hardwick twisted the plan round on the table. "There are two other ways, theoretically. An outsider—I suppose you mean a burglar?—might have climbed up the fire-escape to the window at the end of the wing. But, as it happens, that particular window is not only solidly locked on the inside: it was reported to me yesterday as being so stuck in its frame that it couldn't be opened at all. A man was to have seen to it this morning. The only other way in would have been for your burglar to have climbed up the face of the building—either on the outer side towards Piccadilly, or else inside by way of the air-well—barged through someone else's room without be-

ing seen, and got out the same way. Knowing what I do of
this hotel, I should say it's so unlikely as to be nearly impossible."

"You see where these questions are leading?"

"Oh, yes. I see it."

Hadley turned to Betts. "Well, excluding outsiders, did
anybody go in or out of that wing during the night? What
about employees of the hotel?"

"Nobody except the chambermaid, sir. She went off duty
at half-past eleven."

"Yes, but——" Hadley scowled at his note-book. "What
about the Boots? Wouldn't there be a Boots, or whatever
you call him? You put your shoes outside the door at
night, and they take them away to be polished————"

Betts nodded. "Yes, sir. But the Boots—he's actually an
under-porter—wasn't in the wing until early this morning,
a good many hours after the murder. It seems they don't
pick up your shoes and take them away during the night,
in case someone comes in very late. They wait until five
o'clock in the morning; then they gather up the lot, polish
them, and put them back. The Boots went through at five
o'clock, and spoke to the men working on the lifts. But
only one person in the wing had put out a pair of shoes—
Mrs. Kent. And the Boots knew there was some mistake."

"Mistake?" said Hadley sharply.

"In the first place, they were a pair of brown suède
shoes; and you can't polish suède. In the second place,
they weren't a pair, though they looked alike at first
glance. One was a lighter brown than the other, and had a
small flat buckle on it. The Boots knew there had been a
mistake somewhere, so he left the shoes there and came
away."

Dr. Fell interposed, with an expression of painful interest on his face. "Just one moment. I'm interested in the
mechanics of this citadel. Just how is a hotel run? Who
would be in and out of the place at that time of night?"

"There are some three hundred people employed here,"
said Hardwick, "and it would take some time to explain

how everything is run. But I can tell you this: after eleven-thirty at night, nobody would have any business upstairs at all—nobody—except one of the four under-porters.

"It's like this. The maids, who are on duty to answer bells and the rest of it during the day, go off for the night at eleven-thirty. That's for moral reasons," he explained blandly; "you don't want a crowd of girls about when you're turning in. At that time, also, any employees who would have had occasion to go upstairs during the day (like waiters or page-boys) are also off duty. The upstairs is left to the four under-porters on the staff of the night hall-porter."

"There are two shifts, I suppose?" asked Hadley.

"Oh, yes. The night men come on at eight o'clock, and go on until eight the next morning. Each man takes care of one or two floors, according to how full we are. If a bell rings from his floor, he answers it. If luggage has to be carried up, or a guest forgets his key or comes home tight —all the odd jobs, you see. They also collect the shoes at five in the morning, as the sergeant says."

"The point is," insisted Hadley, "*did* anyone go upstairs last night except the maid?"

"No, sir," said Betts. "That seems to be pretty certain."

With a very brief preliminary knock, the door opened and Dan Reaper walked in. After him came Francine Forbes, as though for a rear-guard.

Kent got up automatically. She saw him, although Dan did not notice anything. More than ever, in London, Kent realised that Dan was built on a large scale like a relief map of Africa, and he required room in which to breathe. Yet, despite Dan's buoyant energy, he looked ill; there was a part of his brain which for ever worried and worried and worried. His hair, turning dry and greyish at the temples, was cut short in the Teutonic style; his very light eyes, in a face whose brick-dust tan had not faded, were sur-rounded with little wrinkles which made the heavy face seem to have been gone over with a nutmeg-grater. His mouth, which expressed at once generosity and suspicion, had been pulled in so that the lower lip was drawn over the lower teeth.

In appearance Francine offered a contrast, though in a few mental features she might have been his daughter. She was calmer than Dan, possibly even more determined: it was that determination which brought her and Christopher Kent into conflict whenever they met. She was slender, with that very fair skin which does not tan or burn, but seems to keep a kind of glow in its whiteness: emphasised by fair hair curtly bobbed, and dark brown eyes with long lids. She looked—there is no other word for it—overbred, though the overbreeding seemed to have run to vitality rather than anaemia. You knew that her brown dress was an extreme in fashion less because it was so plain than because it was so completely right for her.

"Look here, Hardwick," said Dan, with restraint. He put the palms of his hands flat on the desk, and then he saw Kent.

Dan whistled.

"How in the world—?" he added, with a subdued roar.

"I think," said Hadley, "that you know Mr. Kent?"

"Lord, yes. One of my best—" said Dan. He stopped again, and looked up quickly. "Did you tell him who you were, Chris? Because, if you did————"

"I know: I lose. Never mind the bet, Dan. Forget the bet. We're in the middle of too serious a mess for that. Hello, Francine."

Dan flushed, rubbing the side of his jaw. He looked at a loss, the other thought, because his innate tact was struggling with his innate desire to explain himself.

"Rotten," he said. "Rottenest nightmare I ever stumbled into. We tried to find you, Chris, but of course— Don't worry, though; don't worry a bit. I took care of everything. He was buried in Hampshire; you know his people came from there; everything of the best; cost me over five hundred, but worth it." After these jerky utterances, even Dan's strong nerve seemed to falter. He spoke querulously. "But I wish I were back having a nice comfortable drink at the SAPC. Now it's Jenny. Have you got any idea what's been happening to us?"

"No."

"But you can tell them, can't you, that nobody would want to kill Rod or Jenny?"

"I can and have."

Hadley let them talk, watching both of them. After barely acknowledging Kent's greeting, Francine Forbes waited with that same air of just having emerged from a cold bath; it was a glow of the skin, he thought, as well as a mental atmosphere. But she was not at ease. Although the long eyes did not move, her hands did: nervously brushing the sides of her dress.

"If we are through discussing Chris's gallant gesture," she said in her brittle voice—it made him hot and angry in a fraction of a second—"perhaps we'd better tell you, Mr. Hadley, why we are here. We form a deputation of two to tell you that we're jolly well not going to stay caged up in separate compartments, like isolated cases, until we know what has happened. We know Jenny is dead. And that's all we do know."

Hadley was at his suavest. He pushed out a chair for her, although she declined it with a turn of the wrist which indicated that she saw nothing except the matter in hand.

"I'm afraid it's all we know ourselves, Miss Forbes," the superintendent told her. "We were coming round to see each of you as soon as we had gone over the room where the murder was committed. Yes, murder: the same as the other one, I'm afraid. By the way, let me introduce Dr. Gideon Fell, of whom you may have heard."

She nodded curtly: a salutation which the doctor, who had got up with vast wheezings, acknowledged by sweeping his shovel-hat across his breast. He also surveyed her through his eyeglasses with an expression of vast and benevolent interest which she seemed to find irritating. But she kept her eyes fixed on Hadley.

"Was she—strangled?"

"Yes."

"When?" asked Dan. He seemed to wish to assert himself.

"We don't know that yet; as I say, we haven't been to the room or seen the doctor. I know," pursued Hadley smoothly, "that it's difficult to remain in your various rooms just now. But, believe me, it would help to keep matters quiet and prevent attracting attention to what's happened—and to yourselves as well—if you would just follow my advice and go back there now. Unless, of course, you have anything important to tell us about last night?"

"N-no," said Dan, clearing his throat. "Not that, God knows!"

"I understand your party came back here from the theatre about a quarter past eleven last night?"

"Yes, that's right."

Hadley paid no attention to his suspicious glance. "When you came back, Mr. Reaper, did you visit one another's rooms or did you all go directly to your own rooms?"

"Straight to our own rooms. We were tired."

By this time Francine had assumed so bored an expression that Kent longed to administer a whacking in the proper place. What he could never determine was whether these moods of hers were quite genuine or an elaborate shell of affectation.

"Well, then: did you see or hear anything suspicious during the night?"

"No," said Dan rigorously.

"You, Miss Forbes?"

"Nothing, thank you," said Francine, as though she were refusing something to eat or drink.

"Did either of you leave your room at any time?"

"No," answered Dan, and hesitated. "No; that still goes. I didn't leave the room. I put my head out and looked into the hall, that's all."

"Looked out into the hall? Why?"

"To see the clock. There's a clock on the wall in the hall there, near Francine's door. My watch had stopped. I called out to my wife to ask her if she knew what time it was; but she was in the bathroom with the bath running, and couldn't hear me. So I opened the door," said Dan, making a heavy gesture of lucidity, "and looked out at the clock. That's all."

"At what time was this?"

"At two minutes past midnight," replied the other promptly. "I set my watch then."

Sergeant Betts moved unobstrusively round behind Hadley's chair. He wrote a few words on the margin of his note-book and held it out. Kent, who was sitting nearest, could read it before Hadley noncommittally passed the note-book to Dr. Fell. It read: *Doctor says she died about midnight.*

"Did you see or hear anyone then, Mr. Reaper? Anyone in the hall, for instance?"

"No," said Dan. "Nobody," he added, "except one of the hotel-attendants, outside Jenny's door, carrying a big pile of towels."

Chapter 5

The New Iron-maiden

WHAT Kent could not understand was whether or not Dan realised what he had said—even whether he threw it off deliberately, and had come here to do so. It was difficult to think that a man of Dan's practical intelligence would not think of it. But he spoke with his own casual air of flat positiveness, as though the matter were of no importance. Something brushed the atmosphere of that room, and they all felt it.

"But—" protested Hardwick suddenly; then he adjusted his expression and remained polite.

"Sit down for just one moment, Mr. Reaper," Hadley said. "At two minutes past midnight you saw a hotel-attendant in the hall carrying towels? A man?"

"Yes."

This time the atmosphere in the room brushed Dan like a touch on the shoulder. His look responded to it.

"A man in uniform?"

"Yes, naturally. I think so."

"What kind of uniform?"

"What kind have they all got? Dark blue; red stripe on the cuff; brass or silver buttons; something like that."

Abruptly Dan's heavy eyes grew fixed, and then opened slightly like those of a man making out something from a great distance away. "Oho!" he said.

"You realise it, then. At the time Mr. Kent was murdered, a man in the dress of a hotel-attendant was seen at Sir Gyles Gay's house————"

Dan summed it up. "Ah, *vootzach!*" he said. After a pause he went on: "I see what you're getting at, of course. But do you think it surprised me to see a hotel-attendant *in* a hotel? Do you think I'd regard it as suspicious? What the blazes should I expect to see? I didn't even notice the fellow, particularly. I simply looked out—saw it out of the tail of my eye—and shut the door again. Like that."

Dan used many gestures when he argued. He was arguing now, with some heat. And there was reason in his position.

"That's not the point, Mr. Reaper. We have evidence, or seem to have evidence, that no employee of the hotel was in that wing between half-past eleven last night and five o'clock this morning."

"Oh," said the other. He assumed his buttoned-up "business" expression, and he had assumed it suddenly. "I didn't know that, superintendent. All I can tell you is what I saw. What evidence?"

"The men working on the lifts say that nobody went upstairs or came down during that time."

"Staircase?"

"Nor by the staircase."

"I see," said Dan abruptly. "Well, what does that make me?"

"An important witness, possibly," Hadley answered without heat. "This man in the hall: did you see his face?"

"No. He was carrying a big pile of—bath-towels! That's it! Bath-towels. Must have been a dozen of 'em. They hid his face."

"He was facing towards you, then?"

"Yes, he was walking along. . . . Just a minute—I've got it now! I was standing in the door of the bedroom of our suite, looking towards the left—towards the clock on the wall, naturally. He was coming towards me. As I was saying, he was just about outside Jenny's door."

"What was he doing?"

"I've told you," replied the other, in a tone as expressionless as Hadley's own, "that I hardly noticed him. I don't suppose I had the door open more than a couple of seconds, just long enough to see the clock. I'd say he was either walking towards me or standing still."

"Which? All I want is your impression, Mr. Reaper."

"Standing still, then."

It was no very terrifying ghost to be found in the halls of an ordinary hotel; but it was a patient kind of ghost which strangled its victims and then battered their faces in. Kent found himself thinking that it was all the more unpleasant because it had been described as "standing still" near Josephine's door.

"Bath-towels," said Hadley. "A number of bath-towels, we've heard, were found in the room where the murder was committed. It looks as though your mysterious man had at least gone into that room. . . ."

"Was her face—?" Francine cried suddenly.

"Yes. And a face-towel was used to strangle her, as in another case we know about," said Hadley. The girl did not falter, or anything of a dramatic nature; but her eyes suddenly grew so bright they thought she was going to cry. Hadley was not uncomfortable. He turned to Dan. "About this man: didn't it strike you as odd to see an attendant carrying bath-towels? Wouldn't it have been a job for the maid?"

"I don't know whose job it was," retorted Dan. "It certainly didn't strike me as odd, and wouldn't have done even if I had noticed all the subtleties you're putting into it. At home, in the hotels, you hardly ever find a maid at all. All the work is done by boys—Indians, mostly. I can see now that it's queer enough; but why should it strike me then?"

"Can you give us any description of this man? Tall, short? Fat, thin?"

"Just ordinary."

Hardwick interposed. He had been standing unobstrusively on the fringe of the group as on the fringe of thought; but he looked so solid and so dependable that Dan turned to him as though he were going to shake hands.

"You have been speaking about a uniform," he said slowly. "What sort of uniform was it? We've got several, you know."

Hadley swung round. "I was coming to that. What uniforms have you got, to begin with?"

"For that time of night, not many: as I told you a moment ago. If this had happened during the day, there would be a pretty broad range. But when you get to a time as late as midnight, there are only three kinds of employees who wear a uniform at all; everybody else, from car-starter to page-boy, is off duty. First, there's the night hall-porter, Billings, and his four under-porters. Second, there are the two liftmen. Third, there are the two attendants in the lounge—you know, serving late drinks. That's all."

"Well?"

"The hall-porter," replied Hardwick, half shutting his eyes, "wears a long blue tunic, frock-coat effect: double-breasted, silver buttons, opening high at the neck: wing collar and black bow tie: red stripe on cuff and collar. The four under-porters wear a double-breasted coat with wing collar and black four-in-hand tie; red insignia. The liftmen wear a short single-breasted coat high at the neck; silver buttons, shoulder epaulets. The lounge attendants have a uniform like blue evening clothes, with silver buttons and red insignia. But as for the last two being upstairs————"

"I had no idea there were so many of 'em," growled Dan. "It's no good. If I try to keep on thinking, I'll only put ideas into my own head and probably lead you wrong. I remember the coat and the buttons; that's all I can swear to. You could see the buttons under the pile of towels. He was holding up the towels in front of his face."

Hadley frowned at his note-book.

"But can you tell us, for instance, whether it was a long or a short coat? Or an open or a closed collar?"

"I couldn't see his collar. I've got a fairly strong impression that it was a short coat; but I wouldn't swear to that either."

Hardwick interrupted with abrupt explosiveness.

"This is a worse business than you think. There's something you'd better know, superintendent, though it won't help you much. Some years ago we had a night under-porter who turned out to be a thief—and as neat and ingenious a thief as I've come across. His method of robbing the guests was very nearly fool-proof. He would have his two floors to attend, as usual. In the middle of the night he would go upstairs to answer a bell, or to 'look round' as they often do. Up there he had hidden a pair of pyjamas and slippers, and sometimes a dressing-gown as well. The pyjamas would go on over his uniform. He had, naturally, a master-key to the rooms in his circuit. So he would simply slip in and steal what he liked. If the occupant of the room woke up, or was disturbed in any way, he had a magnificent excuse which never failed, 'Sorry; wrong room; I've barged in.' In any case he would be taken for a guest. If he were seen coming out of a room, or walking in the halls, he would excite absolutely no suspicion; he was a guest going to the lavatory, or wherever you like. When the robbery was discovered a guest would naturally be suspected. Well, he did that for some time, until one victim refused to accept the 'wrong room' excuse, and grabbed him."[1]

---

[1] It is unwise, I know, to thrust out an editorial head from behind the scenes; but, in case it should be thought that I am plagiarising from fiction, I should like to say that this really happened. For obvious reasons I cannot give the name of the hotel, but it is a large one in Bloomsbury.—J. D. C.

Hardwick paused.

"Don't," he added, with dour amusement, "run away with the idea, please, that you're in a wayside den of thieves. But I thought I had better mention it. It's what made me put up those signs in every room, 'Please bolt your door.' "

Francine took up the challenge—if it was a challenge. "It seems to me that there is a moral there," she said without inflection. "If an employee can dress up as a guest, a guest can also dress up as an employee."

There was a heavy silence, while the room seemed very warm.

"I beg your pardon, Miss Forbes," said Hardwick, not too quickly. "I honestly did not mean that at all. I—um—merely mentioned it. In any case, I can check up on the movements of all those people last night."

"You might do that immediately," Hadley suggested, and got up with decision. "In the meantime, we'll have a look at the body. Just one more question. You were speaking about 'master-keys.' Are the locks on the doors the same in every room?"

"Hardly. The locks are something of a fine art in gradation. As a rule, each maid has assigned to her a certain number of rooms to do: usually twelve, though it may be less. She carries only one key, which opens any door in her group. And each group of rooms has a different lock. Lock-patterns may be repeated in different parts of the hotel, of course, but there are nearly twenty different combinations. The under-porters carry a master-key which will open any lock on their two floors; and so on up in gradations, until I have a key which will open any door in the building. *But* that general rule does not apply to our top floor, the new addition. We're trying out an experiment, probably not successful, of having Yale locks on all the doors, and no two locks the same. It will be a hundred times more trouble, and cause a lot of confusion; but it's absolutely impossible for any unauthorised person to open even so much as a linen-closet."

"Thank you. We'll go round to 707, then. You had better come along, Mr. Kent." Hadley turned to Francine and Dan. "Will you wait here for us, or would you rather go back to your own rooms?"

For answer Francine went to the chair he had previously drawn out for her, and sat down in it with the air of one who folds her arms. Dan—rather deprecatingly—said that they would stay.

It was very warm in the corridors outside, crossed in zebra-fashion with cold where someone had left open a window or raised a skylight in this hive. The raising of windows gave brief glimpses deep into the life of the hotel, and brought together the noises that make up the hollow hum which is its background. Ghostly voices talked in the air-well. You heard a plate rattle, and the buzzing of a vacuum-cleaner. Indistinct figures crossed the line of vision at windows; Kent felt certain that there would be roast chicken for lunch. All this was built up layer upon layer below them, leading to the sedate modernness of Wing A. The three of them, with Sergeant Betts following, looked down that wide corridor, with its bright mural decorations and each of its lights enclosed in a chrysalis of frosted glass.

"Well?" prompted Hadley.

"I have found the essential clue," said Dr. Fell earnestly. "Hadley, I'll let you into the secret. It's the wrong sort of bogey-man."

"All right," said the other with some bitterness. "I was wondering when it would commence. Fire away, then."

"No, I'm quite serious. For a murderer deliberately to dress up as a hotel-attendant is wrong; and therefore—I say, therefore—it means something."

"I suppose you wouldn't consider the startling theory that the murderer was dressed like a hotel-attendant because he really is a hotel-attendant?"

"Perhaps. But that's what I want to emphasise," urged the doctor, plucking at Hadley's sleeve. "In that case the business becomes much worse. We have here a menace which is undoubtedly peering round corners and dogging this party. Now, a menace may or may not be frightening; but it's usually appropriate. Unless it is appropriate there's no point to it. For the first murder we have as a setting an isolated house by a churchyard in Sussex: a setting appropriate to nearly every kind of lurking menace except a hotel-attendant in full canonicals stalking through the passage with a salver. Considering what has happened here in the hotel, I don't think we can dismiss that business at Northfield as a coincidence or the mere hallucination of a drunken man.

"You see, these two murders were committed either by a real hotel-attendant, or by a member of Reaper's party dressed up to look like one. But if it is the first, why should the murderer deliberately put on his workaday uniform to wander through a Sussex country house in the middle of the night? And, if it is the second, why should a member of Reaper's party put on the infernal costume at all?"

Hadley was troubled.

"Here, stop a bit!" he protested. "Aren't you jumping to conclusions all over the place? It seems to me you're being hag-ridden by the idea of a double-murderer in fancy dress. Suppose what Bellowes saw at Northfield was a hallucination: suppose the attendant carrying the towels, here, was an innocent member of the staff who somehow escaped being noticed as he came upstairs—" He stopped, because he could not convince himself of this. But about the principle of the thing he was dogged. "I mean, there's not a shred of actual evidence to show that either Mr. or Mrs. Kent was killed by someone dressed up like that. It seems probable, but where's the evidence?"

"Well," said Dr. Fell mildly, "our friend Hardwick should be able to check up on the movements of his staff last night at midnight. Eh?"

"I should think so."

"H'mf, yes. And suppose they can all account for their whereabouts? That would mean, I think (let's face it) that it was somebody in masquerade? Ergo, what becomes of your innocent figure who is first a hallucination and then an accident?" The doctor was lighting his pipe, and his vast puffs sent the smoke skew-wiff round his face. "I say, Hadley, why are you so opposed to the idea?"

"I'm not opposed to the idea. Only, it seems ruddy nonsense to me. Why should anyone dress up like that? Unless, of course————"

Dr. Fell grunted. "Oh, yes. We can always say (soothingly) that the murderer is a lunatic with a complex for doing his work in that particular kind of fancy costume. I can't quite believe that, because to my simple mind the dress of a hotel-porter is hardly one I should associate with an avenging angel or any form of secret violence. But look at your cursed evidence! The crimes appear to be completely without motive; they are wantonly brutal; and there seems to be no reason why the murderer should insist on strangling his victims with his hands wrapped up in a towel, which I submit would be a clumsy and uncertain process. Finally, there's that."

They had come round the turn in the corridor, where Sergeant Preston was on guard. Dr. Fell indicated the "quiet-is-requested" sign still hanging from the knob of the closed door, with its announcement in red ink of the presence of a dead woman inside. Then he reached out with his stick and touched the brown suède shoes a little to the left of the door.

"Shoes that don't match," he said gruffly. "Mind, I must caution you against too many deductions. But kindly note —shoes that don't match."

Hadley turned to Sergeant Preston. "Anything new?"

"Two sets of finger-prints, sir. They're developing the pictures now; the manager lent us their regular dark-room here. The doctor's waiting for you."

"Good. Go downstairs and get that hall-porter; also the chambermaid who was on duty here last night. Bring them up here, but keep them outside until I call."

Then Hadley opened the door. The cream-coloured blinds were now drawn up on the windows, so that Kent had a good view of the room he had first seen in dimness. For a second or two he was not sure whether he could force himself to go in. He knew what was lying on the floor; he knew now that it was Jenny; and he felt a certain nausea choking him. For several hours he had been telling himself that it was not as though he had lost someone very close to him, either in Jenny or even in Rod. He bore their name in law; but other friends, and particularly Francine, were much closer to his feelings than this amiable young couple who had dodged about on the fringes of his life. But it was the meaningless nature of the crimes which took his nerves; suddenly it disgusted him with his own crime-fiction.

Then Hadley touched his elbow and he went in. Two broad windows opening on the air-well, their grey velvet curtains drawn fully back, showed the white tiling outside like the wall of a cold-storage vault; and snow patched the window-ledges. It was a room about twenty feet square, with a ceiling somewhat low in proportion. Its tint was uniformly grey and blue, with light outlines in the panelling, and sleek maplewood furniture after the prevailing fashion. It showed little sign of disturbance. Towards his left were the twin beds, their blue silk counterpanes undisturbed. In the wall on the left was the other door leading to the corridor; and, farther on, a dressing-table. The bureau—as he had good reason to know from his first visit—stood between the windows. In the wall on the right he now noticed a door open on a bathroom, and a large wardrobe. Completing the circuit of the room, the pile of bath-towels still lay on the little table to the right of the door.

Evidently Jenny had been unpacking her trunk when the murderer entered. The wardrobe door stood ajar, and he could see just one frock hanging up inside from the many still hanging in the trunk; there were also several pairs of shoes in the wardrobe. But he saw one great difference from this morning. The trunk stood in its former position, facing the door and some eight feet out from the right-hand window, its leaves well open. Yet the body, which formerly had lain on its right side with the head just inside the trunk, now sprawled face upwards some three or four feet closer to the door. He was relieved to see that the towel had now been draped over her face. Then Kent caught sight of his own face reflected in the mirror over the bureau, and dodged back instinctively.

"I see," he said, clearing his throat, "you've moved her."

A middle-aged man in glasses, who had been sitting across the room with a medical bag on the floor beside him, got up quickly.

"Moved her?" repeated Hadley. "She certainly hasn't been and wouldn't have been moved. That's how she was found—that right, Betts?"

"Yes, sir," agreed the sergeant. "Aside from the constable, I was the first person here; and that's how *I* found her."

"Well, it isn't how I found her," said Kent. He described the position. "I've got good reason to know that. Somebody must have pulled her out this distance after I had gone."

Hadley put his brief-case on the bed. "We want that hall-porter. Where the devil's that hall-por— Ah, I've sent for him. Look round, Mr. Kent; take your time. Does anything else look different?"

"No, not so far as I can see. I didn't get a good look at the room; the blinds were down; but everything seems about the same. I didn't notice that wardrobe, though it's unlikely that *it* wasn't here a couple of hours ago. But there's another point besides the position of the body: that missing bracelet which the woman who vacated the room last was supposed to have left behind in the bureau. If that's the bureau you mean,"—he pointed—"I'll swear again there was no bracelet in it at eight o'clock this morning. Yet according to the manager, it was found by the hall-porter after I had gone. I'd like to know how long it was between the time I left the room and the time he opened the door."

"We'll attend to that," said Hadley. "In the meantime —well, doctor?"

Hadley knelt beside the body, twitched the towel off Jenny's face, and grunted noncommittally; Kent was glad that his back hid the sight. The police-surgeon approached with interest.

"So she's been moved," the latter commented, with a quick look at Kent and a beam of satisfaction. "I'm not surprised. That would account for it. If I'm right, this is a new way of committing murder."

"New way of committing murder? She was strangled, wasn't she?"

"Yes, yes, strangled, asphyxiated, what you like; but with a difference. She was probably stunned first, though there are eight blows on her face and head, and I can't tell which of them might have done the stunning. I should say, roughly, that she died about midnight—allow a margin one way or the other." The doctor peered over his spectacles, and then knelt beside Hadley. "But look here! Look at the front and back of the neck."

"Creases. As though," muttered Hadley, "there'd been a cord or wire tied round. But————"

"But there's no cord or wire, and the creases don't extend round as far as the sides of the neck," the other pointed out. "It explains everything, including the towel, though I should have imagined the fellow would have used a thick bath-towel rather than this. Now take a look at that wardrobe trunk. It's a big trunk—plenty of space at one side where the dresses hung—and she's a small woman. You also notice that the dresses inside look a bit rumpled and tossed about. It's a job for you, of course: but I should say her neck was put between the sharp jaws of the trunk as it stood upright, with the towel round her neck so that the edges wouldn't cut. . . ."

Hadley got to his feet, snapping his fingers.

"Oh, yes. Nasty business, of course," agreed the other. "As I say: the towel muffled her neck, and her body was in the part of the trunk where the dresses are hanging. Then the murderer slowly pressed together the edges of the trunk until she was very effectually strangled. Afterwards she was allowed to drop, and the blows were administered for good measure. Neat idea, though. There's death in everything nowadays, isn't there?"

Chapter 6

Fifteen Bath-towels

THERE was a silence, after which Hadley dropped the towel back on the face and drew a deep breath. The big trunk, very suggestive despite the pink frock that hung uppermost in the space to the left, drew all their eyes.

"This is one murderer," said Hadley, closing his hands deliberately, "that I'm going to see hanged if it's the last thing I ever do. Look here, doctor: you examined the other one—her husband—didn't you? *He* wasn't killed with any such hocus-pocus as that, was he?"

"No, that seemed to be a straight case of strangling with the hands wrapped in a towel. Pretty powerful hands, too; or else—" He put his finger to his temple and made a circling motion with it. "Dementia praecox, superintendent. The whole case smells of it; or has so far. The trouble is that this looks like too reasoned and deliberate a plan of campaign. However, that's your job. Unless you want me for anything more, I'll be pushing off. They'll bring the body along whenever you say."

"Thanks, doctor. Nothing else," said Hadley. For a time he moved slowly in a circle, studying the body and the trunk, and making careful notes. "Betts!"

"Yes, sir?"

"That 'quiet' sign on the door: could you find out where it came from?"

"It came from here," said the sergeant. "There's one of them supplied to every room; it's put in the bureau drawer, in case the guest wants it. New-fangled notion, apparently. And as for the writing in red ink on it—here you are, sir."

He walked across the room to a small writing-desk, placed cater-cornered in the far right-hand corner near one window. The dark-blue carpet was so thick that no football sounded here when either Hadley or the sergeant moved. Kent also suspected that these new walls were sound-proof. Drawing away the chair before the desk, Betts indicated the blotter. In addition to the hotel pen and inkwell, with stationery in the rack above, there was a small agate-coloured fountain-pen.

"Probably hers," the sergeant suggested. "It's got her initials on the band, and it's filled with red ink."

"It is hers," said Kent, who recognised it even at a distance. The stuffy warmth of the room was growing heavy on his forehead. "She had two of them, one filled with blue and the other with red ink. They were something like— mascots."

Hadley frowned at the pen. "But why red ink?"

"Capable business-woman. She had a part interest in a dress-making shop in Pritchard Street, although she never let it appear. Apparently she thought it wasn't dignified." Suddenly Kent felt tempted to laugh. Many images rose in his mind. The term "capable business-woman" seemed the last to describe Jenny, for it did not convey the extraordinary attractiveness which (in a purely spiritual way) turned so many people's heads. Harvey Wrayburn had once remarked that she appealed to the adolescent mentality. Through those memories he heard Hadley's voice:

"Finger-prints on this?"

"No, sir."

"But if she had two pens, where's the other one?"

"Must be in her trunk," said Betts. "It's not in her handbag, over on the dressing-table."

Disturbed, Hadley examined the trunk. Though solid, it was an old, worn one; and her maiden name, "Josephine Parkes," had almost faded out in white lettering on one side, the surname now being replaced with a bright white, "Kent." The top compartment on the right-hand side of the trunk formed a kind of tray, filled with handkerchiefs and stockings neatly arranged. In the middle of a pile of handkerchiefs Hadley found the second pen, together with a little gold box, the key in its lock, containing costume jewellery. He juggled the two pens in his hand, muttering.

"This won't do. Look here, Fell, what do you make of it? She was undoubtedly beginning to unpack the trunk when the murderer got her. She'd begin with the dresses— my wife always does, anyway, to see that they don't crumple. But she had taken out only one dress and some shoes; the shoes apparently to change them, for she's wearing bedroom slippers. The only other thing she removed was this red-ink fountain-pen, which was buried under a pile of handkerchiefs. Unless, of course . . ."

During this whole examination Dr. Fell had been leaning back against the wall, his shovel-hat over his eyes. Now he roused himself, putting away his pipe.

"Unless the murderer took it out himself. And in that case he knew where to look for it. H'mf, yes," said Dr. Fell, wheezing in slow laborious breaths. "But I say, Hadley, I should be very much obliged if you would just recapitulate what you think happened here. It's rather important. Again we have one blessed gift from heaven. The guests seemed to have remained quietly in their rooms— except the murderer. We are not obliged to remember a complicated time-table of people treading on each other's heels through the halls, or who met whom in going to post a letter at 9:46. What we have got to do is merely to read the indications of the physical evidence. But, oh, Bacchus, I've got an idea it's going to be difficult! Begin, will you?"

"Where?"

"With the entrance of the murderer."

"Assuming that the murderer is the 'attendant' Reaper saw outside the door at midnight?"

"Assuming anything you like."

Hadley studied his note-book. "I know that tone of yours," he said suspiciously. "Just let me tell you this: I'm not going to stand here and get a whole analysis worked out while you merely wave your hand and say you knew it all the time, but that it's not the important point. By the Lord Harry, I'm going to have one case where you play fair. Agree or disagree, I don't give a damn which; but no misleading. Is it a go?"

"You flatter me," said Dr. Fell with dignity. "All right; fire away."

"Well, as I see it, there's one main difficulty. There are eight blows on the face and on the front of the skull, and no blow or bruise on the back of the head. But she certainly couldn't have been conscious when she was put into that Iron-maiden trunk over there; she had to be fitted into the machine; and she'd have cut up a row that would have been heard. I know the walls look fairly solid, but sound-proof walls are like noiseless typewriters: you can still hear through them. This seems to mean that the murderer must have attacked her face to face with our blunt instrument, and that one of the blows from the front stunned her."

"Undoubedly. Whereas, you remember," Dr. Fell pointed out, screwing up his face, "Rodney Kent was hit on the back of the head."

"If the murderer, then, used a weapon large enough to do what's been done to that face afterwards, how was it that she didn't sing out, or run, or put up some kind of struggle, when she saw him coming? And—in a brightly lighted hotel—how was he able to carry the weapon about without being observed?"

Dr. Fell pushed himself away from the wall. Lumbering over to the tall pile of bath-towels on the table, he began picking them up quickly one after the other, shaking them out, and letting them fall. At the sixth towel, when the floor was littered with them, something dropped with a soft thud and rolled to Hadley's feet. It was an iron poker some two feet long; its head was covered with lint where stains had made it stick to the towel.

"Look here, my boy," said Dr. Fell, turning to Kent apologetically; "why not go downstairs and get a drink? It can't be very pleasant for you to see her like that, and ————"

"I'm all right," said Kent. "It was the way the thing jumped, that's all. So that's how it was done?"

Drawing on his gloves, Hadley picked up the poker and turned it over.

"It's what we want, right enough," he said. "I see. It was not only a good concealment; but, with your hand on the grip of this thing, and the towels hiding the sight of it from the other person, you could whip it out and hit before the other person knew what you were doing."

"Yes. But that's not the only consideration. It is also reasonable to ask: why are there *so many* towels? There are fifteen of the blighters; I counted. If your purpose is merely to hide the poker, why do you stack them up like that and badly encumber your movements when you have to strike? But fifteen towels would not only serve to hide the poker: they would also hide————"

"The face," said Hadley.

Again Dr. Fell got the pipe out of his pocket and stared at it blankly. "The face. Quite. Which leads us to the question: if the murderer is a real hotel-attendant, why should he bother to hide his face either in the halls or before Mrs. Kent? In the halls he is in his proper sphere; open to no suspicion so long as he is not seen entering this room; and carrying such a great pile of towels will actually serve to call attention to him. Before Mrs. Kent, when he knocks at the door, he is a hotel employee with an obvious errand. But if he is some member of her own party—some person she knows very well—he *must* hide his face. He cannot run the danger of being seen walking about in that elaborate uniform with his well-known face bared. Mrs. Kent will certainly be surprised and probably alarmed if she opens the door and sees a friend in fancy-dress: particularly the same sort of fancy-dress that appeared in the house when her husband was murdered. And he must get inside that room before she is suspicious. Add to all this the fact that the liftmen swear no real attendant came up here last night between eleven-thirty at night and five in the morning: you begin to perceive, my boy, that the Royal Scarlet Hotel houses an unco' dangerous guest with an odd taste in clothes."

There was a pause. Hadley tapped on his note-book.

"I've never suggested," he returned, "that she was killed by a complete stranger. But in that case—unless he pinched a real attendant's uniform, the clothes he wore must still be in one of these rooms?"

"So it would appear."

"But why? Why carry about an outfit, and wear it only for murders?"

Dr. Fell clucked his tongue. "Tut, tut, now! Ne'er pull your hat upon your brows. There are other things to claim our attention. Since you won't recapitulate, I will.

"Several things were done in this room besides murder. First, someone picked up a pair of mis-mated brown shoes and put them outside the door. It seems unlikely, to say the least, that Mrs. Kent would have done it. They were not only shoes that did not match; they were suède shoes that could not be cleaned. So the murderer did it. Why?"

"At first glance," replied Hadley cautiously, "you'd say it was because the murderer didn't wish to be interrupted by anybody, as he might have been. He was in the midst of a clutter of shoes. So he picked up a pair, which looked alike to a man in a hurry, and put them outside the door so that it would be assumed Mrs. Kent had gone to bed. That was why he also—hold on!"

"Exactly," agreed Dr. Fell. "That was why, you were going to say, he also hung a 'quiet' sign on the door. But there we take a dismal header. The murderer takes a (hidden) 'quiet' sign out of the bureau drawer; he takes a (hidden) fountain-pen out of Mrs. Kent's trunk; on this card he writes 'Dead Woman' in large letters, and hangs it on the door-knob. It seems rather a curious way of making sure you avoid interruption. Why does he appear to need so much time, and to take so many precautions?"

"Any suggestions?"

"Only to conclude this account by indicating what happened this morning. We assume,"—he pointed his stick towards Kent, who had been swept aside in the backwash of this argument—"we assume that our friend here is telling the truth. H'mf. At about eight o'clock he comes up here with the hall-porter. At this time the bureau does *not* contain a bracelet left behind by an American lady who departed yesterday, the body is lying with head almost inside the leaves of the trunk. While the hall-porter waits, our friend gets out. Presently the porter has the door opened again. The missing bracelet is then found in the bureau, and the body has been moved some feet out from the trunk. The conjuring entertainment is over: ladies and gentlemen, I thank you."

Kent thought that the glance Hadley turned towards him was speculative enough to be ominous.

"If I were judging the matter from outside," Kent admitted, "I should say I was lying. But I'm not lying. Besides, what about that bracelet? I certainly didn't come here last night, pinch a bracelet I'd never seen from a woman I'd never heard of; and then come back here this morning and return it. Where does the bracelet fit in?"

"The alternative being," said Hadley, ignoring this, "that the hall-porter is lying?"

"Not necessarily," said Dr. Fell. "If you will look _____"

There was a knock at the door. Preston brought in the hall-porter and the chambermaid.

The girl was an earnest blonde in a starched blue-and-white uniform which made her look stout; she seemed to jingle like the bunch of keys (all Yale keys) at her waist; but she appeared excited rather than frightened, and a nerve twitched beside one eyelid. Myers, the hall-porter, stood in massive contrast. Though Kent again noted his pointed moustaches and slightly pitted face, the most conspicuous thing in all their eyes was the porter's costume: notably the long double-breasted frock-coat with the silver buttons. Myers, after one glance, affected not to notice Kent's presence. That glance was not belligerent; it was one of dignified but hideous reproachfulness.

Hadley turned to the maid first. "Now there's nothing to worry about," he assured her. "Just look here, please, and answer a few questions. What's your name?"

"Eleanor Peters," said the girl, hardly lifting her eyes from studying the figure on the floor. She seemed to carry an atmosphere of strong soap.

"You were on duty here last night, weren't you, until half-past eleven?"

"Yes."

"Look up at me, please; never mind that!—Now. You see these towels? Do you know where they come from?"

A pause. "From the linen-closet down the hall," she answered, reluctantly following instructions. "Or at least I suppose they do. There was fifteen of them gone from there this morning, and the place was pulled all about, sir."

"Do you have charge of that linen-closet?"

"Yes, I do. And I locked it up last night, too, but somebody got in and pulled it all about."

"Was anything else gone?"

"Nothing but one face-towel. That one, I'll bet." She nodded in a fascinated way towards Jenny Kent's body; and Hadley moved over to obscure her sight of it.

"Who else has a key to the linen-closet?"

"Nobody, far as I know."

"What time did you come on duty this morning?"

"Quarter-past seven."

Hadley went over to the door, opened it, and detached the "quiet" sign from outside. Standing well back in the room, Kent could now see out diagonally across the corridor towards the door which, on the plan, had been marked as that of Sir Gyles Gay's sitting-room. This door stood part-way open, and a face was looking out with an air of alert and refreshed interest. If this were Sir Gyles Gay, Kent was conscious of surprise. He remembered Dr. Fell's mention of interest in names, whatever might have been the significance of it. The name itself had a spacious Cavalier ring, as of one who would down tankards on the table and join a businessmen's chorus in full Cavalier style. Actually, he was a little wizened, philosophical-looking man with an air of interest in everything and a complete lack of embarrassment. After giving Hadley an amiable, somewhat marble-toothed smile reminiscent of the portraits of Woodrow Wilson, he withdrew his head and shut the door. The mural design on that wall was a representation of a cocktail party. Hadley closed the door of 707.

"You came on duty at a quarter-past seven," he said to the maid. "I suppose you passed this door?"

"Oh, yes, sir. Naturally."

"Did you notice this card on the door?"

"I noticed the card, but I didn't notice what's written on it. No, I did *not*," said the excited Eleanor, who evidently wished she had.

"Between the time you came on duty and the time this gentleman came upstairs with the porter," he nodded towards Kent, "did you see anyone else in this wing?"

"No. That is, nobody except a page. He came up about half-past seven and looked at the door of number 707 here, and turned round and went away again."

Myers, the porter, was about to come into action. He had been waiting with several slight clearings of the throat, like a nervous orator who has several speakers before him. Now he began, with massive respectfulness, to explain; but Hadley cut him short.

"Just a moment. . . . About last night. Were you in this part of the wing when Mr. Reaper's party got back from the theatre?"

"That's the handsome one in 701," said the maid; and stopped, covered with a pouring confusion. She added rapidly: "Yes, I was."

"Did you see—?" Hadley stood aside and indicated Jenny.

"Yes, I did. I saw them all except the one with the moustache, in 705."

"What was Mrs. Kent wearing then? Do you remember?"

"Same as she's wearing now, but with a mink coat over it. Except that she'd got on shoes instead of slippers," added Eleanor, after another careful inspection. "The other, the fat one"—Melitta Reaper, undoubtedly—"was in evening dress, gold lawn, with a white fur wrap. But this lady, and the hoity-toity one in 708 were both in ordinary clothes."

Myers, evidently furious, was about to quell this style of talk with cold authority; but Hadley's glance at him was even colder.

"Did you hear them saying anything?"

"Only good night, that I remember."

"Did they go directly to their rooms?"

"Yes, sir. They all stood with their hands on the knobs of the doors, looking round, as though they were waiting for a signal or something; and then all of a sudden they all turned round together and went into their own rooms."

Hadley studied his note-book; then he turned to Myers.

"First, about this bracelet: when did you hear it had been left behind in this room?"

"Eight o'clock this morning, sir, when I came on duty," replied the other instantly. He had a good parade-ground manner of giving evidence, and he was on his mettle. His answers bristled up as though you had given him a shake by the shoulders. "I'm the day-porter, you see, and I come on duty at eight. But Billings, the night man, told me about it when he went off duty. Mrs. Jopley-Dunne, who occupied this room last, had telephoned last night about the bracelet. Mrs. Jopley-Dunne was then staying overnight with friends in Winchester, intending to go on to Southampton next day to catch the *Directoire*. But she telephoned so late that Billings would not disturb Mrs. Kent at that hour."

"What hour? Do you know when the call came through?"

"Yes, sir, there's always a record. At 11:50."

"At 11:50?" the superintendent repeated quickly. "Was anyone sent up here to inquire?"

"No, sir, nor even telephone. As I say, he would not disturb Mrs. Kent at that hour."

"Where were you at that time, by the way?"

"Me sir? I was at my home, in bed." A new, somewhat hoarser tone, had come into Myers's voice; he showed a kind of Gibraltaresque surprise.

"Go on: about next morning."

Myers retold the familiar story. "—so you see, sir, Billings had already sent up a page-boy at seven-thirty, and the page said there was a 'quiet' sign on the door. When I came on duty, and Billings passed the word along to me, Hubbard (that's one of the under-porters) said he thought the gentleman in 707 was just finishing his breakfast in the dining-room. I took the liberty of asking this gentleman, thinking naturally—you understand.

"We went upstairs. I got the chambermaid to open the door, and he went in. He asked me to wait outside, of course. When he had been gone about two or three minutes, and there was no sound out of the room, I tapped on the door: meaning to tell him, you see, sir, that the matter could wait if he could not find the bracelet. There was no answer to that. A minute or so later I tapped again; I was beginning to think it was queer. Then my coat or something brushed that sign on the door. It had been turned round so that the dead-woman part was facing the wall, and I hadn't seen it until then." Myers drew a quick whistling breath. "Well, sir, I knew I was taking a responsibility, but I asked the maid to open the door. And I went in. This gentleman—wasn't there."

"Where was the body lying then?"

"Just where it is now."

"What did you do first when you went in?"

"I went to look for the bracelet."

"For the bracelet?"

"Sir," replied Myers, in a sudden lofty passion, "I had been told to go and get that there bracelet. I did it; and I

306 TO WAKE THE DEAD

don't see why everyone should think it was so out of the
way. I walked across, like this"—he illustrated—"I opened
the right-hand bureau drawer, like this; and there it was,
stuck down by the paper lining. I put it in my pocket. Then
I went and told the manager I had got it, and that the lady
in here was dead. I know there's been mistakes; and I
don't *say* this gentleman here killed her; but I've heard
nothing about nothing; that's all *I* say."

Hadley turned to Kent.

"How long should you say you were in here before you
slipped out that side door into the other angle of the corridor?"

"It's hard to tell. About three minutes, I should think."

"And you?" the superintendent asked Myers. "How
long between the time Mr. Kent came in here and the time
you followed him?"

"Well, sir, say five minutes."

"While you were waiting outside what we'll call the
main door, the one with the sign on it, I suppose nobody
went in or out past you?"

"Not by that door they didn't! No, sir!"

"Then here is the order of events, if we say both of you
are telling the truth. Mr. Kent comes into this room. After
three minutes he goes out by the side door. At the end of
five minutes you come in. During the space of two minutes,
then, someone has entered by the side door—must have
been, because you were planted in front of the only other
entrance—someone has put the bracelet in the drawer,
moved the body, and gone out the same way. This, I repeat, happened in the two minutes between the time Mr.
Kent left the room and the time you entered it. Is that
right?"

Myers was aggrieved. "I can't speak for him, sir, that's
all I say. But I can speak for myself, and what I say's the
truth."

"Just one last thing. While you were outside the main
door, you could see the doors of all the rooms in this angle
of the corridor?"

"Yes, sir," replied the other—and stopped, evidently taken backwards by a rush of thought.

"During that time, did any of the guests come out of their rooms? Would you have noticed?"

"I should have noticed. And, sir," said Myers, with massive simplicity, "none of 'em did. That I'll swear to."

"What about you?" inquired Hadley, and turned to the maid.

"Stop a bit!" urged that young lady, examining the past. "Yes, I'll agree to that. *I* should have noticed, I'm sure. But there's one door I couldn't see from there; I mean it was round the corner. That's the side door to 705, facing the side door of this one across the hall."

Hadley shut up his note-book. "That's all, thanks. You can go; but don't talk about this, either of you." When they had been dismissed, he looked for Dr. Fell with some satisfaction. "This looks dangerously like a bit of luck. It's what you would call a logical certainty. Either this one is lying—" he put his hand on Kent's shoulder—"which I don't believe. Or *both* the porter and the maid are lying, which I don't believe either. Or—we come to it—the person in this room must have been Harvey Wrayburn, from 705."

Chapter 7

A Square Black Stone

DR. FELL had again played his disconcerting trick of never being in the place you expected him, which was a physical as well as a mental trait. When Hadley looked round, the doctor was bending over the dressing-table at the other side of the room, so that they could see only a vast expanse of back and black cape. A red face now turned round and rose to the surface like Leviathan, while he blinked over his eyeglasses.

"Oh, it's possible," admitted the doctor, with a petulant wheeze. "It's still more possible since—" He flourished a snake-skin handbag.

"Since what?"

"Since I can't find her key. The key to this room. I've been looking all over the place for it. You remember, we heard a very interesting account of the spring-locks with which all the doors on this floor are supplied; no two locks alike. Except, I dare say, when one room has two doors, like this one: then the same key would open both. But where is the key? If someone used that side door to sneak in here and return the bracelet in two minutes—well, he had to get in. On the other hand, there are certain curious suggestions which occur to me, especially after a closer examination of that trunk, and they do not fit in with your friend Wrayburn."

There was the sound of an argument outside the partly-open main door to the hall, cut short by a faint "Pah!" Into the room, with the utmost composure, came the wizened and calm-faced man whom Kent had seen peering out of the doorway across the hall. Though he was of middle height, he seemed much shorter by reason of his bony lean-ness; he was carefully dressed, to the point of the dapper, in a blue double-breasted suit and (very) hard collar. That collar, like the set if pleasant expression which suggested false teeth, seemed to give him a high glaze like the polish on a tombstone. While preserving the most careful de-corum, he nevertheless contrived to suggest the same air of refreshed interest. His thin hair, carefully parted, was whitish at the top and dull grey over the ears; its smooth-ness contrasted with his wizened face. He stopped by the body, as though performing a conventional rite; he shook his head, cast down his eyes, and then looked at Hadley.

"Good morning, superintendent."

"Morning, Sir Gyles."

"And this, I think," the other went on gravely, "will be the celebrated Dr. Fell. And the other—?" Introductions were performed, while Gay's shrewd eye appraised them. "Gentlemen, I have come for you, and I will not be de-nied. You must come over to my rooms and———

"—and take a cup of China tea," he added, when by some mysterious power of eye he had got them out of the room. "I could not say it in there. I don't know why."

Despite his poise he was a trifle white. Dr. Fell beamed down on him as though on some interesting phenomenon.

"Heh," said the doctor. "Heh-heh-heh. Yes. I particu-larly wished to speak to you. I want a fresh viewpoint on character, so to speak; the others are able judges, I don't doubt, but they have lived too close to each other to be free from bias."

"You flatter me," said Gay, showing the edge of a marble-toothed smile. "I am entirely at your service."

While Hadley remained behind to give brief instructions to Betts and Preston, Gay took the others into his sitting-room. It was a pleasant place, furnished (surprisingly) in eighteenth-century fashion, though the noise of traffic from Piccadilly boiled up below the windows. From this height you could see far down the slope of grey barrack-like roofs, past the curt solidness of St. James's, to the bare trees of St. James's Park. The dapper old man fitted into this. On a table by the window there was a steaming tea-service; and, when the others refused tea, their host poured a cup for himself with a steady hand.

"You will find cigars in the box beside you," he told Dr. Fell. "And now, gentlemen, to business: though the business will be mostly theory. One thing, though, I can tell you at the start," he said vigorously. "I know no more of this—this bloody business than when that young man was murdered in my house. I did not leave my room last night, and I don't know who did. All I *know* is that we seem to be pursued by an exacting and business-like murderer."

"H'm," said Dr. Fell, who was endangering a frail-looking chair. "Well, look here: what do you think of Mr. Reaper's party in general?"

Gay drew a deep breath. There was an expression of pleasure on his bony face, which faded as he seemed to reflect.

"Up to the time young Kent was murdered," he answered gravely, "I had never had so much fun in my life."

He paused to let this sink in.

"I must explain. In business I have been known as a terror, a spoiler of the Egyptians and everyone else; and I confess that my conduct in the City, as the Wodehouse story puts it, would have caused raised eyebrows in the fo'c'sle of a pirate sloop. Also, I have been a successful government official: hence my surprising knighthood. Also, there is no arguing with the mirror—and the mirror displays a stern and shrivelled look. Therefore it is taken for granted. Therefore people, coming in contact with my bleak atmosphere, talk about the weather. I think it has been years since anyone invited me to have a second drink.

. . . Well, Reaper's party paid no attention to that, or never thought of it. They came into my house, and after a decorous interval they cut loose. They banged the piano. They got up games in which I found myself blindfolded, inadvertently pinning a paper donkey's tail to the posterior of Mrs. Reaper. Young Wrayburn, and even the Grim Reaper himself, when he forgot he was an M.A. and a business man, introduced the novel note of 'Ride 'em, cowboy!' In short, they made the damn place resound!—and I loved it."

He ended with a surprising and deep-throated crow of mirth, lifting his neck to do so, and showing an extraordinary animation which twinkled up to his eyes.

"And murder came next," said Dr. Fell.

The other grew sober. "Yes. I knew I was enjoying myself too much for it to last."

"You're an intelligent man," Dr. Fell went on, in the same sleepy and abstracted fashion. "What do you think happened?"

"Oh, I don't know. If this hadn't happened to me, I should have said, Read your psychology: but those books don't apply—to personal cases. They never do."

"Was Rodney Kent one of the persons who promoted the hilarity?"

Gay hesitated. "No, he was not, though he tried to be. It was not in his nature, I think. He was too conscientious. I think you have met the type. He is one of the persons who stand, smiling but uncertain, on the edge of a group who are enjoying themselves; and you think over and over, 'What in blazes can I do to amuse so-and-so?' till it amounts to a point of desperation. But you never succeed."

It was, Christopher Kent reflected, a perfect description of Rod, who was really in his element only when he had facts to dig out.

"But he was murdered," said Gay.

"What about Miss Forbes?"

"Ah, Miss Forbes," said Gay dryly, and again showed the edge of the marble-toothed smile. "I think you misunderstand her, Dr. Fell. You should have seen her, when *she* forgot herself, standing by the piano and singing a ballad whose drift I need not repeat." He turned to Kent, and added: "She is in love with you, you know."

As startled as though he had got two successive blows in the wind, Kent sat up.

"She's— What makes you think that?"

"Secrets," said Gay reflectively. "You would be surprised at the number of secrets that have been confided to me in the past fortnight. Nothing damaging, nothing helpful, I am afraid; but I was surprised and pleased and a little touched. It is flattering. In the old days nobody would have thought of confiding a secret to me. That person would have been afraid I should use it to extract his back teeth or collar-stud. And I fear he would have been right. But I mention this particular secret in the hope that it may be helpful." He considered. "Now listen, and I'll sum up. In South Africa to-day there is a minority political group called the Dominion Party. They are excellent fellows, although they haven't a dog's chance; the government is eighty per cent *Afrikaans*. But they try to keep up English traditions—including the wholly mythical one of English reserve. Nearly all the members of Reaper's crowd are touched with that brush. Reaper himself is, though he professes to be a United man." He looked at Kent. "*You* are, I suspect. But I don't think Miss Forbes realises that it is not really necessary nowadays to stand on her dignity. The spectacle of me lapping up sherry out of a saucer as a forfeit for failing to do something else equally dignified—I forget what—should have corrected that. You understand, Dr. Fell?"

The doctor chuckled, though he kept a speculative eye on their host.

"I'm not sure I do understand," he rumbled. "Are you trying to tell us something? Do I detect, as a sinister undertone to these games, a suggestion that there is a repression or neurosis which takes the form of murder?"

Gay's face did not change, though it was a second or two before he answered. "I'll be quite candid," he said with a broad air. "I don't know what I bloody well do mean."

"H'mf. Still, there's one person, you know, whose character you haven't described. I mean Mrs. Josephine Kent."

Gay got up, with his dapper walk, and passed round a humidor of good cigars. Each accepted one; and, in a perplexity of thought, Kent looked out across the grey roofs patched in snow. The scratching of a match, and the ritual of cigar-lighting, roused him. Their host was again sitting quietly on the edge of his chair; but his face had hardened.

"You forget," he continued, "that I met the lady for the first time last night, and that I knew her only a few hours before this happened. She was with her aunts during the other business; she met us in London. Nevertheless, I'll tell you what she was. She was a dangerous girl."

"Nonsense!" exploded Kent. "Rod's wife?"

Sir Gyles Gay's face was alight with a great pleasure, so that it seemed to shine as at the discovery of a toy.

"Hadn't you discovered that?"

"Yes," said Dr. Fell. "But go on."

"I don't mean," said Gay, with a quick and sharp look at the doctor, "I don't mean a crooked girl, or an evil one. (By the way, she must be rather older than she looks, you know.) I don't suppose there was ever a consciously crooked thought in her head; I doubt whether she would have recognised one of her worst and most radiant thoughts as being crooked, even if such a thought had been there. Since you object to the term 'dangerous,' though, I'll describe her in another way. She would have made an ideal wife for me. And she knew it."

Kent grinned in spite of himself. "Was that why she was dangerous?"

"You still don't understand. The sort of character she had is common enough, but it's elusive and difficult to describe. So I'll merely tell you something. I met her last evening for the first time. Within fifteen minutes she was making up to me. Object, matrimony. For my money."

There was a pause. "Sir Gyles," Kent said, "you're a very intelligent man, as Dr. Fell has said; but don't you think that's rather an asinine statement?"

The other did not seem offended, though there was a gleam in his eye. On the contrary, he appeared pleased as at more confirmation of a theory. After taking several deep pulls at his cigar, and savouring the smoke, he leaned forward.

"And," he insisted, "I should have fallen. Oh, yes. Was I attracted? Damme, yes! Even though I knew—well, I have now got the phrase that describes her. She was the ideal Old Man's Darling. Hadn't you realised all this?" His calm certainty on the point sent through Kent a sudden discomfort that was like a touch of belief. "Tell me if I've read her character correctly on other points. I judge that she was an excellent business woman: probably with a business of her own: very likely something to do with clothes or millinery. I also judge that nobody ever saw her disturbed or out of countenance: that nobody ever really knew her. She slid through things. That little—er—*half pint* (a word I've picked up) could not actually be touched by anything. That, gentlemen, is the quality which would drive our sex crazy; and she had the particular kind of attractiveness, blessed-Damozel and kiss-me-lightly style, which turns a lot of heads to begin with. Of course she would marry a well-meaning chap like Rodney Kent. Of course she would sweetly expect all the favours; and get 'em. But when she saw the possibility of a better match, or was merely tired, she would say he was too gross, or something; that she had been entrapped or sold into the marriage; that her soul had been snatched; and she would pass on to what she wanted amid general murmurs of sympathy. Dignity she had, I've no doubt—and for some curious reason there persists among our countrymen a belief that if you have dignity you're probably right."

It was a thrust so straight and deep that Kent stirred again. Jenny, instead of lying over there with her face covered by a towel, now seemed to walk in the room. Dr. Fell seemed to be half asleep; but you could see the steady shining of intentness in his eyes.

"Forgive the long oration," Gay concluded abruptly.

Dr. Fell examined the end of his cigar. "Not at all," he said with offhand affability. "Do you think that quality had anything to do with her murder?"

"I didn't say anything about the murder. You asked about her character."

"Oh, here! Do you mean that a person's character has nothing to do with his or her murder?"

"Undoubtedly. But I haven't had a chance to deduce anything about the murder yet. I haven't even heard about the circumstances. So I must stick to what I know."

At this invitation Dr. Fell merely opened one eye. "Yes, but—" he said with an air of stubbornness. "Tell me: is there anything you know, or can deduce, which would lead you to suspect that Mrs. Kent wasn't what she seemed?"

"Wasn't what she seemed? I don't understand."

"Then I won't ask it. It is another of those subtleties which grieve Hadley. 'For *nutu signisque loquuntur* is good consistorial law.' It also has some reference to a blind horse, which I may be. I take it you regarded Mrs. Kent, then, as a kind of painted Roman statue, hollow inside?"

"That's it exactly. If you knocked on it, you'd get the same kind of sound. Knock, knock—" Gay paused with another interested expression, as his agile brain seemed to go after a new line of thought. "Ahem! By the way, doctor, I have been introduced in my old age to a game which offers considerable possibilities. It consists in taking various good English words and twisting them out of the shapes God gave them. For example! I say to you, 'Knock, knock.' You are now to reply, 'Who's there?' "

"All right. Who's there?" inquired Dr. Fell, with interest.

"Beelzebub. You now say, 'Beelzebub who?' "

"Beelzebub who?" said Dr. Fell obediently.

What particular gem of this genus was about to be perpetrated Kent never learned, although he was interested by the spectacle of the two grave philosophers playing it. At this point there was, in actual fact, a knock at the door, and Hadley came in. The theories were dispelled. Kent wondered whether the superintendent had been listening at the door, for his face wore a curiously exasperated look.

"Wrayburn," he said to Dr. Fell, "will see us in a minute. He's just getting up, it seems." Then Hadley looked at Gay. "In the meantime, Sir Gyles, would you mind answering a few questions? Also, would you have any objection to this suite being searched?"

"Searched? Not at all; go right ahead. But may I ask what you're looking for?"

"For a hotel-attendant's uniform." Hadley waited, and Gay put down his cigar on the edge of the saucer; he tried to flash his marble-toothed smile, sardonically, but he displayed the first sign of uneasiness he had yet shown.

"Ah, I thought so. I knew it. The ghost has been walking again. I tried, by applying the spur of silence, to extract some information from Dr. Fell. But it doesn't seem to work as well with schoolmasters as with business men or lesser breeds without the law."

Hadley gestured to Sergeant Betts, who went towards the bedroom. "—and also, if possible, we hope to find a key."

"Key? What sort of key?"

On the polished round centre table a key was lying now: a Yale key through whose thumb-hole was threaded a little chromium tag bearing the number 703. Hadley picked it up.

"A key like this. This is yours, naturally?"

"Yes, it's the key to the suite. Why?"

Hadley was at his most offhand. "Someone, presumably the murderer, stole the key to Mrs. Kent's room. It must be somewhere in this wing now, unless it was—thrown out of the window, for instance." The tone of the last few words was curious, though he looked amused. "*You* haven't see it, have you?"

Their host was thoughtful. "Sit down, superintendent; make yourself comfortable. No, I have not seen it. Not since last night, that is."

"Last night?"

"Yes. I noticed Mrs. Kent opening the door of her room with it."

"How was that?"

"It is customary," explained Gay, with icy testiness, "to open doors with a key." He had adopted a harder guard with Hadley than he had attempted with Dr. Fell. "No, see here—it was like this. I don't know whether you've heard it; I suppose you have; but we all went to the theatre last night, and when we came back we turned in immediately. We made a kind of military drill of saying good night, each standing in the door of his own room. Well, Mrs. Kent's room is directly across the hall. She opened the door with her key. She turned on the light just inside. Then, just after she went inside, I remember that she dropped the key in her handbag."

Dr. Fell woke up. "I say, you're sure of that?" he demanded with some excitement. "You're certain she put the key in her handbag?"

"Yes, I'm quite certain of that." Gay's interest was aroused again. "Why do you ask? She was standing with her back to me (naturally); but turned round a little towards the left, so that I could see her left arm. I think she was holding the door open with her right knee. She wore a fur coat, and her handbag was snake-skin. She turned round to say good night over her left shoulder; she went in—I am following this carefully—and at this time the bag was in her left hand. She dropped in the key and closed the bag. I remember that left hand because on the wrist she was wearing a white-gold bracelet, with a square black stone in it, and I noticed it when the sleeve of the coat fell back."

He stopped abruptly, aware of the expression on his companions' faces.

Chapter 8

The Card from the Window

I SEEM to have startled you," Gay observed, picking up his cigar. "Is anything wrong?"

Though Hadley remained impassive, he wore a heavier look. "A white-gold bracelet with— Are you telling us that Mrs. Kent was wearing Mrs. Jopley-Dunne's bracelet?"

"No indeed, superintendent. I never heard of Mrs. Jopley-Dunne, and I can't say I like the name. I merely said she had on *a* bracelet of that kind. It had a Latin inscription on the stone, I believe; though I didn't get close enough to examine it. I'm fairly sure she had it on at the theatre. One of her friends ought to be able to identify it."

Dr. Fell, after spilling cigar-ash down the ridges of his waistcoat, spoke in a hollow voice. He said:

"That has torn it, Hadley. That has most definitely torn it. Oh, my sacred hat. We grope through a spiritual abyss; and all because, by the innate mental workings of guests at hotels, Mrs. Jopley-Dunne drops a brick. It's a curious fact, worthy of consideration by psychologists, that whenever someone away from home mislays anything, he or she is always firmly convinced that it was Left At The Hotel.

Don't you see the sinister significance of it now? The elusive Mrs. Jopley-Dunne didn't leave her bracelet. It wasn't her bracelet at all. It was Mrs. Kent's. . . . There ought to be a house-telephone here somewhere. I strongly advise you to get hold of Hardwick, bring him up here with the bracelet and Reaper and Miss Forbes, round up Mrs. Reaper as well: and if one of them can't identify that thing as belonging to Mrs. Kent, I'm a son of Boetia."

"But, according to everybody, Mrs. Jopley-D. seemed pretty positive she had left it," Hadley muttered. "And why are you so excited? Even if this is true, how does it help us?"

"Help us?" roared Dr. Fell, who was stirring with spark and cigar-ash like the Spirit of the Volcano. "Help us? It is the most enlightening and stimulating thing I have heard this morning. It solves a good many of our difficulties. Grant me the fact that the bracelet belonged to Mrs. Kent," he argued, "and I'll take you a little farther along an exceedingly murky road."

"How?"

"Just tell me this, Hadley: what happened in that room last night?"

"How the hell should I know? That's what————"

"No, no, no," said Dr. Fell testily. "I've had occasion to tell you about this before. You're concentrating so exclusively on the murder that you don't stop to ask yourself what *else* happened there. Why, we were asking a while ago, did the murderer need so much time in that room? Why did he need to be free from interruption for a fairly long time? What was he doing in there?"

"All right. What was he doing?"

"He was making a very careful and intensive search of the room," replied Dr. Fell, making a hideous pantomime face by way of emphasis. "Without, apparently, finding what he wanted or pinching anything. Consider the following points. He found a fountain-pen which had been hidden under a pile of handkerchiefs in the tray of the trunk: therefore he had been through at least that part of the trunk. He found a 'quiet' sign hidden in the bureau drawer:

therefore he had been into the bureau. He got the key of the room out of Mrs. Kent's handbag: therefore he had been through the handbag. So much it requires very little cerebral activity to determine, and we are pretty safe in postulating a search. The trouble was that, so far as I could see, nothing appeared to be missing. If we prove that the bracelet belonged to Mrs. Kent, and that for some reason the murderer pinched it last night————"

Hadley was staring at him. "After which the murderer came back and returned it this morning? You call that making things clearer? And, anyway, what's the point of the bracelet? You were making a great fuss about its being one of the most ingenious devices of the ancient world, or some such nonsense; but you haven't said a definite word about it yet."

"Oh, I know," said Dr. Fell despondently. "And yet— and yet—well, I still think you'd better get on to that telephone."

"There it is, on the table," suggested Gay.

Hadley roused himself to the fact that he was indiscreetly talking before witnesses. After asking to be put through to the manager's office, he showed the newspaperman's trick of speaking to the telephone in such a way as to be inaudible four feet off. The others shifted uncomfortably until he put back the receiver again.

"Hardwick will phone through to Mrs. Jopley-Dunne," he said. "Then he'll come round here with Reaper and Miss Forbes. We may as well have them all here. Mr. Kent, you know Mrs. Reaper. Will you go down to their suite and ask her to come here?" (Kent suddenly realised that the superintendent found Melitta a difficult proposition.) "In the meantime, Sir Gyles, those questions . . ."

"I am at your service," assented Gay, with a sort of ancient vivacity. "Though, as I told Dr. Fell, I am afraid I can't help you. Nothing suspicious happened last night so far as I know. I turned in immediately, and read in bed until half-past twelve; but nothing disturbed me in any way. . . ."

That smooth, hard voice was the last thing Kent heard

as he went out into the hall. But he did not go immediately to Dan's suite. He stood for a time in that muffled corridor, the stump of the hot cigar almost burning his hand, and tried to rearrange his thoughts.

Two things were becoming apparent now. In spite of himself he was beginning to credit Gay's deadly sharp analysis of Jenny. He had always been credited with being unobservant about people; and certain vague scenes, gestures, inflections, returned to trouble him now. It was like trying to remember a passage or a quotation in a book, in which you can remember the appearance of the book, the page on which the passage occurred, and even the part of the page on which the passage occurred; but you cannot remember the quotation itself. But, even granting all Gay had said, this did nothing to explain her murder—and certainly gave no ghost of a reason why Rod should be killed.

Next, Harvey Wrayburn was in a bad position. You had only to look at this corridor in order to see that. The maid and the hall-porter had been outside one door; they were in a position to testify that nobody else could have stirred out of a room, and Wrayburn's side door was the *only* one they could not see. But why? Why? Why? He thought of Wrayburn, with his brushed-up moustache, his bouncing energy, and his vast mine of information on all the most useless subjects: in appearance a little like that Laughing Cavalier who does not (you recall) really laugh. Then there was this odd business of Wrayburn being still asleep at eleven o'clock in the morning; so far as Kent could remember, he had never done that before.

From hotel-attendant to bracelet to Iron-maiden trunk, it was all a bogging mass of whys. Kent walked slowly down the hall; and, about to knock at the door of Dan's suite, he stopped to inspect the linen-closet. Its door was now ajar; through a frosted-glass window, partly raised, the dull light showed that it served another purpose besides housing the neat shelves of sheets and towels. Other shelves contained tea-services, evidently for those guests who wished early-morning tea before breakfast. He inspected it gloomily, without much enlightenment. Then he knocked at the sitting-room door of Dan's suite, and Melitta's voice told him to come in.

Well, you would not unduly upset Melitta even by the presence of murder, for Melitta lived in a perpetual state of being mildly and stoically upset. It was as though she had taken a tonic which kept her always in the same state of disturbance, and her voice at the same monotone. Twenty years ago she had been a very beautiful woman. She would still have been a beautiful woman if it were not for her soft stoutness, or a certain expression by which the angles of her face seemed to have drooped plaintively out of line: as though the whole woman had been pushed down squatly from above.

But her eyelids were reddish this morning. She sat in a deep chair by a table on which were the remains of a large breakfast, and a box of chocolates. She seldom touched the chocolates, however; she remained bolt upright as a Sphinx, her hands flat along the arms of the chair. The large body was exceedingly well if a little hastily dressed. Her voice struck him like a familiar tune; she showed no surprise at seeing him, but simply picked up the conversation as though it had been broken off five minutes ago, while the handsome blue eyes never left his face.

"—and it is all very dreadful, I know, and of course I know how dreadful it must be for you, and I quite sympathise; but what I say is that it seems so *inconsiderate*, when we had been looking forward to such a nice holiday; but it just does seem as though there would always be something wherever I go. Did you have a nice trip out?"

"Melitta," said Kent, "do you know what's happened? The superintendent wants to see you."

Her monotone never noticed a change of subject; she accepted it, and slid into it as easily as though they had been discussing it all the time. But, even while seeming to regard him vacantly, she showed her frequent disconcerting shrewdness.

"My dear Christopher, I got it all out of the maid a little while ago, and gave her a shilling for it too. Not that I begrudge the shilling, heaven knows; though I do think that things in England are *too much*, and when I see the prices on things in the shops I simply gasp, and I cannot understand how they can pay so much when at home I could get that same hat for twenty-seven and six. Poor Jenny; her shop was much nicer, and Parisian models too. Poor Jenny: my heart does bleed for her, it does really," —and undoubtedly it did—"but I wish Dan would not let them talk such nonsense as they do. But you know how men are, and Dan especially, wanting to get on well with everybody————"

In conversation with Melitta, Kent had discovered, the best policy was to find some train of thought you could understand, and trace it back to its devious beginning: at which time you usually found something worth hearing.

"Nonsense? Nonsense about what?"

"Christopher, you know perfectly well what I mean. Why should any of us do anything like that to Rod or Jenny? We never did at home, did we? I have said before, and I say again, though you needn't repeat it, I do *not* trust that Sir Gyles Gay, even if he has got a title. I have heard about him at home, though of course Dan wouldn't listen, and in business he has the reputation of being nothing better than an absolute Twister. But of course Dan is easy and soft-headed"—it was hardly a description Kent himself would have applied to Dan—"when he finds someone he thinks is a good fellow. Yes, I know what you're going to say, but all men are like that; and I admit he made me laugh, but, as my grandfather used to say, beware of people who make you laugh, because they're usually up to no good."

"That," said Kent, a trifle stunned, "is just about the most cynical remark I've ever heard. But what has it all got to do with Jenny or Rod?"

"I'm sure I don't know," she told him placidly. "But what Rod knew, Jenny knew; you can be sure of that."

"Meaning? It doesn't seem to make any sense."

"Oh, fiddle-de-dee!" cried Melitta, losing a little of her injured air and showing some of that sparkle which could still make Dan Reaper beam with pride. "Who wants to make sense? *I* don't pretend to, thank heaven, though I've always been more sensible than most, and a good deal more sensible than any of you. If you want to know what happened, you just think of everything that could have happened; and one of them is the right explanation; and there you are."

Kent looked at her with a certain reverence. If she had taken just two glasses of champagne at that moment, the hump would have lifted from her face as well as from her feelings, and she would have been a genuinely beautiful woman.

"I suppose it's a sound principle in detective-work," he admitted. "But, since you have a suspicious mind and secrets are coming out all over the place, how did Jenny strike you?"

"Strike me?" she asked quickly.

"I mean what's your version of her character?"

"Version fiddlesticks. People do not have versions of character in families: they take what they can get, and thank heaven it isn't worse, as Uncle Lionel used to say. I do think you ought not to talk in such a silly way, Christopher, though I dare say it's all very well in novels. Jenny was a sweet girl, or as much as could be expected."

"Well, you'd better make up your mind before you see Superintendent Hadley and Dr. Fell." This was the sort of talk from Melitta which always stung him. "There seem to be more niggers in the woodpile than you'd think. As old friend to old friend, Melitta, you're only fifty; don't try to talk like a grandmother before your time."

He was sorry a moment later, that he had said it. It pierced something that was not a fancied complaint. But there was nothing now that could be done. When he took her down to Gay's room, he asked only one more question.

"Did you ever notice in Jenny's possession a white-gold bracelet with one black stone, like an obsidian?"

"No," said Melitta, her first monosyllable.

Yet she was complacent, amiable, even cheerful in Gay's room, where Hadley was concluding his questioning. Gay preserved towards her an attitude of great gallantry, and, when he presented her to Dr. Fell, she was almost effusive. Hadley, his note-book on his knee, forged ahead as steadily as an army lorry.

"—and you did not wake up, Sir Gyles, until half-past nine this morning?"

"That is correct," agreed the other with great gravity.

"How did you first learn of the murder?"

"From one of your men. Sergeant Somebody. I rang for the maid to get hot water for my tea," he nodded towards the table. "The maid answered the bell, but the sergeant came with her. He told me Mrs. Kent had been killed, and asked if I would stay in my suite. I obeyed orders."

"One last question. I believe it is the usual thing, when you take a room at this hotel, for them to issue a little folded card with the number of the room, the price, and so on?"

Gay frowned. "I don't know. It certainly is so at a number of hotels. This is the first time I have ever been here."

"But didn't you get such a card?"

"No."

Hadley's pencil stopped. "I'll tell you why I ask. Mr. Kent here was standing in front of this hotel between seven-twenty and seven-thirty this morning. One of those cards—let me have it, will you?—dropped down out of a window; from up here somewhere, anyhow." He took the card Kent handed him. "This, you see, is for room 707, Mrs. Kent's room. But her room looks out on the air-well. This card, apparently, could only have come from your suite or Mr. Reaper's. What we want to know is how the card for 707 came to be in here, and why it was dropped out of a window at seven-thirty in the morning."

There was a pause. Gay returned the look unwinkingly.

"I don't know, superintendent. So far as I know, it was not dropped out of here."

"Can you tell us anything, Mrs. Reaper?"

"My husband attends to all that," Melitta said vaguely. The lines of dissatisfaction pressed down her face again, so as to make its expression unreadable; Kent guessed that she and Hadley were not favourites of each other. "I remember quite well that there were a number of those little cards. And naturally they gave them to my husband in a batch, because of course he was the host and paid for all the rooms. I am quite *sure* he put them all down on the bureau in our bedroom. And, though I cannot and do not expect to be consulted about it, I should think it was easy. It blew out."

"Blew out?"

"The card blew out," she told him with an air of patience. "Out of the window. And since my husband will insist on sleeping with both of the windows wide open, and they always put the bureau between the windows, I cannot say I am surprised. There must have been a high wind this morning,"—this was true, Kent remembered, for he had been standing out in it when the card whirled down,—"because I know he got up at some time to close the windows, and things were blown all about on the bureau."

Hadley wore a look of unspoken profanity. If this attractive clue turned into a mere gust of wind, it would be a final bedevilment.

"Are you certain the card for 707 was among them?"

"I am not certain; I don't know anything about it. All I know is that I simply glanced at them, to make sure my husband had told me the truth about what the rooms cost. I never noticed the numbers at all. I am afraid, as usual, you will have to ask my husband."

There was an opportunity to ask him. Dan, shouldering in at that juncture, stopped short and seemed disturbed to find her there. Francine was behind him, with a worried-looking Hardwick, the latter carrying a sheet of notes.

"That bracelet—" exploded Dan. "No. You tell 'em, Hardwick. Fire away."

The manager gave a careful and courteous greeting to

everyone before he took up a task he did not seem to relish. He resembled a grizzled clerk studying a ledger, and had a pencil poised.

"About the bracelet, as Mr. Reaper says. It belonged to Mrs. Kent; Miss Forbes has just identified it. But we're not through with the other one yet. I've talked to Mrs. Jopley-Dunne on the telephone. Her bracelet is a silver linked one set with small diamonds; it's worth three thousand dollars, and she says that beyond any doubt she left it in that bureau." He looked up. "I think she means it, Mr. Hadley. She—er—she can't claim any liability; but, all the same, we don't want this unpleasantness and I have got to find the bracelet somehow."

Dr. Fell sat up. "Steady!" rumbled the doctor. "Let me understand this. You say there were *two* bracelets in that bureau?"

"It looks like that," admitted Hardwick.

"Two bracelets. Both were stolen, and then one was returned. But the one that was returned was Mrs. Kent's bracelet, which very probably has some meaning in this case. And the one that was taken and *not* returned was a bracelet belonging to Mrs. Jopley-Dunne, a woman whose belongings have absolutely nothing to do with the case at all. If it had been the other way round, we should have had sense. But it isn't and we haven't. Oh, my eye, Hadley! This won't do."

Hadley gave a sharp glance round.

"Not so fast," he snapped. "Anything else, Mr. Hardwick?"

"Yes. I've checked up on the night-staff. I take it," inquired Hardwick, "Mr. Reaper saw this 'hotel-attendant' in the hall at two minutes past twelve?"

"That's right. Well?"

The manager peered up over his eyeglasses. "Then every solitary soul employed on the night-staff has what you'd call a complete alibi. It's a long story, but it's all here for your convenience in checking. I've had them routed individually out of their beds as quickly as I could. Shall I read this out?"

"Fine," said Dan without enthusiasm. "I hope that clears the air. But, since I'm chiefly interested in my own tight little circle— You haven't got any mechanism, have you, to prove an alibi for all of us?"

"As a mater of fact, in one case I can." Hardwick forgot himself and put his pencil behind his ear. "It goes along with the alibi of Billings, the night-porter, who was in his lodge downstairs. A telephone-call from up here came through at just midnight. Billings answered it. The guest wanted information, and they talked until three minutes past. Billings is willing to swear to the voice of the guest who spoke to him; and an under-porter heard Billings's side of it. So—er—well, it's your affair; but that seems to let both of them out of it."

"Who was the guest?" demanded Hadley.

"Mr. Wrayburn, in 705."

Chapter 9

Men in the Case

HADLEY did not comment; for a short time it was as though he had not heard. But he avoided Dr. Fell's eye and studied the ring of faces which, blank or interested, now included all of the *dramatis personae* except one. A very clever person (had he known it) was then within sound of his voice.

"We'll go into that later," he observed. "Thanks for the information, though. At the moment, have you got that bracelet? Good! Miss Forbes: you identify this as belonging to Mrs. Kent?"

Kent had been looking at her ever since she had come in, wondering about Gay's maunderings, wondering about the nature of the mess in which they had been landed. Francine's expression baffled him as she regarded the bracelet; it was not an expression he knew.

"Yes. She was wearing it last night."

"Will someone else identify it? Mrs. Reaper? Mr. Reaper?"

"I'm sure *I* never saw it before," said Melitta.

"Neither have I," Dan asserted, wheeling round as though surprised. "Funny, too. You'd notice a thing like that, with the inscription and the rest of it. Do you suppose she bought it since she landed over here?"

Hadley gave a quick look at Dr. Fell, who did not respond. "It doesn't look the sort of thing you could buy in Dorset; or possibly even in London, according to the doctor. However! She was wearing this at the theatre last night?"

"Yes, she was," Francine said in a cool tone which gave the impression that her truthfulness might be doubted. "Perhaps the others didn't notice it because she wore her fur coat all last night. But I saw it beforehand. I————"

"We don't doubt you, Miss Forbes," Hadley said at that curious tone, as though to prod her. "When did you see it?"

"Before we went to the theatre, and just before we went out to dinner. I went to her room to ask her whether she was going to dress for the theatre last night."

"Time?"

"About seven o'clock."

"Go on, please."

"She said she was much too tired and queer inside to dress. She said she wouldn't even go to the theatre if it weren't for sticking to the party; she said she thought it wasn't decent." Francine stopped. Under the long eyelids her dark brown eyes, which gave vitality to the too-fair complexion, flashed towards Hadley as though pondering. "She said————"

"Just a moment. She talked about 'sticking to the party.' Do you mean she was alarmed or frightened?"

"No, I don't think so. It would have taken a great deal to frighten her." Another pause. The emotional temperature was so low that Kent wondered about it. "When I went in her trunk was open but not unpacked; she said she would unpack after the theatre. She was standing in front of the dressing-table, with her wrist out, looking at that bracelet. I admired it, and asked whether it was new. She said yes. She also said, 'If anything ever happens to me, which I don't anticipate, you shall have it.' "

Hadley looked up quickly.

"She was a great friend of yours?"

"No. I'm not sure whether she liked me. But I think she trusted me."

This was a curious remark from Francine; both Dan and Melitta Reaper seemed to find it so, for there was a shifting and muttering in the group.

"Anything else, Miss Forbes?"

"Well, she looked very hard at me, I thought, and asked if I had ever seen anything like the bracelet before. I said I hadn't, and looked at it closer. I asked her whether the inscription had any meaning; any personal meaning, that is. She said, 'Only if you're able to read it; that's the whole secret.'"

Again Hadley glanced at Dr. Fell, who seemed intrigued and sardonically amused. "'Only if you're able to read it; that's the whole secret.' Wait!" muttered the superintendent. "You mean that Latin inscription is, or contains a cryptogram or cipher of some sort? Oh, Lord, haven't we had enough————"

"Be careful, Hadley," warned Dr. Fell. "I rather doubt that. Anything else, Miss Forbes?"

"No, that was all. I don't know what she meant. I certainly never suspected her of subtlety. So I went back to my room, and she didn't refer to the matter afterwards. May I have it now?"

"Have what?"

"That bracelet. She promised————"

This was so frankly and blatantly out of character that even her voice sounded wrong. Francine corrected herself, with a little husky cough, and tried to assume her earlier impersonal air. Hadley, with a smile that was not pleasant, closed up his note-book; he sat back with a look of luxurious patience.

"Now let's have it, Miss Forbes. What is it you're hiding?"

"I don't think I understand."

"But I do think you understand," said Hadley patiently. "You ought to know the consequences. I'm not going to sit here and howl at you; I simply warn you that I'll act on the assumption you're keeping something back. Some exceedingly dirty work has been done in this hotel and I mean to find out what. I'm going to ask your friends some questions; and then I'm going to ask you again. See that you have something to tell me."

"Oh, really?" said Francine in a high voice. "You don't know how you frighten me. Well, I still have nothing to tell."

Hadley ignored this. "Some general questions, please. I got you all together because, if anyone can add anything to the pool, we want to know it. You all swore to me two weeks ago that there was no reason why Mr. Kent—Mr. Rodney Kent—should have been murdered. Now his wife is killed. You all must know quite well that there is a reason somewhere. Mr. Reaper!"

Dan had sat down in a chair opposite Melitta, with Sir Gyles Gay between them like a referee. When Dan got out his pipe, unrolled an oilskin tobacco-pouch, and began to press in tobacco with a steady thumb, it was as though he were loading a gun: say a twelve-bore shotgun.

"Fire away," he invited, shaking himself.

"I think you told me that Mr. and Mrs. Rodney Kent lived in your house in Johannesburg?"

"Right. They had the top floor."

"So you and Mrs. Reaper must have known Mrs. Kent as well as anybody?"

"Yes, certainly."

"Do you share this general belief that nobody knew her very well?"

"I don't know," said Dan, and stopped. "I never thought of it. What do you mean by 'knowing' her, anyway? Term makes no sense. I didn't watch her go to bed at night and get up in the morning."

Sir Gyles Gay interposed, with Cheshire-cat effect. "I think the superintendent is wondering, though, whether anybody else did. The seeds are taking root."

"*You* put them there," said Hadley. "What I mean, Mr. Reaper, is this. Do you know of any love affair Mrs. Kent may have had before her marriage—or afterwards?"

"Good God, no!" said Dan, who seemed to be genuinely shocked as he dug back into his memory. "That's the last thing I should have thought of Jenny. Afterwards, I mean. I know you hinted at something like that after Rod's death; but I knew you didn't mean it seriously. She wasn't like that. She was a—a kind of sister. Wasn't she, Mel?"

Melitta nodded with such earnestness that she seemed to be waggling her head like a China figure.

"What was her attitude towards divorce, Mr. Reaper?"

"Divorce?" repeated Dan with a blank look.

"She was absolutely and unalterably opposed to it," interposed Melitta suddenly. "She told me so any number of times; she said it was shocking and disgusting the way they go on in Hollywood because someone drops a shoe on the floor or something."

"But what are you getting at?" asked Dan.

"The devilish respectability of many murderers," Sir Gyles Gay put in with the effect of a pounce. "Now that I have got a policeman in a corner, I should like to get his practical opinion on the matter. It's the only thing that's puzzled me about murderers. I don't care what causes crime in general, whether it's the thickness of a gland or the thinness of a lobe or anything that the doctors wrangle about. To my forthright mind the explanation of most crime is simple: somebody wants something and so he simply goes and grabs it————"

Dan grunted approvingly. Hadley did not stop this oration; he was watching the group while Gay, with the pleased expression of a wizened small boy, continued:

"—but one kind of crime is plain nonsense. It's this: A. falls in love with Mrs. B. So, instead of separating from Mr. B., instead of doing anything rational about it, Mrs. B. gets together with A. and they murder Mr. B. This seems to me to be carrying respectability too far. I know it isn't an original thesis. But I'll make an extra point: it's the only kind of murder case which is certain to cause a big splash of noteriety in the Press, to be eagerly followed and read by everyone, and to be remembered for many years in the public mind. Millionaires are shot, chorus-girls are gassed, matrons are dismembered in trunks; that kind of case may or may not attract great notice. But the case of A. and Mrs. B. always does. Think of the criminal cases which most readily jump to your mind, and you'll see what seven out of ten of them are. Now, that seems to indicate that it strikes home. It's close to the great British household. It affects us—a disturbing thought. Maybe A. and Mrs. B. are prowling closer round our own doors than we think. Mrs. B. doesn't get a separation, or a divorce, or go and live with A.; she simply has her husband murdered. Why?"

Francine could not keep out of this. "Because," she said curtly, "most people aren't well off and can't afford emotional luxuries. Get a decent social state, and you'll change all that. Under our present state the only emotional luxury the poor can afford is murder."

"They don't really intend to do any dreadful thing like that," said Melitta with the same air of suddenness, "though I suppose most women have thought about it at one time or another, like that terrible woman who wrote all the letters that are shocking, but you wish more of them had been printed in the book. But all of a sudden they get drunk or lose their heads or something, and before they know it it's all over: like adultery, you know."

"What do *you* know about adultery?" said Dan with restraint. He blinked at her, after which a grin crept over his face. "Here! If the parade of epigrams has finished, I'd like to know just what all this has to do with Jenny. She wouldn't—er—lose her head."

Francine, folding her arms, looked straight at Hadley though she addressed Dan.

"Don't you see what they're hinting at? The background of the idea is that someone has fallen in love with Jenny, but *she* knows Rod will never give her up under any circumstances; and above all things she mustn't be touched by any scandal. That would horrify her. So she encourages this man to kill Rod. But for that reason she won't go down to Sussex and stay in the house while the killing is done; so she remains with her aunts. It may be delicacy or caution. Then she discovers that she can't stick the man—possibly she says her soul is revolted, or possibly she wanted Rod killed for some other reason, and now that it's done she needn't encourage the murderer any longer—so she tries to send him about his business. But he kills her."

"Could you believe that about *Jenny*?" demanded Dan. "Didn't she make Rod a good wife?"

"Oh, uncle, my darling," said Francine, "I didn't say it was my theory. But, as for the last part of it, yes. I've watched her making him a good wife, and, frankly, it made me sick. She cared no more for Rod than I do for that lamp-shade."

"I am glad to have my judgment," observed Gay, tilting up his chin with shining pleasure, "confirmed by outside witnesses. I warned Dr. Fell, and later Mr. Hadley, that she was that very dangerous and insidious thing, a sweet and dignified woman."

"Well, I'll be—" said Dan. "What kind of a woman do you want, then? Sour and undignified?"

"*Hey!*" roared Dr. Fell.

There was an abrupt silence after that thunderous blast. Dr. Fell pounded on the floor with his stick, but his eye twinkled over eyeglasses coming askew on his nose. Then he cleared his throat for pontifical pronouncement.

"Much as I dislike to interrupt," he said, "this discussion appears to have turned into an argument about matrimony. I am always willing to argue about matrimony; or, in fact, anything else; and at any other time I shall be happy to oblige. Both murder and matrimony are stimulating and exciting things: in fact, an analogy could be drawn between them as regards the interest they excite. Harrumph! Ha! But Miss Forbes has made at least one point —point of fact—which is so good that we can't let it drop. Eh, Hadley?"

"Thank you," said Francine. Her chilly manner was in contrast to the fervor with which she had spoken last; but in spite of herself she smiled under the beam of Dr. Fell's presence. "I didn't say it was my theory."

"H'mf, no. That odious burden shall rest elsewhere. But in this theory, how did that bracelet fit into it?" He pointed his stick towards the table where the bracelet lay. "Was it a kind of pledge or token given by this X, this unidentified man, to Mrs. Kent?"

"Well—yes."

"Do you believe that to be actually the case?"

"Yes. I—oh, I don't know! That's just it: I don't know anything! I've already said a dozen times more than I intended. . . ."

"Yes," agreed Hadley placidly, "I thought you would." He seemed to gain his point by ignoring her. "Mr. Reaper: let's get back to the subject we started on, before we continue about this. What do you know *about* Mrs. Kent? I met her only once, and she was ill then, or said she was; so it's little enough I got out of her. For instance, where was she from? Johannesburg?"

"No, she was born up country, Rhodesia. I knew her parents well, when she was a kid in curls. Good old stock; gentlemen-farmers; not very go-ahead."

"Are her parents living?"

"No. I lost touch with them some years ago. They left her very well provided for, though I shouldn't have suspected that. She came to Johannesburg about three years ago; she and Rod have been married for two."

Dr. Fell interposed a sleepy question. "I say, was she fond of travelling? Did she do much of it?"

"No," said Dan, sighting behind his pipe. "Funny you should ask that. She detested it; never did any. Trains and ships made her sick, or something; even coming from Salisbury to Johannesburg was something to set her teeth about. Didn't want to make this trip, either. As it happens," he added, staring down at the packed tobacco with a heavy and lowering embarrassment, "I wish she hadn't. I wish nobody had. And then—" He spoke quietly. "Right down to brass tacks: did you mean all that about A. and Mrs. B.?"

"That was Sir Gyles's suggestion." Hadley was still

prodding, and he saw Dan look sideways with abrupt suspicion. "I'm merely trying to get at the truth. But do you think someone in your party is a homicidal lunatic?"

"My God, no!"

"Then we've got to look for a motive, if you'll help. Think. Was there *any* reason why someone should have killed both Mr. and Mrs. Kent? By this time you've all got to face it: it wasn't an outsider or a member of the hotel staff. So was there any reason? Money? Revenge? You shake your head—you all do. Then, Mrs. Kent being the sort of person some of you think she was, the only indication we've got is a possible affair in which Rodney Kent is killed by X in collusion with Mrs. Kent, and X later kills Mrs. Kent herself. If," Hadley's tone grew sharper, "Miss Forbes will now tell us what she knows. . . ."

"Which is still nothing," said Francine. "The sum and substance of it is this. I wasn't actually told a word. I inferred, from the way she talked, that some man she was very much interested in had given her the bracelet; someone she either loved or———"

"Or———?"

"Feared, I was going to say. There you are. I couldn't tell you because I didn't want to sound silly," she drew in her breath with hard effect, "like one of Chris's melodramatic novels. Maybe I was imagining it all, because it seems a little too melodramatic to be true. But I did understand that if I looked hard enough at that bracelet I might learn something."

"About what? About the person who gave it to her?"

"Yes."

"And that is why you wanted me to give it to you a while ago?"

"Well, yes."

Hadley picked up the bracelet and turned it over in his hand. "You can see for yourself that there's not a scrap of writing, or place for writing, or any secret hanky-panky, except that Latin inscription. Do you mean there's a secret hidden in that, like an acrostic or some such thing? *Clau-*

dite jam rivos, pueri, sat prata biberunt. This is more in your line, Fell."

"I still think," Gay urged, "that you're making too much of a small thing. If I may suggest it, the inquiries should be broader. If there has been a man in the case, there ought to be traces of him. Find that man, and you'll be a good deal closer to finding the murderer."

"No, you won't," said a new voice.

The door to the hall had opened and Harvey Wrayburn came in. He did not come with his usual bounce or bustle. In appearance he was stoutish and undistinguished, except when some enthusiasm animated him—as it often did. Then his gingery hair and moustache, his alert eyes under a bump of a forehead, would all take on a vividness of self-assurance in which few could disbelieve. He had a fondness for wearing old grey worsted suits, and a habit of jamming his fists into the coat-pockets so that the coat always looked bulging and long. At this time he was self-assured enough, except for a look of strain round his eyes. He seemed poised on the edge of speech, as though he had just been put in front of a microphone and told that the red light would flash on in half a second.

"For the last five minutes," he said, "I've been listening outside that door. Who wouldn't?" he added, raising his neck up a little. "The question was whether I should get our friend Hadley in a corner and explain, or else get it all off my chest in front of all of you—and have done with it. I've decided to get it off my chest. All right: I'm the man you want."

Hadley jumped to his feet. "Mr. Wrayburn, you may make a statement if you like, but I must caution you ———"

"Oh, I didn't kill her," said the other rather irritably, as if he had been robbed of an effect. "I was going to marry her; or she was going to marry me. Your grand reconstruction also misfires on one other point: that bracelet. I didn't give the bracelet to her. She gave it to me."

Chapter 10

Shipboard Idyll

WRAYBURN'S next statement was in a slightly different key. "I feel better," he said in a surprised tone. "No balloon or aneurism seems to have burst. You don't look any different. Oh, hell."

After a violence of expelled breath, he perched himself on the edge of the table as though he were addressing a class, and went on:

"I know about the penalty for suppressing evidence. And that's not all. I've always hated the silly fathead who shoves an important clue into his pocket and causes everybody trouble because he (or usually it's a she) won't speak; and then, when you find it, it's not worth the hunt. All right, here I am. And here's your clue."

From his waistcoat-pocket he took a Yale key with a chromium tag bearing the number 707, and tossed it across to Hadley.

"You mean," said Dan, "that you and Jenny have been _____"

"Have been what? Six kisses," said Wraybrun gloomily. "I counted 'em. She said the last one was for luck."

Hadley was curt.

"I think we'd better hear about this from the beginning," he said, only less satisfied than exasperated. "You didn't say anything about it when Mr. Rodney Kent was murdered."

"No, of course I didn't. Why should I? I didn't kill him."

"And yet, if you intended to marry her, his being dead must have simplified matters, didn't it?"

"This isn't going to be as easy as I had hoped," said Wrayburn, fixing his eyes grimly on the door-knob after a quick look at Hadley. "Try to understand this. I didn't think about it simplifying matters at all. I thought about it as an infernal shame and a piece of senseless brutality done by that fellow Bellowes when he was drunk. That's all I thought. It—woke me up."

"How long has this been going on? I mean the affair with Mrs. Kent."

"Well—it only really started on shipboard. Oh, Lord, these ships. The weather was cutting up rough, and only Jenny and I, and sometimes Dan, had our sea-legs. You know how these things happen."

"Mrs. Kent wasn't sea-sick?"

"Not a bit."

"We heard just a minute ago that she couldn't stand ships in any kind of weather."

Wrayburn glanced over his shoulder. As a rule, Kent knew, he was fond of the limelight; but he seemed to regret that he had perched on the table.

"Then all I can say," he retorted querulously, "is that somebody is mistaken. You ought to have seen her. That old tub was jumping about like a ball in a roulette-wheel, and Jenny would stand as cool as though she had just walked into a drawing-room. It was the—the humanest I ever saw her. How that woman liked to see things smashed up! Once the wicker furniture, and the gramophone, and all the rest of the stuff got loose in the palm-room when the ship was pitching badly. It sailed round from one side to the other, and simply busted the whole show to blazes. It was one of the few times I ever saw Jenny really laugh."

There was a stony kind of silence, while some members of the group shifted in their chairs. Dr. Fell was the first to speak.

"You ought to know, Mr. Wrayburn," he said, "that you're making rather a bad impression. That look on Hadley's face—I know it. In other words, you don't show any signs of being a broken-hearted lover."

"I'm not," said Wrayburn, moving off the table. "Now we're getting down to it."

He looked round the circle.

"You must be Dr. Fell. Will *you* explain what happened, even if I can't? I don't know exactly how it came about on that ship. The trouble with sirens, like Jenny, is that they win half their victories by their very reputations. They're attractive; you know they're attractive; but you have no intention of being attracted by them. Then they let you know—inadventently—how much interested they are in you; and you're so flattered that, like a chump, you wonder if you're not falling. Then you do fall. Finish. You're anaesthetised; for the time being."

"You needn't look so crushed about it," rumbled Dr. Fell cheerfully. "It happens, you know. When did you begin to wake up?"

His manner was so casual that Wrayburn stopped pacing.

" 'Begin.' 'Begin.' Yes, that's the word," he admitted. He dug his hands into the usual pockets; and once his animation had gone, he looked undistinguished again. "Let's see. It was—maybe just after the ship docked. Maybe it was when she told me she wasn't going down to Sussex because she couldn't trust herself to be with me. All of a sudden that struck a wrong note. Bing! I looked at her and knew she was lying. Finally, maybe it was when Rod died."

Dan had been waving a hand for silence.

"Will somebody explain this business about Jenny's 'reputation'?" he insisted. "What reputation? All I can say is that it's complete news to me."

"Of course," said Melitta.

"You mean to say you knew it?"

Melitta's thin voice kept to its monotone. "Of course, my dear, you will *not* listen to anyone; and you say everything is gossip, as it often is, and you're so terribly concerned with your own ideas—you and Chris, too—that naturally nobody ever tells you anything." Melitta was full of impatience. "All the same, I stick to my opinion, and I don't alter it. Jenny was a Sweet Girl. Of course, I know there has been a certain amount of gossip, and my grandfather always used to say that most gossip is probably true because it is what the people would like to do even if they are not doing it. But in Jenny's case there was *absolutely* nothing against her, and I was quite sure she could be trusted not to do anything foolish. And it was really most interesting to see what happened."

"Murder happened," said Hadley.

A wrathful superintendent had been trying to break through this screen of talk.

"It won't be necessary to explain your state of mind, Mr. Wrayburn. Just tell me what you did. Were you in Mrs. Kent's room last night?"

"Yes."

"Very well; let's get that clear. What time did you go in?"

"About twenty-five minutes to twelve. Just after the maid left, anyhow."

"At what time did you leave the room?"

"Midnight—I was also in there at seven, and again at eight o'clock this morning."

"And you tell us you did not commit this murder?"

"I did not."

During a strained pause of about ten seconds he met Hadley's eye. Then Hadley turned briskly and nodded to Dr. Fell and Kent.

"Good. Then just come across the hall with me to 707, and explain how you managed it. No! The rest of you, with the exception of these two, will remain here."

He very quickly shut off the protests. Opening the door for the other three, he ushered them out ahead of him and closed the door with a snap. Wrayburn, breathing hard, went out with a stiff gait which suggested that he might have been walking through a more evil doorway than this. In the corridor Hadley beckoned to Sergeant Preston, who was just coming out of the Reapers' suite. From room 707 the body had now been removed, leaving only a few stains on the floor.

"We've nearly finished searching, sir," Preston reported. "And so far, there's not a sign of that unif————"

"Shorthand," said Hadley. "Mr. Wrayburn, your statement will be taken down, and you will be asked to initial it afterwards. Now let's hear just what happened in here."

After looking round quickly, Wrayburn leaned against the foot of the nearest twin-bed and seemed to brace himself. His moustache was not now brushed up, either literally or metaphorically; he looked heavy and a little shabby.

"Well, it was like this. It's no good saying I was entirely out from under the ether. That's partly camouflage for the benefit of—" he jerked his head towards the other side of the hall. "But I was beginning to wonder whether I might have made a fool of myself aboard ship. Besides, we had had a roaring good time at Gay's."

"Wait. Had there been any talk of marriage between you and Mrs. Kent?"

"No, not then. She wouldn't bring it up, and I didn't. You understand, there was always Rod." He looked at Kent. "I swear, Chris, I never meant any harm to him."

"Go on."

"So, you see, I saw Jenny again for the first time last night. Considering what had happened—naturally, I didn't expect her to fly to my shoulder or anything of the sort. I was beginning to wonder whether I wanted her to; I didn't trust her. But I couldn't get an opportunity to speak to her alone. She seemed odd. At the theatre she arranged matters so that we were sitting at opposite ends of the row of seats, and between the acts she monopolised Gay. I had never seen her look—brighter.

"As you can understand, the only time I could get to see

her alone was after the others had gone to bed. I waited for fifteen or twenty minutes after we had all closed our doors. Then I nipped across the hall to there," he indicated the side door, "and knocked."

"Yes?" Hadley prompted, as he hesitated.

"I can tell you this. She was frightened about something. After I knocked there was no answer for a second or two. Then I heard her voice very close to the door, asking who it was. I had to repeat my name twice before she opened the door."

"Had she seemed frightened earlier in the evening?"

"No. At least, not noticeably. There was a stealthy kind of air about this; I don't know how else to describe it. And the door was bolted—I remember the noise of the bolt when she drew it back.

"She had changed her shoes for slippers, and was just beginning to unpack her trunk. The trunk, everything, looked just about as it does now. I don't want you to think I'm any more an ass than necessary. But when I saw her again, I didn't know what to say. I simply stood and looked at her; and my chest hurt. That's a devil of a confession to have to make, but it did. She sat down in a chair and waited for me to speak first. She was sitting in that one, over by the writing-desk."

He nodded towards it. The room was now grey with early-afternoon shadows, and the maplewood gleamed faintly.

"So I started in to talk—chiefly about Rod, and how bad it was. Not a word about ourselves. I knew she was waiting for me to do it. And she was listening with a kind of composed expression, as though she were waiting to have her photograph taken. You know: cool, and the corners of the mouth turning down a bit. She was wearing that bracelet with the black stone and the inscription. It was the first time I had ever seen it. As I told you, *I* didn't give it to *her*; she gave it to me, presently.

"There's something else I must tell you, because it fits into the story. I kept on talking, inanely, and wondered why I talked at all. During this time she got up once or twice; in particular, she went over to the dressing-table there, picked up her handbag, and got a handkerchief out of it. I noticed, when she ran through the things in the handbag, that the key to the room—the key with the chromium tag—was inside.

"By the time I was wondering if I ought to make jokes, she came to a decision. You could see it; all at once. Her face softened up a bit. She asked me straight out, in that trustful way of hers, whether I was in love with her. That broke the barriers. I said I was. I said a whole lot. Whereupon she said she was going to give me a keepsake, a pledge, all that kind of thing. She unhooked that bracelet and handed it to me, and I can remember exactly what she said. She said: 'You keep that for always. Then nobody will try to wake the dead.' Don't ask me what it means. I thought it was a high-flown kind of thing to say. Because, mind, one part of my intelligence was still awake. In these romantic moments—arrh!—I didn't seem any closer to her than to a clock ticking beside you. Also, she brightened up immediately afterwards. She said it was late, and what would anybody think if I were found there at that hour?

"I was still fuddled; I wanted to keep on with a good thing. So I had a romantic idea. I said, why shouldn't we get up early in the morning, and have breakfast together and go out and see the town on our own before any of the rest could join us? It would have to be early, because Dan Reaper is always up and roaring round the place just at the time I like to take the best part of sleep. I recklessly said seven o'clock. You understand. I didn't really *want* to go out at seven o'clock. God love you, I wouldn't want to get up at seven o'clock in the morning to walk through the Earthly Paradise with an unveiled Houri. But I stood there and said fool things. She welcomed the idea, with an out-you-go expression. Finally, she asked me whether I wasn't going to kiss her good night. I said of course. Instead of grabbing the wench, as I would have grabbed any other woman, I gave her a couple of chaste and tender salutes.

. . . Stop looking so damned embarrassed, coppers; you wanted the truth—and drew away. Then she put out her swan-like neck and said, 'And one for luck.' Then was when I saw her eyes sort of slide past my shoulder. There wasn't much in them; it was an expression like that of a woman in a foyer waiting for the lift to go up; they were blank and blue as marbles. And in that one second the cable was cut. My cable. In short, I saw————"

There was a click, and the wall-lights over the beds came on; Sergeant Preston was no longer sure with his shorthand notes. Nobody except Wrayburn, Kent thought, would have had the nerve to pour all this out to a note-book. He was now regarding them with sour poise and flippancy, his hands dug deep into his coat-pockets. The wall-lamps, behind their frosted-glass shades, made a sleek, theatrical light in the sleek, theatrical room.

"That's it," Wrayburn said complacently, nodding towards them. "Crafty little devil! I knew then; I felt it; though I couldn't imagine what the game was. I might have pursued the subject then, because all of a sudden it was beginning to hurt. But I couldn't—because that was when we heard the knock at the door."

Hadley jerked up his head.

"Knock at the door? Which door?"

"At what I suppose you'd call the main door: the one that had the sign hung on it later."

"What time was this? Do you know?"

"Yes. It was just a few seconds short of midnight. I know, because I looked at my watch when Jenny said good night."

"You were actually *in* the room when you heard this knock?"

"Certainly I was in the room—" Wrayburn was beginning with some asperity, when he stopped, and for the first time his eyes shifted. He added in a lower tone: "Oi! Here! You don't mean it was— Nobody told me————"

"Go on; what happened when you heard the knock?"

"Jenny whispered to me to get out in case I should be

found there. So I ducked out of the side door, with the 'keepsake' in my pocket. I think Jenny bolted the door after me. I walked straight across to my own side door and went in."

"The time being————?"

"Oh, midnight. It couldn't have taken more than ten seconds. I admit I was feeling a bit mixed-up, and not too good-humoured; but I was going to see the thing through. In case I should forget it, I rang up the porter on the telephone (or at least I put through a call downstairs) and told him I was to be waked up at a quarter to seven next morning. I also wondered, with a few less romantic fumes in my head, where we should get breakfast at that time; and what in the name of sense we were going to *see* at that hour. Most people get over calf-love by the early twenties. I waited for a brief, bad bout of it until the early thirties. I suppose I saw us riding on a bus in the snow. Anyhow, I asked the porter a lot of questions, and I must have talked for three or four minutes on the phone."

Kent found himself fitting together the pieces of evidence. Wrayburn's story coincided exactly with the ascertained and ascertainable facts as regarded the man himself. He had been speaking on the telephone (according to Hardwick's schedule) from midnight until three minutes past. If any wonder might have been felt as to what could have been the reason for such a fairly long call at so late an hour, there was now a strong and plausible motive behind it. Wrayburn also spoke with an air of weary earnestness which was difficult to disbelieve. The question was now how far this evidence coincided with Dan's. Dan had seen in the hall this goblin, the figure carrying bath-towels, at exactly two minutes past midnight—standing outside Jenny's door. If Dan's statement were accepted (and nobody had questioned it), Wrayburn could not possibly be the elusive figure in uniform.

But there was one extra question. Someone, undoubtedly the figure in uniform, had knocked on the main door at a few seconds before midnight. Would it have remained there for two full minutes after the first knock, without going into or being admitted into the room? Why not? At least, so it appeared to Kent, who was watching Hadley and Dr. Fell.

Hadley drew a design in his note-book.

"Did you see anything of the person who knocked at the door?"

"No," said Wrayburn shortly. "No gratuitous information. I'll answer what you like; but I'm not bubbling over any longer. Thanks."

"Are you sure your watch was right about the times?"

"Yes. She's a good timekeeper, and I set her early in the evening, by the big clock on the wall outside this room."

(The same clock Dan had seen. Well?)

"Just continue your story," Hadley said. "You left this room at midnight, with Mrs. Kent's bracelet————?"

"*And* I didn't sleep. I couldn't. There was no need to ring me; I was awake long before seven. I got dressed, feeling seedy. At seven o'clock I went over and knocked at Jenny's door. There was no answer, even when I knocked harder. That made me mad, rather. It occurred to me that, since she would be sleeping in one of the twin beds, she would be closer to the main door, and would hear me better if I knocked there. I went round to the main door. The shoes were outside it, and the 'quiet' sign was hung from the knob. Now begins the story of my derelictions. I looked at the sign, and saw 'Dead Woman' scrawled on it. I picked up the sign to look at it closer; then I could see, behind it, the key still stuck in the lock outside the main door."

Dr. Fell puffed out his cheeks. So far he had been shutting out the view of one window, but now he lumbered forward.

"The key," he said, "was in the lock outside the door. Kindly take note of that, Hadley. The night before it had been in her handbag. Well?"

"I opened the door with it," said Wrayburn obediently,

"and took the key out of the lock. Automatically, I suppose. I stuck my head inside the room, and saw her."

"That door wasn't bolted on the inside, then?"

"Naturally not, or I couldn't have got in. There was a heavy stuffy smell inside the room, and I thought, 'Doesn't the little so-and-so put her windows up at night?' Then I saw her; she was lying on the floor with her head inside that trunk. I went over and touched her. She was cold. I didn't investigate further; I didn't want to. But now comes the hardest part of the story to tell. I walked back out of the room by the way I had come, with the key in my hand, and stood in the hall. My first impulse, naturally, was to set up an alarm; to go and wake Dan, or wake somebody. But I'll admit it: I got the wind up. My trouble is that I always want to know what's going on, and I won't act until I do. Without saying a word I went back to my room and tried to think. This was about five minutes past seven o'clock.

"At a quarter-past seven I heard the maid coming on duty; I heard her jingle. And I was still racking my brains. Somebody had killed Jenny. I knew something queer had been going on last night, but *I* wasn't going to find that body. I had been the last person alone with her, and— you know. What bothered me most, and kept on bothering me, was *how* she had been killed. I wondered why on earth I had not stopped to make sure. There had been something done to her face; that's all I could tell, because it was early morning and very nearly dark. I felt I had to know, but I couldn't screw up quite enough nerve to go back to that room.

"It was going on towards eight o'clock when I remembered something that was nearly the last devilment. *I* had Jenny's bracelet. It's a distinctive-looking thing; it undoubtedly cost a lot of money; it would be certain to be missed; and if they found it in my possession————

"Well, no frills. I felt like that, anyhow. On top of this, I heard two men coming along the corridor saying something about 707. I got my door open a crack, and saw them go round, and heard them talking about a master-key in front of the main door of 707. How the devil was I to know one of 'em was you?" he demanded, turning to Kent. "I heard the door to 707 being opened, and closed, and then dead silence. The other man—the porter—was still out in the hall talking to the maid. On top of all this, the side door of 707 opened, and the first man (you) slid out with his head tucked into his overcoat collar. He didn't give an alarm; he hurried down the hall and got away."

Dr. Fell interposed again, this time turning to Kent.

"Hold on! When you got out the side door, Mr. Kent, do you remember whether or not it was bolted on the inside?"

"It was bolted," said Kent. "I remember that quite well —drawing the bolt back."

"H'mf, yes. Go on, Mr. Wrayburn."

"I'll tell you exactly what it was like for me," said the other, who had been reflecting, and could not stop his own garrulousness. "It was like standing in the street before oncoming traffic, and wanting to get to the other side. You think you've got good clear margin to get across before the traffic bumps you; but, all the same, you hesitate. Then, when it's almost too late, you suddenly make up your mind and dash for it. And the traffic nearly bumps you to glory after all. That's what I did. I had Jenny's bracelet in one hand, and the key in the other. Just after that fellow—you—had gone, I made up my mind to do what I should have done before. If the key opened the main door of Jenny's room, I was sure it would open the side door as well: my own key did. I went across the corridor and got in there while the porter was still outside, Mind, I kept *some* sense. I touched things only with a handkerchief. All I wanted to do was dispose of that bracelet, so I simply dropped it in the bureau drawer. That took only a few seconds; and there was Jenny on the floor. I had to see her and find out what was wrong, now I'd got my courage to the sticking-point. It was broad daylight, though the blinds were drawn. I wanted to see her face, but I couldn't because her head was still inside that trunk. I dragged her out. I took one look—and then bolted. I was back in my own room again, closing the door, by the time the porter barged into 707. And, of course, I walked off with the blasted key after all. There it is.

"That's what I did, and that's all I did. Call it what you like; I claim it was only natural and human. The trouble is that I'm a ruddy rotten criminal. I once picked up a pound-note off the floor in the foyer of a theatre and kept it; and afterwards I was convinced everybody in the place had seen me, and was ready to denounce me. That's how I felt to-day. I couldn't keep it down. So I decided, in the words of your favourite film-star, to come clean. I've now come so clean that I feel I've been through a wringer. Thus spake Zarathustra."

He ended with a deep breath, and sat down on the bed with enough violence to make it creak. He had sketched out a perfect characterisation of himself, Kent thought.

Dr. Fell and Hadley looked at each other.

"It it too early to inquire," said Wrayburn, "whether you believe me? Or is it handcuffs and bread-and-water. Arrh!"

Hadley looked hard at him. "It certainly fits all the facts," he acknowledged. "And coming clean, I don't mind telling you, was very wise. Well, Mr. Wrayburn, if your story about the telephone-call at midnight is confirmed, I don't think you've got much to worry about. One other thing. While you were in this room on any of those occasions, did you come across a silver linked bracelet set with diamonds, and belonging to a Mrs. Jopley-Dunne?"

"Eh? No. I never heard of it or her."

"For the moment, then, that's all. You might wait across the hall."

When Wrayburn had gone, Hadley whistled softly between his teeth. "So that's the story of the reappearing bracelet. Yes, I don't think we can doubt that the murderer was looking for it, and made a thorough search to find it. Only, it wasn't here. And therefore, presumably ——————?"

"The murderer pinched Mrs. Jopley-D.'s property, wondering if it might be an old friend in disguise," said Dr. Fell. "Why not? The background of both, so to speak, is similar. Both are linked bracelets, and silver looks much like white gold. H'mf, yes. The murderer was looking for the bracelet with the black stone, all right. But that's not, I think, the really important point of the story. And, oh, Bacchus, Hadley, the real point is important! I mean the key left behind in the door."

"You think it clarifies anything?"

"I know it does. Look here!—Eh? Yes? What is it?"

A knock at the door was followed by the entrance of Sergeant Betts.

"Just finished, sir," he reported to Hadley. "And it's no go. I've been over every room, cupboard, cranny, and rathole in this wing; and there's no uniform hidden anywhere."

Chapter 11

The Solution According to Fiction

A WINTER evening, when there is good food behind plate glass, money in the pocket, and a warmth of light to be seen on snow from inside, may be considered the best of all times for argument. Christopher Kent, entering the Restaurant des Epicures in Lisle Street at seven o'clock that evening, was ready for all of them. It had been a long day—which, for him, only began when Hadley and Dr. Fell finished their questioning at the Royal Scarlet Hotel.

The most important business had been the establishing of his own alibi for the night before, and the cashing of a cheque to bring him to the surface again. The first was not difficult; the second enabled him to pour largesse on the clubmen at the coffee-stall who swore to it, and to redeem his suit-case from the landlady in Commercial Road, East. Once his alibi was beyond question, Superintendent Hadley became genial and almost talkative. Kent was accumulating facts, facts, facts. He felt somewhat surprised at this: facts had never before been a great concern of his. But, relaxing under the ministrations of the barber, and spending a fine hour steaming in the Turkish baths at the

Imperial, he began to tabulate the discoveries for reference.

1. The writing-printing in red ink on the "quiet" sign, which might have been so promising a clue, ended in nothing. It was so much printing and so little writing that it had to be classified as the former; and could never be identified.

2. The two sets of finger-prints found in the room were his own and Jenny's. Since the room had been cleaned and dusted by the maid just before Jenny moved into it, there were few old prints beyond smudges. Wrayburn, evidently by accident the first time and design the second, had left no prints at all.

3. Wrayburn was proved to have been speaking on the phone between midnight and three minutes past. Hadley, nothing if not thorough, set half a dozen persons to speak anonymously over the wire to Billings, the night-porter, and Billings had again identified Wrayburn's voice at once.

4. There was nothing wrong with the clocks, and no possibility of tampering with them. They were all electric clocks, with glass fronts which did not come off; all were operated on Greenwich time from a central switch. If Dan had seen the figure in uniform outside Jenny's door at two minutes past twelve, the time was exactly two minutes past twelve and no other.

5. Nothing, so far as could be ascertained, was missing from Jenny's possessions. Melitta Reaper went through them and said she was certain of this. There were several good pieces of costume jewellery in Jenny's trunk, in addition to £30 in notes in her handbag and travellers' cheques for £400 on the Capital Counties bank. But there was no silver or loose change whatever in her handbag.

6 The batch of small folded cards, bearing the room-numbers of each guest, had in fact been handed to Dan. He did not definitely remember seeing the card for 707 among them, since he had not looked at them. But he

confirmed Melitta's statement that he had put them down on the bureau in their bedroom.

7. A detailed deposition from each of the persons concerned, regarding where they were at about two minutes past midnight, produced the following statements: Sir Gyles Gay had been reading in bed. Melitta Reaper had been taking a bath in the private bathroom of their suite. Francine Forbes had been "doing her hair" in her own room. Wrayburn and Dan were accounted for. Kenneth Hardwick, the hotel-manager who had been questioned along with the others, provided another alibi: from midnight until ten minutes past, in his own rooms, he had been going over the next day's menus with the head-waiter of the Royal Scarlet dining-room.

Thus the facts stood; and Christopher Kent had been tinkering with them as though for a story. To be near the party, he had reserved the only vacant room in Wing A, and he wondered about a number of things. He had invited Francine, Dr. Fell, and Hadley to dinner that night. Hadley (as usual) would be detained at the Yard, but Dr. Fell accepted with heartiness and Francine after some consideration.

When he entered the Restaurant des Epicures at seven o'clock, he found Francine waiting for him. She looked rather lonely in that crowd, and he suddenly felt protective. They sat down by a shrouded window, with a yellow-shaded lamp between them, and he ordered cocktails; but, instead of taking advantage of this mood, he said, "Well?" —which was definitely the wrong thing.

"Well, what?" she said instantly, and put down her glass.

He had meant nothing by it, merely a sort of clumsy opening to start a conversation: which causes much difficulty. He admitted this.

"Look here, what's wrong between us?" he inquired in some desperation. "I'm not your worst enemy: I swear it. I'm not trying to put one over on you or do you in the eye. But———"

After a time she spoke in a reflective tone. "Oh, Chris, if you weren't so beastly intolerant!"

His own glass slid on the table as he put it down.

"Intolerant? *Me*?"

"If you could only hear yourself say that," said Francine, and was amused. "Oh, come on, let's face it. You think being intolerant merely means persecuting somebody for moral or religious reasons, or not liking lowbrows and fish-and-chips, or all the rest of it. But it doesn't. It doesn't!" she said fiercely. "It means that you simply go your own sweet way, and pay absolutely no attention to anything that isn't in your ken. You're tolerant on moral grounds because you sympathise with most of the offences, you're tolerant on religious grounds because you haven't got any religion, you're tolerant of lowbrows because you *like* Wild West stories and band music and merry-go-rounds. But if there's something that doesn't come into your ken, like doing some real good in the world—all right: I won't say that: I'll take something in your own province—like the work of certain great authors whose beliefs you don't agree with, then you simply don't discuss them as being beneath contempt. Grr! Your idea of being generous is merely to be ridiculously generous with money, that's all."

"Sorry," he said. "Is that really it? All right. Honestly, if it will make you any happier, I will even admit that Blank Blank or Dash Dash is a great writer; but privately ————"

"There. You see?"

"And if, in the latter part of the indictment, you were referring to certain gifts which you practically threw back in my face————"

"Trust a man," said Francine icily, "to take the conversation straight to the personal. You always do, and then accuse us of doing it." She paused. "Oh, I don't mind, really!" she cried in a different tone. "But you will *not* notice things, Chris; you sail through the world in your own sweet way, and you never do! For instance—Jenny."

The evil subject was back again; they could not keep it out. Francine spoke in an off-hand tone:

"I don't suppose you even noticed she was making a play for you, did you?"

"Nonsense."

"She jolly well was!" cried Francine, firing up.

He sat back and stared at her. Into his mind, doubtfully, had come a gleam of light; and with it a feeling of uproarious happiness sang through him. They looked at each other, each knowing the other knew.

"I wish I could persuade *you*," he said, "that I am the fair-haired prize-package you seem to believe other women think. Jenny? That's impossible! I never————"

"Thought of it? Neither did poor old Harvey Wrayburn, as decent a sort as there is, until she got after him during a long sea-voyage. She really was a terror, Chris. She did it as much to amuse herself as anything else. What annoys me is that I can't see how she did it, or how she had the knack. But she was most definitely going out to make a play for you."

"But I hope you don't think I—? To begin with, she was Rod's wife————"

"Your cousin's wife. Yes. And you wouldn't think of making love to the wife of a friend of yours, would you? In fact, the idea rather shocks you, doesn't it?"

"Frankly, yes," he admitted with what he hoped was dignity. "Your friends' wives are—well, damn it, I mean ————"

"Not-to-be-thought-of-like-that," said Francine. "Oh, Chris, you are an old mossback!"

"Very interesting," he said coldly. "I suppose that in Russia————"

"Don't you say anything about Russia!"

"I was merely about to point out————"

"Don't you see, Chris," she urged with great sincerity, "that the moral issue involved is precisely the same whether the woman is your friend's wife or the wife of someone you don't know? You wouldn't make love to

Rod's wife; but you'd have no compunction—not you!—about making love to the wife of some poor devil who's making maybe two pounds a week, and has to stay at a factory all day, and hasn't your leisure to————"

"One moment," he said, rather dazed. "So far as I remember, I never said one word about roaring round the country after other men's wives. As a menace to the home I am practically nil. But will you explain to me how it is that we can never touch on any subject without your somehow coming round to the political and economic aspect of it? I'll swear you and the world and Davy Jones seem to have gone politics-mad————"

"Indeed," observed Francine with sweet savagery. "It must be so nice, it must be so stimulating, for you to sit on your Olympian height and watch all the little imbeciles crawl about in the valley. I was attempting to explain, in as elementary a way as I could, that it is your kind of outworn, stupid codes and shibboleths which have made such a mess of the country————"

"Well, would it please you any better if I made love *both* to my friend's wife and the factory-worker's wife? Do you think we should be happier then?"

"My God, Chris Kent, there are times when I could kill you. You go and make love to whom you like! You————"

"That's what I am trying to do, my dear. Only————"

"*Ahem*," said Dr. Fell.

They stopped. The vast presence of Dr. Fell towered over the table, beaming down with doubtful but benevolent interest, and following the thrusts with his head as you follow strokes in a tennis match. Now he cleared his throat. Francine, radiant with cold anger, put a handkerchief to her lips; but she burst out laughing instead.

"Ah, that is better," beamed Dr. Fell. "Heh-heh-heh. I dislike to interrupt; but the waiter has been hanging about the table for the past five minutes with the *hors-d'œuvre* wagon, and hesitating to say, 'Sardine?' for fear it should seem to have a personal application."

"He's a pig-headed—" said Francine.

"I have no doubt of it, my dear," said Dr. Fell, cheerfully. "In fact, it is a very good sign. The woman who does not think her husband is pig-headed is already beginning to dominate him, and that would be bad. I beg your pardon: I do not wish to begin an argument about equality or inequality in marriage. As the Frenchman said about love-making, 'Never before the fish!' But, if I might make a suggestion here, I should suggest that you get married; then you could stop being on the defensive and begin to enjoy yourselves."

"Jenny got married," said Francine.

"Not now," interposed Dr. Fell, with sudden strong authority. "Not that—just now."

That meal was like a loosening or unbuckling of armour, while the doctor's face grew redder and redder, and his chuckles more explosive behind the wine-bottles. However unbelievable his anecdotes became, however his rapid paradoxes gave his listeners the impression that they had just been whirled round a particularly fast switchback after having drunk two Seidletz powders, it was all directed towards one thing: putting these two at their ease. What a master of ceremonies he made Kent never fully realised until afterwards. But it was not until they were padded round against night and the things of night, over the brandy, that the subject was introduced again.

"Harvey should have heard that story—" began Francine.

Dr. Fell trimmed the ash off his cigar, and blinked sideways at her.

"Yes. Now is the time," he said. "What do you think of the whole affair, Miss Forbes?"

"I can answer that. It's the idea of—someone close to you—doing all that," she told him quietly. "Someone you've known a long time, but who's got a hinge loose. I don't think I'm afraid, though. I think it's all over."

"Why?"

"Because the poker was left behind this time." She took

a deep inhalation of her cigarette, and spoke in the same even tone. "It wouldn't have been left stuck in those towels if somebody had had a further use for it. Unless, of course—well, unless someone has grown too fond of blood. But I can't credit that. I was trying to tell Chris what I thought, a while ago."

She considered.

"Some people might have been able to take Jenny, and Jenny's ways, lightly. I could, for instance. Probably most people could. But the tenth person mightn't be able to see her in so light-hearted a way. I've often wondered what Rod thought of her. Oh, she managed him, and her noted devotion to him, beautifully. Do you know, it was all so skilful that it was rumoured—and many people believed, at the time—*Rod* was marrying *Jenny* for her money?"

The glasses almost dropped off Dr. Fell's nose; he gave one wheeze through that nose. Then he said:

"Repeat that, please."

"It's true! It went all round our crowd in South Africa; and it's the first thing Sir Gyles Gay joked Rod about (subtly, of course) when we came over here; so the version was pretty broad and pretty garbled. It hurt Rod a good deal, though he simply said nothing about it and never even bothered to deny it. But I think some people even in our crowd believed it."

"Was she wealthy?"

"Well-off, anyway. I think."

"From what source?"

"From her parents, we thought, though a stony veldt farm isn't usually—and then her dressmaking business must have been very profitable. She had wonderful taste in clothes, there's no getting away from that."

"But why are you so interested in that piece of gossip?" demanded Kent.

"Because it's merely the motive for your cousin Rodney's murder," groaned Dr. Fell. "Oh, Lord, what a duffer I've been! What a thundering idiot! And yet there was no hint—!" He knocked his fists against his temples. "You see, the first murder was the one which wouldn't fit into any rational scheme of things. It wasn't rational sense; it wasn't even rational insanity. But Rodney marrying the woman for her money: that provides a very deadly and sane explanation."

"How? If you know anything," urged Francine, her too-fair skin flushed with wine, and looking less poised and more beautiful than Kent had ever seen her: "if you know anything, or guess anything, *won't* you tell us? It isn't just curiosity. It's to keep the devils out."

"That's fair enough," said Kent.

It was a little time before Dr. Fell answered.

"No!" he roared. "No, by the temple of Eleusis! And there's one main reason why I don't. I think (mind you, I say I think) I know just half this affair; with luck I may be able to get the other half. But there's a strong possibility, on which I am balanced at the moment, that the explanation may be exactly opposite to what I think it is: for that reason I haven't even dared to explain fully to Hadley. And he has some new information. I don't want to raise your hopes, and put you off-guard in case————"

"Eleusis," repeated Kent, as Dr. Fell stopped in mid-sentence. "If Wrayburn were here, with his mine of good-for-nothing lore, we might get that explained. Didn't the Eleusinian mysteries celebrate the descent of Persephone into the underworld, and her return to the light of day? System of rewards and punishments?" He added, " 'To wake the dead.' "

Dr. Fell chuckled. " *'Pale beyond porch and portal, Crowned with calm leaves she stands—'* It's a curious thing about Swinburne, but the more intolerably doleful the poem, the more the rich gusto with which you can recite it. *'Who gathers all things mortal, With cold immortal hands————' "*

"Who does?" inquired Francine, who had a practical mind. "What on earth are you talking about?"

"Yes, we had better stop it. But the character of Mrs. Kent fascinates me as it unfolds. If we had only seen her, if we had only known after Rodney Kent's death what we know now, we might have been able to prevent Mrs. Kent's death." Dr. Fell brooded. "Or could we? I don't know. I doubt it."

"You think there's still—danger?"

"There's no danger," said Dr. Fell, "if you keep your door locked at night. I'm sorry if I seem to act as a Job's comforter; but we have got to take care of all possibilities. Can either of you help me? You must have some ideas. Where would you look?"

Kent thought of his sheaf of notes.

"My trouble is," he replied despondently, "that even now I can't look at the thing with an eye of human reason. All I can think of is how I should make it work out if I were writing the story. That's the phobia of all fiction-writers. I tell you, according to the laws of fiction there's only one possible solution and only one possible murderer! But it's not only guessing at an artistic solution; it's a very strong case. And yet————"

Dr. Fell looked at him with interest. "I know," he said guiltily. "I thought of that, too."

"You thought of what?"

From the breast pocket of his coat Dr. Fell began to take out an enormous collection of old papers and envelopes (there were enough of them to stuff a waste-paper basket) until he found the stub of a pencil. On one comparatively clean surface of paper he wrote a few words. Then he turned the paper over and pushed it across to Kent.

"Write down," he suggested, "the name of the person who springs to your mind as the murderer. That's it: thank you. Now, Miss Forbes, take this piece of paper and look at both sides."

Francine stared at it.

"But you've both written down the same name!"

"Of course," agreed Dr. Fell gloomily. "Kenneth Hardwick, the manager of the Royal Scarlet Hotel."

Chapter 12

Above Suspicion?

FRANCINE, it appeared, could not understand whether they were joking or whether Dr. Fell's glum face was as serious as it looked.

"But you don't honestly mean that? Or is this another of Chris's ridiculous—That nice quiet man?"

"You really will throw suspicion on him if you talk like that," Dr. Fell grunted. "Let's hear the case against him."

"To begin with, it's a question of keys," said Kent. "Somebody got into that linen-closet and took out fifteen bath-towels and one face-towel. Therefore somebody had to open the door of the linen-closet: unless the maid failed to lock it last night. There's no sign of burglarious entry, so apparently the door must have been opened with a key. But, according to this new system of locks—here I'm quoting Hardwick himself—it's impossible for any unauthorized person to open even so much as a linen-closet. Now I remember it, he used the word 'linen-closet.' On the other hand, again quoting him, he alone can open any door in the whole building. That's a short and simple point to start with."

"Good," said Dr. Fell. "Go on."

"Next, the question of disguise. There couldn't be any more admirable disguise for him than the uniform of one of his own attendants. It's like the story he told about the porter who dressed up in pyjamas and pretended to be a guest. If Hardwick were seen by one of the real guests, he wouldn't be recognised even if someone got a glimpse of his face: the uniform would do the trick. He would know, furthermore, that he ran very little danger of being spotted by one of his own employees: the only employee who could come upstairs after eleven-thirty would be one of the under-porters, and on such large floors he wouldn't have much difficulty in hiding himself if he saw the under-porter coming. As two additional points, I might mention that his private rooms are on the seventh floor; and that he would have easy access to any kind of uniform he chose to wear. You notice that the mysterious costume hasn't been found. But, if it were a real uniform belonging to the hotel, why should it be found?"

"Chris, that's awfully good," said Francine. "Do you think it's true?"

He reflected.

"I don't know; I'm only saying it's the way a story should work. For the crux of it is this: the production of an alibi."

"The clocks!" said Dr. Fell with a wheeze of great pleasure.

"Yes. You think of the dozens of wall-clocks in that hotel, all worked from a central switch, and you've got it first shot. I remember we had the same sort of system at school. One day, in the Schoolroom, roars of delight were caused when the clock on the wall went crazy: its hands began to whirl round the dial and point to all hours like something in a pantomime. What had happened—a master informed us acidly—was that all the clocks in the building had stopped, and were being re-set from a controlling-station in the headmaster's study.

"Now, you can see the beauty of that device. Suppose a murderer wants fifteen minutes out for an alibi, and this person has access to the master-clock. Well, he gets hold of the dupe who is later to swear to his presence; he talks to the dupe between (let's say) 11:55 and 12:10; then he dismisses the witness. Whereupon he goes to the master-clock and sets it back to 11:55: *thereby altering every clock in the building.* Out he goes to commit his murder. He may even let himself be seen. Afterwards he returns to his office, and puts every clock right again. He has created a hiatus in time of ten to fifteen minutes; and his dupe will later swear to his alibi during the time the murder was committed. The excellence of it is that he runs no risk of being caught out, or having anybody notice a discrepancy in time; no matter who looks at no matter what clock, they will all have precisely the same time. And, at the Royal Scarlet, in whose charge would the master-clock be? I'll lay you a fiver it's the manager. Hardwick, you observe, has an alibi for just those minutes."

He stopped in some doubt, and finished his brandy with a feeling of defiance.

"It really is good," admitted Francine. "It's so horribly ingenious that I can't believe a word of it."

"I am afraid that will be the general impression," beamed Dr. Fell. "Though I like the idea very much myself. It might, you see, cause some curiosity if a chance guest glanced at one of the clocks and saw its hands suddenly jump fifteen minutes in one way or another."

"At midnight? How many people were abroad in the halls then? I'll acknowledge," said Kent, hunching his shoulders, "that it still leaves much to be explained." The grizzled, amiable figure of Hardwick rose in his mind. "Where's the motive? Unless he's somebody out of Jenny's dark past; you appear to think she has one. What's the reason for all that hocus-pocus with shoes and 'Dead Woman' signs? Why, after getting into the room, does the murderer take Jenny's own key and shove it into the lock outside the door———"

"H'mf, yes. I told you that was an intriguing point."

"———and, lastly, which in sequence was firstly, why was

the same uniform worn at Gay's place in Sussex? Every explanation of the case, as you said this morning, takes a violent header over the first apparance of the uniform in a country house at two o'clock in the morning. Unless ————"

"Keep at it!" urged Dr. Fell. "You're going great guns. That's the point on which I vary badly need help. Why?"

"Symbolic meaning in a uniform?"

"Harrumph—well. Maybe."

"I believe I've got it," said Francine, putting down her cigarette and looking at the lamp in a startled fashion. "Did Hardwick know Dan had booked rooms for all of us at the Royal Scarlet?"

"Yes, naturally. Dan arranged it a long time ago, before any of us left South Africa."

"The murderer," she told them, "was seen at North-field in a uniform because he *wanted* to be seen. That was the reason for it! He wanted to draw attention to the uniform. If he hadn't been observed by the drunk on the sofa, he'd have said Boo to someone else. Think of him walking straight down the hall, like—like someone behind footlights, do you see? It was easy. He shook the drunk by the shoulder, and then let himself be seen much too obviously. But that must mean—no, don't say anything, Chris!—that must mean he was preparing everybody's mind for his appearance later, when he came to kill Jenny —preparing our minds to see—but where is there any indication in just a coat and a pair of trousers?" She paused. "I'm afraid that's the best I can do."

Dr. Fell studied her with an odd frown. "I should not be surprised," he commented, "if that remark came closer to the truth than anything we have heard."

"Meaning?" asked Kent.

"Meaning that Hadley and I are trying to work out a plan of campaign. To-morrow we are going down to Northfield; and we're—h'mf—well, we're going to ask all your party to go down there as well. In the first place, Sir Gyles Gay's house interests me. In the second place, I want to go to the jail and see Mr. Ritchie Bellowes; specifically, I want to find out what he was really supposed to see."

"Supposed to see?"

"Yes. Isn't it fairly obvious?" inquired Dr. Fell, opening his eyes. "I think you're quite right in one respect, Miss Forbes. There had to be a witness to see our figure in uniform walking down the hall. What do you think of the theory that Ritchie Bellowes was deliberately chosen?"

"Hold on," protested Kent; "I don't follow that. How do you mean, deliberately chosen? The murderer couldn't have known that the village toper would have come wandering in conveniently on the very night of the murder."

"Oh, yes, he could," said Dr. Fell, "if the village toper had been summoned."

For a time he remained wheezing, his eyes half-shut, and then he went on in an abstracted tone:

"Very well, I'll give you a hint; and you can see what you make of it. Not enough attention, I think, has been paid to the first murder. First tell me this: did any of your party ever meet Bellowes before he was found in the house that night?"

"No, we didn't exactly meet him," said Francine. "Our amiable host brought him in one night during the first week we were there, as a sort of hired entertainer, to show us his mental tricks. You'd riffle through a pack of cards in front of him and he'd afterwards tell you each of the cards in the order he saw them. You mix up several dozen articles on a table, and he identifies them all after one second's look; that sort of thing. Tall, hollow-eyed chap, very pleasant-spoken. He talked to us casually. Then our host took him out to the kitchen and sent him home full of whisky. I thought it was rather rotten of Sir Gyles, because that used to be Bellowes's home, you know. That was why, when Rod was killed, we thought at first————"

Dr. Fell shook his head, fiery with argumentativeness.

"Now consider the following indications! I pointed out to Hadley this morning Bellowes's importance in the case.

You see, his presence there on the very night of a particularly brutal murder was a little too fortuitous. The man himself was unquestionably dead drunk and incapable of mischief. His presence there might be a coincidence, a somewhat painful tearing of coincidence; but there were certain indications against it.

"First (you recall), when he was found on the sofa at two o'clock in the morning he had a key to the house in his pocket. That meant either that someone had given him a key, or it was an old one of his own; but, in either case, it meant he had left his lodgings early that evening intending to go to his old home—and intended it before he had taken a drop to drink! What, then, becomes of the homing pigeon reeling back by instinct?

"Second, he concluded his evening at the pub, contrary to custom, by drinking whisky and going away with a pint of it. Now, I don't know whether you know anything about the habits of village pubs. I, to my joy, do. The drink there is beer, because spirits are too expensive. Whisky is a luxury reserved for rare and mystic occasions. Bellowes, we know, was almost penniless; his usual tap was beer; but on this occasion, *with* a key to the house in his pocket, he orders whisky. It looked as though someone had been supplying him with extra cash. Why?

"Third, you recall that Bellowes's finger-prints were actually found in the room where Rodney Kent was murdered—which made it look very bad for him—although Bellowes absolutely denied ever having been in that room. He had at least looked in there, since the prints were round the light-switch. But he didn't remember it.

"Suppose Bellowes had been summoned or invited to the house at a certain hour. But why? It assuredly was not to be a scapegoat for the real murderer. If this had been so, he would have been made a far more thoroughgoing scapegoat. The poker, instead of vanishing mysteriously from the house, would have been found in his hand. There would have been blood on him; and finger-prints in more damning places than merely round the light-switch.

Furthermore, the real murderer would have known—stop; or would he wonder?—that Bellowes's nearly paralysed left arm would make it impossible for him to have strangled Rodney Kent in the crushing two-handed grip that was used.

"Yet, the more I turned it over, the more it seemed to me certain that Bellowes had been invited there. In short, he was to be a witness: as he was. A far from sober witness: as he was. An incurious witness: as he was. A witness with a photographic memory: as he was. And a complete witness to some skilful and evil design for strangling, planned to throw suspicion on the wrong person: as, alas, he was *not*. He got too drunk. What might he have seen when he looked into the room where Rodney Kent was killed? In other words, what lies just under the surface of this first crime, which is rather more devilish than the second? Bellowes saw part of what he was meant to see. But was there anything else? Archons of Athens! I wish I knew! And we are going down to Sussex to find out."

Ending on a note of some savagery, Dr. Fell drew out a large red bandana handkerchief, mopped his forehead with it, and blinked at the other two from under its folds. He added:

"I trust you take my meaning?"

"But if someone invited or got Bellowes to the house," muttered Kent, "it must have been the murderer. Consequently, Bellowes must know who the murderer is?"

Dr. Fell put away the bandana. "I wish it were as simple as that. But I'm afraid it's not. Bellowes, you see, could hardly have been paid to keep silent when he himself was in danger. I don't think he suspects at all; if he did, perhaps it's just as well that he's safely in jail. What I am going to do, you perceive, is find out what he was supposed to see on the night of January 14th. I am going to dig into the subconscious; and digging into the subconscious, we are assured by the tenets of the newest science, inevitably produces a nightmare. Shall we have a final brandy?"

Their cab prowled up Piccadilly, the chains on its wheels clanking faintly. Dr. Fell had gone home, more silent than was usual with him; and Kent had told the driver to take a turn anywhere he liked. It was warm enough to be pleasant inside the cab. Pale lamps looked in on them; the street was churned to slush, but by the time they turned into the high dimness of the Park, there were lawns of snow outside the windows and the bare trees wore bonnets. Francine, a bundle of furs topped by yellow hair that fluffed out over them, leaned against his shoulder and stared straight ahead. He had just put his hand on a cold hand when she spoke.

"Chris, do you know who he suspects?"

"Who—?" For a moment Kent was puzzled; it seemed incongruous at such a time. Though she pressed his hand, she did not turn round. "I don't know," he confessed. "Harvey Wrayburn seems out of the running, and my elaborate case against Hardwick was, I admit, sheer fireworks. I don't like to think of anyone else."

"He suspects Melitta Reaper."

It was so abrupt and so startling that he dropped her hand. Of her face he could so far see only the tip of her nose; now she moved, turning towards him squarely.

"Meli—rubbish!"

"It's not, Chris. I know. I can feel these things." She spoke with fierce intensity. "You think a minute and you'll realise it. Do you remember? I was maundering along, trying to find a reason for someone wearing the uniform. I hardly knew what I was saying—but I saw his eyes. I said, 'But where is there any indication in just a coat and a pair of trousers?' A pair of trousers, Chris; it was as though I had made some kind of slip of the tongue. And he didn't thunder out. He just said it was closer to the truth than anything else. It was enough to give me gooseflesh, because I saw. Why would a murderer be so horri-

bly anxious every time to print a picture in our heads of a
man, a man in an especially mannish kind of uniform?
You see? Because it's a woman."

He looked at the white face over the furs, with the
large, long brown eyes shifting slightly. The run and
crossing of car-lamps among the trees shifted like her
eyes; and the wheels seemed to hammer loudly.

"But that's crazier than any of my guesses! You don't
believe it, do you?"

"No; I suppose I don't, really, but————"

"But what?"

"Chris, I've been a beast. I suppose, from now on, I'll
tell you every thought that's in my head; because I'd like
to; but I'm always having them." She seemed rather incoherent from the strain of the past weeks, but she spoke
in a quiet voice, looking up now and again. "Suppose it's
Dan himself who's been tied up with Jenny? It's quite possible, you know: living in the same house, and Jenny being what she was. To say nothing of the fact that Dan's
close to being a millionaire. You saw how queer Dan was
to-day when we talked about Jenny's real nature, didn't
you? And didn't it strike you that Melitta was just a little
too quick to defend Jenny, and say bah-bah-my-dears-
there's-nothing-in-it, and act in a way that's not exactly
like her? If Dan is the man in the case, the one from whom
Jenny has been getting all the cheques————"

He felt cold, though he would have nothing to do with
the idea.

"Well, old girl, in my opinion it's still raving lunacy.
Melitta: definitely not. Why should she?"

"You say I'm mad on economics. But you know how
Melitta is about plain money."

"But how does Rod fit in?"

"Jenny lived off Dan; Rod was supposed to live off
Jenny————"

"Come here," he ordered. "And forget that gibberish.
If we go on like this, there'll be nobody at all we can dare
trust. We can't go on feeling that everybody round us is a

hobgoblin. Why not Dan himself? Why not me? Why not you?"

"Why not?" she said, and plucked at a button of his overcoat. The bundle of furs stirred; the cab jolted slightly, and moved on into the darkest curve of the park. "I wonder," she added in a small voice, "just what that chap Bellowes will say?"

Chapter 13

A Welcome at Four Doors

ALL I can say," replied Ritchie Bellowes, "is what I have said. I'm sorry I went there, but I don't see that I did any great harm."

He sat back on the bunk of the cell and regarded his visitors with an air of polite cynicism which was not even marred by the stubble on his face. He was that rare product, a gentleman; and it was all the more odd to meet him in a jail in Sussex. Tall, with dark hair in a wide parting, he looked even more hollow-eyed from his fortnight's enforced sobriety. He wore a grey shirt open at the neck, and a pair of brown braces with one button missing made him hitch his shoulder frequently.

They had gone down to Sussex early on the morning of February 1st, Christopher Kent accompanying Dr. Fell and Hadley, and the others arranging to follow on a faster train. The nine-fifteen from Charing Cross idled through the succession of tunnels which make the Kentish hills seem to shut away London as though with a wall. The flat lands beyond were stiff with snow. Dr. Fell was occupied with a vast series of notes, spreading over from one small piece of paper to the other, so Hadley gave up any attempt to talk to him and settled down glumly with a crossword puzzle. They changed at Tonbridge; and, the nearest station to Northfield being Eglamore, a police car was waiting for them there.

Northfield, an attractive enough village in summer, now carried out its reputation sufficiently to look like something off a Christmas-card. Great pillars of yew-hedge before the church, and arching over the lychgate, were powdered with snow. The village green, hard earth, sloped down to the public-house of the Stag and Glove, as though tilting its inhabitants there; it was fronted by low houses of white weather-boarding and others of that faded half-timbering which looks brittle to the touch. The visitors, after having been inside several of the houses, thought that they had never seen so many oak beams; oak beams seemed to sprout and crowd, to the manifest pleasure of the owners; but living inside too many oak beams, Kent decided, must be like living inside the stomach of a zebra.

They did not go to Four Doors, Sir Gyles's house, since Gay himself had not arrived. After (at Dr. Fell's insistence) testing the local brew at the Stag and Glove, and finding it good, they went on to the district police-station on the road to Porting. The station consisted of two converted semi-detached houses, and was presided over like a householder by Inspector Tanner. Dr. Fell—one or two of whose great sheaf of notes had suffered from having fallen into the beer—was determined to conduct the examination of Bellowes. After a great unlocking of underground doors, they found Bellowes reasonably courteous, but apathetic and cynical.

"Look here, I'll be frank," said Dr. Fell, getting down to business with a directness which pained Hadley. "We're here because we're not satisfied you told the whole truth about the night of January 14th."

"Sorry," said Bellowes. "But I've already said it a hundred times. *I—did—not————*"

"Now, steady!" urged Dr. Fell, with a redder tinge in his face. "The question is not what you did; the question is why you did it. Quick! Did someone tell you to go to Four Doors on that night?"

Bellowes had been reading a well-thumbed Wild West magazine. Now he put it down on the floor beside the bunk; and, stirred out his apathy, regarded the doctor with what Kent could have sworn was genuine surprise.

"No," he said.

"You're sure of that, now?"

"I'm certain of it. What's all this? Why should—well, why should anybody want me there? Why should anybody want me anywhere?" he added, with a rush of bitterness which was dangerously near self-pity.

"You still maintain you wandered there of your own accord, while you were drunk, and had no intention of doing it beforehand?"

"I don't know why I went there. Yes, I suppose I do know; but you understand what I mean. But I hadn't any intention of doing that early in the evening. I honestly don't go about breaking into people's houses as a rule, and I can't understand how it happened."

"How do you explain the fact that there was a key to the house in your pocket?"

"Key? But I always carry that key; I've carried it for years," replied Bellowes, bringing his heel down with some violence on the floor. "Ask my landlady. Ask anybody. I don't suppose I'm entitled to it; but Sir Gyles knows I have it————"

"Forgive my mentioning this: but you were rather in funds on the night of the fourteenth?"

The other's face grew pinched.

"I was."

"Well?"

"You may have heard," said Bellowes gravely, "that I gave a little tame conjuring entertainment for the guests at Four Doors. As I was leaving Sir Gyles pushed an envelope in my pocket. There was more in that envelope than I deserved; and, just between ourselves, than I had—hoped for. We used to learn a lot of tosh about people being too proud to accept charity. I was not."

"Damn and blast!" said Dr. Fell. He opened and shut his hands; he would have surged up with oratorical thun-

der had the size of the place permitted it. After a curt remonstrance from Hadley, he subsided to mutterings, and
pursued the subject with almost ghoulish hopefulness.

"Would you maintain in court that nobody prompted
you to go to that house?"

"I would."

"Humph. Ha. If you don't mind, I'd like to take you
over that statement of yours. But, first, as a general thing:
you know Sir Gyles Gay fairly well?"

"I'm acquainted with him. That is, I've been to the
house two or three times in the past year."

"When you went there to entertain the guests, I suppose
you met all of them?"

Bellowes frowned. "Yes, I was introduced to all of
them—I think. I didn't talk much to them, barring when
they asked questions: except to Mr. Reaper. I liked him,"
said Bellowes, staring at the past. "He's my style, somehow. He asked me if I'd like to get a new start in South
Africa, and I think he meant it."

"Did you meet Rodney Kent, who was later————"

"It's a queer thing about that. I suppose he must have
been there, because he was one of the party: as I have
good reason to remember, God knows. But I can't remember seeing him at all."

"Did you ever see any of the others on any subsequent
occasion?"

"Yes, but not to speak to. Mr. Reaper dropped in at the
pub one evening later, but he was in the private bar and I
was in the public. I didn't have—have the nerve to walk
in and say good evening. Then another of them was in the
pub early on the night—the night it all happened; but
that was very early in the evening."

"Which one was it?"

"I think the one named Wrayburn. But he was only
there to order half a dozen of sherry, and didn't stay more
than a minute or two."

Dr. Fell made another note. Hadley was growing restive; and Bellowes, whose long sobriety had done him no
good, was beginning to twitch.

"Now, about the night of the 14th in question," rumbled the doctor. "Let's begin with the time you were in the bar of the Stag and Glove. What made you change to whisky and go away with a bottle of it?"

"Oh, I don't know. Why do you ever do anything like that? I thought of it, and so I did."

"Yes. I know," admitted Dr. Fell. "With the idea of going out to this clearing called Grinning Copse and drinking the bottle?"

"That's right. If I take a bottle home, Mrs. Witherson always starts to preach. She waits up for me. I hope you find this helpful," said Bellowes between his teeth.

"How drunk were you?" asked Dr. Fell blandly.

"I was—padded. Muzzy."

"Have you got a strong head?"

"No."

"You started for Grinning Copse, I understand, at closing-time: ten o'clock? H'mf, yes. You sat down on an iron bench or chair in the copse and began on the whisky. Never mind; I know you've made a statement; but just tell me everything that comes back to you in connection with it."

"There's nothing more I can tell," answered Bellowes, with a duller colour in his face. "Things began to run together and mix up then, but that was what I wanted them to do. I've got a hazy idea that at one point someone was talking to me; but don't take this too seriously—I was probably speaking aloud myself. Reciting or something. I'm sorry; that's everything. The next thing I knew I was sitting on some different kind of surface, which turned out to be leather; and in some different kind of place, which turned out to be the upstairs hall at Four Doors. You know what I did. I thought it was as good a place as any, so I just lay down on the sofa."

"Can you put a time to any of this; even an approximate time?"

"No."

"You say in your statement to the police—where are we?—'At this time I do not think I went to sleep immediately. While I was lying there,' and so on to describe the appearance of the figure in uniform. Are you certain you did not go to sleep?"

"No, I'm not sure."

"What I am endeavouring to establish is this," persisted Dr. Fell, with such unwonted sticking to the point that Hadley was disturbed. Every wheeze seemed to emphasise a word. "Were you conscious of an interval, any time between your lying down on the sofa and the time you saw the figure?"

"I don't know," groaned Bellowes, massaging the veins in the back of his hand. "Don't you think I've been over all that a hundred times? I think there was an interval, yes. Something to do with the light—the moonlight. But I'm not sure what." He broke off. "Are you a lawyer, by the way?"

Dr. Fell certainly sounded like one, though it was a suggestion which at any other time he would have repudiated with some heat.

"You'd call it a kind of semi-conscious state, then?"

"Yes, that's a polite way of putting it."

"While you were lying there, do you remember any sounds, anyone moving, anything like that?"

"No."

"But what roused you? I'm digging in here, you see. Something must have made you look up, or stirred you in some way?"

"I suppose it did," the other admitted doubtfully. "I have a vague impression that it may have been someone talking, or maybe whispering. But that's the closest I can get."

"Now listen. I'm going to read over a part of your statement again.

I should describe him as a medium-sized man wearing a uniform such as you see in the big hotels like the Royal Scarlet or the Royal Purple. It was a dark-blue uniform with a long coat, and silver or brass buttons; I

could not be sure about colours in the moonlight. I
think there was a stripe round the cuffs, a dark red
stripe. He was carrying a kind of tray, and at first he
stood in the corner and did not move.

Question: What about his face?

I could not make out his face, because there seemed
to be a lot of shadow, or a hole or something, where
his eyes ought to be.

Dr. Fell put down the sheet. In the light and warmth of
a town, in a soft-carpeted hotel, such a figure had seemed
merely fantastic. Here in the sealed countryside it was beginning to assume hues of something else altogether. Kent,
who had not before dwelt too closely on that description
of the face, felt a sensation very similar to that with which
he had first seen Jenny's body.

"Have you anything to add to that, Mr. Bellowes?"

"No. I'm sorry."

"Would you recognise the face if you saw it again?"

"No, I don't think so. It was a fattish kind of face, I
think; or the shadows or something gave it that effect.
Man," cried Bellowes, and, to everyone's acute discomfort, the tears of raw nerves or self-pity overflowed his
eyes, "what do you think I am? I wasn't in any condition
to see it. If I hadn't been what they call a camera-eye observer, I shouldn't have seen anything at all, probably,
and maybe I'm all out of focus as it is."

"Now, steady!" urged Dr. Fell, disturbed. He wheezed
violently. "You make a reference here to the 'Blue Room.'
Was that where Mr. Kent was killed?"

"So they tell me."

"And you didn't go in there?"

Bellowes grew more quiet. "I know all about those
finger-prints, or alleged finger-prints. But, in spite of them,
I don't honestly think I did go in there, even when I was
drunk. From the time I was a kid I never liked that room.
It was my grandfather's, you see, that's the reason for all
the old-fashioned furniture, which went when I disposed

of the house: and to keep me quiet, when I was a kid, my father turned the old man into something like an ogre."

"One last point, Mr. Bellowes. Do you remember this tray or salver?"

"I remember seeing it."

Dr. Fell leaned forward. "Was there anything on it?"

"On it?"

"Carried on it. Think! A number of small articles are put out in front of you, and you remember them all. It's your gift. You must use it. Was there anything on that tray?"

Ritchie Bellowes put up a hand and rubbed his forehead; he stared down at the Wild West magazine; he shuffled his feet; and nothing happened.

"I'm sorry," he apologised for the dozenth time. "No. There may have been. I don't remember."

"Thank you very much," Dr. Fell said in a dispirited voice. "That's all."

But even so he had not finished. When they were on their way out he went back to ask the prisoner still one more question; whatever it was, Bellowes seemed to return a decided negative, and this appeared to cheer the doctor somewhat. During this interview Hadley, who had been corking himself down, had with some effort managed to keep silent. But when they were driving back to Northfield he let himself go.

"All right," said the superintendent grimly. "Let's hear it. I asked you much the same sort of question once before. What was being carried on that salver? Somebody's head?"

"Yes," replied Dr. Fell with every evidence of seriousness. "Mine. A sheep's head, and a whacking great one, too. You know, I never realised until last night the purpose or meaning of that salver. It presented a real problem; and yet it's quite simple. I must be running on senile decay."

"Good," said Hadley. "I mean, I'm glad you find it so easy. I confess that so far it escapes me. But that's not the main point. You're not going to divert me from the solid information I got from South Africa. You were bombarding me with a hell of a lot of 'suggestive' points yesterday evening, among them your new idea that somebody invited Bellowes to the house early in the evening on the night of the murder. What becomes of that now?"

Dr. Fell made a handsome concession. "I withdraw it in the form in which it was presented. I also call your attention————"

"More suggestive points?"

"Didn't you see any?"

"As soon as I begin to hear the call of mumbo-jumbo," Hadley snapped, "I begin to have an idea (yes, I'll admit it) that you're probably on the right track. But I still don't like it. One of these days, my lad, you're going to come a cropper; and it will be the world's most outstanding cropper. Why do you want our party buried down here again? If you want a look at the house, couldn't you do it without bringing them back here? When they're in London, at least I've got an idea I could keep my eye on them. But I've got no such comfortable feeling about Northfield."

For a moment Dr. Fell did not reply. Their car circled the green at Northfield, and eased its way down a gravel road beside the church: a road dusted with snow as lightly as you might dust finger-print powder. At the end of a gradual descent the hedges curved and opened on the small grounds of Four Doors. The house was of that style of Queen Anne architecture which seems at once massive and yet squeezed together, as though the designer had tried to crowd too many arched windows into deep walls. The bricks were of a grimy colour; the front door, painted white like the window-facings, was as square as the house's heavy length; and dead wistaria clung to its face. An abrupt little garden, with a herbaceous border and a sundial in a brick path up the centre, also clung to the front of it. The party from London had evidently arrived from the station: a big black sedan, cut ropes hanging from its luggage-grid, was slewed round in the drive. Behind the house you could see the slope of the hill, and one great elm against the sky. A wind blowing down from the east brought, very distinctly, the sound of the church clock striking noon.

They looked at it for a time; while that wind rattled in the bushes and a little dust-devil of snow danced round the sundial.

"You see what I mean?" inquired Hadley.

"I do not see what you mean," said Dr. Fell. "Will you accept my assurance that there is absolutely no danger?"

The door was opened for them by Sir Gyles Gay, before their car had even come to a stop. Gay stood on the threshold with that slightly shivering air, as of one on the edge of a pool, with which many hosts either welcome or bid good-bye. He seemed still interested, even smiling, his hands behind his back as though in meditation. But his very correct tie was rumpled, and he greeted them with a certain gravity.

"Come in, gentlemen. I was wondering how long you would be. We have been here only an hour, but even in that time there have been certain happenings. Country air seems to have a curious effect."

Hadley stopped dead on the doorstep.

"No, no," their host assured them, with wrinkled amusement. "Not what you may be thinking; nothing serious. I mean that country air seems to bring about a sense of humour. But it is an unusual and perverted sense of humour, and,"—he looked back over his shoulder into a warm, comfortable hall—"I can't say I like it."

"What's happened?"

Again Gay looked over his shoulder; but he made no move to go inside.

"You remember my telling you yesterday that we played all sorts of parlour games down here, including that of pinning a paper tail on a paper donkey?"

"Yes; well?" said Dr. Fell.

"I did not know, when you asked whether we would all come down here, whether you wanted us for the day only, or for several days. Anyhow, I set aside rooms for you gentlemen, in case you should care to honour me with a visit." He looked at Dr. Fell. "It concerns the room which is at your disposal, doctor. Within the last half-hour, someone has had the highly humorous notion of taking a paper donkey's tail and pinning it to the door of your bed-room."

They looked at each other. But nobody was amused.

"That, however, is not all," Gay went on, sticking out his neck and looking round each corner of the door. "The humorist has gone even further. Put in a highly ingenious place—where somebody was certain to find it soon—I discovered this."

He took his hands from behind his back and held out a piece of stiff paper. It was a group photograph some eight by ten inches, taken by one of those professionals who lie in wait at amusement resorts and persuade you to buy the photograph afterwards. Kent recognised it easily as being the inside of the "fun-fair" at the Luna Park outside Dur-ban. He remembered the slope of a rafter, a lemonade-stand by a window. The picture was taken from the top of the broad platform of one of those big slides or chutes by which you sail down into darkness. All the members of Dan's crowd were standing at the top of the chute, most of them turning laughing faces towards the camera—though Melitta was looking dignified and Francine an-noyed. Someone, who could not be seen because Dan's body blocked the view, appeared to be sitting on the edge of the slide and making a sudden protesting gesture against the descent.

"Now look at the other side," said Gay, turning the photograph over.

It was scrawled in exactly the same printing-handwrit-ing they had seen before. It was in red ink, and had a sloppy look. It said:

THERE IS ONE MORE TO GO.

Chapter 14

Red Ink

VERY funny, isn't it?" asked Gay. "I was inclined to split my sides when I saw it. But you had better come inside."

Four Doors, centrally heated, was as warm as the hotel had been. Gay took them across a comfortable hall and into a lounge where an additional fire had been lighted. Though the house was of massive build, with fan-lights over the pillared doors and white woodwork round high ceilings, Gay had overlaid it with furniture of genuine comfort. There was no sight or sound of anyone else about. But Gay closed the double-doors.

"Where did you find this?" Hadley asked quietly.

"Ah, there's another piece of subtle humour," said their host. "I went into the bothroom to have a wash. Then I reached out after a towel off the rail, and this fell out from among the towels."

"When did you find it?"

"Not ten minutes ago. By the way, I have established one thing. When we arrived here at eleven o'clock, there was no such delightful piece of mummery hidden in the towels. You see, I keep a cook and two maids. When we got here Letty had just finished tidying up the bathroom and putting out fresh towels. Consequently————"

"Who knows about this, besides yourself?"

"Only the humorist who put it there. I hope you do not think I was indiscreet enough to tell Letty anything. I also pulled that donkey's tail down off the door before (I hope) anyone spotted it. I don't know when it was put up. I noticed it when I was coming out of the bathroom, on the principle that jokes never come singly."

"Yes. And what do you think this means?"

"My good friend," replied Gay, drawing himself up and looking Hadley in the eye, "you must know very well what I think it means. I am fond of good crimes in the abstract; but I do not like funerals. This has got to stop." He hesitated, after which his face altered, and he addressed Kent with great gravity. "Sir," he added, "I beg *your* pardon."

"Granted readily," said Kent, who liked him. "But why?"

"Because I was more than half inclined to suspect you. Er—you have been with Dr. Fell and the superintendent? Between eleven and twelve o'clock, I mean?"

"Yes. We were at the police-station then. But why suspect me, in particular?"

"Why, frankly," responded Gay, with an air of candour, "because your turning up at the hotel yesterday seemed almost too good to be true. Also, because there has been a persistent rumour that you were more than a little interested in Mrs. Josephine Kent———"

"That can wait," snapped Hadley. He turned to Dr. Fell and held out the photograph. "So you'll give me your assurance that there's no danger? How does this fit in with it?"

The doctor put his shovel-hat under his arm and propped his stick against his side. Settling his eyeglasses with a vaguely troubled air, he studied the photograph.

"I don't mind the donkey's tail," he said. "In fact, I think it rather moderate. There are times when I feel I deserve the fate of Bottom the Weaver. But this, honestly, is not one of them. On the other hand, it's a complication I definitely do not like. Someone is growing frightened." He looked at Gay. "To whom does this photograph belong? Did you ever see it before?"

"Yes, it's mine. That is to say, I don't know whether you're aware of Reaper's passion for having photographs taken. He sent me on a batch of them, showing his friends on aqua-planes, and his friends holding up glasses of beer, and so on."

"H'mf, so. Where did you see it last?"

"I think it was in the desk in my study, with the others."

"What is more, this isn't ordinary writing-ink," pursued Dr. Fell, scratching the nail of his little finger across the thick and flaky surface of the inscription on the back of the photograph. "It's too viscid. It looks like————"

"Drawing-ink. That is what it is," supplied Gay. "Just come with me."

He seemed much stiffer than yesterday; he retained that hard glaze like the polish on a tombstone, even to his smile. As though coming to a decision, he led them to another pair of double-doors at the end of the room, and into a room fitted up as a study at the back of the house. Its windows looked out on a back-garden raked by the wind: on a gate in the brick wall, and the elms in the churchyard. But the study also was cheerful with firelight. It was conventional enough, with its bookshelves and busts above, except for an inner staircase ascending along the end wall: a room antiquated rather than ancient. Their host glanced towards this inner staircase before he indicated an open roll-top desk.

"There are, as you can see, four or five bottles of drawing-ink. Various colours," he pointed out. "I seldom or never use them; but the winters pass slowly for me, and, one winter, my hobby was architecture. By the look of that printing, I should think the pen used was this."

He lifted the stopper out of a bottle of black ink. To the stopper, inside, was attached a broad pen-nib—a feature common to bottles of drawing-ink—for testing it before use. He waggled it at them. Kent did not like the expression of his face now.

"I suppose you can guess where that staircase leads?

The door at the top of it is beside the bathroom door upstairs. This humorist, this *slim* fellow, can simply walk down here, scrawl on that photograph like a child on a wall, and walk up with it."

For the first time Hadley was indecisive. Apparently he did not like it either, and there had been a strain ever since they entered the house, but he was studying Gay in a very curious way.

"Do you keep the desk locked?"

"No; why should I? There's nothing of value in it. Half the time the top is not even closed, as it is now."

"But where are the photographs?" asked Dr. Fell. "I've come a long way to see those photographs, you know."

Gay turned round quickly. "I beg your pardon? You've what?"

"Come a long way to see the photographs. Where are they?"

Their host reached towards his trouser-pocket; then he shrugged his shoulders and pulled open a drawer in a tier at the right-hand side of the desk. "I am afraid you will not be well rewarded," he said sardonically. "There is very little to—good God!"

He had jerked back his hand quickly. What oozed out from between his fingers, what he moved back to avoid in case it should splatter on his clothes, was not blood. It looked like blood. But it was red ink. Gathering round him, they saw that the inside of the drawer was what Dr. Fell literally described as an incarnadined mess. In the drawer there had been photographs: some loose ones of all sizes, and others which had obviously been taken of or by Gay himself, for they had been pasted into an album. All were ripped and torn into many shreds, a kind of pudding, over which had been poured some half a bottle of red drawing-ink.

Dr. Fell groaned. Sir Gyles Gay did not. Standing with his hand stiffly outstretched while he swabbed at the fingers with a handkerchief, he began to curse. He cursed with such careful, cold-voiced, measured authority that it showed a new side to the man, a new use for marble teeth. He cursed in English, *Afrikaans* and Kaffir, the sort of thing which would have skinned the hide either from an offending houseboy or a Government department: yet Kent could not help feeling he had heard exactly the same tone of voice on a golf-course when someone has just foozled about the sixth easy stroke. Kent saw the veins in his neck.

"I hope," Gay continued, without changing his even tone, "I can be called a good host. I like my guests. I have enjoyed their presence immensely. But this—by God! this is going too far. That ink is still running in the drawer. It hasn't been put in for much more than half an hour. And where are my guests now? Why, I'll tell you. Without a doubt each is sitting or standing in his own room. Without a doubt nobody has ventured out, as on other occasions. It is all beautifully quiet; by the so-and-so it is."

Dr. Fell scratched his chin. "Do you mind my saying," he observed, "that you're rather a rum sort of bloke?"

"Thanks very much."

"No, I mean it. When a murder is committed—even one in your own house—you are helpful, philosophical, and all good things. It is an intellectual problem. It stimulates you. But you go off the deep end, with one majestic volplaning sweep, when someone plays a senseless practical joke that makes you mess up your hands. You don't mind a throat being cut; but you can't stand a leg being pulled."

"I can understand murder," said Gay, opening his eyes. "I cannot understand this."

"You don't see any meaning in it?"

"Ah, there I am not qualified to judge. But I want to know what has been going on. Up to this time 'somebody' has confined his or her inane scribblings to nighttime. Now this humorist walks about in the light of day and writes—Chequebook!" said Gay, breaking off.

Now not minding the confusion in the drawer, he began to grub in it. With some relief he produced a leather-bound cheque-book on the Capital Counties Bank; it was by some chance not stained at all, and he put it gingerly on the desk. Then he drew out a small leather purse, of the sort used by countrymen for carrying loose change, and snicked it open.

"Something wrong here," he added in an altered tone —a natural tone. "There's some money missing."

"Money?" said Hadley. "I thought you said you kept nothing valuable in that desk."

"Quite true, superintendent; I don't. All this purse ever contains is a little silver in case I have to pay for a parcel, or hand out a tip, or the like. There's never more than a pound here at any time."

"How much is missing?"

"Twelve shillings, I make it," said Gay with competence. "Is this some more highly subtle humour, do you think?"

Hadley took a deep breath and studied the room with a vindictiveness that equalled Gay's own. With his hand in a handkerchief, he picked up the bottle of red drawing-ink from the desk. It had undoubtedly been used to deluge the drawer; it was nearly empty.

"Yes," he growled, "yes, I'm taking precautions about finger-prints in going after a practical joker. I remember a time, Fell, in the Mad Hatter case, when the answer to a piece of tomfoolery was the answer to a murder. You know—" Hadley stopped and cooled off. "We'll settle this up right now. Will someone—will you," he looked at Kent, "go and round up all the others? No, never mind sending a servant, Sir Gyles; I want all the servants here now, if you'll send for them. We'll begin with them. If you've got two maids, I don't see how it's impossible for someone to have raised the devil like that without *any-thing* being seen." He added to Kent, grimly: "Yes. Tell 'em what you like. It won't do any harm."

Kent went up the inner staircase to the hall of the floor above. He went quickly, because he did not want time to think. Four Doors, according to the plan of its (would-be) period, was severely oblong, with a central hall running broad-wise through the building. And he had no difficulty in finding three out of four of his quarry. Francine, Dan, and Melitta were sitting together in a sort of upstairs den whose big oriel window looked out over the main door. They sat round a gas-fire in an atmosphere of grousing.

Dan greeted him peevishly.

"I must say you're a fine sort of friend. You walked out last night with the wench here—well, that's understandable enough. But this morning you up and walked out with the police————"

It was the home atmosphere again.

"I walked out with the police," Kent said, "because Dr. Fell countenanced it, and because I wanted to see whether I could find anything to help us out of this mess. And there's a lot more to say now." He looked round; Wrayburn's absence was a noticeable gap. "Where's Harvey?"

Dan's intuition was disconcertingly keen: keener, perhaps, than Melitta's. He had been sitting with his elbows thrust out and his hands on his knees; now he got up as though he were levering up a boulder. On one side of him sat Melitta in stout discontent and a Chanel dress. On the other, Francine smoked a cigarette and looked properly attentive. He always remembered them at that moment, because of the home atmosphere which seemed to connect this with bright-hued villas in Parktown. What had happened this morning was like a home-bickering become distorted: a clash of wills or a bad joke, like breaking into somebody's liquor-cabinet or setting a booby-trap. The worst of it was that it was real. It could happen, and did happen—on a scale that ended in murder. And Dan guessed. He was standing so close to the gas-fire that you could smell the fire scorching a tweed suit.

Dan said: "Harvey? He went up to the pub after cigarettes. What's up?"

"Somebody's been acting the fool." Kent stopped. It was not actually that, in spite of every ludicrous attempt at a jeer in the actions that had been done this morning. "How long have you three been in here together?"

"Mel and I just came in. Francine has been here all the time. What's *up*?"

Kent told them.

The way in which they received it might or might not have been considered curious. They were very quiet. It was like Melitta's what-a-holiday mood, as though they had taken seaside lodgings where it rained steadily for two weeks. Only at the end did something appear to rouse Dan.

"I never heard of such tomfoolery in all my born days!" he said, looking for the perpetrator in corners of the room. "Let me see if I have this straight: somebody takes that photograph, writes on the back of it, and puts it in among the towels. Somebody tears all the other photographs to pieces and douses them with red ink. Then someone steals twelve shil—oh, here! Why steal the money?"

"You've got it," said Kent, realising. He knew at last what was wrong with the picture. "I've had a feeling that something didn't ring true, and you've got it. It's the money. The rest of it might have been perverted humour, or there might be an explanation for most of it; I think I can see one. But stealing the money doesn't fit in."

"May not have anything to do with it," Dan pointed out. "Suppose one of the maids took the money, or something like that?"

"Jenny had none, you know," interposed Melitta.

"Jenny had none of what?"

"No silver, coppers, small change of any kind," she answered obediently. "In her handbag at the hotel. I know, because they asked me to go through her things."

It was true; Kent remembered having written it down in his notes. Melitta, whose handsome nose was pink this morning, warmed up.

"Now do not tell me I don't know what I'm talking about. I thought it was awfully queer at the time, and I told Mr. Hadley so; because whoever travels, you know, *always* carries some change, and I am quite sure Jenny always did. When I saw it was not there I felt somebody must have taken it, though of course I knew it was no good saying anything."

"But she had thirty pounds in notes, and that wasn't touched."

"So she had, my dear; but how did you know that?"

"Because I took charge of it," Dan returned grimly. He had evidently noticed no implication. "Somebody's got to take the responsibility here. I'm the fellow who cleans up afterwards. That's all right; I'm the executor; but I want this nonsense stopped. Do you mean that there's someone who goes around consistently stealing loose silver and coppers, and letting big banknotes alone?"

"I'm sure I don't know, my dear," said Melitta with her infuriating placidness, and smoothed her skirt. "As my grandfather used to say————"

Dan lowered his head for a moment.

"Mel," he observed, "there's something *I* want to say. And don't misunderstand me in saying it. I'm your husband. I'm fonder of you than of anyone in the world, if you'd only Snap Out Of It. What I want to say is this, man to man. Damn your grandfather, and your Uncle Lionel, and your Aunt Hester, and your Aunt Harriet, and your cousin Who-is-it, and all their garnered wisdom. There never was a man so afflicted with relatives as I am; and every single one of 'em is dead."

"Easy!" Kent urged, as Dan stalked gloomily across to the window. "This thing has got all our nerves to such a pitch————"

"I suppose so," admitted Dan. "Sorry, Mel. Only I'd give anything I've got just to hear you laugh again. Well, what do we do now?"

"If you could show, to Hadley's satisfaction, where you were between the time you arrived here at eleven o'clock and, say, a quarter to twelve————"

"Library," said Dan promptly. "I was fooling about

with the books, and wondering where everybody else was and why we were here at all."

"You don't mean Gay's study?"

"No, no; the library at the other side of the house."

"And you say Harvey went to the pub after cigarettes? When did he leave?"

"Almost as soon as we got here. He walked back with the chauffeur who drove us. So he's out of it—again."

They both looked at Francine, who had been unwontedly silent. "I hope, Chris," she said, and smiled while she contemplated the fire, "you haven't got round to suspecting me. I told them all about your grand case against Hardwick, so I imagine nobody's safe."

"I didn't mean that." What he meant was that he could not straighten out last night, when each had so very nearly spoken, and then there had come between them the dead wall of her mood. But he was not speaking of what he meant. "The police are going to ask you in about one minute———"

"Oh. Yes. I was up here, between my old room and this room. I didn't go downstairs at all."

"Melitta?"

"I was having a bath."

There was a silence. "You were having a bath?" repeated Dan. "You always seem to be having baths when these things happen. When? I mean, where?"

This time she did laugh, an honest and homely sound. "Well, really, my dear, there is only one place I do, usually. Though I remember, when we were first married, you used to have them in the water-butt, and nearly drowned the parrot each time. I was in the bathroom, of course. You got us up so terribly early to come down here, and I didn't have time at the hotel. I rang for the maid—Letty or Alice; Letty, I think it was—and she drew it for me. That was just after we got here. I know, because she was just finishing tidying up the bathroom, and putting new towels there when I asked her to start the bath running."

"Then—" said Kent. "How long were you in the bathroom?"

"I'm afraid it was well over three-quarters of an hour, really." She wrinkled her forehead. "I renewed the hot water twice. And then there was that nice church clock, and I think it is so nice that you can hear it from here. It struck the half-hour after eleven, and then the quarter-hour, before I was out of the tub————"

"Did you use the towels?"

"Fiddle-dee-dee! Of course I used the towels. Two of them. And that photograph was not there."

He spoke slowly. "We got here at just noon by that clock; we heard it strike. Gay met us at the door with the photograph. He said he had found it in the bathroom ————"

"You certainly got here at noon," interrupted Francine. "I was sitting up here at this window watching you; and I saw him standing down there with the photographs behind his back. But *I* wasn't going down to inquire. I didn't wish to be told to mind my own business."

"Wait!" he said, feeling as though he were half mesmerised. "Gay said he had found it in the bathroom ten minutes ago; or, in the exact words, 'not ten minutes ago.' "

Melitta smoothed her skirt again. "Well, I'm sure I don't wish to say anything against anyone's character; but you remember, Chris, and you too, Dan, I *warned* you. Of course he may have found it there, but I don't really see how he could have. Because I wasn't out of the tub until after I heard the quarter-hour strike: that was what made me get out, now I come to think of it: and then I dried myself, and tidied up the bathroom, and opened the upper part of the window to let the steam out, and actually, you see, I've only just got dressed."

Dan's face changed colour.

"You think the old devil wrote it himself?"

"I think," Kent said decisively, "we'd better go downstairs and Melitta had better tell this, before they get the idea that we're up here inventing a story to stick to. There's something damned funny about every move that's been made this morning. Gay's behaviour was odd. But so was Hadley's. He's got something on his mind. He made no objection to my coming up here and telling you everything. In fact, he practically directed me to, though I should think he'd want to spring it on you and see what happened. I tell you, there's something going on under the surface, and I wish I knew what it was."

In just two minutes he found out.

Chapter 15

Duello

IT WAS Hadley's voice which made him stop with his hand on the knob of the door. The voice was not raised; it had the unimpassioned tone of one discussing a business-deal; but Kent had not heard just that different tone in it before.

The door, at the head of the private stair leading down into the study, was open some two or three inches. He could look down on them with a tilted, theatre-like view, which was yet close enough to follow every movement of a wrinkle or turn of an eye. He saw the brown carpet spread out below, its ancient pattern of roses faded. Past the chandelier he saw Superintendent Hadley's head. Hadley was sitting by the fire-place, facing outwards, his back to the watcher above. Opposite him sat Sir Gyles Gay—his hands lifted, the fingers lightly interlocked as though he were inspecting them—a business man listening to a business proposition. The firelight shone fully on Gay's face, on his alert little look. There was no sign of Dr. Fell. Round the house the wind deepened in a winter afternoon; from the back of it drifted the smell of hot food being prepared for lunch.

What Hadley had said was:

"—and, since we're alone, I feel inclined to tell you a little of what I know."

It did not need Kent's fierce gesture to stop and silence the three persons following him. They all waited, and they all listened.

Gay assented to the proposition with a slight nod.

"You have just heard the testimony of the maid, Alice Weymiss?"

Again Gay nodded.

"You heard her say that that drawer in the desk, where the photographs were kept, is always kept locked by you?"

"I heard it."

"Was it true?"

"You see, superintendent, Alice has no business to know whether drawers are kept locked or not. If she does know, it puts her trustworthiness in doubt. You can see for yourself that the drawer is unlocked now."

Hadley leaned forward.

"Have you a key to that drawer, Sir Gyles?"

"I believe so, somewhere."

"Are you carrying that key in your right-hand trouser-pocket now?"

Gay answered neither yes nor no; he waited, and shook his head slightly as though the question were of no consequence.

"You also heard what the other maid, Letty King, said? She said that she prepared a bath for Mrs. Reaper at shortly after eleven o'clock: that Mrs. Reaper remained in the bathroom until five minutes to twelve: that she knows this because she kept an eye out in case the bathroom should have to be tidied up afterwards."

Their host looked puzzled. "Naturally. I don't deny any of that. When I told you I found the photograph there within the last 'ten minutes,' perhaps I should have consulted my watch. Perhaps I should have said five. But I did not consult my watch. I went downstairs and questioned Letty about whether the photograph had been there when she laid out the towels earlier."

"Therefore your position is that Mrs. Reaper put the photograph there?"

"Come, come, man!" said Gay, as though mildly disappointed. "My position is nothing of the kind. I don't know who put it there; I wish I did. To put the photograph there would have taken perhaps ten seconds—after Mrs. Reaper left, if you like. Or whenever you like."

After a pause there was a certain sort of amusement in Hadley's tone; it was not pleasant to listen to.

"Sir Gyles, I wonder if you think everyone who opposes you is blind. I wonder if you think we've been blind from the beginning of this case. Now, I've had instructions not to trouble you more than was necessary. You know, you're being favoured. So I've hesitated to come out with it until I had enough to trouble you a whole lot. But, after what you've said this morning, I've got no choice. The plain fact is that you've been telling me a pack of lies."

"Since when?" inquired the other, interested.

"Since yesterday. But we'll begin with to-day. Your story about this 'donkey's tail' on Fell's door was rubbish. Don't try to play with flourishes like that. Had you told any of your other guests that you expected to entertain either Fell or myself here overnight? Think before you answer. They will remember, you know."

"No, I suppose I didn't."

"Of course you didn't—sir. Then how could any of the others be expected to know even that he would be here at all; let alone what room you had 'set aside' for him?"

It is a sober fact that a reddish patch showed across Gay's forehead, though he kept the atmosphere of a business discussion.

"I think it was well known," he answered without hesitation, "that you both were coming down here. This house, as you know, boasts eight bedrooms. The others would have their old rooms; and I assuredly would not put anyone in the room where Mr. Kent was murdered. That leaves only two. There is not much margin for error. It is possible, you know, that the donkey's tail was meant for *you*."

"Just between ourselves, do you still stick to that flap-doodle?"

"There is nothing 'between ourselves.' You will see to that. Incidentally, I stick to the truth."

The fire was built of somewhat slaty coal; it crackled and popped, distorting the light on Gay's calm, interested face. Hadley leaned down beside his chair, picking up the photograph.

"Let's take this printing on the back. Even without calling in a handwriting man, I think we can decide that this was written by the same hand that wrote 'Dead Woman' on another card. Do you agree? Yes, so do I. Was this message written this morning between eleven and twelve?"

"Obviously."

"It was not. That's definite, Sir Gyles," Hadley returned. "Fell noticed it—maybe you saw him scrape his little finger across the ink. This thick stuff takes a very long time to dry. And this particular printing was not only dry; it was so flaky that it shredded off when he touched it. You saw that. That message has been written on the card for well over a week, if not more."

Again Gay would not be drawn. A dawning anger showed in his eyes, as (Kent remembered) he had shown before in that odd impression of a man foozling an easy golf-stroke, and knowing it. But he regarded his clasped hands from several angles.

"I gave an opinion, my friend."

"I give a fact—sir. Unless that writing was really done this morning, there seems no point at all to torn photographs and splattered ink. And it was not made this morning. So far, I understand, Fell and I disagree about this case. But we both agree about this, I think. . . . We'll go on to something else. Your maid swears that you always keep that particular drawer locked. You maintain that it is always open. Fair enough. But, when you were asked to open it and get the photographs out, you automatically reached for the key—in your right-hand pocket—before you remembered the drawer was supposed to be unlocked. You then jabbed your hand, much too ostentatiously, into the drawer, in order to get red ink on it and show how surprising the thing was. Anybody would have looked before doing that. You didn't. I know two burglars and a screw-man who made the same mistake."

After some deliberation, Gay crossed one leg over the other, shifted in his chair, and seemed to grow comfortable.

"You have talked for a while," he murmured. "Now let me talk. Do I understand that you accuse me of faking the whole thing? That I put the photograph in the towels; that I tore up the other photographs in my own drawer, and poured ink over them?"

"Yes, that ink was fresh."

"Quite so. Then am I accused of insanity? For there are two sides to your attack, and they won't fit. First you inform me that I did all this within an hour or so ago. Then you turn round and say that the printing on that photograph was made well over a week ago. Which is which and what is what? I'll try to meet your charges, Mr. Hadley, if I can understand them."

"Very well. To begin with————"

"Wait. Am I, by the way, accused of stealing twelve shillings of my own money?"

"No. You were really surprised when you discovered that: it was different from the other acting."

"Ah, then you acknowledge that someone else besides myself could have got into that drawer? So far, you've been building a good deal on the fact that I'm the only person who has a key to it. Excuse this insistence on small points," begged Gay, beginning to show his teeth; "but, since all your charges are built on nothing else, I want you at least to be consistent."

Hadley's tone changed again; Kent would not have liked to look him in the eye then.

"I'll give you a big one, Sir Gyles. You were acquainted with Mrs. Josephine Kent, then Miss Josephine Parkes, when she was in England four years ago."

Again the fire crackled and popped in a gush of light; a grain of burning slate exploded out towards Gay, but he did not notice it. His eyes were wide open.

"That, I concede, *is* something; if you think it is true. But what makes you believe even that she had ever been in England? You heard all her friends, her relatives, everyone say that she had never been out of South Africa in her life."

"Yes," said the superintendent grimly, "I heard it. I also heard them swear she never did any travelling at all, that she hated travelling, and could not stand even a short journey in South Africa. Then, yesterday, I saw her trunk —Fell called my attention to it. Have you seen that trunk?"

"No."

"I think you have. It is an old, battered, worn one; it has seen years of good service in trains and ships, as it shows by its handling. That trunk was certainly Mrs. Kent's own: she did not, for instance, inherit it from someone else who had done the travelling. Her maiden name, Josephine Parkes, was painted in it in chipped, faded lettering that was as old as the trunk; it had certainly got its knocking-about at the same time as the trunk itself. You see what I mean. The trunk had been used by her."

At the top of the stairs Kent turned round and glanced at Dan, who was looking guilty in the gloom of the hall. He heard Dan breathe. Nobody hesitated in the ancient practice of eavesdropping; they were listening with all their ears. And Kent remembered only too well the worn lettering on the worn trunk.

"We heard also how badly she was affected by train and sea-sickness; though she was one of the few who stood up to bad weather on the voyage out. Never mind that. But we learned that she 'turned up' unexpectedly in Johannesburg three years ago: she had come, she *said*, from her old home in Rhodesia. It surprised everyone that she had a great deal of money, which she had 'inherited' from her dead parents."

"But still————"

"Just a moment, Sir Gyles. It was worth looking up. I looked it up. I had her passport: or, rather, a joint husband-and-wife passport made out to Mr. and Mrs. Rodney Kent. Last night I cabled Pretoria about it, and got an answer. In order to obtain that joint one, she had to turn in a previous passport on the Union of South Africa, Number 45695, made out in the name of Miss Josephine Parkes." Hadley again opened his brief-case, without haste, and consulted notes. "Here I've got the immigration stamps on it.

"She landed at Southampton on September 18th, 1932. She then, at various times, paid any number of visits to France: here are the dates: but she was domiciled in England. She left England on December 20th, 1933, and landed again at Capetown on January 6th, 1934. Are you satisfied?"

Gay shook his head a little, as though fascinated.

"I won't deny your facts, of course. But still what has it to do with me?"

"She came to England to see you."

"Er—can you prove that?"

"I have proved it. Here are the papers. You were then, if you recall, Under-Secretary for the Union, and you should recognise this. Mrs. Kent said that she intended to take some kind of employment. She was given a form to fill up. She rather grandly wrote on it just this—here's the form—'To see my friend Sir Gyles Gay, who will arrange it for me.' Would you like to see it? I got it from South Africa House last night."

"I wonder, my friend, if you have any idea of just how many people passed through my office, in the course of a season, while I was on executive duty?"

"She was not a friend of yours?"

"No, she was not. I never saw the woman in my life."

"Then just take a look at this. They tell me it's a very unusual thing, nearly unheard-of, and shows direct personal intervention. Across here is written, 'Personal interview, satisfactory,' written and signed by you. Will you acknowledge this as your handwriting?"

Gay did not take the paper which Hadley was holding out. Instead he got up from his chair with an abrupt movement, and began to walk up and down the room under the dead marble busts on the bookshelves. The fire was simmering now, its light not so bright. Stopping by a humidor on a side-table, Gay tapped his fingers on the lid, opened it, and took out a cigar. He did not seem so much alarmed as very thoughtful. He spoke without turning round.

"Let me see. You think I knew, before Reaper's party got here, that a certain Mrs. Josephine Kent was really a certain Miss Josephine Parkes?"

"You might or might not. She had a different surname."

"Yet I must have known who she was? I had the photographs there, which Reaper sent on recently."

Hadley allowed a pause before he answered.

"Yes, you had the photographs, Sir Gyles. That was why they all had to be torn up and made unrecognisable with red ink."

"I confess I don't follow that."

"I mean," said Hadley, raising his voice a little, "that the photographs Mr. Reaper sent weren't the only ones you had in that drawer. There were a lot of old ones belonging to you, in your album. I'm suggesting that some of them showed you and Mrs. Kent together. That's why they had to go."

Gay closed the humidor with a snap and turned round.

"Damn your ingenuity. All very clever, all very beautiful, and—basically—all wrong. Whatever I am, I'm not as much of a lunatic as all that. It won't hold water, my friend. If what you say is true, I had week upon week's time to destroy everything long beforehand. Yet you say I waited until this very morning to do it; and then I went

out of my way deliberately to call attention to it. How do
you explain that?"

"I'm waiting for *you* to explain it."

"You mean that you cannot? Then there is that photograph with the obvious threat written on the back of it.
According to you, the ink has been dry for over a week.
Yet I am supposed to make use of it this morning, for
some purpose which escapes me. Have you anything else?"

Evidently he was recovering his mental wind, after a
bad attack of cramp, and had begun to fight back. But, in
clipping the end off the cigar, he almost got his own finger.
Hadley was not impressed.

"I have. We were rather busy last night. Sergeant Betts,
following this lead, went down to Dorset to see Mrs.
Kent's two aunts. We can rule them out so far as suspicion goes. They really never had seen her before. She
hadn't thought it necessary to visit them when she was in
England before: it seems she had other business. But they
were very convenient. When she wanted to avoid meeting you, and keep up her pretence that she had never been
in England, she decided to stay with them————"

"Curse it all," said Gay, in such a melodramatic way
that he seemed to be shaken clear through, "why should
she want to pretend she had never been in England before? Answer that, if you can. Had she committed a
crime? Also, I think you forget that I did meet her, on the
evening before last."

"The night she was murdered," agreed Hadley, as
though merely confirming the fact. "Yes. I told you we
had something else. While she was with her aunts, Mrs.
Kent received two letters written from here. One was from
her husband—the aunts had seen that handwriting before. One was in a handwriting they did not know."

"You have the letters, of course?"

"We have the letter from Rodney Kent. The other she
destroyed. Why? But she answered both of them." Hadley
leaned forward. "I'm suggesting to you, Sir Gyles, that
you recognised Mrs. Kent from the pictures Mr. Reaper

sent on. (No wonder she objected to making the trip to England.) You then wrote to her to assure her that you would be prepared to meet her as a stranger. And, the night before last, you did."

Gay lit his cigar. He said:

"You started on me with a charge of playing senseless pranks. Somewhere along the line the gears were shifted. It's beginning to dawn on me that you're running me straight into a charge of murder." He spread out his hands, crisping the fingers, and spoke past the cigar in his mouth. "My God, man, do you really think I"—the fingers opened and shut—"I took these and killed two inoffensive—" His voice ended in a kind of deep yelp. "It's p-p-preposterous!"

"I asked you for an explanation of certain things, Sir Gyles. You haven't so far answered one straight question. If you don't give me an explanation, I shall have to ask you to come back with me to London for further questioning. And you know what that is apt to mean."

Across the room Kent saw the white-painted door leading to the lounge at the front of the house. From outside this door there abruptly began a fusillade of knocks. Kent knew why it startled him: it was the first sign of life, of bouncing movement, that had echoed up in this house. The knocks were not really loud; but they seemed to have a heavy and insistent din in the quiet afternoon. From outside the door rose up Harvey Wrayburn's hearty voice. He did not stop for replies: he asked the questions and sang out the answers himself.

"Knock, knock," said Wrayburn.

"Who's there?

"Jack.

"Jack who?

"Jack Ketch," said Wrayburn, suddenly opening the door and grinning at them. "Sorry; I know it's a rotten one, and doesn't even keep to the rules: but I'm just back from the pub, and I thought it was applicable."

Gay's face had gone muddy pale. You could see the Adam's apple move in his neck.

The others did not wait to hear what Wrayburn, apparently in careless fettle, would say when he saw Hadley. Behind Kent's shoulder Dan whispered: "Lets' get out of here," nor did any of them care for the smell of boiled lamb for lunch, coming up the back stairs across the upper hall. Melitta and Francine were the first to turn back. They all went on tiptoe like thieves: which, in fact, was what Kent felt like.

And the first thing they encountered behind them, towering up in the hall as though it would block the way, was the vast presence of Dr. Fell.

Chapter 16

The Woman on the Slide

I HAVE just been looking at the famous Blue Room," said Dr. Fell amiably. "And I think you're wise; you're not really wanted downstairs now, any more than I am. Why not sit down for a minute?"

He indicated the open door of the den looking out towards the front, and shepherded them in with his stick like a master of ceremonies. Kent, with a vague and warm feeling that he was being made a fool of, followed in some perplexity. For a few seconds nobody commented. Then Melitta Reaper, who had gone by instinct towards the gas-fire, turned round and summed it up (if inadequately) in one explosive word:

"Well!"

"You never heard Hadley run out his masked batteries before, eh?" inquired Dr. Fell, settling his chins in his collar. "Yes, it's an improving process. And anyone who can break down Sir Gyles Gay's guard has my sincere admiration. I wonder if he's done it? I wonder if he will do it?"

Dan regarded the doctor with a wary eye. "You heard all that, did you?"

"Yes, indeed. I was as interested as you were. Of course

I knew what was up his sleeve—in fact, I helped to stuff the sleeve myself—but I wasn't sure when or how he would produce it. Harrumph."

He beamed on them.

"Then Gay is guilty after all?" demanded Dan, who seemed on the edge of an explosion that never quite came off. "I never thought it. By God, I never did: down inside. And Jenny seems to have made roaring fools out of all of us with her past history. But even if he did it, why should he?"

Dr. Fell grew quiet. He lowered himself on the edge of the window-seat.

"Would it make you feel any happier if you knew he was guilty? Eh?"

"It would clear the air," said Dan, with a quick glance. "Every time I go round a corner or open a door, I've been feeling I ought to look a leedle oudt. The trouble is that it's nothing you can hit back at."

"But is he guilty?" asked Francine quietly. "You don't think so, do you?"

The doctor considered this.

"I merely wish to know more about it, you see. Being afflicted with a real scatter-brain, I am full of a hideous curiosity about very small details, and tend to let the main picture go hang. Hah!" He folded his hands over the head of his stick. "And I'll tell you the impression I got from that little episode," he added impressively. "Supposing always that things are what they seem, on every major issue Gay was floored. On every minor issue he floored Hadley. You might be able to make out a case against him as a murderer. But you cannot make out a case against him as a practical joker. You see, I am one of those people who honestly think it is funny to paint a statue red; and I can see the force of it."

"What's that got to do with it?"

"Well, look here! If that drawer full of photographs had really contained a picture of him with Mrs. Kent, or anything of a betraying nature, why should he have waited until this morning to destroy it? Why wasn't it destroyed quietly instead of being joyously besprinkled with red ink to call attention to it? Burning would have done it in one minute, with nobody the wiser. Gay made those points himself. And they were so pertinent that Hadley had to dodge them.

"Then there is the question of the fun-fair photograph. Hadley was quite right: the ink on the back of that picture is at least a week old, and probably a good deal more. Now, psychologically, that rather unpleasant-sounding threat, 'There is one more to go,' was inspired by precisely the same motive as a joke. But the whole point of such a trick is its immediate execution and its full, fine flavour while you are in the mood. I will give you an example. Let us suppose that I am a member of the House of Lords. One day, musing dreamily on the back benches, it occurs to me what an excellent thing it would be if I were to inscribe a piece of paper reading, 'Just call me Snookums,' or 'Ready-made, £1 3s. 6d.'; to pin this paper to the back of the unsuspecting fellow-peer in front of me; and to study the interesting effect as he stalked out afterwards.

"Now, either I decide not to do this, or (if I am made of nobler stuff) to do it. There is only one thing I assuredly do *not* do. I do not write out the sign and put it carefully away in my pocket, saying to myself: 'I will hang this paper on old Plushbottom's back exactly a week from next Thursday, the proper time for it, and meanwhile I will keep it always ready at hand, guarded against all ravages.' Why on earth should I? It takes only a second to scribble: I may have a different mood or a brighter thought: it is an utterly useless sort of thing to carry about, and may cause surprise if it falls out at the dinner-table.

"Don't think I am not serious because I use such an example. Exactly the same principle applies here. But it applies much more strongly. If I am caught, all I risk from old Plushbottom is a dirty look or a punch in the nose. The person who wrote this, and kept it about him, risked the hangman. So why should Gay do any such non-sensical thing as write it weeks ago and keep it at hand for a possible opportunity?"

There was a silence.

"I've wondered," Francine said demurely, "just where in this affair you would live up to your reputation and really begin to lecture. But, I say, I don't see that it applies only to Sir Gyles. It applies to anybody else as well, doesn't it?"

"Exactly. And therefore I have wondered why Hadley has neglected to ask the only really important, the only really significant question about the photograph."

"What question?"

"Why, the question of who is *in* the photograph, of course!" thundered Dr. Fell, and brought his hand down on the head of the stick. "Or, more properly, who isn't in it. It's not very complicated, is it? If this means a menace at all, it means a menace to someone in the group. And if it follows the distortedly jesting symbolism which is the only symbolism it can have, the victim indicated is the person who is being pushed down the slide in the picture: the one who seems to be making a protesting gesture about it. But that is the only person in the group whom you can't see. Mr. Reaper's back is in the way, and hides the view." He paused, wheezing, and added mildly: "Well, that's what I'm here to find out. Do you remember that picture being taken? And, if so, who was being pushed down the slide?"

He looked at Dan, who nodded.

"That's smart," said Dan thoughtfully. "Yes, naturally I remember it. It was Jenny. She didn't want to go down the chute; afraid she'd show her thighs or something; but I gave her a push."

"But that means—!" cried Francine, with a sort of inspiration.

Dr. Fell nodded. "It was Mrs. Kent. I thought so. And that's the whole sad, ugly story. Do you begin to see why the message, 'There is one more to go,' was written a fortnight ago? Eh? When Rodney Kent was killed, the murderer scrawled this message on the back of the photograph and intended to leave it on the scene of the crime: just as later he sardonically scrawled, 'Dead Woman' when the threat was fulfilled. 'There is one more to go' *applied to Mrs. Kent.* But the murderer changed his mind about leaving it: this murderer you see, can never seem to make up his mind about anything—that's what has betrayed him. But he was wise in not leaving it. That would have been incautious. And the photograph-cum-message has been calmly reposing in this house, probably in Gay's desk, ever since: until it was hauled out for some very curious monkey-tricks this morning. Well, do these heavy cogitations lead you on to deduce anything else?"

He watched them with grim affability. Getting out his pipe, he unscrewed it and blew through the stem as though he were blowing a particularly seductive whistle. He was still whistling for something, certainly.

"In Gay's desk," muttered Christopher Kent. "The heavy cogitations show that Gay can't possibly be the murderer."

"Why not?"

"It's pretty plain. If the picture was intended to represent a threat to Jenny, the murderer knew that the person being pushed down the slide *was* Jenny. But you can't tell that just by looking at the picture. She's hidden. You can't even tell it's a woman. So the murderer must be somebody who is either in the picture or was there when it was taken; and that rules out Gay."

"Won't do," objected Dan, shaking his head with decisiveness. "I remember telling Gay who it was, or writing about it, or—here! Seems to me I've seen that picture more recently, somewhere—seen it—seen it————"

"Yes," chimed in Francine abruptly. "And so have I. We saw it————"

Their voices stopped: that mutual jump at thought seemed to defeat itself as they came into conflict, like two people trying to open a door from opposite sides. Dr.

Fell's whistle piped enticingly, and piped again. Nothing happened.

"It's no good," said Dan. "I've forgotten."

"H'mf, ha! Well, never mind. But still is there anything else that strikes you?" prompted the doctor.

"But still, about Gay's innocence," persisted Kent. "I'd like to—er—yes, I'd like to think he's guilty. All the same, it comes back to what we were arguing about a while ago: the blazing fathead who would keep the thing in his possession for a couple of weeks. You say you think it was probably in Gay's desk. But, if he were the murderer, wouldn't he have destroyed it?"

"Warm," said Dr. Fell. "Unquestionably warm. Therefore?"

"The only thing I can think of was that it was planted on him." Kent started; it was as though his sight went into another focus, and he could see the other face in the moon. "I believe I've got it! Listen. Someone planted it in the desk two weeks ago. But Gay hadn't found it because he hadn't looked in that drawer in the meantime. When he came back home to-day, he did look in the drawer, and discovered it among the other photographs. Now, listen!———"

"Chris," said Francine coldly.

"He was properly scared out of his Sunday trousers, because he wondered whether it would be found or whether somebody mightn't have seen it among his things already. It was all the worse because he really had been tied up with Jenny in the old days; and, for some reason, has persistently denied it. So he pretended to 'find' the photograph-and-message somewhere else. To cover up its sudden appearance, and pretend that the murderer had been up to funny business again, he tore up the rest of the pictures and sloshed them with red ink. He invented a story about donkeys' tails and pinched some silver out of his own drawer. That's it! It would explain both his guilty and innocent actions; his behaviour to-day and the rotten badness of his acting when———"

"Warmer and warmer yet, I think," beamed Dr. Fell. "But not, I am afraid, quite on the mark. It is significant that the only picture left completely intact did not contain a likeness of Mrs. Kent. True enough, I managed to dig one out of the mess, one that had not been effaced by tearing or ink; but————"

He stopped. There were heavy footsteps outside. Hadley, with a depressed-looking Wrayburn who was not now inclined to bounce, glanced in at the door. He gave the others a perfunctory good morning.

"May I see you alone for a minute, Fell?" he said.

When Dr. Fell had lumbered out, Hadley was careful to close the door. There was an uneasy silence, while they all looked at each other. Wrayburn, jamming his hands again into the pockets of his coat, attempted a light note in speech. His face was glossy.

"It may interest you to know," he remarked, "that I've just dropped one of the world's heavier bricks. The trouble being that I haven't got the remotest idea what it is. I made quite a study of psychology once; but I still don't know. I came back from the pub enlivened with a couple of pints, and charged back to the study, and said something asinine: still, I don't see how it could have been as asinine as all that. Hadley rather prefers the measles to me. Our host, after a conference with Hadley, is sitting downstairs with his head in his hands, looking like death. Poor old cuss: I felt sorry for him. I knew a fellow once, fellow named————"

"Shut up," said Dan briefly.

"Oh, all right. But fair's fair, and somebody ought to talk to me. If I'm still in disgrace for making a fool of myself over Jen————"

"Shut *up*," said Dan.

There was another silence.

"Yes, but all the same," argued Wrayburn, "isn't that what's making everybody so frosty? I had to get a couple of pints inside me to ask it; but what have I done that others haven't done? You know, I've been wondering about something I never thought of before. Just why did we call her *Jenny*? Is it natural? The ordinary diminutive for 'Josephine' is 'Jo' or even, save the mark, 'Josie.' But she always referred to herself as Jenny, you know. Would it be Jenny Wren? No, I've got a better idea————"

"What the devil are you burbling about?" asked Dan, out of the thick wool of reflection.

Both of them broke off when the door opened, and even as Kent remembered Dr. Fell's remark that his first interest in the case had been in names. It was Dr. Fell who opened the door. He was alone.

"I am afraid," he said gravely, "that some of us will not be staying to lunch. But—hum—before we go, will you do me one favour? Believe me, it is necessary. Will you all come up to the Blue Room with me for just a short time?"

There was a noticeable shuffling of feet when they went out. The long hall which bisected the house, of rough plastering and beamed ceiling, had a large but small-paned window at each end. The windows were of slightly crooked glass, and held a reflection of snow. Kent knew which door would be the door to the Blue Room, since the famous leather sofa stood near it. They were all awkward about getting through the doorway.

The room in which Rodney Kent had died was at the back of the house, its windows looking out over the garden wall and the elms of the churchyard. Like the other rooms it was large but narrow, papered in velvety dark-blue stuff which now merely succeeded in looking dismal. The furniture, old-fashioned without being ancient, was of the fashion of some seventy years ago: a great double bed in oak, its headboard and footboard pointed at the top but sloping down shallowly to a curve by the little posts, showed much scroll-work and aggressively dominated the room. A bureau, and a dressing-table with a very tall mirror, both had marble tops like the round table in the centre. There were two chairs trying to break their backs with straightness, and a wash-hand-stand (marble-topped) bearing blue-and-white china. Face towels hung neatly from a rack beside it. On the dark-flowered carpet near the table there was a broad greyish mark of scrubbing. Tasselled draperies on the windows were not drawn close enough to shut out a view of a headstone or two, or of the church tower, whose clock now made the glass vibrate by striking one. Dr. Fell stopped by the table.

"Is this room," said Dr. Fell, "except for one exhibit, now just as it was when Mr. Kent was murdered?"

It was Dan who answered yes.

"There were no signs of a struggle?"

"None."

"I have seen it in the police photographs," rumbled Dr. Fell, "but they did not show what I wanted. Will you get down on the floor as nearly as you can in the position the body was lying? . . . H'mf, thank you; that's fairly clear. Right side; head almost touching the left-hand caster of the bed; feet near the table. The bruise on the back of the head was rather high up, I take it?"

"Yes."

"Where was the towel?"

"Draped over the shoulder."

"As in Mrs. Kent's case?"

"Yes."

There was a heavy finality in question and answer which was like the striking of the clock.

"All right, there's that," growled Dan. "But what does it show, now you've seen it?"

"I'm inclined to think it shows a great deal," said Dr. Fell. "You see, up until this morning I wondered if I might be wrong. Now I know I must be right. At least we know one thing that was in the dark before. We know how Rodney Kent really died."

There was not as much light as there should have been, either in the room or in their minds. They stared at him.

"This is really a lot of most unnecessary nonsense," interposed Melitta, who had been sniffing as though she were going to cry. "You are perfectly well aware we *know* how poor Rodney died."

"The murderer was talking to him amicably enough," said Dr. Fell. "Then the murderer distracted his attention to something, so that he turned his head away. The murderer struck him on the back of the head with a weapon smaller than a poker. When he was unconscious, the murderer first strangled him to death and then beat his face with the poker. Yes. But what I said before is still true: we did not know, before, how he was really killed. It is not a riddle. You see, the murderer was someone who hated Rodney Kent very much. And therefore the murder of Josephine Kent————"

"Jenny," said Wrayburn.

"*Will* you be quiet?" requested Dan, turning in exasperation.

"No, I mean it," said Wrayburn. "We all know how attractive a—a woman Jenny was. Excuse me: I was going to say 'piece of goods,' but that doesn't fit. With all the inane crookedness in the little piece of goods's heart and soul, it still doesn't fit. There are women like that. They sort of—hold on."

"You're drunk," said Dan.

"Not on two pints. No. I'm myself. I was telling them, doctor (or trying to tell them) that it occurred to me a while ago how she came to be called Jenny. Of course she liked it. But she didn't coin the name for herself. No. It was some man who did that. God knows who he is or where he is—and if I had an idea, I wouldn't tell you. But he's middle-aged, the sort Jenny liked. She was the ideal Old Man's woman; or has someone said that? And he's probably not far off now, wondering why he killed her and what life will be like now that he hasn't got anything to hate."

"Oh, brace up," growled Dan. "We're all getting soft-headed. Why don't you begin on verse?"

"I will," said Wrayburn. He nodded gravely, his hands jammed into his pockets and his eyes on the window.

"Jenny kissed me when we met,
  Jumping from the chair she sat in,

Time, you thief, who love to get
   Sweets into your list, put that in!
Say I'm weary, say I'm sad,
   Say that health and wealth have miss'd me,
Say I'm growing old, but add————"

Chapter 17

The Questions of Dr. Fell

MURDER—" began Dr. Fell affably.

"Hold on," said Hadley, putting down his tankard and giving the doctor a suspicious look. "There is something in your expression,"—it was, in fact, one of fiendish and expansive pleasure—"which tells me you're about to begin a lecture. No! We don't want to listen to any lectures now. We've got too much work to do. Furthermore, when Gay gets here————"

Dr. Fell looked pained. "I beg your pardon," he rumbled with dignity. "So far from demeaning myself to lecture to you, I was about to submit myself voluntarily to the intolerable process of listening to you lecture. I gather that for once in your life you are inclined to agree partly with me about a case. At least, you are willing to give a sporting chance to a belief. Very well. I have some questions for you."

"What questions?"

It was nearly ten o'clock, and a rush of last-minute customers at the bar penetrated through from the other side of the door. Dr. Fell, Hadley, and Kent sat alone in the comfortable, raftered bar-parlour of the Stag and Glove.

There was ample living-accommodation at the pub, and they had taken rooms there for the night. This Kent knew; but it was all he knew. That day had consisted of cross-currents and mysterious conferences about whose import he had been given (and had asked for) no hint. Dr. Fell had disappeared for a long time during the afternoon. When the doctor returned, Hadley disappeared. There was also a conference with the long and saturnine Inspector Tanner. What was to be done about Sir Gyles Gay, or whether anything was to be done, Kent had not heard. He had not seen Sir Gyles after that episode of eavesdropping. To get away from the atmosphere of tension at Four Doors, he and Francine had gone for a long walk in the snow; but the tension was still there, and the silver of a winter sunset looked merely angry. The only memory he carried away from it was of Francine, in a Russian-esque kind of astrakhan cap, sitting on a stile in her fur coat, with the low grey hills beyond.

That same tension had not even disappeared in the bar-parlour of the Stag and Glove. They were waiting for something. Yet Dr. Fell showed it much less than Hadley. It was a bitter night, though without wind. A big fire had been built in the bar-parlour, so big that its reflections were almost wild: they flickered on Dr. Fell as he sat enthroned in the window-seat, with the leaded panes behind him and a pint tankard in front of him, beaming with pleasure.

He took a deep pull at the tankard, and assumed an argumentative air.

"Murder, I was about to say," Dr. Fell pursued, "is a subject on which my views have been somewhat misunderstood: largely, I confess, because I have muddled them in the telling or in the enthusiasm of controversy. I feel inclined to rectify this, for a very good reason.

"I have admitted to a weakness for the bizarre and the slightly fantastic. I have, in fact, worn it as a badge of pride. That affair of the Hollow Man, and Driscoll's murder at the Tower of London, and that wild business aboard the *Queen Victoria*, will always remain my favourite cases. But this does not mean that I, or any rational person, would take pleasure in a mad world. It is precisely the opposite, in fact, of what I do mean: and this is the only reason why I mention it at all.

"Now, to the quietest human being, seated in the quietest house, there will sometimes come a wish for the possibilities or impossibilities of things. He will wonder whether the tea-pot may not suddenly begin to pour out honey or sea-water; the clock point to all hours of the day at once; the candle begin to burn green or crimson; the door to open upon a lake or a potato-field instead of a London street. Humph, ha. So far, so good. For a reverie or a pantomine it is all very well. But, regarded as a scheme of everyday life, it is enough to make a man shiver.

"I have enough difficulty in finding my eyeglasses as it is, even when they remain where I last put them down. If they suddenly went sailing up the chimney as I reached for them, my language would be difficult to control. The precise book I am looking for on a shelf has no need of magic to elude me. A malevolent spirit already dwells in my hat. When a person goes from Charing Cross to Bernard Street by underground, he can think himself jolly lucky if he gets to Bernard Street. But if he makes the same journey—say for an urgent appointment at the British Museum—and gets out at Bernard Street, and suddenly finds himself not in Bernard Street, but in Broadway or the rue de la Paix, he would be justified in thinking that matters had become really intolerable.

"Now, this principle particularly applies to criminal cases. It would be a very dull business to have a calm, sane criminal in a mad world. The criminal would not be interesting at all. You would do much better to go and watch the nearest lamp-post dance the rumba. Outside things must not act on the criminal: he must act on them. That is why the eternal fascination is to watch a slightly unbalanced criminal—usually a murderer—in a quite sane world.

"This is not, of course, to say that all murderers are

mad. But they are in a fantastic state of mind, or they would not be murderers. And they do fantastic things. It would be, I think, an easy thesis to prove.

"We all know, in any murder case, the questions *who*, *how*, and *why*. Of those three, the most revealing, but usually by far the most puzzling, is *why*. I don't mean merely the actual motive for the crime itself. I mean the why of certain other actions, eccentricities of behaviour, which centre round the performance of the crime. They torment us at the time: a hat placed on a statue, a poker removed from the scene of the crime when by all reason it should not have been removed. More often the why torments us even when we know, or think we know, the truth. Why did Mrs. Thompson write those letters to Bywaters? Why did Mrs. Maybrick soak the fly-papers in water? Why did Thomas Barlett drink the chloroform? Why did Julia Wallace have an enemy in the world? Why did Herbert Bennett make a sexual attack on his own wife? Sometimes they are very small points—three rings left behind, a broken medicine-bottle, an utter absence of blood on clothes. But they are fantastic, as fantastic as mad clocks or the real crimes of Landru; and, if we knew the answers to the why of them, we should probably know the truth."

"What questions?" inquired Hadley.

Dr. Fell blinked. "Why, the questions I've just been indicating to you. Any of 'em."

"No," said Hadley. "I mean what questions were you going to ask me?"

"Eh?"

"I've been patiently waiting to hear. You said you were not going to lecture; you said it was an honour you passed on to me, and that you had some questions to ask me. Very well: let's hear 'em."

Dr. Fell leaned back with an evil dignity.

"I spoke," he retorted, "by way of preface to the document I am going to lay before you. I have noted down here, on various small sheets, a number of questions. They are mostly 'whys'; any of the 'what' variety are of the why nature. All of them must be answered and answered satisfactorily, before we can say we have a complete solution to this case. Look here, we'll put this up to an umpire." He turned to Kent, and went on doggedly:

"Between last night and this morning, Hadley became convinced that Gay was our man. I was not so sure. I doubted it then, and I am now certain he isn't; but I was compelled to regard it as a possibility. Gay has been given a few hours' grace to answer certain matters: he should be along any minute. We are then—um—going to test a theory of mine, which Hadley regards with at least an open mind. It is now ten o'clock. By midnight we may have the real murderer. Now, both of you, how are the following questions to be answered? How do they fit in with Gay's guilt, or anyone else's guilt? It is your last chance to have a shot at it before the gong."

He spread out his multitudinous note-sheets.

"1. Why, on both occasions, did the murderer wear the costume of a hotel-attendant? An old question, but still a stimulating one.

"2. What happened to that costume afterwards?

"3. Why, on both occasions, was a towel used in strangling the victim?

"4. Why was it necessary for the murderer to hide his face from Josephine Kent, but *not* from Rodney Kent?

"5. Why did Josephine Kent first begin to wear a curious bracelet, having a square black stone cut with a Latin inscription, only a few hours before she was murdered?

"6. Why did she pretend she had never been in England before?

"7. What is the explanation of her words to Miss Forbes, in reply to the latter's question about whether the inscription on the bracelet meant anything? Her reply, you recall, was, 'Only if you're able to read it; that's the whole secret.'

"8. How did the murderer get into a locked linen-closet at the Royal Scarlet Hotel?

"9. Similarly, how did the murderer—supposing it to be some person other than Gay—get into a locked drawer in the desk of the study at Four Doors: a drawer to which only Gay had a key? You observe that the murderer seems able to go anywhere without difficulty.

"10. Why was a small amount of loose change stolen from Mrs. Kent's handbag, and also from the desk in Gay's study?

"11. It must be presupposed, in Mrs. Kent's case, that the murderer placed a pair of odd shoes outside the door of 707, and also hung the 'quiet' sign on it. If he wished to make sure of not being disturbed, this is understandable. But he wrote 'Dead Woman' in red ink, as though to call attention to his presence while he was there. Why?

"12. Perhaps the most intriguing 'why' in the whole case. We believe (I think correctly) that the murderer, dressed as a hotel-attendant and carrying his pile of towels, was admitted to room 707 by Mrs. Kent herself. Very well. At this time, we know from another witness— Wrayburn—Mrs. Kent's key to that room was in her handbag. But the next morning this same key was found by Wrayburn in the lock *outside* the door. You follow the fascinating double-turn of that? The murderer goes in. For some reason he takes the key out of the handbag, having found it there in his search of the room, and puts it in the outside of the door. Why?"

Dr. Fell put the sheaf of notes together and made a mesmeric pass over them.

"Eh bien?" inquired the doctor. "Or which of them appears to you the most interesting?"

"As umpire," answered Kent, "I should say the second one. In other words, what has happened to that infernal costume? It applies to everyone else as well as to Gay. But the uniform seems to have disappeared like smoke. The murderer couldn't have got rid of it in any way I can follow. He couldn't have tossed it out of the window, or burnt it, or hidden it: I suppose you took care of that. We seem to be reduced to the logical certainty that it must be in the hotel somewhere. Which would make it a genuine uniform, borrowed or pinched from somebody. It's unlikely that the murderer went roaming about looking for a uniform at random: it looks like collusion. And so we get back to the hotel again—like my case against the manager."

"And nothing else suggests itself to you?" inquired Dr. Fell, with a curious look at him. "Hasn't any member of your crowd ventured on a suggestion? Come! Surely there would be an ingenious theory somewhere. A theory from Wrayburn, for instance?"

"No, I've seen very little of him. There's been no suggestion except————"

He stopped, having made a slip.

"Except what?" asked Dr. Fell quickly.

"Nothing at all. It was only————"

"It was enough. At a conference of the powers, I think we had better hear it."

"Some far-fetched idea about the possibility of the murderer having been a woman. I suppose you hadn't thought of that?"

Dr. Fell and Hadley exchanged glances. The doctor chuckled.

"You wrong me," he said with offhand geniality. "It was one of the very first thoughts that did occur to me. You mean as regards the uniform, to make us postulate a man from the sight of it?"

"Yes. But you see the reason why it couldn't be so? I mean," said Kent, "the suède shoes. In the first place, it's unlikely that a woman would have taken two odd shoes; she'd have selected a pair. Second and more important, she'd never have put out suède shoes, which can't be polished. That means it was a man. I can realise—once I think about it—that you don't polish suède. But, if I had been the murderer and simply wanted to shove a pair of shoes outside the door, I question whether I should have thought of that at the time. I'd have picked up the first shoes that came handy, as the murderer evidently did."

"Unless," Dr. Fell pointed out with relish, "it was the double-twist of subtlety. The murderer is a woman. She wants us to believe it is a man; that, I think you will acknowledge, would be the whole point of the deception. Therefore she strengthens it by deliberately choosing a pair of shoes which no woman would choose."

Kent regarded his tankard moodily.

"I know," he admitted. "It's a very useful device in fiction, because you can prove very nearly anything by it. But, deep down inside me, I've never really believed in it. You remember the famous passage in which Dupin shows how it is possible to anticipate the way a person's mind will work, and uses as an example the schoolboy's game of evens or odds. You have a marble concealed in your left or your right hand, and the other fellow gets the marble if he picks the correct hand: so on as long as your marbles last. After estimating the intelligence or stupidity of your opponent, you put yourself mentally in his place, think what he would do, and win all the marbles. Well, it won't work. I've tried it. It won't work because, even if you have two minds exactly adjusted, the one thing they will differ over is what constitutes strategy. And, if you try any such games when the other fellow is probably only leaving it to chance, you'll build up such an elaborate edifice that you can't remember where you started. . . . Don't you honestly think that most murderers are the reverse of subtle? They haven't got time to be; and I should think they would be pretty nervous about being misunderstood."

Across the room, the private door leading to the stable-yard opened, and Sir Gyles Gay came in.

By the expression on his face, it was evident that he had heard the last few words and was turning them over in his mind. Cold air blew in with him, making the firelight dance. Ten had struck loudly from the church clock. They were turning the last customers out of the bar; you could hear a noise of firm-shutting doors and final good nights.

Gay wore a soft hat pulled down on his forehead, and a heavy herring-bone coat. He carried a stick under his arm.

"I am a little late, gentlemen," he said formally. "You must excuse me."

"Will you drink something?" asked Dr. Fell, reaching for the bell. "We're putting up here, you know, and we can order it."

"Yes. I know," said Gay, stripping off his gloves. He studied them. "You prefer to come here rather than accept my hospitality. Does this mean that you cannot dine with a man you mean to arrest?—In any case, I cannot accept yours."

"There's no question of arrest yet, Sir Gyles," Hadley informed him sharply. "You were asked to tell us certain things. For some reason you wanted a few hours to 'think it over.' At Fell's insistence, I was willing to agree. Have you anything to tell us now?"

Gay put his hat and stick on the table, smiling at the hat. Drawing out a chair, he sat down with some care; he seemed to be listening to the chimney growl under a cold sky.

"Yes, I am prepared to tell you the whole truth." He turned round. "I warn you that you will find it disappointing. After I have told you, you will, of course, take what steps you like. What I wanted was time for reflection. I wanted to remember whether I had ever met Mrs. Kent before in my life. Wait!" He held up his hand. "I am aware what your evidence shows, superintendent. I know that I must have met her in the sense that I must have encountered her. You would not believe me this afternoon, when I assured you that a woman could have come to England claiming acquaintance with me—in fact, many people do just that—and such a staggering number of persons go through an Under-Secretary's office in the course of a year that he would require a card-index mind to remember a quarter of them. The plain truth is still this: I do not remember that woman. I have gone over very carefully in my mind everything I can remember for the year in question. I was then living in Norfolk. With the aid of my diary I can almost reconstruct the whole year. Mrs. Kent does not fit into it anywhere. I never had any 'dealings' with her, of the sort you mean; and I shared with her no secret which would have obliged me to kill her. That is my last word."

There was a silence. Hadley rapped his fingers on the table with slow indecision. Such seemed the sincerity of the man's manner that Hadley was evidently impressed.

"And that's all you have to say?"

"No, not quite all. Now comes my confession. I did put that photograph among the towels in the bathroom; or, rather, I did not put it there, since I never went into the bathroom at all and only pretended to find it. I also ruined the inside of a drawer with red ink. But that is *all* I did."

For some obscure reason, Dr. Fell was rubbing his hands with pleasure. Hadley studied Gay, who returned his look with a sardonic smile.

"Oh, yes, it was quite asinine. Was that what you were going to say?"

"No," interposed Dr. Fell. "A more important matter. Did you tear up the other photographs?"

"I did not."

"Good. In that case," said Dr. Fell, "I think you had better tell us about it."

"It is to be conceded that my first and only venture into crime was not a success," observed Gay. This seemed to sting him more than anything else. He was prepared for an attack; he did not appear to be prepared for the casualness of his hearers. "I suffered from the delusion that, if I made the thing grotesque, it would therefore be believed. It is a weakness of mine, which————"

"We can omit that," said Hadley. "Why did you do it?"

"Because I was not going to be framed," retorted Gay, with the blood now in his shrunken face, and a certain violence about his dry fingers. He leaned forward. "If you can ever believe me again, listen to the sober truth. I had not your eye or flair for detecting that the ink on the back of that picture was so old; it occurred to me afterwards, and made me curse myself. I thought it had been put there this morning.

"We returned to Four Doors at eleven o'clock. Good. That at least you don't dispute. And there is something I fear you missed, for all your deductions. I don't keep a regular chauffeur. I hire the same man when he is needed. This man—Burns—drove us back from the station this morning. Consequently, I had to pay him. I was going to pay him out of the small-change-purse in the drawer of my desk. Shortly after we arrived, and the others had gone upstairs while Burns was taking the luggage off the grid, I went back to my study————"

"Wait. Is that drawer, as the maids say, usually kept locked?"

"It always is. I was not aware, however, that my inquisitive staff knew it. I shall remember such possibilities when I commit my next crime. Very well. I went back to my study. As I passed through the lounge I heard somebody moving about in there. And, when I opened the door of the study, I was just in time to see somebody on his— or her—way out, slipping through the door at the head of the inner staircase."

"Who?"

"Ah, there we are. I honestly do not know. I want you to believe that. I was just in time to see the upper door closing."

"But noises, footsteps?"

"Yes, I believe there had been footsteps. But I can't describe them. I called out, and there was no answer. If I said I was not uneasy, I should be lying; I *was* uneasy, particularly as I had no idea what might be up. While I was thinking of this, I unlocked the drawer of the desk. I found all those photographs torn to pieces; and, on top of them, the picture announcing another—murder. Or so I interpreted it."

"How long had it been since you looked in that drawer last?"

"Probably three weeks."

"Go on," said Hadley quietly.

Gay's voice grew cold. "You are not a fool, my friend. You know what I thought and what I still think. It was a plain, barefaced attempt to saddle me with the blame for these crimes. You wish to know why I burst out against my guests this afternoon? That is the reason. Somebody had put that there. In a very short time somebody would have had it 'found.' That is how some genial friend repays hospitality." His fingers twitched, and he put them flat on his knees. "Wasn't it obvious? I am the only person with a key to that drawer. Yet someone else had got one. How, I don't know. Why, I know only too well. If you can think of any better evidence of a premeditated attempt to throw the blame elsewhere, I should be interested to hear it."

"And so————"

"Well, there is an ancient truism about beating someone to the punch. Possibly I acted like a fool. I don't know. I know that I was more furious in that moment than I can remember being since the days of my encounters with official stupidity in the Government. I compressed several years' rage into my feelings then, nor have I even yet recovered my usual child-like good temper."

He exhibited very little sign of child-like good temper. Yet it seemed evident that he sincerely believed in this quality as belonging to himself. Nobody commented; and, after a wheezy breath Gay went on:

"If I had known who put the picture in the drawer————"

"A picture," interrupted Dr. Fell dreamily, "on which the message had been printed two weeks ago."

"And a fact," replied Gay, "which I did not know. There was certainly a prowler in my study just after eleven, and up to no good. I repeat: if I had known who did it, I should have been after him with great pleasure. I should have tried my hand at counter-framing. But I did not know, and I was unwilling to make a guess which might be wrong. You see, I am more charitable in several ways than the real murderer. But above all I was exceedingly curious to mark the effect if I should fight back with a return stroke against 'somebody.' Perhaps it would have been more sensible to have got rid of the picture and the torn fragments. But I was not willing to have the matter drop altogether. Being innocent, I wanted the police to find such clues. But, by God, gentlemen, I was unwilling for the police to find such clues in my desk!"

"It didn't occur to you to come to us and tell the truth?"

"It did not," said Gay quite simply. "That was the only course which did not occur to me."

"Go on."

Gay cocked his head on one side. Amusement crept into his wizened face, the sort of amusement which had been absent from it for some hours.

"I concede that I was a trifle too spectacular. The donkey's tail, too, was an error; and I am not sure that I gained much by ruining the inside of the drawer with red ink. But I wanted to draw attention to it. Believe me, gentlemen, there was absolutely no thought in my mind of making the snapshots in the drawer unrecognisable. I admired, even when I felt my hair rise on my scalp, the ingenuity with which you dove-tailed these bits of evidence to-day. Can you understand this?—that I was stunned into a kind of detached interest, a contemplation of myself, by the way in which you spun a case out of nothing? I was Pickwick listening to Sergeant Buzfuz, and hearing my chops and tomato sauce used against me."

He paused.

"I think that's all I have to say. You understand, I did not have to create a prowler. There really was someone in my study. You have got a valuable piece of evidence, even if you got it in a way for which I am heartily sorry. I have no dark and terrible secrets connected with the past of Mrs. Kent. There is my story; you may believe it or not; and (just between ourselves) be damned to you."

Hadley and Dr. Fell looked at each other. Hunching

his neck into the upturned collar of his overcoat, Gay blinked at the fire.

"You don't find the atmosphere so hostile now, do you?" asked Dr. Fell amiably.

"Well—no. To tell the truth, no."

"Just a question or two," suggested the doctor, as Hadley scowled at his note-book. "Can you think of any reason why this person should have torn up all the pictures in that drawer?"

"No. I cannot. *That* could not be for throwing suspicion on me. Or at least I don't see how."

"H'mf, no. Would it be easy to have got a duplicate key to the drawer?"

"I shouldn't have thought so. It's something of an elaborate and intricate lock, for a desk drawer. But it's quite possible, since it was done. I am not exactly aware how these things are done. From a wide acquaintance with sensational fiction, I know that it is customary to use wax or soap; but if somebody handed me a sheet of wax or a bar of soap and said, 'Get on with it,' I don't think I should know how."

"You say you heard footsteps when someone was in your study. Light or heavy footsteps?"

"The best I can do," answered Gay, after reflection, "is the old and unhelpful 'medium' of this whole affair."

"It could not have been one of the maids?"

"Why should it be? They would have told me."

"Has your staff of servants been with you for a long time?"

"Oh, yes. They came with me from Norfolk. I—er—well, yes, I trust them absolutely, in so far as I trust anybody in this world."

"I think you told us you were living in Norfolk at the time Mrs. Kent was in this country?"

"Yes, if I have the dates down right."

"H'mf. Well—just at a guess, Sir Gyles, have you any notion as to who is responsible for all this?"

Gay shook his head without taking his gaze from the

fire. An odd smile twisted his mouth. "That is your business. Mine, too, I acknowledge; but in a different way.
Will you answer me, truly and freely, one question?"

Hadley was cautious, and interposed before Dr. Fell
could speak. "All depends on what it is, Sir Gyles. What
question?"

"Why," said Gay, still without taking his eyes from the
fire, "why have you two got a police-officer watching Miss
Forbes?"

Chapter 18

Hands Across a Grave-stone

KENT remembered the thump as he put his own tankard of beer down on the table. He glanced quickly round the little group; and he realised by the quiet that Hadley and Dr. Fell had taken the words with the utmost seriousness.

"What makes you think that?" Hadley asked.

"I see," said Gay, half humorously. "Don't you ever give anybody information on any subject whatever? When Miss Forbes and Mr. Kent here went for a walk this afternoon, you had a man following them. I am not certain who it was, but it was one of the sergeants I saw at the Royal Scarlet Hotel. When they came back to Four Doors, he followed Miss Forbes. I'm inclined to suspect that the reason why you—hum—lured me here to the pub to-night, instead of coming to my home, was for the purpose of getting a man inside. I don't object. But if my house is to be used for any purpose, I think I have a right to know what is going on. The place seems to be full of policemen. There was another in the bar to-night. You can't expect to disguise things like that in a village, you know; and I've been wondering what is going on."

"You'd better tell him, Hadley," said Dr. Fell. "I've

been urging it all along. He could give us a lot of help; and, if things went wrong in any way, he might wreck the plan."

"Why," interposed Kent, "have you been having Miss Forbes watched?"

Hadley smiled without enthusiasm. "Not for the reason you think. Just to see that she doesn't get into any trouble. As she might." He turned to Gay. "Very well. The whole story is that, with luck, we may get the murderer to-night."

Gay whistled two notes and sat up. "Interesting—also attractive! Where and how?"

"Your house is unusual," said Hadley. "It really lives up to its name. Unlike Seaview and Parkside, it really does have four doors, one on each side of the house. All those doors must be watched. If Fell is right, we hope to meet someone coming out of the house by one of those doors in the middle of the night."

"Leaving the house? Why?"

"That," said Hadley, "is as far as the story goes now."

Gay looked puzzled. "But I still don't follow this. If you merely caught somebody sneaking out of the house in the middle of the night, would that, *per se*, prove it was the murderer? I have always thought"—he frowned in a meditative manner—"that, when these traps were laid and someone is caught suspiciously prowling, the person caught is almost too ready to break down and admit his guilt. Suppose he were to fold his arms and say, 'This is a frame-up; I refer you to my solicitors?' Where would your evidence be?"

"We've got reason to hope," said Hadley, "that it would still exist." His tone changed. "What I'd like to ask of you, Sir Gyles, is this. If you should happen to see a police-officer in the house: in fact, no matter what you do see or however suspicious it appears: do nothing and say nothing to anybody. Let the household go to bed in the ordinary way, just as usual. At some time early in the morning you may be waked up; but by that time, if we have any luck, it may be all over. Will you promise that?"

"With pleasure. I—er—take it you accept my own story as being true?"

"If I didn't accept it, would I confide this to you?"

"I don't know," said Gay, with candour. "However, you can depend on me. If I scent the presence of dirty work, I also like the presence of dirty work. Good night, gentlemen. I hope I shall see you soon."

He pulled down his soft hat on his forehead, got up, and put the stick under his arm. By the door—the same door as that by which he had entered—he studied them for a moment before he made a brief salute and slipped out. The night, which remained cold and almost absolutely still, sent in hardly a chill after him.

Hadley looked at his watch.

"I'd better see the landlord," the superintendent commented. "We want none of *that* interference."

And he reached up and switched off the electric lights.

While the uncertain firelight rose up, and they heard Hadley blundering out into the bar, Kent looked at Dr. Fell. Dr. Fell drained his tankard without comment; he seemed to be listening for the sound of the church clock, which should be close on the half-hour.

"Am I allowed to know what's up?" demanded Kent, yet speaking in little above a whisper. "What's this about Francine? I've got a right to know————"

He could not see the doctor clearly, though he heard the wheezy breathing. "Miss Forbes," declared Dr. Fell, "is in no danger of being hurt. Set your mind easy about that."

"But if she's in any danger I want to————"

"H'mf, yes. That, I believe, is a part of the idea."

"I mean, I want to be on the spot to————"

"No," said Dr. Fell. "Never again. I allowed it in that case of the Eight of Swords; and I swore a mighty oath that it should never happen again. It merely meant tragedy. It's a professional's job, my lad; and a professional's doing it. But you can make yourself useful, if you will. We want two men on each of the four doors, and we're short-handed. If you like, you can share the watch. Without stretching the matter in the least, I can tell you that we may run foul of someone who is apt to turn infernally nasty if certain schemes go wrong."

The church clock struck the half-hour.

Hadley returned with the tankards filled. Very few words were passed. Sitting down close to the fire, so that he could keep his eyes on his wrist-watch, Hadley bent over it. Nor were there many sounds except the scrape of pewter on wood, the watch ticking, and the fire: which had turned to a red-glowing bank. The quarter-hour rang, and then the hour. Northfield was asleep.

At a few minutes past eleven Hadley, who had been going from one window to the other to pull back the curtains, moved across to the door opening on the stable-yard. He opened the door wide and stood peering out. A patch of cold crept over the floor like a carpet, widening against the walls, while the smoke of Hadley's breath blew back over his shoulder. There was a creak in the stable-yard, and a whisper.

"Tanner!"

"Superintendent?"

"Men in position?"

"All ready, sir."

"Hold on."

Hadley moved out on to a creaking board, and there was the mutter of a conference. When he returned he picked up his own overcoat from a chair. He faced Kent.

"Your beat," he said, "will be with the inspector at the back door of the house. He's got his instructions, so you just follow the leader. You're not to go into the back garden. Miss Forbes's room overlooks the back, and you might be seen if the moon should come out. Stay just outside the iron gates to the back garden, on the edge of the churchyard. You'll have a clear view of the back door from there. Haven't got the wind up, have you?"

"I don't think so."

"In any case—" Hadley bent down, picked up the poker from the hearth, and handed it to him. "In any case, just take this along. You're a private citizen, so you can be armed. All right."

Hadley went with him to the door. Inspector Tanner was waiting, his flat cap looking belligerent; but he muttered little beyond issuing directions. They moved out quietly through a gate opening on the green.

Or, at least, Kent supposed it must be the green. It was his first experience of that puzzling, disquieting phenomenon, the complete pitch-blackness and silence of an English village at night. We use terms loosely. Few urban streets, few parts of the remotest town in the deadest hour of the night, are ever without *any* light or *any* sign of movement. There is always someone awake. The African veldt is lighter and more aware than this core of a well-populated district, a village. Venture into one after nightfall, and you will never know you are there until you are in the middle of it: a house is as startling as a ghost. Your impression is that people must fall into a drugged sleep at nightfall. Even when a public-house remains open until ten o'clock, the blinds are so sealed or the lights so remote that it looks as dead as the rest; it might be a public-house in Pompeii.

Though he walked slowly beside the inspector, Kent heard his own footsteps sound with such distinctness on the frosty ground that he might have been making footprints for trackers to follow. It was a night of smoky cold, in which you could smell mist without seeing any of it. Later there might be a moon. Their own heavy footfalls went ahead of them round the green. There did not seem, Kent thought, to be any dogs in Northfield.

Instead of going down the dim road past the church Inspector Tanner softly opened the lych-gate of the church itself. Kent followed him through under the great pillars of yew. The poker had grown blistering cold in his hand; he was gripping it too tightly; so he thrust the end of it into his deep overcoat pocket and crooked his arm round it. They moved down a flagged path, still slippery with snow, and round the church. Beyond it was so dark that each of them kept a hand out in front. Then they went into the churchyard, which sloped down with some abruptness and in whose maze flat stones made obstructions.

"Which way?"

"Down here. Look sharp!"

Great elms were materialising out of the sky in front of them. Beyond ran a wall pierced by iron gates, and he could see a faint light. Evidently someone at Four Doors was still awake.

Kent, who had had it drilled into him as a boy that you must never step on a grave, had been doing some unusual walking to avoid them. He barked his chilled knuckles several times on the stones. Then, just as they stopped on the edge of the churchyard, the light at the house went out. But his eyesight was now growing accustomed to the dark; he had lost that naked feeling such as is experienced on groping into a dark theatre, and losing the usher with the flashlight half-way down the aisle. He could see a sort of shine on the iron gates. Beyond that, the white window-frames and white back door of the house loomed up with some clarity. He could even pick out the line of the chimneys. If it were not so infernally cold——

The church clock struck the quarter-hour.

He was leaning, incongruously, against the headstone of a grave, only a few feet from the gates. Objects were now assuming a night-time clarity; he made out the steps to the back door, the dust-bin, and all white paint seemed to shine. But he wished he had brought a pair of gloves. His hands felt raw, and a shiver went through him. "Walking over somebody's grave" was the thought that occurred to him: it was the same sort of feeling.

All the same——

What was going on in that house? Who or what did they expect to slip out of a door, when only the church clock was allowed to talk? He put the poker, which was beginning to irk him, down in the rimy grass by the headstone. Bending forward, he made certain that the rear gates had been left unlocked. They creaked softly, and he drew back. It seemed to be the consensus of opinion (good old sober phrase) that there was no danger. But there must be danger inside, or they would not have surrounded the place with a ring of guards. If they had let him go in to Francine, he would have felt better. The roles (he mused) were reversed. Those inside the house, those tucked into stolid steam-heated walls, were the persons who ran a risk; the people outside, in loneliness where there was no cover, were safe.

After touching the padlock on the gates, he crouched back to the headstone. He would get a crick in the back if he stood long like this. Sit down? That would be the easiest thing. The damp headstone, worn to a wafer by time, was scrolled along the top like the bed in the room where Rodney Kent had died. His fingers brushed it as he bent down to pick up the poker. And the poker was not there.

The poker was not there. His fingers groped in sharp patches of snow. He squatted down, moving his hand wide. He remembered just where the end of it had lain, and it was not there.

"What the devil—?" he whispered to his companion beside him.

"I have it," whispered the other voice.

Kent turned round in relief. His companion was standing just where he had stood when they took up their posts, still motionless and large. Kent's eyes, accustomed to the gloom, could not pick out details. He saw the blue coat, no overcoat being worn; he saw the silver buttons shining dimly; and he saw something else.

It was not an inspector of police who had been walking through the churchyard with him.

Then it moved. The noise of the poker in the air was a kind of *whup*; it sang in brittle air, and struck the headstone as it was intended to strike a head. Kent had not dodged: he had stumbled, or so he always remembered it afterwards. He heard his own knee strike the ground. He rolled, and bounced to his feet like an india-rubber cat, as the poker rose up and fell again. Then they were standing, breathing hard, with the headstone between them.

Now it seemed a very long time, minutes by the church

clock, before any other movement was made. The longest adjustment is an adjustment of thought. In front of him, at not much more than arm's length, was the person they had been looking for. How this person had come there was not the question. The question was what to do. It never once occurred to Kent to cry out and call for help. And this was not bravery, for he was frightened green and he could hear a thick beating in his ears. It is possible that he did not have time to think. He stood looking at the other through the mist of his own breath.

"Put that down," he whispered. "Who are you? Put it down."

The other did not reply. Instead he began to edge round the headstone.

"Put it dow————"

If it had been a longer weapon that his adversary carried, he might have risked a grab at it. But it was too suitable for murder at close quarters; that last blow, if it had landed, would have smashed his skull like an orange. As the indistinct figure shuffled round, Kent moved back. His adversary was moving the poker a little, like a boxer about to feint. Then he struck again—and overshot his mark.

Both were turning at the time. Kent felt no more than a faint burning sensation, as of pins-and-needles, in his thumb: which then seemed to be warm and soft and numb. It was the mound of the grave itself, wiry and slippery underfoot, which tripped the other in his forward drive. His body struck the headstone. His feet, off-balance, clawed for support. Thrown almost against Kent's chest, his neck was across the stone; and the poker rattled on stone as he tried to swing it. Kent, out of sheer fear, struck once the worst blow he knew. He struck with the closed fist, in the form of the rabbit-punch, across the back of the neck; and it caught the back of his adversary's neck on the gravestone as you might catch iron on an anvil.

Even as he heard the poker drop and roll in wiry grass, there was another and more rapid rustling. Three men came into the dimness under the bare elms; and two of them carried flashlights. He heard them breathe. And he recognised the heavy but not quite steady voice of Superintendent Hadley.

"No, don't call me anything," Hadley said. "I didn't turn him loose on you. I didn't know he was anywhere near here. The swine stole a march on us————"

He paused, drawing in his breath. Kent coughed, and kept on coughing for a moment.

"Whatever happened," he said, "*I've* probably committed the murder this time. There wasn't anything else to do. You'd better see if his neck's dislocated."

The figure had slipped down and rolled like the poker. Hadley bent over it as more heavy footsteps sounded, and Dr. Fell wheezed into the group.

"No, he's all right," said Hadley. "He'll be in proper shape to have it dislocated in another way. But he nearly got just about what he gave his victims. All right, boys. Roll him over. Make sure nothing has fallen out of his pockets."

Kent stared at his late adversary as the flashlight moved, and turned round again.

"Is that—?" he said.

Dr. Fell, who had been mopping his forehead with the bandana, got his breath. He ran the bandana through his fingers, blinked, and looked down in a disconsolate way.

"Yes," he said. "That's the real murderer, of course— Ritchie Bellowes."

Chapter 19

The Gentler Crime

AND he wore—?" asked Kent.

At the head of the lunch-table Dr. Fell leaned back expansively.

"He wore," said Dr. Fell, "for reasons which will be indicated, the spare uniform of an inspector of police; which is so exactly like that of the liftmen at the Royal Scarlet Hotel that I have sometimes been tempted to address them as 'officer.' You have not forgotten the description of the liftmen's uniform as given us by Hardwick? 'A short single-breasted blue coat high at the neck; silver buttons, shoulder epaulets.' You observe that they were the only uniformed men who wore *short* coats, like a police officer: the others had frock coats or tails. The only true and honest witness who had seen our phantom in blue (Mr. Reaper) said that he believed the phantom wore a short coat. Thus the field was tolerably narrow in drawing analogies. But all Ritchie Bellowes wanted anybody to notice (and calculated on anybody noticing) was the blue coat and silver buttons. You will see."

"But how did he get out of clink?" roared Dan. "And why———?"

To say that an atmosphere of tension had lifted from this group: to say that a hobgoblin had drifted away and a bad smell faded, would be to understate the case at Four Doors on that frosty morning of the second of February. Melitta Reaper was said to have cried all night, a proceeding which was generally thought to reflect great credit on her. A brittle sunlight showed at the windows of the dining-room, where Gay had provided a lunch that was something in the nature of a celebration. Kent's thumb, it is true, had given him a bad night after catching the weight of the poker in Ritchie Bellowes's hand; but he was too easy with wine and relief to be troubled about that. Dr. Fell presided at the head of the table like the Ghost of the Christmas Present. And Dr. Fell, wagging his cigar drowsily, said:

"Ahem. Yes, I am inclined to lecture, if only because I have so far had no opportunity satisfactorily to oil the wheels of my eloquence. But there is another and (if this can be credited) even more cogent reason. Academically, I like this case. It affords one of the better opportunities for gathering up pieces of evidence into one whole; and, to such of you as enjoy deductive orgies, it should prove of interest. The superintendent and I," he waved his cigar towards Hadley, "followed its tail together. If it is I who tell you about it, this is not because I have any great farsightedness; it is simply that I am the more enthusiastic and inexorable talker.

"The most satisfactory way to approach it will be to outline it to you from the first as we followed it. Now, when I went to the Royal Scarlet Hotel at first, I had only one firm idea in the welter: that Mrs. Josephine Kent was not what she seemed. Hadley, in his sharp brush with our host yesterday, outlined the reasons for investigating this; they began with the scuffed condition of the lettering on the battered trunk, and they did not end with some suggestive information we received from South Africa. They woke certain doubts to ally with others.

"At the inception, again, I had little doubt of Ritchie

Bellowes's story. The police were fairly sure he was not guilty; there were too many physical objections to it—notably his paralysed left arm, which would have made it impossible for him to have strangled Rodney Kent. Again, he certainly was very drunk at two o'clock when he was found. If he had committed a murder at midnight, he would not have gone to sleep on a sofa outside his victim's door and waited to be found at two o'clock. Again, the weapon was missing. Again, there was a complete lack of motive. Finally, I was inclined to credit his story of the 'man in the hotel-attendant's uniform' simply because it was too preposterous not to be true. This is not merely a congenital sympathy with the preposterous. I mean that it was not the *sort* of story which would do a deliberate liar any good. If Bellowes were the murderer, he would try to shield himself with a lie; but presumably not a lie so (apparently) meaningless and unrelated to the whole affair. At first glance the story of the hotel-attendant had no point unless it were true. If he were a liar, he might say he had seen a burglar in the hall: but not that he had seen an Arctic explorer, a ballet-dancer, or a postman.

"Thus, when we first came to the hotel, I was inclined to believe the murderer was actually in the hotel. More specifically, that it was one of the guests on the seventh floor. Then two points appeared to trouble me very badly about this.

"First, the utter disappearance of that uniform. Where in blazes had it got to? It was not hidden, burnt, or tossed out of a window; we should have found it, or traces of it. If a guest wore it, how was it conveyed into limbo afterwards? You see, it amounted to that. You might say that a guest was in collusion with an employee of the hotel, and had borrowed a real uniform for use in the masquerade, to return it later. Even if this were true, how was it spirited out of Wing A? The only entrance to that wing was watched all night, and up until the time the police arrived, by the three men working on the lift. Was it dropped out of a window by the guest, to be picked up in

Piccadilly or in the air-well by an employee in the conspiracy? This seemed unlikely; and yet the uniform was gone.

"Second, a circumstance which brought much light. Musing, it occurred to me that a door had been found strangely open. This was the spring-locked door of the linen-closet. Now, we had heard much of these varied new locks, which cannot be opened from the outside by any unauthorised person. The linen-closet was locked by the maid on the night before. It was found open in the morning. Therefore (and not unnaturally) ominous sideways glances were directed towards Mr. Hardwick, the manager.

"But my own mind is of a simpler nature. Nobody could have unlocked that door from outside. But anybody on earth can open a spring-lock from *inside*. You turn the little knob on the lock; and the thing is done. It therefore interested me to glance into the linen-closet. H'mf, ha. By the way, has anybody else here done that?"

Kent nodded.

"Yes. I looked in there when the superintendent sent me down to get Melitta," he answered, with a vivid recollection of the place. "What about it?"

"Good," said Dr. Fell. "Now, at the beginning of the whole case, we brought up the various ways by which an outsider could have got in and out of the hotel without being seen by the men working on the lifts. These were (1) climbing up and down the face of the building into Piccadilly; (2) climbing up and down the face of the building from inside the air-well; (3) by means of the fire-escape outside the window at the end of the corridor. All these were ruled out as 'so unlikely as to be very nearly impossible.' There were obvious objections to (*a*) and (*b*). As for (*c*), this would have been a broad highway of entrance and exit—an obvious lead, a dazzler of an easy way—but for one apparently overpowering fact. The locked window guarding the fire-escape was stuck and could not be opened; hence a sad eye passed over (*c*). But we looked into the linen-closet and got a shock. You," he turned to Kent, "looked in there on the morning after. What did you see?"

"A window," said Kent.

"Open or shut?"

"Open."

"H'mf, exactly. Since it would be a nuisance to take you back to the hotel in order to demonstrate this," pursued Dr. Fell, "we might just glance at the plan of Wing A. You see the window in the linen-closet. You also see that the commodious fire-escape outside comes within a foot—one foot—of that same window. A man would scarcely have to be a steeple-jack in order to stand on the fire-escape and climb in through the window.

"I stared. I saw. I was uneasy.

"For values had shifted backwards. Unless Hardwick or the maid had opened it, that linen-closet door could not have been unlocked from outside in the corridor: not by a guest, that is. And, if Hardwick or the maid opened it, they must first have got upstairs past the lift-workers: which they did not do. Therefore the linen-closet door was unlocked from inside the linen-closet itself, by the simple process of turning the knob. Therefore the murderer came into the linen-closet from outside. Therefore the murderer was (not to be too painfully repetitive about it), an outsider."

Dr. Fell put his large elbows on the table, seemed in danger of scratching his head with the lighted end of the cigar, and frowned at his coffee-cup.

"I hesitated, let me confess, on the brink of the deduction. I was not amused. Cases are not solved by one flying leap. The man who says, '*Only* this can be true; there can be no other explanation,' excites my admiration as much as he inspires my regret. But of the twelve major queries to be answered—the queries I propounded last night to Hadley and Christopher Kent—this theory would take care of two. These were (7), 'How did the murderer get into a locked linen-closet at the Royal Scarlet Hotel?', and (2) 'What happened to the costume afterwards?' The answers being, 'He came in from outside,' and 'He walked away in the uniform when he left the hotel.'

"But, if it might—might, you understand—be an outsider, what outsider? Our little coterie was all under this roof. Every person who had been at Four Doors on the night of the first tragedy, the night the uniformed figure had first been seen, was in the Royal Scarlet Hotel that night; and therefore segregated. Everybody— H'mf, well, not quite. Ritchie Bellowes was missing, for instance. And this for a good reason, since he was locked up at the police-station. In any case, he had never met Mrs. Josephine Kent—for she had not come to Northfield.

"This had been a fascinating query from the first: why did she rush away to riot in the home of her aunts? Why did she refuse to go to Northfield at any time, even after her husband had been murdered? We had then reason to suspect, and shortly afterwards reason to know, that she was not what she seemed. She had been in England for well over a year; she had returned to South Africa with a packet of money; but this visit she carefully concealed, and swore she had never been here before in her life. Why? Now note: she makes no real objection to travelling: she makes no objection to coming to London: she makes no objection to meeting people (such as Sir Gyles Gay, for example); but she will not *go to Northfield*. In a woman whose real character we were already beginning to see, that attack of 'utter nervous prostration' after her husband's death seemed to be overdoing it.

"This, then, was what one part of our simple minds registered. The other part of our minds registered still another question.

"As troublesome as the uniform was the murderer's consistent weakness for towels. Why, in the case of both murders, was a towel used to strangle the victim? As I pointed out to Hadley, it is assuredly a cumbersome and clumsy kind of attack, an unnatural kind of attack. Above all, it was unnecessary. The murderer assuredly did not use it for fear of leaving finger-prints: he would know what anybody knows, that you cannot leave finger-prints on human flesh, and that the marks of hands on a throat cannot be identified. We also know, from the universal lack of finger-prints on furniture or other surfaces, that the murderer must have worn gloves. We are therefore faced with the incredible spectacle of a murderer who uses *both* gloves and a towel to avoid leaving marks. And that will not do. We must look for another reason.

"Kindly note, to begin with, that Mrs. Kent was not strangled. No. She was put into the Iron Maiden trunk, and it was closed on her throat, with the towel wrapped round her throat so that the edges should not cut: so that it should leave bruises on the throat *like* strangulation. But why again, such a clumsy device? It would have been much simpler to have strangled her in the ordinary way, as (presumably) Rodney Kent had been strangled. This unnaturalness plus the unnaturalness of the towel began to make such a tower of inconsistencies that there must be method in them. What, off-hand, would that Iron Maiden device suggest to you?

"Why, it would suggest that the murderer was of too weak strength for ordinary strangulation—or a person who had the full use of only one arm.

"The full use of only one arm, the right arm.

"What else? The body is propped inside the trunk. The trunk is supported and propped against the left leg; the right hand pulls it powerfully together against that support of the murderer's left leg, and the thing is done.

"But this did not square with the murderous two-handed grip which was used on Rodney Kent. It seemed to put the matter out of court as a fantastic suggestion, until I reflected dimly on the subject of Rodney Kent's murder. Hadley had already described the furniture in the Blue Room here at Four Doors. The matter was not a certainty until I came here and saw for myself, but I could envision the scene. I have seen furniture of a much similar type. Just recall the foot-board of the bed. It is a heavy piece of work, pointed at the top and sloping down shallowly to a curve or round depression by the little posts. Thus."

He took up a pencil and drew rapidly on the back of an envelope.

"Like, you might say, the neck-piece or collar of a guillotine, in which the condemned man's neck lies. Rodney Kent was lying with his head almost touching the leg of the bed. Suppose the neck of an unconscious man has been put sideways into that homely guillotine. Suppose that neck were wrapped in a face-towel: not a bath-towel, which might be too thick and woolly to leave the proper sort of marks. Suppose the murderer stands over him; and, with one hand gripping one side of the neck, lets the other side be gripped by that broad curve of the wood, the victim's windpipe being pressed against the edge. When the murderer's work is finished—the marks being neatly blurred and made unrecognisable *as fingers* by the towel —you will have bruises in evidence of a crushing two-handed grip which went round both sides of his throat.

"Once might be coincidence. Twice could not be. It would explain the use of the towels. It would indicate that the murderer was a man who had the complete use of only one arm.

"Humph, hah! Well! I began to see the indications expanding like the house that Jack built, into (*a*) the murderer came from outside the Royal Scarlet Hotel; (*b*) he wore a uniform and went away in it; (*c*) he is, to all intents and purposes, one-armed. The only person who corresponded to this description was Ritchie Bellowes. The very thing which had so operated in his favour at first— namely, the partially paralysed left arm—was the thing which now rebounded against him. Everything began to rebound against him, once you considered. For, even if you still believed him to be ruled out as a suspect because he had been locked up at the police-station, the next connection was clear to any simple straightforward mind: I mean the connection between police-stations and blue uniforms.

"This point I indicated a while ago. 'A short single-breasted blue coat high at the neck, silver buttons, shoulder epaulettes.' Ladies and gentlemen, you have seen that costume on the streets every day; if the connection did not occur to you, it was because the prowling intruder was without any head-covering. If I wished (as I do not) to coin a bad riddle, I should cryptically inquire: When is a policeman not a policeman? And I should answer, amid universal groans, but quite sincerely: When he is without his helmet. This astonishing difference will have been noted by anyone who has ever gone to a trial and seen the police in court without their hats. Wearing their own hair, they are a different race. They look like attendants: as a matter of fact, in that capacity they *are* attendants.

"But to return. Ritchie Bellowes was locked up at the police-station. It was not reasonable to think that he said to his jailers: 'Hoy! Let me out of here and lend me a spare uniform, will you? I've got to go to London and commit a murder; but I'll be back later to-night.'"

"Nevertheless, we begin to reflect on one feature of national life—the village police-station. Like the village bank, it sometimes surprises observers. It is not a great grim temple of stone, erected in some city for the especial purpose of housing a hundred drunks overnight. No; it is an ordinary converted house (like the one at Northfield) such as you and I might live in. It has been taken over for the purpose of turning it into a police-station. But somebody had to build it. And, whispering back through the halls of consciousness, we hear the information that Ritchie Bellowes's father, the grand old man and 'character,' was a builder—who, as Hadley had informed me, had put up half the modern houses in the whole district.

"We heard of old Bellowes's taste for doing the work with his own hands. We heard in particular of his very particular sense of humour, much of which has been twisted and burnt to more ugly purposes into the soul of his son. We heard of the old man's fondness for tricks and gadgets and ingenious deceptions: in particular the trick door or passage. We heard of the 'greatest joke in the world' he was going to bequeath to the village. Since I share the same liking, I can have a radiant vision of what *would* seem a private joke of this kind: a joke of the ripest vintage: a use to which such a device, so far as I know, has never before been put: I mean, ladies and gentlemen, a trick door in the cells of a police-station."

Dr. Fell sat back, musing.

"Of course we have one precedent several thousand years old. You recall Herodotus's story of the sardonic builder who did the same sort of thing in King Rhampsinitus's treasure-house? But, with regard to young Ritchie Bellowes, observe one suggestive fact. This story he told —of the hotel-attendant seen at Four Doors at the time of Rodney Kent's murder—when did he tell that story first? Did he tell it immediately after he was nabbed on the night of the murder? Not at all. He only told it late next day, when he found himself in the police-station. Eh? Not only in the police-station, but in a particular cell of that place. Suppose he knew quite well that he could get out of that cell whenever he liked? Suppose he had badly bungled and ruined the first crime, for reasons I will indicate in a moment? But, if another crime is committed, he is now safe from suspicion. And so, with a hysterical cleverness I cannot help rather admiring—for adolescent hysteria, as you may have observed when we talked to him, was the keynote of his character—he told a certain story. . . .

"A story which, as Hadley said, was either delirium tremens or prophecy or truth. And, by thunder, but it was prophecy! Calmly considered, it was too prophetic. It not only put the cart before the horse: it set the cart running uphill without any horse to push it. Not only did he describe a hotel-attendant, but he actually and barefacedly gave the name of the hotel at which the attendant was employed. You recall: 'I should describe him as a medium-sized man wearing a uniform such as you see in the big hotels like the Royal Scarlet or the Royal Purple.'

"Of course this was necessary to implant the image in

our minds. If it is definite to a nearly damning extent, it had to be; and he had, fortunately, his reputation as the camera-eye observer to sustain him. He had to turn a blue coat and silver (or brass) buttons—which might have meant anything, and to an innocent observer would probably have suggested something altogether different—into a concrete figure. Hence the salver. The meaning of the salver plunged me into a spiritual abyss until I had hit on Ritchie Bellowes's guilt. Naturally, it was merely an extra flourish to limn out and establish his picture; there never had been any such salver or any such figure. But I am afraid I am running ahead of the actual evidence. Incidentally Hadley, where did you find the trick entrance in the police-station?"

Hadley glanced round the table as though reluctant to speak of matters in mixed company. But he saw only interested faces: the refreshed alertness of Gay and Harvey Wrayburn, the heavy admiration of Dan Reaper, Melitta's surprising cheerfulness, and the blank absorption of Francine.

"Find it?" growled Hadley. "We've been finding nothing else all morning. There were three of 'em; and nobody ever knew. This is going to cause a number of smart remarks in the Press when it all comes out. Of course it wasn't quite as simple as it looked for Bellowes. The trick doors to the cells, you know, connected only with the cellar of the inspector's private house next door. He didn't have the run of the station. Consequently, though he could walk through the inspector's house and out of the place, he couldn't go————"

"Go where?" asked Gay.

"Where he really wanted to go," said Dr. Fell, "and needed to go. That is, up from the cells into the charge-room and waiting-rooms of the station itself. There were several barred doors, including that of his own cell, in between. Also, there were men on duty at inconvenient hours in that part of the station. It was a nasty knock because, to a man planning what he had planned, two things are vitally necessary. He needs clothes, and he needs money.

"Bellowes, as you know, was being charged with burglarious entry. Well, there are certain formalities attached to that. They had put away his money, they had put away his tobacco, they had put away his overcoat. All these things were safely locked up upstairs in the station, where he could not get at them, and he was naked without most of them. Do you begin to see? He could not return to his own lodgings in Northfield without exciting some curiosity on the part of the landlady. He could not wake up a friend in the middle of the night and ask to borrow a mackintosh or ten shillings for train-fare. He was either in jail or he wasn't: there could be no middle course: and he must *not* be seen. The only thing he could take for the night, without being detected, was a spare uniform from the inspector's place next door. He must take it, for, oh, Bacchus, he needed that uniform! You recall, when we talked to him in his cell, he was in his shirt-sleeves on not too warm a day. There was no sign of a coat or jacket or sweater in the cell, because he hadn't been wearing one when he was arrested. Now the cells were heated and warm enough for him to stay there without discomfort. But he couldn't walk about on a snowy January night without discomfort, to say nothing of the more vital necessity to attract no attention. Hence the inception of his rather brilliant triple-barrelled scheme of the uniform; first as covering, second as an excellent disguise, third as the phantom attendant at the Royal Scarlet. Between the night of January 14th, when Rodney Kent was murdered, and the night of the 31st, he had plenty of time to explore; and to prepare the ground. He knew what everyone else knew (as you shall see) that the whole party was going to the Royal Scarlet: that Mr. Reaper had specifically insisted on booking rooms in Wing A of the new seventh floor: that Josephine Kent was joining them there on a specified date————"

"But how could he have known it?" cried Francine.

"H'mf, wait. One moment. Finally, to kill small Josephine had become the deepest and strongest obsession of his life. You can guess the reason why."

"Well?"

"She was Ritchie Bellowes's lawfully wedded wife," said Dr. Fell. "But she could hardly be very garrulous about anything without admitting that she had committed bigamy."

Chapter 20

The End of the Stone

ONCE that tumbler falls into place," said Dr. Fell, "the safe-door opens by itself. You understand why she was so positive in pretending she had never been in England before. You understand why she was so anxious to keep away from Northfield, where she had previously lived. You understand why, though she knew quite well that Ritchie Bellowes had killed Rodney Kent, she had no intention of denouncing him or his motive. You understand why she was not unduly apprehensive about her own safety, since she thought Bellowes was in jail. And the hub of it is this: Josephine Parkes Bellowes was supposed by everyone except her husband to be dead. But I beg your pardon. I must give you the reasons which led us to think this."

Kent, at that moment, was remembering a face. He was remembering Ritchie Bellowes sitting on the edge of the bunk in the cell, fidgeting. Tall and thin and hollow-eyed, Bellowes seemed to look back at him now as he had looked back last night across a gravestone. But most of all Kent remembered an atmosphere and two gestures. The first gesture was that of Bellowes's fingers massaging the veined hand of his withered left arm. The second was Bellowes's suddenly stamping his foot on the floor, when there was addressed to him a question he did not like: stamping his foot on the floor of the cell like a child in a tantrum. It was an oddly revealing gesture like the whole atmosphere of this man who had never quite grown up.

"I have told you," said Dr. Fell, "reasons for believing in Bellowes's guilt and Josephine Kent's past connection, in some fashion, with Northfield. If we looked for a motive, it could only be in some relationship which had existed between this woman and Bellowes in the past. What, offhand, did we know about Bellowes himself? I knew from the beginning—Hadley told me—some pertinent things about his past history, and the sudden moral collapse of this well-to-do builder's son. He had been married, and his wife had 'died of typhoid at the seaside': a term which stirred my interest when I heard it. She did not die under the eyes of the Northfield villagers, then. In any case, from this time on began the abrupt disintegration of Bellowes into a thoughtful, polite, sober-pacing toper. Beware of such, my lads: especially when they go out to wintry copses to drink alone and 'recite' in the moonlight, as Bellowes admitted he did. But you will note that Bellowes's change was not merely one of stamina: it was a crashing financial collapse as well. One moment he was tolerably well off, and the next he was stony. It surprised people. In murder trials they are fond of quoting the Latin proverb. 'No one ever became suddenly the baset of men.' I will affirm that nobody ever became suddenly the brokest of men, unless there had been a snatching away of great proportions somewhere.

"And 'Miss Josephine Parkes' arrived back in Johannesburg from England with— Well, let us consider her and certain of her actions. On the evening she was murdered, the first evening she had ventured out from the shelter of her aunts, she was wearing a bracelet of an extraordinary sort. Nobody had ever seen it before. It seemed unlikely that she had got it in the country. To a

simple mind it seemed much more likely that the bracelet
was something out of her past life: something which, up
to that time, she had carefully concealed. Why? Why bring
it out now? She herself throws out hints which convince
Miss Forbes that it had been given to her by someone she
fears. She hints that she may be in danger, and that the
bracelet is a safeguard against danger, because it contains
a clue to the identity of the man she fears. To Miss Forbes
she says 'If anything ever happens to me, which I don't
anticipate, you shall have it.' Then she changes her mind,
and in a fit of night-terrors she turns it over to Mr. Wrayburn with the words: *'You keep that for always. Then nobody will try to wake the dead.'*

"To wake the dead———

"That her fears were justified, and that the murderer
also thought it was a danger to him, are indicated by his
frantic ransacking of her hotel-room to find the bracelet:
even to the extent of stealing another linked bracelet resembling it, in the ghost of a hope that it might be the
right one in disguise. But I couldn't help thinking of Bellowes's 'dead' wife at the seaside. Was she dead? Or had
she quietly kissed sad finger-tips and slipped away with
Bellowes's money in her pocket: leaving him to explain
as best he could how he had been made a laughing-stock?
That also was worth investigating."

Wrayburn made a wig-wagging gesture as though he
were trying to stop a bus.

"Wait!" he urged. "What's the point of that damned
bracelet anyhow? What's the secret?"

"I will deal with the bracelet," said Dr. Fell, "shortly.
Here I feel inclined to tell you in a few words the facts, as
we have got them now, of the Bellowes-Parkes marriage.
Hadley got them this morning, from Ritchie Bellowes himself. He does not deny his guilt. Considering the evidence
against him, I don't see how he could.

"He met her and married her after two weeks in London in March 1933. It was, perhaps, inevitable. She had
come to England looking for fresh woods and pastures

new; and she had failed. Her bluff of knowing Sir Gyles Gay, and of being put on to something good in the way of employment, had succeeded only in getting her an interview with him————"

"Thank you," said Gay gravely.

"It must have been a sore setback, for I think she had great confidence in herself. A man like Ritchie Bellowes was her obvious move. He was quiet, he was obscure, he was emotionally immature, he was idealistic, he was content to worship; and he was moderately well off, which could be useful. In short, I think you will find his outward semblance much like that of Rodney Kent. She married him in her real name; but she did not tell him she came from South Africa. If she should wish to change her plans later, it would be a snag to let herself be traced. So they married, and they went to Northfield, and she made him an excellent wife (admired by all for her devotion) for eight or nine months. But she could not stifle here; and besides, being an abstemious woman, she disliked his fondness for drink. At her suggestion, and as a sound business principle in case anything should happen to the somewhat shrunken business he had inherited from his father, most of his money had been transferred into her name. She went for a seaside holiday. Just before doing so, she withdrew six thousand eight hundred pounds in cash; she left him a gentle, reproachful letter; and she disappeared. Well, you cannot do that without running a man into debts he can't pay, and nearly everything he has got must be sold to meet them. But banks, you know, don't tell.

"And there is one thing you must not do to a man of Ritchie Bellowes's type: you must not make a fool of him.

"These facts, night before last, I did not know. But, suspecting that Bellowes would do anything else in the world before letting this be known, suspecting that he had gone to some trouble and frenzy to create a mythical 'death' for the benefit of the neighbours, we had new questions ahead. How would Ritchie Bellowes learn that

'Josephine Kent'—the attractive wife of a South African who was coming to visit Sir Gyles Gay—was in reality his own nimble lady? The photographs, of course.

"You, Sir Gyles, were not living in Northfield at the time Josephine Bellowes-Kent was in England. You lived in Norfolk, as you told me, and moved here when Bellowes was compelled to sell this house. (You observe, though, how it brings our dates into line with the departure of the lady out of England?) But you were well acquainted with Bellowes. He had been several times to see you here. You were full of the subject of your visitors. You showed him all the photographs, didn't you?"

"I did," said Gay grimly. "*And* I talked. He seemed interested."

"On the other hand, it was not likely that many people from Northfield would see these photographs, and have their curiosity roused by the strange reappearance of Mrs. Bellowes. By your own confession, people are kept away from you by your manner; though Bellowes—drawn here by the fondness for his old home—you made hearty friends with as you are willing to be friends with anybody. The servants, usually local people, would not stumble on anything; you brought them from Norfolk. But Bellowes could not risk anything. Sooner or later, he had to see that those unfortunate pictures were destroyed—for when she died there must be no picture of her in a newspaper.

"Unfortunately it was you—the night before last—who threw a sizable spanner into *our* machinery. Just before I went out to dinner with those two"—he glanced sadly at Francine and Kent—"I had a conference with Hadley. He had got his cable from South Africa and his information from South Africa House. It threw light on Mrs. Kent; but, by all the top-hats of hell, it also threw suspicion on you. My stride was interrupted by you. It was possible that my idea was as wild as wind; that one Sir Gyles Gay was the man in the case and the murderer at the Royal Scarlet Hotel. Harrumph. Heh. Hah. Therefore, Miss Forbes, when you said to me, 'Won't you tell us who is guilty so that we can sleep soundly,' or words to that effect, I had to————"

Francine sat up.

"Yes," she said, "I've been waiting to ask you about that. Why did you deliberately sit there and make out (partly, anyway) a case to show that Bellowes was innocent, and had been brought as a witness to Rod's murder————?"

"I don't think you understand," said Dr. Fell humbly. "I deliberately sat there, as you put it, and tried to make out the strongest case I could in favour of Bellowes, in order to convince both myself and you that he *must* be guilty. Particularly to convince myself."

"What?" said Kent. "Hold on! The paradoxes are coming a bit too————"

"It's not very complicated, is it? I prayed that you would knock holes in my case. An intelligent sneer would have been manna to me. But you didn't, worse luck. You see, I was quoting all the points which in my mind told against Bellowes—(1) his having a key to this house in his pocket, with deliberate intent beforehand; (2) his whisky-drinking to screw up his courage for the murder of Rodney Kent, which drinking made him foozle the job after all; (3) the fact that his finger-prints were in the Blue Room—and I was trying to see whether innocent explanations of them could be found. If Bellowes were *not* guilty, those facts had innocent explanations. I raked my wits to find 'em. For these innocent explanations did not satisfy me. I hoped you would say, 'Bosh,' as I felt b-o-s-h. I hoped you would say, 'Gideon, *mon vieux*, all this is the merest eyewash. Your facts damn Bellowes; your explanations do not exculpate him. Witness? Do you expect us to believe that a murderer is so fond of witnesses to his crime that he pays one to come in and watch it? In all your fog of words, where is the sense?' I should then have said, radiantly, 'Good. Excellent. That is what must be so.' But you didn't. You appeared to accept it. Perhaps you noticed my strange behaviour, which caused me to mop my forehead resolutely; and I went home, a most unusual thing, before it was time for the party to break up.

"I was particularly despondent because you, Miss Forbes, had almost burnt your fingers a moment before on just what I believed to be the reason for the masquerade in the blue uniform. I can hear you yet, 'That must mean,' you were saying, 'he was preparing everybody's mind for his appearance later, when he came to kill Jenny —but where is there any indication in just a coat and a pair of trousers?' I came close to uttering a cheer; I stimulated you with my fiery glance; but the light went out.

"For this is what I thought, and know now, had really happened—beginning with the first murder:

"Bellowes coolly determined to kill Rodney, in a quiet and workmanlike manner. There was to be no flourish of hotel-attendants. Bellowes had met all of your party at his memory-entertainment; he knew Rodney; it would be easy to find out which room Rodney occupied. By the way, he made one more hideous slip when he told me an unnecessary lie at the police-station: Bellowes told me that he (the memory-expert) couldn't remember a single feature of Rodney's face. And his motive? You, Miss Forbes, told me about that at our celebrated dinner. It was believed by many people—and well known to Sir Gyles here, who liked to joke about it—that Rodney Kent had married Josephine for her money. Her money? Ritchie Bellowes's money. You must not tamper with men of Bellowes's kind. I can imagine him looking at the colourless figure of Rodney, the pleasant and colourless Rodney; and I can imagine the inside of his mind turning black with pure hate. Conjure up before you a picture of Bellowes's face, and you will see what I mean.

"But the murder was to be a workmanlike job. It was to be a murder by 'strangling,' since Bellowes's arm is paralised and he can strangle nobody. He had had a long time to think about it, you know. Did he know about the useful furniture in the Blue Room, which would enable him to do it? Of course he knew about it; that furniture was there in his father's time, and Sir Gyles Gay must have bought it with the house; Bellowes told us so himself.

"Bellowes left the pub at ten o'clock, with just the right amount inside to steady himself, and a bottle of whisky to keep him at it. He waited until the household at Four Doors had gone to bed at about midnight. He allowed a few minutes more, and then let himself into the house with his key. He went upstairs quietly. He was then wearing gloves; he was carrying a life-preserver in his pocket, and a poker under his overcoat, supported by his more-or-less useless left arm. He went into Rodney's room. Rodney, just retiring, would be surprised to see him; but not startled or alarmed. Any excuse for his presence would suffice. He distracts Rodney's attention, and knocks him unconscious with the life-preserver. Then he does what has to be done.

"Afterwards (at, say, about twenty minutes past twelve) he slips downstairs. His work in the house is not finished. He goes to—why, the study, of course, where his father's old-fashioned furniture remains in the house exactly as it remains in the Blue Room upstairs. He opens— the locked drawer of the desk, certainly, with the paternal keys he has kept as he has kept everything else he can. Who else could have opened that (admittedly, by Gay) elaborate lock? That is where he knows he will find the photographs.

"The whole scheme is arranged. Josephine is to go next. In fact, he has already written to her, announcing coolly that he will do this; for he knows it is one letter she will never dare show to anyone. (You recall, she received two letters postmarked Northfield, one from her husband and the writer of the other unknown?) She replied to this. She replied with equal coolness that he had better not try any tricks, for if anything happens to her she still has a bracelet which will hang him. Hence the reappearance of the bracelet. Meantime, Bellowes will give a turn of the screw to her feelings by killing her bigamous husband, Rodney; still knowing that she will not dare to speak.

"After the murder of Rodney, then, Bellowes crept down to the study. He closed the curtains and turned on one small lamp. It will interest you to know what we heard this morning, the place he had chosen to hide his murder-properties—the poker, the life-preserver, the gloves, the key to the desk, and so on—until he should need them again. Well, they were actually in the desk all the time. They were in a false compartment at the back of it, another of the devices of his father. It was the best of all hiding-places for them: if by any remote chance they were found, they would only serve to incriminate Sir Gyles or some member of the party.

"After stowing them away, he proceeded systematically to tear to pieces every photograph in the desk drawer, Sir Gyles's own as well. But a new idea occurred to him. I told you this man could never be satisfied with anything. I told you he could never let well-enough alone; and that is what betrayed him. The only photograph he did not destroy was the big group one, the slide at the fun-fair ————"

Gay interposed.

"There is another question here," he said. "I suppose he kept that picture because he could use it as a threat against Mrs. Kent without ever leaving behind a view of her face. But how did he know it *was* Mrs. Kent in the photograph? I imagine I must have shown him the picture, at one time or another; but I didn't learn who it was until you people had actually arrived here————"

"The memory-test!" said Francine.

"I beg your pardon?"

"That's it," agreed Dan, opening his eyes. "Damnation! I've been trying to remember just where I'd seen that picture recently. We were both trying to remember it yesterday. The memory-test, of course. When Bellowes gave his demonstration, I mean. One of the inevitable tests is to shove a photograph under somebody's nose, a group photograph with lots of details, and ask him to quote the smallest detail after one look. We used that picture! And somebody remarked that the unseen figure was Jenny. All right. Go on."

"The sight of the bottles of coloured inks," resumed Dr. Fell obediently, "put into his head the idea of writing, 'There is one more to go,' and of putting it beside his first victim. He did write it. But he rejected the idea as much too dangerous. He wanted the woman to know she was in danger. But he didn't want anybody else to know it. So he sat there by the desk in the middle of the night, puzzling the matter through his little brain—and at the same time (now his job was finished) gulping down steady pulls at a bottle of neat whisky.

Wrayburn stared. "You mean, with a dead body upstairs, he sat as cool as anything in somebody else's house————"

"You forget," said Dr. Fell, "that he wasn't in somebody else's house. That's the keynote to the whole affair. He was in his own house, the only place familiar to him. The others were interlopers, whom he hated. And, instead of hurrying out of the house, the fool proceeded to get drunk. As you might have guessed, the more he took the more indecisive he became, the more uncertain; for he could *not* let well-enough alone. Was everything all right upstairs? Was there anything he had omitted? It was Ritchie Bellowes's form of self-torture. And, when he was three parts gone, he had to see. He left the photograph in the desk. He went upstairs in the dark, with no glove on his hand and hardly a thought of precaution in his head. Scarcely in a condition to see, he opened the door of the Blue Room wide—as it was found—and proceeded to leave finger-prints by turning on the light. He had enough sense left to realise that he had been a fool; but it was too late. He had no sooner turned out the light and gone out (in the moonlight) when you, Mr. Reaper, opened your own door. He couldn't run; he could barely walk. So he did the instinctive thing. He tumbled down on a sofa and pretended to a stupor which was only half pretence.

"That, in the wrecking of the plan, was the story of the first crime and the reason for the second.

"I have told you how, out of necessity and his own cunning, he got the scheme for the second. He was going to kill Josephine at the Royal Scarlet, and he was going to be an 'attendant' in uniform; hence his story. He knew you were all going to the Royal Scarlet, he knew about the new top floor, he even knew the date: heaven knows you all talked enough about it. Then you altered the date, and went one day earlier; a piece of information which was kindly passed along to him by Inspector Tanner in Tanner's daily questionings.

"They lock up the cell-row for the night at nine-thirty. Before a quarter to ten he was out of jail, dressed, in one of those pitch-black village nights where nobody would have noticed him even if he had been seen. If he were going to London, as I told you, he would need money. But nothing could be simpler. He still had his key to Four Doors. There was nobody here except servants. In the drawer of the study desk, as he knew from his visit two weeks before, there was a purse containing at least enough money to pay his bus-and-train fare to town.

"And, of course, he had to come here to get his invaluable poker as well. . . .

"Hence the mysterious theft of loose change. With good connections by train and bus, the time from here to town is an hour and ten minutes. This would get him to Charing Cross at just gone eleven. A bus to the hotel, the poker wrapped in a newspaper; now (invaluable!) the status of his police uniform, which is not only a passport anywhere, but will allow him—unsuspected—to question car-starters or outside-porters about where fire-escapes lead; and within fifteen minutes he is on the fire-escape outside the corridor of Wing A in time to see your party return from the theatre.

"He had to wait until the departure of the maid before he could get into the linen-closet through the window. But even then, he waited until midnight before he attacked: why? Because he was patiently waiting for someone to *see* him. With his cap off, he was now disguised; he was transformed into an employee. He mustn't be seen by a real employee, of course, which will blow the gaff immediately. But he wants a guest to catch a glimpse of him —and they obstinately remain in their rooms. The linen-closet will be his refuge if anyone should come too near. It was lucky for him, however, that he did not attack. Wrayburn was in the woman's room, though he couldn't tell that because Wrayburn had entered and left by the side door to 707; and, as it was, they narrowly missed each other.

"They would have missed each other by a still narrower margin if Mrs. Kent had not prudently waited a couple of minutes to make sure the coast was clear before she opened the door to the attendant, who murmured, 'Extra towels, madam.' She was not afraid then. Her attacks of tremors had passed; Bellowes was safely under lock and key; and Wrayburn was within call. In this brief interval you, Mr. Reaper, glanced out to set your watch. If you had looked a second longer, you would have seen an attendant walk into 707 with the towels—and he wouldn't have minded if you had. In fact, it was what he was hoping for. He posed for you.

"Mrs. Kent, with a comforted heart, opens the door to a mound of towels. She says, 'Yes?' He gets just across the threshold and lowers the towels, and she has one good glimpse of his face before he does what has to be done. He couldn't catch her on the back of the head as he had caught Rodney. She knew him.

"But, above all things, he must find that bracelet. It will require, as we decided before, an intensive search of the room. To keep himself secure against interruption, he hastily puts a pair of shoes (or what he thought to be one) outside, and hangs the 'quiet' notice on the door. He is wearing the same old gloves he used for Rodney's murder. But he can't find the bracelet! He comes across the key to the room, and he pockets all the loose change in her handbag; he is not (he will now point out to you, somewhat frenziedly) a thief, and he doesn't want any other money. But still he can't find any bracelet except

Mrs. Jopley-Dunne's. Do you know what he did with that bracelet later, by the way? He threw it down a drain out of sheer spite, proving that there are vagaries to the character of even the most altruistic murderer.

"Next observe how the technique of this crime is exactly like the first. Again, though with better reason this time, he cannot let well-enough alone. He is convinced that the right bracelet isn't anywhere in the room. Yet he is nearly wild with indecision. Once he actually does leave the room—and takes the key to 707 with him—because he knows he's going only as far as that linen-closet; and he will come back. He wavers exactly as he wavered here. Yet he can't delay too long, or he will miss the last train back. Back he goes to that room for one last look. The little devil has tricked him, even if she's dead. Where in the name of Satan is that bracelet? In the same kind of jeer at her as he had thought of once before, he takes the 'quiet' sign off the door, he scrawls 'Dead Woman' on it with a pen he has found in the trunk. Leaving the key in the door, he goes at last."

Dr. Fell drew a deep, wheezing breath, and put down his dead cigar.

"Well, you can guess our plan of campaign. If our views about Bellowes were correct, we already had enough evidence to convict him. But he would be damned beyond excuse if we could once more entice him to come out in that uniform. I had to handle him warily when I spoke to him at the police-station; I wouldn't let Hadley get in a question edgeways. It was all the worse because Bellowes was in a bad state of nerves: he hadn't had a drink in two weeks, and he really was in a state of enforced sobriety as great as though he had been locked up there beyond any getting out. You see, he couldn't get out except at night when the watch was withdrawn; and, by the time he could reach a pub where he wouldn't be recognised, our beautiful licensing hours had closed the pubs.

"I gave him firmly to understand I believed in his innocense. I outlined to him my bogus theory of himself as a 'witness.' He was so surprised at the novel idea that for a minute he was thrown off balance, and couldn't play up to it; believe me, I cursed in my sleeve at that. By the time he was tentatively agreeing to it, it was too late. What I had to do was bring the missing bracelet into the conversation somehow, without exciting suspicion. I finally got round it by the wild expedient of suggesting that the 'phantom attendant' had been carrying something on a salver at Four Doors. I couldn't go further without making the thing apparent. When we were leaving, you recall, I went back and spoke to him. I said that we had found a piece of evidence which the late Mrs. Kent had said would be important, a bracelet: I described it: I asked him if it might have been in the possession of the blue-coated phantom. He said no. I said, with a thoughtful shrug of my shoulders (which could, I fear, only be measured with a seismograph) that we were sending it for expert inspection, and showing it about to a few persons: I said Miss Forbes was keeping it for us.

"I believed, you see, that he would be fool enough and in a bad enough state of nerves to have one more go at that bracelet, and wouldn't hesitate if he thought he was dealing with a woman. He didn't hesitate. But the plan nearly miscarried. Everything was all right—we were going to let him get into Four Doors, let him pinch the bracelet, and catch him with it coming out—as we saw it. I assure you (cease this uproar) that Miss Forbes was in no danger: there were two men in her bedroom, although she didn't know it, and would have been at him if he had come within two yards of her. Things went well until Bellowes, who knew Hadley and I were staying at the pub, came close to reconnoitre on his way down. Hadley (quite naturally, in that dead blackness) mistook him for Tanner. And Bellowes couldn't run again. From what Hadley said, he knew the game was up. The only question was what he should do about it. I think he pondered it very carefully in his usual quiet style. After reflection he decided that, since he was going to be caught, he would sim-

ply take somebody with him; and he was not particular
who. When the real Tanner turned up at the pub ten minutes later, your humble undersigned turned suddenly ill.
That there was no casualty was not our fault. I salute
your courage, sir; I congratulate your future wife; and I
think that's all."

They looked at each other, and Wrayburn smote the
table.

"No, by the gods, it's not all," said Wrayburn. "What
about that bracelet? Where is the secret writing on the
bracelet or the acrostic or whatever it is? I've made a fairly
extensive study of puzzles; but I can't make head or tail
of it."

"The secret," said Dr. Fell, "is that there is no secret
writing."

"But there's got to be! You've quoted what Jenny said
to me. What about the things she told Francine, particularly: 'Has the inscription any meaning?' 'Only if you're
able to read it; that's the whole secret.' "

Dr. Fell chuckled.

"She was quite right, correctly and literally right. I am
not here referring to one fact which does not concern us:
namely, that originally there was an inscription 'J.P. from
R.B.' engraved on the inside, which she had had removed
some time ago. Bellowes, of course, thought it was still on
there, covered over in some way. The real secret is something quite different. Josephine thought it was quite sufficient to damn Bellowes, if it were found, and she was
right. There were only two of those black stones—originally belonging to Bellowes's father—and set in rings.
Ritchie had one of them put into a bracelet for her, keeping the other himself. Many people had seen them; and
the secret was so curious that it would be remembered.
Do you know what the secret was? It lies in two words, a
description not of the jewel itself, but of the device which
that jewel represented."

"Well, what was it?"

"It was a sober-stone," said Dr. Fell.

After a pause Wrayburn struck the table more softly. "Of course," he said. "By Xenophon's ten thousand, of course! Why didn't I ever think of it? To wear a sober-stone ring was the mark of the well-bred Roman at banquets. Suetonius is very serious about it." He grew excited. "Hang it, it's such a good and practical device that it ought to be revived to-day. The sober-stone was a semi-precious jewel of any kind on the flat surface of which could be engraved a few lines of writing. Some good text: this one was especially applicable, and in clear but small print. The noble Roman began drinking at a banquet, and from time to time he consulted his ring. Whenever he could not clearly read the text written on it, he knew he had got over the line of being sober and that it was time to stop. '*Claudite jam rivos, pueuri, sat prata biberunt.*' 'Stop singing; enjoyment has been taken.' And, 'Only if you can read it; that's the whole secret.' Oh, my *eye!*"

"Exactly," said Dr. Fell with benevolent placidness, "though the device, far from commending itself to me, is so conscientious that it makes my flesh creep. The interesting point is that Ritchie Bellowes gave it to her. They plighted their troth to each other with the stones. It was her good influence, you know, her sweetness and light, which turned Bellowes from a potentially sound and likeable man into a murderer with a fixed idea. I don't think I blame him, morally."

Dan Reaper drew a deep breath. "All I've got to say is," he declared, "that I wouldn't go through that again for—well, for a lot of money. I didn't know what to think. Half the time————"

"Whom did you suspect, my dear?" asked Melitta placidly.

They all started a little, and looked at each other. It was the letting out of a secret, a releasing of tension, which made them all sit back with a jerk. And then, gradually, a shamefaced grin appeared on several faces.

"Yes," said Wrayburn. "Let's have it. Who?"

"I suspected *you*, you cuss," Dan told him with some

violence. "Maybe I had been reading too many of Chris's tomfool ideas. But, since you had a cast-iron alibi and were ruled out of it practically from the start after having been once suspected—well, it looked funny. Sorry about my rotten manners————"

"Oh, that's all right. Here, what about another glass of wine? To tell you the truth, I should have voted for our good host————"

"The notion," agreed Gay, "seems to have occurred to several persons. For myself, since frankness seems not to be resented, I first favoured Mr. Kent there. But I very quickly shifted to Miss Forbes————"

"Me?"

"Especially since," insisted Gay, "it was you who were prowling about in the study yesterday, just before I found that long-lost photograph in the desk. I saw you closing the door at the top of the stairs————"

"But I was only looking in there to see what had happened to everybody! I never even thought of it afterwards."

"—and, when I saw the police had a man following you," pursued Gay, "I was sure of it. I should have been very sorry. You observe that I shielded you. Have you any views, Mrs. Reaper?"

Melitta, almost beaming, had already wound herself up. "Well, of course, I shouldn't like to venture any opinion, but I felt sure my husband must have something to do with it. I do not say, mind you, that he is any worse than other men; but then that is what other men do, and I have felt most horribly unhappy about it. As my grandfather used————"

"So now I'm guilty," said Dan. "Well, you're luckier, old girl. With Chris's case against the hotel-manager, that makes a pretty big round, and you're the only one who has escaped suspicion."

"No, she hasn't," Kent pointed out. "Melitta has been suspected by Francine here————"

Francine looked at him sadly. She said: "Chris, you

didn't really believe that?" and she stared at him in genuine perplexity.

"Believe it? Why, you told me yourself————"

"Chris, you are a blockhead! Of course I thought it was you. Why do you think I've been acting like such a harridan? I thought you were carrying on with her. I always thought so. That's why I was so terribly anxious to get that bracelet and find out if it concerned you. And at the restaurant, and afterwards much harder in the taxi, I was trying and trying to get you to tell me if you had killed her by saying it might be Melitta————"

Kent stared round.

"Let me understand this," he said. "Things have come to a fine pass. You don't know what people are thinking even when they tell you. What do you call that?"

From the head of the table Dr. Fell put down his glass and spoke.

"I call it," he said, "a detective story."

THE SKELETON IN THE CLOCK

LOCKED ROOMS:
A Mystery Guild Lost Classics Omnibus

THE SKELETON IN THE CLOCK

by

John Dickson Carr

Mystery Guild
Garden City, New York

THE SKELETON IN THE CLOCK

Printed and manufactured in the United States of America
ISBN: 978-0-7394-9089-1

Chapter 1

The policeman, passing through Moreston Square at three o'clock in the morning, saw lights still burning in the windows of the top-floor flat at 16. And he smiled to himself.

That would be Miss Ruth Callice's flat. The chimes from St. Jude's Church rang the hour, rippling through the little eighteenth-century square and lapping it in security. Police-Constable Davis glanced up at a quarter-moon over the rooftops. No more, he thought, of *one* thing. These narrow red-brick houses, these white-painted window-frames and pane-joinings, wouldn't burst or burn amid a nightmare of noise. At least, P. C. Davis amended with the skepticism of all his tribe, not just yet.

In front of the door of number 16 stood a heavy shiny car, a new one to rouse envy. Again he looked up at the lighted windows, lulling against rooftop and sky.

Miss Callice was—nice. And he didn't mean it in any smug or smarmy way, either. Young, good-looking, but (still his mind would find no better word) nice. There were people up there, the men in black ties or white, the women in high-cut or low-cut dresses, sometimes as late as three in the morning, like this. But never any disturbance; seldom any drunks. They went in talking; they came out talking. What did they find to talk about?

At that moment, in the living-room on the top floor, John Stannard, K. C., was employing his most measured tones.

"Let's suppose, Ruth, your theory is correct. In that case, what would be the most dangerously haunted place in the world?"

Miss Callice, on the sofa under silver-shaded wall-lamps, made a protest.

"I didn't say it was my theory," she pointed out, and looked at her two companions. "It doesn't necessarily mean I believe in—"

"Say it," Stannard urged dryly. "Don't be afraid of a word; or you'll never get near the truth. Say it. 'The supernatural.' "

It would have been difficult to tell Ruth Callice's age, though she could not have been more than twenty-eight. And P. C. Davis's definition of niceness would be hard to analyze even by closer observers.

Frankness? Honesty? True; but these qualities, when too strongly observable, are suspect because they may be assumed. It may have been that she completely lacked coquetry; never thought of it, never noticed herself; though she was undeniably pretty and her rounded body, in the oyster-coloured evening-gown, was far from unnoticeable as she sat coiled on the sofa.

The light, smoke-misted, glistened on her light-brown hair. She rested one elbow on the arm of the sofa, her arm straight up, fingers turning over a cigarette that had gone out. When she changed her position, the light altered the complexion of her face and shoulders from pale to pink-pale. Her straight-forward eyes, dark-brown, regarded Stannard deprecatingly.

"I only said—" she began again.

"Let me put the case to you."

"Oh, my lord of the law!"

"My dear Ruth, it's not necessary to mock at me."

Ruth Callice was genuinely astonished. She sat up. "Stan! I never thought any such thing!"

"Never mind," chuckled John Stannard, K. C.

He had one of those heavy voices, roughened into what for him was unjustly called a whisky-voice, which can make any statement sound abrupt. Thick-bodied, not overly tall, he picked up his cigar and settled back in the easy-chair. Out of a roundish face, roughened like his voice, the brilliant black eyes peered sardonically. Though he had reddened during those remarks with Ruth, this may have been a matter of the drinks.

"A man dies," Stannard went on, after a gust of cigar-smoke. "His soul is heavy with evil; with spiritual poison; call it what you like. He may die a natural death; more probably, he commits suicide or is killed. In any case—"

Here Stannard made a chopping motion with his hand.

During this time neither Ruth Callice nor John Stannard had glanced at the third person in the gilt-and-silver room: a young man who sat some distance away from them, his head down and his hands on his knees, near the empty fireplace and the grand piano. At the barrister's last words he did look up.

"Your dead man," continued Stannard, "in a spiritual sense is chained there, He's what the books call earthbound. Is that correct?"

Ruth gave a quick little nod of absorbed attention.

"Yes. That, you see," she threw out her hands, "*is* what would make some of these houses so horribly dangerous, if it were true. It wouldn't be like an ordinary haunting. It would be like . . . like a man-eating tiger."

"Then why don't your psychical researchers do the obvious thing?"

"The obvious thing? I don't follow you."

With the cigar Stannard gestured round at the bookshelves.

"You tell me," he retorted, "that at Something-Old-Hall there's a psychic strangler, and at Somewhere-Low-Grange there's an earthbound force that can crush you to death. It may be so; *I* can't say. But I can tell you a far better place to look for evidence. If what you say is true, what *would* be the most dangerously haunted place on earth?"

"Well?"

"The execution shed of any prison," replied Stannard.

He paused, letting the image sink in. Then he got up and went to the coffee-table beside the sofa. His black hair, showing no grey and brushed to a nicety round his head, gleamed in contrast to the reddish, roughened face. The white shirtfront bulged and crackled. Picking up the decanter, he poured a very little whisky into his glass.

"But that's—horrible!" Ruth cried.

"No doubt," Stannard agreed dryly. "All the same, think of it for a moment."

The sofa-syphon hissed.

"Your human tiger, at the very high point of his rage and desperation, is dragged to the execution shed and has his neck cracked on a rope." The strong, faintly husky voice pointed it vividly. "If anybody would leave an earth-bound soul in that place, he would.

"Believe me," Stannard added abruptly, "I've defended too many murderers not to know that many of them are decent honest fellows. There-but-for-the-grace-of-God, and all the rest of it. When you hear the foreman of the jury say 'not guilty,' you feel half sick with relief. You pat yourself on the back for the rest of the week."

Ruth's eyes were fixed on his face.

"I've heard," she said, "that only two persons you defended on a murder charge were ever . . . well, executed."

"Much exaggerated, my dear. Much!" Stannard chuckled; then his expression changed. "But I've seen the other kind of murderer too. That's why I don't scoff at spiritual evil."

He lifted his glass, drained its contents, and put it down.

"By God, it *is* true to say they don't know the difference between right and wrong. Not at that time. Mostly they go to the rope with indifference; outwardly, that is. But not inside. They're boiling crazy. Society hasn't understood them. Society has persecuted them. They want to tear . . ." Stannard spread out his hands. "That's why I say, Ruth, that a place like Pentonville or Wandsworth must be deadly. Hasn't any psychical researcher ever thought of spending a night in the execution shed?"

Ruth lifted her shoulders.

"I don't know," she confessed. "I never thought of it." And she turned towards the young man who was sitting near the fireplace and the grand piano. "What's *your* opinion, Martin?"

Martin Drake looked up. Like Stannard, he was dark. Unlike Stannard, he was tall. But his cat-green eyes, now absent minded, had a sardonic quality which sometimes matched Stannard's. He looked thin and he looked ill.

"Oh, I suppose they've thought of it," Martin Drake answered. "But they wouldn't be allowed to. The Prison Commission would have a fit."

"Right," chuckled Stannard.

(He missed no glance Ruth Callice turned towards Drake. There were currents in this room, not quite like a usual social evening.)

"But I wish we could do it," the young man said unexpectedly, and struck his clenched fist on his knee. "Lord, how I wish we could do it!"

Ruth's voice went up. "Spend a night in a . . . ?"

"Oh, not you!" Drake smiled at her; it lightened the illness of his look to kindliness and affection. "I suppose, actually, I meant myself."

"But whatever for?"

Stannard, who had returned to the chair with his cigar, spoke gravely.

"You mean, Mr. Drake, that since the war you have found life in England dull and intolerably frustrating?"

"If—you want to put it like that, yes."

"Will you forgive me, Mr. Drake, for saying you are very young?"

"Will you forgive me, Mr. Stannard, for saying that you are a little pompous?"

Again Stannard chuckled. Perhaps he was doing this too much. His lips were drawn back from the teeth in a fixed, pleasant smile; his small black eyes glittered.

"Of course I forgive you," Stannard said heartily. "I have achieved—" he glanced at Ruth, evidently himself feeling young and callow at forty-five, and hating it—"I have achieved some small success in this world. That breeds pomposity sometimes. God knows I try to avoid it." His tone changed. "Are you serious about wanting to meet earthbound spirits?"

"Quite serious."

"Ah? Suppose I arranged it?"

Ruth Callice was now sitting bolt upright on the sofa. Her lips opened as though in expostulation, but she did not speak.

"It couldn't be done!" Martin Drake said.

"Not at the prisons I mentioned, no. But what about Pentecost?"

"Pentecost?"

"You've never heard of Pentecost Prison, Mr. Drake?"

"Never."

Stannard crossed his knees comfortably and addressed Ruth.

"Fifty years ago Pentecost was one of our model local prisons." He paused. "I use the word 'local' prison to distinguish it from 'convict' prison. At local prisons, offenders serve sentences only up to two years; executions are always performed there.

"In '38," Stannard pursued, "Pentecost was closed. It was to be enlarged and modernized. Then came the war. The Government took it over with the usual rubber-stamp excuse of 'storage purposes'. Ever since then it's remained the same. It's not under the control of the Prison Commission; it's controlled by the Ministry of Works. I—ah—have some slight influence at the Ministry. I might get the keys for a night or two. *Now* do you begin to understand?"

"By George!" the young man said softly. His long, lean figure grew tense; his upper lip was partly lifted as though at the scent of danger. "I'd be eternally grateful, Mr. Stannard, if you could."

Stannard, too, seemed to have been struck by a startling new thought. Seeing that his cigar had gone out, he dropped it into a standing ashtray beside the chair.

"Extraordinary!" he said, and his face grew more red. "I've just remembered something else."

"Remembered what?" Ruth asked quickly.

"Pentecost is in Berkshire. It's under a mile or so from a place called Fleet House, a big Georgian house with a flat roof." His little black eyes stared at the past. "Eighteen years ago—or was it twenty? yes, twenty!—a man named Fleet, Sir George Fleet, pitched off that roof within sight of a lot of witnesses. It was accident, of course. Or else . . ."

"Or else?"

"It was a supernatural murder." He spoke without smiling.

Martin Drake brushed aside this reference to Fleet House.

"Do you honestly think you can get the keys to the prison?"

"Oh, I think so. At least I can try. Where can I reach you tomorrow?"

"I'm afraid I've got to be at Willaby's Auction Rooms all morning. With a friend of mine named Merrivale." Unexpectedly, a reminiscent grin lit up Drake's dulled eyes. Then he became sober again. "But I can make a point of being at my rooms in the afternoon, if that's convenient? I'm in the 'phonebook."

"You'll hear from me," Stannard assured him.

Loud in night-stillness, the clock at St. Jude's rang the quarter-hour after three. Stannard got up, brushing a trace of cigar-ash from his waist-coat. He drew a deep breath.

"And now, my dear," he said to Ruth, "you must excuse me. Middle-aged barristers can't keep late hours like you young people. I'll ring *you* tomorrow, if I may."

Throughout this conversation Ruth had kept her eyes fixed on Martin Drake. Doubt, uncertainly, showed in them .and troubled her breathing under the oyster-coloured gown. Stannard noticed that Drake, though he got up politely, made no move to leave. It was a dead hour, dull on the wits and opium to the emotions. Yet something wrenched in Stannard's heart as his hostess followed him to the door.

In the little hall of the flat, every inch of wall-space was occupied by shelves of bright-jacketed books. Ruth Callice was the owner of a fashionable bookshop in Piccadilly, which she managed herself; that was how she and Stannard had met. A dim little ceiling-lantern burned in the hall. Stannard picked up hat and rolled umbrella from an oak chest.

"It was awfully nice of you to come," Ruth said.

"Not at all. The pleasure was mine. May I see you again?"

"Of course. As often as you can."

She extended her hands. Stannard, the suave, had considerable difficulty in managing his hat and umbrella.

"Thanks." He spoke gruffly. "I'll remember that. No; I can manage the front door. Thanks again. Good-night."

The door, closing heavily after him, made a hollow vibration. For a moment Ruth stood staring at the door. Then she returned to the sitting-room. Though both windows were wide open to the warm July night, she made a feint of attempting to push them higher to let the smoke out. Martin Drake, his back partly turned, was standing by the fireplace lighting a cigarette. Ruth went softly over to the grand piano and sat down.

She hesitated. Common-sense, practicality, shone in the dark-brown eyes as she lifted her head; a perplexity verging on impatience. But this expression faded, with a wry twist of the mouth, as she began to play.

The tune was *Someday I'll Find You.* Its saccharine notes riffled and rippled, softly, through the room and faintly out into the square.

"Ruth!"

"Yes, Martin?"

"You're one of the finest persons I ever met," said the young man, and threw his cigarette into the fireplace. "But would you mind not playing that?"

Ruth closed her eyes, the lids shiny and dark-fringed, and opened them again. "I'm sorry, Martin." Her fingers rested motionless. Without looking round Ruth added, "Still searching for her?"

"Yes."

"Martin, dear. Isn't that rather foolish?"

"Of course it's foolish. I know that. But I can't help it. There it is."

"You met her," Ruth pointed out dispassionately, "for just one evening."

"Long enough, thanks."

"And you haven't seen her for . . . how long?"

The other's reply was immediate, almost mechanical. "Three years. One month. And four—no, five days. I'll tick off the calendar this morning."

"Oh, *Martin!*" The piano-keys jangled.

"I've admitted it's foolish. But how many things, the closest things, are governed by reason? Answer me that!"

"You were both in uniform," Ruth persisted gently. "It was in that scramble and hectic whirl just after D-Day. You don't know anything about her, except that she wore a Wren's uniform. You don't even know her name, except the first, and she admitted that was a nickname."

It was as though, in remonstrance, Ruth attempted to press and prod with every detail.

"A station buffet at Edinburgh!" she said. "A station platform! A train tearing through the blackout, with you two," her voice strengthened, "kissing and swearing you loved each other. Martin! Lots and lots of people have had adventures like that."

Martin Drake's face was white. Ruth, with her consummate tact, should have noticed this.

"It wasn't an adventure," he said quietly.

"No. Of course not. I didn't mean that. Only—suppose you do find her, and she's married?"

"Curiously enough," retorted the other, with a brief return to his mocking air, "that possibility had occurred to me in the course of three years, one month, and five days." He lifted his shoulders. "What could I do? Murder the husband?"

"Well, but . . . suppose she's engaged. What would you do then?"

"Try to cut him out," Drake answered instantly. "Not that I could, probably. But—" he lifted a clenched fist, dropped it, and then cleared his throat—"use every trick, fair or unfair, to cut the swine out and get her back again. That needn't lead as far as murder, of course."

There was a silence. Still Ruth did not look round. The doubt, the indecision in her eyes, had grown stronger.

"Ruth!" her guest began apologetically.

"Yes?"

He went across to her, stood beside her at the piano, and put his hand on her bare shoulder. "Thanks," he added, "for not asking the obvious question."

"What obvious question?"

"How many Wrens," he went on, with a kind of fierce and shaky cheerfulness, "how many Wrens, at a time like that, must have said, 'Oh, just call me Jenny.' Jenny! Jenny! I know it. So do several of my friends, who think it's funny. But it's not funny. That's the trouble."

Ruth reached up and disengaged his hand from her shoulder; rather quickly, he thought. She did not admit or deny that she had thought of asking any such question. She looked straight ahead, unseeingly, at the music on the piano-rack.

"What did you think," she asked, "of our friend tonight?"

"Stannard?" Martin Drake's face clouded. "Stannard's a damn good fellow. I'm sorry I called him pompous. Nerves. If he can really get permission to spend the night in the execution shed at that prison . . ."

"If you two go there," Ruth interrupted quickly, "I'm going too. Did you notice that Mr. Stannard seemed rather—embarrassed?"

Drake was startled.

"The Great Defender? Embarrassed? Why?"

"Oh, no reason," said Ruth, with a lift of her head that made the soft brown hair gleam. "No reason! No reason at all!"

And again her fingers moved over the piano-keys.

Downstairs, under the moon, the sleek black car still waited before the door of number 16. Inside the car, his thick arms round the steering-wheel, John Stannard sat where he had been sitting for some minutes. Once more he heard the strains of *Someday I'll Find You* drifting down from the lighted windows on the top floor.

This time Stannard trod on the starter. As the motor throbbed into life, he revved it to a hum which deepened into a roar. Then, very gently, he put the car in gear and drove off towards Kensington High Street.

Chapter 2

On the following morning, Friday July 11th, the blue-and-white flag was up at Willaby's in Bond Street to show that there would be an auction that day.

Martin Drake saw it as he turned out of Brook Street at a quarter to eleven. London in 1947, dazzling under its first really warm summer since the beginning of the war, winked with show-windows against dingy brick or stone. It heated the body and strengthened the spirits. Martin, freshly shaven and as well-dressed as clothes-coupons permitted, felt his own spirits lift.

But that always happened on a sunny morning. It was the night he dreaded.

He hadn't, Martin reflected, been drunk at Ruth Callice's flat last night. Merely a trifle muzzy, and blackly depressed. He had an impression that some remark, some reference made by Stannard (he could not remember it now) ought to have had significance. But his mind was closed to so many things. He had almost become maudlin in the presence of Ruth Callice's obvious sympathy. He was so fond of Ruth that under any other circumstances . . . but there were no other circumstances.

Jenny!

The silent oration he addressed to himself ran something like this:

You are London's prize fool. You admit that. At the age of thirty-four you have had, to put it very conservatively, some slight experience. Your conduct is not made more supportable by those people, two or three friends at the Savage Club, who know about it.

"My dear old boy," one of them had said, "all you need is thus-and-so. With so many willing dames about . . ."

Or old Hook, with his touch of grey side-whisker and his twinkling eyeglass, who always quoted Leigh Hunt:

> *Jenny kissed me when we met,*
> *Jumping from the chair she sat in—*

And this, though you had to smile, touched a raw spot. It was, in so many ways, expressive of Jenny. Jenny, blonde and slender, in the blue uniform and hat which at first glance made her seem unapproachable. Jenny's eagerness, her sincerity, almost her naïveté.

"*A station-buffet at Edinburgh!*" Ruth had said. "*A station platform. A train tearing through the blackout, with you two kissing and swearing you loved each other.*"

Hell!

When such things happened to other people, Martin reflected, or even happened in stories, they had at least a trace of dignity. This hadn't.

In the hush just before dawn on a summer morning, the express from Edinburgh stops at Rugby. Heavy boots clump and bumble along the wooden platform. Misshapen shadows, interweaving, loom up against the dim blue station lights and the faint glow from the services' tea-canteen. Captain Drake of the Gloucesters, and (rank and unit unknown) Jenny, hand in hand, stumble out to get a cup of vile tea. In the confusion and milling on that dark platform—every private's kit seems to swing and bang for a yard in each direction—you lose Jenny's hand.

That was all.

Eight minutes later, when the whistle blew and the doors slammed, Martin jumped into the train. He staggered along the corridors, over kit and luggage and bodies, calling Jenny's name. Two or three times he was answered, not seriously. There were cheers. The drugged dawn-wind blew drowsily. When they reached King's Cross, he swore to himself, it would be all right. But, when that mob charged through the barriers, he couldn't find her either.

That was all too, except for the long waiting.

Ahead of him now, on this brilliant morning of July 11th, loomed the dun-coloured premises of Willaby's. Sedate and solid, hushed and holy, Willaby's yet wore an air of expectancy. How many treasures from the houses of the great and the near-great, of furniture and china and silver, of tapestries and pictures and armour: how many of these have passed under the hammer at Willaby's, perhaps, no man can compute. The porter—who recognized Mr. Martin Drake as a black-and-white artist of something more than national reputation—respectfully held open one door.

"Morning, sir!"

"Good morning." The image of Jenny, held in abeyance, started up again like a toothache we think vanished overnight. "Er—have they started yet?"

The porter eyed him reproachfully.

"Not till eleven, sir. *As* usual. Got your catalogue?"

"No. I'm just looking on today. What's up this morning?"

"Furniture and carpets, sir. Mainly seventeenth and eighteenth century."

To judge by the subdued murmur of voices from upstairs, there must be a fair-sized crowd. A number of persons were mounting the broad, dingy staircase. At the top it opened into a large, square room, walls panelled in some material which resembled faded brown burlap, where they displayed specimens of future auctions. Beyond it lay another large room, with towering bookshelves. Both of these rooms opened, at right-angles, into the main auction-room.

"Hel-*lo*, Drake!"

A face, half-remembered, drifted past and was lost. Martin returned the greeting vaguely. He heard a fashionably dressed woman talking, with greed and not for antiquarian reasons, about the display of carpets. An old man with a white moustache, obviously a dealer, stood hunched over his catalogue.

The main auction-room was long and high. Sunlight sparkled against its grimy glass roof. At the rear, blue-smocked attendants lounged or stood with arms folded in front of a line of ticketed exhibits. The auctioneer's desk, like a high-set rostrum, faced out over a very long horseshoe-shaped table, covered with green felt, round which would gather the chairs of the eagerest bidders. Martin had loathed crowds—no matter how soft-voiced or shuffling—ever since that night on the train. The whole room seemed to hiss at him.

"*Get it dirt-cheap if the dealers don't . . .*"

"*Jump in at the beginning! That's when people are cautious, and . . .*"

No!

Just off the main hall, at the right, opened another showroom smaller and narrower than the others. Here were displayed the items for the next sale, which would be on

Monday. Arms and armour, of course! That was why he was here!

On two tables along the narrow sides of the room, and a long one down the centre, they had thrown rapiers, daggers, hand-and-a-half swords, even two-handed swords. Many were tied in bundles, most of them unpolished. Round the walls there hung, very highly polished, the more obvious of the choice items. The only other person in the room was a girl, at the other end of the centre table, her back towards him, searching through a handbag.

Martin looked round.

The walls glittered with steel in low, dim-burning electric light. Halberds and guisarmes with long light shafts and undulled points. A wicked-looking main-gauche. What seemed to be—he took a step forward—a Thomas cup-hilt. This was Martin's hobby; he wished he had a Monday's catalogue.

Then the girl at the other end of the table turned round. And he saw that it was Jenny.

Silence.

Martin Drake was faintly conscious of a murmur of voices from the other room, and the ticking of his wrist-watch. But he felt alone, and amid the stuffiness of the arms-room, with Jenny. At first his chest seemed light, light and hollow; then he felt a sensation almost like physical sickness.

Jenny, blonde and slender. Jenny, with the wide-spaced blue eyes, the eagerness and the—no! not naïveté! some other expression! With intolerable vividness he remembered her, in the corner of the railway compartment, her arms round his neck, and moonlight draining colour from her face, the rattlety-clack of the train dimming speech. Even now she was wearing a dark-blue tailored suit with a white blouse. Martin tried to speak. All he could force out was the inanity of, "Hello."

"Hello," said Jenny in a voice hardly above a whisper.

He started to walk towards her. Though they were separated only by the length of the green-felt-covered table with its weapons, it seemed an enormous distance. Then he noticed something else.

You are not permitted to smoke at Willaby's. Fumbling in her handbag, Jenny found a tortoise-shell cigarette case, the kind that contained only very small cigarettes. Jenny took out a cigarette; and automatically he reached in his pocket for a lighter. But her hand was shaking so badly, as she lifted it, that she hastily put back the cigarette in the case.

Emotion caught these two like a net; it made them flounder;

it kept them half deaf and partially blind.

"Where were you on that train? I couldn't find you!"

The blue eyes flashed up.

"I—I stayed behind on the platform. I thought you would too, so we shouldn't miss each other. —But it's too late!" she added. "It's too late!"

"How do you mean, it's too late?"

Jenny turned away from him, but he swung her back again. The softness of her shoulder under the blue coat, the brushing of the yellow hair in a long bob against his hand: he had to remember where he was. Then he lifted her left hand. Though there was no wedding-ring on the third finger, it held an engagement ring both costly and in good taste.

(Well, you've been expecting this, haven't you? You've been prepared for it? Steady!)

"Do you love him?"

Jenny looked away.

"No. But I'm afraid he's very much in love with me. And then grandmother—and, of course, Aunt Cicely—"

"*Do* you love him?"

Still without looking round, Jenny shook her head violently.

"Who is he?"

"He's awfully nice. He was one of the original Battle-of-Britain pilots. And his record since then . . ." The soft, sweet voice, perhaps over-cultured in accent, trailed away. "Did you ever try to find me?" Jenny asked accusingly.

"Jenny, I've done nothing else ever since that night! But all I knew was your nickname!"

"Jenny is short for Jennifer. Surely you could have guessed that?"

"Yes, of course. Only I thought . . ."

"You thought—you thought I gave that name on some kind of casual adventure." She clenched her fists.

"No, so help me! But it was the only clue I had. Did you ever try to find *me?*"

"Yes, of course. And I did: easily."

"Oh?"

"You're Martin Drake. You're a famous artist. You live at the Albany, and you're not married. Only grandmother said—and, of course, Aunt Cicely—"

"Look here," said Drake with restraint. "Who the devil are these two powerful jujus, grandmother and Aunt Cicely? Can't they be tipped over like any other savage idols?" He glanced round. "And, by the way, can't we get out of here?"

"No! Please. Sh-h!"

"Why 'sh-h'?"

"Grandmother's here. She wants to get something at the auction. How on earth did you know *I* was here?"

"As a matter of fact, I didn't. I came here for a pre-view, to recommend one or two rapiers for Sir Henry Merrivale."

"Sir Henry Merrivale!" exclaimed the girl.

Jenny raised one hand as though to shade her eyes. On her flushed face, with the short nose and the rather broad mouth, was an expression he could not read. Martin noticed, absently, that beyond her was a stand of armour—a Cavalier half-suit, much blackened, with lobster-tail helmet—and behind it, on the wall, a picture depicting one of the loves of Aphrodite.

"Sir Henry Merrivale!" Jenny exclaimed. "You know him?"

"Slightly, yes. I went to him last week about tracing you. He said he'd help, but just for the moment he was too much engrossed in studying the subject of reincarnation."

"The subject of . . . *what?*"

"Reincarnation," explained Martin. "He thinks he may be the reincarnation of— Hold on! Wait! I've got it!"

For the rush of happiness at seeing Jenny, it seemed to him, had loosed a spell from his wits. He knew now why a certain cloudy reference should have been clear.

"Got what?" asked Jenny, with that eagerness he knew so well.

"Last night a barrister named Stannard mentioned a place in Berkshire: Fleet House, I think it was. He said there'd been some ugly business, twenty years ago, which was either an accident or a supernatural murder. And that's it, of course!"

"How do you mean?"

"A friend of Sir Henry's, Chief Inspector Masters, has been pestering him to take up the case. Masters wants to re-open it. It seems there's new evidence, anonymous letters or the like." Martin stopped short. "What is it? What's wrong?"

He interpreted Jenny's expression, now. It was fear. Again he became conscious of the room's stuffiness, and the weapons glittering round the walls. Jennifer said:

"Richard Fleet, my *fiancé*, is the son of the Sir George Fleet who died. Aunt Cicely, who's only an aunt by courtesy, is Lady Fleet. My grandmother is their closest friend."

"Listen, Jenny," said Martin, after a pause during which his throat felt dry. "There's only one question I'm going to ask you, but it's got to be answered."

"Yes?"

"Do you still feel as you did—in the train? *Do you?*"

"Yes," replied Jenny and lifted her eyes. "Yes!"

"Jennifer, dear!" interrupted a calm, authoritative female voice. It cracked their idyll to bits. Jenny started; Martin swung round guiltily.

And it is now time, in this chronicle, to introduce none other than Sophia, Dowager Countess of Brayle.

She had approached unheard. She was a large, commanding woman, her grey-white hair confined under a rakish fashionable hat, and her body so compressed into a dress of garish design that it almost, but not quite, failed to make her seem fat. Her voice, which forty-odd years ago had been called a 'pure contralto' as her nose had been called 'sweetly aquiline,' could often be heard speaking on public platforms.

The Dowager Countess, in fact, occasionally showed habits rakish and even skittish. At these same public meetings, for instance, she had a trick of taking two sweeping steps backwards, while raising her right arm and exclaiming, "Here's three chee-ah-s." Sometimes she even did this in private, to the mild-voiced protest of Aunt Cicely.

All her friends would testify to her good qualities: that she was fair, that she was generous, that she even had a sense of humour. She had perhaps every good quality except that of being likeable. But that did not matter. The Dowager Countess meant to get her own way, always got her own way, and accepted this as naturally as she expected a lamp to light at the click of a switch. Whether you liked her, or didn't like her, simply did not matter.

"When you see my composure ruffled," she would say comfortably, "*then* will be the time to criticize."

This imposing lady, a faint smile on her face and an auction-catalogue in her hand, stood before the two culprits and waited with endless patience for someone to speak.

Jenny, pushing back her yellow hair, blurted it out.

"C-Captain Drake," she said, "may I present you to my grandmother? Captain Drake, Lady Brayle."

The latter's nod and glance flickered over Martin as though he had not been there at all.

"The auction," she said to Jenny, "has begun. Lot 72 should come up in a few minutes. I feel sure, Jennifer, that you will wish to be present? Follow me, please."

She swung round, her somewhat ample posterior conspicuous in the flowered dress, and moved majestically away. Jenny, on the other side of the long centre table, followed her almost parallel. Martin, with a raging heart, could only follow Jenny. At the far end of the table, however, Lady Brayle wheeled round with her back to the open arch into the main auction-hall. She glanced at the weapons on the table.

"Ah—Jennifer dear," she continued with a sort of cold archness. "It occurs to me we must not forget our *fiancé*. Now must we?"

Jenny made an incoherent noise.

"Richard, or dear Ricky as we call him . . ." Lady Brayle paused. "Captain Drake. Let me see. You were in the Guards?"

"No. The Gloucesters."

"Oh. The Gloucesters." Her eyebrow indicated that she had momentarily scanned the army-list and found no such name. "How interesting. Richard, or dear Ricky as we call him, is one of our new breed of chivalry: our heroic and fearless knights of the air. Don't you think so, Jennifer?"

"Grandmother, he'd pass out if he heard you talk like that!"

But grandmother's contralto was now warming up with platform eloquence.

"You might give him, I think, some small present of arms. This fine old English blade," exclaimed Lady Brayle, picking up a Turkish scimitar of about 1885, and waving it in the air, "would surely be suitable. I am informed that the air-force seldom carry swords. But the spirit of it! You agree, Jennifer?"

"Yes, grandmother. But . . ."

"*You* agree, Captain Drake?"

Martin swallowed a heavy lump in his throat. This calm and indomitable old lady was trying to get his goat. He longed to take one dig at her, just one. But he feared its effect on Jenny. Just how much influence this doubtless-benevolent Gorgon exercised over Jenny, who three years ago had given her age as twenty-two, he could not yet estimate.

"Quite," he agreed.

"It is no use, Captain Drake," she smiled at him. "It really is no use."

"I beg your pardon?"

"But any criticism you might make of the weapons, of course!" said Lady Brayle, deliberately avoiding the issue and raising her eyebrows. The cold, shrewd grey eyes expressed astonishment. "This cute little dagger, now, with the sheath!" she broke off. "Perhaps *that* might appeal to dear Ricky, Jennifer. Or here, better still . . ."

Martin gritted his teeth. His glance wandered past her into the main auction-hall. For the most part the spectators, either in chairs or standing up, had pressed close to the long horseshoe table below the rostrum. In the cleared space outside and beyond them, approaching slowly and at a lordly pigeon-toed walk, moved a figure which sent Martin Drake's hopes soaring up.

"It's the Old Man," he breathed.

Chapter 3

The auctioneer's voice was small, thin, and at this distance all but inaudible.

"*Lot 55. A fine Queen Anne table, grained mahogany, drawers richly gilt, date circa 1721, originally . . .*"

The figure Martin had seen was a large, stout, barrel-shaped gentleman in a white linen suit. His spectacles, usually pulled down on his broad nose, were now in place because he held his head up. On his head was a Panama hat, its brim curiously bent, and in his mouth he clamped an unlighted cigar.

As he advanced, his corporation majestically preceding him, there was on his face such a lordly sneer as even the Dowager Countess could never have imitated. Indeed, a close friend of Sir Henry Merrivale would have noticed something a little odd in his behaviour. The brim of the Panama hat, to an imaginative observer, might have been arranged so as to carry sweeping plumes. As he rolled the cigar round in his mouth to get a better grip, his left hand rested negligently in the air as though on the pommel of an imaginary sword. Aloof, disdainful, he sauntered towards the armour-room.

"Or this, for instance!" cried Lady Brayle.

Martin drew his gaze back. Into the room, unobserved, had slipped another figure: the tiny old man, with the white moustache, whom he had seen hunched over a catalogue in the outer room.

From the table Lady Brayle had fished up a heavy iron shield—round, convex, its outer side scored with dull embossments—and balanced it on the edge of the table.

"Really, Jennifer, I might defy you to find a better present than this shield of our lives and homes! This monument of antiquity, this holy . . ."

The apologetic little man cleared his throat.

"I trust you will forgive the intrusion, madam," he whispered in a soft and creaky voice. "But the shield is not genuine."

"Not genuine!"

"No, madam. I could give you reasons at length. But if you will look in the catalogue you will find it described only as 'Scottish type,' which of course means . . ."

"Scotland," said Lady Brayle. "I believe the Fleets were originally Scottish. That will serve well enough. Look at it, Jennifer! Observe its beauty and strength of purpose!"

Lady Brayle was really thrilled. Also, she must have been a powerful woman. She caught up the shield with one hand on each side of the rim. Inspired, she took two sweeping steps backwards and swung up the shield with both arms—full and true into the face of Sir Henry Merrivale just as he entered the room.

The resulting *bong,* as H.M.'s visage encountered the concave side of the shield, was not so mellifluous as a temple-gong. But it was loud enough to make several persons in the auction-room look round. The Dowager Countess, for a moment really taken aback, held the shield motionless before H.M.'s face as though about to unveil some priceless head of statuary.

Then she lowered it.

"Why, Henry!" she said.

The great man's Panama hat had been knocked off, revealing a large bald head. Through his large shell-rimmed spectacles, undamaged because the concavity of the shield had caught him mainly forehead and chin, there peered out eyes of such horrible malignancy that Jenny shied back. His cigar, spreading and flattened, bloomed under his nose like a tobacco-plant.

He did not say anything.

"I suppose I must apologize," Lady Brayle acknowledged coolly. "Though it was really not my fault. You should look where you are going."

H.M.'s face slowly turned purple.

"And now," continued Lady Brayle, putting down the shield, "we must not be late. Come, Jennifer!" Firmly she took Jenny's arm. "I see Lord Ambleside and it would be *most* discourteous not to speak to Lord Ambleside. Good day, Captain Drake."

All might still have been well, perhaps, if she had not turned for a last look at Sir Henry Merrivale. Mention has been made of Lady Brayle's sense of humour. She looked at H.M., and her face began to twitch.

"I am sorry, Henry," she said, "but really——!" Suddenly she threw back her head. The once-pure contralto laughter, refined but hearty, rang and carrolled under the roof.

"Haw, haw, haw!" warbled the Dowager Countess. "Haw, haw, haw, HAW!"

"Easy, sir!" begged Martin Drake.

He seized H.M.'s quivering shoulders. Taking the squashed cigar out of H.M.'s mouth, in case the great man should swallow it, he threw the cigar away.

"Easy!" he insisted. "Are you all right?"

With a superhuman effort, no one knows how great, H.M. controlled himself or seemed to control himself. His voice, which at first appeared to issue in a hoarse rumble from deep in the cellar, steadied a little.

"Me?" he rumbled hoarsely. "Sure, son. I'm fine. Don't you worry about *my* feelin's."

"You—er—don't hold any malice?"

"Me?" exclaimed H.M., with such elaborate surprise that Chief Inspector Masters would instantly have been suspicious. "Oh, my son! I'm a forgivin' man. I'm so goddam chivalrous that if I was ever reincarnated in mediaeval times, which I probably was, some old witch must 'a' copped me in the mush with a shield practically every day. You lemme alone, son. I just want to stand here and cogitate."

Martin, so intent on Jenny that he could think of little else, for the moment forgot him. Jenny and her grandmother were standing on the outer fringe of the crowd, their backs to the arms-room: though Jenny, peering round over her shoulder, tried some lip-message which he could not read.

H.M., cogitating deeply with elbow on one thick arm and fingers massaging his reddened chin, let his gaze wander round. Presently it found the halberds and guisarmes, their long shafts propped upright against the wall. Slowly his gaze moved up to their points. Then, musingly, the gaze travelled out into auction-room and found the ample, flowered posterior of the Dowager Countess.

"Ahem!" said the great man.

Elaborately unconcerned, he adjusted his spectacles and took down one of the weapons. Holding it horizontally on both hands, he ran his eye along the shaft with the critical air of a connoisseur. But it was obvious, from his blinkings, that he needed more light. That was why he strolled out into the auction-room.

"One hundred and fifty . . . Sixty? . . . Seventy? . . . Eighty? . . ."

The auctioneer, a sallow dark man with a pince-nez and a cropped moustache, had an eye that could follow lightning. He never missed; he never misinterpreted. A nod, a mutter, a pencil or catalogue briefly raised: the bidding flickered round that horseshoe table, or out into the crowd, more quickly than the senses could determine. Nobody spoke; all bent forward in absorption.

"Two hundred? Two hundred? Do I hear . . ."

"Oh, my God!" breathed Martin Drake.

That was where he saw what was approaching, on stealthy and evilly large feet, the unconscious back of Lady Brayle.

The only other person who noticed was the timid little man with the white moustache, who had observed all these proceedings in silence. But the little man did not cover ground like Martin. Silently, in loping strides, he reached the side of the avenger; firmly he gripped the other side of the shaft, and looked at H.M. across it.

H.M.'s almost invisible eyebrows went up.

"I dunno what you're talkin' about," he said in a hollow voice—though Martin, in fact, had not uttered a word. He uttered one now.

"No," he said.

"Hey?"

"No."

H.M. altered his tactics.

"Looky here, son," he pleaded. "It's not as though I'm goin' to hurt her, is it? I'm not goin' to *hurt* the old sea-lion. Just one little nip and bob's-your-uncle."

"H.M., don't think I disapprove of this. I'd give a year's income to do it! But one little nip and I may lose the girl."

"What girl?"

"Two hundred pounds! Do I hear more than two hundred pounds?"

"The girl I told you about! There! She's Lady Brayle's granddaughter!"

"Oh, my son! You stick Sophie in the tail and this gal's goin' to adore you."

"No!"

Faintly the hammer tapped. *"Lord Ambleside, for two hundred pounds."*

"Sold!" cried Lady Brayle, in the midst of that shuffling and mist of murmurs which greet the tap of the hammer. "Did you

hear that, Jennifer? And to our good friend Lord Ambleside
too! Here's three che-ah-s!"

Playfully Lady Brayle threw up her arm like an opera star.
She took two swinging steps backwards. And she landed full
and true against the point of the shaft gripped by Martin and
Sir Henry Merrivale.

The sound which issued from the lips of Lady Brayle at that
moment would be difficult phonetically to describe. If we
imagine the scream of bagpipes, rising on a long skirling note
of shock to burst high in a squeal and squeak of outrage, this
somewhat approximates it. For about ten seconds it petrified
the whole room.

Jenny, after one horrified look, put her hands over her eyes.

The auctioneer, in the act of saying, "Lot 71," stopped with
his mouth open. Two blue-smocked attendants, who carried
each exhibit into the open space inside the table so that it could
be exhibited during the bidding, dropped a Sheraton writing-
desk bang on the floor.

"Mr. Auctioneer!"

Shaken but indomitable, Lady Brayle made her voice ring
out.

"Mr. Auctioneer!"

Up from a hidden cubicle, to the auctioneer's right, popped
that bald-headed gnome who at Willaby's takes your cheque or
bobs up at intervals to see whether you are one whose cheque
may be taken. He and the auctioneer seemed to hold a flashing
pince-nez conference.

"Mr. Auctioneer," screamed Lady Brayle, and pointed
dramatically, "I demand that these two men be ejected from
the room!"

The auctioneer's voice was very soft and clear.

"Have the gentlemen been guilty of unbecoming conduct,
my lady?"

"Yes, they have!"

"May I ask the nature of the conduct?"

Truth, stern truth, will not be denied.

"This old trout," bellowed Sir Henry Merrivale, snatching
the weapon from Martin's hands, "thinks we stuck her in the
behind with a halberd."

The meek little man with the white moustache, appearing at
H.M.'s elbow, tapped him softly on the shoulder.

"No, no, no!" he protested. "No, no, no, no!"

H.M. turned round an empurpled visage.

"What d'ye mean, no?" he thundered. "Didn't you hear

Beowulf's Mother yellin' for the chuckers-out?"·

"Not a halberd, my good sir! Not a halberd!"

"Ain't it?"

"No, I assure you! A fine seventeenth-century guisarme."

H.M., his feet wide apart, the shaft of the weapon planted on the floor like a noble Carolean soldier, now made the situation perfectly clear.

"This old trout," he bellowed, "thinks we stuck her in the behind with a seventeenth-century guisarme."

Through the audience ran a sort of suppressed shiver. Martin Drake noted, with amazement and pleasure, that it was not a shiver of horror. It was the spasmodic tension of those who try, by keeping face-muscles rigid, to avoid exploding with mirth. One elderly man, with an eyeglass and withered jowls, had stuffed a handkerchief into his mouth. Another lay face downwards across the table, his shoulders heaving. Even with the auctioneer it was a near thing.

"I feel sure, my lady, that there has been an unfortunate accident." He made a slight gesture to the blue-smocked attendants. His voice grew thinly colourless. *"Lot 71. Here we have . . ."* And H.M. and Lady Brayle were left alone in a sort of closed ring, surreptitiously watched.

"Henry," the old lady said calmly.

"Uh-huh?"

"I am compelled to tell you something. For nine generations," declared Lady Brayle in a shaky voice, "your family have held the baronetcy in a direct line. Yet speak I must. — Henry, you are not a gentleman."

"So I'm not a gentleman, hey?" inquired H.M., getting a firmer grip on the guisarme.

"No, you are not."

"Listen, Sophie," said H.M.., tapping her on the shoulder. "I'm going to show you just how goddam gentlemanly I really am. I've had a reincarnation. Got it?"

Lady Brayle, whose confused mind evidently connected this with some sort of surgical operation, stared at him. Swiftly, silently, the bidding rippled round the table, followed by the tap of the hammer. It was the words, *"Lot 72,"* followed by a sudden loud murmur to drown out the next part, which galvanized Lady Brayle. The spectators, though interested, seemed reluctant to bid.

"Shall we start it at five pounds? . . . Five? . . . Will anyone say five?"

"I really," cried Lady Brayle, "cannot continue this childish discussion any longer." In haste and anxiety, which often happens at such moments, her contralto rang loudly. "Five pounds!"

"I was a Cavalier poet," said H.M. "TEN POUNDS!"

A horrible suspicion seemed to strike Lady Brayle as she whirled round.

"Henry, you are not bidding? —Twenty!"

"Lord love a duck, what d'ye think I'm here for? —Thirty!"

"Henry, this is *too much*. —Forty!"

"It's no good gettin' mad, Sophie. —Fifty!"

Lady Brayle, instead of directing her bids at the auctioneer, advanced her face towards H.M.

"Sixty!" she hissed.

H.M. also advanced his own unmentionable visage.

"Seventy!" he hissed back.

The buzz of voices, never before heard in such volume at Willaby's, rose like a locust-storm. Twisting and swaying, the crowd pressed forward to get a look at what was being exhibited. It is recorded that one lady, maddened, climbed up on a stranger's back so that she could see. Martin, his own sight obscured, tugged at the great man's coat-tail.

"Listen, sir! Take it easy! You don't even know what it is!"

"I don't care what it is," yelled H.M. "Whatever it is, *this* old trout's not goin' to get it."

"This is malice," said Lady Brayle. "This is insufferable. This is pure childishness. I will end it." Her voice rose in calm triumph. "One—hundred—pounds."

"Oh, Sophie!" grunted H.M. in a distressed tone. "You're playin' for monkey-nuts. Let's make it really interesting. — *Two* hundred pounds!"

"Gentlemen," observed a voice in the crowd, "here we go again."

"Two hundred and ten? Two hundred and ten?"

But Lady Brayle, a very shrewd woman, clamped her jaws. Undoubtedly she knew that the old sinner in front of her, whose cussedness was without depth or measure, would cheerfully have gone to a thousand. Catching the auctioneer's eye, she shook her head. Then she adjusted the rakish fashionable hat on her grey-white hair.

"Jennifer!" she called.

But Jenny did not reply, nor was she in sight.

"You will meet me," her grandmother spoke carefully to the air, "at Claridge's for lunch. One o'clock." Then she turned for a final remark to H.M.

"I must tell you something else," she continued. Martin Drake saw, for the first time, the very real ruthlessness of her mouth, and of the wrinkles round mouth and eyes. "You, and in particular your friend Captain Drake, are going to regret this for the rest of your lives."

And, drawing a pair of white gloves from her handbag, she marched slowly towards the outer room and the stairs.

There no longer appeared to be any comedy in this. Open war. All right!

Searching round for Jenny, Martin saw her signal. Along the long right-hand wall, where stood exhibits overflowing from those at the back, Jenny looked out from between a high lacquered wardrobe and a row of gilt-and-satin chairs. He went to her, and they regarded each other in silence.

"I ought to be furious with you," Jenny said. "I ought to say I'd never speak to you again. Only . . ."

Again he saw the contrast between the placidness of her appearance and the extraordinary violence of her emotions. Ancient Willaby's was treated to the spectacle of a girl throwing her arms round a young man's neck, and the young man kissing her with such return violence as to endanger the equilibrium of the wardrobe.

But the spectators had returned intently to their bidding. Nobody saw them except an attendant of thirty-five years' service, who shook his head despondently.

"I *do* love you," said Jenny, detaching herself reluctantly. "But—however did you have the nerve to take that halberd or what-do-you-call-it, and . . ."

"I didn't," he admitted. "When your grandmother let out that yelp—"

"Darling, you shouldn't have done it." (This was perfunctory.)

"—when she yelped, and everybody looked round, I felt about two inches high with embarrassment. Then I took one look at H.M., and I felt about nine feet high. There's something about the old ba . . . the old boy's personality. It's like an electric current."

The gentleman in question, having detached himself from the spectators, was now lumbering towards them in the aisle between bidders and wall. From the arms-room he had retrieved his Panama hat. He carried the guisarme like a mighty man of war, thumping down its shaft at every step. But, when an attendant took it from him, it was with such a deferential, "*If* you please, sir," that H.M. only scowled. Then he surveyed Martin and Jenny.

"Not for the world," he said querulously, "would I show any curiosity. Oh, no. But, burn me, I'd like to have *some* idea of what it is I paid two hundred quid for. They say it's back there somewhere," he nodded towards the rear of the room, "and I can't get it till the end of the sale."

"Please," urged Jenny. "Lower your voice. I can tell you what it is."

"So?"

"It's a clock. A grandfather clock."

"Well . . . now!" muttered the great man, and scratched his chin. A vast load seemed lifted from him. "That's not bad. That's not bad at all. I was sort of picturing myself goin' home with a fine big bit of needlework labelled, 'Jesus give you sleep.' "

"The clock," Jenny explained, "hasn't got any works inside it. There's only a skeleton, fastened upright to the back, with its skull looking out through the glass clock-dial."

The effect of this remark was curious.

Instead of showing surprise or even sarcasm, H.M.'s big face smoothed itself out to utter expressionlessness. His small, sharp eyes fastened on Jenny in a way that evidently disconcerted her. He did not even seem to breathe. The thin voice of the auctioneer sounded far away.

"A skeleton in a clock, hey? That's a bit rummy. Do you happen to know any more about it, my wench?"

"Only—only that they say it used to belong to a doctor in our neighborhood. Years ago he sold it, or gave it away, or something. Then he died."

"Uh-huh. Don't stop there. Go on."

"Well! Aunt Cicely, that's Lady Fleet, saw it in Willaby's catalogue. She thought it would be nice as a present for Dr. Laurier; he's the son of the old doctor, you see. Aunt Cicely is kind. But she's so vague, though she's still very pretty, that she asked grandmother to bid."

"Oh, my eye!" breathed H.M. "Oh, lord love a duck! I want a look at that clock. Excuse me."

"But—"

"Sure, sure. I can't take it away. But a little largess, I think, ought to get me just a look at it. You two stay where you are!"

Martin made no objection. His blood was beating with the nearness of Jenny, his wits whirling, his entire universe concentrated on Jenny; and, he knew, she felt in much the same way.

"Now listen," he said. "Before the wires can get crossed again: what's your full name, and where do you live?"

"My name is Jennifer West. Grandmother—grandmother's made me hate titles so much we won't bother with the rest of it. My mother is dead. My father's lived abroad since the beginning of the war: in Sweden. I live at a place called Brayle Manor."

"Is that anywhere near Fleet House?"

"About half a mile south of it. Why?"

"Look here." Martin hesitated. "This engagement was— arranged. Wasn't it?"

Jenny hesitated too, and would not meet his eyes.

"Yes, I suppose you could call it that. We're practically broke; haven't a bean. The Fleets are very wealthy. Aunt Cicely . . ."

"Go on!"

"Well, Aunt Cicely's only weakness is that she *is* a bit of a snob about titles. Her husband gave I don't know how much to party-funds so he could get his knighthood. But that's not all! Richard is really . . . fond of me. Richard—"

"Or 'dear Ricky, as we call him.' "

"Darling, you *mustn't* talk like that!"

"Sorry. Do you know what black bile is? It's jealousy. Sorry."

"He really is nice. He's a great athlete, and very intelligent too: a double-first at Cambridge."

Fierce, tense, lowered whispers! Their voices were so soft, as they stood against the brown wall between the gilt chairs and the lacquered wardrobe, that no bidder could have complained of disturbance. Over a grimy skylight the sun alternately strengthened and darkened.

"If you don't mind," said Martin, "we'll omit the list of Richard's accomplishments. Jenny, I'm going to smash this marriage to blazes. Is that all right with you?"

"I think I should hate you if you didn't. But grandmother . . ."

"There is a technique with grandmother. You saw it used today by a master hand. How long are you staying in town?"

"We've got to leave this evening. I'm—I'm to spend Saturday and Sunday at Fleet House."

"Richard?"

"No! Not particularly!" The blue eyes grew puzzled. "It's something rather mysterious."

"How so?"

"Well, there's a friend of Aunt Cicely's, and mine too, named Ruth Callice. This morning, very early it seems, Ruth rang up Aunt Cicely. She asked if she could come down for the week-end, and bring two guests. I don't know who the two men are; but Ruth said Aunt Cicely would like them. Ruth said she had some tremendous project, about the old prison. She said it *might* not work, but she'd know for certain today whether some Ministry would say yes."

Then, very quietly, Jenny added: "Why did you jump when I said 'Ruth Callice.'"

Martin had not jumped. But, as they stood together negligently against the wall, their hands were locked together. Each tremor, each blood-beat, almost each thought, seemed to flow from one into the other. And women, at times like these, have an emotional power which is almost like mind-reading.

"Yes?" murmured Jenny.

"Because I'm one of the two men. I was in Ruth's flat last night."

"Oh," murmured Jenny, and her gaze moved away. He felt, in the literal sense of touch, something wrong. "Do you know Ruth well?"

"I've known her for years! She's one of the finest persons I ever met!"

"Oh. Did you ever tell her anything about—us?"

"Yes, several times. I'm afraid I got rather emotional about it last night. She cheered me up."

"How nice," said Jenny, and suddenly tried to wrench her hands away. He held tightly. "Then didn't she ever tell you who I was? Who 'Jenny' was? Why didn't she?"

"Probably because she had no more clue than I had."

"Oh, yes, she had. She knew who I was. She knew all *I* knew about you, because I told her. Three years! And in the meantime, I suppose . . ."

It occurred to Martin Drake, quite accurately, that Jenny must feel about Ruth Callice much as he felt about Richard Fleet. He must stop this nonsense. But such talk is contagious.

"If it comes to that, why didn't you get in touch with me and tell me yourself?"

Jenny's pale complexion was flushed, and she was trembling.

"Because you thought it was just a casual adventure. Oh, yes, you did! Or else you'd have found me—somehow. *You* had to come to *me,* don't you see? Won't anybody leave me a little pride? Please let me go."

"Jenny, listen to reason! You know how I feel, don't you?"

"Yes. I think so."

Jenny's resistance fell away. It was trivial, a brushing of the wing in those fierce whispers. The hands of the clock on the far wall stood at a quarter past twelve; the morning's auction would soon be over. And yet, in the state of mind of these two, all unintentionally they were precipitating tragedy and disaster which moved closer as steadily as the ticking of the clock.

"And now," she said, "you've been invited to Fleet House."

"Ruth and Stannard can go there. *I* can't.'

"Why not?"

"Damn it, you can't accept a man's hospitality and then tell him you're going to break up his marriage. Isn't there a hotel or a pub somewhere near?"

"Yes. There's one almost opposite Fleet House. That's where—" Jenny paused. Into her eyes came the same fear he had seen once before. She threw the thought away. "What are you going to do?"

"I'm going to put up at the pub. Tomorrow I'll see Mr. Richard Fleet, and Aunt Cicely, and as for grandmother: this afternoon, I think."

"No! You mustn't! Not this afternoon!"

He gripped her shoulders. "If I could only tell you, Jenny, how much—"

"*Oi!*" said the voice of Sir Henry Merrivale.

H.M. was standing very close to them. How long he had been there Martin could not tell, but it might have been a long time. H.M.'s hat was in his hand, and his expression was malevolent. Martin bumped back to reality.

"Well? Did you see the clock?"

"Uh-huh. I saw it. And it seems my first wild and wool-gatherin' notion," here H.M. massaged his big bald head, "is no more use than a busted kite on a calm day. But there's got to be *some* explanation! Or else—" With no change he added: "So you're putting up at the pub, son?"

"You listened?"

"I'm the old man," said H.M., austerely tapping himself on the chest as though this constituted all necessary explanation. "And I'm a bit glad you *are* stayin' there, if there's room for you. Masters and I will be there too."

Somewhere, noiselessly, an alarm-bell rang.

"Chief Inspector Masters?"

"Yes. Y'see, son, this business is not all bath-salts and lilies on the pond. It's messy. It's got claws. Pretty certainly in the past, and maybe in the future, we're dealin' with murder."

Chapter 4

Martin Drake did not see the skeleton in the clock until late on the following afternoon, when he saw it in the bar-parlour of the Dragon's Rest near Rimdown.

The Dragon's Rest, to be exact, boasted two bar-parlours in its long frontage. The inn, in that remote corner of Berkshire, faced westwards over a road running north and south. From the windows of either bar-parlour you could see, almost opposite—set well back from the road behind trees and clipped lawns—the white Georgian facade of Fleet House. By craning to the left, you could just make out in the distance the two square towers of Brayle Manor. By craning to the right, you could more distantly discern the round greyness of Pentecost Prison: six stone wings like spokes inside a stone wheel.

Both Pentecost and Fleet House, Martin felt, would hold bitter dreariness at night. Also, he was on a wire of nerves.

For he could not forget yesterday's events. Jenny had permitted him to go with her only as far as the foyer at Claridge's, where she was to meet grandmother. She had made him promise, solemnly crossing his heart, that he would see Richard Fleet first, Aunt Cicely second, and grandmother third.

Martin returned to his rooms at the Albany. After putting through a complicated and exasperating series of 'phone-calls, he managed to book a room at the Dragon's Rest. Then, under the huge arched window which had served a Regency artist, he tried to make new sketches of Jenny from memory. They displeased him. Presently the telephone rang.

"Stannard here," announced the hoarse, hearty, half-chuckling voice.

He could picture Stannard leaning back in a swivel-chair, the black hair plastered with nicety on his round head, the black eyes twinkling. Martin could almost hear the pleased creak of the swivel-chair as Stannard shifted his stocky bulk.

"I hope, Mr. Drake, you haven't forgotten our little talk last night?"

No, he hadn't forgotten it. But he could think only of Jenny.

Why, and in what crazy moment, had he insisted on this vigil in the execution shed?

"Because I'm glad to say," Stannard pursued, "that I have been successful. For a night or two at least we are masters of Pentecost Prison."

"Good! Good! Good!"

"Our good friend Ruth has helped us. A friend of hers has been kind enough to invite us all to spend the week-end—"

"Yes. I know."

"You know?"

This time an edge did get into Martin's voice.

"Mr. Stannard, it's a vitally personal matter; I'll explain when I see you. I can't stay at Fleet House. But you'll find me at the pub just across the way."

There was a slight pause.

"You'll travel down with us, of course?" inquired Stannard. "Noon train from Paddington to Reading, change for Newbury, then bus for the rest. Devilish awkward, being without petrol."

"Sorry. I'm afraid I've got to take an earlier train."

Now there was a definite pause. He knew Stannard had detected something odd in his tone, and that Stannard was examining the 'phone curiously.

"Shall I—ah—make excuses to our hostess and young host?"

"No. They'll have learned about it when you arrive."

"Shall I make excuses to Ruth?" This was said very casually.

"No." Martin clipped off the monosyllable.

"Ah. It should be very interesting to visit Fleet House," mused Stannard, "especially as I once had some slight acquaintance with its late owner. Just as you like, my dear fellow. Good-bye."

Martin replaced the telephone. He looked round his sittingroom, on whose walls much of his own work hung framed amid his collection of rapiers. It *had* occurred to him that afternoon to ring Ruth Callice and ask her what the devil Ruth had meant by her secrecy about Jenny. But Ruth was a good fellow; Ruth must have had some real reason; he put the thought aside.

That was how, next morning, a grey bus with dropsical wheels rattled him up in Rimdown crossroads at half-past eleven. Not far ahead he could see the Dragon's Rest, with its three tall and broad gables in a straight line, set up on a little rise on the east side of the road.

The Dragon's Rest was a beamed house of great age. Behind

it lay rolling fields, the glitter of a stream, and the largish oak-wood he later identified as Black Hanger. Not a blade of grass stirred, nothing stirred, in that hollow of silence and heat.

Mr. Puckston, the landlord, took him up to a first-floor bedroom facing west. Then Martin's first move was to clatter downstairs again to the telephone at the back of the saloon bar, and get in touch with Fleet House. He was answered by an informal and chatty maid.

"Mr. Richard? Oh, he's driven over to the races at Newbury."

Martin's heart sank. He put obvious questions.

"No, not back to lunch. But he'll be back in the afternoon, because there's people coming. Would you like to speak to his mother? She's in the garden."

"No, thanks. You say he drove over. Can you describe the car?"

"Oh, it's just an ole black car. Makes a lot of noise."

"Do you happen to know the number?"

"Are you kidding?" asked the maid, who had evidently been out with American troops.

"As soon as he comes back, will you ask him to ring Martin Drake at the Dragon's Rest? It's very important. Will you give him that message?"

"You have a nice voice," said the maid. "I sure will!"

Martin went back to his room fuming. To follow Richard Fleet in the crowds at Newbury races would be certainly to miss him, even if there were a photograph for identification. The minutes ticked on. He had lunch in the scrubbed oak dining-room, the food being incredibly good. But always he prowled back to the bedroom, also clean and surprisingly comfortable despite the humps of age in the floor.

Pulling back the thin white curtains at one window, he kept glancing across the road to where—some three hundred feet away—Fleet House raised its square, uncompromising face of white-painted stone. Being on higher ground, he could look across almost to the topmost row of windows. Over trees and clipped lawns, he could see a flagstone terrace before the front door.

Flagstones. That was probably where Sir George Fleet had
. . .

Martin saw no sign of an ole black car. But someone was moving on the terrace, woman in a long filmy dress with a red sash and a broad straw sun-hat.

And Martin yielded to temptation.

On a table beside his bed, with its spotlessly mended white

counterpane, lay an old-fashioned brass telescope of the short and folding sort. He pulled out its few bands and focussed the end one. The image sprang up close and clear, just as the woman turned her head round and up.

Aunt Cicely.

He remembered Jenny's soft voice: "Aunt Cicely *is* kind. But she's so vague, though still very pretty." The westering sun was in Martin's eyes, though the telescope shielded it. Aunt Cicely must be into her fifties. Yet she had an Edwardian air, Martin thought: the sort Sargent had painted so well. With her pale blonde hair under the broad sun-hat, face turned up, she seemed (through the telescope, at least) almost young and rather fragile.

Furthermore, she had recently been crying.

Martin shut up the telescope. What *was* the air of sheer coldness which seemed to breathe out of Fleet House? Probably his professional imagination. But . . .

This situation was getting to be damned awkward. He had not seen Ruth or John Stannard. But then he had not seen H.M. or Masters either, though the landlord told him they had booked rooms. Half-past two and a quarter to three.

It was past four, the cigarette-tray full of stubs, before he made a guess which he should have made before. He hurried down, fumbled with the small 'phone-directory, and rang Brayle Manor.

If grandma came to the 'phone? All right! But it was a male voice which answered, evidently a butler.

"Is Mr. Richard Fleet there?"

"Yes, sir. Whom shall I say is calling?"

Martin spoke deliberately. "This," he said, "is an enemy. Tell Mr. Fleet that an enemy is waiting for him at the Dragon's Rest to give him a message of great importance."

If young Fleet had an ounce of sporting blood in his body, Martin thought, that ought to fetch him. He expected further questions. But the unruffled voice merely said, "One moment, please." And then, after a long minute, "Mr. Fleet will be with you immediately."

Got it!

At this hour of the day, the whole inn was so quiet that you could hear the wainscot creak. Mr. and Mrs. Puckston must be enjoying their afternoon nap. The Dragon's Rest had three front doors, one in each gable. As Martin unlocked the first one, which was in the saloon bar, the snap of the key sounded like an act of guilt.

Moving on to the first bar-parlour, on his right, Martin

unlocked the front door there. This was a cosy room, its walls thickly hung with sporting prints and with quite genuine antique hunting horns of the early nineteenth century. Somewhat decaying leather chairs stood at the tables, and at either side of the black marble mantelpiece.

Then Martin turned round, and saw the skeleton in the clock.

The clock stood in the angle of the wall, south-east, beyond the mantelpiece. It was about six feet high, including its platform-base, and of dark polished wood elaborately wrought at the top. Through a round glass dial, with gilt numerals and hands, the skull-face looked out.

And the clock was ticking.

No! Wait a minute! It couldn't be ticking. The clock-case had another glass panel, oblong, so that you could see the skeleton behind a brass pendulum: which was motionless.

The illusion had been produced by a large square metal-cased clock, with a small pendulum, on the mantelpiece. Its slow *tick-tick* animated the hush of an atmosphere flavoured with the smell of beer and old stone. But the tall clock said nothing.

Yet it gave the watcher a slight start, the skull face a smug look in its dusky recess. Martin was conscious of golden shine lying through the windows behind him, of Fleet House across the road in its aloofness. He went over to examine the clock. As he had expected, the oblong lower panel opened on little hinges. He peered inside, he peered up.

With fine wires, and a heavier wire drilled into the head, the skeleton had been fastened to the back of the case; its feet and ankles partly concealed by a wooden fitting evidently designed to help the upright position. The clock-hands, like the pendulum, were dummies held by screw and spindle. You could adjust them to any position you liked. The hands now stood at ten minutes past twelve.

Tick-tick, tick-tick, tick-tick.

Richard Fleet would be here at any moment.

Martin drew back his head and closed the glass panel. How this reminder of mortality had got there he did not know. And it didn't matter.

He went through another door into the second bar-parlour. Dominated by a large iron stove rather than the usual fireplace, full of wicker chairs, this room was distinctly a comedown from the first. Nevertheless, Martin unlocked its front door. He had just turned the key when distantly, from the saloon-bar two rooms away, that particular door opened.

A voice called, "Martin!" He heard light, quick, running footsteps in tennis-shoes. And in the doorway of the second parlour, breathing hard, stood Jenny.

She wore a white tennis-blouse and white shorts, with a light pullover thrown over her shoulders. With her yellow hair somewhat tumbled, the colour of exertion tinted her face to more than mere prettiness. He stared at her.

"How did you get here?"

"On my bike." Choking a little to get her breath, she made a gesture towards the outside of the inn. "Darling, why did you send that message about being an enemy?"

"I had to get him here somehow."

"Grandmother was in the room when you rang up."

"Yes. I thought she might be."

"You hadn't said three words to Dawson before grandmother said: 'That is Captain Drake, I suppose.' Ricky said, 'Who's Captain Drake?' Grandmother said nothing at all. She just picked up her knitting and walked out of the room. Then I had to tell Ricky it was only a joke, but it was terribly serious. Afterwards I got old Riddle to insist the front tire of Ricky's car needed air—which it did—so I could get here before him."

"But you don't want to be present while we have it out, do you?"

Jenny's breathing was still quick. But the blue eyes regarded him steadily.

"If you want me to," she answered, "I'll stay here. I promise that. But I don't want to. I don't want . . . oh, God, no!" She shuddered. "The trouble is, you see, that I've got to know what happens. Just as soon as it happens." Jenny spread out her hands. "I'm sorry. That's how I feel."

"That's how a lot of us feel. Jenny! Do you still—?"

This was when they heard the loud cranking of a motor-car, emphasized by a loose mud-guard, approaching and drawing up outside the south wing. Once more the door of the saloon-bar, after a tentative rattle at its knob, was opened. Martin motioned Jenny (confound this sense of guilt!) to go out by the second-parlour door to the road.

"Hoy there!" called a male voice. "Hullo!"

Footsteps scuffled, hesitated, tramped through one room and then through two. In the doorway, inquiringly, appeared a tallish young man in sports coat, flannels, and with a blue tie skewered under one wing of his soft collar.

His mop of dark-blond hair was uncombed and unruly. He was on the lean and muscular side, carrying himself well. But first of all you noticed the quality of good-humour, which was so genuine that it flowed from him and made friends immediately. His grey eyes, his bump of a chin, made it a strong face as well as a good-humoured face.

"Well," he said, "are you the enemy?"

"Yes." Martin could not help smiling back. "But not a personal enemy, if you follow me."

"Ah. That's good. Well, what's up?"

Selecting a wicker chair by the door into the first-parlour, the newcomer dropped into it and threw one leg over its arm. He began to fill a pipe from an oilskin pouch.

There was a long silence.

"Look here, old boy," expostulated Richard Fleet, who was fishing after a pocket-lighter.

"Yes?"

"Stop pacing up and down like a Norman baron. Get it off your chest. Spit it out. You're making me nervous."

"All right," agreed Martin. "It's about Jenny. I've been in love with Jenny for more than three years, though I've only seen her twice. I have reason to think she feels the same way about me. I haven't formally asked her to marry me, but we intend to get married. I hate to tell you this, but there it is."

Again silence. Richard sat partly sideways, motionless, his leg over the chair-arm, pipe and lighter also held motionless, looking up at his companion. His grey eyes were without any shade of expression. *Tick-tick, tick-tick* went the clock in the other room, noticeable now as well as audible.

"I'm sorry to tell you this!" Martin shouted. "But . . ."

Then he saw that there was a shade of expression, slowly moving in like a new blood in Richard's face, though for a second he could not interpret it. It was tinged with incredulity, but this did not predominate. Then Martin realized. The feeling was relief. Slowly young Fleet sat upright, and expelled his breath.

"Thank God!" he said.

Chapter 5

The words were so startling that Martin backed away until he bumped into the iron stove in the middle of the room. Richard Fleet hastened to correct any wrong impression he might have made.

"Mind!" he said, jumping to his feet and pointing with the pipe. "Jenny's the world's best. I'd do anything for her. I'm so fond of her that sometimes I've almost thought this plan would work. But—"

"But?"

"I grew up with her," the other retorted with extraordinary intensity. "Jenny was always *there,* from five to seventeen and onwards. Let's face it: I'm not physically attracted by Jenny. Whereas you, it's plain, have gone completely overboard physically; and that's the main thing. Yes, I know!"

He held up a hand, forestalling objection. He dropped pipe and lighter into his pockets. The grey intelligent eyes regarded Martin as though they knew, or thought they knew, the whole universe.

"They tell us a lot of things about companionship and community of interests and so on. Well, old boy," he grinned, "let's wait until we're old enough to have to bother with such things. The glorious part of all this is that I've gone overboard too. *I* want to get married."

Martin's sense of relief, he thought, completely overshadowed that of his companion.

"Congratulations! And very hearty congratulations! Who is she?"

Richard went over and carefully closed the second-parlour door.

"Susan Harwood. She lives on the other side of Brayle: the town, not the Manor." A shadow of worry crossed Richard's face, but his animation burst through it. "By God," he breathed, "this is the most magnificent . . . shake hands!"

They shook hands, fervently.

"Look here," said Richard, "what would you like?"

"Like?"

"Well," said the other, whose first impulse on feeling pleased was to give something to somebody, "what about my car with fifty gallons of best Black Market petrol? Or your choice from the gun-racks? Or I've got the finest book of telephone-num . . . no, you won't want telephone-numbers if you're going to get married. Neither will I." He pondered. "You know—by the way—what's your first name?"

"Martin."

"Right! Ricky here.' Again he pondered, "You know, if we plan this carefully, I'm damn sure we can wangle it."

" 'Plan carefully?' What have we got to plan?"

"You don't know what you're up against," Ricky said

quietly. "No, wait! You think you do; but you don't."

"Family opposition?"

"You say that fairly contemptuously. Maybe Jenny hasn't told you everything." Ricky brushed the palms of his hands together; then gripped them in sinewy fingers. "I don't suppose you've ever played chess with Grandmother Brayle? *I* have. She ought to have been a man. She wants money, and she means to get it."

Though the sun was sinking, the many little panes of the second-parlour window were still tinged with gold. With both doors and windows closed, the room was hot and stuffy. Ricky went over to the window and stared out unseeingly.

"My mother," he continued, "is wonderful. But Grandmother Brayle has got mother"—he put his thumb in the palm of his left hand, and twisted it—"like that. And Dr. Laurier has more influence than anybody knows. As for Jenny . . ." He broke off. "Great Scott, there *is* Jenny!"

Martin hurried to his side.

In front of the Dragon's Rest, a slope of sun-glowing grass stretched down to the road. Across the road, beyond a short strip of grass, ran the low stone boundary-wall of Fleet House's park. Near the wall stood Jenny and Ruth Callice, apparently in casual conversation.

They made a contrast, against the trees and, somewhat towards the left, the white, square solidity of the house. Ruth wore a silk frock as though she were in London; her light-brown hair was done in some new upsweep style, with earrings. Jenny, in her white blouse and white shorts, lifted one shoulder as she spoke.

Ricky Fleet leaned his weight on the window-sill with both hands.

"You know," he said, "there's a row going on over there."

"A what?"

"A row. Don't ask me how I know; can't you feel it? Besides, I've been expecting one."

"Why?"

"I suppose," Ricky grunted, "I ought have been at home to greet the guests. But I start gassing, and time gets mixed up. Then Ruth rang up the Manor just before you rang me. Jenny talked to her." He hesitated. "Jenny wasn't any less gentle than she always is. But she sounded too—sugary. Like a woman waiting for a time and place to blow up. You know what I mean?"

Even as he spoke Jenny said a last few words, lifting her

shoulder, and moved away. She glanced towards the window where Ricky and Martin were standing. Her gait faltered and grew slow, but she continued; and automatically swung the thin blue pullover at her side. When Martin saw his companion's shoulders grow rigid, he realized something else.

"What the hell," Ricky blurted, "am I going to tell her?"

The door opened, framing Jenny against sunlight. Pouring embarrassment flooded into that room, holding all three motionless. Martin saw Ricky brace himself for an actor's role in some heroic speech of renunciation; he even saw Ricky glance at himself in a flyblown mirror to make sure the posture was right. But it was Jenny who spoke.

"It's all right," she said, looking at the floor. "I knew it was all right as soon as I saw you two shake hands."

The embarrassment remained, but the tension had gone.

"It wouldn't have worked, you know," growled Ricky.

"Ricky here," Martin said, "has been so decent about the whole thing that I don't know how to thank him."

"Nonsense, old boy! Nonsense!"

Jenny's eyes brimmed over as she regarded her (they hoped) ex-fiancé.

"You *are* a dear, Ricky."

"Not a bit of it, old girl! Not a bit of it!"

In another minute, Martin thought, he'll convince himself he really has made a heroic sacrifice.

"Martin," said Jenny, and hesitated. "Will you take me out somewhere tonight?"

At this change of subject, Ricky became natural again.

"That's not a bad idea! You can take my car. But where would you go for a beano in unexplored wilds like these?"

"That's not it." Jenny shook her head vehemently, still looking at Martin. "Will you just take me somewhere, and drive and drive and drive? I don't care where. Will you?"

"You know I will, my dear."

Jenny advanced into the room. Sinking into one of the wicker chairs beside a round table, she threw her pullover on the table. At this change of subject, abruptly introduced but well received, more emotion should have been drained away. And yet, in Jenny's case at least, it was not.

"Ruth Callice," she bit at her underlip, "Ruth Callice says you and she and this barrister had some horrible idea of spending a night in the execution shed at Pentecost, to see whether there were any ghosts of hanged people. Ruth says you suggested it."

"Well . . . in a way I did, yes."

"She says you promised. But you won't go now, will you?"

Martin laughed.

"Under the circumstances, Jenny, I think they'll make no difficulty about releasing me from the promise." He turned to Ricky. "Would you like to substitute for me?"

"*Would I!*" exploded Ricky. The words 'prison' and 'ghosts' had powerful effect. Again taking out pipe and lighter, his dark-blond hair falling over his forehead, he snapped on the lighter and kindled the tobacco with deep inhalations.

"Listen," he went on, with a waving gesture of pipe and smoke. "I've been trying to get a look inside that place for nearly ten years, ever since they hoicked the convicts out. But you can't *get* in, any more than the poor devils could get out. How are you going to do it?"

"Ricky!"

Jenny's small voice stopped him. He looked at her curiously. She was half lying back in the chair, the yellow hair thrown back, her face with a little more of its customary pallor.

"All the p-pleasant things," she stammered, gripping the arms of the chair, "have got mixed up with the dreadful ones. It was awfully kind of you to . . . to . . ."

"Rubbish. Let's get back to the subject of ghosts."

"All right," Jenny answered unexpectedly, "I will. Ricky, your mother's been very upset all afternoon."

Into Martin's head came an image of Aunt Cicely, with her tear-reddened eyelids, seen through a brass telescope from a bedroom window. But mention of Aunt Cicely seemed to act on Ricky as mention of Grandmother Brayle acted on Jenny, though in a different way.

"I know! I ought to have been at home in the afternoon!"

"No, Ricky. It wasn't that. Have you ever heard of a man named Stannard?"

"I don't think so. Why?"

"He's one of the guests. He and Ruth came down by an earlier train than they'd expected to. Ruth said she ought to keep an eye on Martin—"

(Here Ricky turned a surprised face, but Martin was looking at Jenny.)

"—and they got here about lunch-time. During lunch, Mr. Stannard started talking about the day your father . . . died."

Ricky took the pipe out of his mouth.

"Blast his impudence!" Ricky shouted.

"I honestly don't think it was impudence."

"No? It always upsets mother, though."

"You see," Jenny frowned, "Mr. Stannard said to Aunt

Cicely something like, 'I'm afraid we've met before, Lady Fleet.' Aunt Cicely laughed and said, 'That's not very complimentary.' Then Mr. Stannard said, 'Forgive me: I only meant I was at Fleet House on the day your unfortunate husband met his death.' "

"What did mother say?"

"Well, Ruth Callice tells me it wasn't a very merry lunch."

"Damn him!"

"Ricky, do you remember or did you ever hear of any 'Stannard' being there at the time?"

"No. Never."

"Nor I. In anything I've ever heard, or—read."

"But what is all this?" demanded Ricky. His pipe had gone out, and he put it down on the table. "You're as fretted as though you'd seen a whole crowd of ghosts. My governor's been dead for twenty years. It's a pity about mother; I'd like to wring Stannard's neck; but a little tact and we'll smooth it over."

"We can't smooth over the police," Jenny said.

She rose to her feet and appealed to Martin.

"I—I haven't said anything about what Sir Henry told us yesterday. I mean, at Willaby's. Partly because I was afraid of the rumpus, and partly because I never can tell whether he's serious or not."

Jenny turned to Ricky, and nodded towards the closed door of the other parlour.

"The police are here," she added. "They're in that room now. I saw them go in when I came here. There's a Chief Inspector from Scotland Yard, and the other man—well, they call him the Old Maestro. They're here to investigate. Sir Henry thinks your father was murdered."

The word, on Jenny's lips, sounded incongruous.

"Nonsense!" said Ricky. "He got vertigo and pitched over the parapet."

"Yes; but suppose someone did kill him?"

"Look here! Wait a minute!"

"I want to know who was at the house that day," Jenny went on, "and where everybody was when it happened. I was only five years old then. Ricky, how well do you remember?"

The other tousled up his hair, digging the fingers in.

"Some parts of it very plainly, and others not at all. Because they get mixed up with different years. I was barely twelve myself. Besides, I didn't see it happen. I was in the back garden with Miss Upton. She had a head-lock on me."

"Ricky, please do be serious!"

"I am serious! Can't you remember Miss Upton the governess, with a build like Sandow and yet that refined la-di-da accent coming out of her mouth?"

"Yes. I remember. She was with your family four years."

"Well, I mean quite literally she had a wrestling-hold on me. Because I wanted to watch the hunt go past." Ricky paused. "You know, Jenny-angel, this subject . . ."

"Yes! It's been taboo in our families for all these years. Let's tear it apart!"

"But why?"

"Have you thought," asked Jenny, and looked at Martin, "what the upset of a police-investigation would be in your house? And my house?"

Clearly Ricky hadn't. Up to this moment, it was clear, he had regarded the matter as nothing very important. 'The governor's been dead for twenty years; we've forgotten it; why bother?' Such might have been his phi'osophy. Now he sat down heavily in what had been Jenny's chair by the table, and picked up his dead pipe. The sun's glow was dimming to a pale, clear after-light through the open door to the road.

"Tell it," Jenny almost whispered. "Tell it!"

"It was October or November. I'm sure of that, because the trees were mostly bare and there were leaves on the ground. Also because they'd given me a new cricket-bat; and the governor asked what I wanted with a new one when the season was over; but cricket has no season for you at that age. There was some kind of special treat promised for tea, because a number of people were to be there.

"As I say, Miss Upton and I were in the back garden. Near the house, I think. There was a red sky to the west, with the bare branches of trees up against it. It wasn't very cold, and there was a clean autumny-tanging kind of wind. Then we heard the Ascombe Hunt.

"We'd heard faint noises before. But nothing to the uproar like this. We couldn't see anything, because the house was between us and the road. But the hounds were ding-dong and hell-for-leather on a breast-high scent. I knew they'd broken out of Black Hanger and across Guideman's Field just back of this pub here, and I guessed they were running to view.

"I started to make a bee-line for the front of the house. Miss Upton grabbed my arm. She was afraid I would run across and get among the field in front of somebody's horse, which had happened once or twice before. I kicked up a devil of a row until she got a head-lock on me. Then she said: "Richard, you may go to the front if I keep hold of your hand.""

"I said yes, and meant it. We started round the north side of the house, on the broad gravel drive. Then we heard a . . . well, a shout."

Ricky paused.

"I didn't think of anything being wrong, or even connect it with the house particularly. I knew my governor was up on the roof, trying to follow the hunt through a very powerful pair of field-glasses. As he always did when he had the rheumatics and it was agony to sit on a horse. But—

"Well, just as we were nearly to the front of the house, where there's a tap for the garden-hose, I distinctly heard Dr. Laurier's voice."

Jenny interposed. She had crept into a chair opposite Ricky, both of them with their elbows on the table.

"Was it old Dr. Laurier?" she asked. "Or the Dr. Laurier we have now?"

Ricky made a fussed gesture with the pipe. His eyes were hypnotized.

"Old Dr. Laurier, with the beard. The hounds were yelling, and there was the hallo-forrard. Only the hunt-servants had followed through the wood. Most of the field had ridden round; you could see a flash of pink coats coming round the edge of Black Hanger, and hear the horses. But I distinctly remember Dr. Laurier's voice saying, 'Get the table-cloth out of the hall.'

"In the front hall there used to be a piece of tapestry, worked with what I then considered very funny-looking knights; they had it on a table. That's the most distinct thing of the lot: *Get the table-cloth out of the hall.*'

"Then we got round to the front terrace. There was my governor, lying face-down on the flagstones, looking just as usual: except that old Dr. Laurier, with the beard, was spreading the tapestry-piece over his head and I think his shoulders.

"I was so excited I looked across the road first: there were two men sitting on the roof-gables of this pub, and the hunt streaming beyond. Then there was something: I don't know what. Dr. Laurier straightened up. Your grandmother was standing beside him. When you're a kid, you never really know there's something wrong until you see the look on their faces. Dr. Laurier said, 'Miss Upton, take the boy away from here.' I could feel Miss Upton shaking through all her fifteen stone, and all of a sudden I felt as frightened as hell without knowing why. She turned me round and took me back. Then . . ."

Again Ricky paused. He put the pipe into his mouth and chewed at its stem.

"On my word of honour," he declared in that same hypnotized tone, and dropped the pipe again, "I haven't thought of this for years. Maybe you jogged it into my head. Maybe it's sheer imagination. But I have an impression that I looked *up*."

"Towards the roof?"

"No, no! I didn't connect the governor with anything like 'death' or all the terms you might imply. It was a vague kind of wonder what he was doing down here instead of up there. I looked at an upper window, I think to the right of the front door. And I saw . . ."

There was a sharp rapping on the inside of the open door to the road.

Martin Drake—shut out, almost forgotten, feeling a sharp twinge of jealousy at the absorption of these two in each other and their long familiarity—Martin jerked up his head at that rapping. The other two started as though they had been burnt.

In the doorway stood a wiry, middle-sized man whose pince-nez, except for its gold nose-clamp, seemed to fit into his eyes rather than advance outside them. His hair, cut *en brosse*, was iron-grey. In an ascetic face, with somewhat hollow cheeks, showed a narrow fastidious mouth. His whole air was one of fastidiousness and extreme precision; and he carried a medicine-case in his right hand.

Despite the bloodless mouth, his voice was vigorous if soft. He smiled at Jenny and Ricky, making the countenance pleasant and human, and then looked towards Martin.

"Captain Drake, I imagine?" he inquired. "I am Dr. Laurier."

(So he's been talking to grandma, eh? Why did Lady Brayle persist with that 'captain' when they'd finished another war two years ago? Gossip, flying and twisting! How much was known?)

"Just Mr. Drake," Martin said, "if you don't mind."

Dr. Laurier bowed slightly. Next he turned to Ricky. You could imagine him, at a desk, pushing a group of small articles carefully into line.

"In my opinion, Richard, it would be very wise if you returned home at once. Your mother is not well."

Ricky twitched up his head. "You've been over there?"

"Yes." Dr. Laurier, not moving from the doorway, fired softly from a distance. He inclined his head. "I don't know how many times I have told you that your mother has a definitely serious heart-condition. An unpleasant shock of any sort—" very slightly emphasizing the words 'of any sort,' Dr. Laurier's almost invisible pince-nez moved towards Jenny, and then Martin—"would be . . . most undesirable."

"Then if she heard—" Ricky checked himself. He also looked at Jenny and Martin. Wretchedness laid hold of him and shook him as though with hands.

"I'll go straightaway," he said, and got up.

"I hope," interposed Jenny politely, "my grandmothe. is well?"

And this was a different girl from the timorous one of yesterday. Martin saw that with a shock of hope. Though she seemed outwardly placid, her breast rose and fell under the white blouse.

"Your grandmother, Lady Jennifer," Dr. Laurier returned her smile, "is in excellent health. She was a bit disappointed, however . . ."

Jenny's tone expressed immense surprise. "Were you at the Manor too?"

"For a cup of tea; no more. As I say, she was a bit disappointed you were not there for tea. She wondered where you were."

"Oh, I've got to be out much later tonight. I shall have to go home and change, of course. But I've got to be out much later tonight."

Deliberately Jenny rose from her chair. Deliberately she slipped over to where Martin was standing, and took his arm. He put his hand over hers. Dr. Laurier made no comment and no sign: a grey-headed statue in the doorway, his pince-nez opaque, the medicine-case in his hand.

"And—Ricky!" the ex-*fiancée* called.

"Eh?"

"You will lend us your car for tonight, won't you?"

"Of course. And . . ." Despite his perturbation, the old smile kindled Ricky's face. "Look here, old boy. This man-of-honour business is all very well. But is there any real reason why you shouldn't stay with us instead of putting up at the pub? Can't you at least come over for dinner tonight?"

"I've been a fool," Martin blurted. "I'm always being a fool. But I had some wild sort of notion that everyone here was an enemy .. ."

"Who can tell?" murmured Dr. Laurier.

The words fell with soft, chilling weight. It was as though a dagger had thudded into a door; not too melodramatic a comparison, because Dr. Laurier had a certain hobby. Martin felt Jenny's soft arm grew rigid against his coat-sleeve. And then: "I *beg* your pardon!" added the doctor, and stepped aside.

Ruth Callice, brushing past him with apology, stepped into the room.

In her unobtrusive way Ruth was urban charm, urban fashion, invading a country pub. Her grey dress, the dull-twinkling ear-rings, set off her dark-brown eyes and the full roundness of her neck. Ruth regarded everyone with smiling apology.

"Martin, dear," she said. "I've come to remind you about your promise for tonight."

Chapter 6

Some half an hour before Ruth's appearance, in the other bar-parlour with the clock containing its skeleton, Sir Henry Merrivale sat in a leather chair near the fireplace. Chief Inspector Masters stood opposite, behind a table on which lay a brief-case stuffed with documents.

And these two were carrying on in a way which would have sounded familiar to any friend of theirs.

"Now, now, Masters, keep your shirt on!"

Masters, large and burly, usually bland as a card-sharper, his grizzled hair brushed to hide an increasing bald-spot, was buttoned up in a blue serge and had assumed his witness-box manner. This indicated that his words would have weight and dignity.

"It might interest you to know, sir, that I've *got* my shirt on."

"That's right, Masters. Be like Me."

"These impossible situations," said Masters. "What do I care for 'em?" He reached out and snapped his fingers. "Not that! Oh, ah! And why? Because I'm resigned."

"*I* got a spiritual nature too."

Masters's blood-pressure soared, as was evident in his countenance. "But what I DO object to——"

"Easy, son!"

"But what I do object to," continued the Chief Inspector,

swallowing hard, "is the Assistant Commissioner wanting to dig up a twenty-year old case, because: first, he was an old friend of Sir George Fleet; and, second, he recently gets three anonymous postcards straight out of Colney Hatch. Now I ask you! Is that fair or reasonable?"

Delving into the neatly packed brief-case, Masters drew out three cards and pushed them across the table towards H.M., who did not even glance at them. H.M., with a malignant scowl, had folded his hands across his corporation and was twiddling his thumbs.

These cards, the ordinary twopenny-halfpenny sort you buy at any post office, had both address and message printed in small block capitals, with a pencil. They were postmarked in the town of Brayle, about two miles southwards, on July 5th, July 6th, and July 7th, and addressed, 'Chief of the C.I.D., Scotland Yard, London W.1.' The first card read:

Re Sir George Fleet: examine the skeleton in the clock.

The second card read:

Re Sir George Fleet: what was the pink flash on the roof?

The third card read:

Re Sir George Fleet: evidence of murder is still there.

"Lummy!" breathed Masters. "I've seen some scatty messages in my time, but this beats the lot." He squared himself. "Now I'll just take each point, sir. This clock, to begin with."

Both of them, in the old room hung with hunting prints, surveyed the tall clock. Standing cater-cornered in its southeast angle, its gilt hands and numerals faintly shining, the glass dial conveyed an impression that the skull had its chin tilted up so that the skull could see better. Like Martin Drake, Masters experienced the illusion that the *tick-tick* of the mantelpiece clock issued out of that dead case. It made Masters uncomfortable, which in his staid soul he resented.

"Sir," he demanded, "what's wrong with that clock?"

"Nothin'," H.M. answered simply.

"What's wrong with the skeleton?"

"Nothin'."

"Then why in lum's name do you want to bring it down here and stick it up in a bar-parlour?"

"Because, son, I can't do everything at once. I want to take that blighter out of his case—" H.M. pointed to the skeleton— "and put him on a table, and examine him thoroughly. I dunno who he is, son. But I can tell you who he's not. He's not Sir George Fleet."

"Oh, ah!" muttered Masters, with a sideways look. "So you thought of that?"

"Oh, my son! It was the very first wild and wool-gatherin' notion I did have, for no reason at all. But it won't work. Now the overall height of that clock, includin' platform and fancy top, is six feet. And the late lamented?"

"Six feet one inch tall," grunted Masters, with the heaviness of one who has studied much, "and with big bones."

"Right. Whereas the chap who's watchin' us," H.M. indicated the clock again, "was a little feller. Five feet five, about. Well-proportioned, small bones. Masters, I'll tell you what it is. That's an ordinary medical-school skeleton: varnished, articulated . . ."

"Meaning strung together with wire?"

"With fine cat-gut, usually. Besides, you couldn't possibly conceal the injuries to Fleet's head. Who'd want to?"

"Ah, and that's just it. What *about* the skeleton?" exploded Masters. "In all this record—" he brought his hand down slowly on the brief-case—"there's not a word to do with any skeleton in a clock. What's it supposed to mean?"

"I dunno. But an anonymous letter, postmarked Brayle, tells you to examine it. Five days later Our Sophie, on instructions from Cicely Fleet, waddles up to London to buy it for Dr. Laurier: son of clock's former owner. Don't you find that rather fetchin' and interesting?"

Masters took several paces up and down. The ticking of the clock seemed to trouble him.

"If we had one bit of evidence that this was murder—!"

"Oh, Masters. It was murder. Tell me something about George Fleet."

"Lummy, haven't you read this stuff in the brief-case?"

"Uh-huh. But I want to see what impressed *you*."

H.M., his spectacles pulled down on his broad nose, closed his eyes. An expression almost of serenity crossed his unmentionable face. Masters, deeply suspicious of being done in the eye again, studied him warily. At length the Chief Inspector cleared his throat.

"Hurrum!" he said. "Sir George Fleet? Came of a well-to-do family in the Midlands, with a cotton-business. Family wanted him to be pukka Army; so did he. Boarding-school when he was a tiny 'un, then Harrow, then Sandhurst. Never finished Sandhurst; father died, and he had to take over the business.

"But he acted Army all the rest of his life, though he didn't join up in '14. Upright carriage, cropped moustache, dead-keen on sport. Roared at everybody. Wanted a knighthood; got it; wanted a baronetcy so his title wouldn't die with him; didn't get it."

Still H.M. did not open his eyes, though his look was now evil. He grunted.

"Yes. That's why it's so rummy that . . . h'mf. What about his wife?"

"She lives just over the road, sir. You could go see her."

"I meant twenty years ago."

"Bit of a beauty, I'd say." Masters considered. "You've seen her photograph. Yes, bit of a beauty in the fair-haired, blue-eyed way. Completely gone on her husband. Idolized him. Do anything he said, and like it."

"Wait a minute, son. Does that mean she was all coos and clucks in public, and in private wept and twisted him round her little finger?"

Masters repressed a guffaw.

"No, it does not," he retorted dryly. "Old Chief Inspector Radford: if you've read his notes of that time—"

"I have. I've gone over other things too. Y'know, Masters, I may have been doin' you in the eye. Just a little bit."

Masters stiffened. Once more he became as wary as a heavy-game hunter near a somnolent water-buffalo.

"But it was only a telephone-call," pleaded H.M. in a bumbling way. "And it don't (burn me, it don't!) help with our real problem."

"If you hadn't sent that ruddy clock on ahead of us, and we'd got here—"

"You were tellin' me, Masters. About Fleet's wife."

"Now get this, sir! At that time there was only one person who ruled the roost in *that* house: it was her husband. Why, sir, he once tore up her favourite morning-room, or whatever they call it, and put in new panelling and a billiard-table. And she never said a word. I know what *my* old woman would have said.

"Changeable sort of gentleman, too. One time he had a collection of old swords and daggers. Got tired of 'em, and bang! overnight they went, and she had a room with nothing on the walls but hooks until he could put up antique guns instead. Now," Masters added grimly, "we'll come to the day of the accident. Because it was an accident, and I'll show you why. Come over and look at the house, Sir Henry. Just look out of the window!"

"I got a picture in my mind's eye, son. You just gush on."

Returning to the table, Masters sat down, took a blue-bound

folder of typewritten sheets out of the brief-case, and opened it.

"The date," he continued, "was November 4th, 1927. Just so. Let me emphasize a few points about that roof.

"It's a very big roof, flat and perfectly square. It's floored with cement; they used it for sun-bathing. On the edge of the south side there's a low chimney-stack, narrow and oblong, flat on top. In the middle of the roof there's another chimney-stack just like it, and a third on the edge of the north side. All in a straight line dead across the middle of the roof. Got it?"

"Got it. Sure."

"Just so. At the time this happened, there was nothing at all on the roof except two beach-chairs and a wicker settee, all of 'em pushed back dead against the little chimney-stack in the middle."

H.M., eyes closed, blew out his cheeks hideously.

"Stop a bit, son. What were beach-chairs doin' there in November?"

"It'd been a warm autumn, and still wasn't cold. They'd just been left there."

"Any smoke from the chimneys?"

"No. Not a fire lighted. Gas-range in the kitchen."

"What colour were the beach-chairs?"

Masters stared at him.

"How in lum's name should *I* know? This report deals with—"

"Now, now, Masters! Keep your shirt ōn!"

Again the Chief Inspector's forefinger, somewhat agitated by his blood-pressure, travelled down the typewritten lines.

"I don't have to explain this hunting stuff. You've read it. Sir George Fleet, even if he did act like a comic-paper colonel, really was a sport. First-class horseman and A-1 shot. He hunted except when he had (don't I know it?)˙the rheumatic pains in his side. On November 4th, about two o'clock in the afternoon, he was sitting in his study reading *The Field* when the gardener came to see him. This gardener said the Ascombe Hunt was 'drawing,' whatever that means, a big wood called Black Hanger."

H.M. sat up with ghoulish thoughtfulness.

"I say, Masters. Did you ever see me on a horse?"

"I daresay," the Chief Inspector said with heavy sarcasm, "you were one of the greatest horsemen in England too?"

"Well . . . now!" said H.M., with a deprecatory wave of his hand. "I wouldn't like to say that, no. But I had a steeplechaser, named Whoozler, who could take fences like the cow jumpin' over the moon. Besides, it'd fit in—burn me if it wouldn't!—with a former existence where . . ."

Masters stiffened.

"So help me," he swore, and pointed at H.M., "if I hear one more word about your reincarnation, just one more word, then back I go to tell the A.C. I'm through. I tell you straight: it gives me the creeps."

H.M. pondered. He peered round carefully, to make sure both doors were closed.

"Y'see, Masters, I'm not just sure I believe it myself, exactly."

"Ah!"

"But some of those books sound awful plausible, son." H.M. shook his head. "And it stirs you up, sort of (wouldn't it anybody?) to imagine . . . I say, Masters: couldn't you see me as a Cavalier poet?"

"In a pig's eye I could."

"But the feller was my own ancestor, curse it! His picture's the spittin' image of me. And I've just got a book on swordsmanship. And," added H.M., suddenly drawing himself up and glaring at his companion with awful dignity, "are we goin' to get on about Sir George Fleet, or aren't we?"

Masters shut his eyes, counted ten, and opened them again. There was a brief silence, under the ghost-clock and in the room of sporting prints. Then Masters went on.

"The gardener," he said, "told him the hunt was coming. So he picked up a pair of field-glasses, and started up for the roof. Now the only way to the roof is through a covered door at the very back, or west side, of the roof.

"Sir George walked straight to the front of the roof, a position just about over the front door below. He raised the field-glasses, and focussed them. It seems there was a lurid kind of red sky behind him, but it was clear light. Now get this, sir. The chimney-stacks were fifty feet behind him. He was alone on a concrete floor, *without anybody or any object within fifty feet of him.*"

Masters paused. He riffled over several pages, flattening them down with his fist.

"Stop the bus again," muttered H.M. "What about the field-glasses? I seem to remember readin' a story where there was hokey-pokey with field-glasses, and they stuck somebody in the eye."

Masters was now cat-like and bland.

"The fact is, sir, I thought you might bring that up. The

glasses were just plain field-glasses, as you'll hear in a moment. Accept that?"

"Uh-huh. Go on."

"Our *real* evidence," Masters continued, "comes from six witnesses on this side of the road. Two of these witnesses," he pointed upwards, "were sitting astride the gable-tops of this pub. And these two witnesses are clinchers.

"The Ascombe Hunt is disbanded now. But in those days, it seems, everybody hereabouts was keen about it. It beats me to know why. You'd think it'd make country people mad as hops to have a lot of horses and dogs tearing over private property and mucking it up. But they tell me it didn't. These six men, they were down in the bar. They heard about the kafuffle coming just about when Sir George did. And up *they* went.

"Our two chief witnesses are Arthur Puckston and Simon Frew. Mr. Puckston, who's still the landlord here, was astride one gable with an old brass telescope that belongs to the house. Simon Frew had a pair of big new binoculars he was very proud of.

"This pub's on high ground, sir. From the top you can see straight over and across Fleet House, covering the roof. During this time there was an unholy row in the wood. First one dog—"

"HOUND."

"—started to yell, then another, then a lot more, and before long: smack! out they came from Black Hanger, tearing across in the open. Now listen to what Simon Frew said, when he was astride the middle gable with his binoculars. All this question-and-answer stuff has to be polished up and made smooth into a statement. But here you are."

Again Masters smoothed out the turnover pages with his fist.

"'The field—'" he began, and stopped. "This 'field,' it'd seem, would mean the gents in the red coats."

"I got it, son. Well?"

Masters read slowly.

The field had just started to come round the far side of Black Hanger, almost facing us. It is a good distance away there and on higher ground than us. I put my glasses on them. The first few men were smiling and waving their hands. They seemed to be waving straight in my face. I knew it could not be me. So I turned my glasses round.

"Towards Fleet House," Masters interpolated grimly. "About three hundred feet, that's all."

Sir George was there. I could see all round him. He had his glasses to his eyes in one hand, and was waving with the other. Then it looked like somebody gave him a hard shove in the back. He stood there for a second. He shouted. He fell head-first. I did not follow him with the glasses because I was too surprised. I just kept looking round to see who could have pushed him. '

It was a shorn statement. Yet Martin Drake, had he been there, would have seen the red sky with the silhouetted figure, and scented the autumn air, and sensed the rush and crash.

"I won't trouble you," Masters said drily, "with what you know. But just to hammer it home, sir! A bit of what Puckston said, the man with the telescope. His attention was caught by this yell Sir George gave."

And then spoke Mr. Puckston.

I looked round. I saw something pitch over the little ledge, but it was so quick I did not see what it was. I looked all over the roof, but did not see anybody or anything. I looked down. Sir George was lying there, and something was wrong with his head. Dr. Laurier ran out of the front door. Bert Hartshorn—

"Bert," Masters explained, "was the constable. He'd been at the pub, but naturally he (hurrum!) couldn't climb on the roof."

—Bert Hartshorn was coming up to the terrace. Dr. Laurier said something, and Bert picked up Sir George's binoculars and walked into the house. Dr. Laurier said something else, and Lady Brayle came out with some kind of cloth. I said aloud, 'The bastard is dead.'

To Masters it was one more case, with nothing more of drama than a blueprint. He closed the blue folder.

"There's more of Puckston," he explained. "And four others who were lower down in between the gables. But it needn't trouble us. Eh?"

H.M. groaned.

"Let's sew it up," suggested Masters. "The 'little ledge' Puckston talks about is a stone coping, just six inches high, which runs round the whole roof. You agree nobody could have hidden there? Or, if we accept the witnesses, attacked a big powerful man without some kind of struggle?"

"Uh-huh. I'm afraid I got to agree."

"You admit the fact that the roof was as bare as a biscuit-tin?"

"Well . . ."

"Sir George's injuries, for instance." Masters remained affable and bland, if anything more affable. "They were to the head, the arms, and one shoulder. That's not unusual, when somebody pitches from a comparatively low height. There wasn't another fracture or another mark on him. Not even," Masters lingered on the word, "a bruise."

H.M. made fussed motions.

"Don't leer, Masters. I hate leerin'. What's on your mind?"

"You were going to ask, weren't you, whether there was a bruise? Whether something might have been thrown or fired at him? Eh?"

H.M. only grunted.

"If it hit him hard enough to knock him over the edge," Masters pointed out, "it must have left a mark or a bruise. But it didn't. Finally, there's the evidence of the post-mortem."

Reaching with infinite effort into his hip pocket, H.M. fished out a case of his vile cigars and lighted one with relish. He seemed to have little relish for anything else.

"There was a possibility, just a bare possibility," Masters goaded him, "that somebody might have given him a drug—poison, even!—to make his head swim so he fell. But there was no drug, no poison, nothing."

"As I understand it, Masters, the post-mortem was performed by old Dr. Laurier. The family friend. So! Was there anybody assistin' him at the post-mortem? To sort of look on?"

Masters grinned.

"As a matter of fact, there was. A doctor from Newbury. I forget his name, but it's in the record. He confirmed the finding."

"O tempora," said H.M. "O mores. Oh, hell!"

Masters rubbed his hands together.

"Here's your victim," he explained, "on a concrete floor with no person or thing within fifty feet of him. He wasn't pushed. He had nothing thrown at him. He wasn't drugged in any way. What happened to him?"

"Son, I just don't know."

"You bet you don't. But I can tell you. Sir George was a man over forty, who'd just climbed some long flights of stairs. He got excited waving to the hunt; he came over dizzy, as anybody might; and he fell. Do you still want to know the colour of the beach-chairs?"

"Sure I do," retorted H.M. instantly, taking the cigar out of his mouth. "What's the pink flash?"

"Pink flash?"

"Certainly. See the second anonymous postcard on the table in front of you. Quote: *Re Sir George Fleet: what was the pink flash on the roof?* Go on, Masters: say it's a pink rat and I ought to be makin' faces at it."

"But there's not a word about a pink flash in any of this evidence!"

"No," returned H.M., "and there's not one word about a skeleton-clock either. But you'll find one standing just behind you."

Masters strode over to the middle of the room, where he jingled coins in his pocket.

"This chap Puckston," mused H.M. "I didn't realize he was still the licensee here. By that statement, he didn't seem to like Fleet much."

"There's nothing to that," Masters snorted. "It was only . . ."

Whether by coincidence, or at mention of the name, there was a discreet tap at the door to the bar. The door opened, to reveal the Puckston family: father, mother, and daughter.

To a befuddled Martin Drake, Arthur Puckston had been little more than a name and a voice. He was, in fact, a lean man with a freckled bald head, a harassed but conscientious smile; tall but stooped, with stringy powerful arms. Mrs. Norma Puckston, though stoutened and rosy, had fine black hair and was not unattractive. Miss Puckston, dark-haired and sixteen years old, was not unattractive either.

"I 'ate to disturb you, gentlemen," said Mr. Puckston, making an apologetic motion. "But it's five minutes to opening-time, and . . . well, do you really want this parlour for a private room?"

"We sure do, son," H.M. assured him. "If that's convenient?"

"Oh, it's *convenient*. But I shall 'ave to charge you a good bit extra. This being Saturday night, and other things. Even for the police . . ."

Three pairs of eyes surreptitiously watched Masters.

"Well, well!" said Masters, suddenly urbane and in his most cheerful manner. "How would you have learned I was a police-officer, now?"

"Things," said Mr. Puckston thoughtfully, "get about." He glanced up. *"You* ought to know that."

H.M. intervened.

"He's a copper, son. But he won't bother you. I'll see to that. Anything else?"

"Well, sir. If you wouldn't mind keeping the doors locked and the curtains drawn? It's that clock. You told me you were going to take the skeleton out . . ." Puckston's voice trailed away; his throat seemed to be constricted.

"Yes, I see your point," nodded H.M., taking several puffs of his (to others) venomous cigar. "You think it might put the customers off their beer if they saw me sittin' here with a skeleton on my lap like a ventriloquist's dummy?"

Miss Enid Puckston suddenly giggled, and was shushed by a look from her mother. The father, for some reason, took the girl's face between his hands.

"I'll be careful," H.M. promised. Behind smoke and spectacles, his eyes had taken on a faraway look. "I don't want to be chucked out of here. I'm always being chucked out of places, though burn me if I can think why. This is a fine old house, this is. Antiques, and real antiques."

"Oh, yes!" cried Mrs. Puckston in one gush. "Arthur always tries to—"

The doors of the Dragon's Rest, unlike those of most pubs, were solid and close-fitting. Little could be heard through them unless you bent close. But now, from beyond the closed door to the far bar-parlour, arose a sudden babble of angry voices, all clamouring together. One voice, a man's, clove through the tumult.

"I can't do it, I tell you! What's more, I won't!"

H.M. abruptly snatched the cigar out of his mouth.

"That sounded like young Drake." His own big voice boomed out. "Does anybody know who's there with him?"

It was the dark-haired and well-spoken Enid who answered.

"Lady Jennifer, sir. And Mr. Richard Fleet. And a lady from Fleet House; I don't know her. And Dr. Laurier."

"So!" grunted H.M., and surged to his feet. "That's a combination I don't like." And, with his white linen suit rucked up and the gold watch-chain swinging across his corporation, he lumbered towards the door and opened it.

The heat of strained feelings was as palpable in the other room as its atmosphere of beer and old stone. But, except for Martin Drake, it was now empty. Martin stood by the stove, his dark eyebrows drawn together and the green eyes enraged. H.M., after giving him a dismal look, lumbered over to peer out of the open door into the road.

Some distance to the left along the Dragon's Rest, Jenny was detaching a bicycle from the ivy and steadfastly refusing to look round. A light-haired young man in a sports-coat had just opened the central gate in the wall round Fleet House. Sauntering, her head high, a girl in a grey silk frock walked in the same direction. Though there was no visible sign of Dr. Laurier, you could hear a car-motor start up close at hand.

It had been a swift, decisive exodus. The emotional echoes still swung like bells inside your head. H.M., the corners of his mouth turned down, turned and surveyed Martin.

"You been havin' a good time?" he demanded.

"Listen, sir," Martin began. He paused for a few seconds, and tried again more calmly. "Yesterday, before Jenny and I left Willaby's, we told you pretty well everything."

"You did, son. Well?"

"But you didn't hear about the execution shed. You didn't hear—" Again Martin stopped. "*Women!*" he added, with one savage and sweeping gesture.

Then, shouting something, he also plunged out through the open door.

Chapter 7

Martin had slowed his run to a walk before he reached the central gate of Fleet House.

Well to the north and well to the south in the low stone wall, there was a wide iron gate through which a gravelled carriage-drive curved up to the front terrace and returned to the road again like the arc of a bow. In the middle of the wall there was a smaller central gate; from it a narrower path, between lines of trees, ran straight up to the terrace like an arrow to the bow.

Martin, his footsteps rasping on gravel, overtook Ruth Callice just as she reached the terrace. Ricky had already hurried inside to see his mother. This terrace was only a broad stretch of flagstones, with four shallow flagstoned steps leading up to it. Ruth hesitated at the top, and turned round at his call.

"Ruth!"

"Yes?"

He stood at the foot of the steps, looking up at her. Her softly rounded face had that clear-flesh tint he associated with youth and health. The dark-brown eyes were inquiring.

"Martin," she smiled, "you needn't apologize." Her expression grew whimsical. "I've been yelled at so often in my business career, especially by men, that I hardly notice it."

"I haven't come to apologize, Ruth. For the first time since I've known you, I think you ought to be put over a convenient knee and walloped."

Ruth's colour receded to pallor, and slowly returned.

"I won't quarrel with you, Martin."

"As a second point of fact, I didn't yell at you."

"You were fairly audible, dear. And please remember *only* what I said. I merely reminded you of your promise. Whereupon you and Jenny and Dr. Laurier began arguing as to whether or not it was a good thing to go ghost-hunting. All I said in the whole discussion was: would you come and see John Stannard before you decided. Then you yelled at me."

"That's why I'm here. To see Stannard."

He ran up the four steps and faced her. Round and above him stretched that white, and still cold, face of Fleet House. Four smallish Corinthian pillars were set flush into the facade, two on each side of the broad front door. Except for a small close-in balcony on each of the windows above, these were the only ornamentation. Eight windows on the ground floor, eight windows on the floor above, eight smaller windows on a smaller floor above.

Very high ceilings in the rooms, too. High, breathing cold like a prison! This Martin noted somewhere at the back of his mind as he ran up the steps.

"Jenny . . ." he began.

Ruth laughed. "Jenny thinks I've been your mistress for years and years. Isn't it exquisitely silly?"

"Not if she thinks so. Look here: if you knew who 'Jenny' was for all this time, why didn't you tell me?"

"Perhaps I had my reasons." A pause. "Perhaps I still have them." Another pause. "Perhaps I'll tell you tonight."

"Oh, no, you won't I—"

"Aren't you forgetting something?" Ruth asked sharply.

"Forgetting what?"

"That *I* was the one who arranged for us to stay here? That *I* was the one who deliberately arranged to throw you and Jenny together?"

This, it occurred to him, was true. It checked him in mid-flight, while Ruth smiled.

"Oh, Martin!" Her tone softened. "We've been such good —" the trailing of the voice implied 'friends.' She put out her hand, and he took it. "Now let's go in and see John Stannard!"

"Where is he?"

Ruth nodded towards the second two of the four windows to the left of the front door.

"In the library. Cicely, I'm sorry to say, hasn't been very well. You may not meet her yet."

"Tell me, Ruth. Do you know anything about what happened here nearly twenty years ago?"

"Yes. Almost everything."

With a common impulse they glanced over their shoulders. In the middle of the gravel path, down towards the gate, stood Sir Henry Merrivale. But he did not see them. H.M.'s fists were on his hips, his big bald head raised; and he was glaring with malignancy at something which appeared to be just over their heads.

Martin, looking up, could see nothing except the white-painted iron frame, crossing near the tops of the Corinthian columns, and folding flat a large old-fashioned awning, coloured orange. It could be let down to shade a long space before the front door. Then Ruth hurried him into the cool, not to say chilly, front hall. But her hand suddenly fell on his arm, warning him to say nothing as they saw what was ahead.

Fleet House had been built in the very early nineteenth century, in that pseudo-Greek classicism which began with the French Revolution and was continued by Bonaparte. The wide, dim hall had at its far end an arched window. A staircase had been built against that wall, sideways as Martin and Ruth faced it.

A little way up the stairs, outlined against the tall arched window, stood Aunt Cicely. Just below her was Ricky, asking questions. They were oblivious to any newcomers.

"Really, Ricky. It is nothing at all. I only wish to lie down."

The voice floated, with whispering-gallery effect, through the cool dim hall.

"But they said—"

" 'They said.' They always say." Seen closer at hand, in Aunt Cicely's faded prettiness there was some quality which was eerily familiar to Martin. Was it a faint resemblance to Jenny? Jenny thirty years older? "But there is something," she continued, "that you have got to learn. Very soon, I'm afraid. I have telephoned to Lady Brayle. Now don't detain me, please."

In her filmy Edwardian-looking dress, against the pallor of the arched window, she hurried upstairs. Ricky hesitated, irresolute, and then followed her. Ruth Callice almost impelled Martin to the left.

They went through a high, square, green-painted room, on

whose walls hung a collection of ancient fire-arms ranging from the match-lock to the Brown Bess. They emerged into a well-appointed library, of the same size and shape, with gilt cornice mouldings.

"Ah, my dear fellow!" said a familiar husky, powerful voice.

Stannard, in somewhat ungainly plus-fours, stood with his back to a white marble mantelpiece. On a round Regency table in front of him lay a large crackling document, once folded into many squares, now pressed open.

"Our hunt for man-eating tigers, in the psychical sense," he went on, "is almost ready. I have here—" he tapped the document with a pencil—"a plan of Pentecost Prison. I've investigated it this afternoon. Come here, my dear fellow! Let me show you the condemned cell and the execution shed."

Martin braced himself. "Mr. Stannard, I can't go with you."

"Can't go with me?"

"No."

For some seconds Stannard did not reply. Lowering his dark head, he put the pencil with great care in the middle of the plan. Martin sensed the hidden quirk at the corner of his mouth. Vividly he remembered Stannard at Ruth's flat on Thursday night: the chuckle, the too-fixed smile, the glitter of the black eyes, Stannard's too-frequent glances at Ruth. 'Will you forgive me, Mr. Stannard, for saying that you are a little pompous?' Martin remembered that too.

Then Stannard straightened up. "To tell you the truth, young man, I am not altogether surprised."

"Look here! Will you just let me explain?"

"Of course." Stannard inclined his head courteously.

"On Thursday night I didn't know something I know now. There was a certain girl—" here he saw Stannard's eyes narrow—"I'd lost for three years. On Friday I found her. There's what you might call family opposition, and everything is upset. I promised to take her driving tonight."

And now Martin recognized the other's posture. In imagination he saw Stannard, in wig and gown, standing behind a desk on counsel's bench: his head a little inclined to one side, listening in cross-examination with that air of polite incredulity and amusement which is all the more effective because it keeps a perfectly straight face.

"Indeed," Stannard observed. "You promised to take her driving." The inflection he put into the words was masterly.

"Yes!"

"When was this appointment made?"

"This afternoon."

"I see. You consider it sufficient excuse for breaking a previous engagement which has entailed some time and trouble, and which you suggested yourself?"

Fleet House, the chilly and wicked Grecian house which to Martin was beginning to seem like a prison, might have laughed.

"The circumstances are unusual," retorted Martin. He was conscious, under the black glitter of the eyes, how flat these words would have sounded in court. "I hoped you would release me."

Stannard slowly shook his head. He sent a surreptitious glance towards Ruth, who was sitting on a sofa turning over the pages of an illustrated paper as if she had heard nothing.

"I can't force you," smiled Stannard. "But 'release' you: no, I will not. The fact is, young man, you've lost your nerve."

"That doesn't happen to be true."

"Truth has many guises," said Stannard, dryly scoring a point while appearing to concede one. "It's unfortunate, too. I had devised a special test for your nerve."

"Nerve?"

"And for mine too, of course. Now it will apply only to me. Still," he chuckled, "I hope to survive."

"What's the test?"

"Does it matter? Since you are not interested . . ."

Martin took a step forward. *What's the test?*

Stannard's movements were deliberate. From a tapestry wing-chair beside the mantelpiece he took up a thick blue-bound book with faded gilt lettering on the back.

"I have been looking through Atcheson's *History of the Penal System*," he continued. The round face, roughened as though by a nutmeg-grater, looked pleased. "This was written in 1912, and there's a chapter on Pentecost. I hadn't realized what a fine lot of man-eating tigers were executed there. Old Mrs. Gill, for instance. And Bourke-Smith. And Hessler, who mutilated the bodies of women; Hessler actually tried to escape from the condemned cell.

"About ghosts," Stannard went on, "let me repeat my dictum. I don't say yes; I don't say no. What I can credit are the influences, released emotions. Haven't we all had the same experience, in a small way? We go into a house, usually an empty house. And for no reason at all someone says, 'I can't stand this place; let's get out.' "

Martin was about to say, "Like this." He also noticed Ruth looking furtively around, and wondered if it touched her too. Yet the library was a well-lighted room, two windows east and two south, though green-shaded by the trees.

"The vibrations in that death-house," added Stannard, "must be like lying under a tolling bell."

"Never mind the vibrations. What's this test?"

"Ah!" murmured Stannard. He threw the book back into the chair and took up the pencil. "Observe this architect's plan of the prison!"

"Well? What about it?"

"You notice that the wings are like spokes in a wheel, with the outer wall as its rim. These shaded spaces between the spokes—" the yellow pencil moved briefly—"are exercise grounds, gardens, and so on: open to the sky. Our concern is Wing B—" again the pencil moved—"which is here. Wing B, on the ground floor, contained mainly offices for clerical work. But at the far end of it, *here*, is a self-contained unit. Behind an iron door it housed the condemned cell and the execution shed."

Ruth Callice had abandoned the paper and joined them by the table, where Stannard leaned on the crackling plan.

Ruth, Martin was thinking, couldn't have been brushed by any emanation from Fleet House. She had been here too many times before; she was a friend of Aunt Cicely; she would have remarked on it. Yes; but had Ruth ever said anything at all about Fleet House?

Stannard's yellow pencil was moving again.

"Pentecost, please remember, was not abandoned until 1938. It had the most up-to-date of neck-cracking methods."

"Stan," Ruth began in an uncertain voice, "do you think it's necessary to dwell so . . ."

But Stannard was looking at Martin.

"There was none of that hideous walk across a yard, into a shed, and up thirteen steps. The condemned cell at Pentecost is *here*. Opposite it, directly opposite across a passage eight feet wide, is the execution shed. The condemned man never knows it is there. He can be trussed up, marched across the passage, placed on a drop worked by a lever—"

Here Stannard made a chopping motion with his hand.

"—and plunge on a rope into a brick-lined pit. All in a merciful matter of seconds.

"My point," he added, after a slight pause, "is that these two rooms and the passage form a separate unit, a kind of self-contained flat, shut off by the iron door of the passage. Here is the key to that passage."

And he held it up. It was a large key, though it fitted easily into the pocket of his brown tweed plus-four suit.

"All the inside doors of the prison, of course, were unlocked at the time the government took it over for the infernal 'storage purposes.'" Stannard's face mocked them behind the big key. "However, I got this one. Shall I tell you how my test *would* have worked if you (most unfortunately!) had not decided to go driving?"

Martin, himself white as a ghost with wrath, merely nodded.

"The vigil," mused Stannard, *"would* have begun at midnight, outside the iron door to the self-contained flat."

Another nod.

"You and I," pursued Stannard, "would then have drawn lots. Whoever lost would have gone to the execution shed and closed the door behind him. The other would have locked the iron door, so that the loser would be shut into the flat.

"The winner," Stannard's mouth quirked, "would sit down outside the iron door, and wait. The locked-up man, of course, could move from the execution shed across to the condemned cell. But I cannot think that any swirling and pressing influences would hammer his brain less hard in the condemned cell than in the execution shed. He would be a rat in a spiritual trap. If he cried out for help, the man outside must unlock the iron door and let him out.

"The man outside, it is true, even the so-called winner, would have no easy time. If any spiritual evil raged there, he would be very close to it. You and I—one inside, one out—would remain there alone from twelve o'clock to four o'clock in the morning, when it begins to grow daylight. 'Spend the night' was I think the term you used?"

"Something like that, yes."

Stannard threw the key up and caught it.

"There it was," he concluded, with a husky sigh of regret. "What a pity you can't accept."

"Pardon me," Martin told him. "After you said you insisted on holding to it, I never said I wouldn't accept."

Stannard caught the key with a flat smack against his palm, and looked up.

"Meaning what?"

"That I do accept, with great pleasure."

There was a silence. If a short time before Fleet House might have laughed, now it seemed to be listening. Ruth, her white teeth fastened in her under-lip, hesitated.

"You mean that?" Stannard demanded.

"Naturally I mean it." Martin reflected. "We do all this, of course, in the dark?"

Stannard was slightly taken aback.

"No," he answered, after a slight hesitation. "Even in the best ghost-hunting tradition, that's not necessary. I have brought several portable electric lamps, with plenty of spare batteries. Each of us may have a lamp. If only," he added, "to read and pass the time."

"You know, Martin," Ruth said dreamily, "this means you won't see Jenny tonight."

Jenny! How to explain that he couldn't back out, literally and physically couldn't, if Stannard insisted? You touched a switch, you touched an emotion; you set forces moving, and you must go with them. Jenny would understand it. Surely Jenny would understand it! He could telephone her, and then go out to Brayle Manor.

"All the same," Ruth was saying in a troubled voice, "I almost wish I hadn't encouraged this. Or—arranged it."

"Arranged it?" said Stannard, and looked at her with genuine astonishment. "My dear girl, Mr. Drake suggested it. *I* arranged it." The blood came into his already reddish face. "I wanted to show you, my dear, that these young men, with their war-records and their infantile prancings, are not the only ones to be depended on."

Abruptly he pulled himself together, as though he had said too much.

"But—Stan." There was an affectionate note in Ruth's voice. "You didn't tell me these 'conditions.'"

"A little surprise."

"You see," Ruth braced herself, "*I'm* going to the prison. And other people are wild to go too. Ricky Fleet and even Dr. Laurier. When they were having that argument at the Dragon's Rest, Dr. Laurier said he'd consider himself insulted if he didn't get an invitation."

Stannard lifted his thick shoulders.

"I see no reason why a dozen shouldn't go," he said. "*If* they all consent to leave the prison at midnight when the test begins. You agree, my dear fellow?"

"I do."

"This affair is between the two of us?"

"By God, it is!" said Martin. "And, as Ruth says, you imposed the conditions. Now *I* impose one."

"Ah!" murmured Stannard, casting up his eyes in sardonic melancholy. "I fear, I very much fear, someone may be backing down again. However, what is the condition?"

"That both of you tell me," Martin replied unexpectedly, "what you know about the death of Sir George Fleet some twenty years ago."

Again there was a silence. Ruth, her dark-brown eyes wide with wonder, merely seemed puzzled. Stannard, his eyes quizzical, seemed to hold behind locked teeth some chuckle which shook his stocky body. It was at this point that Ricky Fleet, his hair troubled by ruffling fingers, came into the library.

"I second that motion," Ricky declared. He went to stand by Martin.

"Ricky, darling!" cried Ruth. He kissed her perfunctorily on the cheek, and pressed her shoulder. All this time his eyes were fixed in a puzzled, troubled way on Stannard.

"But you haven't met Mr. Stannard!" Ruth added, and performed introductions. "How is your mother?"

"Pretty well, thanks. She's taken a sedative. But it hasn't had much effect, and she'll probably be down to dinner. You know—" Ricky tugged his necktie still further in the direction of his ear—"a lot of talk about my governor's death always upsets her. But she never minds a reference or a comment, and we cured her long ago of any dislike about going up to the roof."

Still he was looking in that same puzzled way at Stannard.

"On my word of honour, Mr. Fleet," the other assured him gravely, "*I* made no more than a casual reference. Ruth will verify that."

"Then it must have been something else. She was all right at breakfast; though, come to think of it, she did look a bit disturbed and disappointed at breakfast. But nothing *wrong*. She keeps talking about . . .'."

"Mr. Richard!" called a weary female voice from the doorway.

Martin recognized the voice, very quickly, as that of the maid who had answered him on the telephone, and who had evidently met more than one American G.I. She was a brown-haired girl in her twenties, combining an air of boredom with conscientiousness. Though she wore cap and apron, she lounged in the doorway with her weight on one hip.

"Yes, Phyllis?"

"Your mother," said Phyllis, "don't like trespassers. There's been a trespasser out on the lawn for one hell of a long time."

"Please don't bother me, Phyllis!"

"This trespasser," continued Phyllis, jerking her thumb over her shoulder in a way which may be seen on the films, "is a fat old guy with a big stomach and a bald head. I think he's nuts, because he gave the gardener some money. Now he's arguing with the gardener about how high you can grow tomato plants and still get the best tomatoes."

"That's H.M.," said Martin. "Sir Henry Merrivale."

Stannard dropped the big key on the plan beside his discarded pencil. "Merrivale!" he exclaimed.

"Does that mean anything?" asked Ruth. "I think I heard the name from Jenny, but—"

"My dear Ruth." Stannard paused. "If I had that man against me in a criminal case, I'd think I had a walkover from the beginning and then suddenly discover I hadn't a leg to stand on. He's the craftiest old devil on earth. If he's here now, it means . . ."

Martin hurried to the nearer of the east windows and peered out sideways. He saw the crafty old devil almost at once. On the smooth lawn stood a tall stepladder, with a pair of pruning-shears near it. Beside it stood H.M. and a dour-faced man in overalls. H.M., glaring, was holding his hand in the air to indicate a tomato-plant of improbable height. The dour-faced man shook his head with a fishy smile. H.M. levelled a finger at him in question. The dour-faced man still smiled fishily. Whereupon H.M. climbed nearly to the top of the stepladder, turned round, and indicated a tomato-plant of such height that it could have been credited only by a believer in Jack and the beanstalk.

But Martin saw something else. Towards their left was the gravel path, tree-shaded, leading to the front door. Up this path marched the Dowager Countess of Brayle.

Martin swung round and addressed Ricky. "Do you by any chance want peace and quiet in the house?"

"God knows I do," answered the harassed Ricky, who was still glancing at Stannard to remember where he had seen the man before. "It's all I do want. Why?"

"Lady Brayle," Martin told him, "is coming up the path. Sir Henry is on the lawn."

"What about it?"

"Those two," said Martin, "act on each other like a lighted match in a box full of fireworks. Go out and grab 'em! Go out and bring 'em in here, where we can keep an eye on both! Quick! Hurry!"

Chapter 8

At one side of the broad leather-topped desk in the library stood H.M. At the other stood Lady Brayle.

Ricky's good-natured charm had worked, aided by the fact that he seized each by one arm. So they stood there, with their backs to the high glimmering-coloured books in the tall shelves, facing the group by the white marble mantelpiece across the room.

Grandmother Brayle had been at her haughtiest—"I *think* I have met Captain Drake—" during the few sketchy introductions. Today she wore heavy horsy tweeds, her grey-white hair without a hat. Without a flicker towards H.M., she looked steadily across and up at her own reflection in a mirror over the fireplace, and (incidentally) over the other group's heads as she faced them. It was H.M. who broke the thick silence.

" 'Lo, Sophie," he volunteered with surprising meekness.

"Good evening, Henry."

"Nice weather we're havin', ain't it?"

"That," murmured Lady Brayle, "is not altogether unexpected in July."

The length of the broad desk, with its inkpot and blue quill pen, separated them as though a leprous touch might be infected.

"Y'know, Sophie, we've been on speaking-terms for a good many years."

"Are you trying to appeal to my sentimentality, Henry? How amusing!"

"I say, though. Do you remember the night I took you to see Lewis Waller play *Beaucaire* at the old Imperial Theatre?"

"Please don't be ridiculous. Besides," Lady Brayle added suddenly, "your behaviour in that hansom was so utterly disgusting that . . ."

H.M. was stung. "Burn it, Sophie, I only put my hand—"

"It will not be necessary to go into details."

"But you didn't tell your old man so he'd come whistlin' after me with a horse-whip, which you said you were goin' to. What I mean: you were an A-1 sport in those days. Now you've turned into—" H.M. swung round. "Sophie, will you believe me if I tell you that honest-to-God I'm trying to help you? And your family?"

Lady Brayle hiccoughed with mirth. "When, yesterday, you . . ."

"But I didn't know I was buying the clock, did I?"

"You must excuse me," the other said crisply. "I was summoned here by an urgent 'phone-call from Cicely Fleet. I do not know why. I—"

"Do you want the clock back?"

What effect this conversation was having on Ruth, Stannard, and Ricky, who were gathered with him beside the round table with the map, Martin could not tell. Ricky, he quite accurately guessed, had been told nothing about any attempt to buy a clock; and the water grew deeper. But Stannard, as a detached and sardonic observer of human life, sat down in the tapestry chair and, with pleasure, placed his fingertips together.

"Your behaviour yesterday," announced Lady Brayle, "was so despicable! So puerile! So childish—"

"Sure. Do you want the clock back?"

"Really, Henry." Lady Brayle seemed bewildered. "*I* have no interest whatever in the clock, except that I was asked to bid for it as a present for young Dr. Laurier." Her mouth tightened amid wrinkles. "And I should never allow Cicely to pay any such ridiculous price as . . ."

"Oh, Sophie! I'm not selling anything. It's yours if you answer me a few questions."

The other stared at him. "Questions? What questions?"

"Well," he said argumentatively, "when was the date you got that Willaby catalogue of the auction on Friday?"

"Really, Henry, I don't see—"

"I know you don't. That's because I'm the old man. Date?"

"Everybody knows," retorted Jenny's grandmother, "that Willaby's post their catalogues from London just a week before the sale. I must have received mine," she computed, "on July 5th."

"That's what I thought. But I had to be sure. Who else in this district subscribes to a Willaby catalogue?"

"Cicely, of course. And I think young Dr. Laurier. He is interested in arms and armour."

"What about Arthur Puckston, over at the Dragon's Rest?"

The wrinkles round Lady Brayle's mouth deepened, as though she were about to say she had no interest whatever in the Dragon's Rest. But human curiosity, it appeared, would not be stifled.

"Incongruous as it seems," she conceded, "Puckston does.

He is . . . one of our fine old yeomen. He is not well off, as few
of us are; but he wants genuine antiques for his inn."

"Uh-huh. It was a possibility. Y'see . . ."

Aunt Cicely herself, in what seemed to Martin some
informal pinkish robe with lace over it, interrupted them then.
Her entrance was flurried and apologetic, but with such real
charm that it seemed to lighten the chill of Fleet House.
Though she had perhaps a trick of archness and rapid speech,
not quite in keeping with her faded beauty, the personality
triumphed.

Ricky sprang forward.

"Mother, I want to present—"

"Of course. How delightful of you all to come!" smiled Aunt
Cicely, sweeping aside introductions, new ones or forgotten
ones, by giving each of them a look of such pleasure that they
all felt warmed.

"You must forgive me," she raced on, "for popping in here,
like a cuckoo out of a clock, and not even dressed. But I *do* so
want to have a word with Sophia, and she didn't come
upstairs."

Lady Brayle seemed anxious to forget what she and H.M.
had been talking about.

"We were merely discussing," said Jenny's grandmother,
plucking a subject out of the air, "Dr. Laurier's interest in arms
and armour. Come to think of it, yesterday in the arms-room I
saw a shield and a fine old English blade which I thought of
commissioning someone to buy as a present."

Sudden horror showed in Aunt Cicely's eyes, an expression
which startled Martin Drake until he imagined it was one of
her exaggerations.

"But you must never . . . !" she cried. And then: "Oh, dear,
what am I saying? Dr. Laurier is *so* conservative that it really
doesn't matter. Do come and talk to me."

They went. Yet not without a parting shot from the
Dowager Countess as she turned at the door.

"Captain Drake," she said.

(Martin thought: shall I let them have it now, both of them?
About Jenny and me? Ricky probably wouldn't mind. But the
old dragon undoubtedly knows or guesses already; whereas
Aunt Cicely would sob and call for sal volatile. Better hold
your fire until you can blast the old dragon).

"Yes?" he said.

"Without doubt," said Jenny's grandmother, "you were
thinking of telephoning to the Manor?"

"I was thinking of doing just that."

"When you ring," said Lady Brayle imperturbably, "you will be told that Jennifer is not at home. This, of course, you will disbelieve. Yet it happens to be true. I tell you so to save you trouble."

Fear, irrepressible however you tried, began to crawl through Martin.

"I pass no comment," said Lady Brayle, "on what does not concern me. Still! When Jennifer left the inn, I believe you were rushing in a somewhat frenzied manner across the road. You were calling the name of a young lady whom—ah—I think I have met in the past as well as today."

The old dragon's eyes seemed deliberately to seek Ruth without finding her. Martin, with a sick sensation, felt the props kicked out from under him.

"Jennifer, no doubt for some good reason, wished to visit some friends in London. Their address would not interest you. She left for the train in one taxi, while I came here in another."

Now, as Lady Brayle looked very hard at his own imperturbability, there was a grudging respect in her tone.

"Captain Drake, I have little respect for law. I would cheerfully steal and if necessary I would kill. But I am not a liar. Good-day."

Her flat-heeled footsteps, and Aunt Cicely's light ones, faded away. Stannard still sat motionless, watching the scene with less than amusement behind the pyramid of his finger-tips. Ruth kept one hand pressed to her breast, watching Martin. It was Ricky who spoke.

"You understand now what I meant, old boy?"

"Yes. I've understood that all along."

"What are you going to do?"

"Get that address in London, somehow."

"Phooey!" exploded Sir Henry Merrivale.

It was such a bellow that they all were touched by it except Stannard. Ever since that remark about Martin rushing across the road after Ruth, Stannard had been faintly smiling. Sir Henry Merrivale was standing behind the desk, surveying the quill pen with its blue feather. Ricky went over to him.

"Look, sir." He spoke with directness. "There's a lot more going on here than most of us can understand. Can you help?"

"Well, son, that's just what I was goin' to tell you." H.M. raised his head and spoke with the same directness. "Across the road," he indicated, "there's a snake named Masters. Chief Inspector Masters."

"Yes. I heard my gov—my father's death was being

investigated again. It's my mother I'm . . ."

H.M. shook his head.

"Masters won't bother your mother, son. He thinks it's all eyewash. I'm the one who believes there was hokey-pokey."

"It's a funny thing." Ricky had the same desperately undecided look. "Today I was giving Jenny and Martin here my personal reminiscences of what happened on the day of—well, the day it happened."

H.M.'s interests quickened. "So? You remember it?"

"Very plainly; but by fits and starts. Anyway, in telling them, I had just got to the point where Miss Upton and I came round the side of the house and saw him lying there with the tapestry-piece over his head. Then, as I told them, we started back. And I looked up at a window, the upstairs window on the first floor just to the right of the front door."

"You'd just got to there," interposed Martin. "What did you see?"

"The face," answered Ricky, "of somebody I'd never met. The face of a total stranger. Looking down like God. Even this afternoon I might have imagined I'd invented it, if I couldn't half-swear I've met the same man in this room."

Ricky swung round.

"Excuse me, Mr Stannard," he added, "but I think it was you."

Stannard's black eyes twinkled above the pyramided fingertips. He smiled, and Ruth smiled as one who shared the secret.

"Don't apologize, Mr. Fleet," the barrister urged him. "What you say is quite true. You *did* see me."

H.M. regarded him curiously. "So!" he muttered. "Then why is it there's nothin' about you in the record?"

"Because there is no reason why there should be."

"How d'ye mean?"

"I came down here, for one day, on a matter of business."

"Specifically?"

"Sir George wished to begin certain legal proceedings. He went to a solicitor in London, who hesitated and took counsel's opinion: meaning myself. I told the solicitor his client had no case. Would that do for Sir George? Oh, no. I must come down here and explain why. Being the rawest of young juniors then," Stannard spread out his hands whimsically, "I bowed."

"Uh-huh. What happened then?"

Stannard's eyes narrowed. His voice appeared to come from deep in his soft collar, where his chin was pressed. He glanced up at Ricky.

"If memory serves," he remarked, "that window you speak of is, or was, the window of your father's study."

"It's still a study, in a way," said Ricky. Ricky's eyes were fixed on Stannard with hard, cold, uncompromising, hostility. "The governor's trophies are still there, and one or two of mine. And the guns."

"Go on," H.M.'s very soft tone prodded Stannard, and the latter's shoulders lifted.

"Sir George raved," he went on, and now Ricky was pale with anger. "I talked. Some one came in to tell him about the hunt. He asked me if I were interested in hunting. I replied, I fear with truth, that nothing on earth interested me less. He took up a pair of field-glasses and excused himself to go up on the roof for a few minutes. Shortly afterwards I heard a shout and an unpleasant sound on flagstones. I went to the window."

The old, friendly, engaging expression kindled Stannard's face.

"Don't think me callous or unfeeling, I beg. I was shocked, of course. What struck me," his mouth twisted, "was the utter pointlessness of this tragedy. I stood there for perhaps five minutes. The dead man's pipe was still spilled on the desk-blotter. There were his guns behind folding glass cases. Then round the house came the large woman and the boy: that I remember as a symbol. The large woman and the grubby boy looking on horrified, looking on stupefied, as though they had seen the end of the world. Whereas they had seen the end only of (forgive me) an overbearing man who would be little missed."

Ricky started to speak, but H.M. shushed him fiercely.

"I gave my name and address to the local policeman," Stannard added. "But I was not needed. I took the train from Newbury: giving (I recall) a very callow statement to a newspaper reporter at the train. I have no connection with the Fleets, and never met any of them from that day to this."

"And that's all?"

"That's all," smiled Stannard, and Ruth joined the smile.

"Stung!" said H.M.

From the desk he picked up the pen with the long blue feather, and seemed to meditate aiming and firing it at one of the brass andirons opposite.

"Whole great big beautiful bloomin' possibility," he said, "and yet—" H.M. threw down the pen. He adjusted his spectacles, peering at Ricky over them. "I say, son. That roof. It's our last hope. Is there any possibility of seeing it?"

"Certainly. We use it more nowadays, for parties, than we

ever did. Like to come along, Martin?"

"Not for a minute," replied a bedevilled man whose thoughts churned round and round Jenny. "If you don't mind: in spite of what the old poisoner said—"

"*Poisoner?*"

"Lady Brayle. I was speaking figuratively. In spite of what she said, I'd like to use your telephone."

"At your service, old boy. Beside the stairs in the hall."

That was how, a few minutes later, Sir Henry Merrivale and Richard Fleet climbed several flights of dark steep stairs, and emerged under a metal hood with a door opening on the northwest corner of the roof.

Clear evening light, with a softness of air which could be felt like a touch, lay over the concrete surface. The roof, a hundred feet square and perhaps forty-five feet from the ground, had its floor painted light brown. At equal intervals, from north to south across the middle, stood the low white oblongs of the chimney stacks.

Just-before-the-war porch-furniture, of dulled chromium tubing and orange canvas seats, stood scattered about the roof. There were tables with orange tops, like the colour of the awning down over the front door. Two beach-umbrellas lay on the floor, ready to be put up. All these H.M. surveyed with displeasure.

A faint breeze moved here. Some distance over across the road you could see the three higher gables of the Dragon's Rest; and, on slightly rising ground behind them, the vast expanse of Guideman's Field and the wood called Black Hanger. To the north, much farther away, you could distantly study the round grey bulk of Pentecost Prison: its tiny windows unwinking, its air repellent even from here.

H.M., fists on hips, turned round.

"Oi! Son!"

"Yes, sir?" Ricky, the muscles tight down his lean jaws, kicked moodily at the floor.

"Don't let Jack Stannard get your goat." H.M. hesitated. His face seemed to swell and grow cross-eyed with embarrassment. "Looky here. Did you like your old man very much?"

"It wasn't that." Ricky shrugged it away. "The governor's very dim in my mind. He had his faults; he could wallop you like blazes. But—"

"But?"

"Well, he never minded how filthy dirty you got, or if you were in a fight. If you wanted something to do with games, he'd buy it for you before the words were out of your mouth."

Ricky dismissed this. "No; I was thinking about Mother. That swine of a lawyer must have said something . . . no, he couldn't have! Ruth swore he didn't upset her, and Ruth's as honest as the Bank of England. Never mind. What did you want to know?"

"I want to know," roared H.M., "the colour of the beach-chairs."

At this particular point the roof-door in the corner opened. Chief Inspector Masters, wearing a bowler hat and carrying the brief-case, overheard the last words as he stepped out on the roof.

"Goddelmighty," said Masters, very softly and wearily.

"By the way," H.M. told Ricky. "This weasel is the Chief Inspector I was telling you about. Don't pay any attention to him."

Ricky, though considerably more impressed by Scotland Yard than he could ever have been impressed by H.M., nevertheless turned back.

"You mean—the beach-chairs *then?*"

"Yes! Not this chromium stuff now. Do you remember?"

"Ho! Do I remember!" snorted Ricky. "The old lot stayed here from the early days practically to the time I was at Cambridge."

"Well? Colours?"

"The beach-chairs were striped green and black. There was a combination of settee and wicker chairs, also striped green and black."

"What about the floor?"

"It was painted dull grey, like the chimneys then."

"Nothing pink?"

"*Pink?* No; not unless it was carried up here like a coat or something."

H.M.'s expression grew murderous. "Looky here, son. I'm not doubtin' your word, but it was a long time ago. Can anybody verify what you say?"

Ricky considered.

"Miss Upton—no, she left two years later and they pensioned her off. MacAndrews, the gardener and handy-man? No: Crawshay! Crawshay was the butler. Nobody has a butler nowadays except Grandmother Brayle. But he still lives at Reading; Mother can give you his address. And he'll tell you it's gospel truth!"

"Very interesting, sir," Masters observed satirically, to the surrounding air. "Are we getting on the track of that pink flash at last?"

H.M. stood for a moment, blinking. Then he turned round and lumbered towards the front of the roof, standing at the very edge. Masters, on the spot, could see the impossibility of anyone attacking Sir George Fleet in that fifty feet square beyond the chimneys of what had been bare concrete.

H.M. faced front, his feet apart and his bald head glistening. Then he turned round. His mouth was open.

"What a cuckoo I've been!" he breathed in a hollow voice. "Oh, my eye! What a thundering dunce!"

Now Masters had heard this tone before. And Masters, even with his mind made up, started a little. Both he and Ricky joined H.M. at the edge.

"Do you mean—?"

"No, no, dammit! I'm not *quite* on to something yet. But there were two pieces in the evidence I was forgetting. Was there anything *white* on the roof?"

Masters and Ricky exchanged glances. "No," the latter said, "unless—"

"Unless, as before," growled Masters, "somebody carried it up?"

"Y'see, I was forgetting that very bright-glowin' and lurid red sky everybody commented on. It might make something white seem pink, if only . . ."

Again H.M. paused.

"Also," he plodded on doggedly, "I had the whole conception and direction maybe a bit scrambled. I'll admit, fully and with a spit, that it's still an impossible crime. But look across at the pub there!"

"Ah, ah. Well?"

"Our witness named Simon Frew, the one with the powerful binoculars, was sittin' astride the centre gable. Just opposite us. Now Arthur Puckston, with the brass telescope: where was *he*?"

Masters pointed to their left.

"Astride the north gable. There!"

"That's right. Therefore he was lookin' sideways. Sideways." H.M. ruminated, like an ogre with a bone. "And there was nobody on the south gable. And . . . y'see, Masters, I didn't like Puckston's testimony one little bit. He didn't like George Fleet either."

Masters gestured impatiently with the brief-case.

"I told you there wasn't much in that! Sir George thought a pub across from his house was undignified and spoiled the view. But he couldn't even get Puckston's license revoked by the magistrates, let alone snaffle the land by some legal . . ."

"Legal, hey?"

"Maybe you've heard the word, sir?"

"Once or twice. That's what Stannard was doin' here on the day it happened, as sure as Moses had a beard." H.M. nodded vaguely. "Finally, you were goin' to tell me something more about George Fleet's field-glasses, only you didn't."

"For the last time," Masters said with powerful restraint, "there was NOTHING wrong with those field-glasses. They fell on the grass and weren't broken. Bert Hartshorn, the constable, took them into the house only a second or two after the gentleman fell. No murderous devices. No—"

"H.M. turned to Ricky. "What about you?"

"I didn't see them," retorted Ricky. "I . . ." He told his story briefly, much as he had told it to Martin and Jenny. "All these years the thing has seemed perfectly simple. Now you've got it so tangled up I don't understand it myself. Field-glasses, for instance."

"Pink flashes," amplified Masters. "Skeletons in clocks. God's truth!"

"I want to know what's wrong with Mother," persisted Ricky. There were lines of strain drawn from his nostrils to the corners of his mouth. The powerful hands and wrists dug into the pockets of his sports-coat. "I'm released from a marriage-obligation, or I'd hoped so; but am I released? Then this expedition to the prison tonight . . ."

"What expedition to the prison?" H.M. asked sharply.

They had all, by instinct, gone to the middle of the roof at its edge. Now, also by instinct, they moved back towards the furniture of darkened chromium and orange canvas.

At the rear of the roof, the staircase-door opened. Martin, somewhat drawn of face but with a gleam in his eyes, walked quickly towards them. Ricky signalled, "What did you find out?" and Martin signalled back, "Tell you later."

"You—" H.M. pointed his finger at Martin—"were shouting some gibberish about an execution shed, now I remember. What's this game tonight? All of it?"

Martin told him.

"I see," commented H.M., keeping an indecipherable poker-face. "Resistin' the powers of darkness and cryin', 'Ho!' All right. You two just nip downstairs, will you. Masters and I have got to have a little *causerie*. Don't argue, burn it! Hustle!"

Presently the staircase-door closed behind Martin and Ricky. It was very quiet on the roof, though a very faint murmur of voices floated from the Dragon's Rest. All about them the countryside, dark-green and somnolent, called a visitor to lounge and drowse from worry. All, that is, except Pentecost Prison.

"Masters," said H.M., "we've got to stop this 'expedition.' "

The Chief Inspector, though uneasy and no longer satirical, remained practical.

"We can't stop it," he pointed out. "If they've got permission from the Ministry, there's nothing anybody can do."

H.M. lifted both fists. "Then we got to . . . stop a bit! What do you know about the inside of this jail?"

"Not much. We got the wire, a year or two ago it was, that Shag Fairlie was hiding out there. Remember when Shag broke Dartmoor? But it wasn't true."

" 'Storage purposes.' What have they got stored in the place?"

"Paper," grunted Masters. "Bales and boxes and tied-up bundles! Stacked as high as your head and higher, through practically every corridor and cell and room! Only a little space so you can move between them and the wall. Oh, ah. I expect," his eye wandered round, "I expect anybody (hurrum!) anybody who was on the stout side wouldn't be able to get in at all."

Then every superior air dropped away from him.

"Fair's fair," snapped Masters, "and messing about is messing about. I ask you—straight, now—is there anything in all this 'pink flash' business?"

"There is. But that's not the main reason why we're here, Masters. We're here to prevent another murder."

Masters straightened up. The breath whistled through his nostrils.

"Another . . . ?"

"That's right."

"But whose murder?"

"Decide for yourself, son. In this whole case, where there are as many women as there are men, who would you say is practically certain to get murdered?"

Chapter 9

There was a bright quarter-moon, that night, in a soft blue-black sky without stars. The darkness caressed, it invited, anyone who sat under the hedgerows or followed the broad winding road. Its warmth would have stirred the blood of lovers, and doubtless did, somewhere under those trees.

The side road which led to Pentecost Prison had once been paved. Now, between the tall grass on each side, it lay cracked and broken and ridged because it had not been repaired for decades. The motor-car, with one wing banging, jolted badly on its surface. But, since the road was straight, the car's headlamps picked up far ahead the high iron double-gates against a rounded face of bricks once painted grey.

A few seconds more the car jolted off the asphalt to a gravel circle now thick-grown with weeds. The handbrake ticked back with a decisive wrench and the clanking engine was shut off, letting in stillness.

First John Stannard jumped out of the car, from the front seat. Then Ricky Fleet from behind the wheel. Then, from the back, Martin Drake, Ruth Callice, and—still to the surprise and very faint discomfort of the others—'young' Dr. Hugh Laurier.

"I am extremely grateful . . ." Dr. Laurier began. But his voice rang out loudly, and he stopped. The clock on the car's dashboard indicated the time as twenty-five minutes to midnight.

Footsteps swished among weeds. Someone laughed nervously.

"Got the lamps?" called Ricky's voice.

"Here," came the husky assurance of Stannard; and he chuckled.

"Shall I leave these car-lights on?" Martin demanded.

"Yes," assented Stannard's voice. "After all, three of you will be leaving in twenty-five minutes."

Seen only by car-lamps, magnified by darkness and a quarter-moon, the grey-brick roundness of Pentecost appeared immense. Its air of intense desolation was heightened, towards the north-west, by the ghost-village which still straggled towards its wall.

When men fretted out their sentences here, when they heated their brains and assured everybody they would be free next week, there grew up round it that huddle of cottages which lie near any country prison. Here lived the married officers, the non-convict staff, their wives and relatives and children: all the residue from that force which made the machine-shop hum, the food-tins bang, the endless line shuffle round and round the exercise yard. These houses, now, were as dead as Pentecost.

"Is everybody ready?" asked Stannard.

All five had gathered round the car-lights. Stannard had told them to wear old clothes: which Ruth interpreted as meaning black slacks and a red sweater, Stannard his ungainly plus-fours, the others sports-coats and flannels.

Ruth laughed softly. So did Dr. Laurier.

"You know," Ruth observed, "I thought this evening would never end. I almost choked over dinner."

"So did I," said Ricky, for some reason deeply impressed by this coincidence of thought. "I'm sorry Mother didn't come down after all."

"I assure you, Richard," declared the precise and conservative Dr. Laurier, "that Lady Fleet is in no danger. I have given her half a grain of morphia. We, on the other hand, have a stimulant."

All five were strung up, each of them not quite his or her normal self, which may account for much that happened afterwards. Each would have denied this. But if anybody had been watching them—and there *was* someone watching—that person would have seen it in a quick movement, a turn and gleam of an eye against the head-lights.

"I should have thought," said Ruth, "that you people who lived in this district must have been terrified. I mean, of escaped prisoners."

Stannard chuckled, his lips folded back from gleaming teeth.

"My dear, you are still confusing local prisons with convict prisons."

"I'm afraid I don't remember the difference."

"Come, now! If a man's sentence is anything from six months to two years, with time off for good behaviour, he won't endanger it by trying to escape. Some of them go mad, of course. But an attempted break is rare." Then Stannard's eyes narrowed. "Stop, though! There *is* an alarm-bell, aside from the ordinary main bell."

"What for?"

"You can see for yourself. Shall we go?"

From a bulging pocket he produced three flattish electric lanterns, of the sort carried on the belt by a policeman. Taking one himself, Stannard handed the second to Martin and the third to Ricky.

As they approached the high iron gates, the bright pale-white beams of the lamps flickered and roved. They touched the spikes atop the brick wall. They swept past the lettering. 'Fiat Justitia, MDCCCXCVI,' carved in stone over the doors. They raked the ground. Except for the ruts of heavy Army lorries trundling paper-bales, no approach marred Pentecost's weedy gravel.

From his other side pocket—"Don't worry; I oiled the lock this afternoon!"Stannard brought out an immense old-fashioned key, rust-coloured but not rusty. To his annoyance he had to use two hands in turning it. Then the lock clicked with a heavy snap like a game-trap.

"Now!" he ordered, a little out of breath. "One of you at each door. Push!"

The big doors moved soundlessly (oiled hinges too?), and fairly easily. The breath of the prison, which at one time might not have been too pleasant, blew out at them. Now it was only a thick warmth overlaid by a mustiness of dried paper-bales. A little way ahead their lights caught a large arched barrier of vertical bars, with an opening in it like an ordinary door.

"Swing the gates shut," called Stannard. "We don't want intruders."

Martin and Ricky, their lamps hooked on their belts, complied. Inside they saw a heavy and complicated pattern of bolts, which they did not touch. The next moment they were shut up inside Pentecost.

Nerves sang a little more thinly, pulse-beats were a trifle faster.

"Just a minute." Ruth's quiet voice rose hollowly.

"It's all right, old girl!" Ricky assured her.

"But Stan told us at dinner," continued Ruth, "that they've stored this place full. If they've filled up the—the condemned cell and the execution shed, what are you going to do?"

"They haven't, my dear." Stannard's chuckle, echoing, sounded huge. "Either they were respectful or they hadn't the stomach. Our little self-contained flat is empty. Now follow me closely, and don't lose my light."

Martin Drake glanced at the luminous dial of his wrist-watch. Eighteen minutes to twelve.

Behind the barrier of vertical iron bars, they saw a mountain of brown-paper bales. Holding his lamp ahead, Stannard slipped sideways through the opening in the barrier, and edged to the left. Ruth, with an appealing glance at Martin, followed Stannard. Martin followed her. Dr. Laurier came next, with Ricky at the end.

Then they made a sharp turn to the right. They were in a narrow aisle—just broad enough for walking in a straight line—between the bales on one side and a grey-brick wall, with doors, on the other.

"You'll get used to the atmosphere," Stannard called from

ahead, where his light bobbed and splashed. His voice went up in reverberations, which seemed to roll back at them through dust-puffs from the bales. "They had a ventilating system. Quite a good one."

And Martin's imagination, heightened and tautened, began to bring this prison to life: with doors opening, bells ringing, the blank-faced men in the grey garb.

Just before the war he had visited Eastaville, a local prison like this one. He had been given only glimpses, which came back as much in sounds as in visual images. The wing they called B Hall: with its high tiers of cells facing each other across an open space, and a steel-woven net slung between to prevent suicides. Each oak cell-door painted yellow. Stung by bells, the unending shuffle, shuffle, shuffle, or march, march, march. A sense of suffocation; and the voice of a blue-uniformed prison officer: "Quiet, there!" A workshop: "Quiet, there!" A line of grey men, stiffly at attention near the door of the Governor's room, to get punishment or make complaint: "Quiet, there!"

"Turn to the right, here!" called Stannard.

Martin, peopling unseen corridors and galleries with old shades out of Eastaville, realized that they had all been shuffling as the aisle narrowed. Ruth coughed in the dust.

Their turn led them through an aisle of bales, then into another one between bales and wall, with another line of doors (*not* cell-doors) to the right.

"Why," Martin asked, "do cell-doors look so repulsive when they're painted yellow?"

"I beg your pardon?" demanded Dr. Laurier, adding to the burst of echoes which rolled to upper and outer air.

"Never mind!" said Martin.

Ruth, a gallant little figure in red sweater and black slacks, not quite so tall as Jenny, turned around and smiled at him.

"Here we are," announced Stannard.

Martin's heart jumped a little, then went on (it seemed to him) normally. With the image of Jenny in his mind, with what he had heard about Jenny over the 'phone, he told himself he was the calmest person there. This was going to be easy.

They emerged, one by one, into a completely cleared space. The beams of the three lamps converged. You could see that the corridor was ten feet wide. Ahead of them, cutting off the corridor, was a grey-brick wall; and into this was set an iron door, with a very small barred opening in it so that you could peer and talk through.

Stannard's breath was noisy in his nostrils. "Here are the

premises," he explained. "I have not even looked into the rooms. I have done nothing except oil the lock of this door."

He held up the key he had shown to Ruth and Martin that afternoon. He fitted it into the lock. And, with a squealing creak of hinges, the iron door swung inwards.

A sudden animation seized that whole group, and they began talking twenty to the dozen. Martin afterwards supposed he must have talked too.

The babble of their voices carried them through into a passage some eight feet wide and twenty feet long, ending in a dead-wall facing them. It was floored with very dirty asphalt. In the wall to the left, eternally the grey-brick, was a door which faced across to a corresponding door on the right.

Stannard, taking one of the lamps from Ricky, propped it up a little slantways against the floor and the dead-end wall so that it should shine straight down the passage.

"Would you like first—" he put his hand on the knob of the left-hand door—"to see the execution shed first?"

"No!" cried Ruth. "The other one. I mean, the beginning. I mean, after all, the condemned cell is the beginning."

Stannard turned to the other door.

"I have always understood," rattled Dr. Laurier loudly, "the condemned cell really is a room, with wall-paper and religious pictures."

"Oh, yes," said Stannard. (Damn the man, thought Martin; his voice rasps on you like a lecturer's). "Oak door," he went on. "Notice the little glass peep-hole high up. The condemned man had two warders—or wardresses, if it happened to be a woman—with him or her every instant of the time. That peep-hole was for the hangman."

"Hangman?" Ricky's voice went up.

"To judge weight and height for the proper drop."

Stannard had difficulty with the iron knob. Ricky wrenched open the scraping door. The first thing their lights picked up, inside, was a dilapidated rocking-chair.

And now the pull and swirl, of what Stannard had called atmosphere or vibrations, began to creep round Martin Drake. He could imagine someone sitting in that rocking-chair, someone who started up and cried, "Get out!" No, this wasn't going to be too easy. Martin subconsciously felt that, when he and Stannard drew lots, he would be the one to be locked up.

"Look there!" Stannard was saying. "Over in the corner. The rope."

"Rope?" Ruth almost screamed. "Not—?"

"No, of course not. Easy, my dear!"

"I'm all right. How dare you say I'm not all right?"

"Do you remember, this afternoon, when I told you about Hessler, the multilator of women's bodies? That he tried to escape from the condemned cell?"

"Yes. No! What about him?"

"The mercy and tact of our Prison Commission," cried Dr. Laurier, "are beyond praise. That picture of Our Saviour on the Cross is truly moving."

"Hessler, Ruth, managed to smuggle potassium cyanide into this room. He used it—"

"To k-kill himself?"

"No. On the guards. In cups of cocoa. When they staggered and tried to shout, he made a break. My *History of the Penal System* is very discreet. Undoubtedly they knew how he did it, but they won't say. In some fashion he got from here into the garden between this wing and the next. He had a rope thrown over a spike in the wall. They winged him with a revolver as he was climbing, and he fell back into a flower-bed. Hessler . . ."

"Listen, old boy," Ricky's voice hissed in Martin's ear. He seized his companion's wrist, and twisted it. "Over there! To the right!" A pause. "Well, damn me to perdition if . . ."

Ricky's exclamation drew round the slightly glazed eyes of the others.

"Afterwards," continued Stannard, "the prison governor insisted an alarm-bell be installed here. Idiot! Prize, thundering idiot! Look at that hanging rope over there! As if . . ."

But the others were not listening. They saw what seemed a crowning incongruity.

In the far corner, grimy but only a few touched with rust, lay a much smaller but better collection of rapiers and daggers than Martin had seen at Willaby's on Friday.

The rapiers were flung down in a heap, as they had lain for many years. The white lamp-beam played over cup-hilts, swept-hilts, ring-hilts, both the pointed and the double-edged. Ricky's eyes were fixed on a little ivory tag attached to one handle. Behind the rapiers stood a row of ancient dusty medicine-bottles, corked, and several empty bottles of whisky.

"Either I've got hallucinations," snapped Ricky, "or those swords belonged to my father."

"Your father?" exclaimed Ruth.

"Ages ago," Ricky tugged at his collar, "my father had a collection. Did you know that?" (Sir Henry Merrivale, had he been present, would have growled assent). "He got tired of 'em; Grandmother Brayle said he gave the stuff away; he put up those old guns you can see in the Green Room. But I could swear, from that writing on the tags . . ."

He hurried over, catching his own reflection in a dust-furred mirror where so many of the despairing must have looked, and bent down.

"*You* remember, Dr. Laurier?" he added.

Dr. Laurier, for a moment hypnotized, uttered what for anybody else would have been a cry of delight. He darted over to the rapiers, pulling at one so that others rattled and tumbled down.

"Surely," he cried, "this is a . . ."

"It's damn funny," said Ricky. "How did this stuff get here? Why?"

Up went the influences or vibrations, up and up! Stannard inflated his thick chest and laughed.

"Are you a swordsman, Mr. Fleet?"

—"No," said Ricky, standing up. "I never liked it. It seems—Dago, somehow. Like sticking a man with a knife. But," and sheer vanity bubbled out of him, "there was a time when I couldn't fly a plane, either. Fencing? I could learn it as easy as winking!"

"Indeed?" mocked Stannard, showing teeth against the red face. "When I saw you, you were such a *very* little pious boy."

Ricky whipped round, his grey eyes wide open in the dazzle of cross-light.

"I may have been no giant then," he said. "But I could put-the-weight twenty-seven feet three inches when I was eleven years old, and I've got a cup to prove it. How would you like to try a little strength-test now?"

"Thank you. But I have another kind of test in about ten minutes."

"Unquestionably," declared Dr. Laurier, "a Toledo blade. Note also the 'Christus Imperat' engraved on the blade near the hilt, and the beautifully wrought pattern on the cup-hilt itself. I must have more light. Excuse me."

And he almost ran out of the room into the passage.

Martin too, having handed his lamp to Ricky, had drawn out a rapier to his taste. Like Laurier's, it was no clumsy double-edge blade; like Laurier's it was thin and tapering, for play with the point. It had a large plain cup-hilt with broad quillons, so finely balanced in the hand that it seemed to bear its own weight.

"Excuse, *me*," Martin said—and also hurried out of the room.

It wasn't, he told himself, that he felt fear. But he felt shut up in there. The condemned cell, twenty feet square, with its flowered peeling wallpaper, boiled with hatred and despair. He could have sworn (though he knew this for an illusion) that the rocking-chair swung a little.

But one touch of panic, real or only half-real, acts on human beings as on animals. Ruth, Stannard, and Ricky crowded after him.

At the far end of the passage, where the lamp stood slightly tilted on the floor, Dr. Laurier was bending over the thin Spanish blade to examine it. For some reason, his prim pince-nez and iron grey hair and hollowed cheeks looked grotesque above the sports costume, like a clergyman's head on a clown. He was trembling. He straightened up, with a flash of pince-nez, when he saw Martin with the other cup-hilt.

"Captain Drake!" he said eagerly. "Do *you* fence?"

"Yes. Most rapier-collectors do."

"Ah!" said Dr. Hugh Laurier.

He advanced slowly, silhouetted against the eye of the lantern, its white glow spreading round and behind him. Turning his body sideways, he bent his knees tentatively and swept out the still-sharp point in insinuating challenge. His wrist turned in that short semi-circular movement, engage and disengage, by which fencers feel, as though by antennae, for an opening.

Insinuating, insinuating, moving forward . . .

Martin, without any sense of incongruity in time or place, instantly crossed points.

All of them, now, were far from normal.

"This is good," Ricky threw at Martin. "Give him hell, old boy!"

"Take your pleasure, gentlemen!" said Stannard.

"Stop it!" cried Ruth.

Her voice was not loud, but it pierced and begged. She had dodged round to the door of the execution shed. If anyone had looked at her then (nobody did) that person would have seen Ruth was far more terrified of these sharpened points than of any forces in Pentecost Prison.

"Look here, Ruth, we're only playing!" said Martin. "Ricky!"

"Yes, old boy?"

"Put that lamp of yours at the other end, against the iron door. Propped up behind me just as the other one is behind him."

Tick-ting went the blades, circling and feeling round each other.

The two facing lights sprang up, silhouetting both fencers

and somewhat clouding each other's sight. *Tick-ting, tick-ting.*

Of course, Martin knew, this was only playing. Feint-lunges, as harmless as the hop of insects; much threatening and scrape of feet; cats darting with sheathed claws. Yet he could feel his own heated excitement, and feel through the thin blades the tensity of Dr. Laurier's arm.

"Only playing!". cried the latter, in a kind of ecstasy. *Tick-ting.* His eyes never moved from Martin's through the crossing-line of the points. "Only playing!" He made a feint of darting in.

"For God's sake stop," shrilled Ruth. "I can't bear swords! I can't stand it! I—" Then, in horror, she pressed one hand over her mouth.

The *tick-ting* ended abruptly. Dr. Laurier disengaged and lunged.

It was a full lunge, with stamp of foot on asphalt. Martin saw the glint on the blade; his wrist snapped two inches in parry; the point, scarcely rasping above a whisper, flicked past his right sleeve.

Hugh Laurier, slow and clumsy on return, stood wide open to a riposte that would have skewered him like a fowl. Movements are automatic, as in boxing; Martin checked his lunge in time, he felt the sweat start out on his body, and then stood staring at the Doctor, who had lowered his point.

"Captain Drake."

Dr. Laurier's husky voice, impeded as though by too-large a tongue, faltered. "I slipped!" he said with great earnestness. "I slipped!"

And he pointed to the gritty asphalt, where there was in fact a long gouge in grit from his right foot. The source of the accident was plain enough.

"But," said Dr. Laurier, fumbling at his pince-nez, "I should not have lunged even half so far. It is incredible. I can't think what made me do it. If any of my patients had seen me tonight—" He ran a hand over his long, hollowed face, exploring it in wonder. Then he added, in appeal, just five words.

"My life is very dull," he said.

Martin, however, had become somewhat light-headed with wrath.

"It's quite all right," he said. "But, if you want to play like that, I'll teach you how. Give me a hand, Ricky?"

"What's up?"

"There were a lot of old medicine-bottles in that room. The corks will do as buttons for these rapiers. Bring the light."

Ruth cried out in protest. Martin did not want to go into that condemned cell again, where to him the air was like a physical touch of evil. But in comparatively few minutes he might be in a worse place—across the passage—and locked into these rooms at that.

He fought it to the back of his mind, while he and Ricky stumbled again over the heap of swords and daggers. More of them clanged and rolled as the light moved. Martin put down his cup-hilt ready to hand.

"Big corks or little corks for the ends of the swords?" demanded Ricky. "There'd be more sport in little ones. If the point—" He paused, and Martin did not reply. They were both looking down at what had been revealed among the scattered swords.

It was an Italian dagger of the sixteenth century, of plain steel for blade, crosspiece, and handle, in a metal sheath of engraved design. It was not so large as we usually imagine such weapons. The blade, shaken almost out of a loose sheath, was so stained with blood that splashes smeared the crosspiece, and somebody evidently had tried to wipe off the lower part of the handle. It was fresh blood.

"Don't touch it!" said Ricky. "They tell you never to . . ."

"Got to touch it." Martin, far less bothered by this than by the evil old room, lifted it by the top of the dagger and the end of the sheath. He inspected it. "Antique," he said. "But—"

"But what?"

"The one cutting-edge has been ground to an edge like a razor. The point's just as sharp." He raised his voice. "Both the lawyer and the doctor had better come in here. Keep Ruth behind you; don't let her look."

There was a long silence, followed by a rush.

Stannard and Dr. Laurier carried the lamps. The former's black eyes were hard with suspicion. Dr. Laurier, dropping the Toledo blade with a clang on the other weapons, seemed miraculously transformed: any of his patients would have recognized him as Martin held out dagger and sheath half-together.

"We found it," Martin told the doctor, "in with the other things. Is that blood—recent?"

"Very." The pince-nez edged round the blade; the long, delicate fingers touched it. "I should say," he drew in his cheeks, "within the last half-hour. Of course, it may not be human blood."

"If you're anything of a pathologist?" Stannard suggested. Dr. Laurier nodded as though startled. "Then," Stannard added, "you can discover whether it's human blood in a very few minutes."

"A very few minutes?"

"Yes, my dear sir. You and Ruth and Mr. Fleet are going home."

Stannard took a deep breath. He thrust out an elbow and looked at his wrist-watch. Then he smiled.

"It is two minutes to twelve," he told them. "Time, I think, that Mr. Drake and I drew lots."

Chapter 10

A moment more, and they were all outside again in the passage between the doors: both closed now. The sheathed dagger, wrapped in a handkerchief so that he should not get blood on his clothes, had been thrust into the pocket of a dazed Dr. Laurier.

The tendency towards hysteria was mounting again.

"You quite understand the terms?" Stannard persisted.

"Quite." Martin tried to speak with a careless air, though his nerves were jerking like an alcoholic's. "Whoever wins the toss locks the other in, keeps the key, sits outside, and doesn't let him out until four o'clock—unless he yells for help."

"Exactly!" Stannard beamed. Then he looked at Ricky, and hesitated. "You recall the rope of the alarm-bell? In the condemned cell?"

"Yes. What about it?" snarled Ricky.

"It's very old. It probably doesn't work. But if you should hear the alarm-bell in the night, it will mean we are in serious trouble."

"What kind of trouble?"

Stannard nodded towards the door of the execution shed.

"Probably that Mr. Drake has gone mad in there," he replied.

"What makes you so infernally sure," demanded Martin, "that I'm going to lose the throw?"

"My luck," Stannard told him. "It never fails."

It was evident that he quite seriously believed this. Self-confidence radiated from him like a furnace; he kept patting his stomach, as though the luck rested there. Then, as he caught Ruth's eye, his tone changed.

"Not that it matters. In humanity, I should like to be the one who is shut up here. It would not, I think, trouble me much. My friend Drake has a disadvantage that will always beat him."

"Meaning what?"

"Your imagination, my dear fellow. You will see nothing, hear nothing; but you will feel. It is only when you *imagine* you see them crawling up from the gallows trap—men-eating tigers like Hessler and Bourke-Smith and pretty Mrs. Langton —that the brain will crack like a china jug." He turned round. "Have you got the folder of matches, Ruth?"

"I have them," said Ruth. "I wish I hadn't."

"Turn your back. Tear out one match, and tear off another much shorter. Give us the heads to choose. The short match is the loser."

Suddenly Dr. Laurier threw back his head and laughed, like a clergyman at a funeral. "This is most amusing!" he said. "This is really extraordinarily amusing."

Stannard bowed slightly.

"Have you got reading-matter, my dear fellow?" he asked Martin briskly, and produced from his conjuror's coat a pocket edition of the plays of Chekhov. "Come! Let's compare reading-matter!"

Martin took out a pocket edition of stories.

"What's this?" fussed Stannard. "*The Beach at Falésa. Markheim. Thrawn Janet. The Sire de—*" His bright black eyes grew incredulously chiding, then gently chiding. "Come, now! Stevenson!"

"If you," Martin said slowly, "are one of the clod-heads who don't appreciate Stevenson, then nobody can make you see his fineness of touch. But did you note the title of the first story? It's called *A Lodging for the Night.*"

Stannard handed the book back. "Touché," he said.

Ruth swung round, holding up her hand with the match-heads above her clenched fist. The hand trembled slightly.

Only Martin and Stannard wore wrist-watches; these could be heard ticking in the pressure of silence. Martin moistened his lips. Stannard, comfortably smiling, nodded towards the matches.

"Won't you go first, my dear fellow? If not—"

"No, you don't!" said Martin.

They both lunged together for a different match. Ricky Fleet, his fists dug so deeply into the pockets of his coat that it seemed to stretch almost to his knees, watched with eyes round and fixed in a kind of incredulous hope. Both contestants, after a glance, opened a hand side by side; and Ruth expelled her breath.

Stannard had drawn the short match.

"Believe me," he said quietly and with evident sincerity, "it is best."

Then he became brisk.

"My dear Drake, here is the key to lock the iron door; together with your lamp and two spare batteries. Mr. Fleet," he indicated a lamp on the floor, "there is your light to guide your party to the main gate. It's a shade past midnight."

Martin felt Ricky clap him on the back at the result of the draw.

"That's all very well, Mr. Ghostmaster," said Ricky, leaning one elbow on the wall and making no pretense of liking Stannard, "but you led us in here. How do you expect us to get out?"

"Ah. Did you observe the floor as we came in?"

"Not particularly."

"In the aisle leading out you will find a length of heavy white string. I put it there this afternoon, a clue to the Cretan labyrinth. Follow the string; it will take you to the main gate."

In spite of everything, Martin thought, Stannard's all right. He's all right!

In a very short time he and Stannard were alone. The other three, obviously very nervous, watched while Martin stood outside the iron door, turned the key, and dropped it into his pocket. They saw the white splash of Stannard's lamp as he stood inside, close to the tiny square barred opening in the iron door.

"It's amusing," the barrister said, "that nobody's asked to see the execution shed. You and I can speak to each other through this opening. If," he added very pointedly, "it is at all necessary."

The trembling echoes fell away to sharp-pointed quiet.

Ricky's bobbing light, Ruth's red and black slacks, Dr. Laurier's smile all faded amid rustles against bales. Martin switched off his own lamp. For a little time he watched Stannard, without speaking, through the little barred opening.

Holding the lamp ahead, Stannard opened the door of the execution shed. He raked the light inside. He started a little, though he must have guessed exactly how the room looked. It would look—

Stop that! Martin Drake shut up his own imagination.

Stannard, not quite so ruddy in the face, contemplated what lay inside. He turned back, entered the condemned cell, and after a moment emerged carrying an ugly-looking rocking-chair which Martin well remembered. Hoisting this awkwardly on one arm, Stannard returned to the execution shed, maneuvered in backwards, and closed the door. Utter darkness and silence descended on Pentecost Prison.

Martin hastily switched on his own lamp. The space between the iron door and the line of the piled paper was about ten feet clear. Brick walls and a brick floor. He set the lamp in a corner.

Got to sit down.

Standing on tiptoe, and with a heavy lift, he brought down one of the long paper bales. Pushing the lantern to one side with his foot, he thumped down the bale almost in the corner with its back to the wall at right-angles to the iron door. He glanced at his wrist-watch, thinking vaguely that Stannard's watch must be slow: his own registered a full fifteen minutes past twelve.

Only when he sat down and relaxed back against the wall, letting his arms and legs go as limp as a straw, did he realize.

God!

His head swam dizzily. His heart beat hard, though it was slowing down. There was sweat on his forehead, and his shirt stuck to his back. He hadn't quite realized the heat and oppressiveness in there. The others had been the same as himself, dust-grimed figures—except for Ruth, who in some inexplicable fashion preserved her freshness, the trim up-swept hair-do—but at the time he hadn't noticed it.

You couldn't call this place exactly soothing; yet it was soothing by contrast to that force which had put the black dog on his back in the condemned cell. Soothing! The lamp shed a thin beam at his feet across the floor. With Stevenson, and tobacco, he could easily pass less than four hours until dawn.

Smoking here? Yes; the paper bales were a good distance away. He lit a cigarette, drawing in smoke deeply and again relaxation; and out of the smoke swam Jenny, and Jenny's look, and Jenny's present address.

Well, Martin thought grimly, he had got that address.

Vividly he remembered how, at the telephone in the hall of Fleet House at well past seven that evening, he had got in touch with Dawson the butler at Brayle Manor. Dawson couldn't be overheard. The Old Dragon was upstairs at Fleet House with Aunt Cicely.

"I am sorry, sir," the voice told him. "I'm not at liberty to say where Lady Jennifer is."

"Yes, I appreciate that," Martin had answered. "But I'll pay you five hundred pounds if you do."

The telephone, so to speak, shook at its moorings.

If you want to bribe anybody, Martin thought, don't mess in small craftiness with ten-bob notes, or there'll only be haggling and you'll lose. Hit your man in the eye with a sum so staggering that he'll fall all over himself to get it.

"Go on!" jeered the telephone, in a startlingly different tone, but much lower-voiced. "How do I know you can pay that?"

"The banks are closed. But did you ever hear of Mr. Joseph Anthony? He's the biggest art-dealer in London."

"Yes, sir," the voice muttered respectfully. "We've had to—" the word "sell" seemed to tremble on his lips.

"His private 'phone-number is Grosvenor 0011. Confirm it with Information if you doubt me. I'm going to 'phone him now. You ring him in about fifteen minutes. Ask him then if he's ready, on my say-so, to send you his own personal cheque for that amount. The cheque will reach you tomorrow, and won't be stopped unless you've given me a fake address."

"The . . . the address is not on the 'phone, sir."

"Never mind. Get it!"

Then he had 'phoned Joe Anthony; and waited in agony, twisting his knuckles, for Dawson's return-call. Curious, too: once or twice he imagined he had heard somebody whispering in the background while he spoke to Dawson. Then the telephone pealed its double-ring.

"That's all right, sir," Dawson muttered. "The address is not exactly in London."

"I didn't suppose it was, or the old—she wouldn't have told me so."

"Care of Mr. and Mrs. Ives, Ranham Old Park, Ranham, Hertfordshire."

Serene satisfaction animated Martin when he wrote it down, and put it in his pocket. He was still sitting by the telephone in the hall when Lady Brayle herself came downstairs past the dying light from the tall arched window.

Martin, startled, did not get up. She did not look at him; was not conscious of him. On her face was an expression he failed to read. She marched on her flat heels, shoulders swinging a little, to the front door; and departed without a word to anybody.

Then there had been dinner in the high square room at the

back of Fleet House, candle-flames on polished wood making a shimmer against daylight through garden trees. H.M. and Masters had somewhat hastily departed after the interview on the roof, saying they were going to see the local police at Brayle. Ricky insisted on Martin's bringing his bag across from the inn. Then the long sitting in the back garden—Dr. Laurier arriving in his own car from just outside Brayle, Ricky rushing into the house to see how his mother was—until the position of the quarter-moon above rustling darkness told them it was time to . . .

Yes; he had got that address!

Sitting back relaxed, the cigarette-end glowing red against the darkness of Pentecost, Martin felt cool in temperature as well as mind; and he smiled. Tomorrow morning, very early, he would see what train-connections he could make for Ranham in Hertfordshire.

"With luck," he said aloud, "I might get there at breakfast-time."

The sound of his own voice startled him. By the Lord, he was jumpier than he'd thought! Not a whisper of noise had come from beyond the iron door. Stannard must be sitting in the rocking chair, perhaps wheezing a little as he read Chekhov, near the closed gallows-trap. Martin reached down for the Stevenson; and then flung his head round.

Something was moving and rustling among the paper bales.

Steady, now!

He dropped his cigarette on the floor and ground it out with his foot. Reaching down for the lamp, he directed it towards the aisle between bales and wall. Whoever it was, the person carried a light. Out into the open emerged Ruth Callice: her face anxious, her finger at her lip.

"What the devil are you . . . ?"

"Sh!" Ruth tiptoed over. "I know I'm breaking my promise. But I *had* to talk to you alone."

This was the Ruth he had known on Thursday night, and for so long: the dark-brown eyes softened and upturned, the lips half parted, that sense of "niceness" which so many persons found impossible to describe. Her sweater-and-slacks costume, Martin observed for the first time, became her very well. She looked at the iron door.

"Can Stan hear us?"

"I don't think so, unless you shout. The door of the—that place is thick oak, and he's got it closed. Where are the others?"

"They went home. I knew *I* was perfectly at home, if I had

a lamp and that thread guide-line." Ruth's smooth forehead slightly wrinkled; a smile curved up the corner of her lip. "Sit down," she invited, "and move over. Have you a cigarette?"

Martin put down the light in its old position with Ruth's lamp beside it, and lit cigarettes for both of them. With his eyes becoming accustomed to near-darkness, he could see that the paper-mountains had been built up on the side of windows. He was acutely conscious of something else: Ruth's physical nearness.

"I suppose," Ruh said softly, when the cigarette had several times pulsed and darkened, "you thought I behaved very badly today?"

He had forgotten all about it. "No, not in the least."

"Well, I did."

"Never mind your behaviour. Why didn't you ever tell me you knew Jenny? You knew I'd been searching for three years . . ."

"Pardon me," Ruth corrected. "I learned it just under a year ago. You got horribly drunk and told me all about it."

"Yes. That's true. I remember. Even so!—"

"Oh, I wish I could make you understand!" The cigarette glowed and darkened nervously. Ruth half turned. In near-darknss he could see the sincerity, the deep earnestness, in the gleam of her eyes. "I had to know whether it was right for both of you, and that wasn't easy. I had to decide what was best."

"You had to decide what was best for us?"

"Yes."

"Forgive me, Ruth. But can you, or I, or anybody else in this bloody Socialist world, say what's best for his neighbour?"

"I knew you wouldn't understand. You see, I'm very fond of Jenny, and I—am rather fond of you. Jenny's had a queer upbringing. Her father and mother, the Earl and Countess, never got on well. Her mother's dead. Her father lives abroad: in Sweden, I think."

"Yes. So Jenny told me."

"She's been brought up by this stately grandmother . . ."

"And you think the old she-dog can stop Jenny from loving me?"

"Oh, she'll love you." Ruth laughed. "She'll love you so desperately that in a year or two you'll be bored to death. Also, Jenny's terribly jealous. And she has almost no sense of humour."

Ruth dropped her cigarette on the floor and trod on it. Martin watched her.

"How many times have you been in love, Ruth? Did you

ever find a sense of humour much of a help?"

Ruth ignored this. She seemed about to add something else about Jenny or Jenny's family, but checked herself.

"And take you, for instance!" she went on, with soft and tender satire. "Do you remember what you said on Thursday night?"

Now the ability of a woman to remember some trivial remark, made possibly decades before, is a weapon which cannot be met.

"You said if you ever found Jenny again, and she was engaged, you'd use *any* trick, however underhand, to get her back again. And what, as it happened, did you actually do?

"Darling, your fair-play-and-no-advantages attitude was ridiculous. If Ricky Fleet hadn't been up to his ears with Susan Harwood, there'd have been trouble. You insisted on keeping your word about the vigil here, though I was a cat and tried to make Jenny even more jealous than she is.

"Look at your best, or rather your most popular, work! Look at your fencing! Look at Stevenson! You're an old-fashioned romanticist, that's what you are, only temperamental and a bit crazy."

Ruth said all this in a low voice, speaking more quickly as she went on. Martin dropped his own cigarette and crushed it out.

"What you say," he retorted, "may be true. If it is, it's no very deep damnation. Your friend Stannard . . ."

"Oh, Martin!"

"Why do you say, 'oh, Martin' like that?"

(Yet all the time he was becoming more heavily, acutely aware of Ruth's physical presence.)

"Poor Jack Stannard is only showing off, that's all. He despises younger men, and wants to show them up as ignorant louts. And he's rather tremendous, you know. And that grave bearing of his, shaking hands just as though I were made of fragile china, is so touching that sometimes I—" She paused. "Do you know why he arranged this whole expedition?"

Martin hesitated. "Well! I suppose because he thought you were, you know, more interested in me than you were."

"So you've guessed *that*," Ruth mocked softly.

(They were both breathing with a little more quickened beat.)

"I'd have known it, of course, if there hadn't been a kind of spell on my brain. In any case, since it happens to be wrong . . ."

"Who says it's wrong?" asked Ruth coolly, and turned round. "Suppose you kiss me."

Now here, it may be submitted, what is any man to do under such circumstances? Besides, human nature is human nature: to put the matter politely. Furthermore, ordinary social behaviour . . . Anyway, he did not treat her like fragile china.

Suddenly Ruth struggled and pushed herself away.

"This doesn't mean anything," she said. After waiting a while, she repeated in a calmer tone: "This doesn't mean anything."

The thought of Jenny, even in Martin's present state of mind, partly sobered him.

"I know!" He got his breath back.

"I wouldn't have an affair with you," said Ruth, "and I certainly wouldn't marry you, for anything on earth."

"I know that!—But, for the sake of academic clearness, why not?"

"Because you have your way of life; you're an idiot; and you wouldn't change it one little bit. I have my way of life; I'm practical; and I wouldn't change it one little bit. It would be horrible."

"Jenny—" he stopped. "There's Stannard, you know."

"Do you think you're joking?"

"No!"

"Because I might, just conceivably might, be able to care a good deal for him, if only," said Ruth with intensity, "if only he were more of an idiot!"

"For God's sake," exclaimed the other, taken aback by what seemed to him the deep seriousness and complete illogicality of this remark, "isn't that the deadly charge you've been levelling at me?"

"Oh, you don't understand." Ruth was almost crying. "I shouldn't have come here. You shouldn't have let me talk to you. It's your fault."

She reached across, took up her own lamp, and stood up. She moved softly away from him, turning round only at the aisle. Her dark-brown eyes were soft again. Her lips made a movement of lightness.

"I shall get over this very shortly," she told him. "In the meantime, I warn you by your own code that I'm *rather* jealous of Jenny. Against that, I *am* trying to do the decent thing and what's right. What I really came here to tell you . . ."

"Yes?"

"I *can* tell you, because it hasn't directly to do with Jenny herself. Years ago," said Ruth, "a child was found murdered and mutilated at a place called Priory Hill, not very far from here."

Then she was gone.

The old brick prison might have echoed with ghostly occupants shaking their cell-doors. Was Hessler, who also murdered and mutilated, listening with his ear to the little grille of the iron door? Across and beyond the paper bales Martin could see the tops of high windows, with vertical bars; but the lighter sky beyond made darkness here more dense.

Ruth . . . he must forget that subject, Martin told himself. Suppose Jenny had seen them? No harm in it, only natural; but hard to explain. Lord, suppose Ruth told Jenny? "I'm *rather* jealous of Jenny." Stop! Mentally he closed the lid of the incident with a bang.

Still not a whisper, not a chink of light, from beyond the iron door. Under the rules of the test, the man inside was permitted to get up and walk about. Could anything have happened to Stannard?

Martin would have shouted to Stannard, except for the practical certainty that it would bring the barrister to the iron door, sardonically to inquire whether his friend outside needed help.

Yes, Ruth—careful!—did right to respect Stannard. Aside from anything else, the Great Defender was as clever as Satan. Another memory stirred in Martin's head: a festal occasion at his club, viewed through a gauze of whisky, in which a certain eminent judge had spoken with great indiscretion. He spoke of Stannard, who had been briefed for the defence in the Cosens murder case.

"Gentlemen," His Lordship had declared, his speech being rendered here as free from alcoholic slur, "gentlemen, counsel for the defence produced an unexpected alibi. It was not only, gentlemen, that we couldn't prove the flaw in it; we couldn't even *see* the flaw in it. And that thus-and-so Cosens, as guilty as Judas, walked out a free man."

Well, there was no question of ali . . .

Great Scott, no wonder Stannard hadn't become restless! Martin, blinking hard at the luminous dial of his watch, saw that the time was only half-past twelve. It should have been two o'clock, at least. But he held the watch to his ear, and it was ticking.

Swung round once too often in the emotional bowl, exhausted, Martin sat down heavily on the paper-bale. His head felt very heavy. The light of the lamp began to grow yellow (somebody using it too long before?), and he hastily replaced the battery with a spare one.

With heavy movements he groped along the wall, found a nail there, shifted along the bale, and hung the lamp sideways so that its beam should shine past his shoulder. He groped down again for the Stevenson he had found in the library at Fleet House.

Begin with the first story, yes. Title-page, table of contents, foreword, so! Begin with the fine scene of the snowflakes sifting over mediaeval Paris. Begin . . .

The type blurred before his eyes. He had a hazy consciousness that the book was there, the light was there, and he was there; but not for long. His head and shoulders lolled back against the wall. Martin Drake, with the lines of tiredness drawn slantwise under his eyes, was asleep.

What woke him he did not know at the time, or for nearly twenty-four hours afterwards.

But it was a noise. It made him start up, nerves twitching; it made him jump to his feet, miry-eyed, and peer round until he realized where he was. His first impression, possibly created by a dream, was that the alarm-bell on the roof was ringing.

"If you hear the alarm-bell in the night," someone had said, "it will mean we are in serious trouble."

But a bell would have gone on ringing. Besides, a deeper memory suggested, this had been something like a crash: not very loud, yet loud enough to jolt thin sleep. Martin's head remained mazy. By concentration on his wrist-watch, he saw the hour was two o'clock. Then Stannard flashed through his mind. Yanking the lamp off the wall, he hurried to the iron door and played the beam inside.

"Stannard!" he yelled.

The oak door to the execution shed was still closed. So was the other one.

"Stannard! Are you all right?"

To his relief he heard the "Yes! Quite!" of the other's unmistakable tones, muffled by the oak door. But in the voice was a curious wild inflection which in his relief he did not stop to analyze.

He groped for the key in his pocket, but hesitated. He would not offer Stannard the insult of asking whether he wanted to be let out.

What vaguely puzzled Martin, as he returned to his seat, was the fact that he had been able to sleep in the place of bogles. But this wasn't the place of bogles. Wasn't there some legend about iron, cold iron, keeping them off?

It was within the rules, both stated and implied, to sleep if you could. You could drowse in the rocking-chair, or even on the ruddy gallows-trap. Martin hung the lamp on the wall again, his hand heavy.

When he leaned back against the wall, he felt no sense of crick in the neck or stiffness in the back. His senses were padded. Once more, from here, he bellowed out at Stannard; and very faintly Stannard's voice told him to mind his own damned business.

Right you are, Mr. Great Defender.

Sleep coiled insidiously, sleep soothed with shadow narcotics.

Though it might have been unusual under such circumstances, Martin afterwards remembered his dreams as being cozy and pleasant. He became somehow entangled with the love-scene between Blanche and Denis in *The Sire de Malétroit's Door;* and the old Sire de Malétroit, who was going to hang somebody in the morning, bore a baffling, dissolving resemblance to Lady Brayle. The old Sire de Malétroit . . .

Look out! *Thud!*

This time what woke him was toppling off the bale, his hands and arms in semi-consciousness saving him as he struck the floor. It was an ugly feeling, that sense of a helpless fall. But he was awake, chilly and sharply wide-awake, when he crawled up from the dirt-sting of the floor.

The corridor swam in a dim grey twilight which seemed as dingy as the prison. Outside the tall barred windows he could detect a white mist, wisps of it, past grime-speckled panes. Once more he consulted his watch. Two minues to four o'clock.

A great exultation sang in him, though he felt as if he had slept in a barrel. It was nearly all over. Give it dead to the time—exactly to the ant-busy travelling of the watch's secondhand—and then unlock the door.

The beam of the lamp still shone straight across, against murky daylight. Stevenson, unread, had sprawled open on the floor. If there could be degrees of silence, Pentecost Prison seemed more utterly silent now than at any time during the night. And Stannard?

Martin let the full two minutes tick round. Then, drawing the large key out of his pocket, he went over to the iron door.

"Stannard!" he shouted.

Chapter 11

Shading his eyes, Martin peered through the grille.

Grey traces, very faint, showed a vertical glimmer along the edge of the execution shed door, which stood about an inch open. Obviously, as in the case of the condemned cell, that room must have some kind of window.

"Stannard!" he called, with the same formula. "Are you all right?"

"I'm here. I'm—" The voice seemed to answer somewhat hollowly, and from a distance away, though the oak door stood a little open. Odd, perhaps. Who cared?

"The time's up," Martin shouted back, "and I'm unlocking this door."

He did so, after which he pushed the iron door partly open with a squeak and squeal of hinges. There was a ringing clatter as he threw the key inside on the floor.

"Thanks," he added, "for an entertaining evening. You're free, and I'm free too."

The thought of Stannard's company, on the way back, almost revolted him. In his exuberance he felt like talking to empty air instead, so that he could use rich words unheard. Putting Stevenson in his pocket, and picking up the lamp, he took long strides to get away from there.

Faintly, once, he thought he heard Stannard calling something after him. But the light found the white-string guideline with ease; amazing he hadn't noticed it before! Nevertheless, in his daylight mood, it was of a pattern with all the other incidents of last night.

Every action, every speech, had seemed quite natural at the time; even inevitable. Yet now, when the images unreeled before him—those evil forces (imagined?) in the condemned cell, a fencing-match in which he had nearly been murdered by the sedate Dr. Laurier, a blood-stained dagger, an alarm-bell with its rope in the cell, an amorous passage with Ruth Callice—it became a phantasmagoria which struck him with wonder. The little talk with Ruth seemed to him inconsequential, as though it had never happened; even amusing. He would tell Jenny about it.

In less than two minutes, at rustling quick-step through what was now only a dreary storage-building, he reached the main gate. All phantasmagoria, like that skeleton in the clock. Briefly he wondered what Sir Henry Merrivale might have been doing with the skeleton in the clock.

Through the arched frame of bars like a portcullis, he saw that the tall iron gates stood wide open. Beyond lay thick white mist, drifting and with rifts in it; the mist would presently vanish before heat and sun, but meantime it muffled the world in eeriness.

As he passed the opening in the portcullis, switching off the lamp and putting it in his pocket, Martin laughed aloud at this so-called "eeriness." He could have danced or hit the air a right-hander. Then, just outside the prison gates as a rift in the mist floated past, he saw Jenny herself. She was obviously waiting.

For a moment he stood still, with a notion that this might be part of the fantasy.

By coincidence, Jenny also wore slacks and a sweater: coloured brown, with a light coat thrown over her shoulders. As soon as he saw her, other considerations of feminine appeal were forgotten. Her yellow hair curled to her shoulders. She was smoking a cigarette, which she instantly threw away. They ran towards each other.

"How the devil did you get back here?"

"I was never away," Jenny confessed. "I thought I could take that train. But I couldn't face it. I told the taxi-driver to come back. Because—" She stopped. "So you'd have paid five hundred pounds just to learn where I'd gone?"

"If that butler has blabbed, the old lady will sack him."

"Dawson," said Jenny, "isn't a butler. I suppose he is, in a way, and Grandmother insists on calling him that. He's butler and handy-man too; we don't employ much of a staff of servants. Anyway, I caught him when he was going to take your money. I was afraid you could hear me whispering in the background."

Realization bumped him. "Come to think of it, I heard something."

"Of course I rang up Mr. Anthony after you did, and said it was all a joke and he wasn't to send any cheque. Dawson nearly wept. Then I made him ring you and give the address, or you might have come to the Manor. But—"

Here, raising her blue eyes, Jenny began such a bitter denunciation of her own character, such a writhing of self-loathing, that it would have been considered strong even by her worst enemy.

"Martin, I knew you had to go through with that 'bet.' I wouldn't have you back out. That's what makes me so vile. There's one excuse," her eyes looked at him oddly, "that perhaps helps, and I've got to tell you soon. But Ruth had got me absolutely furious. Then, when I saw you running across the road after her . . ."

He ended her rush of speech in the appropriate way, which was an effective way. At the back of his mind it occurred to him that he wouldn't just yet tell Jenny about that small brush with Ruth last night. Presently, of course! But not just yet.

Presently Jenny spoke.

"So I had to sneak out this morning and meet you. Otherwise," she said happily, "you'd have been ripping away or chartering a special plane or heaven knows what. Where do you want to go now?"

"Anywhere you like. We might go and throw a bucket of water over your grandmother?"

"Martin! You mustn't . . ."

Jenny stopped. Suddenly she began to laugh, with such full infectiousness and delight that Martin joined in without knowing why. It warmed his heart to see this girl growing healthier and more exuberant at every minute, as though she had been let out of prison.

"If you think the idea is as funny as all that, Jenny, it would be still better to use a fire-hose."

"Wait!" cried Jenny, shaking all over and wiping the tears of joy from her eyes. "Do you mean to say you haven't heard about the perfectly awful thing that happened last night? In the public road between the Dragon's Rest and the Manor?"

"No."

"Well, Grandmother and Sir Henry Merrivale . . ."

"Godalive, don't tell me those two had *another* knock-down row?"

"Yes."

"*He* threw a bucket of water over her, I suppose?"

"No, no, it wasn't anything like that." Jenny, the wings of her yellow hair falling forward, pressed a hand over her mouth and began to shake again. He straightened up her shoulders. "Darling," she assured him, "I shall be a perfect model of prim correctness. I've been trained to that. You're at the Dragon, aren't you?"

"No; at Fleet House."

"If you don't mind wading in wet grass, there's a wonderful short-cut over the fields."

"We will roll and revel in the wet grass. Lead on."

About them the white mist so muffled sight that even the prison was hardly visible twenty feet away. Sometimes the mist would drift past Jenny, obscuring her until the smiling face emerged. Their footsteps crunched in weedy gravel; once, on the edge of the gravel approach, Jenny hesitated.

"Good heavens, what about Mr. Stannard? What about everything?"

"Stannard," he replied, "is A-1. He'll be out in a minute, so let's go ahead. *I* saw no ghosts. In fact," concluded Martin, telling one of the more remarkable lies of his life, "there was practically no excitement. Let's hear about this row."

The wet grass swished and soaked to their knees as they went down across an almost invisible field in the mist. The shape of a tree swam dimly past, to be blotted out as though by magic. They walked happily, arm and hand linked; but Jenny was now frowning.

"You see," she explained, "Grandmother's now got the skeleton."

"She's got . . . you mean the skeleton-clock?"

"Not the clock. Just the skeleton. Heaven alone knows why she wants it," Jenny bit her lip, "or why anybody wants it. It all started very seriously. Grandmother had gone to visit Aunt Cicely, and got back home about a quarter to eight."

"Yes. I remember."

"I was a bit uneasy when she got home. I shouldn't have been, and I won't be again. But I wondered what she'd say when she found I hadn't gone to visit Mr. and Mrs. Ives after all. She just looked at me in the oddest way—" Jenny hesitated—"as though it didn't matter. She said: 'Jennifer dear, I must think hard for five minutes.'

"Whenever she says that, I know it means she's thinking about legal proceedings. Grandmother's got a passion for law suits. She's always trying to prove something from old documents of 1662, or things like that. *I* imagined she was thinking about the fair (you'll hear about it) that opens on Monday.

"Anyway, she came back in fifteen minutes looking grim and sort of triumphant. She made me sit down in a chair. She said: 'Jennifer, mark my words! The unspeakable Merrivale —'"

(Martin could hear Lady Brayle saying it.)

"'—the unspeakable Merrivale,' Grandmother said, "in the

presence of no less than four witnesses, distinctly promised to give me the clock if I answered "a few" questions. These questions I did answer, as the witnesses can testify.' "

To Martin's memory returned a view of the library at Fleet House, with H.M. and Lady Brayle standing on either side of the desk like offenders in a magistrate's court. He saw Ruth, Stannard, Ricky and himself with their backs to the white marble mantelpiece.

"Jenny," he said, "that's true. He did say so!"

"Anyway, I'm afraid I couldn't follow the legal lecture she gave me. Something about possession of the clock including possession of its contents: as, *par example*, and to wit, when it is sold at Willaby's with a skeleton inside. Then she called for Dawson to get out the electric car. Do you know what an electric car is?"

Martin reflected.

"I dimly remember having seen, or at least heard of one. It looked like a two-seater carriage with a dashboard, but no horses; nothing in front except the dashboard and a glass windscreen. You steered with a handle instead of a steering-wheel. Yes! And it was used by stately ladies who didn't want to travel fast."

Jenny nodded.

"That's it exactly. Grandmother has one, and it still works. But it's never used except on *very* special occasions. I asked Grandmother what it meant, but she only smiled that peculiar smile and said I should understand in good time. What's more, she told Dawson she would drive herself, because she wanted me as a witness.

"It was broad daylight, not more than half-past eight. Along we went in the electric—'brougham,' Grandmother calls it— with Grandmother sitting bolt upright and never looking more grand, and *me* sitting bolt upright, eyes ahead, and feeling *awful*. We got as far as Fleet House, and then turned round in a graceful curve to the main bar of the Dragon's Rest."

Martin Drake was beginning to taste ecstasy.

"Is that the one she usually patronizes?"

"Martin!" said Jenny. Her eyes belied her seraphic countenance.

"I beg your pardon. Go on."

"Of course Grandmother wouldn't let me go in. She stationed me just outside the door. It was Saturday night, and they were pretty noisy. They're not supposed to sing, but the constable doesn't interfere much. A group in one corner were harmonizing on a pirate chantey with a refrain like, 'Skull and bones, skull and bones; ho, the Jolly Roger.'

"When Grandmother walked in, every man of them looked up as though he'd seen the hangman. But Grandmother loves—" Jenny's voice poured with bitterness—"*how* Grandmother loves being the lady of the manor. She raised her hand and said, 'Please, my good men, be at ease.' Then she beckoned to poor Mr. Puckston.

"I couldn't hear much of what they were saying. Mr. Puckston seemed to be telling her the first bar-parlour was used as a private sitting-room by Sir Henry Merrivale, and H.M. was out, and the door was locked. Of course you can guess how Grandmother dealt with that. Mr. Puckston unlocked the door, Grandmother went in; and in a minute Mr. Puckston followed her with a pair of wire-cutters.

"Then the door opened again. Out marched Grandmother, with the skeleton slung over her shoulder. The head was hanging down her back, and she had the legs in her hand.

"One poor old man, who must have been eighty, spilled a pint beer-glass straight into Miss Partridge's lap. Grandmother never stopped or looked round. She marched straight out to the brougham, sat the skeleton up in the seat like a passenger, and told me to get in.

"That's where the fireworks really started. As I was getting in, I looked round. In the middle of the road, about thirty feet behind us—well, there was Sir Henry.

"His eyes were bulging out behind his spectacles, and his whole corporation was shivering like a mountain. I can't reproduce the tone, and, anyway, nobody could reproduce the volume, of what he said.

"He said: 'You stole my skeleton.' Then he turned round to the people in the door, who'd crowded out with their glasses in their hands, and said: 'Boys, that goddam hobgoblin stole my skeleton.' By this time we were off to a flying start.

"There wasn't any motor-car outside the Dragon at all. Only a lot of bicycles, and a farm-cart with Will Harnaby's horse. H.M. was so mad he really and literally couldn't see straight, and he fell all over the farm-cart when he tried to get up. But he did get there, and he did grab the reins and whip, and off we all went.

"Grandmother was bending tensely over the steering-lever, putting on every ounce of speed; and Sir Henry was standing up and whirling the whip round his head like a charioteer in *Ben-Hur*. Only, you see, that electric car couldn't possibly do twenty miles an hour. And Will Harnaby's horse couldn't do fifteen.

"That's where—" Jenny faltered a little—"Grandmother gave me the instructions. She said, with that smile of hers, I was to stick the skeleton's head out of the side-window so it faced H.M. And I was to move the lower jaw up and down as if the skeleton gibbered at him.

"Well, I did. I made the skeleton stick its head out and gibber about every twenty yards. And, every time the skeleton gibbered at him, his face got more purple, and his language was awful. Truly *awful*. I never heard anything, even in the Navy, that could . . ."

Jenny stopped. "Martin!" she said, in an attempt at reproachfulness which broke down completely.

He couldn't help it. He knew it wasn't really funny; it was funny only because you could visualize the expressions of the persons concerned. He had collapsed against a tree, beating his hands on the bark. Jenny collapsed as well..

"But, Martin!" she insisted presently. "You've got to see the serious side as well!"

"If you can see the serious side of that, my sweet, you'd appeal greatly to Sir Stafford Cripps. Besides, you haven't told me the ending."

"The ending *is* the serious side."

"Oh? Who won the race?"

"We did. By yards and yards and yards." Jenny reflected. "I'm perfectly certain Grandmother told Dawson to be ready. He was there at the lodge gates, where there's no lodge-keeper now. But the wall is fifteen feet high, and there are big iron-barred gates."

Prisons, it suddenly occurred to Martin: striking the amusement from his heart. Pentecost, Fleet House, Brayle Manor, all were prisons; though for the life of him he could not think how this applied to Fleet House, where the impression had come only from feeling.

He and Jenny were walking again through the mist. A white tide of mist-under-mist washed across the grass, then revealed it, ever moving. Its damp could be felt and breathed.

"Go on," he prompted. "What happened after your electric flyer got through the gates?"

"Dawson closed and locked them. Grandmother drove the car a fairly long way up the drive. After that she walked to the gates again. By that time she and H.M. too must have done a little thinking, because . . . well, because it was different. H.M. was sitting outside the gates on the seat of the farm-cart, with the whip across his knees and no expression on his face at all.

"Grandmother put her own face almost against the bars,

and (don't think I've forgotten a word!) she said: 'It may be conceded that you won the first round, Henry; but can there be any doubt about who won the second?' "

Martin whistled.

"Jenny," he declared, "something tells me there is going to be a third round. And that the third round will be a beauty."

"But that's just what mustn't happen!" Jenny, peering at him past the side of her yellow hair, was again the eager and the breathless. "Oh, I suppose it doesn't matter if it's something silly, like making skeletons gibber. Though even there I doubt whether your H.M. is as clever as Grandmother."

"You think that, eh?"

"Yes. I do."

"Wait," advised Martin.

"But the skeleton-in-the-clock," Jenny told him, her thin and arched eyebrows drawn together, "is a different thing. It's serious, and—it may be deadly. Do you realize, from what H.M. said at Willaby's and from every bit of gossip floating about, that H.M. thinks this skeleton is a vital piece of evidence?"

"But evidence of what?"

"I wish I knew. And he told us straight out what he thought about Sir George Fleet's . . . death."

"*You're* sure it was murder too. Aren't you, Jenny?"

She stopped short and turned round, her lips apart. "Martin! What makes you ask that?"

"Because every single time you've mentioned it, you hesitate before you say 'death.' Besides, for some reason yesterday you started to be passionately interested all of a sudden, and wanted to learn all about it. Why, Jenny?"

Instead of lessening as they walked, the mist was becoming thicker. Already, some distance back, a hedgerow had loomed unexpectedly in their faces; they groped for the stile. Now a fence emerged with almost equal materialization from the white twilight. They reached the fence, and Jenny put a hand on it.

"Martin. Did you ever wonder why I didn't offer to go with you on the ghost-hunting expedition?"

Martin felt uncomfortable. "Well! I thought you were . . ."

"Jealous? Yes, that was true. Afraid of ghosts? Also true, a little." Her lips and eyebrows apologized gently. "But I told you there was another reason. Martin, I want you to know *everything* about me. I do, I do! But I can't tell you now because if I'm wrong it's not merely being mistaken; it's—it's sordidly stupid."

"Jenny, I don't care. I'm not a detective."

She shook her hair violently, and settled the coat over her brown sweater as though more conscious of mist-clamminess.

"It all comes back to that utterly meaningless skeleton," she said. "And now Grandmother's got it locked up somewhere."

"For innocent reasons, of course." He tried hard to make this a plain statement, without any inflection of question.

"Naturally. You see, under everything, Grandmother is just a sentimentalist."

Martin found his reason rocking. "*Your grandmother*," he said, defining the words with care, "you call a sentimentalist?"

"Oh, she isn't easy to live with. I hate her sometimes. But she *is* kind-hearted, and you'd see it if it weren't for the arrogance. Grandmother is shielding somebody." Jenny hesitated. "She says the skeleton is legally her property. She also says nobody, not even the police, can take it from her unless they can show *why* it's a vital piece of evidence. Is that right?"

"You'd better ask Stannard. But it sounds reasonable to me."

"Then that means," cried Jenny, her eyes shining under lowered lids, "the police don't know themselves. It means . . ."

Here Jenny, whose gaze had wandered along the line of the fence, uttered a cry and ran to Martin. Some little distance down beside the fence, a man was standing motionless.

A drifting mist-veil hid everything except his legs, as he stood sideways to the fence. Then the moving veil slowly swirled past and up. Martin saw clearly a large and somewhat burly figure, with its blue serge suit and its ruddy face dominated by a boiled blue eye, under a bowler hat.

"Chief Inspector Masters!" Martin said.

Masters lifted one foot experimentally, and set it down with a faint squelch. If he did not happen to be in a good temper, the Chief Inspector never showed this in his professional countenance.

"Morning, miss. Morning, sir," he greeted them, as offhandedly as though he were in a London office instead of a mist-wrapped Berkshire field at half-past four on Sunday morning. Bland as ever, poker-faced as ever in public, he walked towards them and looked hard at Martin.

"Still alive, I see," he added.

We talk with scorn of prophetic instincts. Martin felt one then, as sharp as the twinge from a bad heart; but, like the mist-movings, it drifted away and was lost in an instant.

"Still alive?" he repeated, and laughed. "Is there any reason why I shouldn't be alive?"

"We-el!" smiled Masters, with a tolerant and amused wave of his hand. "As you described it to Sir Henry and me, this execution shed business was to be a swell affair. But *you* don't seem to be hanged by the neck or snuffed out by any ghost, do you?"

Martin, studying him, saw that Masters had the appearance of a man who has walked hard to keep just ahead of somebody. In addition to his reddish eyelids, there were certain familiar dust-stains on the blue serge which had not quite been erased by a handkerchief or the mist-damp.

"Chief Inspector," he said, "were you at that prison too?"

"We-el!" said Masters, as though he debated this himself. "That's a very interesting question, sir. I might have been, and then again I might not have been." He drew closer, confidentially. "The fact is, a minute ago I heard you two saying something about a skeleton and a clock."

"Please don't start to browbeat me," begged Jenny. "Go and see my grandmother."

"Browbeat? Now, miss!" Masters was reproachful. He grew more confidential, like a Balkan diplomat. "I'll just tell you something about that skeleton, if you like. It wasn't Sir George Fleet."

Jenny's eyes opened. "Who on earth ever said it was?"

"Still, miss, one or two people seem to have got the idea." His eye swung towards Martin. "What about you, sir?"

"It did occur to me, yes. But not very seriously."

"Oh, ah. And that's right. Yesterday evening at the police-station, we got a message from London. From a supply-firm that keeps records as far back as the Flood, it'ud seem. Dr. Pierre Laurier, the old one who's dead, bought the skeleton as an anatomical specimen in 1912.

"Also last night, before he went to join you on the (hurrum!)

ghost-hunt, Sir Henry and I talked with 'young' Dr. Hugh
Laurier, who's forty-eight years old. Lives just outside the
town-limits of Brayle."

"This was after the Ben-Hur chariot-race, I gather?" Martin
asked.

Masters frowned at him slightly, and addressed Jenny.

"Dr. Hugh, miss, told us all about it. When it became
(hurrum!)—well, what you might call not fashionable to have
skeletons hanging about in doctors' offices, his father put it
away in a cupboard. It wasn't till shortly before his death in
1936, when he was old and maybe a bit fanciful, that this
Pierre Laurier . . . was he French, miss?"

"Yes. His name was formerly De Laurier. That means,"
Jenny spoke wearily, "he was a nobleman, and Grandmother
simply— Never mind. And the Fleets! He was supposed to
have a hopeless passion for Aunt Cicely."

Masters made a broad wave of the hand.

"Anyway, miss, the old doctor with the beard took this
skeleton, and put it in a clock after he'd taken the works out,
and stuck it up in his back parlour as a kind of . . . kind of . . ."

"*Memento mori?*" suggested Martin.

Masters considered this.

"Oh, ah. Just so. If that means what I think it does. Like the
people who put up sun-dials with a motto, '*It is later than you
think.*'"

'It is later than you think.' Yes, Martin had heard that
before. When Masters leaned towards Jenny, his head
suddenly emerged out of a mist-wreath like a fatherly Spanish
Inquisitor.

"Now come, miss!" he urged persuasively. "That's the living
truth. And there's no harm in anything; I'll take my oath to it.
Why does her ladyship, your good grandmother, want to cause
a lot of unnecessary fuss and bother? Just why does she want
the thing anyway? Eh?"

"If it comes to that," said Martin, instantly putting a guard
between Jenny and Masters, "why do you want it yourself?"

"Ah! I'm afraid that'd be Official Secrets, sir."

"But there was nothing secret about why Lady Brayle
wanted it: as a present for Dr. Hugh Laurier. She was bidding
for it at Willaby's, until H.M. topped her. Afterwards he gave
it to her. That's all."

"Is it, now?" Masters asked affably. "Then why did she take
the skeleton alone? And not the clock?"

Too late Martin saw the flaw in his argument. But Masters
dismissed the matter.

"What I really wanted to say," he declared, this also being a lie, "was I've got lost in this ruddy mist. How can I get back to the Dragon?"

"This is a landmark," Jenny assured him, putting her hand on the fence. "Follow this, no matter how far it seems to go, and you'll come to the main road. Then turn right and follow the main road. You can't miss it."

"Well, now, miss, I'm much obliged!" Masters' fatherly heartiness was overpowering. "The fence, eh? Not a country-man myself." His look at Martin was almost a sardonic wink. "Good day to you!" He followed the line of the fence a few feet; then turned round.

"By the way, Mr. Drake. Have you got the time?"

"It's getting on towards five."

"Ah!" Masters shook his head regretfully. "Pity! Bit too early to wake up Dr. Laurier. I wanted to know whether that blood on the dagger is human blood."

"What blood?" cried Jenny.

But Masters, at the deliberate walk he had never lost since he was a policeman on a beat, had disappeared into the mist. Jenny's eyes asked Martin the same question.

"It's a joke," he growled. Like other things, he had forced the matter of that dagger out of his consciousness; shut the lid on it. "Just some horseplay at the prison. That fellow," he snarled, "was only trying to scare you when he didn't know a thing. Let's forget it."

They climbed the fence, navigated several ditches, and walked for some time in silence when his words seemed to ring with vibrations in Jenny's voice.

"You're quite right," she said. "Let's forget it! Today is— Sunday, isn't it? Let's forget it! Let's enjoy ourselves!"

"And tomorrow," said Martin, "you go to London with me. You must have *some* friends who aren't under the eye and grip of Grandma, and you can stay with them. We can get a special license soon, if you don't mind being married in a registry office. Will you do that?"

"Of course," Jenny said simply "Anywhere, any time. I *did* think it would be better to get Grandmother's approval, because she says she's beginning to like you; but—"

Martin stopped short.

"Listen, Jenny angel." He touched her moist cheek, and looked down at the eager blue eyes. "It's a good thing I'm reasonably honest. Anybody you like seems able to deceive you. I can no more imagine your 'good grandmother' giving us her approval than I can imagine her canoodling with Sir Henry Merrivale."

He felt a compression in the chest; such an immensity of tenderness that he could not have expressed it.

"It'll be all right, you know," he said. "You needn't worry. I'm not exactly broke, and . . . damn it, come on! We're nearly home!"

For the white, square solidness of Fleet House loomed up ahead in a mist-rift, seen partly from the north side and partly from the back. They were nearly on the edge of a flowergarden, whose paths they managed with care, until they emerged across a clipped lawn at the back of the house. To Martin Drake, this morning, Fleet House had no forbidding quality at all.

"I suppose," Jenny said, in a voice which asked to have the supposition denied, "you'll want to sleep for hours and hours?"

"Sleep? Sleep!" He chortled from deep springs of happiness. "No, Jenny. What I want is a bath, a shave, and a change. But first I want quantities of very black, very strong tea."

"I'll make it for you."

Martin surveyed the back of the house. "But how do we get in?"

"Darling, nobody ever locks doors hereabouts. Anyone can walk in anywhere."

"But we'll wake the whole house up, won't we?"

"Wait; I've got it!" breathed Jenny. She pointed to a middle door hardly discernible through mist. "I'll go into the kitchen and make tea; Aunt Cicely won't mind. You go on up to the roof."

"The roof?"

"It will be above the mist, and clear air. We can do it without disturbing anybody, and we'll have the whole place to ourselves. I'll be up as soon as the kettle boils."

"That," declared Martin, "is one of the better ideas. But can't I help you?"

"*Please* let me do it myself," begged Jenny. Her look was irresistible . . . "If you knew how much I want to . . . to show . . . *Please* let me do it myself, and bring it up to you!"

"Yours to command, Jenny." It pleased him immensely. "Can I get up to the roof from here?"

Jenny indicated a small door at the north-west corner.

"The stairs," she said, "are enclosed. It's a kind of thin box. Do be careful, because they're nearly as steep as a carpeted ladder."

"I know. I've gone up there from another floor." He looked at the kitchen, and then at Jenny. "Ten minutes?"

"Less, if I can make it."

With even more acute exhilaration, Martin sauntered through mist-wreaths towards the door. It was set up well above ground-height, on five concrete steps. The stairs, if he remembered correctly, were very narrow; they turned back the other way at each landing, which had a window and a door. Though half expecting to find the door bolted, he discovered it was open. He had shut himself into the cramped stair-well, whose dingy carpet showed holes and whose window-light filtered through mist, when another door at his right hand opened.

Framed in the doorway, against the dim-lit background of the dining-room, stood Dr. Hugh Laurier.

From his hard white collar to his polished shoes, from the precision of the dark necktie to the pressing of the dark blue suit, Dr. Laurier was so immaculately groomed that Martin felt like a tramp dragged out of an areaway. On Dr. Laurier there might never have been a speck of dust in his life.

"Capta—I beg your pardon: Mr. Drake."

His voice had the pleasant, engaging professional level.

"Ordinarily," Dr. Laurier uttered a short laugh, "it would be hard to explain my presence at this hour. It would, indeed. But I was like the boy with the serial story. After going home, I returned here. I *had* to know what happened."

"You'll have to ask Stannard," replied Martin, feeling at his unshaven chin. "He'll be along in a moment."

"Mr. Stannard didn't come back with you?"

"No."

"Isn't that rather odd?"

"Nothing odd about it. I didn't feel like having company, that's all."

Martin started to take a step up, but the doctor detained him.

"Mr. Drake. One other matter. I could not—" Dr. Laurier emphasized the words more than italics can convey—"speak of this in the presence of others. I want to say a word or two; then ask you not to remember it."

"Of course."

Dr. Laurier peered behind him. In the dining-room, the tall curtains of heavy red velvet were still drawn closely. The light of a single small bulb in a wall lamp touched his grey hair, his pince-nez. Martin remembered him silhouetted against a different radiance.

"Mr. Drake. My slip with the rapier was honestly an accident."

"But, man! I never thought it was anything else!"

The other smiled whimsically.

"So many times," he said, "I have thrown myself under my opponent's guard. Or dropped sideways, on one knee, to cut with the double-edged blade!"

If this referred to the rules of fencing, it was weird talk. Dr. Laurier saw Martin's expression.

"In imagination," he explained dryly. "Are you well read in the history of small-arms?"

"I'm afraid not."

"There was the 'Fifty-fifty,' where you threw yourself in to catch his unedged blade in your left hand and kill him with the right. If your left hand in the least slipped, you were a dead man. There was the Spanish 'Low-High' with double-edgers: you parried a cut low to the right; you dropped on one knee to cut across the back of the knees above the ankles; then rose and thrust him through the side. There was the 'Vanity': a very narrow mirror set into the blade along its length. Only a thread of it, unperceived till play began; but it blinded him with its flash.

"There was the *botte de Jésuite*, mentioned in *Esmond*. It really existed, and was a perfectly fair device of swordsmanship, unlike the others; they were outlawed.—But I bore you," Dr. Laurier added evenly.

"Not a bit. But some other time . . ."

"I speak," said the doctor, "of what interests me privately. It is the hobby of a lonely man. Do you understand?"

"I do."

"Nor am I a good swordsman as yet. Who can be, with so little opportunity to practice? My father fought two duels."

Martin, who had been about to get away as politely as possible, felt the tangle of ugly incidents catch him again like a net of hooks.

"By the way," he said. "Chief Inspector Masters wants to see you."

Dr. Laurier looked frankly puzzled.

"Chief . . . ah, yes! He and some other man came to my home last night before I joined you here. They asked some questions, completely mysterious to me, about a clock formerly owned by my father."

"That's not on his mind now. He wants to know," Martin cleared his throat, "whether what we found on that dagger was human blood."

Dr. Laurier remained silent for a brief time.

"I regret to say," he answered, "that it was human blood."

Martin climbed the treacherous stairs. Would the lid bang on memory this time? Not quite, perhaps; but enough. Oh, to the devil with it anyway! In a very short time, any minute now, Jenny would be here. And he emerged on the roof.

Jenny was right. The roof-top lay just a few feet above the mist. In every direction it swam and hovered, so that only a few tree-tops showed green like islands. Far over across the way, the front of the Dragon's Rest lay submerged well above its gable-windows, the three gables rising to steep peaks with plaster faces and window-curtains drawn close.

The sky was clear and warm; no sun, but the hint of a sun. Dead stillness here, and it seemed as lonely as Pentecost.

As Martin took a few experimental steps to see how they sounded on concrete in this mist-world, the thought of Pentecost made him glance round.

Pentecost Prison—the observation occurred to him quite gravely—had not moved. Though it was a very long distance away, he could see the mist lapping nearly to the top of its circular wall. He could pick out no details, and wished he could.

By the way, oughtn't Stannard to be showing up soon? As Dr. Laurier had asked, where *was* Stannard?

Martin made a complete circuit of the roof, studying the short chimneys and the plentitude of garden furniture. A flick of disquiet touched him when he thought of Stannard. But the man had distinctly said he was all right; he must have lost his way in the mist.

Hold on! What's wrong with this roof-top?

Nothing *wrong*, exactly. Yet . . .

Martin was now standing towards the front, but turning slowly round to study it eastwards. There stood the orange-and-chromium chairs, settees, and tables, vivid against brownish concrete and a pale sky. When he had come up to the roof yesterday evening to see H.M. and Masters, he had taken no particular account of the furniture. Yet it seemed to him now that it was now arranged—especially the folding beach-chairs—in a different pattern.

Nonsense! The furniture didn't get up, sportively, and rearrange itself overnight. Such furniture, which suggested cocktail glasses and a portable gramophone, could hold no suggestion of the sinister. Then why was he having this damnable feeling of being watched?

Watched from where?

This was only reaction from last night. That exhilarated mood couldn't have lasted anyway. A number of people were peacefully sleeping underneath him.

"But I've seen the other kind of murderer too," he could remember Stannard saying, at a time which now seemed weeks instead of days ago. "That's why I don't scoff at spiritual evil."

Very well. Yet, whatever constitutes spiritual evil, it is confined to the dark and the unseen way. It has no strength, it is even ludicrous, in the calm early hours of a Sunday morning, on a commonplace roof-top where the furniture suggests a place for a party.

Martin strolled towards the northern side—careful of that ledge, now!—near the front. Again he looked towards Pentecost Prison, wondering about Stannard. As he did so, two sentences went through his head.

"*I regret to say that it is human blood.*"

And, recurring from another time, another he had remembered before:

"*If you should hear the alarm-bell in the night, it will mean we are in serious trouble.*"

He would like to see that alarm-bell. It would show the exact position of the condemned cell, where its rope hung. But, at such a distance, this was impossible. Idly he had noticed beside him a square table with a glassy-looking orange top. It might do for the tea-tray when Jenny arrived. On the table, he now suddenly observed, lay a pair of field-glasses.

Martin laughed aloud. This was like making a wish and having it answered by a flick of the lamp. They were very old glasses of antiquated pattern: the leather scuffed and peeling, the leather strap worn thin. But they might, as a matter of curiosity, find the bell on top of the prison. He picked up the field-glasses.

"Jenny, where's that tea?" he called aloud.

Easy! Mustn't go bawling 'where's that tea' when people are trying to sleep on a lethargic morning with all the windows open. He had said it only because again he felt that someone, with steady and shining eyes, was watching him. Never mind! He turned back to the field-glasses.

It is later than you think.

What made him hesitate, and inspect the glasses more closely, was not the motto on the sundial. It was an idea. He was not well posted on the facts of the Fleet case; H.M. and Masters had said little or nothing. But he did know, from two persons' accounts, that Sir George Fleet had come up to the roof with a pair of field-glasses.

Martin's first idea, characteristically, was a recollection of that grisly ghost-story by M. R. James, in which such glasses contain a fluid brewed from dead men's bones. Then, with a hot-and-cold sensation, he wondered if he might have solved the Fleet mystery while still knowing only a part of the facts.

You could, they said, play strange tricks with optical illusions.

As for the technical side—curse the technical side: he had no knowledge—that could only be guesswork.

"But suppose," Martin said aloud to the mist-world about him, "there's something wrong with the lenses that make distances wrong. He walks towards the front of the roof. He thinks he's farther from that six-inch parapet than he really is. He comes nearly to the edge, starts to take another step, stumbles as though he'd been pushed . . ."

It could be tried. Martin, facing towards Pentecost Prison and well back from the edge, lifted the field-glasses to his eyes. The lenses were polished, in focus for about a hundred yards, and very clear. Yet such is the power of suggestion, in such fashion can it poison, that he could not keep the glasses at his eyes for more than a brief look. He rattled them down on the glassy-looking table.

This infuriated him. Were those glasses left here, so very obviously, either to entrap or hoax him? Nonsense; it was all nerves.

Very deliberately, to show himself it was so, he turned round. He sauntered to the front of the roof at the middle, and stood just inside the little ledge. Deliberately he looked out over a countryside submerged in mist: left, right, and across to the gables of the Dragon's Rest.

Then two things happened.

A distant sound—on its first tremor faint and creaky, but gathering volume, gathering voice—shook out with a creak-and-clang, creak-and-clang, metallic bell-notes banging across a hush of morning, clang-and-call, clang-and-call, so that Martin stood rigid with realization of what it was. The alarm-bell at Pentecost was ringing.

He did not turn round. He had not time to turn round.

A pair of human hands, just behind him, lunged out and gave him a violent shove in the middle of the back.

Martin had just that flash-hundredth of a second, with the bell-note in his ears, to understand he had been pitched forward—head foremost, but a little sideways—pitched forward over the ledge into a sea of mist. After that he felt no pain; he felt nothing at all.

Chapter 13

From the right came a faint, steady ticking, just outside the circle of a shaded light. The ticking grew stronger (it was a watch on a table) just as did reality. Consciousness looked out through almost-closed eyelids.

The first thoughts of Martin Drake were those which he had once or twice entertained during war-time. They were as follows:

Well, here I am again. What the hell's happened *now?* Pause for long reflection. Either this is damn serious or it's not serious at all, because I don't feel much. Ah, clever idea. I'm not flat on my back; I'm propped up somehow.

Still with his eyelids open only a slit, Martin sent tentative movements through his body. He felt stiff and shaken, but he wasn't bound up in anything. His right shoulder and a part of the chest pained, but his exploring left hand found no splint or bandage. He had a slight headache; yes, but only what felt like a smallish, narrow, oblong bandage.

Whereupon memory returned like an electric shock.

This wasn't war-time. He had been jabbed in the back by somebody's hands; he had taken a half-turning dive over the ledge into mist, with a bell-note in his ears and panic in his vitals. Sheer incredulity at the fact of being alive shook him fully alert; and he looked round wildly.

At his bedside, to the right, was a large face, squarish and wrinkled, with an acquiline nose and a steady grey eye.

"Captain Drake," said the Dowager Countess of Brayle.

Martin shut his eyes, and opened them again.

(And upon thy dazzling face, O madonna, I must first rest my eyes after being picked up off the flagstones and somehow pieced together. It couldn't be Jenny. It couldn't even be a good-looking nurse. It had to be You).

"Captain Drake," pursued Lady Brayle, "I will tell you very briefly what you wish to know. First: you are in the bedroom of the late Sir George Fleet. Second: the time is nearly ten o'clock on Sunday night. Third: Dr. Laurier has had to put five stitches across your forehead. Aside from this and some bad bruises, you have suffered no hurt."

Martin, propped up on both elbows, was staring at her incredulously.

"No—hurt," repeated Lady Brayle, with measured emphasis. "Dr. Laurier has kept you under opiates all day, in case there were effects of shock. *I* thought it unnecessary; and indeed," she glanced at him, "that appears to be the case."

Martin leaned back on his pillow, head aching, to consider this. Then he pushed himself up again.

"Let's get this straight," he begged. "I fell off a forty-odd-foot roof on to flagstones? And all I've got are some bruises and five stitches in my head? How did *that* happen?"

"You owe your life to Providence. Remember that, Captain Drake, in your prayers tonight."

"Yes, but how did Providence operate?"

Lady Brayle's lips tightened.

"Also," she said, and looked away, "to an accident. I believe your acquaintance, the unspeakable Merrivale, was somehow concerned in it."

"Old H.M.? What did he do?"

"You may or may not have observed," said Lady Brayle, "that outside this house, some distance above the front door, there is a very large awning coloured orange. This is usually kept folded up on an iron frame."

"Wow!"

"I beg your pardon?"

Only too well Martin remembered that orange-coloured awning; and, yesterday, H.M. standing in the middle of the gravel path, his fists on his hips and an expression of malevolence on his face, looking up at the awning above Martin's and Ruth Callice's heads.

"As for Henry," continued Lady Brayle, now with a handkerchief at her lips, "I sometimes think, you know, he must be feeble-minded. According to the maid Phyllis he actually gave money to the gardener—"

"I know! I was there when Phyllis said so!"

"Ah, but for what purpose? The gardener was to go out in the middle of the night—the middle of the night, if you please!—and lower the awning so as to shade the terrace!"

"By such acts of stupidity," said Lady Brayle, her voice rising strongly, "does good come about in this world. When you fell, I am informed, the loose canvas of the awning broke your fall like a firemen's whatever-the-term-is. Then the awning ripped, and let you slide through. You have had a most extraordinary escape, Captain Drake."

"The Old Maestro!" Martin said softly.

"I'm afraid I don't understand," said Lady Brayle.

On the bedside table there were cigarettes and his lighter. Martin, in the act of stretching out a painful right arm for them, stopped and looked at her. His glance said, 'Whatever is going on in that twisty brain of his, he saved my life and you know it.' Lady Brayle's lofty stare replied: 'Kindly refrain from mentioning objectionable subjects.'

This duel of glances became, as it were, so silently audible that anger gathered round Lady Brayle's mouth. Martin's stare did not fall. Instead Lady Brayle rose up from her chair, shaking shoulders which appeared massive in heavy tweed, and paced up and down the room.

"It may be conceded," said Lady Brayle, "that Henry sometimes possesses the vulgar cunning to outwit criminals."

"Thank you."

"But he is despicable," said Lady Brayle, breathing hard.

"I hadn't observed it."

"Constantly he consorts with low company. Never once does it enter his head—" this was the real grievance—"that their station is in any way inferior to his. His childish vanity, which makes him seriously imagine he is a model of deportment like Lord Chesterfield, is infuriating. On his vile tempers and obscene language I need not dwell. Even now, I believe, he is downstairs explaining to poor Cicely how he was once a Cavalier poet."

"Lady Brayle," Martin interrupted, "where's Jenny?"

Lady Brayle flowed into this without even seeming to notice the change of subject.

"Jennifer," she corrected him, "has gone home. On my specific order. Her behaviour here today was unladylike and even disgusting. No less than twenty times, by my own counting, Dr. Laurier had to assure her you were not at death's door. The speech she addressed to you—well, I make no comment."

This bedroom, uncompromisingly masculine, was a large square room with striped wall-paper and heavy oak furniture, dimly lighted by the bedside lamp. Lady Brayle stopped short in her pacing and loomed over the bed.

"Captain Drake," she began formally.

There was something strange in her tone. Martin, in the act of lighting a cigarette, blew out the lighter-flame.

"Yes?"

Lady Brayle seemed to be pushing, pushing hard against some door inside herself, to struggle out. It was a difficult business.

"I sat here tonight," again she pushed at the door, "for one specific purpose. I wished to say—" She stopped. "From what I had heard of your behaviour from certain sources, I was beginning to believe you possessed the qualities (and also the imperfections, which are just as necessary) of a gentleman."

There was a pause.

At this point (perhaps) Martin might have ended the feud. But he didn't trust the old girl an inch, not one inch. And his face showed it.

"Thank you," he said gravely. "You sat here tonight to tell me that?"

"Yes, yes, of course!" retorted his companion, with rather too much haste, "What other reason could there have been?"

"I can't say."

"But I no longer," snapped Lady Brayle, "think my belief to have been a true one." Her voice became colourless. "It remains only for me to give you your orders. On the table beside you you will find a yellow pill. Take that, with water from the glass, and lie back. Tomorrow you will be perfectly fit."

Martin, putting down cigarette and lighter, instantly threw back the bed-clothes and slid his legs out of bed. He was wearing his own pyjamas, and his slippers were beside the bed.

"If you don't mind, Lady Brayle," he suggested pointedly, "I'd like to get dressed. —You've guessed, of course, that Jenny and I are to be married."

"That, Captain Drake, can await discussion later."

"Can I reach you tomorrow morning?"

"Fortunately or unfortunately," replied Lady Brayle, taking up a handbag from the chest of drawers, "no. I am driving tonight to visit some friends at Priory Hill, and I shall not return until the afternoon. Then there will be the fair."

"The fair?"

"Has Jennifer told you nothing of the fair?"

Martin drew his hand down over his face. "She did say something . . ."

"Among my records," Lady Brayle informed him triumphantly, "there is a document, dated 1662. By permission of the King, an annual fair may be held within the park of Brayle Manor. The town-council," she shook her shoulders, "have opposed this project. I have informed them that I will sue them for five thousand pounds if one of their representatives sets foot inside the park.

"Cromwell, by which I mean the vile Oliver, sought to suppress these fine old wholesome English customs. Doubtless there will be grinning-matches through horse-collars, and quarterstaff bouts; perhaps even a Maypole."

Lady Brayle, having reached the door, spoke as though she were addressing a public meeting. Then her face seemed to close up; to retreat.

"Now," she said, "you must excuse me. My friends at Priory Hill wish to hear the details of a—of a most unpleasant affair at Pentecost Prison this morning."

"The bell!" exclaimed Martin.

Until this moment, his own grace-of-God escape from death had swept away everything else.

"The alarm-bell," he said, "was ringing from Pentecost. The alarm-bell from the condemned cell. Stannard . . . What happened there?"

Lady Brayle regarded him coolly.

"You have had your orders," she informed him. "You must not excite yourself." And she went out and closed the door.

Martin stumbled over his slippers when he sprang forward. Then he stopped and put them on. Pain knifed across his forehead, the effect of opiates still lingered, and (to tell the truth) not many of his joints seemed to work well. But he had his wits with him.

Thank the Lord he had brought that suitcase across from the inn last night. Across the room stood a gigantic wardrobe, with a long mirror. As he reached out to open the door of the wardrobe, he saw his own face.

Wow! Though the bandage was small enough, he had not counted on the swelling and discolouration of the forehead, which made him resemble someone out of a horror-film. Never mind appearances; and somebody had given him a shave. Inside the wardrobe were clothes: clean, fresh clothes.

When Lady Brayle opened the door, it had disclosed a modern bathroom. Martin brushed his teeth, doused and doused his face and head in water, and felt better. Physically, that is. While he dressed, automatically putting on his wrist-watch, the full implications of this business spread through his mind.

Whatever had happened to Sir George Fleet, his own fall had been no accident. Some person, man or woman, had lunged with a solid pair of hands and sent him over the edge to crush his skull on flagstones. Someone hated him that much.

Why, for God's sake? And who?

It was nonsense. It couldn't be anybody he had met hereabouts. In imagination, their faces all smiled at him. And yet Stannard's 'spiritual evil,' his 'man-eating tiger' of fancy, might be close. What made Martin Drake shiver was not so much the attempted murder as the consciousness of all that hatred directed against himself.

H.M. had somehow foreseen this. He must get to H.M. And the old man, Lady Brayle had said, was downstairs now.

Trying to find the position of his own bedroom, Martin threw open the window-curtains on windows wide up in the breath of a perfect summer night deepening from dimness into dark. Sunday would be early closing for the Dragon; across the road he could see the last customers being turned out against a background of lighted door and small-paned lighted windows.

His bedroom was at the north-east corner front. Hence—

Martin went through the bathroom, obviously an addition making two rooms smaller. The room beyond was dark. Groping across it, he felt his knees begin to shake and the sensation that someone was following, just behind, to push him over an edge.

"Steady!" Martin said. But you can't argue with feelings like that.

Groping wildly, he bumped into a desk and after a moment found the chain of a desk-lamp. When the light sprang up, healing to nerves, he sat back heavily in the desk's swivel-chair.

And Martin waited to get his breath back.

He was in Sir George Fleet's study, no doubt of it. That was where Stannard had sat with his host before Fleet hurried up to the roof, just as Martin had heard Stannard speak of it.

Along the west wall were the gun-racks, behind folding glass doors. A ledge of silver cups, kept bright, ran round the other walls. Cricket-bats, once the whitest of white ash and now brown-grey from use and age, were inscribed in red with the dates when George Fleet had made a century. Between the windows, where the desk stood sideways, hung a picture of a man who must be Fleet himself. Aunt Cicely—old ghosts, old and deep loves;—must have put it there.

Stern kind of bloke, Martin thought. Thin military-looking face, ridged hair parted in the middle, cropped moustache. Then Martin glanced down at the desk-blotter, and in a few seconds began to grin.

It was only a grey-covered book, open and face down. But its title, which was *The Cavaliers, 1625-1649,* made it seem an odd book for this particular room. Martin turned it over and glanced at the flyleaf. He was greeted by the following formidable and menacing announcement of ownership, done in red crayon:

ME—H.M.

The old maestro himself seemed to scowl out of that flyleaf, warning with ferocity an attempted book-pincher to keep away. Martin's grin became a laugh, and he got up. It was infernal nonsense, letting these bugbears weaken his knees and letting him grow soft. Noting the position of the door, he switched off the lamp and walked slowly to the door.

The upper hall outside was luxuriously furnished and softly lighted. At the rear was the staircase, beside its tall arched window. He went downstairs without a tremor, walked to the front of the lower hall with its polished hardwood floor; and hesitated. But he did not hesitate long.

Green Room and library, which were on the right as you faced the front door from inside, showed no light. But a faint glow filtered out from the left-hand door at the front.

Also, Martin heard a familiar voice.

"Honest-Injun," the voice rumbled with a faint note of surprise, "you'd like to hear all about it?"

"I'd love to," said the attractive and still-young voice of Aunt Cicely.

"You want to know what Charles the First said about me?"

"I do, really."

"Ahem!" said the other voice, beginning to take on a stern, stuffed air.

Martin peered round the edge of the door.

In a drawing-room rich with the luxury of twenty years ago, Aunt Cicely was sitting at one side of the tall mantelpiece just opposite. In her upraised face there was no trace of amusement; she was, Martin saw, deeply fascinated. At the other side of the mantelpiece, his back to it, Sir Henry Merrivale stood swelling with the same stuffed, heroic look.

The muffled lamps, dull red or white, struck gleams from a wine-coloured carpet. It was a setting for romance.

"This here," said H.M., whipping out a pocket-book and extracting a typewritten slip, "is a quotation from the *Dictionary of National Biography*, edition of 1889. It ain't there now, because a lot of people have got born since and they don't pay any attention to the arts. But here's just what it says.

" '*Merrivale, Sir Curtius, first baronet. (1583-1645?). Knighted by James I., created baronet Charles I. Poet, duellist, and lover of fair women.*' "

Here H.M. gave a short cough, and glanced sideways behind his spectacles.

" '*He is best known for his lyric poetry, later collected by Anthony a Wood. Many present-day critics, including Mr. Andrew Lang, consider his best work—notably the lyric called,* "Come rest in this bower, my honey-haired bride,"—*to be the equal of Herrick.'* How's that, hey?"

"It's lovely!" said Aunt Cicely, her eyes far away. " 'Come rest in this bower, my honey-haired bride.' Could you recite it?"

H.M. touched his neck and made a long challenging noise.

"You got a throat-spray?" he inquired.

"Really, I . . ." Aunt Cicely looked round vaguely. "I'm afraid . . ."

"Never mind," H.M. consoled her. "We'll come back to that. Lord love a duck, I'll give it all the organ-stops I had when I played Richard the Third for Henry Irving. You just lemme go on with this."

"Of course, Sir Henry."

" *'Charles the First'*—are you gettin' this, hey?—*'Charles the first is said to have remarked of him: "No man of fairer manners was ever about us." His tragic marriage to Lucy Baimbridge, and the duel that followed, are well known. In the middle years of his life there is a long gap, which Anthony à Wood was evidently unable to trace."*

"A gap in his life?" exclaimed Aunt Cicely. "What tragic fate was it?"

"Well," said H.M., "they stuck him in the coop."

"I . . . I beg your pardon?"

"Into the 'foul, heynouse' jail of Newgate they stuck him," roared H.M., beginning to fire up. "Three times they did. It was a put-up job, of course. The Cecils did it."

"You mean they persecuted him?"

"Oh, my wench!" said H.M., momentarily forgetting the heroic atmosphere and shaking his head dismally. "It was the scummiest piece of work in history, and I'm goin' to write a monograph to prove it.

"Looky here!" he went on with inspiration. "You just imagine him (or, as it might be, me) standing up at the Old Bailey to face his accusers the first time. You imagine him (or, as it might be, me) in a big lace collar, with his Cavalier hair down to his shoulders, lookin' up at the bench like this."

Here H.M., with his arms hooked out at his sides, squared off and directed a glare of martyrdom about half way up the opposite wall.

"The place," he added, suddenly turning round to explain in a normal voice, "was as full of Cecils as the Café Royal is of drunks on Saturday night. Got that?"

"Yes, I follow you! But . . ."

"But Curtius Merrivale (or, as it might be, me) folded his

arms, like this. And he looked up at the judge. And: 'Me lord,' he says, 'this is a frame-up.' 'Have no fear, Sir Curtius,' says the judge, who was an honest man; 'for well I know,' he says, 'that there is hokey-pokey goin' on in this court.'"

"Stop it!" cried Aunt Cicely.

"Hey?"

"You're joking. You're teasing me! I don't like it."

H.M. was completely taken aback with amazement.

"Honest to God!" he said in purple-faced earnest, and lifted his right hand to take the oath.

"But they didn't say it in those words, surely?"

"Well . . . now! I was only giving you the gist of it, sort of. The original's in a manuscript I got at home."

"But you make it sound so terribly *unromantic!*"

H.M. considered this. "H'm, yes. Maybe I did make it a bit on the dry and legal side, at that."

Aunt Cicely leaned her head sideways against a wing of the chair. The dim lamp-light, in that corner dark red, made her blonde good-looks seem those of thirty instead of over fifty. One frail-looking hand trailed down over the arm of the chair.

"I've always half-believed in reincarnation," Aunt Cicely murmured. " 'His tragic marriage to Lucy Baimbridge, and the duel that followed,' she quoted softly, from H.M.'s slip of paper. "Was she beautiful?"

"Uh-huh. Absolute stunner. I got her portrait at Cranleigh Court."

"My own marriage," continued Aunt Cicely in the same faraway tone, "was very happy. The world didn't understand George. He was dominant; I love dominance. Of course, with George, there was always the terrible responsibility of . . ."

"Aunt Cicely, seeming to wake up, paused. Only now did you notice that she wore rather heavy make-up, because of the pallor underneath. A bright, arch animation swept round her an aura of charm; and she almost bounced in the chair, hands clasped, to pour eager questions at H.M.

"You were saying, ma'am?" asked H.M., in a sharply different tone of voice.

It was here that Aunt Cicely caught sight of Martin in the doorway. She sprang up in consternation and solicitude; and, as he advanced in what seemed to him a steady manner, she extended both hands with their flowing sleeves.

"Mr. Drake!" she exclaimed. "You shouldn't have got up!"

Martin touched the cool fingertips.

"There's nothing wrong with me, Lady Fleet," he told her. "It was very kind of you to take such trouble." Then he turned to H.M., the rush of gratitude showing in his face. "Sir," he said, "I don't know how I'm going to thank . . ."

H.M., to conceal an exploding embarrassment which he would have denied under torture, raved and bellowed and shouted at him (for getting up) to such an extent that nobody could understand what the great man was saying. But Martin cut it short.

"H.M., how did you know someone might try to—to—" he hesitated.

"To push you off the roof?" H.M. supplied.

"To . . . *what?*" cried Aunt Cicely in horror.

H.M., his expression wooden, replied only by extending his own hands and making a lunging motion.

"But it was an accident," pleaded Aunt Cicely, retreating. Her eyes and mouth begged them to reassure her. "Sophia said so. Dr. Laurier said so. I've always thought something might happen when the young people used that roof for parties, with drinks and everything. But they get older, you know, and you simply can't do anything with them."

Her voice ran on, telling them Sophia said it only went to show, but Martin was not listening.

"H.M.," he insisted, "how did you know?"

H.M. looked uncomfortable.

"Oh, my son! I didn't know! It was only one of about eight possibilities, where I had to block the approach-shot somehow. Though, mind you, I thought it was the most probable."

Where I had to block the approach-shot somehow . . .

"Very early this morning," said Martin, clearing his throat, "Jenny and I met Masters in a field near here. I asked him if he'd been at the prison during the night. Was he by any chance keeping an eye on *my*—welfare?"

"That's right, son. All night."

"Are you trying to tell me—" the words sounded wild, but Martin could not help using them—"that I've been a kind of focus for murder?"

"Uh-huh."

"But that's impossible!"

"Son," returned H.M., without any swelling of dignity, "I'm the old man. I've got to believe," scowling ferociously, he rapped his knuckles against his bald head, "what this cokernut tells me is true. Even when Masters thought I was loopy and you won't believe it even now. I couldn't tell *you*, because— well, never mind the because. You were in a sweet whistlin' ring of danger. And you still are." H.M.'s tone changed. "Did you see who shoved you off that roof?"

"No."

"Got any idea who it was?"

"No. What's more, I'll swear my side of the roof was empty!"

Then Martin flung this aside.

"Never mind the roof," he said. "What about the alarm-bell? I heard it ring as I went over. What happened?"

"Lord love a duck, didn't old Sophie tell you?"

"No! Either she was cantankerous, or she thought it wouldn't be a good thing to tell me. Is Stannard all right? I'll never forgive myself if anything happened to Stannard. Where's Stannard?"

"Stannard?" echoed H.M., in a huge puff of astonishment. "Oh, my son! Stannard's as right as right as rain. Though," H.M. added in a curious tone, "he did get a bit of a shock. Something like you, only in a different way."

"Then if he . . . what did happen?"

H.M. looked at the wine-coloured carpet; teetered bulkily back and forth on his heels; hesitated, as though he could not quite place what he meant to say in the scheme of things; and looked up again.

"Murder," he answered.

And, at the same moment, the front door knocker began to rap sharply.

Chapter 14

To the sleek room, in tone dull-red and white and dark gold, these dim lamps lent at once an intimacy and a kind of religious hush. In a far corner stood a grand piano, with Sir George Fleet's framed photograph on its dull-gleaming top.

The questions which rushed from Martin—"Who was murdered? Where in the prison? When?"—were shushed by a particularly meaning look from H.M. Martin sank down into a deep sofa, feeling the pain-throbs above his eyes. All of them heard the nonchalant maid, Phyllis, saunter through the hall to open the front door.

"It's the cops again, m'lady," rose the bored voice of Phyllis from outside.

The cops, on this occasion, were represented only by Chief

Inspector Masters. Masters, holding a brown cardboard file in his left hand as well as the brief-case in his right, coughed with discomfort at the door of the drawing-room. His bowler hat was held under his arm.

Aunt Cicely responded automatically. Though clearly still frightened and shocked, it was apparent she had resigned herself to the belief that somebody, somehow, would take care of this matter. In white, with flowing sleeves, vivid against a Burgundy carpet, she turned to the newcomer.

"Mr. Masters! It was *so* kind of you to come!"

"Well, ah—" said Masters, completely off balance by this reception of a police officer, "I'm not here on official business, as you might say. I just wanted to pick up Sir Henry."

"*Do* please make yourselves at home!" urged Aunt Cicely, with such sincerity that even Masters believed it. "I shall have to run along to bed now, but do make yourselves comfortable. Have you got the Ovaltine, Phyllis? That's a good girl! And I must have someone to talk to before I . . . Phyllis! Where is Lady Brayle?"

"Gone home, m'lady. Long ago."

Aunt Cicely fretted. "Then I wonder . . . Mr. Masters! Is Ricky over at the Dragon?"

"Not there now, Lady Fleet. It's been closed for half an hour."

"Then I suppose," Aunt Cicely said, "he must be with Susan Harwood." And she gave a bright, inquiring smile at Martin Drake.

(Careful, now! But you don't know anything about Susan except that Ricky wants to marry her and Ruth says he's deeply enamoured, so you're safe in admitting ignorance. Besides, the maddening questions . . .)

"Susan is a dear girl," said Aunt Cicely. "But, of course—!" She laughed deprecatingly. "I mean; her father being a farmer. Not serious; and what matter? No woman can resist Ricky. I've always told him so. And I must confess," her attractive laughter rang again, "I've always been rather proud of it. It seems to reflect credit on me, somehow. What was I thinking of? Oh, yes! Retiring. Of course. Will you say good-night for me to everyone?"

Radiating charm with her smile, giving a whisk of the loose sleeve, Aunt Cicely left them.

It was just as well, Martin thought, that a harmless if somewhat feather-headed siren had gone. The tension which invaded that room, when H.M. and Masters faced each other, set his nerves tingling again.

"Got the stuff?" demanded H.M.

"All of it," Masters growled. "I'm fair sick of interviews, and that's a fact." He dropped hat, brief-case, and cardboard file into a chair.

Murder.

Thanking Grandmother's Providence first of all, Martin's thoughts raced on, the person killed couldn't have been Jenny. Jenny had been here today, hovering over him, her behaviour being 'unladylike and disgusting.' Lady Brayle and Aunt Cicely were both very much alive. So was Dr. Laurier, whom he had met here in this house early in the morning.

(In front of him, like mumbled voices heard in a crowded room, he was conscious of H.M. and the Chief Inspector talking away. Masters was pointing at Martin, and asking questions about the fall off the roof. H.M. was growling that the victim seemed to have no evidence; and up went Master's blood-pressure again. But little of this penetrated to Martin.)

The person killed, he was thinking, couldn't have been Stannard either. Stannard was as right as rain. Now he knew it couldn't have been Ricky, because Ricky's mother had just asked whether her son was at the pub. That left only . . .

"Look here!" Martin exclaimed, and jumped up. "Was it Ruth Callice?"

Both the others—Masters with his face red instead of ruddy, H.M. taking out a cigar—swung round.

"Burn it all, son, don't start shoutin' like that," complained the latter, making fussed gestures. "Was she what?"

Martin felt a hollow of dread, with a pulse to it, inside his chest.

"Was she the victim? Did somebody kill Ruth?"

Yes, his voice had been loud. In the north wall of the room towards the west, a door opened. It opened to show a glimpse of a billiard-room, corresponding with the library on the other side of the house.

Ruth Callice came out of the billard-room, and John Stannard after her. They were noticed neither by H.M. nor by Masters. But Martin saw them, and slowly sat down again.

"Listen," said H.M., standing in front of Martin. "The victim hasn't got anything to do with you; and I'm trying to drive it through Masters's head that the victim hasn't got anything directly to do with the case either."

"Ho," said Masters, and snorted like a bull. "A murder slap-bang in our laps, and it hasn't got anything to do with the case."

"Regardin' motive," H.M. insisted over his shoulder, "no."

He turned back to Martin. "You put up at the pub, didn't you? Didn't you meet the Puckstons?"

"Puckstons? That's the—?"

"Yes. Father, mother, and daughter."

"I met Puckston, yes, and I think I saw his wife. I don't remember any daughter."

"Enid Puckston," said H.M. His expression was not pleasant. "Only a kid . . ."

"Oh, ah," muttered the Chief Inspector. "Only a kid. Like the one twenty-two years ago."

"She was the pride and joy," said H.M., slowly and heavily, "of those people's hearts. Goin' to a fancy school, she was. Not harming anybody."

"Last night at Pentecost," Masters interrupted, "she was stabbed through the heart and (hurrum!) pretty badly mutilated. What's more, for a fair-to middling certainty, she was killed with that dagger your crowd found in the condemned cell."

For some time nobody spoke.

To Martin, Enid Puckston was only a name, not even a person to be visualized. Yet the ugliness and brutality struck through. At this point, too, he became aware that Masters was speaking not for information, but for effect; that the corner of Masters's eye had caught Ruth and Stannard over there by the billiard-room. Martin shook his head to clear it.

"Stabbed and mutilated," he repeated. Then he looked up. "Was she—?"

Masters now spoke almost blandly.

"No, sir. She wasn't violated, if that's what you mean. Or any attempt like it. Might have been anybody's crime. Might have been—" here Martin could have sworn the Chief Inspector was about to say 'man or woman,' but checked himself—"might have been anybody who'd got what they call a strong sadistic nature. With their flummy talk nowadays," he added.

"Where was she found?"

"Ah! As to that, now!"

Straightening up, with an air of surprise and grave welcome, Masters turned round in the direction of Ruth and Stannard.

"Evening, miss! Evening, sir!" he intoned, as though he had just seen them. "Didn't notice you in the dark. I'd be glad to have a bit of a chat with both of you, if it's convenient."

"Yes, of course," answered Ruth, whose eyes were fixed on Martin. Abruptly, as though breaking loose, she ran across the room and took Martin's hands.

"So you're up and about!" Ruth added, scanning his face
and forehead. She added, as though in reproach: "Martin, you
look *horrible*."

He grinned at her. "No worse than a hangover. Honestly!"

Stannard approached more slowly. H.M. had spoken of him
as having had a shock, and you could well believe it. Some of
his strong vitality—not too much, but some—seemed to have
ebbed from him. The black eyes had no glitter; he smiled,
though with visible effort. As he moved towards them he put
one hand on the back of a dark-red wing chair as though his
ankle hurt him.

What had he seen in that execution shed last night?

But, for that matter, Ruth herself looked far from well. She
was as trim as ever, the small light-brown curls gleaming above
the rounded face, her dress a close-clinging green. Yet she
looked physically ill. And Martin began to understand the
strain which had been growing on everybody all day.

The strain grew and grew. They seldom spoke of it. And yet
. . .

"Martin," Ruth began, and braced herself. "Some people are
saying what happened to you was an accident. It wasn't, was
it?"

"No. It wasn't."

Very much, now, he was conscious of H.M. and Masters in
the background.

"What did happen?" asked Ruth. Then, without waiting for
a reply, as though afraid of a reply she went on:

"All *I* know is that I was waked up about a quarter to five by
that alarm-bell going. Then I heard a crash—"

"Great Scott, Ruth, did I fall as hard as that?"

"It was the tea-tray!" said Ruth, and snatched her fingertips
away from him in a reproachful way as though he had
somehow insulted her.

"What tea-tray?"

"Jenny," Ruth explained, "was carrying a loaded tea-tray
through the dining-room to those little back stairs. She heard
you—she heard that thud on the awning, and the awning
ripping wide open, and something hitting the flagstones. And
would you believe it?"

Here Ruth turned to Stannard, who, though he must have
heard the story half a dozen times, only nodded.

"Would you believe it?" Ruth said to Martin. "Jenny says
the front door was partway open, with mist in the hall. Jenny
simply threw the whole tea-tray to one side and rushed out.
She found you lying on the terrace in the mist, with blood

coming out of your forehead. Then Jenny began screaming. By
that time I was there, and Ricky came flying downstairs in his
pyjamas. Poor Cicely was tired out and slept through it.
Fortunately Dr. Laurier was on the spot."

Stannard, smiling, had been examining the trim of his
fingernails and polishing them on the sleeve of his dark-grey
suit. He grew grave now. He approached Martin, limping a
little, and formally extended his hand.

"My dear fellow," he said in his husky hearty voice, "real
congratulations on a lucky escape."

Everybody I meet, Martin thought, seems to want to shake
hands.

"It *was* you ringing that alarm-bell?"

Stannard's look was wry. "Yes. For my sins."

Well, then, here was one hand free from attempted murder
and one face without hypocrisy. Martin already liked
Stannard; he liked the man better now.

"But," Ruth prompted. "Up on the roof?" She made a
tentative gesture.

Martin thought he had better get it over. He told them
everything, from the time he and Jenny walked through the
mist to the time somebody's hands lunged out. He could see
Master's black notebook, the shorthand travelling steadily.
H.M. had sat down near the tall white marble mantelpiece,
with its dull-gold clock and its dull-gold candelabra against
dark-red walls.

When the recital was finished, neither Ruth nor Stannard
commented. They did not even speak. Too much repression!
Dangerous! The person who did speak, after studying Martin,
was Chief Inspector Masters.

"Field-glasses, eh?" ruminated Masters. "A pair of old field-
glasses, on an orange-topped table near the north-west side of
the roof!"

"That's right."

"Would it interest you to know, sir, that other witnesses who
went up there later didn't see any field-glasses?"

"I can't help that. They were there earlier."

"I say, Masters." H.M. raised his head briefly. "Could they
'a' been the same glasses George Fleet used on the famous
day?"

Masters simmered. "For the *last* time, Sir Henry—"

"Will I stop babblin' about field-glasses, you mean? Oh,
Masters, I know there were no hokey-pokey spikes to stick him
in the eye! But I gather the field-glasses weren't busted; they

fell just wide of the terrace and on the grass. And that's why the policeman picked 'em up and carried 'em inside."

"Yes!"

H.M., an unlighted cigar in his fingers, craned round in his chair to blink at Martin.

"Now tell me, son," he said. "Supposing (just supposing!) these were the same glasses! Were they a good pair? Good lenses? Easy focus? No blurrin' that would . . ." He paused. "Were they?"

"As I told you," Martin returned, "I didn't look through them very long. But they were in first-rate condition. I'll swear to that."

"That's good news," breathed H.M. "Oh, my eye! That helps a lot."

Masters was unable to yank down his bowler hat on his head, since he was not wearing it, but his gesture conveyed this.

"The field-glasses," he said, with strong self-control, "were in A-1 order. They had nothing wrong with them. And *therefore* (eh?) they're a great big smacking-sure help to us?"

"That's right, Masters."

"Er—just so." Masters addressed himself to his notebook and to Martin. "Anything more you can tell us, Mr. Drake?"

"I don't think so." This atmosphere had become dangerously explosive, and Martin tried to lighten it. "I woke up with Lady Brayle sitting beside me. I annoyed her, and she annoyed me, so I decided to dress and come downstairs. In here I found H.M. telling Aunt—telling Lady Fleet about his previous existence as a Cavalier poet and duellist." He grinned. "By the way, sir, you ought to talk to Dr. Laurier."

"What's that, son? Hey?"

"Dr. Laurier. He's an authority on old-time fencing. He can tell you all about the 'Fifty-fifty' and the 'Low-High' and the 'Vanity' and everything else. Incidentally, he says his father fought two duels in France."

Masters barked him back to attention. But Masters himself had a grievance, and was annoyed enough to air it.

"A fat lot of good," he growled, "this gentleman Laurier did us last night!"

Martin, knowing a question would shut him up, said nothing.

"All *he* kept talking about," Masters growled, "was his father, with the big grey beard, when the gentleman was old and a bit scatty, sitting in a rocking-chair in front of that infernal skeleton-clock, rocking back and forth and muttering something in French that Sir Henry says means, 'Would a man of honour have done it?'

"Ah, but not done a murder," Masters added. "Because, according to the record, he was in this very room talking to the butler when Sir George Fleet pitched off the roof." Masters started, and woke up. "Hurrum! Sorry! Off the subject! Now, Mr. Drake! What I wanted to ask—"

But he never asked it.

Masters's gaze had strayed towards H.M.; and, after a pause, Masters's expression became that of one who sees a prayed-for portent in the sky.

H.M. had sat up straight. His mouth fell open, and the unlighted cigar dropped out and rolled on the carpet. His look was fixed straight ahead behind the big spectacles; his hands were on the arm of the chair, his elbows hooked as though to push himself up. His voice, astounded, started from deep in the cellar and was at the same level when it emerged.

"Wait a minute!" H.M. begged. "Lemme think! Stop babblin' and lemme think!"

Nobody spoke. Martin, Ruth, and Stannard exchanged inquiring glances; Masters remained very quiet indeed; and H.M. fiercely pressed his hands over his head.

"But that couldn't be," H.M. addressed the empty air. "It couldn't be, unless . . . yes, burn me there was!"

His hands dropped again to the arms of the chair. With some effort he propelled himself to his feet.

"I got to go and look at something," he explained, with an air of haste and absent-minded apology. "I've been an awful ass; but I got to go and look at something now. You stay here. You play bridge or something." And he lumbered across to the hall door, where he turned right towards the interior of the house.

"By George," breathed Masters, "the old bounder's got it!"

Martin stared after H.M. "Got what?"

"Never you mind that, sir," Masters said cheerfully. "We'll get back to business. Now, Mr. Stannard!"

"I beg your pardon?" Stannard was obviously surprised.

"I said a while ago," Masters told him smoothly, "that I'd like a word with you. If you don't mind, I'd like to take a statement from you as to what happened in the execution shed last night."

The other stood motionless, a vertical line between his black eyebrows.

"If memory serves, Inspector, I gave a statement to the police this morning."

"Yes, sir. But that was to Inspector Drake. County Constabulary."

"True. And what then?"

"The Chief Constable's Office—" Masters was suave—"have got in touch with our people in London. *I'm* in charge of the case, you see. Now, about that statement . . ."

Stannard pushed back his cuff and glanced at his wristwatch.

"It's rather late, Inspector."

"I'm afraid I've got to insist, Mr. Stannard."

Dead silence.

The light of battle sprang across that room as clearly as the opposing lamps had shone behind the fencers at Pentecost Prison last night. And Martin knew why.

Too often had John Stannard wiped the floor with the police, including Chief Inspectors of the C.I.D., in a battle of question-and-answer at the Central Criminal Court. Masters knew this; Stannard knew he knew it. They looked at each other.

Last night, Martin reflected, Stannard could have wiped the floor with Masters in such an engagement. But Stannard was shaky now; there was some horror inside him; his eyes were dull; his movements, perhaps mental as well as physical, seemed slow. Then he glanced towards Ruth Callice.

To Martin's astonishment, Ruth was looking at Stannard with an expression of . . . well, not nearly as strong as hero-worship; but something deeply moved and as near to love as made no difference. What had been happening during the past twenty-four hours? Ruth veiled her look instantly, slipping back into H.M.'s chair.

And Stannard smiled.

"I'm at your service, Inspector," he said. And vitality seemed to flow and expand through him.

He sat down at the other end of the sofa from Martin, crossed his knees, and took from his pocket a cigar in a cellophane wrapper.

"I'll make the statement," he went on, "mainly because," he looked sideways, "I think my friend Drake deserves to hear it."

"The trouble was," Martin blurted, "I thought I might have left you there helpless or dying or—God knows what."

"No. You played the game strictly according to the rules. Unfortunately, however . . ."

Sharply Masters cut across the amenities.

"You might begin," he said, "from the time Mr. Drake locked you up behind the iron door at just past midnight. Well?"

"To tell the truth," Stannard admitted, "I was not as easy in my mind as I led others to think. I have—some imagination too. But there it was: it had to be done, and more than done. So I opened the door of the execution shed." Again he looked at Martin. "You never saw it. Nor did any of the others. I'd better describe it. It was—"

"I don't want to hear any of that, sir," snapped Masters.

"Oh?" Stannard slowly turned his head back. "You 'don't want to hear any of that?'"

"No. Not by a jugful!"

"Thus," Stannard said evenly, "denying a witness his right to give testimony in his own way. The other name is coercion. May God help you if I ever quoted your words in court."

Sting went the mental whip across Masters's face. Masters, dogged and conscientious, was inwardly raving. But he remained impassive, with sheathed claws.

"Hurrum! My mistake. Go on!"

"It was a good-sized room," pursued Stannard, taking the cellophane wrapper off the cigar, "though with not a very high ceiling, as in the condemned cell. Its walls were brick painted white, pretty dirty, with two small barred windows near the top of the opposite side.

"I picked this up, detail by detail, with my light. In the centre of the floor, which was stone, I saw the gallows-trap: two big oblong wooden panels, fitting closely together and set flush with the floor-level. They would drop together when you pulled a lever. An iron beam stretched across the ceiling just over this trap. In the left-hand corner—concealed from a condemned man as he entered by the opening door—was a rather large vertical lever which controlled the drop.

"My dear Drake, do you remember the *feel* of the condemned cell just over the way? Yes; I can see you do. Well, this was worse. I had expected that. As soon as I opened the door of that execution shed, the whole room seemed to jump at me. It did not like visitors."

Chief Inspector Masters interrupted harshly.

"Just a minute, sir!"

"Yes?"

Masters had to shake his own head to clear it of a spell. Like the mist on the countryside that morning, this dim-lighted drawing-room became invaded with the shapes and sounds of Pentecost Prison.

"I ask you!" persisted Masters. "What kind of talk is that?"

"It is true talk, Inspector. Write it down."

"As you like, sir."

"A dirty white brick room, a trap, an iron beam, a lever: no other furniture," continued Stannard. Instead of lighting the cigar, he put it down on the arm of the sofa. "But I had seen a rocking-chair across the passage in the condemned cell. I went over there, fetched in the chair, and, as a matter of honour, closed the door behind me.

"I put the rocking-chair in a corner, the far corner from the door, looking obliquely across the gallows-trap towards the lever. I hung my lamp over the back of the chair and tried to read *The Cherry Orchard*. This became impossible. The influences, previously poisonous, were now devilish.

"No, Inspector! Don't make faces. I saw no ghosts and I heard none. I am prepared to admit the influences *may* have been imaginary, though I don't believe it. Everything centered round that gallows-trap.

"There, of course, the condemned person had dropped on his long or short rope—according to weight—into a brick-lined pit underneath. It was natural that these currents of hatred, of malice, of despair, should come from there or seem to come from there.

"Then I did the worst possible thing.

"I put down my book. I did what I called in my own mind —" a sardonic grin tightened back Stannard's lips—"the act of a boxer riding with the punch. I lit a cigar. I rocked in the chair, and deliberately exposed myself to whatever was here. I tried to imagine what an execution would look like. In short, I did exactly what I said Drake would do.

"I knew I was somewhat rattled; but not how rattled until . . ."

"You remember that I was sitting in the corner of the execution shed. I had been imagining the hanging of Hessler, who had tried to escape from the condemned cell. I had been wondering about this: when the doctor and other officials went down into the pit to make sure the hanged man was dead, how did they get down? Ladders? But I saw no ladders. All of a sudden I woke up from these thoughts.

"My cigar, which for some reason I had been holding near the tip, had burnt down and was searing my fingers. And I was not sitting in any corner. I was sitting in my rocking-chair on the gallows-trap itself."

Stannard paused.

He moved his right hand towards the cigar on the arm of the chair, and suddenly drew back again. Ruth Callice, a little way back from the light which touched Stannard's cheek, sat back with her eyes closed. There were bluish hollows under Ruth's eyes.

"The explanation, of course," said Stannard, "is so simple as to be almost comic. I mention it as a matter of: say unconscious muscular reaction. You're familiar, I imagine, with old fashioned rocking-chairs? And how they moved when you swung? I had simply rocked myself there.

"This sobered me. I threw that chair back and stamped out the cigar. My burnt fingers seemed to pain out of all proportion. It was now getting on towards two o'clock in the morning. And I decided to carry out an idea that . . . well, it had been in my mind from the first. I would try out that idea, and get rid of its fears."

"Idea?" demanded Masters. "What idea?"

Stannard grimaced.

"I wanted to see what would happen," he replied, "if I threw the lever and the trap fell."

Chapter 15

Stannard essayed a smile.

"There was no reason," he said, "why I shouldn't have done this before. One cause of my reluctance," he brooded, "may have been shrinking from mere *noise*. Just as all of us shrink from making loud noises in an ordinary house at night.

"I had some idea, perhaps from fiction, that it would be a boom or a crash. Logical reasoning should have told me that such trap-doors, in use, would fall smoothly and without noise. Or, at a time like this, that the machinery might not work at all.

"In any case, I laid hold of the lever and pulled. It moved a little, but only a little. I pulled again, harder. A rasping noise followed, either from the lever's mechanism or from under the trap-door. Then I laid hold, blind-determined, and put out all my weight with both hands. And the trap fell.

"With luck there would have been no more than a heavy creak. But the right-hand trap-door, too heavy for its old hinges, ripped loose and fell into the pit with a crash which seemed to bring down the roof."

Martin Drake stared at the past.

The crash which had roused him out of sleep—loud, yet not very loud because it was muffled by a heavy oak door and the inside of the pit—the crash which had roused him, at two o'clock, was just that.

But Stannard was speaking again.

"If I had expected a noise," he said, "I never expected a noise like *that*. It dazed me. Immediately afterwards," he turned his head towards Martin for a brief look, "my friend Drake called out from the grille of the iron door: 'Stannard!' And then: 'Stannard! Are you all right?' I shouted back, 'Yes! Quite!' Though I fear my voice showed—never mind.

"While I was tugging at the lever, I had put down my lamp on the floor. Now, in not quite the best state of mind, I went over to the edge, and turned the beam of the lamp down into the pit. It was square in shape, a brick-lined shaft much bigger than the oblong trap."

Stannard paused.

"Well, Mr. Masters," he added, "Inspector Drake must have told you what I saw."

"What you saw?" exclaimed Martin.

"I saw a very young girl," said Stannard, "lying on her back. Her eyes showed whitish slits, and her mouth was open. Her bodily mutilations: well, those are for the morbid. But this I saw; and it seemed to me that all the evil forces in that room were settling down on her like flies."

With a murmured apology Stannard rose to his feet. Limping a little, he went slowly to a gilt table in the middle of the room. On the table-top, of eighteenth-century mottled marble, had been set out a decanter of whisky, a syphon, and glasses. He now faced Martin and Ruth; and Masters, twitching round his own chair, also faced Stannard.

"Enid Puckston," said Masters. "Now we're getting to it!"

Stannard's eyes were glittering darkly as of old. His hand trembled very slightly as he tipped whisky into a glass.

"Enid Puckston," Masters repeated. "Did you recognize the girl, sir?"

"No. Never saw her before."

"But you guessed she was murdered? And recently?"

Stannard, in the act of pressing the handle of the syphon, gave Masters a long and almost affectionate look.

"Yes, Inspector," he answered. "I guessed that." Soda hissed into the glass.

"You were one of a group of people (eh?) who found a blood-stained dagger—with fresh blood—over in the condemned cell?"

"I saw it shortly after it was found, if that's what you mean."

"Just so. Didn't you (hurrum!) associate that dagger with the murdered girl?"

"Not at that moment, I think. Afterwards, naturally."

Masters was snapping at him now; and Stannard, motionless with the glass in his hand, seemed to throw his replies through half-shut teeth.

"Mr. Stannard, do you know what a person is required by law to do when they find a murdered body? —Mind your answer."

"Inform the police, I believe. —Mind your grammar."

"Ah!" said Masters. "Now I understand Mr. Martin Drake was within easy calling-distance of you . . ."

"Come to think of it," Stannard frowned, *"he* called to *me,* for a second time, shortly after I saw the girl's body. His voice seemed to come from farther away, as though he'd moved back from the grille. But he called, 'Are you sure you're all right?' "

"Did you answer that?"

"Yes. I told him to mind his own damned business."

"So you could have called for help. And yet you didn't?"

Stannard's gaze wandered towards Ruth.

"Inspector," he said tenderly, and took a deep pull at the whisky and soda, "I wouldn't have 'called for help,' as you put it, for anything on earth."

"What did you do next?"

Stannard took another deep pull at the whisky and soda, emptying the glass.

"I put my lamp on the floor. I put my hands on the edge of the shaft, opposite the side on which the trap door had fallen. I let myself hang down inside, stretching my arms to full length. Then I let go, and landed on my feet in the blood beside the dead girl."

Masters was badly jarred. "You mean—you thought you might give help of some kind?"

"Never mind my motives. That's what I did."

"Oh, ah. And then?"

"The shaft, as I had noticed before," Stannard's husky voice had grown huskier, "was ten feet deep." His vitality seemed to be ebbing, despite the whisky. "I couldn't get out. I was shut in. And I had no lamp. Consequently, all I could do was sit down in a corner and wait for daylight."

"But *why* in lum's name did you do that? If you knew the shaft was ten feet deep?"

"Chief Inspector!" Martin said sharply. And, though Masters turned a sinister eye which threatened prison or worse, Martin ignored it. "If you'll let me ask Stannard just one question, in my own way, I'll guarantee to get you out of this trouble. Is that fair, or isn't it?"

Masters made a disgusted gesture in surrender. Stannard, who had been leaning his weight with both hands on the marble-topped table, looked up with some attempt at lightness and humour.

"Your question, my dear Drake?"

Martin looked him in the eye.

"You were beginning to have the horrors," Martin said. "But you wouldn't give in. You meant to show these young swine they were pretty small beer when it came to nerve. So you deliberately dropped down into that shaft, and left ·your light behind, to sit in the dark near a—an ugly sight, until you were let out at four in the morning. Is that true?"

There was a silence.

"You put it bluntly," said Stannard. "However, that's true."

Ruth had sat up, her hands clenched. Despite her self-control, the tears stung to her eyes.

"Stan, you idiot!" she raved. "You utter, absolute, and complete *idiot!*"

Stannard, though clearly as blind as a bat regarding women, appeared to sense a new quality here. But he did not believe it.

"Ruth, my dear," he began, and hesitated. He was again sedate and grave. "If any foolishness of mine ever gives you the slightest concern," he said, "it will have been worth it."

And, to conceal the horror growing in him, he blundered back to the sofa and sat down in his old place. Hastily he picked up the cigar and clipped its end with a cutter; Martin passed across a pocket-lighter.

"There's little more to tell," Stannard drew in smoke deeply, "though it was perhaps—no matter. I told you I couldn't get out. There was, of course, a door at the bottom of the shaft."

"A door?" said Martin.

"Yes. Logical deduction, as I sat in my corner, convinced me that there must be one. You know the facts: you should be able to see why the door was there, its purpose, and where it led. But the door," Stannard said thoughtfully, "was locked. I found it after groping round the walls in the dark. Locked!

That, Inspector, should give you a clue to the mystery of the girl's death. As for my plight when daylight came . . ."

"Martin," Ruth cried, "only opened the iron door, and threw the key inside!"

"One moment," Stannard intervened. "It was not Drake's fault. Tell me, my dear fellow: when you fell from the roof this morning, was your wrist-watch smashed?"

The villain of the piece shook his head.

"No. It was the first thing I heard when I woke up. Ticking on my bedside table. I'm wearing it now."

"Tell me the time, will you?"

"It's . . . ten minutes past eleven."

"No," contradicted Stannard. He smiled and coughed out of cigar-smoke. "I examined your watch today. It's something over ten minutes fast. *Now* do you see why I was so badly caught?"

Martin, reconstructing last night, saw himself hauling down a heavy paper-bale to sit on: that was just after the vigil began. He remembered looking at the luminous figures of his watch, and thinking Stannard's own watch must be fast because it was well past twelve. But—Stannard was right—his watch must have been fast.

"Stan, you mustn't keep thinking about it!" urged Ruth.

"But I was never more controlled!" said Stannard. "Would you believe, Inspector, that in my brick corner I alternately dozed and woke up, and dozed and woke up? In darkness the—the poor girl beside me seemed to my imagination worse than she had looked in light. The quiet, the damned quiet! And the influences of people who'd *dropped* there!

"Presently I waked from my doze. My lamp had gone out on the floor above me; but there was a dim kind of grey from the two little windows up above. I kept my eyes on my wrist-watch; it said thirteen minutes to four. Before going down there I had opened the door of the execution shed a little way—you remember?"

"Yes. I remember," Martin said grimly.

"So that Drake would be sure to hear. Thirteen minutes to go. Then . . .

"Then Drake's voice cried, 'Stannard! Stannard! Are you all right?' Bracing myself for those last extra minutes, I was completely off balance. I managed to croak out, 'I'm here. I'm—' Whereupon he said the time was up, and he was opening the iron door. I heard the door open, and the key clatter inside. Then he said something about entertaining evening, and he was free and so was I.

"I was paralyzed. I could not utter a word. Such is the nature of an unexpected voice. Then, since he seemed to be going away . . ."

"Damn it," protested Martin, whose guilty conscience troubled him, "how could I have known you were down there?"

"You couldn't have. It was my own—call it what you like. I did find my voice, and start to call after you. You heard that?"

"Faintly. When I was on my way out."

"So I knew myself in a trap for heaven knew how long. I was there with what remained of Enid Puckston, and the other things. The only possibility was to break down the door I spoke of, the door at the front of the shaft.

"Inspector, have you ever tried this? On many, many occasions in fiction I have read, 'Twice he hurled himself at the door, and on the third attempt the lock splintered.' Well, try it. If this had been a proper prison door, I shouldn't have had a chance. But it wasn't.

"It became an endless series of kicks with a heavy country boot. Once or twice I stumbled over—Enid Puckston. I think it took half an hour. The last frantic kick, which wrenched my ankle and made me think I was done, tore the lock out of the door.

"I had my pocket-lighter, which I had not used except for a cigar or two. In front of me was a short brick passage running straight. Can you guess what it was?"

Masters, who long ago had swung his chair round again, spoke in an expressionless voice.

"No need to guess, sir. I know what it was."

"Oh?"

"It was the way the prison doctor and governor and the rest came down to certify death after an execution. Also the way they carried the body up again, so the prisoners wouldn't get a look at it from windows."

"Ah! So I reasoned! The passage must lead to—"

"To the prison mortuary on the ground floor of Wing B," Masters said slowly. "Along a little passage, turn left to another passage, up a flight of steps into the mortuary. Mr. Drake was sitting all night with his back to one wall of the mortuary."

"I was?"

"Oh, ah. The door's a little way down from where you were sitting, in the wall between the aisle and the paper-bales. Listen, Mr. Stannard!"

Masters held up a pencil and studied its point.

"We know how you got up into the mortuary, pretty well done in," said Masters, "*and* with a bad ankle. You managed to get to the condemned cell, and rang the alarm-bell till the rope broke. The constable found you there afterwards. Now could you give me some *answers?*"

"What the devil do you think I've been doing?"

"Now, now! No call to get excited!"

Stannard's cigar had burnt down raggedly. He dropped it into an ashtray beside the sofa. With some fervency Martin wished that the Chief Inspector, who could at times be as yielding yet as smothering and stifling as a feather bed, would end a questioning which was having such bad effect on—Ruth, for one.

"You smashed the locked door to the underground passage. Oh, ah! You had a pocket-lighter? Oh, ah! Was there a key in this lock on the other side?"

"No."

"Though you'd been told no doors were locked at the prison except the main gates?"

"It *was* the only locked door." Stannard, his black eyebrows raised, leaned forward and again seemed to throw back the words through half-closed teeth. "The hinges of the front gates were oiled, though *I* didn't oil them. The lock and hinges of that door were oiled, though *I* didn't oil them. Are your wits beginning to wake up?"

"Maybe, sir! Maybe! Were there blood-spots in that underground passage?"

Ruth tried to, and only just succeeded in, stifling a gasp.

"Yes," Stannard said briefly. "I didn't tread in them."

"And blood-spots in the other passage? Where it turned left, I mean?"

"Yes."

"And blood-spots on the stairs up to the mortuary?"

"A few."

"What was Miss Puckston's body lying on, sir? On the floor, or on anything else, like?"

"She was lying," Stannard pressed his hands over his eyes, "on a fairly large travelling-robe or lap-robe, plaid in colour, with each corner rather twisted up. As though . . ."

"Ah! As though somebody'd twisted the ends together like a parcel, and carried her there?"

"I can't be expected to answer that."

"Just so. Still—!" Honey flowed in Masters's heavy voice. "Didn't you investigate any blood-spots in the mortuary?"

Stannard stared straight ahead.

"There was a door in the mortuary," he replied, "which led out into a big fan-shaped garden, with a prison wing on each side and a spiked wall at the end. It was on the side of the condemned cell. There was a white moving mist. The garden had gone to ruin, but it was overrun with flowers. Red, blue, yellow; I don't know their names.

"Yes, yes, I went out there! In a square patch of grass there was a scuffed space where the travelling-rug may have been placed. That was the way Hessler must have gone."

"Who's this 'Hessler' you keep mentioning?"

"A mutilating murderer."

"What about him?"

"He poisoned his guards in the condemned cell. Logic, Inspector! He ran to the execution shed, opened the trap that would receive him, and jumped down. He reached the mortuary by way of the passage and the stairs. They shot him in the shoulder as he was climbing the spiked wall, and he fell back into a flower-bed. All this I saw too: in the mist."

With some effort Stannard got up. All his vitality had gone; his jaw sagged. He caught a brief flash of it when he addressed Ruth and the others.

"My dear," he said formally, and took Ruth's hand again as though she were made of china, "Lady Fleet has asked us to stay on tomorrow. I can rearrange *my* engagements to suit it, if you can?"

"Yes! I can arrange it! Of course!"

"Thank you. And now, gentlemen," added Stannard, quite convinced they would believe every word he said, "this country air has a tendency to make me sleepy. Yes. It's past eleven, and I think I'll turn in. We have had—ah—a most interesting discussion. We must continue it soon. Yes. Good night."

And the shortish, stocky barrister, his dark hair gleaming, sauntered to the door while he firmly put down his bad ankle to keep from limping: facing the world with defiance, as though he carried a sword.

There was a long silence, even after they faintly heard his footsteps slacken and slow down on the stairs.

"I didn't think," Martin said slowly, "there were any knights-errant left in this world. But, by God and all honour to him!—there goes one of them!"

Ruth, who was standing and looking anxiously at the door, immediately showed her state of mind by attacking Martin.

" 'Knights-errant,' " she scoffed in her quiet voice. "Don't you see all he needs is somebody to look after him?"

"The Great Defender?"

"Oh, rats!" said Ruth. "All he needs is someone to—to let him be a *little* idiotic but keep him solid and distinguished, which you've got to admit he is. And take you, Martin!"

Again he recognized, as he had recognized last night, that long-lingering if tender note of satire: which, like an arrow on a string, must be drawn to full arc before it is fired. Mentally, he shied back.

"Hold on, now! This is no time for discussing my imperfections!"

"You loathe being taken care of. For instance: are you hungry? You know you haven't had a bite to eat since last night?"

For some reason Martin's gorge rose sickeningly at the very thought of eating.

"Woman," he said, "if there's one thing on this earth I *WILL NOT* stand, it's being pestered with admonitions to eat something. Especially when I'm working. Food!" He was about to say, 'to hell with food,' when the mocking imp at the back of his brain reminded him that he also was shaky, from a fall off a roof, and not quite rational.

"You see?" smiled Ruth, turning up her palm.

"See what?"

"You like the clinging-vine," said Ruth, "who undoubtedly would manage your house so inefficiently, Martin dear, that you'd get furious and run it yourself." Ruth hesitated, and tears came into her eyes. "I don't know what I'm doing here," she said, "I *must* see poor Stan gets safely upstairs."

And, her green dress flashing, she ran out of the room.

During these remarks, which he had not heard, Chief Inspector Humphrey Masters was for once off his official dignity. He leaned back in his chair, his boiled blue eye contemplating a corner of the ceiling. On his face was a trace of reluctant admiration.

"Now if I might ask you, Mr. Drake," he mused, after ruminating for a while, "what did you make of that little 'statement?' "

"With Stannard, you mean?"

"Clever!" said Masters, shaking his head. "Oh, ah! Just as wide as they make 'em; and I've met a few in my time. Did you notice he never once mentioned the alibi?"

"*What alibi?*"

"Come, now! You found that dagger at close on midnight. Even allow a mix-up with watches: 'tisn't much one way or the other. Dr. Laurier testified (and testifies) the blood was fresh within half an hour. Say half-past eleven or a bit later. The police surgeon says Enid Puckston might certainly have been killed round about half-past, though he's like all doctors about allowing much leeway."

"Half-past eleven! But that means—!"

"Now, was she killed with that dagger?" Masters mused.

"Inspector Drake tells me old Sir George Fleet gave away his rapier-collection about November of 1925. Sir George never did like steel; he preferred guns; and after there'd been a knife-murder at Priory Hill he gave the stuff away to Major Colwell, the Governor of Pentecost. But *was* the Puckston girl killed with that dagger?

"There's very strong evidence she was. You can't identify a knife-wound certain-sure like a bullet-wound. But unusual blade; unusual wounds corresponding; fits exactly. Blood-group type's same. Yes; there you are."

Whereupon Masters sat up straight.

"Sir, that girl *was* killed in the garden between the two prison-wings. There's evidence: I tell you straight. She was carried down under the gallows-trap in a travelling-robe. After (mind you) being brought to the garden alive. And that took time. Lots of time. What's the result?

"It's this. Every one of you five people who went to the prison, and were together even before then, has got an alibi as big as a house. Eh?"

"I hadn't thought about it. So that's the perfect alibi, is it?"

"We-el!" said Masters, regarding him with broad and fishy skepticism. "No. I don't say perfect. *I* could pick a flaw in it. But it'd go down with a jury like peaches and cream. You'd want strong evidence to upset it?"

"And you think you can upset it?"

"If you ask me whether I *want* to upset it," Masters said violently, "the answer is: yes. I smacking well do! If you ask me whether I *can* upset it, the answer is: probably. I'll know tomorrow. There's a little camera-trick, Mr. Drake, that might interest you."

Sir Henry Merrivale, at this point, lumbered very slowly into the room and passed them without appearing to see them. H.M.'s big face wore a mottled pallor, and there were beads of sweat on his forehead. It struck Martin Drake with a chill of dread. And Masters—who had sworn at the time of the Bronze Lamp case he would never again be worried by the old man's carryings-on—uttered a roaring oath and jumped up.

"Have you been on that roof?" Masters demanded.

H.M. did not reply.

He went over and stood with his back to the fireplace, his

feet wide apart. Fumbling for a handkerchief in his hip pocket, he mopped his forehead slowly and returned the handkerchief. His eyes were blank. After a long time he spoke.

"Masters," he said, "we're not finished yet. But if we play the cards right we'll finish soon. Masters, we've got the swine good and proper."

And the tone of his voice stung Martin Drake like a red-hot wire.

"We've got a beauty," said H.M., envisaging the murderer. "What sticks in my gorge," he tugged at his collar, "is that Puckston gal being killed just merely for the reason she *was* killed. Masters, we've got a real vicious 'un. And, oh, so innocent!"

"Sir Henry! Listen!"

"Hey?"

"I knew you'd twigged it," Masters said with satisfaction, "as soon as you shouted out to let you think, and then rushed off to the roof. But what have you *got?*"

"I know how Sir George Fleet was murdered."

Masters reached for his notebook.

"And don't you forget that," said H.M., pointing a finger malevolently, "because it's the keystone of the whole business. Everything falls down without it." And, Martin noted with disquiet, H.M.'s face was still pale.

"I won't forget," Masters assured him. "And—?"

"I can tell you the truth about that goddam skeleton in the clock."

"Ah! Just so! Anything else?"

Again there was so oppressive a quiet that they could hear, above H.M.'s head, the almost noiseless gold clock ticking between its two candelabra. The satiny dark-red walls, with their high cream-coloured curtains, seemed to have a stifling quality despite their open windows.

"Y'know," said H.M. thoughtfully, "I've been an awful dummy. Almost as bad a dummy as when I nearly slipped up in that Goblin Wood case. It was because I never connected the pink flash with wood."

"You never connected the pink flash with . . . *what?*"

"With wood," said H.M., reaching over to knock his knuckles on a table.

"Goddelmighty," whispered Masters. "Listen, sir! When Sir George fell off that roof, the only wooden-made things on it were the frames of the beach-chairs and the wicker settee! And all of 'em were fifty feet away from him!"

"I know that."

"Was somebody hiding behind them?"

"No."

Masters wiped his forehead. H.M. was persisting in mazy speculation.

"Y'see, Masters, you've got to find two units, sort of, like the wood here and the skeleton in the clock with old Dr. Pierre Laurier rocking back and forth in front of it. But, burn me, still they don't fit into a pattern until you connect 'em together with a real clue . . ."

Here H.M. roused himself out of his reverie.

"I say, Masters. Am I making myself clear?"

"Curiously enough," retorted Masters, with towering and stiff-jawed dignity, "you are not." Then slow suspicion dawned and grew clear in his expression. "Sir Henry, are you trying to do me in the eye again?"

"Oh, my son! No! I wouldn't do that!"

"Oh, no," said Masters in a hollow voice. "Oh, no. No. You never have, have you? Oh, no. In a pig's ear you haven't!"

H.M. looked at him steadily.

"I'm not doin' it this time son. Honest. It's too serious."

This almost if not quite reassured his companion, who again opened the notebook.

"And I get all the details," he insisted, "straightaway?"

"Every detail," H.M. reassured him, "goes on the table tonight. For our conference. We've been dealt some awful good cards, but a little conjuror's hokey-pokey won't do any harm when it's our turn to deal."

"Then what was all that flummery a minute ago? First you started gabbling about a beach-chair, and then about the skeleton and Dr. Laurier . . ."

"Wait a minute! I didn't . . ."

"And," Masters rode him down, "you said they were connected by a real clue."

"Oh, Masters! The whole place is flooded with clues."

"Maybe so. You talked about a 'real' clue, that bonged down out of the air, like, and hit you on the head. I can't see the wood for the trees. I don't see anything, except that the alibi is a fake. Where did you get this 'real' clue? Where did it come from?"

H.M. pondered.

"Well," he said, "from my reincarnation."

Chapter 16

"Stop," said Masters, extending his arm like a traffic-policeman. "Stop just there."

Despite Masters's effort to be calm, the hoarse and strangled note in his voice betrayed him. He must do more than count teh now. Snapping the rubber band round his notebook, he carefully put it in his pocket.

"Sir," he continued, as one who weighs his words but gets louder and louder, "I've been mixed up in these cases for more years than I'd like to count. *I* get the credit. Oh, ah! But I've got blood-pressure, and I've got a family to think of!"

"Sh-h! Quiet! Don't wake up the house!"

"I've been kicked in the pants," said Masters. "I've been hocussed and flummoxed. I've had poisonous snakes dropped at my feet. I've been told to face a mob of reporters, without a word to say for myself, when you'd promised a world-beater of a story. All right: that's fair enough; I don't complain. *But this is too much.* —Reincarnation!" breathed Masters, and clasped his hands in prayer to heaven.

"Sh-h, now! Sh-h! Sh-h-h!"

Masters subsided. A healing peace settled through the room.

"And now," bellowed H.M., in a voice which made the curtains quiver, "are you goin' to stop being a goop and listen to a word of explanation?"

Masters was silent.

"I've been reading a lot of literature," continued H.M. "I don't believe it as I oughter, because I don't remember as much as I oughter. *But* there was one thing I did read, and it slipped through without more than scratching the surface of the old man's mind, until somethin' was said that made me remember. And it tore the hocus-pocus wide open. *Now* do you see?"

Masters peered at him suspiciously.

"You're not off your chump? You *don't* remember how you wore a big hat and recited limericks to Charles the First?"

"Well. No. Not much. And, Masters, for the love of Esau stop drivellin'. This is a murder case. And I'm scared."

"You?"

"Me," returned H.M., with all the impressiveness this conveyed. "We've got to act fast, son. If we can keep this feller," he pointed to Martin, "if we can keep him alive for just one more night . . ."

(Again that sense of hatred, gathering round and pressing against him! Martin, weak from lack of the food he told Ruth he hated, sat down and lit a cigarette whose smoke made his head swim.)

"If we can do that," said Masters, "he's out of danger?"

"Not necessarily. But a certain innocent-looker will be occupied with other things. We'll be the attackers and not standin' at defence. Now, son!" H.M. pointed. "When you first barged in here tonight, I asked you whether you'd got the stuff. You said you'd got all of it. Where is it?"

Masters indicated the chair where lay his bowler hat, the brief-case, and the brown cardboard folder.

"You don't want to go through all that tonight, do you?"

"I don't want to go through any of it, Masters. I only want to ask you a question."

"Well sir?"

H.M. scowled and adjusted his spectacles.

"You've got," he stated rather than questioned, "you've got from the local police files some testimony from *everybody*, and I mean everybody, who was here at Fleet House on the afternoon of November 4th, 1927?"

From the thick-filled brown folder Masters took out a typewritten slip with pencilled notes.

"I have," he said. "Also what happened to each of 'em afterwards. The word 'here' means within a radius of three or four miles."

"So! Read it out loud!"

"As follows," said Masters, clearing his throat. "Lady Fleet (here), Dowager Countess of Brayle (here), Earl and Countess of Brayle (one dead, one in Stockholm), young Fleet (here), Dr. Pierre Laurier (dead), Lady Fleet's companion (dead), governess (dead), butler (at Reading), parlourmaid (here), first and second housemaids (one here, one in Australia), gardener (dead). In addition to these persons's testimony, Stannard's too."

"Stannard!" interrupted Martin. "But he didn't give any statement then!"

Masters grinned.

"No, Mr. Drake. Still, I'm told that in Sir Henry's presence and yours he said he'd talked to a newspaper reporter at the train. The area's not so large that a few 'phone-calls wouldn't cover it." Masters tapped the cardboard folder. "They sent a copy of the press-cutting by hand."

H.M. pressed his hands hard to his forehead.

"Here's the burnin' question," he snapped. "You or I got testimony, today or yesterday evening, from all the witnesses who weren't dead or out of reach. *Does it agree with what they said twenty years ago?*"

"Ah. Almost to a T." Masters's eye grew thoughtful. "Almost too close, don't you think?"

"No, son. Oh, my eye, no! *You're* not likely to forget the first h.e. bomb that fell close to you; now are you? Or the circumstances? No. And that's a great help."

"It's a great help to know there aren't any contradictions?"

"That's right."

Masters shut his eyes. "Anything else?"

"You don't mention Dr. Hugh Laurier as bein' there. Or wasn't he qualified for medicine yet?"

"He'd qualified a few years before; he was helping his father. But he was in London that day. He missed the train, and didn't get back till later."

"I see," observed H.M. in a colourless tone, and dropped his hands. "Finally, son, in that brief-case you got the Scotland Yard dossier, in a blue folder, with the statements of Simon Frew and Arthur Puckston. One with the binoculars, the other with the telescope." H.M. stretched out his hand and waggled the fingers. "Gimme that folder!"

And now they both saw, with growing alarm, the extent of H.M.'s disquiet.

"This folder? What for?"

"I'm goin' on a little errand," said H.M. "It'll be short, but it won't be sweet. I'm dreading it like the Old Nick." He put the folder under his arm."

"Ready when you are, then!"

"You're not goin', Masters."

Masters stared at him. "In case it's slipped your memory, Sir Henry, I'm the police-officer in charge of this case."

"You're still not goin'," H.M. said simply. "You'd only scare him. Don't argue, burn it! This is the first card we play; and I got to play it. Now that young feller," he nodded towards Martin, "is the one I want to go with me. If he'll do it. Hey?"

Martin staggered up from the sofa, crushing out his cigarette.

"I'll go with you to Land's End," he said, "if you don't mind my ringing up Jenny first. I've been intending to do it all night;

and every time somebody walloped out with something I had to hear."

H.M. spoke sharply.

"You can ring her up, son, but you won't get any answer."

"My God, she hasn't gone away with Grandmother?" Martin thought back. "The old lady said *she* was going away overnight. Did Jenny go?"

"No, no, no," H.M. told him in a fussed and malevolent way. "I made her promise, before the old hobgoblin sent her away from here, to take two nembutal pills as soon as she got home. Son, it wouldn't wake her if the whole town of Brayle fell down. All right: you be stubborn and cloth-headed. Try it!"

Martin did try it. He sat at the telephone-table in the dark rear of the hall, listening to ghostly little ringing-tones which had no reply. Surely Dawson or somebody must be about? Never mind. It was late. He put down the 'phone.

Suddenly Martin realized he was in the dark. A gulf of mist, in his imagination, opened in front of him; somebody's hands lunged out; the solid floor melted away for a plunge outward . . .

None of that! Martin went back towards the lighted drawing-room, timing his steps slowly. Himself: a focus of hatred. And again, everlastingly, why? The atmosphere of the drawing-room intensified this thought, since Masters and H.M. had evidently been talking rapidly. It seemed to Martin that the Chief Inspector, in utter incredulity, had just opened his mouth to protest. Afterwards they did not speak.

They turned off the lights in the drawing-room. They went out of the house softly, Martin slipping the latch of the front door. In a fine night, the quarter moon dimmed by a sweep of stars, they crossed the road.

At the Dragon's Rest, whose front showed no light, what might be called the hotel-entrance was in its south side, the narrower end of the building. As Martin made for the hotel-entrance door, Masters preceding him and H.M. following him, he glanced southwards because Brayle Manor was somewhere there.

It seemed to him that in the distance the sky had a faintly whitish glow, conveying a sense of movement. No sounds; or were there? The glimmer wasn't fire. He could tell that. But . . .

"Oi!" whispered H.M., and shoved him inside.

A narrowish passage ran the length of the inn from south to north. Beyond the left-hand wall lay the three bars. In the right-hand wall was a cubicle for signing the visitors' book, then a door to the dining-room where Martin remembered having had lunch on Saturday, then more doors to the end. The walls, white-painted, had at one side a design of brass warming-pans framing a sixteenth-century crossbow; and the light of a shaded lamp shone on ancient scrubbed floorboards.

"See you later," whispered Masters, and tiptoed up the narrow staircase towards the bedrooms.

H.M., taking Martin by the arm, impelled him down the passage to the far door at the right end. H.M. knocked gently.

"Come in," said a voice which Martin guessed must be Mrs. Puckston's.

Mr. and Mrs. Puckston, whose child had been murdered and hacked last night, were in there. If H.M. had not gripped his arm, Martin would have turned and bolted.

H.M. opened the door.

It was an old-fashioned kitchen-sitting-room, its brick walls painted white. In what had once been the immense embrasure of the fireplace, there now stood a big coal cooking-stove with many lids, and a kettle simmering on one of them. In the middle of the room, with a frayed yellow-and-white cloth and an electric light hanging over it, was a table set for an untouched supper.

Arthur Puckston, back to the door, sat on the other side of the table and faced the stove. His freckled bald head, with its little fringe of grey-reddish hair, and his thin drooping muscular shoulders, were motionless. Mrs. Puckston, dark-haired and stoutening, sat in a corner chair and sewed.

Then Puckston looked round.

The tears were running down his face despite his spasmodic blinkings. His eyes remained gentle. He saw who was in the doorway. First startled, then deeply ashamed, he whipped his head away and began swabbing desperately at his eyes with his coat-sleeves. But grief had beaten him. His arms dropped. He did not care.

"Mr. Puckston," said H.M., in so gentle a tone that Martin could not have thought it possible, "I know we're intruding. Will you believe I only came because I know I can help you?"

Mrs. Puckston, tearless but dull-glazed of eye, looked up.

"Won't you sit down, please?" she asked quietly. "We understand. Arthur suspicioned—at least, he hoped—you'd come."

The two visitors sat down on their side of the table, their eyes fixed on the cloth.

"Norma," Puckston said in a slow, dull monotone, "I've got to explain."

"That's not necessary, Arthur."

"I've got to explain."

With great care Puckston slowly hitched his chair round. He too looked down. His right hand, blue-veined, automatically brushed and brushed and brushed at the table-cloth.

"What I've got to explain, sir, is that we only opened the 'ouse tonight because I'd promised the Choral Society they could have the two parlours for their practice after chapel. Because it was hymns, you see. We thought that was only right and proper. Because it was hymns. And Mr. Bradley, from the Chapel, he said so too.

"Of course, we didn't go out there. But Norma and me, we reckoned it would be right and proper if we sat out in the passage, there, and listened to the hymns through the wall. And we did. And I was feeling fine, I was feeling just as fine as I could be, until it came to that part of the hymn about while the nearer waters roll, while the tempest still is high.

"And I don't know," he went on, shaking his head while he brushed and brushed at the table, "I can't just rightly say, what made me make such a fool of myself. Breaking down like that, and coming in 'ere so they wouldn't know about it. I didn't know I was so soft. I reckon it was just that part of the hymn, that's all."

Both of his visitors, one of whom could not bear this, made an instinctive movement to get up.

"No!" said Puckston, and stretched out his hand. "Don't go, if I've not offended you. Sit down. I was hoping you'd come."

They sat down.

"Don't think about it, Arthur!" said Mrs. Puckston. But there was a heavier glaze in her eyes as she sewed.

"I won't," said her husband. He concentrated hard for a moment, before slowly moving his head sideways. "Norma, haven't you got a cup of tea for the gentlemen?"

The sewing slid from his wife's lap. "Arthur, I never thought of that. I've never been so bad-mannered in all my born days."

"But please don't . . ."

"Easy, son," muttered H.M., and gripped Martin's wrist as the latter started to speak. H.M. looked at Puckston, who had ceased to care whether they saw the tears on his face. "You said, Mr. Puckston, you hoped I'd come here. Was it about anything in particular?"

The other started to speak, but fell to brushing the cloth instead.

"Mr. Puckston," said H.M., "this person who—hurt your little girl."

As Mrs. Puckston moved the kettle from the stove-lid, the white-brick kitchen was as still as death. Mrs. Puckston, an iron hook in her hand to remove the stove-lid and see to the fire, did not seem to breathe.

Puckston swallowed. "Yes, sir?"

"Do you want me to nab that person, and see that there's punishment?"

The lid rattled back. From the stove leaped up a yellow lick of flame, curling high; momentarily it painted the kitchen with yellow brightness; and, had he been facing it, you might have fancied a reflection in Puckston's eyes.

Then the lean man's shoulders sagged.

"What's the good?" he asked dully. "Like old Sir George. Years ago. You can't beat 'em."

"I know this country," said H.M. "It's asinine, sure. It's full of fatheads. But there's been justice here for nearly a thousand years."

"Old Sir George . . ."

"Could *he* take your land from you, when he tried to?"

"No, by God 'e couldn't!"

Rattle went the stove-lid, back into place.

"Arthur," said his wife, herself near to breaking down, "I don't think I'll make tea. I think there's some bottles of the '24 port that the gentlemen would like better. I think I know how to find them."

Then she was out of the room. Her husband, struggling to pull his wits together, pressed his hands flat on the table. His mildness, his weary look, showed he could scarcely do it.

"Can—you help me?" Puckston asked.

"If you help me."

"How? I'll try. Yes; I'll do it."

"Son, I warn you: the first bit is goin' to hurt. It'll keep you thinking about your daughter."

"Go ahead."

From his inside breast pocket H.M. took out three post-cards. One, postmarked July 5th, read, *Re Sir George Fleet: examine the skeleton in the clock.* The second, July 6th: *Re Sir George Fleet: what was the pink flash on the roof?* The third, July 7th: *Re Sir George Fleet: evidence of murder is still there.* Clearing a space on the supper-table, pushing away cutlery and a bottle of Worcestershire sauce, he put down the exhibits.

"Son," he said quietly, "you sent these postcards."

The other's mouth quivered like a hurt child's.

"To be more exact," added H.M., "you dictated the

substance and Enid put it down in correct grammar and spelling, with schoolgirl flourishes."

"'Ow did you know that?" asked Puckston.

"Never mind. It's not important. What I . . ."

"'Ow did you know that?" repeated Puckston, with the insistence of the drunken or the damned. The tears had started again.

"Oh, son! From your antiques here I thought you *might* subscribe to Willaby's catalogue. I asked Lady Br—I asked somebody in this district if you did, and she said yes. She also said she got her last catalogue on July 5th, which is the postmark on that first anonymous card.

"Y'see, that was the catalogue that listed the skeleton in the clock. Somebody got it on July 5th, and fired off an anonymous postcard to stir up the police about the Fleet case. There weren't likely to be two such curiosities as that clock floatin' about."

"I'm not saying I didn't do it." Puckston had the palms of his hands pressed over his face. He rocked back and forth. "But why did it have to be *me* who sent the postcards?"

H.M. expelled a slow, deep breath of relief. They could hear the throb of the fire inside the stove, and Mrs. Puckston moving somewhere in the cellar.

"Well . . . now. That's what we're coming to. And it'll be easier. Because it's about Sir George Fleet's death."

H.M. snapped his fingers down at one side, without looking away from Puckston. Martin rightly interpreted this as an order to pick up the blue Scotland Yard folder, which H.M. had dropped.

Puckston was not composed now, but he was more composed. Any mention of Fleet could rouse him. His light-blue eyes, bloodshot and reddish at the lids, tried to focus on H.M. out of a long, wretched face.

"Do you remember," continued H.M., turning over the typewritten pages of the folder, "what happened the day Fleet died?"

"Do I remember when I first walked out with Norma?"

"You didn't like Fleet. Hey?"

"I wonder," said Puckston, shutting his eyes, "if that man ever thought how much I looked down on him. 'Im, with 'is money made out of the fourteen-eighteen war! Me, whose forbears 'ave owned this inn a matter of two hundred year! But you can't make the nobs see that. They don't notice!"

"Let's come to the day, shall we?"

"Glad to."

"You, accordin' to your testimony, were sitting on the top of the north gable with a telescope. You were watching the hunt. You heard the shout Fleet gave. Now lemme read you a part of your statement verbatim."

H.M. found the passage and ran his finger down it.

I looked round. I saw something pitch over the little ledge, but it was so quick I did not see what it was. I looked—

H.M. paused abruptly. There was a space of silence, while Martin found the sweat stand out on his forehead.

"Y'see," H.M. said very gently, "that second sentence just can't possibly be true."

"Why not?"

"I'll tell you. If there's one thing of general agreement, it's that Fleet gave a shout and immediately fell. If you doubt that, see the testimony of Simon Frew, who had the binoculars on the middle gable and is admittedly an honest witness.

"But what about you? You were on the north gable, watching the hunt: either the hounds streakin' to the north, or the field galloping round Black Hanger to the east. You heard a yell: that's all. You couldn't have known where it came from, except somewhere behind you. You couldn't have known what it meant. By the time you could swing that telescope round, Fleet must have been dead on the flagstones.

"Yet you claim, see, that out of all the space of sky and land comin' round into view through your telescope, you managed to pick out the exact spot where Fleet was standing *just as he fell*. Son, it won't do. It's plain ridiculous."

Again there was a silence.

In Puckston's expression there was no fear, no wrath, no shrinking; only a curious twitch of the mouth which Martin could not identify.

"What did I do, then?" Puckston asked.

"I'm goin' to suggest," pursued H.M., turning back a page and tapping it, "that the same thing which happened to Simon Frew also happened to you."

Puckston shut his eyes.

"*You* saw the field gallop round the side of Black Hanger. Through the telescope they all seemed to be waving and smiling at *you*. You wondered who it could be for: just like Frew. You turned round and raked your telescope along till

you saw your enemy, George Fleet, a few seconds before he
fell. Is that true?"

"Yes," said Puckston without opening his eyes.

"But you were looking at him sideways—a good distance
sideways—instead of face on. That's how you came to see . . ."

"See what?"

"The pink flash. Just like open and shut, wasn't it?"

Were they coming at last, Martin wondered, to the
explanation of that tantalizing obscurity which (Masters
seemed to think) was connected with a wooden beach-chair?
He, Martin Drake, had been pushed by a pair of hands. Or
could he swear he had? The soft, gentle growl of H.M.'s voice
went on.

"To clinch it," said H.M., "here's a final bit of your story.
You tell in this record (Oh, lord love a duck!) about how Dr.
Laurier ran out on the terrace, and the constable came up.
Now you're speakin', son."

And they saw, through Puckston's eyes, the scene played
against the white facade.

Dr. Laurier said something, and Bert picked up Sir
George's binoculars and walked into the house. Dr. Laurier
said something else, and Lady Brayle came out with some
kind of cloth. I said aloud, 'The bastard is dead.'

Puckston stared at a salt-cellar on the frayed white-and-
yellow cloth.

"I never made no bones about what I thought of him.
Maybe I oughtn't to have said that, with the hymns tonight and
all. But that's how I felt. And still do."

H.M. held up a hand for silence.

Dr. Laurier put the cloth over his head. Lady Fleet came
out and started to faint, but they talked to her a while and
she went in. The governess and the boy came round the
house then, but Dr. Laurier yelled so loud you could hear to
go back. Dr. Laurier made as if he was examining all over
Sir George. I did not see anybody at the windows. Bert came
out and seemed to argue with Dr. Laurier about who carried
Sir George. Bert took his head in the cloth and Dr. Laurier
took his legs. They carried him in the house. Lady Fleet
came out again once and looked up. That was all I saw
before I slid down.

Puckston smote the table.

"And there's not a word of a lie in that," he insisted. "Simon could—"

"Sure, son. I know. It agrees with what Simon Frew said, and the other fellers who were farther down on the roof. But, considering what I've read, can you tell me more about the pink flash now?"

Puckston looked vacant.

"I was sure what it was." Again his hand mechanically brushed the table-cloth. "Anyway, I was pretty sure. But . . ."

"But you were glad Fleet was dead. And anyway you didn't want trouble, because you were scared of the nobs."

"Nice lot, aren't they? Lady Brayle . . ."

"Sure, Sophie's one of the bad examples. That's because she's so goddam cloth-headed. She ought to be either ousted or made popular. But when you sent that anonymous card with the fancy words 'pink flash' . . ."

Any reference to those cards, no matter with how gentle probing, seemed to send Puckston frantic.

"Enid didn't know nothing about it," he pleaded. "It was only a lark, don't you see? She loved larks. That's how they got her up to Pentecost, because it was a lark. Because all the gossip was round they were looking for ghosts. Because . . ."

Puckston got up. He stumbled across to a kitchen dresser with an oil-cloth top, fumbled in a drawer, and brought out a table-cloth to dab at his eyes. Then he turned round.

"It was Enid," he said, "who thought of saying 'pink flash.' I—I hemm'd and hawed." Puckston's freckled bald head stood out against the white-brick wall. His thin shoulders, square like a scarecrow's in the old blue-and-white shirt, were humped up.

"I hemm'd and hawed, not wanting to say much. And Enid, she said, 'Well, Daddy, what did it look like?' And I told her. And she thought for a minute and said, 'I know, Daddy! We'll call it a pink flash.' And she put it down."

"Ah!" said H.M. *"Now* we got it!"

"Got what?"

Statement and question were flung across that warm kitchen. Martin knew that a scale-pan hung in the balance, that a gambler prepared to play.

"You've been torturin' yourself," said H.M., "because you thought *you* were responsible for that kid's death. You thought some swine believed she knew too much, and killed her."

Puckston put the table-cloth in front of his face.

"I don't hold many things sacred," said H.M., "but I swear you on what I do hold sacred that you're wrong. Wrong! That wasn't the reason! It wasn't even a reason you or I could understand."

The table-cloth fell to the floor. " 'Ere! Are you trying to . . . ?"

"No. I can prove it, son. And if I do prove it," said H.M., with such a radiance of conviction that the other did not move, "will you help me with something else?"

Ten seconds ticked past. Puckston walked across to the table and extended his hand. H.M. gripped it. After this he slid back in his chair with a Gargantuan thump, and breathed noisily. Slowly his head turned round.

"*You*," he glared at Martin with incredible malevolence. "What are you doin' here, son?"

"But you asked me to—"

"You go out in that passage," H.M. ordered sternly, "and you wait there till I talk to you. You've served the purpose. Now the garden's lovely. Sling your hook."

Martin felt no surprise now when he remembered having heard that Chief Inspectors sometimes came within an ace of murdering Sir Henry Merrivale. He knew why. Deeply he could sympathize. In fact, as his eye caught a bowl of Jell-o on the sideboard, he wondered how its contents would look if they were tastefully pressed down on H.M.'s skull.

But he went out into the passage and closed the door.

"You've served the purpose." What purpose? Why had he been brought to see the Puckstons? He was beginning to suspect H.M. of a purpose in everything, but what purpose in this?

The long passage, with its single dim lamp, lay shadowy and deeply cool. At the other end of it lounged Masters himself, with the hotel-entrance door wide open to the fragrant night. Masters's face was a mask of inquiry as Martin joined him.

"Don't ask me what happened," the latter begged. "He's verified what he wants to verify. Do you understand?"

"Do I!" Masters growled with fervour.

Yet the Chief Inspector, or what could be seen of him in dimness, appeared serene, breathing the fragrant air, almost humming a tune and smiling. Martin pointed southwards.

"By the way, what's that whitish glow away over there? In the direction of Brayle Manor?"

"Can't say, I'm sure."

"Probably doesn't mean anything. Still," Martin was uneasy, "it did strike me he hurried me in here when I tried to look at it. Er—you've heard about his feud with the Dowager Countess of Brayle?"

"Have I!" snorted Masters.

"He won the first round by a thrust with a guisarme. She definitely took the second by making a skeleton gibber at him and insulting him behind locked gates. I've wondered before this if he might—well . . ."

"You know, Mr. Drake," said Masters, shaking his head and folding his arms portentously, "I've tried to stop it; but I can't. It's a sin and a shame how that old bounder carries on!"

"At his age, you mean?"

"Oh, ah! Just so! It'd be a great pity if he (hurrum!) made it worse."

"It would, Chief Inspector! It would! What worries me is that it always upsets Jenny, and I won't have Jenny upset!"

"Of course," Masters observed musingly, after a long pause, "the lady *is* a bit of a handful."

"Are *you* telling *me*?"

"Do you know what she said to me," continued Masters, with his eye on a bright star outside, "when I tried my ruddy best to get that skeleton back?" Here he mimicked heavily. " 'My good man, you are perfectly well aware you cannot remove the article in question until you can show just cause why you need it. Should you set foot inside the park without a warrant, I shall instruct my gardener to use his gun.' —Urr!" said Masters suddenly, making a noise like a dog.

"And do you know," Martin demanded, "what she said to me? Listen!"

Whereupon they both stopped and looked at each other, conscious of a meeting of minds.

"Let's face it, sir," Masters said benevolently, and lowered his defences. "There *may* be trouble."

And the richest and ripest trouble of all, as regards proceedings between Sir Henry Merrivale and the Dowager Countess of Brayle, had its first stir at eleven o'clock on the following morning.

Chapter 17

It was nearly eleven before Martin finished his breakfast on Monday morning.

When he turned in the night before, he had been too tired to bother with the sleeping-pill Dr. Laurier had left for him. He woke to a morning of soft breeze and gentle sun, so stimulated and refreshed that he felt ravenous for food. Certain instructions, which H.M. had made him promise to carry out overnight, now seemed nonsensical.

Martin sang in his bath. A harassed but punctilious Dr. Laurier, who arrived while he was shaving, changed the bandage on his forehead and told him that with luck the stitches would be out in no time.

Somebody had tried to kill him? But he had only to think of Jenny, and other matters for the moment seemed of no consequence. When he went downstairs, he met nobody in the cool house. In the dining-room he was served breakfast by a maid other than Phyllis; and, since Fleet House was supplied with great quantities of food from an unspecified source, he ate with appetite.

But it was the telephone he wanted. Emerging through a series of passages which brought him out opposite the staircase at the back of the main hall, Martin at last heard sounds of life. Voices—apparently those of Aunt Cicely, Ricky, and H.M. himself—drifted down from the direction of the drawing-room.

Then the 'phone rang; and it was Jenny.

The first part of their conversation need not be recorded here. Doubtless Sir Henry Merrivale would have described it as mush, adding that Jenny and Martin seemed to have achieved the seemingly impossible feat of getting into an intimate embrace over a telephone. But there seemed to be a faintly odd note in Jenny's voice.

"You haven't forgotten," he asked, "that this is the day you and I are going to London?"

"We—we can't. Not yet, anyway. Tonight we might."

A sense of impending disaster crept into him. "Why not?"

"Martin," breathed Jenny, *"why* does your H.M. insist on persecuting my poor grandmother?"

(I knew it! By all cussedness and the ten finger-bones of Satan, I knew it!)

"But what's he doing to her now, Jenny? He's here! In the drawing-room!"

Martin, do you know where I am?" asked Jenny.

"What's that?"

"I'm under the main staircase, with a thick oak door closed so I can speak to you. Hold on a second, and I'll push the door open. Listen!"

Martin jumped. The sound which poured out at him, even

over a telephone, made him yank the receiver away from his ear before putting it back to his ear again.

It sounded rather like Blackpool on August Bank Holiday. But the crowd-noises were over-ridden by music, in which Martin (too imaginatively, perhaps) thought he could detect one brass band, a panotrope with a bad needle, and the steam organ of a merry-go-round. High rose the strains of *Waltzing Matilda,* closely contested by *Cherry-Ripe* and *The Daring Young Man on the Flying Trapeze.*

The strains were blotted away as Jenny closed the door.

"Did Grandmother," she asked, "tell you anything about a fair?"

"Well," Martin searched his memory, "she did say something about it, yes. *I* thought she meant some sort of rustic fair with a Maypole."

"So did she," Jenny answered in a weary voice. "But it's the biggest travelling fair in the British Isles. They took half the night to set it up. You see, they—they sent Grandmother some sort of paper, six months ago. She said solicitors cost too much money, when she knew all the law anyway. And she signed it."

For a moment hope began to stir in Martin. After all, six months ago! It had been Grandmother's own fault. H.M. couldn't have had anything to do with this! He said as much.

"Yes," said Jenny. "But have you met a Mr. Solomon MacDougall?"

"Not to my knowledge."

"He's the owner or the man who manages it or something. Anyway, H.M. met him when he was looking over the ground yesterday . . ."

"Oh, my God!"

"And H.M. pointed out something in the contract they didn't know themselves. They intended to use Rupert's Five-Acre, which would have been bad enough. But H.M. said wouldn't it be a wonderful attraction if they had lines of booths and stalls and freak-shows up the main drive to the front door? And that's not the worst, either. Have you ever ridden in a Ghost-Train?"

Martin had. But he wanted to let Jenny pour her heart out.

"It's a big place like a house, dark inside. You ride in a little railway through terrific screams and howls and screeches. Do you know where H.M. persuaded them to put the Ghost-Train?"

"No, my sweet."

"Under Grandmother's bedroom windows," said Jenny.

"Er—yes. What I mean is: I see "

"On the roof of the Ghost-Train house," said Jenny, "there's a papier-maché skull on a pole. It's painted green. It turns round and round. And, every time it turns round, it looks in the bedroom window and chatters *two* sets of teeth."

"Jenny," said Martin, "wait just one minute. Hold the line and wait. The culprit's here. I'll . . ."

With a shaking hand he put down the 'phone beside its cradle. To say that he did not know whether to laugh or swear is to understate a real conflict of mind: it boiled inside him, tearing him both ways. Grandmother Brayle was not due home until this afternoon. To watch her behaviour then would be worth much. On the other hand, H.M.'s craftiness seemed always to separate him from Jenny; and he was resolved to get Jenny away today.

At this point of both murderousness and mirth, he became conscious of the great man's voice from the direction of the drawing-room. It was now raised to a serious and oratorical pitch, holding his listeners.

H.M. said: "What we got to remember, y'see, is the noble *dignity* of Curtius Merrivale. I wish I could paint you the picture of Charles the First sittin' in that noble Banqueting Hall, designed by Inigo Jones, with all his family gathered round just as you see it in the portraits. (Mind, I don't say these are the exact words; it's the idea.) And Charles the First would say, 'Sir Curtius, will you not favour us with some amusing conceit?'

"And Curtius Merrivale would get up, sweepin' off his plumed hat like this, and he'd say:

" 'There was a young girl from Bel Air,
Who used to—' "

"H.M.!" thundered Martin, with full power of lungs. It was enough to bring even H.M. to an abrupt stop. And Martin, torn between two feelings, could only sputter mentally.

"Did you," he shouted down the hall, "put a damn great Ghost-Train under Lady Brayle's bedroom?"

This question, whatever else may be said about it, was at least arresting. It roused attention and curiosity. After short silence, there was movement.

Ricky Fleet, in white flannels and white shirt, with tears of emotion in his eyes after what had been a long narration by H.M., raced and skidded along the hardwood floor. He was followed by Aunt Cicely, now seriously angry with H.M. for his romantic anecdotes. Last of all, with a lofty air, marched H.M. himself.

"Didn't you," Martin demanded, "put the biggest travelling fair in England slap on the main drive of Brayle Manor?"

"Well . . . now," said the culprit in question.

"But what's this," asked Ricky insistently, "about a train running through Grandmother's bedroom?"

At the same moment, in a hall touched by sunshine through the open door to the terrace, Ruth Callice and Stannard appeared at that door, followed by Chief Inspector Masters. Martin, like the skeleton, almost gibbered as he explained while the others gathered round.

"Jenny?" He turned back to the 'phone.

"Yes, dear?"

"How long has this uproar been going on? Why didn't you ring me?"

"But I only discovered it myself," Jenny protested, "about twenty minutes ago. Before I left you last night, you see, H.M. gave me two nembutal sleeping-pills; he got them from Dr. Laurier; and he made me promise to take them as soon as I got home. And I was so worried about you—"

Martin kept the receiver a little way back from his ear. Jenny's small, soft voice was distinctly audible to everyone who had gathered round.

"So," repeated Martin, "H.M. gave you some sleeping-pills, so you wouldn't know. Yes, I remember he said he did."

Sir Henry Merrivale, wearing an incredible air of righteousness, had folded his arms and stood like a statue in a park.

"Dawson and some of the others," pursued Jenny, "tried to wake me in the night, but they couldn't. While we had the lights and the noise, I mean. The first I knew was when I heard someone yelling, 'Get your fresh cockles and winkles.' "

"Did they—er—ring up your grandmother at wherever she's staying?"

"Priory Hill? No. They were afraid to."

"When is your grandmother due to come back?"

"At one o'clock, for lunch. I think she's bringing that clergyman back, the one who's so terribly dead-set against horseracing."

"Holy cats, they haven't got a race-track there, have they?"

"No, no, no! Of course not. And I'm not crying, Martin; I'm only laughing and I can't stop. If you could see this place! Can you please come here soon?"

"I can be there," Martin told her, "immediately. Wait for me!"

"And so can I be there," Ricky declared in ecstasy. "I'll run you over, old boy. I'd heard about this fair, but I never thought it was going to be anything like this."

Martin looked at H.M.

"Y'know," said the latter, taking a reflective survey of the faces round him and then leaning one elbow against the wall, "I think I must be the most reviled, misunderstood poor doer-of-good in this whole floatin' earth! I try to do Sophie some good, I honest-Injun do! And . . ."

"How are you going to do her good by sticking winkle-stalls and coconut-shies all over the lawn?"

"Never you mind," H.M. told him darkly. "They don't understand the old man, that's all. They see the result, when it's all over. Then they say, 'How curious! The silly old dummy did it by accident.'"

His peroration—in which he inquired, rhetorically, whether he was indignant when a skeleton stuck its head out of an electric car to blow raspberries at him; and replied by saying he was the most forgiving soul on earth—his peroration was cut short by the husky chuckle of Stannard.

Stannard looked in fine form this morning, hearty and clear of eye, with hardly a trace of limp.

"Ruth," he said, "something tells me this would be a sight worth seeing. Would you care to go?"

"I'd love to!"

"I'm going too," announced Aunt Cicely, tripping up several steps and running down to look at them, in unconscious pose against the tall window. "Only not until this afternoon, when I'm properly dressed."

Ruth looked worried.

"Cicely, do you think you ought? You heard what Dr. Laurier said only this morning. Shock, or excitement . . ."

"Ruth, I'm not an invalid!" laughed Aunt Cicely. "*I'm* the only person who keeps on talking about my heart. Besides," she nodded at them decidedly, "there's an unanswerable reason. Ricky wants me to"

"Ricky, don't you think you're being a bit inconsiderate?"

"Look here!" said Ricky. "The reason is—"

He hesitated, looked at them, saw in a wall looking-glass that he wore no coat or tie, and took the stairs three at a bound. "Tell you later!" he said.

"You for a sun-hat, my dear," Stannard touched Ruth's

arm, "and I for a suitable cloth cap. I have an instinct that this will be a memorable day."

"Oh, ah," Chief Inspector Masters muttered under his breath, "it will be for somebody."

Masters said this when he and H.M. and Martin stood in an otherwise empty hall. And Martin felt again an unexpected coldness round the heart when he saw him look at him: Masters with the unmirthful smile of one who knows all the facts, H.M. with his fists on his hips.

"So!" the latter growled softly. "You think I'm not attending to business, hey?"

"You don't mean this travelling-fair business is a part of another scheme to . . ."

"It's the same scheme, son."

"To catch the mur—?"

"Quiet, sir!" muttered Masters; and his tone was deadly serious. It was as though the blare of fair-music dwindled in Martin's ears; then grew louder with an implication of what it was to conceal.

"But, H.M.," he protested, "Jenny tells me you saw this man What's-his-name, who manages the fair, yesterday morning or afternoon. If I've got the facts right, you didn't tumble to the whole solution until late yesterday night. Then how could the fair have—?"

"Son," said H.M., "when I talked to that fine feller Solomon MacDougall I was having—hem!—maybe evil thoughts as well as holy thoughts. About skulls that chattered: you see what I mean? But I also saw last night how the cards were bein' dealt straight into our hands. See what I mean?"

"No."

"Anyhow, it's so. If you hear Masters or me say, 'Pip,' you jump to it and ask no questions. Got that?"

"Right."

Their looks were still in Martin's mind ten minutes later when the old car, with Ruth and Stannard in the rear seat, Martin in front with Ricky, moved along the main road southwards under a canopy of mellow sunlight. It moved so slowly that Dr. Laurier's car passed them, the doctor giving a pince-nez flicker of greeting and touching the brim of his hat. At sight of the other car, Ricky blurted out what he had to say.

"I want to explain," he said, "why I seemed to be such a hound towards Mother."

From their previous conversation, it had been clear that Ricky no longer felt any distrust of Stannard. Sheer admiration of Stannard's conduct in the execution shed would have done that. Stannard's friendliness was apparent too, though he treated Ricky as an indulgent uncle would treat a nephew of sixteen.

"My dear boy!" The husky chuckle remonstrated. "You can't be called a hound for inviting your mother to a fair."

"No, that's just it!" Ricky appealed to Stannard as much as to Martin. "But—it's about Susan Harwood."

Stannard whistled. "You don't mean they're going to meet?"

"They've met already, in a way. At charity do's. But this is different. Martin, you'll stand by? You're in the same boat."

"I'll do anything I can, of course."

Ruth, tapping her fingers on her handbag, said nothing.

"Susan knows about it," Ricky explained, with one eye on the road and one eye on his companions, "but Mother doesn't. At one o'clock I'll be strolling with Mother. The place will be near, but not too near, a lemonade-stall or an ice-cream stall or something like that."

"Ricky," Ruth cried, "what *are* you planning?"

"*Will* you be quiet, old girl, and listen to me?"

"Honestly, Ricky . . ."

"I'll introduce 'em," Ricky ignored the protest, "and then I'll out with it. I'll say this is the girl I'm going to marry, and wouldn't they like to get acquainted? Mother can't make a scene in public. Then I'll say, 'Just get you an ice; excuse me a moment.'"

"Ricky," cried Ruth, "you coward!"

Former Wing-Commander Richard Fleet, D.S.O. with bar, did not in this instance deny it.

"I've told Laurier," he confided; "but he's an ass. They'll stroll away, Susan and Mother, and I'll follow. If you see me beckon, crowd in. If you see me motion to keep away, keep away. Anyway, I can't lose 'em when I follow."

"We're with you," said Martin. "But why not simply elope with the girl? That's what I'm going to do, this afternoon or tonight."

"You're . . . *what?*" exclaimed Ruth.

"Never mind. We were talking about Ricky."

"I can't do it," said Ricky, referring to elopement. He was desperately in earnest, so much so that his eyes brimmed as they had brimmed a while ago, though perhaps for different reasons, when H.M. was telling stories. He scarcely noticed the road; the car had gathered speed; yet his instinctive timing never put them in danger. "This is the only way. Mother'll understand it."

"All good luck, my boy!" smiled Stannard. "But, my dear Drake. You were saying—?"

"Martin doesn't mean it," observed Ruth.

(Oh, don't I?)

For now, beyond tall trees at a bend in the road, there rose above a crowd murmur the predominating brass-band strains of *Waltzing Matilda*. In contrast to the stuff which passes for music nowadays, this noble tune must set a stuffed mummy to whistling and tapping its foot. Martin Drake began whistling too. He was going away with Jenny.

Round the curve they swept into the straight. The fifteen-foot-high brick wall of Brayle Manor, which they had seen stretching westwards, now ran past the road on the right. All the noises of the fair were sweeping out at them now.

On the left-hand side of the road, an immense enclosed field had as the sign over its road gate, PARKING, is 6d. Though petrol was supposed to be scarce, you would not have learned this by the glow of sun winking on the backs of so many cars. On the other side of the road seethed mild pandemonium.

The broad iron-grilled gates stood wide open. The head of a perspiring ticket-seller stretched out over the half-door of the gate-keeper's lodge. From the opposite side, hoarsely, rose the chant of a man with vari-coloured balloons and white hats bearing such mottoes as *Kiss Me Quick*.

As Martin crossed the road from the parking-lot with Ricky, Stannard, and Ruth, a police-car containing Masters and H.M. drew up not far from the gates. Then Martin noticed, stuck on each side of the wall at the gates, a huge poster showing an equally huge photograph of the Dowager Countess, wearing a tiara and a smile. Underneath, signed and in red letters, ran what was clearly a quotation from a letter.

"If the civic authorities of Brayle attempt to prevent this fair, or so much as set foot inside the park, I shall sue them for five thousand pounds."

Several newcomers were reading it with stunned admiration.

"Now listen, sir!" Martin heard the Chief Inspector's voice hiss. "You're going to behave yourself?"

An empurpled visage appeared above the shoulder of Ruth Callice.

"What d'ye mean, behave myself?" the face demanded.

This was the last Martin could catch, since they were pressing through the swirl of the crowd. To his surprise he saw Dr. Laurier up ahead. After procuring their tickets, feeling the gravel of the broad drive crunch under their feet, they seemed to be in clearer space while voices and music rolled over them.

"Kick the football! Kick the football, burst a balloon, and win a fine prize!"

"'Ow's yer strength, gen'lemen? 'Ow's yer strength? 'Ere we—"

The churning, tinkling melody of the merry-go-round, blowing hard with steam-pressure, swept across the voices like mist. Another (alleged) melody, made even more ghoulish by a loud-speaker and a deep voice singing, intruded.

"With 'er 'ead TOOKED oon-der-neath 'er arm,
She wa-a-a-lks the bluidy TOW-ER—"

"This, ladies and gentlemen, is the Mirror Maze." A loudspeaker again, with a semi-cultured voice. *"Biggest and finest attraction of MacDougall's Mammoth. The Mirror Maze. If you are unable—"*

"Stan!" cried Ruth. "Where are you?"

"Here, my dear! Take my hand!"

Laughter and giggles broke above them like rockets. Everybody seemed to be eating potato-crisps and then throwing the empty bags in your face. Then they emerged into a comparatively wide open space: where, Martin gathered, two lines of attractions crossed.

"If you are unable to get out of the Mirror Maze," the loudspeaker gave a rasping chuckle, like a loud parody of Stannard, *"directions will be given by—"*

"Sir Henry! Wait! Come back here!"

Martin, getting his breath to plunge towards the house and Jenny, turned round. But nothing appeared to be seriously wrong.

Just to the right was a booth set out as a miniature racetrack with its counter a little higher than waist level. Metal horses, each about five inches long and with its jockey's colours brilliantly painted, stood at the starting-gate of an oval course. Grandstand, spectators, greensward, all were realistically done. Along the front of the counter ran a line of squares, each inscribed with the name of a horse and its colours. Projecting underneath each space was a crank-handle by which you made the horses run.

"It's all right, son!" H.M. assured Masters testily. "Burn it, I'm just havin' a look."

Behind the counter sat a dispirited-looking man, chewing a broomstraw, who had started to get up. Now he sank back again hopelessly.

H.M. inspected the track. He sniffed. He ran his eye

critically over the horses, like one inspecting a parade at Epsom. Then something seemed to take hold of him as though with hands, and he swung round.

"I'll give you five to one the field," he burst out. "And eight to one," he glanced behind him, "Blue Boy." His eyes gleamed. "I'll tell you what I'll do: I'll give you *ten* to one on Blue Boy!"

Ricky sprang forward.

"Here's ten bob on Blue Boy," said Ricky, slapping the money down on the corresponding counter-space. "And, just for luck, I'll have another ten bob on Squaw's Feather."

"For myself," said Stannard, instantly whipping out his note-case, "I fancy Bright-Eyes. With the dark brown colour; eh, Ruth? One pound on Bright-Eyes!"

"Uh-huh. One pound on Bright-Eyes," repeated H.M., who had scrabbled out with a notebook and the stub of a pencil, and was hastily recording. Then he lifted his voice to the whole fair-ground.

"I'll give you five to one the field," he bellowed. "Anybody want to make a little bet?"

"Goddelmighty!" whispered Chief Inspector Masters.

Now there are many words which will instantly rivet or turn the attention of an English crowd. You may say them over to yourself. But perhaps none is quite so potent as the word 'bet.' Materializing and mingling, the crowd pressed in ten-deep towards the counter, with cries and queries.

The man behind the counter, who had swallowed his broomstraw as he leaped up, now appeared to be racked by the convulsions of cyanide poisoning. He was writhing forward across the race-track, his hands outstretched.

"Oi! Gov'nor! The gent with the bald 'ead! For gossake! Oi!"

"What d'ye mean, oi?"

"It's against the LOR."

"What d'ye mean, it's against the law?"

"It's gambling," whispered and blurted the other, his eyes now rolling horribly *in articulo mortis*. "*I* wouldn't mind, see, but it's against the LOR. You'll 'ave the coppers on us!"

"Oh, my son! Don't you know no coppers can get in here today?"

"Whassat-forgossake?"

"This here Lady Brayle—" H.M. was in good voice; it carried far—"thinks people's liberties are bein' interfered with. Couldn't you have guessed that from what she wrote on the posters out there?"

A hum of approval, growing to a roar, spread out over the crowd. Dust and gravel flew. At his last extremity the dying man's eye seemed to catch some flicker beyond, a signal from an arm in a grey-and-black checked sleeve, which said, 'Yes.' The pangs of agony dropped from him.

Whang went the cymbals from an invisible brass-band; and, by one of those inspired coincidences which really do happen, the band crashed into *Camptown Races*. Martin, his head down and pulling Ruth after him, was fighting his way through a pressing crowd with silver in its hands. His damaged forehead took some dizzying knocks, but he got through.

Ruth Callice, her straw sun-hat squashed down, removed the hat and regarded him helplessly.

"Martin," she said, "is H.M. married?"

"Yes."

"Have you ever met his wife?"

"No."

Ruth shut her eyes, puffed out her cheeks, and seemed lost in questions of fancy in her own mind.

"*This stout gen'leman will give you five to one the field; ten to one Blue Boy! Don't crowd, now! Keep back so's the 'andles can be turned. Lady Brayle wants you all to 'ave a fling!*"

"Ruth," Martin said, "I've got to hurry. Excuse me if I go ahead."

He had still fifty or sixty yards of the drive to cover. But the stalls and booths were fewer; he could almost run. A yellow balloon, lost from someone's hand, sailed past on a rising breeze. He could see that the oak trees, set back twenty feet from the drive, allowed room for the stalls inside. But the bigger exhibits, like the Mirror Maze, the merry-go-round, and something which called itself Mermaids' Paradise, raised their garish colours well back on the lawn behind the trees.

Well, the bandage was still on. And he reached the terrace.

Except to glance along the front, Martin hardly looked at Brayle Manor. Between two square grey-black towers, one at each end and of great age, had been built a Tudor or Jacobean frontage, with latticed windows, which seemed almost of yesterday by comparison.

Martin banged the heavy knocker on the front door. There was no reply. He banged and banged until the noise, in his head, grew louder than the band and the loud-speakers and the merry-go-round. He thought he heard some sound from an oriel window, projecting out over the front door, and he stepped back. But a voice spoke from behind the front door.

"Is that Mr. Martin Drake?"

"Yes!"

With a rattle of bolts and the click of a key, the heavy door opened under its low-pointed stone arch. Inside stood an elderly man in butler's canonicals, very shabby and clearly Dawson, with whom he had held that conversation about the five hundred pound.

He was in a dim, polished Tudor hall, low of ceiling and so much in twilight because all windows had been closed, all curtains drawn, against the noise.

"Martin!" said Jenny's voice.

A broad, low staircase, with carved balustrades, ascended along the left-hand wall. A heavy hinged panel at the side of the stairs stood more than part way open, and Jenny's face peered out at him.

"Martin," she said without preamble, "Grandmother's on the telephone."

Chapter 18

Martin strode over, hearing Dawson shut and lock the door behind him. Jenny was now regarding his forehead with far more consternation and concern than seemed possible if he had suffered serious injury.

"Just a minute, Jenny," he said. "What have you told her?"

"She only just started to speak. She said, 'Jennifer, I—' and that was where Dawson opened the door."

Taking the 'phone from Jenny's hands as she moved out from under the stair-opening, Martin sat down on a low little chair and cleared his throat.

"Lady Brayle? Martin Drake here."

To tell the truth, Martin was beginning to feel sorry for the old girl. True, she had brought the whole mess on herself by inviting MacDougall's Mammoth into her grounds. But H.M. was the evil genius. And, in the third round, H.M. had landed such a knockout punch that his adversary was still unconscious after the count. Or was H.M., actually, the evil genius? Martin was beginning to have other ideas. Still, the fact remained . . .

"Indeed," said Lady Brayle. "I was not aware, Captain Drake, that I wished to hold any conversation with you."

Calm and even of voice, conscious of no interest but her

own and not apparently caring who knew it, the lady with the cold grey eye spoke indifferently.

"So?" muttered Martin.

"However! I have heard certain rumours, which I do not believe, concerning the Manor. You will not trouble to comment on the facts. This would not interest me. You will merely be good enough to confirm or deny these rumours."

Martin held the telephone away from him and studied it. His temper, like a red line on a graph-paper, zig-zagged violently and then slowly soared high.

"Where are you now, Lady Brayle?"

"Really, that is not the slightest concern—"

"It may be. Where are you now?"

"I am at the Priory Hill vicarage, about two miles north of Brayle. I am in Mr. Barnham's study."

"Is that the clergyman who's so dead-set against horse-racing?"

Distantly, but still audible, the band-music swayed and jigged:

> *"Oh, I put my money on a bob-tailed nag,*
> *Doo-dah, doo-dah—"*

"Has it occurred to you, Captain Drake, that I am waiting for an answer?"

"Madam," Martin said gently, "I can't answer your question as it deserves to be answered, because I don't know. I have a theory, but it may not be right. Sir Henry Merrivale," he hoped he could keep his promise, "will ring you in half an hour and explain everything."

"You will regret this, Captain Drake. When I return home, I shall carry a riding-crop. It will be most unpleasant for the first half dozen people I meet inside my gates."

Martin put down the 'phone and ducked out from under the stairs. Jenny, her wide-spaced blue eyes filled not only with concern, clutched his arms.

"You didn't say anything to insult her?"

"I don't think so, and I don't care."

"Darling," Jenny asked quietly, "have you any idea how lordly *you* can look and sound, when you get annoyed with somebody?"

"*Me?*"

This, to him, seemed so nonsensical that he put it down to some fancy of Jenny's romantic brain. He glanced round the dim, heavily stuffy hall, where the lean and sallow-haired

Dawson in his shabby butler's-clothes seemed a kind of symbol.

"No," Jenny answered his thought mockingly, with a smile on her entirely irresistible mouth, "we didn't make the house look like a place of mourning because of the noise. It's a sort of gesture: when Grandmother comes back. Upstairs at the window we've been having a kind of signally-game with Mr. MacDougall. I don't know what it means, but he says it's frightfully important. Come along!"

Again the front-door knocker rapped, but far too heavily for it to have been Ruth Callice. Martin had his own guess.

"Chief Inspector Masters?" he shouted; and, at an affirmative reply, he nodded to Dawson.

Masters, having already pushed out a dent in his bowler hat and dusted off his blue serge suit, crossed the threshold with brief-case and cardboard folder under one arm; and he had the air of a tethered bull.

"Sorry to intrude, miss," he said, being not quite sure of Jenny's title and knowing she didn't like it anyway, "but this is business."

Jenny had gone rather white. "Yes," she acknowledged, and pressed Martin's arm. "After all, someone tried to kill Mr. Drake."

"And did kill that Puckston girl," said Martin.

"I wanted to ask——" Jenny began. "Will you come upstairs, please?"

She led them to an octagonal room, of white walls framed in dark oak, above the front door. Here was the big oriel window with its three leaded panes—two slantwise, the other facing straight out—which looked down the gravel drive with its crowd, its gaudy exhibits, the oak-trees, and the green lawns.

Geraniums in flower-pots, as a homely touch, stood just inside the ledges of the diamond-paned windows. The dark oak window-seat ran round all sides of the octagonal room as well; like the chairs, it had flattish flowered cushions. With one window-light partly open, the babble now sounded at its loudest.

"Mr. Masters," Jenny began.

Jenny, in white, her knees crossed, sat at one side of the window. Her elbow was propped on one knee, her chin in her hand.

"I think," she smiled, "I like H.M. far better than Martin likes Grandmother. But doesn't he ask the oddest questions sometimes?"

"Does he, miss?" inquired Masters, who was at his blandest

card-sharper's air as he put down hat, brief-case, and folder.

"He talked to me for ages yesterday at Fleet House. First all about certain things," her eyes moved towards Martin, who was sitting beside her, "when he hadn't been present. Then, if you please, something that seemed to be about Grandmother's influence over me!"

"Is that so, now, miss?" inquired Masters, as though hearing a mildly surprising revelation.

"And that's absurd, of course!" Jenny had some intense purpose behind this; her eyes were lustrous. "You see, my parents were estranged. They sent me away to school from the time I was ten and onwards. Grandmother was always hovering about, it's true. But most of the vacations were abroad with my parents. Then came the war and the Wrens. It's only since the war that Grandmother's had much 'influence.' I was wondering if H.M.—"

"Yes, miss?"

Martin who had got up and was staring out of the window, interposed.

"Where the devil is H.M., by the way?"

Masters's own temper flared as he sat down in a chair opposite Jenny. Everything grated now, everything jarred like a bad slate-pencil on a bad slate.

"Whatever he's doing," the Chief Inspector snapped, "he's not attending to business."

"There's a Derby-Day crowd round that race-track," said Martin, "all waving shillings. Is he still being bookie?"

"When I last saw the gentleman," Masters replied with dignity, "he was starting some kind of darts-contest." Masters looked at Jenny, not without sarcasm. "I suppose, miss, your grandmother doesn't keep a cellar full of beer?"

"Good heavens, no! She used to drink wine, but . . ."

"N-no," intoned Masters, "I didn't think she would keep a beer-cellar. And especially I didn't think she'd keep it in barrels with her photograph pasted on, and 'Here's how from Lady Brayle.' As to what the old bounder's doing . . ."

"I can tell you what he's doing," said Martin. "He told Arthur Puckston last night he'd been thinking for several days Grandmother ought to be ousted or made popular. He's trying to make her popular. And do you know what'll happen?"

Masters didn't care, and said so.

"She told me she'd come back with a riding-crop. And she will. Isn't that so, Jenny?"

"Darling," pleaded Jenny, "she tried to make friends with you. I told you she was beginning to like you, but you wouldn't believe me. I didn't see her last night, because she went straight on to Priory Hill. Surely she tried to make friends with you?"

"Possibly. Anyhow, it didn't work. Now she'll come back with a riding-crop. She'll lay it, right and left, across anybody she sees. Then there'll be a riot and real trouble."

"I don't doubt it at all," Masters agreed, almost with satisfaction.

Then he whacked his hand down on the arm of the chair.

"Mr. Drake," Masters said, "this is a murder case. We had everything planned and even timed to a minute to catch the murderer. But Sir Henry's gone off his rocker, just as he did once at Coney Island, and what chance have we got now?"

"To catch—?" Jenny's face had gone even whiter. "But it couldn't possibly be . . . anybody we know?"

Belatedly, Masters remembered official caution and his usual manner.

"Is that so, miss? Why not?"

"Well!" Jenny laughed, not convincingly. "*I* didn't do it. Grandmother certainly didn't. For the rest, there's the alibi!"

"Oh, ah, miss? What do you know about an alibi?"

"Only what Ruth Callice told me yesterday." Jenny shivered violently; even her mouth seemed distorted; Martin quickly put his arm round her shoulder. "About a blood-stained dagger somebody used to kill poor Enid Puckston, at half-past eleven or thereabouts."

"Anything else, miss?"

"Ruth said Mr. Stannard—he's a tremendous barrister—had suddenly snapped his fingers and said to her, 'You know, I was so tired and groggy I completely forgot to tell Inspector Drake about that alibi. No, wait,' he said, 'let them find it out themselves.' But he told Ruth."

"You can forget the alibi too, miss," Masters remarked quietly. "It's shot to blazes."

From outside the window the churning tinkle of the merry-go-round, silent for a time, began to rise loudly with *We're All Together Now*. In the octaganal room, with its white walls and its red geraniums inside the window, the tune seemed to swirl round as in a bowl, above the babble of voices.

"So you did upset the alibi!" Martin muttered. "How?"

Masters looked complacent.

"We-el! No harm in telling that. You people who were in the condemned cell when you found the dagger, you were doing a lot of talking . . ."

"Chief Inspector, how do you know so much about that conversation?"

Masters eyed him grimly.

"Aren't you forgetting, Mr. Drake, that *I* spent the night in that prison? Oh, ah! Keeping an eye on *you* to make sure nobody nailed you?"

"You could hear everything we said all the time?"

"I'm an old-fashioned copper," Masters said dryly. "I've had trickier jobs when I was a sergeant."

"But where were you during the 'test'? I mean, when I'd locked Stannard behind the iron door, and the others had gone?"

Masters snorted.

"Making myself comfortable," he said, "on top of that mountain of paper. Lummy! We'd get sixteen hours at a stretch in the old days when I was a sergeant. On Saturday night I was facing the iron door. I could see you, Mr. Drake, by your own light, sitting on the paper-bales. I couldn't see down into the aisle, between the bales and the wall with the doors; but I could get there at one jump if I had to."

Here Masters smiled a peculiar smile.

"D'you think I'm a liar, sir? You look a bit funny. For instance! At shortly past twelve, you had a visitor."

The visitor had been Ruth Callice, of course.

Martin, his arm round Jenny's shoulder and the caress of her hair under his cheek, felt such a cold rush of guilty conscience that he was within a quarter-syllable of speaking out and denying it. At the same moment Jenny raised her head round and up, looked at Martin casually, and returned to her former position without comment. After a quick heat of emotional temperature, Jenny's shoulder seemed to become as cool and lifeless as though it did not exist at all; as though it rested there out of mere politeness. If there could have been a mental conversation between them, Jenny would have begun.

(Please don't think I'm annoyed. I knew it would happen *some* time that night).

(What are you talking about?)

(The same thing you're thinking about. How far did it go?)

But Masters, or so the Chief Inspector believed, had no intention of giving away a fellow-male.

"A visitor," he repeated judicially. "Well, no harm in that I could see it in two seconds. Later the—hurrum!—the bloke went back the same way. Then nothing happened until a quarter to one. But at a quarter to one I heard someone else rustle in that aisle."

Both Martin and Jenny were jarred out of their mental conversation. Both sat up. The sound of *We're All Together*

Now, mixed with crowd-babble, seemed to swirl higher.

"Somebody else?"

"Somebody, anyhow. It was just a bit of a faint rustle you could hardly hear, 'Streweth!" said Masters. "If I'd been younger in the force, I might have got the wind up myself.

"You wouldn't have heard it in any case, Mr. Drake. You were sound asleep. I got ready. I thought it was creeping towards you. Anyway, it wasn't. My eyes were enough used to the dark so I could make out the outlines of the doors in the wall. Just so! You remember, I told you last night there was a little camera trick that might interest you?"

"Yes! What about it?"

"Ordinary camera," Masters said, "borrowed from the local police. Infra-red film, infra-red bulb, from the chemist at Brayle. Useful to have along with you. Take photographs in the dark; not a glimmer to show you're taking 'em. *If* you know where to aim a camera.

"I could see that the end door opposite the bale-mountain— Mr. Drake was sleeping against the same wall about ten feet from the door—started to open. Soft as soft! And wider. No sense for me to yell lum's name if nothing was after Mr. Drake. I snapped a picture at the door before it closed.

"We-el," resumed Masters, tapping the brief-case on the table beside him, "I got the print from the chemist this morning. Not a good picture, no. But a picture of Enid Puckston."

"Of . . . what did you say?"

"Of Enid Puckston," repeated Masters, and tapped the brief-case again. "Creeping in backwards. Facing the camera. On tip-toe," Master's face darkened, "and with a 'What larks!' delighted look. Like a kid playing a prank. Somebody's hand was on her arm, drawing her in."

Masters drew a deep breath.

"*And this*," Martin demanded, "*was at a quarter to one in the morning?*"

"That's right. And—come now! Blimy-O'Reilly! Can't you see the trick of it?"

"I can see that the dagger we found among that heap of rapiers . . ."

"Oh, ah! Exactly. It'd been planted there, with fresh blood on it, to make what you think what you did think later.. That somebody'd killed the girl about half-past eleven. But the girl was still alive. Not even in the prison!

"You're the arms expert, Mr. Drake. And that Italian dagger you found, now! I told you knife-wounds can't be identified

certain-sure like bullet-wounds. Would you say that dagger
was (hurrum!) unique?"

"Lord, no. There are plenty of them. I've got one something
like it in my own collection."

Masters bent forward, his fingers spread. Every word he
spoke seemed to pounce.

"Then: a quarter to one. Everything dark and quiet.
Somebody from outside leads Enid Puckston along the aisle.
Creeping; hardly a rustle. Soft as soft. Like a cat! Door opens
(no noise; notice that), door closes. They're in the old mortuary.

"Somebody takes her across the mortuary, out into the
garden under the windows of the condemned cell. Somebody
kills her there with another dagger. Enid's carried the
travelling-robe; it's in the photograph. Somebody carries her
body, soft as soft, down the underground stair from the
mortuary, along the passage, through a door, into the shaft
under the gallows-trap . . ."

Masters, reverting to his normal tone, sat up straight.

"How was I supposed to know," he demanded, "there'd been
a murder in the prison that night? I was uneasy, like: oh, ah!
But my job was to follow Mr. Drake. And I did, when he left
at what he thought was four o'clock. I followed you both," he
looked at Jenny, "down over that field."

Now here was a characteristic of Jenny: that, though she
had been furious a few minutes before over a little matter
concerning Ruth, it seemed swept out of her mind at anything
concerning Martin.

"You said," she exclaimed to Masters, "the murde—this
person—you said this person was 'somebody from outside.'"

Masters pulled himself together, remembering official caution.

"Did I say that, miss?" he inquired, eyeing the brief-case.
"Then I must have meant it, mustn't I?"

"So in that case . . ."

"As for the trick with fresh blood on the dagger that wasn't
used, that's easy. Lummy! The whole alibi-trick was only a
conjuring principle. Sir Henry could tell you that. People won't
believe what's as clear as daylight. People won't believe how
small a space a body can occupy; and, when a dozen girls walk
out of a little cabinet, there's no hocus-pocus: the girls were
honestly there. They won't believe the time a thing happened,
from a coin-change to a couple of bodies, was back-to-
foremost. Sir Henry could tell you that. But will he? Oh, no!
He was supposed to be here fifteen minutes ago . . ."

Martin Drake, stung by memory, fumbled at his wrist-watch.

"Fifteen minutes!" he echoed. "It's more than half an hour!"

"What do you mean, more than half an hour?"

"I promised Lady Brayle—"

"Martin, you did!" Jenny began to move apprehensively.

"—that H.M. would ring her in half an hour. If she doesn't hear from him, she'll be here and start a riot!"

"Agreed," said Masters.

"Then you never will catch your murderer," said Martin, whose brain burned to know the look of somebody's face. "And *I've* got a score to settle too."

"You have," agreed Masters, looking at him in a curious way.

"Isn't there any way to find H.M.?"

"Find him?" said Masters. "That's easy enough. By the signalling system. But get him here? Ho! He's off his chump, I tell you!"

"What's this signalling business?"

Jenny hurried to a writing desk, and took up a sheet of paper with a list typed on it. Hastening to the middle page of the window, she raised her right arm and waved.

From some forty yards down the drive, there appeared the conspicuous sleeve of a grey-and-black checked suit. (Martin had seen that sleeve before, near the race-track booth.) A hand waved. Then, startlingly, the hand held high a square card bearing the large number 7.

Jenny's finger, on the typewritten sheet, found the number 7 and indicated to Martin, opposite the words *Mirror Maze*.

"That's Mr. MacDougall," she said rapidly. "For some reason he thinks H.M. is wonderful. He thinks H.M. was born to the show business. Martin! Wait! Just a moment!"

Martin scarcely heard Jenny's last words as he ran.

Outside the front door, a still-rising breeze swept his face. The sky was overcast, though it did not look like rain. Empty bags of potato-crisps danced past, and a small girl's hat.

"This, ladies and gentlemen," Martin could remember a voice through a loud-speaker, though he did not hear it amid the blatter now, "is the Mirror Maze. Biggest and finest attraction of MacDougall's Mammoth. The Mirror Maze. If you are unable—"

It was half-past twelve. Though a fair number of people still cluttered round the attractions, most of the crowd had retired farther back to eat out of picnic boxes. They sat on the greensward, encamped like an army, with white napkin-cloths and glinting thermos-flasks. As for music, only the band whooshed and boomed softly with Scottish airs. But in the drive, where Martin ran like hell, it was different.

"Get a fish, now! A wood-en fish, with a re-al hook, out of re-al running water. Each third fish contains a number a number, which—"

"See how easy it is? Just throw the wooden ring, like this, over the peg!"

"Come-on-Redjacket! Bill, turn that crank faster! Come-on-Redjacket for 'alf a crown!

This was the place.

Near the race-track, where the crowd bounced him round its edges like a roulette-ball, a wide space had been left between both lines of booths and stalls to form a sort of cross-avenue.

Beyond the open space on his right, set some hundred feet back, was the Mirror Maze. It stood alone; nothing anywhere near it except the Whip and the Dodgem.

"'Ave your try at the coconut-shy!" a voice was intoning, that of a little man who hopped from foot to foot under the spell of his own rhyming. *"'Ave your try at the coconut-shy!"* An arm snapped forward; the wooden ball clacked against the coconut; the coconut toppled and fell. *"That's the stuff, sir. One—cigarette! 'Ave your try at the coconut-shy!"*

It jigged through Martin's head, like the little man jigging back and forth, as he turned off the drive and ran towards the Mirror Maze. The loud-speaker had been right in calling the Mirror Maze its biggest attraction.

The structure was very large, circular in shape (odd, wasn't that, for a mirror maze?), and 'practical' in the sense that it had been built of very light wood painted dull silver. The words MIRROR MAZE stared at Martin in red letters.

But there was nobody at the ticket-seller's place. Nobody to speak into the microphone of the loud-speaker. No visitors. Nobody at all. Over the door hung a curtain of black felt, a good deal heavier and thicker than the under-felt for carpets.

The sky was growing darker, over a buzz and paper-crackle from an army at sandwich-eating. Some female singer, whose voice reminded Martin of Lady Brayle, had joined the brass-band and urged it to softness. Martin heard one line above the heavy lion-purr of the band:

"Ma-a-a-x-wel-l-l-ton's braes are bo-o-n-n-ie—"

Then he ducked past the mattressy black felt, became entangled in another black curtain, and twisted himself free from that.

"H.M.!" he shouted.

Inside the circular structure was another structure: almost as large, but square and painted black. It had only one door, opening into a broad corridor, dimly lighted and lined with polished looking-glass.

To Martin, as he crossed the threshold of the Mirror Maze, it seemed he was walking into a gigantic box-camera.

"Oi! H.M.! Where are you?" he called. But the shout seemed lifeless, flat, stifled, as he strode along the corridor.

(I know it's an optical trick, but this corridor looks as long as something at Versailles. It isn't actually broad, either; I can touch each side by stretching out my hands. Also, I can see the joinings down the mirrors. Of course the corridor's not long! Two turnings here.)

Martin took one turning. He walked a dozen feet farther, and took another.

"H.M., don't try to play the fool! This is only a little place; you can't help hearing me. They know you're here!"

Exasperated, Martin paused. He looked round with curiosity, and then with some feeling other than exasperation.

He was the only living soul in this maze. Yet he was not alone. Everywhere he was pursued, surrounded, and furtively glanced at round corners, by images of himself.

The dim yellow light, from some concealed source along the tops of the mirrors, turned the place into a shiny, shadowy labyrinth, all straight lines and right-angles, short passages and long, with one looking-glass occupant.

Martin Drake, turning to one side, confronted himself: he looked, with the discoloured forehead, exactly like a pirate. He turned to the other, with the same result. He walked forward again, his footsteps clumping, to what seemed to be the junction of four passages. As he circled round, a whole band of pirates multiplied and circled with him.

(All right. If H.M. is up to some crafty game, let it be taken as done. I'm going to get out of here.)

That would be easy, of course. He had only to remember where he came in, which must be comparatively close. But the fact was that he couldn't remember where he came in.

Well, what of it?

All that would be required of him, as Stannard had said, was a little logical reasoning. A sense of direction, too. Here—observe, now!—was the junction of what appeared to be four corridors. One of them looked like a dead-end. Martin edged in, reaching out his fingers to touch his own reflected fingers, and met the glass. Good! He'd established that.

Now the other corridor, opposite, must be fully twenty feet long. It had a mirror there facing him; but a long corridor must have a turn at the side which (now he remembered!) was the direction he had come.

Martin, heated with elation, took five strides forward. And . . .

God!

Out of nowhere, leaping, a full-length mirror rushed at him and banged him full body and face.

Only the sudden vision of his own eyes—appearing hideously magnified by their closeness—made an instinctive recoil and lessened the shock as he smacked full-tilt into his own reflection. What angered him was the real shock to the nerves it had given him in a childish place meant for amusement.

"Now let's consider this!" Martin said, unaware he was speaking aloud.

"Looking-glasses can't suddenly move across in front of you. Any more than a lot of beach-chairs can rush at you and push you off a roof."

That was a grisly thought. What brought such an idea into his head?

"Therefore," he argued, and still aloud to all his ghost-selves, "there's an explanation. This mirror I ran into: it's the end of the passage I was trying to reach.

"Got it! A mirror at the end of the passage gives a double length of reflection. You judge it by the floor. If it looks twenty feet away, it's actually only ten. I went tearing forward, like Grandmother Brayle, and as a result—!" He stopped.

That was a sound, not from his imagination, clearly if very faintly heard, which registered with him. It was, 'Brayle,' or 'Lady Brayle.'

Despite its layers of looking-glasses and its double roof, the Mammoth Mirror Maze was not exactly soundproof. Nobody could mistake the slowly gathering roar from a little distance away, to Martin's heighted senses carrying a note of anger; the shouts; the heavy drumming of crowd-feet across open grass.

The old girl had returned.

She must have returned, he reflected, almost as soon as he himself had dived into this place. She had started raising hell at the main gates, and must have got some way up the drive with her riding-crop before . . .

Well, he'd *got* to get out of this place. Martin tried again.

What drives a man frantic, even under the most ordinary circumstances, is that he cannot make speed even when he refrains from making haste. The more he says it to himself—slowly, slowly, no haste or you'll fumble—the more matters become snarled. The clock-hand crawls; the chance is lost.

"*If you are unable to get out of the Mirror Maze,*" Martin's memory brought back the words from the loud-speaker, "*directions will be given by—*"

Given by whom? Given how? He had heard no more.

Martin, trying to keep from a run and holding out his hands against obstacles, hurried always into a dead-end. His watch kept ticking steadily, tiny digs of urgency: If only he hadn't come in here alone . . .

But he was not alone in the maze.

He discovered this as he whipped round the angle of a corridor, and stopped dead.

This corridor (his eye, used to it now, could judge accurately) was twenty feet long. Ahead of him, back to Martin, walked a man in a brown coat and blue trousers.

A grey soft hat was pulled down on the back of the man's head, concealing even the neck. In the dim light, in the secret silvery cavern, no details could be seen. And, though the man wore heavy boots and walked heavily, he made not a sound. All this went through Martin's head while the man took three steps.

"Hoy! There! Wait a minute!"

Martin ran forward. The air itself took form against him. His outstretched hands thumped into an invisible barrier which jarred him to the shoulder-bones and stopped him in his tracks.

It was a polished sheet of thick plate-glass: invisible, stretching across the whole corridor and cutting it in two. No wonder the man's steps had made no sound!

Martin, his hands against the glass, stood there for a moment and tried to think straight. This wasn't a predicament: it was merely damned ludicrous. He was not in the Cretan labyrinth, or even in Pentecost Prison. He was in a trumpery two-by-four pavilion at a country fair, and yet as excited as though . . .

Whereupon, although the corridor was empty except for Martin, a voice spoke. The voice had a note of slyness; it was not loud; it even whispered. The voice said:

"*You had better leave, Mr. Drake. If you can.*"

Chapter 19

About a quarter of an hour before that voice spoke to Martin, there was at Brayle Manor a scene far more wrenched with emotion, far deeper in the springs of human life.

Sophia, Dowager Countess of Brayle, almost staggered as she moved up the broad oak staircase in the dim house. Her fashionable hat was disarranged on the grey-white hair. The fashionable dress, also a little disarranged, did not now conceal her stoutness. From the limp fingers of one hand dangled a riding-crop. Nevertheless, most noticeable of all was the look of utter stupefaction in her eyes.

Lady Brayle stumbled a little on the top step. She went over to the octagonal room, whose oriel window faced the drive, and opened the door.

In the window-seat, his back to the leaded panes, Sir Henry Merrivale sat smoking a cigar. Chief Inspector Masters stood beside him. Jenny, at the other side of the window, looked at the floor.

Lady Brayle groped for and found a chair. She sat down heavily. She drew her breath heavily through her heavy body. For a few seconds she stared at the carpet, and then looked up.

"They cheered me," she said.

Her tone was one of incredulity, though perhaps she had not meant it as such. It was that of one half-waking from hypnosis.

"They cheered me!" she repeated.

Nobody else spoke.

Lady Brayle seemed vaguely to notice the riding-crop in her hand. As though nobody else in the room knew what happened, she went on.

"I—that is, Mr. Barnham was kind enough to send me over in a car. An open car. With a driver. I gripped *this* in my hand. From some distance away one of the wr-wretches saw the car coming, and ran to tell his fellow—other people. As we swung in at the gates I stood up and gripped *this*. For I could hear them roaring. But . . .

"They were lined up on each side of the drive and beyond. Heaven knows how many of them. Some waved balloons, and some waved Union Jacks. They were shouting and cheering for me. Then, I believe, some wr-wretched band struck up. They began to sing."

It was unnecessary to tell her listeners, even if they did not know. For at that moment, beyond the oriel window, the band struck up with the same tune and the voices joined again.

> "For she's a jolly good fel-low,
> For she's a jolly good fel-low,
> For she's . . ."

Out it rolled, one repetition after another, over the ancient oak-trees of Brayle Manor. Lady Brayle put her hands over her face.

"Sophie," growled H.M., taking the cigar out of his mouth, "you come to this window and wave your hand at 'em. Don't say anything, or I'll wring your neck. Just wave."

"Henry, you fiend!" said Lady Brayle.

"Uh-huh. But you do what I tell you."

Lady Brayle got up, shaking and adjusting her shoulders, and moved over to the window. Beyond the sky showed dull, almost lead-coloured, with the red geraniums in their flower-pots against it. Lady Brayle lifted her arm in the manner of one unaccustomed to do so.

When she returned to her chair, after the tumult subsided, she was still half-dazed.

"As—as the car went up the drive," she said, "I confess I was stunned. I . . . . I could only make some response, as a matter of courtesy, by waving *this*.

"At the terrace there were calls for 'speech.' This, naturally, was a duty I could fulfil admirably. I was about to do so, when my attention was attracted by a revolting noise from that window there. I looked up, and saw projecting from the window a quite horrible face, which I discerned to be Henry's. He was holding a flower-pot.

"He informed me (pray forgive me for repeating such words) that, if I were to speak one word of what I had intended to speak, he would drop the goddam flower-pot on what he described as my onion.

"The fiend told me to do only what he called my routine, which I have always considered somewhat graceful. It consists in calling for three cheers, and taking two steps backwards while raising my hand. I . . . I confess that the volume of the cheering: I never heard it before."

Lady Brayle thought for a while. Then her mood changed.

"This is pure sentimentality," she said abruptly, and

whacked down the riding-crop on the table, where she left it. "How very amusing! The cheers of a vulgar mob!"

"Sure," agreed H.M. "We know you're above all that." He contemplated the glowing tip of the cigar, he frowned down at his big shoes, and looked up again. "But don't you find it just a bit comfortin', Sophie, now that you and I are old?"

There was a pause. Then Lady Brayle heaved herself to her feet.

She went over to the little writing-desk, with her back to them. While the others pretended not to notice, she removed a hat disarranged from (mere) feelings, straightened her dress, repaired her face while peering into the mirror of a compact, and shut up her handbag with a decisive snap.

When she returned to the chair, and sat down with dignity and grimness, she was herself again.

"And now, Henry," she suggested briskly, "shall we have this matter out between us to a finish?"

"Grandmother!" cried Jenny.

But again two strong personalities, with a sort of silent blare, faced each other.

"Sophie," H.M. said mildly, "don't tangle with me again. I'm just warning you."

"'Tangle with' is an expression I have heard before. It is a vulgarism, probably transatlantic. But I will make you pay for your childishness, believe me."

"Uh-huh?" said H.M.

"First of all, I will admit that an error of judgment on my part admitted this revolting display," she nodded towards the booths and stalls outside, "under the impression that it was a simple rustic fair, and . . ."

"Oh, Sophie," groaned H.M., taking the cigar out of his mouth. "You knew smacking well what kind of show it was, or you wouldn't have had correspondence and signed a contract on MacDougall's Mammoth letter-paper. You wanted money; who's blamin' you? But you're spinnin' this little piece of hoo-ha, for your friends, about how you've been taken in."

Jenny, really shocked, uttered an exclamation and sat up straight. Her grandmother regarded her with mild surprise.

"You find this strange, Jennifer?"

"I don't care," Jenny told her with a sort of loathing, "whether you go out in the street with a tin cup and a dancing bear. But why must you be hypocritical about it?"

"One has one's responsibilities, Jennifer. I fear you would not understand that."

"For years," cried Jenny, "you've been saying you would do

this, and you would do that, but you wouldn't stoop to tell lies."

"And I never do," replied Lady Brayle, quite sincerely believing every word she said, "except when I consider it just. As, for instance, telling your friend Captain Drake you had gone to London instead of Ranham Old Park."

Then she whipped round to H.M., coolly.

"But a fair in Rupert's Five-Acre is one thing. A detestable display on the approach to Brayle is quite another. When I heard of it, Henry, I was *quite* prepared to use this riding-crop on the vulgar."

"Sure, Sophie. I know that. What's more," said H.M., with a shadow of huge and ghoulish pleasure on his face, "you're goin' to get another beautiful surprise when you look out your bedroom window."

"And *you*," pounced Lady Brayle, "were responsible. I shall sue—"

"By the way, Sophie, what are they payin' you? The show's here for a week; you bargained for that. What are they payin' you by the day?"

"I believe," answered Lady Brayle, lifting one shoulder with an air of indifference, "it is the beggarly sum of ten pounds."

"Well . . . no. As a matter of fact, you're gettin' sixty."

"Sixty pounds a day?"

"That's right. And fifty per cent of the car-park profits. I had to do some swift work on that first part; but here it is." He fumbled inside his breast pocket and took out a cheque. "This is MacDougall's first of the week's rent. D'ye want it, or shall I turn it back to him?"

"This," Lady Brayle conceded with grace and dignity, "somewhat alters the complexion of matters." She allowed a space of silence. "I accept."

"Here you are, then."

"I am not mercenary," said Lady Brayle, taking the cheque carelessly, scrutinizing it with great care, and then hastily putting it in her handbag. "I do not think," again she brought out the cheque for examination before shutting it up, "I do not think that my worst enemy could call me mercenary. But one has one's rights."

"Definitely, Sophie. Nobody's denying it."

Whereupon Lady Brayle gave him a peculiar smile.

"Another point, Henry. Those photographs of me outside the gates, which by the way are not bad," she adjusted her shoulders, "were no doubt the work of Mr. MacDougall. But this strange popularity of mine, which I had never noticed before: I can guess it might be some of *your* work. Was it, Henry?"

"Uh-huh."

"And why, pray, do you take such trouble on my part?"

H.M. looked embarrassed. "Well, Sophie, there were a lot of reasons."

"As, for instance?"

"You used to be an A-1 sport. You'd still be a human being if you'd only for the love of Esau stop thinking what's vulgar and what ain't. Most of all, I realized—only last night, it was!—why you stole the skeleton out of that clock."

Chief Inspector Masters started to speak, but checked himself.

Against the dark sky outside, the walls of this little octagonal room appeared starkly white. One of the leaded window lights, propped open, rattled at its catch in the rising wind. Masters, heretofore, had been paying small attention to the conversation; he was looking out of the window, on edge, waiting for a signal. Now, as H.M. mentioned the skeleton and the clock, it was as though someone had flung down a coiling snake.

"Ah!" said Lady Brayle, and grew rigid. "I thought we should come to some bargaining-point about your precious skeleton. Well, you won't get it."

"I'm sorry about that, Sophie. Then I got to take it."

"The law, my dear man . . ."

"Didn't you hear what I said?" H.M.'s big voice rose sharply in the little room. "I said I knew why you stole the skeleton. That means I know why it's such vital evidence. And I can take it."

Lady Brayle, with both hands on the arms of the chair, pushed herself up.

"If you think I'm bluffing," H.M. added, "I'll give you a little tip. Masters here has applied to the Home Office for an exhumation-order."

"And what, precisely, does that mean?"

"It means they're goin' to dig up the body of George Fleet."

"Henry, are you entirely mad? The skeleton I have here is not that of Sir George Fleet!"

"I know it, Sophie," said H.M. "It's not Sir George Fleet's," he added, "except for a little bit."

"A little bit . . ."

"Which you can't see," snapped H.M., "until you take it out of the clock."

Lady's Brayle's whole manner and tone altered again.

"For God's sake," she pleaded, "and for the sake of old friendship, let the dead rest! You don't know how horrible it is! You don't . . ."

"MacDougall's signalling," Masters reported, stolidly but with quicker breathing. "It's the left arm for X? Oh, ah!" He lifted his left arm and waved it. A pause. "Card's up. It's number 7." From the window-seat Masters picked up a typewritten sheet of paper. "It's the Mirror Maze, all right. Nobody made any mistake. X is the Mirror Maze."

"So!" grunted H.M., throwing his cigar out of the window. "And pretty near on time, too. Looky here: where's young Drake? *He* ought to be with us."

"How should I know where he is?" demanded Masters "I told you he went charging out of here, looking for you, not two minutes before you got here! I don't know where. The young lady just pointed to some number on the list, and out he went."

"But it was there!" exclaimed Jenny. "The Mirror Maze!"

"Oh, lord love a duck." H.M.'s mouth fell open. "This is bad, Masters. This is bad."

"Eh? What's up?"

"You know what might happen," said H.M. cryptically, "if our dewy-eyed innocent meets the wrong man in that ruddy maze. Masters, come on!"

They paid no attention to protests or entreaties. In a very short time, under the dark sky and with the crowd milling towards shelter against possible rain, they saw the maze ahead. H.M., at a curious pigeon-toed run which made children stare, was able to keep up with Masters.

The circular structure, dull silver with its red letters, loomed up. Out from a fringe of the crowd hastened a lean youngish man, in a grey-and-black checked suit and with a beret on his brilliantined black hair. To a man in overalls he handed a bundle of big numbered placards. The young man had a shrewd, shiny, razorish kind of face, now one focus of eager interest in the eyes.

" 'Owzit, cock?" he asked H.M. affectionately. "Did I do it right?"

H.M. began to rave.

"But you *was* in there," protested Mr. MacDougall, "even if you only looked round. And I wasn't to signal when you come out, was I?" he broke off. "Oi! Charley.' "

A well-dressed young man, in the ticket seller's cage, rose up over the top of the booth.

"I was to drive them out," Charley answered in dubiously refined tones, "at twelve-thirty. I was to come back at a quarter to one. If anybody wanted tickets, I was to tell 'em the maze was full and would they come back later. Except the *right* one. I was to give the right one a ticket, or tickets—"

"Your friend's inside," said Mr. MacDougall. "In we go!"

Though they writhed through the thick felt curtain in a cursing wedge, nevertheless H.M., Masters, and their companion stood still and said nothing on the other side. They were all listening.

The great black box, like a camera with a faintly illuminated door of looking-glasses, stood silent inside its circular wooden shell. Softly the eager MacDougall led the way into the maze. Its soft-gleaming corridors led them on at first one angle, then another.

"Looky here, son," muttered H.M. "We can talk now, can't we?"

"We can talk," said Mr. MacDougall, "until I give you the sign we're near you-know-where. Meantime, we're buried." He looked round at all his reflections. "I don't envy your friend, cock. No fooling: this maze is a bastard. No fooling: it's the best there is. No fooling: ninety per cent of 'em don't get out 'less they take directions from the loud-speaker inside."

"Which loud speaker?" demanded Masters.

The other, hunching up padded shoulders, regarded Masters with exaggerated expression of pity and hopelessness. Evidently he did not like coppers.

"This maze is a square within a circle. See?"

"Well? What about it?"

Mr. MacDougall pointed to the ceiling.

"There's a loud-speaker in every corridor. Only you can't see it (see?) 'less you look close. There's a microphone out in the circle, where it's open space. Bill Fraser keeps talking to the people in 'ere. Bill can't see 'em. 'E can't 'ear 'em. But Bill talks to 'em as if he could, things that'd apply to anybody. And they jump and laugh nervous and Christ how they enjoy it! 'Careful, lady; that's a dead-end.' 'Mind, the gentleman with the bowler hat: you're taking a wrong turn.'"

Still there was no sound in the maze except MacDougall's voice.

"About every ten minutes Bill will say, 'If you can't get out, follow the black arrow.' Them black arrows are painted high up on the glass, see? You can't find 'em 'less you're told about 'em. That leads to . . ."

"*You know me, don't you?*" whispered a thin, faintly husky voice from empty space.

Mr. MacDougall, despite his knowledge, jumped as though

stung. He adjusted his beret over the shrewd, shiny face.

"That's not Bill Fraser," he said to H.M. "That's your murder-party starting now. Come on!"

They gave only one glance towards the fretted circle in the ceiling which showed the source of the voice. Following MacDougall, they hastened and stumbled forward among their own images. They took another right-angled turn—and came face to face with Martin Drake.

Chief Inspector Masters, who expected to meet his own reflection, was even more startled to see somebody else. Martin had just put down on the floor a piece of white paper torn in a thin strip from an envelope. A wave of relief went over his face, and something else as well.

"It's the pipes at Lucknow," Martin said, and flung down the shredded envelope.

"This your friend?" hoarsely inquired Mr. MacDougall. "Good!" He eyed the strip on the floor. "Beg-pardon-I'm-sure; but what the 'ell are you doing?"

Martin looked at him. "For some minutes, now," he said, "I've been putting these down to block up what I KNOW are dead-ends."

"Never mind that," snapped a glowering H.M. "Son, I've been worried. Have you met anybody?"

"Not met," said Martin. "I *saw* somebody with a damned brown coat and blue trousers, walking away from me. Then I ran into a sheet of plate glass. Then a voice; I found afterwards it was a loudspeaker; advised me to get to blazes out of here. That was when I started putting down papers. I wonder if Houdini ever tried this blasted place?"

Mr. MacDougall, immensely pleased, did a little tap-dance; and then nervousness smote him.

"Now look!" he urged. "I'm leading the way. Three more turnings, and we're there. When I give the sign," he made gestures like a temple-dancer, to illustrate, "don't start to speak or mess about. For gossakes don't! We'll be too near 'em!"

"Near them?" repeated Martin. "Near whom?"

"*Go on!*" urged the insistent voice from the ceiling, as though it were eerily feeling its way along the mirror walls. "*Come a little closer! It's not so dark you can't make me out!*"

"Son," H.M. said to Martin, "do you know who's speakin' now?"

"No!"

"It's Arthur Puckston. Puckston was the feller in the brown coat."

"You don't mean Puckston is the . . . ?"

"Puckston's talking to somebody. That somebody killed George Fleet, killed and mutilated Enid Puckston, and almost murdered you: all the same somebody. We're ready, Mac-Dougall."

Though it took them three turnings and one fairly long corridor, it was only a matter of seconds until MacDougall gave the signal. Then Martin tried to straighten out his thoughts.

They all now stood facing down a short passage, not more than six or eight feet deep, with no other passage turning out of it. They stared at a dead-end of looking-glass.

"*I don't say much,*" sounded Puckston's voice from the ceiling. "*I was never one to say much, was I? Would I make trouble?*"

Only a bumbling murmur answered with something like "What do you want, then?" Whoever somebody was, Puckston was crowding the voice away from the microphone. Whoever somebody was . . .

Then Martin realized the presence of something impossible. Straight ahead, reflected in that glimmering dead-end, he saw H.M.'s bulk and impassive eyes, Masters in down-pulled hat and with pencil moving on a notebook, himself like a pirate, MacDougall in beret peering round the angle of the passage. Crowding images of them sprang up wherever you looked. But . . .

"*I know you killed Enid.*" Puckston's breathing was now audible. "*I wanted you to hear that, like. That I know you killed 'er.*"

"You can't prove that." (Whose voice?)

MacDougall had told them almost with tears that they must not utter a whisper, not make a shoe-scrape, or the slightest sound would betray them. But on the floor lay a piece of paper which Martin had dropped there.

He had explored that passage. It was made of solid looking-glasses. If the microphone were outside this mirror maze in the circular shell, you could clump about or talk without being heard.

Then where were Puckston and his companion? Standing there invisibly, by some optical trick?

"*I tell you again, I don't want to prove it. If I did, I'd'a' gone to the police.*"

"With what evidence?" (Come closer! Come closer!)

"*I dunno. I didn't think.*" Puckston's breathing grew shorter and heavier. *"You killed my little girl. That's all I know."*

No reply at all, now. Masters was silently raving.

"You killed my little girl. Why did you do it?"

"I had to. It was a kind of—expression."

"What's that?"

"I said a kind of expression. Don't sob. You—"

"But you did kill 'er?"

"Yes! What's so bad about it?"

Clearly, not loudly, but with smooth and articulated viciousness, somebody's voice moved straight on microphone. Martin Drake realized, with horror, whose voice it was.

"We mustn't worry over these things. They happen," said somebody's voice. *"You seem sensible. I'll take care of you."*

"No, by God!" said Puckston. And every effect was shattered; his voice, with the sound known as blasting, pierced the ear but smothered clearness. *"No, by God! I'll take care of you!"* And through that bubbling blatter there came a faint noise as of a hammer thudded down on meat.

"Stop it!" shouted Masters. "Stop it! The confession is—"

It was too late. And the maze gave up its last secret.

Before Martin's eyes what seemed a solid mirror at the end of the short passage rippled like water, soundlessly, distorting the staring reflections. Then it curled and disappeared. Somebody, back to the watchers, staggered into the passage: reeling out of nowhere, piercing a dead-end, straight into the watchers' faces.

Arthur Puckston, forcing back that reeling figure, no longer stooped. His narrow bald head, his staring blue eyes, loomed like an image of mania. He was hitting for the face with a countryman's blows: unskilled, straight, murderous. Then all the group collided, and flew apart.

Martin, flung backwards, tripped and caught himself as he went down. Master's yellow pencil rolled underneath him as he got up, among reeling reflections less like a mirror maze than like a kaleidoscope. Puckston, still shouting, had driven his adversary into a short passage at right-angles to the other.

But it was all over.

One last blow Puckston landed before Masters locked both his arms from behind. Puckston's adversary, flung back against a mirror at the end of the passage, struck it with too great weight. With a crunching noise, opening in slow cracks, great shards slid down and splintered on the floor as the figure slid down and lay motionless.

"Y'know," said H.M. in a calm and meditative tone, "it's interestin' to nab this feller in a house of mirrors. He may be

the most vicious, he's certainly the most conceited murderer, I've ever met."

And all of them, panting, looked down amid smashed glass-
shreds at the unconscious figure and bloodstained face of
Richard Fleet.

Chapter 20

The policeman, pacing his beat through Moreston Square,
South Kensington, glanced up to see the lighted windows on
the top floor of number 16. It was the Thursday night—or, to
be exact, the Friday morning—exactly a fortnight after he had
seen lights burning so late in Miss Callice's flat.

From St. Jude's tower the chimes rang and rippled with the
hour of three. The policeman smiled and sauntered on.

If he had looked into the comfortable living-room on the top
floor, he would have seen in its easiest chair a large, stout,
barrel-shaped gentleman in a white linen suit, with a cigar in
one hand and a strong whisky-and-soda in the other.

Ruth was there, and Stannard, and Jenny, and Martin, and,
as it happened, Lady Brayle. The light of the silver-shaded
wall-lamps touched unquiet faces. It had taken a long time,
and a very fair amount of whisky, to work themselves toward
hearing what H.M. had begun to say.

H.M. drew deeply at the cigar, scowled, and put down the
glass on the table beside him.

"Y'see," he said, "the boy-murderer is not at all uncommon.
I don't have to tell you that. Usually he's psychopathic, as
Ricky Fleet is. But, as a rule, he's nabbed straightway and
shoved into confinement where he can't do any more harm.

"What's interesting here is to watch the boy-murderer who's
grown up into a man-murderer. Still protected and cosseted by
his mother! Still not believin' a soul now alive has suspected
him! To watch his reaction to grown-up life; watch him
squirm, watch him wriggle, watch him blurt out things, watch
him smile and smile, until he's told his last lie. All that,
y'know, you saw unroll in front of your eyes.

"Now if we're goin' into the grisly details," continued H.M.,
"there are some things we got to understand about Ricky Fleet.

"He really is a charmin' and likeable bloke. His good-nature is absolutely genuine. His generosity and free-handedness are genuine. His bravery, where he could be crazy-reckless but cool-headed at the same time, was genuine too. If you think those qualities can't belong to a murderer just balanced between sanity and insanity, think of Ronald True. Or Patrick Mahon. Or—my eye, how recent this is!—Neville Heath."

H.M. grunted.

At the end of the sofa opposite sat Jenny, her eyes fixed intently on him, and Martin with his arm round Jenny. Ruth sat at the other end of the sofa, with Stannard perched on its arm. He was an effulgent Stannard, beaming.

"To start at the beginning," continued H.M., eyeing a pile of papers on the table beside his glass, "Masters sent me a heap of testimony about the death of George Fleet. Together with three apparently scatty postcards about 'examine the skeleton in the clock' and 'what was the pink flash' and 'the evidence is still there.'

"I'd decided, before we went to Berkshire, that Fleet's death was murder. I argued the salient points with Masters at the Dragon's Rest on Saturday. You people haven't seen these typed sheets, maybe . . ."

Martin intervened.

"I've heard some of it," he said. "I heard you prove to Puckston, out of his own testimony, that he couldn't have swung that telescope round when he said he did. Did that make you suspect it was murder?"

"Oh, my son!" groaned H.M.

"It didn't?"

"Not so's you could notice it. All it showed was that Puckston had been lying, and there might be a lot of hokey-pokey in his statement. But *what* hokey-pokey? No, son. The glarin' give-away is in the testimony of an honest witness, Simon Frew with the binoculars, supported by others. Frew was lookin' straight at Fleet from the middle gable. I'll read what he said, just as Masters read it to me."

H.M. fished among the papers at his side, drew out a blue-bound folder, and grubbed through it until he found what he wanted.

Sir George was there. I could see all round him. He had his glasses to his eyes in one hand, and was waving with the other. Then it looked like somebody gave him a hard shove in the back. He stood there for a second. He shouted. He fell head-first.

H.M. threw the folder back among the papers.

"If somebody gives you a hard shove in the back," he said, pointing his cigar at his listeners, "you don't 'stand there for a second.' You go straight over. As Martin Drake can tell you.

"Nobody pushed Fleet, or the pusher would have been seen. Nobody threw a weight at him. Aside from no weight being found, and no place to throw without bein' seen, it would have made Fleet lurch or stagger even if he didn't pitch straight over. He still wouldn't 'stand there for a second.'

"When I read that first, I felt a frizzlin' kind of feeling,"— H.M. indicated his corporation,—"here. Like devils at work. Fleet was in pain, intense pain. Or weakness. Or both. That look 'like a hard shove in the back' was muscular jerk and reaction which would give the same gestures.

"If you'll think about that for a bit, you'll get the key and the lock together. I didn't get that give-away straight off— being goop-witted, which the same I often am not—but I got it later."

Jenny, under Martin's arm, turned her head up to look at him uneasily, inquiringly, while a shiver went through her. He could think only of unshaped devilries against a lurid-glowing red sky.

"But, H.M.," Martin protested, "that's one of the things we do want to understand. *How was Fleet killed?*"

"You be quiet," H.M. ordered austerely. "I've got somethin' else to tell you."

Before resuming, he also mentioned the fact that he was the old man.

"Honest," he said, "what bothered me most in that bundle of Masters's testimony was the boy. I mean the tow-headed twelve-year old boy, Richard Fleet. The Scotland Yard bloke didn't take a statement from him; only the local police did. But he got into the other statements, and he worried me.

"Whatever else George Fleet was, he was dead-keen on sport and dead-keen on the Army. Take his own career! As Masters said, he'd been sent to boarding-school when he was a tiny 'un—ten or even less—then to Harrow, and then to Sandhurst. He couldn't finish Sandhurst, because he had to take up his dad's business. Oh, my eye! Don't you see a man like Fleet would be dreamin' of a career for his son just like the interrupted one of his own? Dreamin'? He'd have had it planned in detail from the first cradle-squawk.

"But this son, at twelve, was still at home with a governess. Why?

"Was the boy delicate and rabbity? No: he was a pocket

athlete. Thick-witted? That wouldn't have mattered at a school; but, anyway, he was very intelligent. Did the fond mother step in and say she couldn't have her darling away? No: George Fleet ruled that roost and his word was law.

"Then why?

"Let's take the boy's governess, this Miss Upton. H'm. There were bits about *her* in the testimony that bothered me. But let's jump ahead and use what you all knew or heard for yourselves.

"Miss Upton was the rummiest kind of governess I ever heard of. She was sort of immense, with a build like Sandow the Strong Man; and she knew how to put on a real wrestlin'-grip. She was with the family for four years. Correct?"

It was Jenny who answered, Jenny with shining eyes but with the weighted and harassed air of one who has guessed too much.

"Correct," Jenny almost whispered. "I reminded Ricky himself, when he spoke about her."

"And on that roof of gaiety and delight," said H.M., "your Ricky told me—in his careless and laughin' way—she was with him till he was fourteen. Now it's fourteen instead of twelve. And at this time, he added, they *pensioned her off*. A pension after four years' service? I tried to keep from doin' more than blink. Either that was a lie, or else Miss Upton couldn't stand it and Cicely Fleet had to buy her silence.

"I wonder if you've begun to catch the unnatural atmosphere of Fleet House twenty years ago? The nervous, stampin' father, who wallops his son (as the son told me) like blazes. The pretty, well-meanin' mother, who loves everybody and hopes George will get a baronetcy; and there mustn't be any scandal. Lemme give you one reminder: at Priory Hill, in November of 1925, a child was murdered and mutilated. Immediately afterwards George Fleet suddenly tore down his collection of rapiers and daggers from the wall, and gave 'em away. At that time young Fleet was in his eleventh year—Why didn't they dare send him to school? You answer."

A cold shock of horror spread through his listeners and lay inside them like lead, although two of them at least had been expecting it.

"I'm afraid, y'know," H.M. shook his head, "that in a way I did Masters in the eye. I warned him about it at the pub on Saturday afternoon. That little bit about Fleet gettin rid of his weapons was in the original dossier I read in London. It bothered me worst of all. I rang up a friend of mine at the *Evening News*, and asked him if anything unpleasant had happened in this district about November, 1925. Cor! I got a answer.

"Masters learned this later, and told you. I knew beforehand. That was why I told young Drake, at Willaby's on Friday, to keep an eye out for real trouble. Because . . . well, now! You'll see.

"H.M.!" Ruth Callice intervened softly "I've been a friend of poor Cicely for years. I knew she was hiding some kind of secret; but I never guessed it was an awful thing like this. And yet when I first visited there—the impression wore off later—I thought of that house as something like a prison."

(So, thought Martin, you did get the feeling too! Like mine, it wore off).

"And now," said H.M., with a sort of malevolent patience, "I want you to see everything happen from Saturday to Monday. *You!*" He pointed his cigar, long gone out, at Martin. "You went harin' down to Berkshire on Saturday.

"You sent a message to Ricky Fleet, who was at Brayle Manor, that an enemy was waitin' for him at the Dragon. Your gal and Sophie were there when he got the message. I've heard this from a very particular source.

"Didn't it strike you as a bit odd that he should come over there so quickly? The proper reply to you should have been, 'I'm waiting at your service here at Brayle Manor; came and see me.' Above all the sweet fireworks of heaven, didn't it seem odd that your *gal,* should have come flyin' over there on a bicycle, as frightened as blazes, to anticipate him?"

Martin looked at Jenny, who had turned her head away.

"It did seem funny, yes. But Jenny said she had to know what happened between us."

"Sure. And that was true, as far as it went. Now: presto-chango: watch! In the doorway of the second bar-parlour at his most charmin', stands Richard Fleet grown up. At his prime. Intoxicated by his war-success; but modest, not showin' it. Assured by this dotin' mother there's not a woman alive who can resist him. Quite believing it. With conceit runnin' in his veins like blood. Down he sits, takes out his pipe, and asks what's up.

"And you give it to him between the eyes that you love your Jenny, she loves you, and you mean to get married."

H.M. drew a deep breath.

"Son," he went on, "do you remember how Ricky Fleet sat there for a few seconds, with his leg over the chair-arm: not movin', just lookin', without any expression in his eyes: creepy as creepy?"

"Lord knows I do!" Martin answered. "I started to shout out something about being sorry, and I could hear what seemed like the skeleton-clock ticking in the other room . . ."

"If he'd had a weapon then," H.M. observed very quietly, "you'd have been a dead man."

"You mean . . . about Jenny and Ricky and their engagement . . . he really *did*—?"

"Oh, son! He'd fallen head over heels for her. He just couldn't believe, in his vanity, that *any* woman could prefer another feller to himself. Burn it all, when you were at Willaby's the day before, why didn't you take the word of the one person who did know? I mean the gal herself?"

Jenny, her face flushed, still looked away from Martin; but she gripped his hand as she spoke.

"I told you Ricky was in love with me," she said. "That sort of thing—well, you always know. I'm afraid, at Willaby's, I showed I was frightened. I kept telling you about his good qualities and—and looking at you and wondering if you'd see anything wrong. Once, if you remember, I started to talk about Ricky's father's death; but it stuck in my throat."

"Yes. Yes, it did."

"When you mentioned Sir Henry Merrivale, I didn't know what on earth might happen. I'd always heard of Sir Henry as a real sleuth: a strong, silent, unemotional man . . ."

"Hem!" said H.M., endeavouring to look modest. "Thank-'ee, my wench."

"Jenny, listen!" Martin insisted. "Ricky Fleet: you didn't know he was a . . . ?"

Jenny regarded him with horror. "Oh, God, *no!* It was only a feeling of something horribly wrong; of how he might turn on you. I couldn't talk about it. He was our friend. I liked him; but I couldn't endure his touch. As I told you afterwards—if I happened to be wrong, it would only be sordidly stupid."

"We will now," said H.M., "return to Richard Fleet, in the bar-parlour, when he'd just got that staggerer between the eyes. How he did pull himself together! How he *forced* the blood in his face, and that look of relief and 'Thank God.' His charm poured all over the place." H.M. looked at Martin. "But from that moment, in his eyes, you were a dead duck."

(Much, so very much, became comprehensible to Martin now.)

"What did he say?" pursued H.M. "Oh, he was all bounces and smiles! He never in the world could have married the gal, and he was awful relieved. He'd grown up with her! Cor! He gave the impression they'd lived in each other's pockets for about twenty years; and he'd as soon have thought of marrying a sister.

"But what was the truth?

"The gal there," H.M. pointed at Jenny, "told me on Sunday. She'd been at school from the time she was ten. Her holidays were spent with one or the other of her parents abroad. Then came the War and the Wrens. In other words, he couldn't possibly have seen much of the gal for about thirteen years. And what happens then, hey? She comes back at the end of the war.

"And he sees her. He goes straight overboard. Presently, as they say, a marriage is arranged.

"But Ricky Fleet (in the bar-parlour with Drake) is all dewy-eyed innocence. He's mad-keen on a gal named Susan Harwood. She was his newest, ripest conquest. (Of course, son, you heard his philosophy of marriage; you knew he saw himself as a boundin' faun, all Pan-pipes and breathin's in the grove). Oh, he was goin' to marry Susan!—Then in walked our Jenny."

H.M. shook his head. Again Martin saw the dingy bar-parlour.

"She's just been having a blazing row with Ruth Callice here, across the road.—Don't interrupt me, dammit, either of you! Before she came in, Ricky Fleet made a dramatic business of 'what was he goin' to say to Jenny?' Son, do you remember what he did?"

Martin nodded.

"I thought he was acting a little. He looked at himself in a wall-mirror, to see if his posture was right. He was preening a good deal."

"Uh-huh. And Ricky Fleet's passion for looking at himself in mirrors, at exactly the time when nobody except a vanity-swollen feller would, is going to figure in this business again.

"Anyway, in came Jenny. Very soon she asked you would you please, please take her driving that night and not go to the prison. That wasn't merely because she was jealous of Ruth, or

. . .

"*Will you two gals for the love of Esau shut up? Both of you? And lemme get on with this? All right: now put a sock in it!*

"Ahem. Well. If Ricky Fleet did happen to hate Drake, something pretty unpleasant might happen to Drake at the prison. You gather the wench had naturally been listenin' to most of the talk between you and Fleet, even though the windows were closed? All wenches do.

"But most of all she thought she could get these nasty crazy suspicions out of her mind—at least, she might—if she brought up the death of George Fleet and made Ricky Fleet tell about it. Then she could be sure her suspicions were all moonshine.

"He had begun tellin' about it, when they were interrupted first by Dr. Laurier and then by Ruth Callice. There was a rumpus; I came in at the end of it. But just think of Ricky Fleet as he talks about his old man's death!

"I'll take my oath, here and now, he'd practically forgotten about it. It was swept into the dustbin, lost and gone, like a dim sort of prank we remember that *might* have raised trouble in boyhood. His brain's most rational, admittedly; and it's tipped over the edge with hatred for Martin Drake, who's under his charm and thinks he's the best feller in the world."

Martin's feelings, in retrospect, had more of an inward shudder than can be rendered here.

"The coppers are investigatin' that old, dim prank of twenty years ago? Well! What does Ricky Fleet care? They can't do anything. For I'll tell you this much:

"Only three other people, who protected him, ever knew he killed his father and how he killed his father. The first was his mother. The second was old Dr. Pierre Laurier, with the beard, who (we know) cherished a romantic passion for Cicely Fleet. The third was Miss Upton, who told lies by the bucket to save him when the tow-headed boy came babblin' to her with fear.

"Now, twenty years later, Dr. Laurier was dead. So was Miss Upton—see Masters's list of witnesses—and couldn't retract any lie for the boy's alibi. And one more fetchin' point: Ricky Fleet never knew anything about that skeleton in the clock, what it was or what it meant.

"But, shortly after he'd hared away from that explosive argument at the Dragon, and hurried back home, he did begin to get shocks.

"Watch his behaviour now!

"There was something wrong with his mother. Something seriously wrong. Ricky Fleet was worried. He knew it couldn't have been caused by any casual reference made to a twenty-year-old death by Stannard . . ."

"Thank you," Stannard intervened gravely. As he sat on the sofa-arm, bent a little forward, Stannard's black little glittering eyes were absorbed in the story.

"What upset his mother? When young Fleet hurried home, and followed her partway up the stairs (Drake and Ruth Callice saw that scene), all she'd say was that there was something he'd got to learn soon; and that she'd just put in a telephone-call for her now-closest friend, Sophie Brayle. But *we* can guess what was wrong with Cicely Fleet.

"It was the sight of that ruddy great skeleton-clock being carried into the door of the pub just opposite. I'd sent it on ahead of Masters and me, by the carriage-people. Masters and I stopped at a couple of pubs in Brayle and didn't get there till late afternoon. Aunt Cicely must 'a' thought the secret was on the point of coming out.

"But what about Me?

"I was dragged into Fleet House, along with Sophie there, by Ricky himself. I was shanghai'd, I was, and shoved into the library with the rest of you people. And Ricky Fleet had just before that got another shock.

"He'd recognized, or half-recognized, Stannard as being the man standing at the upstairs study window. It jumped at him out of the past: Stannard was the bloke who looked down, when he came round the edge of the terrace that day, and he saw his father lyin' with a smashed head under the tapestry-cloth.

"But let's take the events in their order! In that library, first off I had a bit of a dog-fight with Sophie. At least she gave confirmation to my notion (remember?) that Arthur Puckston might 'a' written the anonymous postcards about the pink flash and the skeleton-clock.

"Whereupon in tripped Aunt Cicely, at her artificial archest and most charmin', to carry away Sophie for a private talk. And there occurred something that was embarrassin' to the point of the horrible."

During all this Lady Brayle might not have been in the room, might not have existed. She sat over by one open window, staring blankly ahead of her, an untasted glass of sherry on the window-sill. She did not seem arrogant or even friendly: only like one who had been lost, and still gropes.

"Do you remember that incident, Sophie?" H.M. called softly.

"Yes." The stiff lips writhed as the grey-white head slowly turned. "I remember."

"What was said?"

"I made some mention of a blade, a sword, which I wished I could have brought back from Willaby's as a present. There— there was real horror in Cicely's eyes. She blurted out, 'But you must never . . .' Then Cicely stopped and turned it off with some reference to Dr. Laurier. What she meant, I imagine, was, 'You must never bring a sharp blade into this house?'"

"That's right," agreed H.M. "And then (hey) she took you upstairs and told you the whole truth?"

They spoke to each other across the length of a room, Lady Brayle with her head turned sideways, trying to control the writhing of her mouth; but they spoke without incongruity.

"Poor Cicely," Lady Brayle went on, "could hardly speak for sobbing. About the skeleton in the clock. About that half-mad, or altogether mad, boy who—" She stopped. "I do not suppose, Henry, you now have much respect for my word of honour?"

"That's where you're wrong, Sophie."

"Never, until that moment," the lips writhed vehemently, "had I the least suspicion, let alone knowledge, of the situation. To think I would allow Jennifer, after that, to be married to . . ." She floundered. "My late husband, who commanded the Grenadier Guards, once said that a person who allowed . . ."

"Yes. Sure. - But Aunt Cicely would have allowed the marriage, hey?"

"Oh, Henry!" The other made an impatient gesture. Again she struggled to free herself from reticence. "You're hardly a person to understand mothers, especially, people like Cicely. That is—"

"Her son was 'cured' of this. It had been only childish aberration. Nothing like it at Cambridge or later. The 'poor boy' had been misunderstood. Cicely wished to believe it so; and it was so. She could not even bear to have him *know* about the skeleton. She ought to tell him; but why remind the boy? The skeleton must be removed. I am Cicely's friend. I could not let her down."

Lady Brayle turned her head away, and looked out of the window. And now Martin remembered her look, on that Saturday evening, when she left Cicely Fleet and walked downstairs past Martin at the telephone table.

"I knew I was right," cried Jenny. "She *was* shielding somebody!"

"God help me," Martin said uncontrollably, "I thought that business of stealing the skeleton was funny."

"Not to me," said Lady Brayle without turning round.

"Looky here," howled H.M., bringing his fist down on the arm of the chair. "Who's tellin' this story? I'd got you people in the library early that Saturday evenin', after Sophie and Aunt Cicely had gone. Ricky Fleet then 'denounced' Stannard as the one who'd been lookin' at him from the study window. Before that he said one thing that gave me a shiver. Can you spot what it was?"

Stannard lifted his shoulders in negation.

"Somebody asked him what he'd seen up there at the window. And it was, *The face of somebody I'd never met. The face of a total stranger. Looking down like God.'*

"Looking down like God.

"Cor! There's your boy-murderer's conscience, leaping out of him and speaking through the mouth of a grown man. That's what he remembered best! That's what he thought all those years ago! And," H.M. looked at Stannard, "he rounded on you pretty savagely."

"I noticed," Stannard pursed his lips, "he was nervous and truculent while you were questioning me. He would have been a difficult witness to handle. And all, you say, because of this repressed—?"

"Ho-ho!" rumbled H.M. "Not so's you could notice it. It was because you said at least one thing that could help to denounce him."

"I did?" Stannard asked in surprise.

"You were in the study when you heard Fleet shout and fall on the flagstones? Right! You then went to the window and stood there looking down? Right!

"But you further said you stood there *five minutes* before the governess and the boy came round the edge of the house to the terrace. In Ricky Fleet's story of it, which he gave me almost immediately afterwards when we climbed up to the roof, he said he and Miss Upton were *just startin' from the back to the front of the house when they heard the shout.* What sort of frozen-snail-with-lumbago takes five minutes to walk from back to front?

"His memory might be bad? Sure! Your memory too? Of course! But there was a certain way of checking it. Across the way, at the pub, there were six witnesses on the roof though only two on the gables. All agreed in their first testimony."

H.M. picked up the blue folder, and stabbed at it with his dead cigar.

"After Fleet's body struck the terrace, Dr. Pierre Laurier ran out of the house. The local policeman walked up the path to the terrace, picked up the field-glasses from the grass, and went in: presumably to 'phone the police-station. Dr. Laurier called to Lady (the Dowager Lady) Brayle, who brought a cloth out of the house. Dr. Laurier put the cloth over Fleet's head and shoulders. Cicely Fleet then came out and started to faint, but they talked to her 'a while,'—I'm quoting, so note the 'a while,'—and she went in.

"Then, and only then, did the governess and the boy come

round the side of the house. Lord love a duck! For the precedin' events, you could easily allow five minutes.

"But did the boy and the governess say the things, twenty years ago when it was fresh in mind, as Ricky Fleet said to me as well as to Jenny and Martin Drake? Including, for instance, that fancy touch about hearin' Dr. Laurier say, 'Get the tablecloth out of the hall?' So I asked Masters to check over their statements made to the local police.

"And they had said the same things. Therefore they were both tellin' a pack of lies. Q.E.D."

Again H.M. threw back the blue folder among the other papers.

"But there was another great big lie," he went on, screwing up his face hideously, "that the old man had to see through before the solution was so blazin' obvious. That lie has caused half the mystery in this case. It had to do with how Fleet was murdered.

"When I went up to have a look at that roof-top for the first time, I was stumped and flummoxed. I couldn't think of anything but colour. I talked more about colour than an interior decorator. Because I'd got my mind fixed on that pink flash.

"So I went to the front of the roof. And then this here venerable scalp did start to stir a bit with wheels workin' inside. I hadn't quite visualized the surroundings. Arthur Puckston had been over on that north gable, in a position to look at Fleet sideways—well sideways.

"It went like this: Puckston probably wrote the anonymous postcards; only a postcard mentioned the pink flash; Puckston had told lies in his statement to the police; Puckston looked sideways . . .

"The pink flash must have been that lurid-glowin' sky on something white or whitish. It must have *moved*, pretty sharply, or there wouldn't have been any flash. It couldn't have been up in the air, or Frew would have seen it. But—stop a bit!—Puckston could see what Frew couldn't see: he could see behind Fleet and a part of the roof-floor. Down on the floor . . .

"Now think! That look of intense pain or weakness, or both, which strikes the victim all of a sudden and holds him there for a second . . ."

"A sword!" interposed Stannard.

"No!" said H.M. sharply. "That's the one thing it couldn't have been, in spite of the tinge of steel in all this case. Because why?

"Because a sword or sharp blade would have meant blood.
Because that's the one thing that couldn't be concealed.
Remember, Fleet's body was lying smack in front of a number
of witnesses. Lemme quote again; and I've been over it so
much I can quote from memory."

H.M. closed his eyes.

Bert (the policeman) came out and seemed to argue with
Dr. Laurier about who carried Sir George. Bert took his
head in the cloth and Dr. Laurier took his legs. They carried
. . .

H.M. sat up.

"Even if old Dr. Pierre Laurier had been up to hanky-panky,
he couldn't have concealed any blood below the shoulders.

"Then: bang! On Sunday night this feller—" H.M. pointed
to Martin—"came weaving his way downstairs after a fall off
that roof, and he tells me I ought to see 'young' Dr. Laurier if I
wanted information about swordsmanship in remembering
(hem!) my reincarnation. He mentioned a cut called the 'Low-
high.'

"Now upstairs I'd got a book called *The Cavaliers*, which I'd
been readin'. As I distinctly told Masters at the pub on
Saturday, it was a blook on swordsmanship. The 'Low-high'
was a cut by which the trickster dropped down and cut
viciously across the backs of both his opponent's legs just
above the ankle. And the only way anybody could have
attacked George Fleet would have been round his feet or
ankles under that six-inch parapet.

"A sword wasn't used. But at the same moment I
remembered what else was hangin' on the wall of the study
upstairs. *You,*" he glared at Martin, "must have seen for
yourself. And I remembered Dr. Laurier in the rocking-chair."

H.M. drew a deep breath.

"Y'see, this wasn't intended to be an impossible crime. Only
one big whitewashed lie made it so. A twelve-year-old young
'un had been beaten too much by a father he hated. He was
goin' to stalk his father just like a red Indian. Only he was goin'
to kill him.

"He knew (he said so) his father was goin' up to that roof to
watch the hunt when it came near. George Fleet always did.
How did the twelve-year-old get up there? By a door, leadin' to
the back garden, and a staircase going straight up there. Could
he stalk the old devil, in all the excitement of the hunt, without
his father seein' him?

"Easy! And why? Because of field-glasses.

"Y'know, Masters kept goin' on at me and raving when I insisted there was only one thing I wanted to know: were they good field-glasses, nothing wrong or wonky about them? .

"That would have been my question no matter how Fleet had been killed. Lord love a duck! Suppose you or I look through a pair of field-glasses, and the vision don't seem to come into focus when we fiddle with the wheel?

"Well, we get mad; we get a vague sort of idea there's something wrong with the scenery and turn 'em somewhere else. We look round. We take the glasses away from our eyes and examine 'em all ways. But, if they're good, we don't notice what's goin' on around us.

"Fleet didn't. That twelve-year-old maniac—with a certain boy's weapon you'll guess—crawled belly-flat like a red Indian under the ledge of the north wall, and then under the ledge of the east wall towards where his father was standing. Remember: not a soul looked round until shortly before Fleet fell. Once the boy was under that front ledge on the east side, nobody could see him; not even Puckston. I think Masters may have told a couple of you that people won't believe how small a space can hide a full-grown adult, let alone a small boy.

"I'd dismissed that possibility at first, because I kept thinkin' of somebody startin' a tussle with the legs or ankles of a powerful man like Fleet. And Masters never dreamed of a kid. But also remember: Ricky Fleet, as he'd told Stannard in the condemned cell at Pentecost, wasn't what you might call ordinary in another way. He could put-the-weight a distance of twenty-seven feet three inches when he was eleven. A lot of grown men couldn't do that.

"On he goes, just as crazy-excited as we've seen him on other occasions, with the music of the hunt to encourage him. The hounds were after the fox; he was after the wolf. He's carrying something out of the realm of sport, but a nasty heavy weapon if you remember it's . . ."

"A cricket-bat!" Jenny whispered. "He told us they'd given him a new cricket-bat that week!"

"And when it's new," said H.M., "it's the whitest of white ash. Don't see it as an ordinary cricket-bat: see the heavy broadness taperin' on each side to the very-narrow-rounded edge that's like the edge of a wooden blade.

"One hand, lyin' flat with his left arm under him, was all Ricky Fleet needed. It was the narrow blade of the bat. Out and back it went: flash! open and shut! It smashed across the back of Fleet's legs just above the ankle, the most painful of all places. It fractured the bone in both legs without drawin' a drop of blood. Fleet jerked in horrible pain; he couldn't stand straight, and—

"That's all. After the first thirty seconds or so, no witness (see testimony!) was studyin' that roof. They all looked down at the terrace, while the boy crawled back by way of the north ledge. But I'm bettin' *he* never thought anybody could see him at any time, except maybe God.

"*You*," H.M. said to Martin. "Burn it, you must have seen the row of cricket bats in Fleet's study! On Sunday night I remembered 'em; I remembered the 'Low-high' cut; I wanted to look it up in my book. And I remembered something else too: Dr. Laurier, old Dr. Laurier, rocking back and forth before the skeleton-clock mutterin', 'Would a man of honour have done it?'

"Done what? We know that after Fleet fell Dr. Laurier (quote) 'made as if he was examining all over Sir George.' *He* ordered the constable to take the head, in spite of an argument, and *he* took the legs. He was the old family friend, the one who cherished Aunt Cicely, and he knew all about the boy's psychopathic traits. He saw in a second this wasn't accident. Finally, remember, he was the police-surgeon.

"The awful creepin' danger was that the coppers, especially Scotland Yard, would tumble to the fracture at the *back* of both legs, when Fleet fell in a way where that couldn't have happened. Then the gaff would be blown.

"At the post-mortem there wasn't much danger—everybody's concentrated on the stomach-contents, as usual—of too-close investigation. Laurier had sworn (which was the lie I told you about) there hadn't been other injuries to the body. But Aunt Cicely intervened, weepin' and pleadin'. And at her insistence old Laurier . . . amputated just above both ankles before burial.

"It was a fat-headed thing to do; but our Cicely pleaded they couldn't *prove* anything against her boy, which was true, if that was done. Also (here I'm on ground I don't know) there had to be hanky-panky with the undertaker.

"I won't go into grisly details," growled H.M., "about how Laurier removed flesh and sinew from what was left. It was only long afterwards, when age wore on him and he got a bit senile, that he built the skeleton-clock for his parlour, *where everybody could see but nobody knew*, as his penance. Anybody here examined that clock?"

"Yes. I have," said Martin out of a thick throat.

"Did you look inside? Look close?"

"There was some kind af platform round the ankles and feet, apparently to keep the skeleton upright . . ."

"Dr. Laurier took his old anatomical-specimen skeleton," said H.M., "He removed what had to be removed, and he attached—what had to be attached. It was a skillful job of fittin'. But any medical man could have seen at a glance that the ankle-bones and feet of a big man don't belong to the skeleton of a small man. *Unless* there's a wooden platform built up round 'em which gives you only a glimpse of the feet and curves round the ankles. You can't probe the truth about that skeleton until you take it out of the clock. And I hadn't time before Sophie stole it.

"So y'see, as regards that nasty business of murder on the roof, there was only a twelve-year crawlin' back unseen, and out to his governess now screamin' what he'd done and how he'd got to be protected. That's why they took five minutes to get round. Nobody'd notice if Ricky Fleet was scared. Nobody'd notice him anyway. But it must 'a' made him nearly faint when he thought he saw God lookin' down from his father's study window.

"*You*," and H.M. pointed to Stannard, "said something else to the grown-up Ricky Fleet that shook his nerve too. You called him a '*grubby* little boy.' It was twistin' and wrigglin' in his mind just later when I asked him about his father and Ricky Fleet blurted out: 'He never minded how filthy dirty you got.' He was thinkin' about how almighty dirty he got when he crawled along that concrete roof to kill his father."

There was a long silence. H.M. picked up his whisky-and-soda, and drained the glass with a volcanic gurgle. Then he set it down.

"There's not much more to tell except what you know already," he went on. "That expedition to the prison on Saturday night . . ."

"Where," Ruth said, "Ricky later killed Enid Puckston. H.M., *why?*"

"Listen, my wench. Young Fleet said himself it was an 'expression.' An outlet. Did you ever see a golfer smash a golf-club against a tree? Or a woman throw a whole breakfast-tray in somebody's face? Well, that's normal; he wasn't.

"Burn it, Ricky Fleet had been hurt. His girl preferred somebody else to *him*. His vanity was scratched raw. There was young Drake, the cause of it all. He wouldn't dare face Drake without a weapon, any more than he'd have dared face his father. (That was still lurkin'; got it?) But he had to *hurt*, had to inflict *pain* on a helpless person, before he killed Drake.

"No, it's not pretty. I warned you long ago it wasn't.

"He prepared it all beforehand. Do you recall, when you were all sitting in that dark back garden just before you started for the prison, how he kept rushin' back to the house—apparently to see how his mother was?"

"Yes," said Martin. "Very well."

"The last time, just before you left, he made his preparations. On this occasion he was goin' to give you a good grown-up sophisticated alibi. He had the dagger and its sheath. He cut his own arm, got plenty of blood for the dagger; and the sheath would hold it without staining him, except for smears on the handle, if he wrapped it in a handkerchief and put it in his pocket. Just as you later did when you shoved it in Dr. Laurier's pocket.

"You went to the prison. Who deliberately called your attention to that pile of rapiers and daggers in the condemned cell? *He* did. You didn't find the dagger, as he'd hoped when he shoved it in there under cover of so much darkness. But back he went with Drake after the fencin' match—"

"By the way," demanded Martin, "was 'young' Dr. Laurier concerned in this?"

"Not in the least, son. He's only a bit of a snob, that's all. His most valued patient is Sophie there, and when he had tea with her on Saturday she must have dropped a hint that 'Captain' Drake was endangerin' Jenny's marriage. Hence the faintly sinister hints in the bar-parlour when he first met you."

"But to get back to—?"

"Sure, if you'll stop interrupting. Ricky Fleet, when you and he went back to get corks, smackin' well made sure you'd find the dagger. He helped tumble over some swords and put his light straight on it. As to how the weapons got there, it's clear he'd been using the prison for some time . . ."

"Using it? He told me," said Martin, "he'd often wanted to explore the place, but he couldn't get in."

"Oh, my son!" H.M. said dismally. "Anybody could get in there. You don't have to be a locksmith to understand that. You just have to go and take a dekko at the main gates. The bigger the lock, the simpler it is. And the easier it is to get a wax impression, if anybody wants to.

"Son, there were too many doors with oiled hinges inside that place, as our friend Stannard pointed out. Even if Stannard himself had been up to some kind of funny business—"

Here the barrister chuckled.

"—why in the name of Esau should he have oiled the hinges

of those high front gates? Admittedly all your party were goin'
there. No; it was somebody who wanted no betrayin' gate-
creaks when he slipped in.

"Ricky Fleet had been usin' the prison for his amorous
adventures, Pan-pipes and nature-worship, which weren't of a
sadistic kind. Masters has discovered he got back the rapier-
dagger collection from the ghost-village . . .

"Ghost-village? You saw it. Built beyond the prison. The
Governor's house was there. George Fleet gave that collection
to Major Colwell, and Major Colwell left it behind when
everybody decamped. So Ricky Fleet had a second dagger,
very like the first, when he led Enid Puckston toward the
prison to kill her."

Martin cleared his throat. "H.M. Was she one of Ricky's
—?"

H.M.'s expression was heavy and bitter.

"No, son. That's the real irony of this case. She liked and
admired him an awful lot, as I could tell when I heard her
mention him at the pub. That's all it amounted to. But—
haven't you wondered why Puckston sent those anonymous
postcards in the first place?"

"You mean she wasn't one of Ricky's conquests, but—?"

"Her father thought she might be," replied H.M.

He was silent for a moment, glowering.

"Mind you, Puckston didn't *know* the boy Richard Fleet
had done that murder years ago. He'd seen what he knew was
the light on a cricket-bat. He guessed nobody but a kid could
have crawled under that ledge unseen. He had no proof and
anyway he didn't want trouble. But if Enid had fallen for this
bloke years later—! So he sent the postcards, with her help but
without her knowin'; and then he thinks she's been killed, by
the same boy grown up, because she knows too much! Do you
wonder at Puckston's state of mind on Sunday night?"

"No," Martin answered. "No. I don't wonder."

"Anyway, Ricky Fleet took that gal to the prison, to see a
'ghost-hunt', at goin' on for one in the morning. He butchered
her with all the hate in him. He left the body under the
gallows-trap, as a rare sight for somebody if the trap was
opened. Masters has told you that story, including the reversed
alibi. Finally, Fleet slipped out again without a whisper to
catch Masters's ear.

"I don't think, though, he slept very well the rest of the
night. And then you two," H.M.'s finger indicated Martin and
Jenny, "had to go yellin' under the windows at going on for

five in the morning, and give him his heaven-gilded opportunity to shove Drake off the roof."

"But why didn't you warn me?"

H.M. drew himself together. He stuck out towards Martin a face of such utter loathing, such indescribable contempt, that the other felt his scalp stir with hostility.

"Look here, you something-something'd thus-and-so," he said. "There's a feller here in London," he mentioned a famous painter, "you think is a friend of yours. I, bein' the old man, happen to know he hates your guts."

"That," Martin said quietly, but with buzzing ears, "is a very bloody lie."

"Darling!" cried Jenny.

"You think so, hey?" inquired H.M., with a contempt which was one vast sneer. "He was in Spain with another feller he hated, and he shot that feller in the back without givin' him a chance. What do you say to *that,* you credulous so-and-so this-and-that?"

"I say," returned Martin, sticking out his own neck, "that I will prove you a thus-and-so this-and-that liar. I will take him to any lonely place you name, with a loaded revolver in my pocket. I will hand him the revolver, and—" Even with badly buzzing head, Martin stopped short.

"Y'see what I mean?" inquired H.M., with a sort of malignant apology.

"I deny that! I . . ."

"Your feelings, son, ring up as plain as l.s.d. on a cash register. Even when," H.M. glanced towards Lady Brayle, "it was half the world to you that they shouldn't. Ricky Fleet would have had to shut you up even quicker than he tried to do.

"And didn't he try! It was a matter of seconds for him to nip up, get the field-glasses out of his father's study where his mother kept 'em, rearrange the chairs on the roof, and . . .

"Are you askin' why? Listen. What's the impulse of anybody who finds a pair of field-glasses on a roof? It's to try 'em, ain't it? People in general (we all did it ourselves on Saturday evening) walk straight to the centre-front of a square roof. You'd have done it on Sunday, with your attention distracted, if you hadn't got suspicious of the glasses. Your bravado took you there instead. The chairs were arranged like a series of rocks for hiding places, while somebody in bare feet crept up behind you.

"To wind it up, on Sunday night I tumbled to the trick of the murder on the roof. And that opened every other door: the skeleton in the clock too. *Puckston*, nobody else but Puckston, was our salvation if we could get him to help.

"He'd written the postcards, probably with the help of his daughter. It seemed to me the poor devil would be over at the Dragon, writhin' in agony with the fear Enid might 'a' been killed because of that. Mind you, I didn't know then he suspected something between Enid and Ricky. And at that time I didn't know old Dr. Laurier, with one too many brandies in his bar, had once given him a hint about what the skeleton-clock meant.

"But—*if* I could show him he wasn't in any way responsible for his girl's death—it seemed to me he'd help us yank a confession out of Ricky. I even took Drake along, as one nearly killed by a maniac. But Puckston didn't even notice Drake's horror-film forehead; and he wasn't necessary.

"The crowds at MacDougall's show were just what we needed. Puckston 'phoned Ricky early in the morning. Ricky arranged to meet him—just as he was willing to meet Drake, with somethin' goading his mind—in the darkish outer-shell of the Mirror Maze.

"But young Richard had plans laid too. He'd arranged a quite genuine meeting between his mother and Susan Harwood, timed for one o'clock. You see why? That was his time to meet Puckston. So he told everybody about it, even Dr. Laurier, with this addition, *'If you see me motion to keep away, keep away.'*

"Neat idea. He could then go where he liked, to meet Puckston, and he could keep any of his friends from followin' him if he waved. All the same, even when we were discussing who was goin' to the fair, he couldn't keep away from his own reflection in the hall mirror. *Just as, on Saturday night and of all places and times, he'd taken a look at himself in the mirror of the condemned cell.*"

"And about his emotional state Monday morning. Did you notice, there in the hall, he had tears in his eyes?"

"But, H.M.!" protested Ruth. "If what Cicely told me was true, he was laughing. You'd been telling some perfectly outrageous anecdotes about your ancestor. Including one about reciting limericks to Charles the First."

"Well . . . now!" said H.M., with a cough and a deprecating wave of his hand. "I didn't really think, y'know, the lofty muse of Curtius Merrivale would ever descend to limericks, even if they'd been invented. It was Masters put the idea in my head by sayin' so the night before."

"Then what—?"

"I was always careful to be very comfortin' and cloth-headed in front of Ricky Fleet. He didn't think he'd got to worry about the old man." Then H.M.'s voice changed sharply. "He wasn't amused then, my wench. He'd been listenin' with all his ears to Drake's end of a do-you-love-me telephone conversation, with that gal there, which didn't amuse him at all.

"When four of you went out there in the car, I heard later, he nearly lost control of himself. He was rigid, nearly ready to burst, hardly keepin' back the tears. That was after Drake had said *he* meant to elope with Jenny if he had to.

"I didn't know this at the time; but cor! I was worried. When I gathered that crowd round the race-track booth, and yelled and bellowed the odds, it was only partly to make Sophie popular. I wanted the jostle of a big crowd so I could make sure Ricky Fleet wasn't carryin' a weapon. He wasn't. But when I heard Drake was in the maze . . .

"You know the rest. Puckston and the dewy-eyed innocent were near a microphone (it was darkish, so the feller didn't see it) outside what looked like a solid mirror. It was only the silver paint usually used over plate glass, for what's known to gamblers as a two-way mirror, but in this case on cardboard and curtain.

"Puckston . . . so! I should 'a' realized, the night before, he was powder packed into a cartridge. He exploded. Ricky Fleet was a first-rate athlete and as strong-built as you'd find; but against that man he hadn't the chance of a celluloid cat in hell. He collapsed in the pieces of smashed looking-glass. And that's all."

There was long silence, extending almost to discomfort. All of them, except Lady Brayle at the window, looked everywhere except at each other. Finally Ruth, smoothing her skirt over her knees and looking steadily down at it, managed to speak.

"There is one thing." Her face was flushed. "Jenny, dear!"

"Yes, dear?" answered Jenny, without looking at her.

"I was in the prison that night. You know what I mean. I made a suggestion to Martin."

"Ruth darling," said Jenny sincerely, "I don't mind. At least—"

"I don't mean *that* kind of suggestion!"

Martin felt like dropping through the floor. Jenny was so surprised she almost looked round.

"About Ricky's—unbalanced state of mind," said Ruth tensely. "I apologize. It was horrible of me. I honestly thought there might be something—well, odd about your side of the family."

Lady Brayle, outraged, turned round majestically. Jenny, with an exclamation of pleasure, put her hand across towards Ruth.

"And that's the only reason you went there?" Jenny did not stop for an answer, which was just as well. "Ruth, everybody thinks that very same thing when your parents are estranged, and everything seems mixed up, and you have a grandmother as reserved and reticent as mine!"

"Ruth," Stannard said softly.

All through H.M.'s recital his strong personality had been repressed, buckled in, to the steady gleam of attention in his eyes. Now, sitting on the arm of the sofa, his husky chuckle seemed to dominate the room. He put his hand under Ruth's chin and tilted it up so that he could look at her eyes.

"What has been," he smiled, "is no longer. What is," he smiled again, "shall continue."

"Always," said Ruth. Her look left no doubt of that.

"By God," Stannard said suddenly, looking up radiantly and lifting his fist, "I can conquer the world!"

He checked himself. His hand dropped, and he looked whimsically at H.M.

"Sir Henry," he said, "it seems an extraordinary thing that only a fortnight ago, in this room, I said I mustn't keep late hours. What is it now? Close on four." He glanced towards Martin and Jenny. "Exactly when, my dear fellow, are you getting married?"

"Tomorrow," Martin answered, "at Westminister registry office. We take the afternoon plane for Paris."

"My new car," chuckled Stannard, "is downstairs. Just as it was a fortnight ago. There's no petrol for long distances. But suppose the four of us drive out to Virginia Water and see the sun come up?"

There was almost a scramble to get up. Much attention from Jenny and Ruth was bestowed on H.M., who endured this with a stuffed and stoical look, like a world-weary Curtius Merrivale. Then it was broken.

"Captain Drake," said Lady Brayle, getting up from her chair beside the window and adjusting her shoulders.

Dead silence.

Martin instantly left the group and went over towards the window so that he could look her in the eye.

"Yes, Lady Brayle?"

"With regard to your proposed marriage with my grand-daughter."

"Yes."

They looked at each other for a full minute, which can be a very long space if you time it. The reason was that Lady Brayle could not speak. She was shaken; emotion tore her; but the lips would not move. Her large, rather flabby hands were folded in front of her. Her shoulders were back. Her eyes wandered in search of determination. Then came firm resolve, and clearly she spoke.

"The Gloucesters, I am informed, are a very honourable regiment."

There was a short silence.

"Very," agreed Martin. He reflected for a moment. "But in my opinion the Brigade of Guards, particularly the Grenadier Guards, must always rank highest of all:"

Then, startlingly, tears came into the woman's eyes.

"Thank you, Captain Drake."

"Not at all, Lady Brayle."

They did not even shake hands. They understood.

And so, as the clock of St. Jude's rang out the hour of four, and white dawn showed faintly behind Kensington, the policeman was on his way back through Moreston Square. The car which had been standing at the kerb was gone. But the windows of Miss Callice's flat were still lighted.

A rumbling voice floated down clearly from those open windows.

"So they framed him, Sophie," the voice said. "And the only reason they framed him was because he killed one of 'em in a duel outside the War Office. But they indicted that fine character on a charge of promotin' fake companies to get Aztec gold out of Mexico, and three times they chucked him into the can. I tell you, Sophie, it was a cryin' scandal against the law!"

The policeman looked up at those windows thoughtfully. But, after all, duels outside the War Office are comparatively rare. And it was Miss Ruth Callice's flat. The policeman smiled and sauntered on.

The End.

ABOUT THE AUTHOR

CARTER DICKSON was the pseudonym for the prolific mystery writer John Dickson Carr. Born in Pennsylvania, he married a British woman and lived in England where he wrote mysteries in the great British tradition and worked for the British Broadcasting Corp. during World War II. Author of over ninety mystery novels, Carr was the creator of the fictional detectives Dr. Gideon Fell and Sir Henry Merrivale. He was considered master of the "locked-room" crime puzzle but also tried his hand at the historical novel, and biography in *The Life of Sir Arthur Conan Doyle*. With Adrian Conan Doyle (Sir Arthur's youngest son), he wrote a series of stories continuing the adventures of Sherlock Holmes, the first of which was published in *Life* magazine. In 1948, Carr, his wife and their three children returned to the United States. In 1949 he was elected for a term as president of the Mystery Writers of America. He was the recipient of that organization's Edgar award in 1949 and 1962, and received the *Ellery Queen* prize twice for short stories. In 1951, he was the subject of a two-part *New Yorker* profile. John Dickson Carr died in 1977.